Ō NO YASUMARO

KOJIKI

RECORDS OF ANCIENT MATTERS

Translated by Basil Hall Chamberlain
Revised and with a Foreword by Matthieu Felt

TUTTLE Publishing
Tokyo | Rutland, Vermont | Singapore

127°30'
130°00'
132°30'
37°30'
35°00'
32°30'
30°00'
The Nether Distant Land ?
The Eternal Land ?
SCARCELY
KARA
KNOWN
KUDARA
SHIRAGI
(SEA OF JA
OKI
IZUMO
MITSU-GO
LEGEN
C. Miho
IZUMO
HŌKI
Riv. Hi
Ō-YAMA
KIBI
AKI
ANATO
SUŌ
SANUK
ŌSHIMA
IYO
IYO
AW
TOSA
Anato Chan.
Hayasui Chan.
TSUSHIMA
TSUKUSHI
LEGENDARY
CYCLE
TSUKUSHI
TOYO
IKI
HI
CHIKA
TSUKUSHI
KUMASO
C. Kasasa
ATA
HIMUKA
(JAPA
(NO
UNKNOWN
The Eternal Land ?

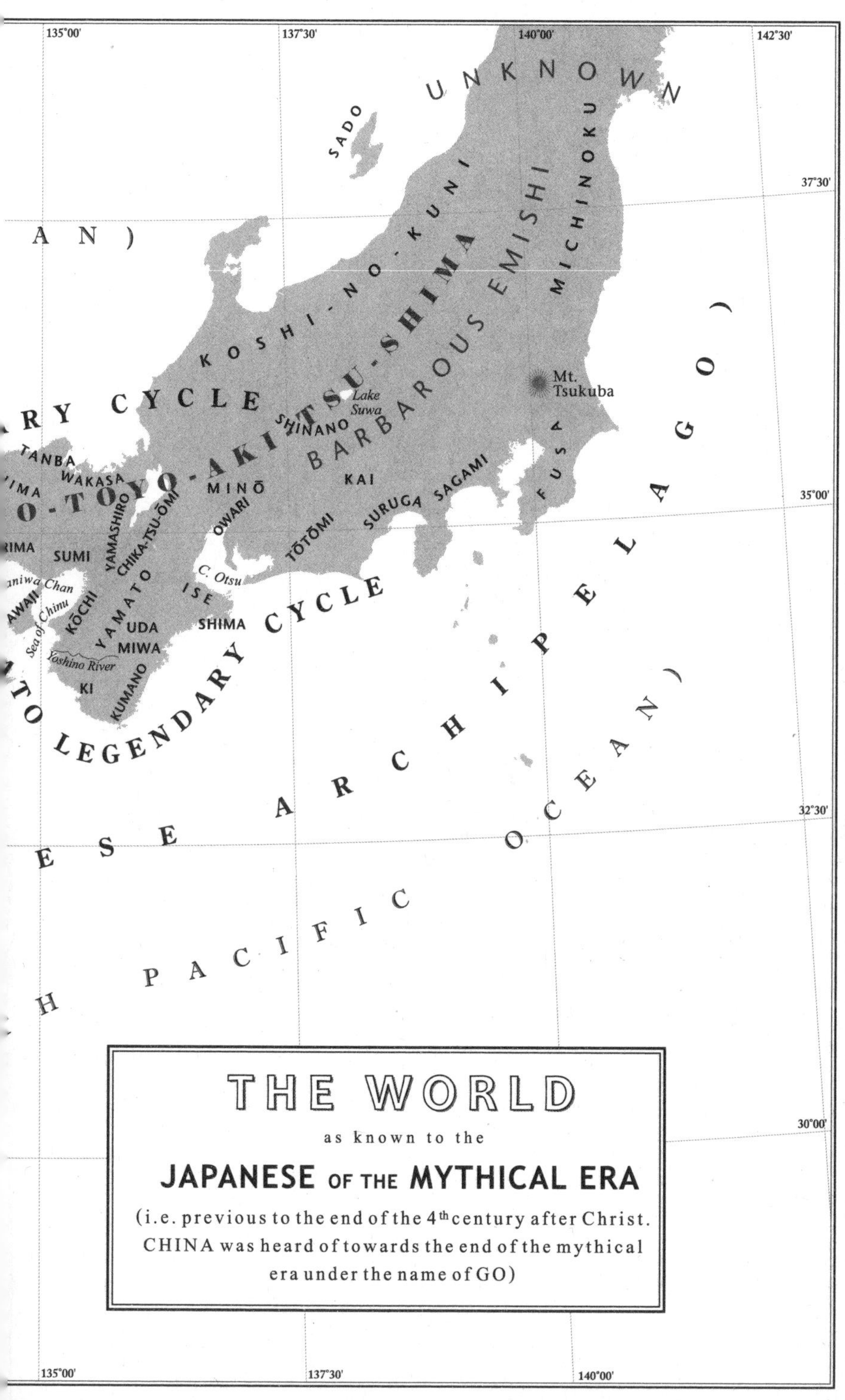

135°00'
137°30'
140°00'
142°30'
37°30'
35°00'
32°30'
30°00'
UNKNOWN
SADO
MICHINOKU
EMISHI
BARBAROUS
KOSHI-NO-KUNI
TOYO-AKITSU-SHIMA
Mt. Tsukuba
Lake Suwa
SHINANO
KAI
MINŌ
OWARI
TŌTŌMI
SURUGA
SAGAMI
FUSA
TANBA
WAKASA
YAMASHIRO
CHIKA-TSU-ŌMI
SUMI
C. Otsu
ISE
SHIMA
KŌCHI
YAMATO
UDA
MIWA
Sea of Chinu
Yoshino River
KI
KUMANO
LEGENDARY CYCLE
PACIFIC OCEAN
ARCHIPELAGO
THE WORLD
as known to the
JAPANESE OF THE MYTHICAL ERA
(i.e. previous to the end of the 4th century after Christ. CHINA was heard of towards the end of the mythical era under the name of GO)

Contents

Foreword

When Basil Hall Chamberlain (1850–1935) translated *The Kojiki, or Records of Ancient Matters* into English, he called it "the most important Monument" of "all the mass of Japanese literature." Now, over 140 years later, the preeminence of *Kojiki* within the Japanese tradition and the relationship of *Kojiki* to the world mythological canon has only grown, in no small part thanks to Chamberlain's 1882 translation. This new edition of Chamberlain's translation recognizes both the importance of *Kojiki* as world literature and world mythology, and the value of Chamberlain's translation, which brought this story to English-language readers for the first time and inaugurated the modern study of Japanese myths.

Chamberlain arrived in Japan in 1873, just five years after a cadre of samurai from western Japan had toppled the Tokugawa Shogunate and installed the emperor as head of state. The Tokugawa clan had ruled Japan for over 250 years, but in keeping with the custom of earlier military governments, had left the imperial family and court intact. Hence, when the emperor returned to power in 1868, the event that might commonly be called a revolution elsewhere was termed, in Japan, a "restoration" of imperial rule. The emperor made 1868 the first year of a new imperial era called "Meiji," meaning "enlightened governance," which lasted until his death in 1912. In the present, it is known as a period of rapid modernization and growing participation in the global economy. Thousands of foreign advisers were employed to assist with technology transfer in fields ranging from agriculture and engineering to philosophy and zoology. In this capacity, Chamberlain began teaching English at the Imperial Naval School in Tokyo in 1874.

Chamberlain was unusual among foreign advisers for his linguistic acumen. While born in England, he was educated at the Lycée Imperial in France and at home by a German tutor. He had planned to continue study at Oxford, but changed course and became a banker instead. The work drained his health, and he resigned his post to travel the world and recuperate. When he ultimately arrived in Japan, his skill with foreign languages led him to quick mastery of both modern and classical Japanese, acquired under private instruction. Chamberlain published his first translations from Japanese, three poems from the eighth-century *Man'yōshū*, in February, April, and October 1874, around only one year after his arrival in May 1873.

Chamberlain's ardor for Japanese study ultimately landed him a new teaching position. When the University of Tokyo was founded in 1877, interest among Japanese scholars in ancient Japan was limited; most focused on mastering foreign languages and fields. But when the university was renamed Imperial University in 1886, university officials created a freestanding Department of Japanese Literature. Chamberlain, knowledgeable in Western philologic methods and, by this time, having translated *Kojiki*, was hired as a professor of Japanese, where his unique knowledge of both modern linguistics and classical Japanese was put to maximum value. Along with diplomats William George Aston (1841–1911) and Sir Ernest Mason Satow (1843–1929), he is regarded as a pioneer of the modern study of Japanese antiquity.

Chamberlain's translation effort was fueled by the hope that it would contribute to a grand discovery about the origins of humanity. Before Watson and Crick's model of DNA, historical linguistics was one of the most compelling methods for identifying ethnic ancestry. In the early 1800s, linguists conclusively determined that Sanskrit, Greek, Latin, Persian, Slavic, and Germanic were all related to each other, resulting in the Indo-European family of languages. By extension, this suggested that peoples across Central and South Asia and Europe shared common origins. Another linguistic hypothesis, the Ural-Altaic language family, attempted to achieve a similar epochal umbrella by linking Hungarian, Finnish, Estonian, Turkish, Mongolian, Korean, and Japanese. While this thesis is now rejected, at the time Chamberlain translated *Kojiki*, the text was thought to be the oldest written record in any Ural-Altaic language then discovered and an indispensable source for scholars searching for evidence of a new, grand language family. As Chamberlain put it, "Japanese mythology remains as the oldest existing product of the Altaic mind."

At the time Chamberlain was translating *Kojiki*, there was also an increasing interest in mythology as an academic field. In one respect, this was driven by linguistics. One of the most influential early mythologists, Max Müller (1823–1900), was a linguist by training and famously defined mythology as a "disease of language," which Chamberlain quotes in his introduction. Linguists combed myths from across the Indo-European language family looking for not only shared vocabulary, but shared narratives. In this same period, myths were also fodder for anthropologists searching for the relationship between myth, ritual, religion, and science in human societies. Chamberlain refers to anthropologist Edward B. Tylor (1832–1917) in his introduction, probably referring to a paper by Tylor from 1877 that was the first English-language assessment of *Kojiki* as mythology. Chamberlain's *Kojiki* translation, along with Aston's translation of *Nihon shoki* (The Chronicles of Japan) and Satow's of *norito* (Shinto Rituals), marked the entry of Japanese myths into world mythological study.

The highlight and enduring value of Chamberlain's translation for contemporary academic study lies in his elaborate set of notes. These notes more than double the length of the actual *Kojiki* translation and are valuable for two primary reasons. First, because no later English translation of *Kojiki* matches Chamberlain's quantity of notes, his translation is still immensely valuable for non-Japanese readers as an academic resource. And in truth, while knowledge and understanding of *Kojiki* has greatly advanced since Chamberlain's day, the modern Japanese editions used by *Kojiki* scholars contain many of the same explanatory notes given by Chamberlain. Second, Chamberlain's notes reveal his relationship to his source material at a level of clarity and honesty rarely seen in translations from any language. Chamberlain makes no secret that his work was only possible by building on the previous efforts of Japanese scholars, especially those from the Edo Period (1603–1868). Chamberlain clearly did not imagine his work as a miracle of modern philology or a work of genius by a Western scholar, but as a sustained engagement with those he calls "native commentators." In the same vein, Chamberlain discusses problems with specific printings and reproductions of *Kojiki* that contemporary translations often elide by clothing themselves as fully commensurate with a nonexistent original text in the source language.

Chamberlain's *Kojiki* translation was first published in 1882 as a

Supplement to the *Transactions of the Asiatic Society of Japan*, the official publication for a group of foreign intellectuals active in Japan from the 1870s through the early twentieth century. This edition was republished in 1919, but the great Tokyo earthquake and fire of 1923 destroyed its remaining stock. A second edition, with annotations by W.G. Aston, was published by J.L. Thompson & Co. (Retail) Ltd., Kobe, in 1932. This edition was based on an 1882 printing that Aston had annotated by hand and returned to Chamberlain in 1892. The 1932 printing transcribed most of Aston's handwritten notes, identified in the text by "W.G.A," and added references to translations by Aston and Satow. Tuttle began publishing the 1932 edition in 1981; the present edition is based on the 2011 Tuttle printing.

Kojiki has now been translated multiple times into English as well as French, German, Italian, Polish, and Spanish. Gustav Heldt's 2014 *The Kojiki: An Account of Ancient Matters* is the definitive English translation. Heldt's translation has no notes and a strong poetic sensibility, making his rendering enjoyable for those with no background in Japanese. A similar focus on readability and prosody characterizes Danno Yoko's 2008 translation *Songs and Stories of the Kojiki*. Conversely, Donald Phillippi's 1968 *Kojiki* is reminiscent of Chamberlain's, with plentiful notes and strong engagement with Japanese commentators. Yet Phillippi's use of transcription, rather than translation, for the names of kami and his use of the Old Japanese alphabet can make his translation confusing and foreboding. In comparative hindsight, Chamberlain's translation sought to balance readability with scholarly rigor, introducing *Kojiki* to an educated readership unfamiliar with Japan and the Japanese language but interested in the points of contention and the unusual details that appear in the notes.

Speaking broadly, the editorial aim for the present edition was, in keeping with Chamberlain's original purpose, to balance readability and scholarly notation for an educated readership. Perhaps the single biggest difference between a contemporary educated readership and a Victorian one is knowledge of Latin, which Chamberlain used for any passage referring to sexual activity or sex organs. While this likely strikes the contemporary reader as overly prudish, it was customary in Chamberlain's era, and Aston's 1896 translation of *Nihongi* does the same. These passages have been translated to English and the Latin original moved to the endnotes. A second issue is Chamberlain's assumption of Western civilizational superiority. This includes occasional identification of Chinese and Indian persons using terms considered wholly inappropriate today; these usages have been amended. Chamberlain refers to the indigenous Ainu people in one instance as "hairy" and another as "barbarous." This is in keeping with common Japanese usage at the time. These expressions are preserved in order to reinforce the imperialistic nature of both *Kojiki* itself, though that text does not speak of Ainu, and of Meiji Japan, which adopted the civilization-spreading rhetoric of *Kojiki* and *Nihon shoki* in order to justify colonization first of Hokkaido, largely populated by Ainu, and then Taiwan, Korea, and beyond. Chamberlain's superiority complex appears elsewhere in his critique of the "uncritical Oriental mind" and the "semi-civilized" state of Japanese scholarship on *Kojiki*. These usages have also been preserved in order to capture the scope and complexity of Victorian Orientalism.

Some of the fundamental assumptions about *Kojiki* that Chamberlain employed are no longer accepted by *Kojiki* scholars. First and foremost, the hypothesis for a Ural-Altaic language family is no longer supported, and so *Kojiki* is not the oldest written document for peoples stretching from Finland and Hungary to Japan. Linguists now classify *Kojiki* as written in Old Japanese, a member of the Japonic language family, which also includes Okinawan. The only language family posited to have any relation to Japonic is Koreanic, and this relationship is hotly disputed. A second major reversal is the history of writing on the Japanese archipelago. At the time Chamberlain translated *Kojiki*, the presumption was that diplomatic contact with China resulted in writing, as a technology, being imported to Japan. Historians of writing now assert that writing first went from China to Korea, and then the distinctive written culture that emerged in Korea was introduced to Japan through both technology transfer and human migration. Finally, the Emishi people of northeastern Japan mentioned in *Kojiki* were considered one and the same as the Ainu; these two people groups are now distinguished.

In contemporary Japan, *Kojiki* is the premier historical record of ancient Japan, but at the time Chamberlain was translating it, *Kojiki* was still rising in esteem. Meanwhile, the 720 *Nihon shoki*, which had been the official record of Japanese antiquity from the time it was completed until the twentieth century, was beginning to fall in fortunes. One important factor was Motoori Norinaga's *Kojiki-den* commentary, whose publication began in 1790. Chamberlain's translation is primarily based on *Kojiki-den*, which dramatically improved access to *Kojiki* for readers of Japanese. While multiple *Nihon shoki* commentaries were published from 812 to 1899, Norinaga's was the first full commentary for *Kojiki*. Norinaga's interest in *Kojiki* stemmed from a conviction that the ancient Japanese language had been better preserved in *Kojiki* than in *Nihon shoki*, which more heavily relied on Classical Chinese written style. When the Imperial University at last created a Department of Japanese Literature and hired Chamberlain, both *Kojiki* and *Nihon shoki* were part of the curriculum. However, one of the major goals for the new department was to create a national canon of Japanese literature, and because the ideals for this canon were linked to the Japanese language, *Kojiki* took precedence over *Nihon shoki*. This perception of the texts and their relative importance spread outside Japan as well, boosting the importance of Chamberlain's translation. For the same reason, *Kojiki* has now been translated multiple times into English, while Aston's 1896 *Nihongi* is still the only full English translation of *Nihon shoki*.

The truthfulness of *Kojiki* was a major difficulty for Chamberlain and the source of most of his tension with the so-called native commentators. Chamberlain was dependent on Norinaga for understanding *Kojiki*. He also relied on commentaries by Hirata Atsutane and Tachibana Moribe, especially when he found Norinaga lacking or suspect. However, Norinaga, Atsutane, and Moribe took the contents of *Kojiki* (and *Nihon shoki*) literally. Chamberlain also worked closely with disciples of these commentators, several of whom were also faculty at the University of Tokyo or the Imperial University. When Chamberlain rails in the introduction and notes against what he calls the outrageous explanations of "Shintoists," he almost certainly refers to the ardent disciples of Norinaga and Atsutane. Still, without these commentaries, Chamberlain had no hope of reading *Kojiki*, and Chamberlain comes across in his notes as conflicted between his deep admiration for the native commentarial tradition and his rejection of the supernatural aspects of Shintoism that seemed, to him, untenable.

In contemporary Japan, *Kojiki* retains its position as the origin story for the Japanese archipelago and a keystone for Japanese culture. There are a wide variety of adaptations in manga, anime, video games, and fiction, some of which delight in irreverence while others attempt to faithfully retell the story. Japanese conservatives celebrate the text as proof of the uniqueness of the imperial line and the Japanese people, and it is not uncommon at Japanese chain hotels to find a *Kojiki* in one's room along with a Gideon Bible, Book of Mormon, and collection of Buddhist Sutras. However, the irreverent and non-literal adaptations of *Kojiki* far outnumber these more serious treatments. Given that in Japan, *Kojiki* is a book that everyone is familiar with but that few have read in the original, these popular adaptations play an important role in making the Japanese origin story accessible and fresh. Similarly, in contemporary Japan, Shinto is more cultural practice than theological doctrine. None of the main reasons that Japanese people attend Shinto shrines today—New Year's Day visits, marriages, visits for children aged three, five, and seven, local *matsuri* festivals, and purification rituals during inauspicious years—have any connection to or basis in *Kojiki*. The singular exception might be *kagura*, dance performances for deities.

Outside of Japan, *Kojiki* is a classic of world literature and an important source in comparative mythology, a position deeply indebted to Chamberlain's translation. As early as 1893, Friedrich W. K. Müller cited this translation when suggesting that an Indonesian myth was related to the Luck of the Mountain myth in Book 1 of *Kojiki*. Claude Lévi-Strauss, the influential anthropologist, refers to the *Kojiki* story of Susano-o in his discussion of South American myths, among others. Whether the Japanese myths are in fact informed by Indonesian ones due to human migration, or even that indigenous South Americans brought some basic form of the Susano-o myth with them across the Bering Strait, is ultimately unproveable, and so we can expect these debates to continue and *Kojiki* to be part of them. In world literature, the new translations of *Kojiki* continue to spread its appeal, no doubt aided by the widespread interest in Japanese culture among young people around the world. In 2024, selections from *Kojiki* were added to the *Norton Anthology of World Literature* for the first time, and hopefully interest in and recognition of this text will continue to grow.

As noted above, Chamberlain's translation of *Kojiki* has academic value for several reasons, but it also has value for world literature generally. One hallmark of a classic is that it can bear several translations. From the Bible to the *Tao Te Ching*, Homer, Proust, or Goethe, it is a joy to rediscover the work in a new translation and to weight the merits and demerits of each translator's decisions. *Kojiki* is undoubtedly one such work for the Classical Japanese tradition, and we hope that this new edition of Chamberlain's translation will return the original to form and dialogue with the other excellent *Kojiki* translations that followed it.

Several formatting changes have been implemented in order to simplify this edition. Chamberlain's original layout included references to the corresponding pages of Norinaga's *Kojiki-den*; these have been removed as that edition of *Kojiki-den* has long been superseded by modern printings. Chamberlain also provided original notes from the *Kojiki* in a smaller font, reflecting the use of half-size characters in the so-called Old Printed Edition of *Kojiki*. These notes are few and the distinction is difficult to see in English, and so these notes are given in this edition in the same size as the original text. Chamberlain's own notes, which were given as footnotes in the original edition, have been split here between footnotes and endnotes. Information required to understand a passage is given in footnotes, with more granular details moved to the endnotes. Aston's notes have been placed in square brackets, attributed to W.G.A as in the 1932 printing. On occasion, I have added further clarifying notes; these are attributed to M.F. Romanization of Japanese words has been converted to the Modified Hepburn system. Japanese prefectures, the geographical system created in 1871, have been added in square brackets following the first mention of Japanese provinces that appear in the notes. Some plant names have also been converted to varieties more familiar to the contemporary English reader. The first and third appendices, which contained transcriptions of poems in *Kojiki* and a list of books on *Kojiki* published after Chamberlain completed his translation, have been omitted here.

Matthieu Felt

Translator's Introduction

Of all the mass of Japanese literature, which lies before us as the result of nearly twelve centuries of bookmaking, the most important monument is the work entitled *Kojiki*[1] or *Records of Ancient Matters*, which was completed in 712 CE. It is the most important because it has preserved for us more faithfully than any other book the mythology, the manners, the language, and the traditional history of Ancient Japan. Indeed it is the earliest authentic connected literary product of that large division of the human race which has been variously denominated Turanian, Scythian and Altaic, and it even precedes by at least a century the most ancient extant literary compositions of non-Aryan India. Soon after the date of its compilation, most of the salient features of distinctive Japanese nationality were buried under a superincumbent mass of Chinese culture, and it is to these *Records* and to a very small number of other ancient works, such as the poems of the *Collection of a Myriad Leaves*, and the *Shinto Rituals*, that the investigator must look, if he would not at every step be misled into attributing originality to modern customs and ideas, which have simply been borrowed wholesale from the neighboring continent.

It is of course not pretended that even these *Records* are untouched by Chinese influence: that influence is patent in the very characters with which the text is written. But the influence is less, and of another kind. If in the traditions preserved and in the customs alluded to we detect the Early Japanese in the act of borrowing from China and perhaps even from India, there is at least on our author's part no ostentatious decking out in Chinese trappings of what he believed to be original matter, after the fashion of the writers who immediately succeeded him. It is true that this abstinence on his part makes his compilation less pleasant to the ordinary native taste than that of subsequent historians, who put fine Chinese phrases into the mouths of emperors and heroes supposed to have lived before the time when intercourse with China began. But the European student, who reads all such books not as a pastime but in order to search for facts, will prefer the more genuine composition. It is also accorded the first place by the most learned of the native *literati.*

Of late years this paramount importance of the *Records of Ancient Matters* to investigators of Japanese subjects generally has become well known to European scholars; and even versions of a few passages are to be found scattered through the pages of their writings. Thus Mr. Aston has given us, in the chrestomathy appended to his *Grammar of the Japanese Written Language*, a couple of interesting extracts; Mr. Satow has illustrated by occasional extracts his elaborate papers on the *Shinto Rituals* printed in these *Transactions*, and a remarkable essay by Mr. Kempermann published in the Fourth Number of the *Mittheilungen der Deutschen Gesellschaft fur Natur und Völkerkunde Ostasiens*, though containing no actual translations, bases on the accounts given in the *Records* some conjectures regarding the *origines* of Japanese civilization which are fully substantiated by more minute research. All that has yet appeared in any European language does not, however, amount to one-twentieth part of the whole, and the most erroneous views of the style and scope of the book and its contents have found their way into popular works on Japan. It is hoped that the true nature of the book, and also the true nature of the traditions, customs, and ideas of the Early Japanese, will be made clearer by the present translation, the object of which is to give the entire work in a continuous English version, and thus to furnish the European student with a text to quote from, or at least to use as a guide in consulting the original. The only object aimed at has been a rigid and literal conformity with the Japanese text. Fortunately for this endeavor (though less fortunately for the student), one of the difficulties which often beset the translator of an Oriental classic is absent in the present case. There is no beauty of style, to preserve some trace of which he may be tempted to sacrifice a certain amount of accuracy. The *Records* sound queer and bald in Japanese, as will be noticed further on; and it is therefore right, even from a stylistic point of view, that they should sound bald and queer in English. The only portions of the text which, from obvious reasons, refuse to lend themselves to translation into English after this fashion are the indecent portions. But it has been thought that there could be no objection to rendering them into Latin,—Latin as rigidly literal as is the English of the greater part.

After these preliminary remarks. it will be most convenient to take the several points which a study of the *Records* and the turning of them into English suggest, and to consider the same one by one. These points are:

1. Authenticity and Nature of the Text, together with Bibliographical Notes.
2. Details Concerning the Method of Translation.
3. The *Nihongi* or *Chronicles of Japan.*
4. Manners and Customs of the Early Japanese.
5. Religious and Political Ideas of the Early Japanese, Beginnings of the Japanese Nation, and Credibility of the National Traditions.

1
THE TEXT AND ITS AUTHENTICITY, TOGETHER WITH BIBLIOGRAPHICAL NOTES

The latter portion of the Preface to the *Records of Ancient Matters* is the only documentary authority for the origin of the work. It likewise explains its scope. But though in so doing the author descends to a more matter-of-fact style than the high-sounding Chinese phrases and elaborate allusions with which he had set forth, still his meaning may be found to lack somewhat of clearness, and it will be as well to have the facts put into language more intelligible to the European student. This having already been done by Mr. Satow in his paper on the "Revival of Pure Shinto,"[2] it will be best simply to quote his words. They are as follows: "The Emperor Ten-mu, at what portion of his reign is not mentioned, lamenting that the records possessed by the chief families contained many errors, resolved to take steps to preserve the true traditions from oblivion. He therefore had the records carefully examined, compared, and weeded of their faults. There happened to be in his household a person of marvelous memory named Hieda no Are,[3] who could repeat without mistake the contents of any document he had ever seen, and never forgot anything that he had heard. Ten-mu

Tennō[A] took the pains to instruct this person in the genuine traditions and 'old language of former ages,' and to make him repeat them until he had the whole by heart. 'Before the undertaking was completed,' which probably means before it could be committed to writing, the Emperor died, and for twenty-five years Are's memory was the sole depository of what afterwards received the title of *Kojiki*[B] or *Funi-ko-to-bumi* as it is read by Norinaga. At the end of this interval the Empress Genmei ordered Yasumaro to write it down from the mouth of Are, which accounts for the completion of the manuscript in so short a time as four months and a half. Are's age at this date is not stated, but as he was twenty-eight years of age some time in the reign of Ten-mu Tennō, it could not possibly have been more than sixty-eight, while taking into account the previous order of Ten-mu Tennō in 681 for the compilation of a history, and the statement that he was engaged on the composition of the *Kojiki* at the time of his death in 686, it would not be unreasonable to conclude that it belongs to about the last year of his reign, in which case Are was only fifty-three in 711."

The previous order of the Emperor Ten-mu mentioned in the above extract is usually supposed to have resulted in the compilation of a history which was early lost. But Atsutane gives reasons for supposing that this and the project of the *Records of Ancient Matters* were identical. If this opinion be accepted, the *Records*, while the oldest *existing* Japanese book, are, not the third, but the second historical work of which mention has been preserved, one such having been compiled in the year 620, but lost in a fire in the year 645. It will thus be seen that it is rather hard to say whom we should designate as the author of the work. The Emperor Ten-mu, Hieda no Are, and Yasumaro may all three lay claim to that title. The question, however, is of no importance to us, and the share taken by Are may well have been exaggerated in the telling. What seems to remain as the residue of fact is that the plan of a purely national history originated with the Emperor Ten-mu and was finally carried out under his successor by

[A] I.e., the Emperor Tem-mu.

[B] I.e., *Records of Ancient Matters*. The alternative reading, which is probably but an invention of Norinaga's, gives the same meaning in pure Japanese (instead of Sinico-Japanese) sounds.

Yasumaro, one of the Court Nobles.

Fuller evidence and confirmatory evidence from other sources as to the origin of our *Records* would doubtless be very acceptable. But the very small number of readers and writers at that early date, and the almost simultaneous compilation of a history (the *Chronicles of Japan*) which was better calculated to hit the taste of the age, make the absence of such evidence almost unavoidable. In any case, and only noticing in passing the fact that Japan was never till quite recent years noted for such wholesale literary forgeries (for Norinaga's condemnation of the *Chronicles of Old Matters of Former Ages* has been considered rash by later scholars),—it cannot be too much emphasized that in this instance authenticity is sufficiently proved by internal evidence. It is hard to believe that any forger living later than the eighth century of our era should have been so well able to discard the Chinese "padding" to the old traditions, which, after the acceptance by the Court of the *Chronicles of Japan*, had come to be generally regarded as an integral portion of those very traditions; and it is more unlikely still that he should have invented a style so little calculated to bring his handiwork into repute. He would either have written in fair Chinese, like the mass of early Japanese prose writers (and his Preface shows that he could do so if he were so minded); or, if the tradition of there having been a history written in the native tongue had reached him, he would have made his composition unmistakably Japanese in form by arranging the characters in the order demanded by Japanese syntax, and by the consistent use of characters employed phonetically to denote particles and terminations, after the fashion followed in the *Rituals*, and developed (apparently before the close of the ninth century) into what is technically known as the "Mixed Phonetic Style" *(Kana-majiri)*, which has remained ever since as the most convenient vehicle for writing the language. As it is, his quasi-Chinese construction, which breaks down every now and then to be helped up again by a few Japanese words written phonetically, is surely the first clumsy attempt at combining two divergent elements. What however is simply incredible is that, if the supposed forger lived even only a hundred years later than A.D. 712, he should so well have imitated or divined the archaisms of that early period. For the eighth century of our era was a great turning point in the Japanese language, the Archaic Dialect being then replaced by the Classical; and as the Chinese language and literature were alone thenceforward considered worthy of the student's attention, there was no means of keeping up an acquaintance with the diction of earlier reigns, neither do we find the poets of the time ever attempting to adorn their verse with obsolete phraseology. That was an affectation reserved for a later epoch, when the diffusion of books rendered it possible. The poets of the seventh, eighth, and ninth centuries apparently wrote as they spoke; and the test of language alone would almost allow of our arranging their compositions half century by half century, even without the dates which are given in many instances in the *Collection of a Myriad Leaves* and in the *Collection of Songs Ancient and Modern*,—the first two collections of poems published by imperial decree in the middle of the eighth, and at the commencement of the tenth, century respectively.

The above remarks are meant to apply more especially to the occasional Japanese words,—all of them Archaic,—which, as mentioned above, are used from time to time in the prose text of the *Records*, to help out the author's meaning and to preserve names whose exact pronunciation he wished handed down. That he should have invented the songs would be too monstrous a supposition for anyone to entertain, even if we had not many of the same and other similar ones preserved in the pages of the *Chronicles of Japan*, a work which was undoubtedly completed in 720 CE. The history of the Japanese language is too well known to us, we can trace its development and decay in too many documents reaching from the eighth century to the present time, for it to be possible to entertain the notion that the latest of these songs, which have been handed down with minute care in a syllabic transcription, is posterior to the first half of the eighth century, while the majority must be ascribed to an earlier, though uncertain, date. If we refer the greater number of them in their present form to the sixth century, and allow a further antiquity of one or two centuries to others more ancient in sentiment and in grammatical usage, we shall probably be making a moderate estimate. It is an estimate, moreover, which obtains confirmation from the fact that the first notice we have of the use of writing in Japan dates from early in the fifth century; for it is natural to suppose that the songs believed to have been composed by the gods and heroes of antiquity should have been among the first things to be written down, while the reverence in which they were held would in some cases cause them to be transcribed exactly as tradition had bequeathed them, even if unintelligible or nearly so, while in others the same feeling would lead to the correction of what were supposed to be errors or inelegancies. Finally it may be well to observe that the authenticity of the *Records* has never been doubted, though, as has already been stated, some of the native commentators have not hesitated to charge with spuriousness another of their esteemed ancient histories. Now it is unlikely that, in the war which has been waged between the partisans of the *Records* and those of the *Chronicles*, some flaw in the former's title to genuineness and to priority should not have been discovered and pointed out if it existed.

During the Middle Ages, when no native Japanese works were printed, and not many others excepting the Chinese Classics and Buddhist Scriptures, the *Records of Ancient Matters* remained in manuscript in the hands of the Shinto priesthood. They were first printed in the year 1644, at the time when, peace having been finally restored to the country and the taste for reading having become diffused, the great mass of the native literature first began to emerge from the manuscript state. This very rare edition (which was reprinted in facsimile in 1798) is indispensable to anyone who would make of the *Records* a special study. The next edition was by a Shinto priest, Deguchi Nobuyoshi, and appeared in 1687. It has marginal notes of no great value, and several emendations of the text. The first-mentioned of these two editions is commonly called the "Old Printed Edition" (旧印本), but has no title beyond that of the original work,—*Records of Ancient Matters*. The name of the other is *Records of Ancient Matters with Marginal Readings* (鼇頭古事記). Each is in three volumes. They were succeeded in 1789–1822 by Norinaga's great edition, entitled *Exposition of the Records of Ancient Matters* (古事記伝). This, which is perhaps the most admirable work of which Japanese erudition can boast, consists of forty-four large volumes, fifteen of which are devoted to the elucidation of the first volume of the original, seventeen to the second, ten to the third, and the rest to prolegomena, indexes, etc. To the ordinary student this *Commentary* will furnish all that he requires, and the charm of Norinaga's style will be found to shed a glamor over the driest parts of the original work. The author's judgment only seems to fail him occasionally when confronted with the most difficult or corrupt passages, or with such as might be construed in a sense unfavorable to his predilections as an ardent Shintoist. He frequently quotes the opinions of his master Mabuchi, whose own treatise on this subject is so rare that the present writer has never seen a copy of it, nor does the public library of Tokyo possess one. Later and less important editions are the *Records of Ancient Matters with the Ancient Reading* (古訓古事言), a reprint by one of Norinaga's pupils of the Chinese text and of his Master's *Kana* reading of it without his *Commentary*, and useful for reference, though the title is a misnomer, 1803; the *Records of Ancient Matters with Marginal Notes* (古事記標註), by Murakami Tadanori, 1874; the *Records of Ancient Matters in the Syllabic Character* (假名古事記), by Sakata Kaneyasu, 1874, a misleading book, as it gives the modern *Kana* reading with its arbitrarily inserted Honorifics and other departures from the actual text, as the *ipsissima verba* of the original work; the *Records of Ancient Matters Revised* (校正古事記), by Uematsu Shigeoka, 1875. All these editions are in three volumes, and the *Records of Ancient Matters with the Ancient Reading* has also been reprinted in one volume on beautiful thin paper. Another in four volumes by Fujiwara Masaoki, 1871, entitled the *Records of Ancient Matters in the Divine Character* (神字古事記), is a real curiosity of literature, though otherwise of no value. In it the editor has been at the pains of reproducing the whole work, according to its modern *Kana* reading, in that adaptation of the Korean alphabetic writing which some modern Japanese authors have supposed to be characters of peculiar age and sanctity, used by the ancient gods of their country and named "Divine Characters" accordingly.

Besides these actual editions of the *Records of Ancient Matters*, there is a considerable mass of literature bearing less directly on the same work, and all of which cannot be here enumerated. It may be sufficient to mention the *Correct Account of the Divine Age* (神代正語) by Norinaga, 3 Vols. 1789, and a commentary thereon entitled *Tokiwa-Gusa* (神代正語常盤草) by Osada Tominobu, from which the present translator has borrowed a few ideas; the *Sources of the Ancient Histories* (古史徴) and its sequel entitled *Exposition of the Ancient Histories* (古史伝), by Hirata Atsutane, begun printing in 1819,—works which are specially admirable from a philological point of view, and in which the student will find the solution of not a few difficulties which even to Norinaga had been insuperable;[4] the *Izu-no-chi-waki* (稜威道別), by Tachibana Moribe, begun printing in 1851, a useful commentary on the *Chronicles of Japan*; the *Izu-no-koto-waki* (稜威語別) by the same author, begun printing in 1847, an invaluable help to a comprehension of the songs contained in both the *Records* and the *Chronicles*; the *Examination of Difficult Words* (難語考, also entitled 山彦冊子), in 3 Vols., 1831, a sort of dictionary of specially perplexing terms and phrases, in which light is thrown on many a verbal crux and much originality of thought displayed; and the *Perpetual Commentary on the Chronicles of Japan* (日本書記通證), by Tanikawa Kotosuga, 1762, a painstaking work written in the Chinese language, 23 Vols. Neither must the *Kō Gan Shō* (厚顔抄), a commentary on the songs contained in the *Chronicles* and *Records* composed by the Buddhist priest Keichū, who may be termed the father of the native school of criticism, be forgotten. It is true that most of Keichū's judgments on doubtful points have been superseded by the more perfect erudition of later days; but some few of his interpretations may still be followed with advantage. The *Kō Gan Shō* which was finished in the year 1691, has never been printed. It is from these and a few others and from the standard dictionaries and general books of reference, such as the *Japanese Words Classified and Explained* (和名類聚鈔), the *Catalogue of Family Names* (姓氏録), and (coming down to more modern times) Arai Hakuseki's *Tōga* (東雅), that the translator has derived most assistance. The majority of the useful quotations from the dictionaries, etc., having been incorporated by Norinaga in his *Commentary*, it has not often been necessary to mention them by name in the notes to the translation. At the same time the translator must express his conviction that, as the native authorities cannot possibly be dispensed with, so also must their assertions be carefully weighed and only accepted with discrimination by the critical European investigator. He must also thank Mr. Tachibana Chimori, grandson of the eminent scholar Tachibana Moribe, for kindly allowing him to make use of the manuscript of the unpublished portions of the *Izu-no-chi-waki* and the *Izu-no-koto-waki,* works indispensable to the comprehension of the more difficult portion of the text of the *Records*. To Mr. Satow he is indebted for the English and Latin equivalents of the Japanese botanical names, to Capt. Blakiston and Mr. Namie Motokichi for similar assistance with regard to the zoological names.

Comparing what has been said above with what the author tells us in his Preface, the nature of the text, so far as language is concerned, will be easily understood. The Songs are written phonetically, syllable by syllable, in what is technically known as *Manyō-Gana, i.e.* entire Chinese characters used to represent sound and not sense. The rest of the text, which is in prose, is very poor Chinese, capable (owing to the ideographic nature of the Chinese written character[5]), of being read off into Japanese. It is also not only full of "Japonisms," but irregularly interspersed with characters which turn the text into nonsense for a Chinese, as they are used phonetically to represent certain Japanese words, for which the author could not find suitable Chinese equivalents. These phonetically written words prove, even apart from the notice in the Preface, that the text was never meant to be read as pure Chinese. The probability is that (sense being considered more important than sound) it was read partly in Chinese and partly in Japanese, according to a mode which has since been systematized and has become almost universal in this country even in the reading of genuine Chinese texts. The modern school of Japanese *literati,* who push their hatred of everything foreign to the bounds of fanaticism, contend however that this, their most ancient and revered book, was from the first intended to be read exclusively into Japanese. Drawing from the other sources of our knowledge of the Archaic Dialect, Norinaga has even hazarded a restoration of the Japanese reading of the entire prose text, in the whole of which not a single Chinese word is used, excepting for the titles of the two Chinese books (the *Confucian Analects* and the *Thousand Character Essay*) which are said to have been brought over to Japan in the reign of the Emperor Ō-jin, and for the names of a Korean King and of three or four other Koreans and Chinese. Whatever may be their opinion on the question at issue, most European scholars, to whom the superior sanctity of the Japanese language is not an article of faith, will probably agree with Mr. Aston[6] in denying to this conjectural restoration the credit of representing the genuine words into which Japanese eighth century students of history read off the text of the *Records*.

2
METHOD OF TRANSLATION.

To the translator the question above mooted is not one of great importance. The text itself must form the basis of his version, and not any one's,—not even Norinaga's,—private and particular reading of it. For this reason none of the Honorifics which Norinaga inserts as prefixes to nouns and terminations to verbs have been taken any notice of, but the original has been followed, character by character, with as great fidelity as was attainable. The author too has his Honorifics; but he does not use them so plentifully or so regularly as it pleases Norinaga to represent him as having intended to do. On the other hand, Norinaga's occasional emendations of the text may generally be accepted. They rarely extend to more than single words; and the errors in the earlier editions may frequently be shown to have arisen from careless copying of characters originally written, not in the square, but in the cursive form. The translator has separately considered each case where various readings occur, and has mentioned them in the Notes when they seemed of sufficient importance. In some few cases he has preferred a reading not approved by Norinaga, but he always mentions Norinaga's reading in a Footnote.

The main body of the text contains but little to perplex anyone who has made a special study of the early Japanese writings, and it has already been noticed that there is an admirable exegetical literature at the student's command. With the Songs embedded in the prose text the case is different, as some of them are among the most difficult things in the language, and the commentators frequently arrive at most discordant interpretations of the obscurer passages. In the present version particulars concerning each song have, except in a very few cases where comment appeared superfluous, been given in a footnote, the general sense being usually first indicated, the meaning of particular expressions then explained, and various opinions mentioned when they seemed worthy of notice. Besides one or two terms of Japanese grammar, the only technical knowledge with which the readers of the notes are necessarily credited is that of the use by the Japanese poets of what have been styled pillow-words, pivots, and prefaces; and those pillow-words which are founded on a jeu-de-mots or are of doubtful signification form, with the one exception mentioned below, the only case where anything contained in the original is omitted from the English version.[7] After some consideration, it has been deemed advisable to print in an Appendix the Japanese text of all the songs, transliterated into Roman. [This Appendix has been omitted in this edition. —M.F.] Students will thus find it easier to form their own opinion on the interpretation of doubtful passages. The importance likewise of these songs, as the most ancient specimens of Altaic speech, makes it right to give them as much publicity as possible.

The text of the *Records* is, like many other Japanese texts, completely devoid of breaks corresponding to the chapters and paragraphs into which European works are divided. With the occasional exception of a pause after a catalogue of gods or princes, and of notes inserted in smaller type and generally containing genealogies or indicating the pronunciation of certain words, the whole story, prose and verse, runs on from beginning to end with no interruptions other than those marked by the conclusion of Vol. 1 and by the death of each emperor in Vols. 2 and 3. Faithfulness however scarcely seems to demand more than this statement; for a similarly continuous printing of the English version would attain no end but that of making a very dry piece of reading more arduous still. Moreover there are certain traditional names by which the various episodes of the history of the so-called "Divine Age" are known to the native scholars, and according to which the text of Vol. 1 may naturally be divided. The reigns of the emperors form a similar foundation for the analysis of Vols. 2 and 3, which contain the account of the "Human Age." It has been thought that it would be well to mark such natural divisions by the use of numbered Sections with marginal headings. The titles proposed by Norinaga in the prolegomena to his *Commentary* have been adopted with scarcely any alteration in the case of Vol. 1. In Vols. 2 and 3, where his sections mostly embrace the whole reign of an emperor, and the titles given by him to each Section consist only of the name of the palace where each emperor is said to have resided, there is less advantage in following him; for those Sections are often inordinately long, and their titles occasionally misleading and always inconvenient for purposes of reference, as the Japanese emperors are commonly known, not by the names of their places of residence, but by their "canonical names." Norinaga, as an ardent nationalist, of course rejected these "canonical names," because they were first applied to the Japanese emperors at a comparatively late date in imitation of Chinese usage. But to a foreigner this need be no sufficient reason for discarding them. The Sections in the translation of Vols. 2 and 3 have therefore been obtained by breaking up the longer reigns into appropriate portions; and in such Sections, as also in the footnotes, the emperors are always mentioned by their "canonical names."[8] The Vol. mentioned in brackets on every right-hand page is that of Norinaga's Commentary which treats of the Section contained in that page. [This information has been omitted in this edition. —M.F.]

The notes translated from the original are indented, and are printed small when they are in small type in the Japanese text. [In this edition, small type is not used. —M.F.] Those only which give directions for pronouncing certain characters phonetically have been omitted, as they have no significance when the original tongue and method of writing are exchanged for foreign vehicles of thought and expression. The songs have likewise been indented for the sake of clearness, and each one printed as a separate paragraph. The occasionally unavoidable insertion in the translation of important words not occurring in the Japanese text has been indicated by printing such words within square brackets. The translator's notes, which figure at the bottom of each page, do not aim at anything more than the exegesis of the actual text. [Some of these notes have been converted to endnotes. —M.F.] To illustrate its subject-matter from other sources, as Norinaga does, and to enlarge on all the objects connected with Japanese antiquity which are sometimes merely alluded to in a single phrase, would require several more volumes the size of this one, many years of labor on the part of the investigator, and an unusually large stock of patience on the reader's part. The notes terminate with the death of the Emperor

Ken-zo, after which the text ceases to offer any interest, except as a comment on the genealogies given in the *Chronicles of Japan*.

Without forgetting the fact that so-called equivalent terms in two languages rarely quite cover each other, and that it may therefore be necessary in some cases to render one Japanese word by two or three different English words according to the context, the translator has striven to keep such diversity within the narrowest limits, as it tends to give a false impression of the original, implying that it possesses a versatility of thought which is indeed characteristic of Modern Europe, but not at all of Early Japan. With reference to this point a certain class of words must be mentioned, as the English translation is unavoidably defective in their case, owing to the fact of our language not possessing sufficiently close synonyms for them. They are chiefly the names of titles, and are the following:

Agata-no-atae	roughly	rendered	by	Departmental Suzerain.
Agata-nushi	"	"	"	Departmental Lord.
Asomi (Ason)	"	"	"	Court Noble.
Atae	"	"	"	Suzerain.
Hiko	"	"	"	Prince.
Hime	"	"	"	Princess.
Inaki	"	"	"	Territorial Lord.
Iratsuko	"	"	"	Lord.
Iratsume	"	"	"	Lady.
Kami	"	"	"	Deity.
Kimi	"	"	"	Duke.
Ma	"	"	"	True.
Miko (王)	"	"	"	King.
Miko (御子)	"	"	"	August Child.
Mikoto	"	"	"	Augustness.
Miyatsuko	"	"	"	Ruler.
Muraji	"	"	"	Chief.
Omi	"	"	"	Grandee.
Sukune	"	"	"	Noble.
Wake *(in the names of human beings)*				Lord.

It must be understood that no special significance is to be attached to the use of such words as "Duke," "Suzerain," etc. They are merely, so to speak, labels by which titles that are distinct in the original are sought to be kept distinct in the translation. Many of them also are used as that species of hereditary titular designation which the translator has ventured to call the "gentile name."[9] Where possible, indeed, the etymological meaning of the Japanese word has been preserved. Thus *omi* seems to be rightly derived by Norinaga from *ō-mi*, "great body"; and "grandee" is therefore the nearest English equivalent. Similarly *muraji*, "chief," is a corruption of two words signifying "master of a tribe." On the other hand, both the etymology and the precise import of the title of *wake*[10] are extremely doubtful. *Hiko* and *hime* again, if they really come from *hi ko*, "sun-child" and *hi me*, "sun-female" (or "fire-child" and "fire-female"), have wandered so far from their origin as, even in Archaic times, to have been nothing more than honorific appellations, corresponding in a loose fashion to the English words "prince and princess," or "lord and lady,"—in some cases perhaps meaning scarcely more than "youth and maiden."

The four words *kami, ma, miko* and *mikoto* alone call for special notice; and *ma* may be disposed of first. It is of uncertain origin, but identified by the native philologists with the perpetually recurring honorific *mi*, rendered "august." As, when written ideographically, it is always represented by the Chinese character 真, the translator renders it in English by "true"; but it must be understood that this word has no force beyond that of an honorific.

Mikoto, rendered "Augustness," is properly a compound, *mi koto*, "august thing." It is used as a title, somewhat after the fashion of our words "Majesty" and "Highness," being suffixed to the names of exalted human personages, and also of gods and goddesses. For the sake of clearness in the English translation this title is prefixed and used with the possessive pronoun, thus: *Yamato-Take-no-Mikoto*, His Augustness Yamato-Take.

With regard to the title read *miko* by the native commentators, it is represented in two ways in the Chinese text. When a *young* prince is denoted by it, we find the characters 御子, "august child," reminding us of the Spanish title of *infante*. But in other cases it is written with the single character 王, "King," and it may be questioned whether the reading of it as *miko* is not arbitrary. Many indications lead us to suppose that in Early Japan something similar to the feudal system, which again obtained during the Middle Ages, was in force; and if so, then some of these "kings," may have been kings indeed after a fashion; and to degrade their title, as do the modern commentators, to that of "prince" is an anachronism. In any case the safest plan, if we would not help to obscure this interesting political question, is to adhere to the proper signification of the character in the text, and that character is 王, "King."[11]

Of all the words for which it is hard to find a suitable English equivalent, *kami* is the hardest. Indeed there is no English word which renders it with any near approach to exactness. If therefore it is here rendered by the word "deity" ("deity" being preferred to "god" because it includes superior beings of both sexes), it must be clearly understood that the word "deity" is taken in a sense not sanctioned by any English dictionary; for *kami* and "deity," or "god," only correspond to each other in a very rough manner. The proper meaning of the word "*kami*" is "top," or "above"; and it is still constantly so used. For this reason it has the secondary sense of "hair of the head;" and only the hair on the *top* of the head,—not the hair on the face,—is so designated. Similarly the Government, in popular phraseology, is *O Kami*, literally "the honorably above"; and down to a few years ago *Kami* was the name of a certain titular provincial rank. Thus it may be understood how the word was naturally applied to superiors in general, and especially to those more than human superiors whom we call "gods." A Japanese, to whom the origin of the word is patent, and who uses it every day in contexts by no means divine, does not receive from the word *kami* the same impression of awe which is produced on the more earnest European mind by the words "deity" and "god," with their very different associations. In using the word "deity," therefore, to translate the Japanese term *kami* we must, so to speak, bring it down from the heights to which Western thought has raised it. In fact *kami* does not mean much more than "superior." This subject will be noticed again in Section 5 of the present Introduction; but so far as the word *kami* itself is concerned, these remarks may suffice.

To conclude this Section, the translator must advert to his treatment of proper names, and he feels that he must plead guilty to a certain amount of inconsistency on this head. Indeed the treatment of proper names is always an embarrassment, partly because it is often difficult to determine what *is* a proper name, and partly because in translating a text into a foreign tongue proper names, whose meanings are evident in the original and perhaps have a bearing on the story, lose their significance; and the translator has therefore first of all to decide whether the name is really a proper name at all or simply a description of the personage or place, and next whether he will sacrifice the meaning because the word is used as a name, or preserve the original name and thus fail to render the meaning,—a meaning which may be of importance as revealing the channels in which ancient thought flowed. For instance *Ō-kuni-nushi-no- kami*, "the Deity Master of the Great Land," is clearly nothing more than a description of the god in question, who had several other names, and the reason of whose adoption of this special one was that the sovereignty of the "Great Land," *i.e.* of Japan (or rather of Izumo and the neighboring provinces in northwestern Japan), was ceded to him by another god, whom he deceived and whose daughter he ran away with.[12] Again *Toyo-ashi-hara-no-chi-aki-no-naga-i-ho-aki-mizu-ho-no-kuni*, which signifies "the Luxuriant Reed-Moors, the Land of Fresh Rice-ears,—of a Thousand Autumns,—of Long Five Hundred Autumns" cannot possibly be regarded as more than an honorific *description* of Japan. Such a catalogue of words could never have been used as a name. On the other hand it is plain that *Tema* was simply the proper name of a certain mountain, because there is no known word in Archaic Japanese to which it can with certainty be traced. The difficulty is with the intermediate cases, —the cases of those names which are but partly comprehensible or partly applicable to their bearers; and the difficulty is one of which there would seem to be no satisfactory solution possible. The translator may therefore merely state that in Vol. 1 of these *Records*, where an unusual number of the proper names have a bearing on the legends related in the text, he has, wherever feasible, translated all those which are borne by persons, whether human or divine. In the succeeding Volumes he has not done so, nor has he, except in a very small number or instances, translated the proper names of places in any of the three volumes. In order, however, to convey all the needful information both as to sound and as to sense, the Japanese original is always indicated in a footnote when the translation has the name in English, and *vice versa,* while all doubtful etymologies are discussed.

3
THE *CHRONICLES OF JAPAN*

It will have been gathered from what has been already said, and it is indeed generally known, that the *Records of Ancient Matters* do not stand alone. To say nothing of the *Chronicles of Old Matters of Former Ages*, whose genuineness is disputed, there is another undoubtedly authentic work with which no student of Japanese antiquity can dispense. It is entitled *Nihon-Gi,* i.e., *Chronicles of Japan*, and is second only in value to the *Records*, which it has always excelled in popular favor. It was completed in A.D. 720, eight years after the *Records of Ancient Matters* had been presented to the Empress Gen-mei.

The scope of the two histories is the same; but the language of the later one and its manner of treating the national traditions stand in notable contrast to the unpretending simplicity of the elder work. Not only is the style (excepting in the songs, which had to be left as they were or sacrificed altogether) completely Chinese,—in fact to a great extent a cento of well-worn Chinese phrases,—but the subject-matter is touched up, re-arranged, and polished, so as to make the work resemble a Chinese history so far as that was possible. Chinese philosophical speculations and moral precepts are intermingled with the cruder traditions that had descended from Japanese antiquity. Thus the naturalistic Japanese account of the creation is ushered in by a few sentences which trace the origin of all things to *Yin* and *Yang* (陰陽), the passive and active essences of Chinese philosophy. The legendary Emperor Jin-mu is credited with speeches made up of quotations from the *I Jing*,[13] the *Liji*,[14] and other standard Chinese works. A few of the most childish of the national traditions are omitted, for instance the story of the "White Hare of Inaba," that of the gods obtaining counsel of a toad, and that of the hospitality which a speaking mouse extended to the deity Master-of-the Great-Land.[15] Sometimes the original tradition is simply softened down or explained away. A notable instance of this occurs in the account of the visit of the deity Izanagi[16] to Hades, whither he goes in quest of his dead wife, and among other things has to scale the "Even Pass (or Hill) of Hades."[17] In the tradition preserved in the *Records* and indeed even in the *Chronicles*, this pass or hill is mentioned as a literal geographical fact. But the compiler of the latter work, whose object it was to appear and to make his forefathers appear, as reasonable as a learned Chinese, adds a gloss to the effect that "One account says that the Even Hill of Hades is no distinct place, but simply the moment when breathing ceases at the time of death";—not a happy guess certainly, for this pass is mentioned in connection with Izanagi's return to the land of the living. In short we may say of this work what was said of the Septuagint,— that it *rationalizes.*

Perhaps it will be asked, how can it have come to pass that a book in which the national traditions are thus unmistakably tampered with, and which is moreover written in Chinese instead of in the native tongue, has enjoyed such a much greater share of popularity than the more genuine work?

The answer lies on the surface: the concessions made to Chinese notions went far towards satisfying minds trained on Chinese models, while at the same time the reader had his respect for the old native emperors increased, and was enabled to preserve some sort of belief in the native gods. People are rarely quite logical in such matters, particularly in an early stage of society; and difficulties are glossed over rather than insisted upon. The beginning of the world, for instance, or, to use Japanese phraseology, the "separation of heaven and earth" took place a long time ago; and perhaps, although there could of course be no philosophical doubt as to the cause of this event having been the interaction of the passive and active essences, it might also somehow be true that Izanagi and Izanami (the "Male-Who-Invites" and the "Female-Who-Invites") were the progenitor and progenitrix of Japan. Who knows but what in them the formative principles may not have been embodied, represented, or figured forth after a fashion not quite determined, but none the less real? As a matter of fact, the two deities in question have often been spoken of in Japanese books under such designations as the "*Yin* Deity" and the "*Yang* Deity," and in his Chinese

Preface the very compiler of these *Records* lends his sanction to the use of such phraseology, though, if we look closely at the part taken by the goddess in the legend narrated in Sect. 4, it would seem but imperfectly applicable. If again early sovereigns, such as the Empress Jin-gū, address their troops in sentences cribbed from the *Shujing*[18] or, like the Emperor Kei-kō, describe the Ainu in terms that would only suit the pages of a Chinese topographer,—both these personages being supposed to have lived prior to the opening up of intercourse with the continent of Asia,—the anachronism was partly hidden by the fact of the work which thus recorded their doings being itself written in the Chinese language, where such phrases only sounded natural. In some instances, too, the Chinese usage had so completely superseded the native one as to cause the latter to have been almost forgotten excepting by the members of the Shinto priesthood. This happened in the case of the Chinese method of divination by means of a tortoiseshell, whose introduction caused the elder native custom of divination through the shoulder-blade of a deer to fall into desuetude. Whether indeed this native custom itself may not perhaps be traced back to still earlier continental influence is another question. So far as any documentary information reaches, divination through the shoulder-blade of a deer was the most ancient Japanese method of ascertaining the will of the gods. The use of the Chinese sexagenary cycle for counting years, months, and days is another instance of the imported usage having become so thoroughly incorporated with native habits of mind as to make the anachronism of employing it when speaking of a period confessedly anterior to the introduction of continental civilization pass unnoticed. As for the (to a modern European) grotesque notion of pretending to give the precise months and days of events supposed to have occurred a thousand years before the date assigned to the introduction of astronomical instruments, of observatories, and even of the art of writing, that is another of those inconsistencies which, while lying on the very surface, yet so easily escape the uncritical Oriental mind.[19] Semi-civilized people tire of asking questions, and to question antiquity, which fills so great a place in their thoughts, is the last thing that would occur to any of their learned men, whose mental attitude is characteristically represented by Confucius when he calls himself "A transmitter and not a maker, believing in and loving the ancients."[20] As regards the question of language, standard Chinese soon became easier to understand than Archaic Japanese, as the former alone was taught in the schools, and the native language changed rapidly during the century or two that followed the diffusion of the foreign tongue and civilization. We have only to call to mind the relative facility to most of ourselves of a Latin book and of one written in Early English. Of course, as soon as the principles of the Japanese *Renaissance* had taken hold of men's minds in the eighteenth century, the more genuine, more national work assumed its proper place in the estimation of students. But the uncouthness of the style according to modern ideas, and the greater amount of explanation of all sorts that is required in order to make the *Records of Ancient Matters* intelligible, must always prevent them from attaining to the popularity of the sister history. Thus, though published almost simultaneously, the tendencies of the two works were very different, and their fate has differed accordingly.

To the European student the chief value of the *Chronicles of Japan* lies in the fact that their author, in treating of the so-called "Divine Age," often gives a number of various forms of the same legend—under the heading of "One account says," suffixed in the form of a note to the main text. No phrase is more commonly met with in later treatises on Japanese history than this,—"One account in the *Chronicles of Japan* says," and it will be met with occasionally in the footnotes to the present translation. There are likewise instances of the author of the *Chronicles* having preserved, either in the text or in "One account," traditions omitted by the compiler of the *Records*. Such are, for instance, the quaint legend invented to explain the fact that the sun and moon do not shine simultaneously,[21] and the curious development of the legend of the expulsion of the deity *Susa-no-o* ("Impetuous Male"), telling us of the hospitality which was refused to him by the other gods when he appeared before them to beg for shelter. Many of the songs, too, in the *Chronicles* are different from those in the *Records*, and make a precious addition to our vocabulary of Archaic Japanese. The prose text, likewise, contains, in the shape of notes, numbers of readings by which the pronunciation of words written ideographically, or the meaning of words written phonetically in the *Records* may be ascertained. Finally the *Chronicles* give us the annals of seventy-two years not comprised in the plan of the *Records*, by carrying down to A.D. 700 the history which in the *Records* stops at the year 628. Although therefore it is a mistake to assert, as some have done, that the *Chronicles of Japan* must be placed at the head of all the Japanese historical works, their assistance can in no wise be dispensed with by the student of Japanese mythology and of the Japanese language.[22]

4
MANNERS AND CUSTOMS OF THE EARLY JAPANESE.

The Japanese of the mythical period, as pictured in the legends preserved by the compiler of the *Records of Ancient Matters*, were a race who had long emerged from the savage state, and had attained to a high level of barbaric skill. The Stone Age was forgotten by them—or nearly so,—and the evidence points to their never having passed through a genuine Bronze Age, though the knowledge of bronze was at a later period introduced from the neighboring continent. They used iron for manufacturing spears, swords, and knives of various shapes, and likewise for the more peaceful purpose of making hooks wherewith to angle, or to fasten the doors of their huts. Their other warlike and hunting implements (besides traps and gins which appear to have been used equally for catching beasts and birds and for destroying human enemies) were bows and arrows, spears and elbow-pads,[23]—the latter seemingly of skin, while special allusion is made to the fact that the arrows were feathered. Perhaps clubs should be added to the list. Of the bows and arrows, swords and knives, there is perpetual mention; but nowhere do we hear of the tools with which they were manufactured, and there is the same remarkable silence regarding such widely spread domestic implements as the saw and the axe. We hear, however, of the pestle and mortar,[24] of the fire-drill, of the wedge, of the sickle, and of the shuttle used in weaving.

Navigation seems to have been in a very elementary stage. Indeed the art of sailing was, as we know from the classical literature of the country, but little practiced in Japan even so late as the middle of the tenth century of our era subsequent to the general diffusion of Chinese civilization, though rowing and punting are often mentioned by the early poets. In one passage of the *Records* and in another of the *Chronicles*, mention is made of a "two-forked boat"[25] used on inland pools or lakes; but, as a rule, in the earlier portions of those works, we read only of people going to sea or being sent down from heaven in water-proof baskets without oars, and reaching their destination not through any efforts of their own, but through supernatural interposition.[26]

To what we should call towns or villages very little reference is made anywhere in the *Records* or in that portion of the *Chronicles* which contains the account of the so-called "Divine Age." But from what we learn incidentally, it would seem that the scanty population was chiefly distributed in small hamlets and isolated dwellings along the coast and up the course of the larger streams. Of house-building there is frequent mention,—especially of the building of palaces or temples for sovereigns or gods,—the words "palace" and "temple" being (it should be mentioned) represented in Japanese by the same term. Sometimes, in describing the construction of such a sacred dwelling, the author of the *Records*, abandoning his usual flat and monotonous style, soars away on poetic wings, as when, for instance, he tells how the monarch of Izumo, on abdicating in favor of the Sun Goddess's descendant, covenanted that the latter should "make stout his temple pillars on the nethermost rock-bottom, and make high the cross-beams to the plain of High Heaven."[27] It must not, however, be inferred from such language that these so-called palaces and temples were of very gorgeous and imposing aspect. The more exact notices to be culled from the ancient *Shinto Rituals* (which are but little posterior to the *Records* and in no wise contradict the inferences to be drawn from the latter) having been already summarized by Mr. Satow, it may be as well to quote that gentleman's words. He says:[28] The "palace of the Japanese sovereign was a wooden hut, with its pillars planted in the ground, instead of being erected upon broad flat stones as in modern buildings. The whole framework, consisting of posts, beams, rafters, door posts and window frames, was tied together with cords made by twisting the long fibrous stems of climbing plants, such as *Pueraria Thunbergiana (kudzu)* and *Wisteria Sinensis (fuji)*. The floor must have been low down, so that the occupants of the building, as they squatted or lay on their mats, were exposed to the stealthy attacks of venomous snakes, which were probably far more numerous in the earliest ages when the country was for the most part uncultivated, than at the present day... There seems some reason to think that the *yuka*, here translated floor, was originally nothing but a couch which ran round the sides of the hut, the rest of the space being simply a mud floor, and that the size of the couch was gradually increased until it occupied the whole interior. The rafters projected upward beyond the ridgepole, crossing each other as is seen in the roofs of modern Shinto temples, whether their architecture be in conformity with early traditions (in which case all the rafters are so crossed) or modified in accordance with more advanced principles of construction, and the crossed rafters retained only as ornaments at the two ends of the ridge. The roof was thatched, and perhaps had a gable at each end, with a hole to allow the smoke of the wood-fire to escape, so that it was possible for birds flying in and perching on the beams overhead, to defile the food, or the fire with which it was cooked." To this description it need only be added that fences were in use, and that the wooden doors, sometimes fastened by means of hooks, resembled those with which we are familiar in Europe rather than the sliding, screen-like doors of modern Japan. The windows seem to have been mere holes. Rugs of skins and rush matting were occasionally brought in to sit upon, and we even hear once or twice of "silk rugs" being used for the same purpose by the noble and wealthy.

The habits of personal cleanliness which so pleasantly distinguish the modern Japanese from their neighbors in continental Asia, though less fully developed than at present, would seem to have existed in the germ in early times, as we read more than once of bathing in rivers, and are told of bathing-women being specially attached to the person of a certain imperial infant. Lustrations, too, formed part of the religious practices of the race. Latrines are mentioned several times. They would appear to have been situated away from the houses and to have generally been placed over a running stream, whence doubtless the name for latrine in the Archaic dialect,—*kawa-ya,* i.e. "river-house." A well-known Japanese classic of the tenth century, the *Yamato Tales*,[29] tells us indeed that "in older days the people dwelt in houses raised on platforms built out on the river Ikuta" and goes on to relate a story which presupposes such a method of architecture.[30] A passage in the account of the reign of the Emperor Jin-mu which occurs both in the *Records* and in the *Chronicles*, and another in the reign of the Emperor Sui-nin occurring in the *Records* only, might be interpreted so as to support this statement.[31] But both are extremely obscure, and beyond the fact that people who habitually lived near the water *may* have built their houses after the aquatic fashion practiced in different parts of the world by certain savage tribes both ancient and modern, the present writer is not aware of any authority for the assertion that they actually did so except the isolated passage in the *Yamato Tales* just quoted.

A peculiar sort of dwelling-place which the two old histories bring prominently under our notice, is the so-called "parturition-house," a one-roomed hut without windows which a woman was expected to build and retire into for the purpose of being delivered unseen.[32] It would also appear to be not unlikely that newly-married couples retired into a specially built hut for the purpose of consummating the marriage, and it is certain that for each sovereign a new palace was erected on his accession.

Castles are not distinctly spoken of till a period which, though still mythical in the opinion of the present writer, coincides according to the received chronology with the first century CE. We then first meet with the curious term "rice-castle," whose precise signification is a matter of dispute among the native commentators, but which, on comparison with Chinese descriptions of the Early Japanese, should probably be understood to mean a kind of palisade serving the purpose of a redoubt, behind which the warriors could ensconce themselves.[33] If this conjecture be correct, we have here a good instance of a word, so to speak, moving upward with the march of civilization, the term, which formerly denoted something not much better than a fence, having later come to convey the idea of a stone castle.

To conclude the subject of dwelling-places, it should be stated that cave-dwellers are sometimes alluded to. The legend of the retirement of the Sun Goddess into a cavern may possibly suggest to some the idea of an early period when such habitations were the normal abodes of the ancestors of the Japanese race.[34] But at the time when the national traditions assumed their present shape, such a state of things had certainly quite passed away, if it ever existed, and only barbarous

Ainu and rough bands of robbers are credited with the construction of such primitive retreats. Natural caves (it may be well to state) are rare in Japan, and the caves that are alluded to were mostly artificial,[35] as may be gathered from the context.

The food of the Early Japanese consisted of fish and of the flesh of the wild creatures which fell by the hunter's arrow or were taken in the trapper's snare,—an animal diet with which Buddhist prohibitions had not yet interfered, as they began to do in early historical times. Rice is the only cereal of which there is such mention made as to place it beyond a doubt that its cultivation dates back to time immemorial. Beans, millet, and barley are indeed named once, together with silk-worms, in the account of the "Divine Age."[36] But the passage has every aspect of an interpolation in the legend, perhaps not dating back long before the time of the eighth century compiler. A few unimportant vegetables and fruits, of most of which there is but a single mention, will be found in the list of plants given below. The intoxicating liquor called *sake* was known in Japan during the mythical period,[37] and so were chopsticks for eating the food with. Cooking-pots and cups and dishes—the latter both of earthenware and of leaves of trees,—are also mentioned; but of the use of fire for warming purposes we hear nothing. Tables are named several times, but never in connection with food. They would seem to have been exclusively used for the purpose of presenting offerings on, and were probably quite small and low,—in fact rather trays than tables according to European ideas.

In the use of clothing and the specialization of garments the Early Japanese had reached a high level. We read in the most ancient legends of upper garments, skirts, trousers, girdles, veils, and hats, while both sexes adorned themselves with necklaces, bracelets, and head-ornaments of stones considered precious,—in this respect offering a striking contrast to their descendants in modern times, of whose attire jewelry forms no part. The material of their clothes was hempen cloth and paper-mulberry bark, colored by being rubbed with madder, and probably with woad and other tinctorial plants. All the garments, so far as we may judge, were woven, sewing being nowhere mentioned, and it being expressly stated by the Chinese commentator on the *Shanhai jing*[38] who wrote early in the fourth century, that the Japanese had no needles.[39] From the great place which the chase occupied in daily life we are led to suppose that skins also were used to make garments of. There is in the *Records* at least one passage which favors this supposition,[40] and the *Chronicles* in one place mention the straw raincoat and broad-brimmed hat, which still form the Japanese peasant's effectual protection against the inclemencies of the weather. The tendrils[41] of creeping plants served the purposes of string, and bound the warrior's sword round his waist. Combs are mentioned, and it is evident that much attention was devoted to the dressing of the hair. The men seem to have bound up their hair in two bunches, one on each side of the head, whilst the young boys tied theirs into a topknot, the unmarried girls let their locks hang down over their necks, and the married women dressed theirs after a fashion which apparently combined the two last-named methods. There is no mention in any of the old books of cutting the hair or beard except in token of disgrace; neither do we gather that the sexes, but for this matter of the head-dress, were distinguished by a diversity of apparel and ornamentation.

With regard to the precious stones mentioned above as having been used as ornaments for the head, neck, and arms, the texts themselves give us little or no information as to the identity of the stones meant to be referred to. Indeed it is plain (and the native commentators admit the fact) that a variety of Chinese characters properly denoting different sorts of jewels were used indiscriminately by the early Japanese writers to represent the single native word *tama,* which is the only one the language contains to denote any hard substance on which a special value is set, and which often refers chiefly to the rounded shape, so that it might in fact be translated by the word "bead" as fittingly as by the word "jewel." We know, however, from the specimens which have rewarded the labors of archaeological research in Japan that agate, crystal, glass, jade, serpentine, and steatite are the most usual materials, and curved and pierced cylindrical shapes *(maga-tama* and *kuda-tama),* the commonest forms.[42]

The horse (which was ridden, but not driven), the barndoor fowl, and the cormorant used for fishing, are the only domesticated creatures mentioned in the earlier traditions, with the doubtful exception of the silkworm, to which reference has already been made.[43] In the later portions of the *Records* and *Chronicles*, dogs and cattle are alluded to; but sheep, swine, and even cats were apparently not yet introduced. Indeed sheep were scarcely to be seen in Japan until a few years ago, goats are still almost unknown, and swine and all poultry excepting the barn-door fowl are extremely uncommon.

The following enumeration of the animals and plants mentioned in the earlier portion[44] of the "Records" may be of interest. The Japanese equivalents, some few of which are obsolete, are put in parenthesis, together with the Chinese characters used to write them:

MAMMALS

Bear (*kuma* 熊); Boar (*i* 猪); Deer (*shika* 鹿); Hare (*usagi* 兎); Horse (*uma* 馬 and *koma* 駒); Mouse or Rat (*nezumi* 鼠); "Sea-ass" [Seal or Sealion?] (*michi* 海驢); Whale (*kujira* 鯨).

BIRDS

Barndoor-fowl (*kakei* 家鶏); Cormorant (*u* 鵜); Crow or Raven (*karasu* 烏); Dotterel or Plover or Sandpiper (*chidori* 千鳥); Heron or Egret (*sagi* 鷺); Kingfisher (*soni-dori* 翠鳥); *Nue* (鵺)[45]; Pheasant (*kigishi* 雉); Snipe (*shigi* 鴫); Swan (*shiro-tori* 白鳥); Wild-duck (*kamo* 鴨); Wild-goose (*kari* 雁).

REPTILES

Crocodile (*wani* 鰐)[46]; Tortoise (*kame* 亀); Toad or Frog (*taniguku*, written phonetically); Serpent (*orochi* 蛇); Snake [smaller than the preceding] (*hebi* 蛇).

INSECTS

Centipede (*mukade* 蜈蚣); Dragonfly (*akizu* 蜻蛉); Fly (*hai* 蠅); Louse, (*shirami* 虱); Silkworm, (*kaiko* 蚕); Wasp or Bee, (*hachi* 蜂).

FISHES, ETC

Pagrus cardinalis [probably] (*aka-tai* 赤鯛) [or perhaps the *Pagrus cardinalis* (*tai* 鯛) is intended]; Perch [*Percalabrax japonicus*] (*suzuki* 鱸); Sea Cucumber [genus *Pentacta*] (*ko* 海鼠); Jellyfish, (*kurage*, written phonetically).

SHELLS

Arca Subcrenata [?] (*hirabu-kai*, written phonetically); Cockle [*Arca Inflata*] (*kisa-gai* 蚶貝); *Turbinidoe* [a shell of the family] (*shitadami* 細螺).

PLANTS

Ampelopsis serianœfolia [?] (*kagami* 蘿摩); *Aphananthe aspera* (*muku*, written phonetically); *Aucuba japonica* [probably] (*awa-gi*, written phonetically); Bamboo (*take* 竹); Bamboo-grass [*Bambusa chino*] (*sasa* 小竹); Barley [or wheat?] (*mugi* 麦); Beans [two kinds, viz., *Soja glycine* and *Phaseolus radiatus*] (thc general name is *mame* 豆, that of the latter species in particular *adzuki* 小豆); Bulrush [*Typha japonica*] (*kama* 香蒲); Bush clover [*Lespedeza* of various species] (*hagi* 萩); *Camellia japonica* (*tsuba-ki* 椿); Cassia [Chinese mythical; or perhaps the native *Cercidiphyllum japonica*] (*katsura*, variously written); *Chamœcyparis obtusa* (*hi-no-ki* 檜); *Cleyera japonica* [and another allied but undetermined species] (*saka-ki* 榊); Clubmoss (*hi-kage* 日景); *Cocculus thunbergi* [probably] (*tsu-zura* 黒葛); *Cryptomeria japonica* (*sugi* 椙); *Eulalia japonica* (*kaya* 萱草); *Euonymus japonica* (*masa-ki* 真賢木); Ginger [or perhaps the *Xanthoxylon* is intended] (*hajikami* 薑); *Halochloa macrantha* [but it is not certain that this is the seaweed intended] (*komo* 海蓴); Holly [or rather the *Olea aquifolium* which closely resembles holly] (*hiira-gi* 柊); Knot grass [*Polygonum tinctorium*] (*ai* 藍); Lily (*sai* written phonetically, *yama-yuri-gusa* 山由理草, and *saki-kusa* 三枝草); Madder (*akane* 茜); Millet [Panicum italicum] (*awa* 粟); Moss (*koke* 蘚); Oak [two species, one evergreen and one deciduous,—*Quercus myrsinœfolia Q. dentata*] (*kashi* 白梼, *kashiwa* 柏)]; Peach (*momo* 桃); *Photinia glabra* [?] (*soba*, written phonetically); Pine tree (*matsu* 松); *Pueraria thunbergiana* (*kuzu* 葛); Reed (*ashi* 葦); Rice (*ine* 稲); Seaweed [or the original term may designate a particular species] (*me* 海布); Sedge [*Scirpus maritimus*] (*suga* 菅); Spindle tree [*Euonymus radicans*] (*masaki no kazura* 真析蔓); Vegetable Wax tree [*Rhus succedanea*] (*haji* 櫨); Vine (*ebi-kazura* 蔔蒲); Wild cherry [or birch?] (*hahaka* 朱桜); Wild chive [or rather the *allium odorum*, which closely resembles it] (*ka-mira* 臭韮); Winter cherry [*Physalis alkekengi*] (*aka-kagachi* written phonetically, and also *hōzuki* 酸漿).

The later portions of the work furnish in addition the following:

ANIMALS.

Cow (*ushi* 牛); Dog, (*inu* 犬); Crane [genus *Grus*] (tazu 鶴); Dove or Pigeon (*hato* 鳩); Grebe (*niho-dori* 鷿鷉); Lark (*hibari* 雲雀); Peregrine falcon (*hayabusa* 隼); Red-throated quail (*uzura* 鶉); Tree-sparrow (*suzume* 雀); Wagtail [probably] (*mana-bashira*, written phonetically); Wren (*sazaki* 鷦鷯); Dolphin (*iruka* 入鹿魚); Trout [*Plecoglossus altivelis*] (*ayu* 年魚); Tunny [a kind of, viz. *Thynnus sibi*] (*shibi* 鮪); Crab (*kani* 蟹); Horse-fly (*amu* 虻); Oyster (*kaki* 蠣).

PLANTS

Alder [*Alnus maritima*] (*hari-no-ki* 榛); Aralia (*mi-tsuna-gashiwa* 御綱柏); *Brasenia peltata* (*nunaha* 蓴); Cabbage [*brassica*] (*aona* 菘菜); *Catalpa Kaempferi* [but some say the cherry is meant] (*azusa* 梓); Chestnut (*kuri* 栗); *Dioscorea quinqueloba* (*tokoro-zura* 薢葛); *Euonymus sieboldianus* (*mayumi* 木檀); Gourd (*hisago* 瓢); *Hedysarum esculentum* (*ogi* 荻); *Hydropyrum latifolium* (*komo* 菰); *Kazura japonica* (*sana-kazura* 実葛); *Livistona sinensis* (*ajimasa* 檳榔); Lotus [*nelumbium*] (*hachisu* 蓮); Musk-melon (*hozochi* 熟瓜); Oak [three species, *Quercus serrata* (*kunugi* 櫪木) and *Q. glanduli-fera* (*nara* 楢), both deciduous; *Q. gilva* (*ichii* 赤梼) evergreen]; Orange (*tachibana* 橘); *Podocarpus macrophylla* (*maki* 檜); Radish [*Baphanus sativus*] (*ō-ne* 大根); *Sashibu* (written phonetically) [not identified]; Water caltrop [*Trapa bispinosa*] (*hishi* 菱); Wild garlic [*Allium nipponicum*] (*nobiru* 野蒜); *Zelkowa keaki* [probably] (*tsuki* 槻).

A few more are probably preserved in the names of places. Thus in Shinano, the name of a province, we seem to have the *shina (Tilia cordata)*, and in Tadetsu the *tade (Polygonum japonicum)*. But the identification in these cases is mostly uncertain. It must also be remembered that, as in the case of all non-scientific nomenclatures, several species, and occasionally even more than one genus, are included in a single Japanese term. Thus *chi-dori* (here always rendered "dotterel") is the name of any kind of sandpiper, plover or dotterel. *Kari* is a general name applied to geese, but not to all the species, and also to the great bustard. Again it should not be forgotten that there may have been, and probably were, in the application of some of these terms, differences of usage between the present day and eleven or twelve centuries ago. Absolute precision is therefore not attainable.[47]

Noticeable in the above lists is the abundant mention of plant-names in a work which is in no ways occupied with botany. Equally noticeable is the absence of some of those which are most common at the present day, such as the tea plant and the plum tree, while of the orange we are specially informed that it was introduced from abroad.[48] The difference between the various stones and metals seems, on the other hand, to have attracted very little attention from the Early Japanese. In later times the chief metals were named mostly according to their color, as follows: yellow metal (gold); white metal (silver); red metal (copper); black metal (iron); Chinese (or Korean) metal (bronze).

But in the *Records* the only metal of which it is implied that it was in use from time immemorial is iron, while "various treasures dazzling to the eye, from gold and silver downwards," are only referred to once as existing in the far-western land of Korea. Red clay is the sole kind of earth specially named.

The words relative to color which occur are black, blue (including green), red, piebald (of horses), and white. Yellow is not mentioned (except in the foreign Chinese phrase the "Yellow Stream," signifying Hades, and not to be counted in this context), neither are any of the numerous terms which in modern Japanese serve to distinguish delicate shades of color. We hear of the "blue (or green), *i.e.* black[49] clouds" and also of the "blue (or green), sea"; but the "blue sky" is conspicuous by its absence here as in so many other early literatures, though strangely enough it does occur in the oldest written documents of the Chinese.

With regard to the subject of names for the different degrees of relationship,—a subject of sufficient interest to the student of sociology to warrant its being discussed at some length,—it may be stated that in modern Japanese parlance the categories according to which relationship is conceived of do not materially differ from those that are current in Europe. Thus we find father, grandfather, great-grandfather, uncle, nephew, stepfather, stepson, father-in-law, son-in-law, and the corresponding terms for females,—mother, grandmother, etc.,—as well as such vaguer designations as parents, ancestors, cousins, and kinsmen. The only striking difference is that brothers and sisters, instead of being considered as all mutually related in the same manner, are divided into two categories, viz.: elder brother(s) (*ani* 兄), younger brother(s) (*otōto* 弟), elder sister(s) (*ane* 姉), and younger sister(s) (*imōto* 妹) in exact accordance with Chinese usage.

Now in Archaic times there seems to have been a different and more complicated system, somewhat resembling that which still obtains among the natives of Korea, and which the introduction of Chinese ideas and especially the use of the Chinese written characters must have caused to be afterwards abandoned. There are indications of it in some of the phonetically written fragments of the *Records*. But they are not of themselves sufficient to furnish a satisfactory explanation, and the subject has puzzled the native *literati* themselves. Moreover the English language fails us at this point, and elder and younger brother, elder and younger sister are the only terms at the translator's command. It may therefore be as well to quote *in extenso* Norinaga's elucidation of the Archaic usage to be found in Vol. 13, pp. 63–4 of his *Exposition of the Records of Ancient Matters*.[50] He says: "Anciently, when brothers and sisters were spoken of, the elder brother was called *se* or *ani* in contradistinction to the younger brothers and younger sisters, and the younger brother also was called *se* in contradistinction to the elder sister. The elder sister was called *ane* in contradistinction to the younger sister, and the younger brother also would use the word *ane* in speaking of his elder sister himself. The younger brother was called *oto* in contradistinction to the elder brother, and the younger sister also was called *oto* in contradistinction to the elder sister. The younger sister was called *imo* in contradistinction to the elder brother, and the elder sister also was called *imo* in contradistinction to the younger brother. It was also the custom among brothers and sisters to use the words *iro-se* for *se*, *iro-se* for *ane*, and *iro-do* for *oto*, and analogy forces us to conclude that *iro-mo* was used for *imo*." (Norinaga elsewhere explains *iro* as a term of endearment identical with the word *iro,* "love;" but we may hesitate to accept this view.) It will be observed that the foundation of this system of nomenclature was a subordination of the younger to the elder-born modified by a subordination of the females to the males. In the East, especially in primitive times, it is not "*place aux dames,*" but "*place aux messieurs.*"

Another important point to notice is that, though in a few passages of the *Records* we find a distinction drawn between the chief and the secondary wives,—perhaps nothing more than the favorite or better-born, and the less well-born, are meant to be thus designated,—yet not only is this distinction not drawn throughout, but the wife is constantly spoken of as *imo, i.e.* "younger sister." In fact sister and wife were convertible terms and ideas; and what in a later stage of Japanese, as of Western, civilization is abhorred as incest was in Archaic Japanese times the common practice. We also hear of marriages with half-sisters, with stepmothers, and with aunts; and to wed two or three sisters at the same time was a recognized usage. Most such unions were naturally so contrary to Chinese ethical ideas, that one of the first traces of the influence of the latter in Japan was the stigmatizing of them as incest; and the conflict between the old native custom and the imported moral code is seen to have resulted in political troubles.[51] Marriage with sisters was naturally the first to disappear, and indeed it is only mentioned in the legends of the gods; but unions with half-sisters, aunts, etc., lasted on into the historic epoch. Of exogamy, such as obtains in China, there is no trace in any Japanese document, nor do any other artificial impediments seem to have stood in the way of the free choice of the Early Japanese man, who also (in some cases at least) received a dowry with his bride or brides.

If, taking as our guides the incidental notices which are scattered up and down the pages of the earlier portion of the *Records*, we endeavor to follow an Archaic Japanese through the chief events of his life from the cradle to the tomb, it will be necessary to begin by recalling what has already been alluded to as the "parturition-house" built by the mother, and in which, as we are specially told that it was made windowless, it would perhaps be contradictory to say that the infant first saw the light. Soon after birth a name was given to it,—given to it by the mother,—such name generally containing some appropriate personal reference. In the most ancient times each person (so far as we can judge) bore but one name, or rather one string of words compounded together into a sort of personal designation. But already at the dawn of the historical epoch we are met by the mention of surnames and of what, in the absence of a more fitting word, the translator has ventured to call "gentile names," bestowed by the sovereign as a recompense for some noteworthy deed.[52]

It may be gathered from our text that the idea of calling in the services of wet-nurses in certain exceptional cases had already suggested itself to the minds of the ruling class, whose infants were likewise sometimes attended by special bathing-women. To what we should call education, whether mental or physical, there is absolutely no reference made in the histories. All that can be inferred is that, when old enough to do so, the boys began to follow one of the callings of hunter or fisherman, while the girls stayed at home weaving the garments of the family. There was also a great deal of fighting, generally of a treacherous kind, in the intervals of which the warriors occupied themselves in cultivating patches of ground. The very little which is to be gathered concerning the treatment of old people would seem to indicate that they were well cared for.

We are nowhere told of any wedding ceremonies except the giving of presents by the bride or her father, the probable reason being that no such ceremonies existed. Indeed late on into the Middle Ages cohabitation alone constituted matrimony,—cohabitation often secret at first, but afterwards acknowledged, when, instead of going round under cover of night to visit his mistress, the young man brought her back publicly to his parents' house. Mistress, wife, and concubine were thus terms which were not distinguished, and the woman could naturally be discarded at any moment. She indeed was expected to remain faithful to the man with whom she had had more than a passing intimacy, but no reciprocal obligation bound him to her. Thus the wife of one of the gods is made to address her husband in a poem which says:

"Thou...indeed, being a man, probably hast on the various island-headlands that thou seest, and on every beach-headland that thou lookest on, a wife like the young herbs. But I, alas! being a woman, have no man except thee; I have no spouse except thee," etc., etc.[53]

In this somber picture the only graceful touch is the custom which lovers or spouses had of tying each other's girdles when about to part for a time,—a ceremony by which they implied that they would be constant to each other during the period of absence.[54] What became of the children in cases of conjugal separation does not clearly appear. In the only instance which is related at length, we find the child left with the father; but this instance is not a normal one.[55] Adoption is not mentioned in the earliest traditions; so that when we meet with it later on we shall probably be justified in tracing its introduction to Chinese sources.

Of death-bed scenes and dying speeches we hear but little, and that little need not detain us. The burial rites are more important. The various ceremonies observed on such an occasion are indeed not explicitly detailed. But we gather thus much: that the hut tenanted by the deceased was abandoned,—an ancient custom to whose former existence the removal of the capital at the commencement of each new sovereign's reign long continued to bear witness, and that the body was first deposited for some days in a "mourning-house," during which interval the survivors (though their tears and lamentations are also mentioned) held a carousal, feasting perhaps on the food which was specially prepared as an offering to the dead person. Afterwards, the corpse was interred, presumably in a wooden bier, as the introduction of stone tombs is specially noted by the historian as having taken place at the end of the reign of the Emperor Sui-nin, and was therefore believed by those who handed down the legendary history to have been a comparatively recent innovation, the date assigned to this monarch by the author of the *Chronicles* coinciding with the latter part of our first, and the first half of our second centuries. To a time not long anterior is attributed the abolition of a custom previously observed at the interments of royal personages. This custom was the burying alive of some of their retainers in the neighborhood of the tomb. We know also, both from other early literary sources and from the finds which have recently rewarded the labors of archaeologists, that articles of clothing, ornaments, etc., were buried with the corpse. It is all the more curious that the *Records* should nowhere make any reference to such a custom, and is a proof (if any be needed) of the necessity of not relying exclusively on any single authority, however respectable, if the full and true picture of Japanese antiquity is to be restored. A few details as to the abolition of the custom of burying retainers alive round their master's tomb, and of the substitution for this cruel holocaust of images in clay will be found in Sect. 63, Notes a and 415, and in Sect. 75, Note 579, of the following translation.[56] If the custom be one which is properly included under the heading of human sacrifices, it is the only form of such sacrifices of which the earliest recorded Japanese social state retained any trace. The absence of slavery is another honorable feature. On the other hand, the most cruel punishments were dealt out to enemies and wrongdoers. Their nails were extracted, the sinews of their knees were cut, they were buried up to the neck so that their eyes burst, etc. Death, too, was inflicted for the most trivial offences. Of branding, or rather tattooing, the face as a punishment there are one or two incidental mentions. But as no tattooing or other marking or painting of the body for any other purpose is ever alluded to, with the solitary exception in one passage of the painting of her eyebrows by a woman, it is possible that the penal use of tattooing may have been borrowed from the Chinese, to whom it was not unknown.[57]

The shocking obscenity of word and act to which the *Records* bear witness is another ugly feature which must not quite be passed over in silence. It is true that decency, as we understand it, is a very modern product, and is not to be looked for in any society in the barbarous stage. At the same time, the whole range of literature might perhaps be ransacked in vain for a parallel to the naive filthiness of the passage forming Sect. 4. of the following translation, or to the extraordinary topic which the hero Yamato-Take and his mistress Miyazu are made to select as the theme of poetical repartee.[58] One passage likewise would lead us to suppose that the most beastly crimes were commonly committed.[59]

To conclude this portion of the subject, it may be useful for the sake of comparison to call attention to a few arts and products with which the Early Japanese were *not* acquainted. Thus they had no tea, no fans, no porcelain, no lacquer,—none of the things, in fact, by which in later times they have been chiefly known. They did not yet use vehicles of any kind. They had no accurate method of computing time, no money, scarcely any knowledge of medicine. Neither, though they possessed some sort of music, and poems a few of which at least are not without merit,[60] do we hear anything of the art of drawing. But the most important art of which they were ignorant is that of writing. As some misapprehension has existed on this head, and scholars in Europe have been misled by the inventions of zealous champions of the Shinto religion into a belief in the so-called "Divine Characters," by them alleged to have been invented by the Japanese gods and to have been used by the Japanese people prior to the introduction of the Chinese ideographic writing, it must be stated precisely that all the traditions of the "Divine Age," and of the reigns of the earlier Emperors down to the third century of our era according to the received chronology, maintain a complete silence on the subject of writing, writing materials, and records of every kind. Books are nowhere mentioned till a period confessedly posterior to the opening up of intercourse with the Asiatic continent, and the first books whose names occur are the *Lunyu* and the *Qianzi wen*[A]," which are said to have been brought over to Japan during the reign of the Emperor Ō-jin,—according to the same chronology in the year 284 after Christ. That even this statement is antedated, is shown by the fact that the *Qianzi wen* was not written till more than two centuries later,—a fact which is worthy the attention of those who have been disposed simply to take on trust the assertions of the Japanese historians. It should likewise be mentioned that, as has already been pointed out by Mr. Aston, the Japanese terms *fumi* "written document," and *fude* "pen," are probably corruptions of foreign words.[61] The present, indeed, is not the place to discuss the whole question of the so-called "Divine Characters," which Norinaga, the most patriotic as well as the most learned of the Japanese *literati,* dismisses in a note to the Prolegomena of his *Exposition of the Records of Ancient Matters* with the remark that they "are a late forgery over which no words need be wasted." But as this mare's nest has been imported into the discussion of the Early Japanese social state, and as the point is one on which the absolute silence of the early traditions bears such clear

[A] 論語 and 千字文 [*Analects of Confucius* and *Thousand Character Classic*—M.F.]

testimony, it was impossible to pass it by without some brief allusion.

5
RELIGIOUS AND POLITICAL IDEAS OF THE EARLY JAPANESE, BEGINNINGS OF THE JAPANESE NATION, AND CREDIBILITY OF THE NATIONAL RECORDS.

The religious beliefs of the modern upholders of Shinto[62] may be ascertained without much difficulty by a perusal of the works of the leaders of the movement which has endeavored during the last century and a half to destroy the influence of Buddhism and of the Chinese philosophy, and which has latterly succeeded to some extent in supplanting those two foreign systems. But in Japan, as elsewhere, it has been impossible for men really to turn back a thousand years in religious thought and act; and when we try to discover the primitive opinions that were entertained by the Japanese people prior to the introduction of the Chinese culture, we are met by difficulties that at first seem insuperable. The documents are scanty, and the modern commentaries untrustworthy, for they are all written under the influence of a preconceived opinion. Moreover, the problem is apparently complicated by a mixture of races and mythologies, and by a filtering in of Chinese ideas previous to the compilation of documents of any sort, though these are considerations which have hitherto scarcely been taken into account by foreigners, and are designedly neglected and obscured by such narrowly patriotic native writers as Norinaga and Atsutane.

In the political field the difficulties are not less, but rather greater; for when once the Imperial House and the centralized Japanese polity, as we know it from the sixth or seventh century of our era downwards, became fully established, it was but too clearly in the interest of the powers that be to efface as far as possible the trace of different governmental arrangements which may have preceded them, and to cause it to be believed that, as things were then, so had they always been. The Emperor Ten-mu, with his anxiety to amend the "deviations from truth and the empty falsehoods" of the historical documents preserved by the various families, and the author of the *Chronicles of Japan* with his elaborate system of fictitious dates, recur to our minds, and we ask ourselves to what extent similar garblings of history,—sometimes intentional, sometimes unintentional,—may have gone on during earlier ages, when there was even less to check them than there was in the eighth century. If, therefore, the translator here gives expression to a few opinions founded chiefly on a careful study of the text of the *Records of Ancient Matters* helped out by a study of the *Chronicles of Japan*, he would be understood to do so with great diffidence, especially with regard to his few (so to speak) constructive remarks. As to the destructive side of the criticism, there need be less hesitation; for the old histories bear evidence too conclusively against themselves for it to be possible for the earlier portions of them, at least, to stand the test of sober investigation. Before endeavoring to piece together the little that is found in the *Records* to illustrate the beliefs of Archaic Japanese times, it will be necessary, at the risk of dullness, to give a summary of the old traditions as they lie before us in their entirety, after which will be hazarded a few speculations on the subject of the earlier tribes which combined to form the Japanese people; for the four questions of religious beliefs, of political arrangements, of race, and of the credibility of documents, all hang closely together and, properly speaking, form but one highly complex problem.

Greatly condensed, the Early Japanese traditions amount to this: After an indefinitely long period, during which were born a number of abstract deities, who are differently enumerated in the *Records* and in the *Chronicles*, two of these deities, a brother and sister named Izanagi and Izanami (i.e., the "Male Who Invites" and the "Female Who Invites"), are united in marriage, and give birth to the various islands of the Japanese archipelago. When they have finished producing islands, they proceed to the production of a large number of gods and goddesses, many of whom correspond to what we should call personifications of the powers of nature, though personification is a word which, in its legitimate acceptation, is foreign to the Japanese mind. The birth of the Fire God causes Izanami's death, and the most striking episode of the whole mythology then ensues, when her husband, Orpheus-like, visits her in the underworld to implore her to return to him. She would willingly do so, and bids him wait while she consults with the deities of the place. But he, impatient at her long tarrying, breaks off one of the end-teeth of the comb stuck in the left bunch of his hair, lights it and goes in, only to find her a hideous mass of corruption, in whose midst are seated the eight Gods of Thunder. This episode ends with the deification[63] of three peaches who had assisted him in his retreat before the armies of the under-world, and with bitter words exchanged between him and his wife, who herself pursues him as far as the "Even Pass of Hades."

Returning to Himuka in southwestern Japan, Izanagi purifies himself by bathing in a stream, and, as he does so, fresh deities are born from each article of clothing that he throws down on the riverbank, and from each part of his person. One of these deities was the Sun Goddess, who was born from his left eye, while the Moon God sprang from his right eye, and the last born of all, Susa-no-o, whose name the translator renders by "the Impetuous Male," was born from his nose. Between these three children their father divides the inheritance of the universe.

At this point the story loses its unity. The Moon God is no more heard of, and the traditions concerning the Sun Goddess and those concerning the "Impetuous Male Deity" diverge in a manner which is productive of inconsistencies in the remainder of the mythology. The Sun Goddess and the "Impetuous Male Deity" have a violent quarrel, and at last the latter breaks a hole in the roof of the hall in Heaven where his sister is sitting at work with the celestial weaving-maidens, and through it lets fall "a heavenly piebald horse which he had flayed with a backward flaying." The consequences of this act were so disastrous that the Sun Goddess withdrew for a season into a cave, from which the rest of the eight hundred myriad (according to the *Chronicles* eighty myriad) deities with difficulty allured her. The "Impetuous Male Deity" was thereupon banished, and the Sun Goddess remained mistress of the field. Yet, strange to say, she thenceforward retires into the background, and the most bulky section of the mythology consists of stories concerning the "Impetuous Male Deity" and his descendants, who are represented as the monarchs of Japan, or rather of the province of Izumo. The "Impetuous Male Deity" himself, whom his father had charged with the dominion of the sea, never assumes that rule, but first has a curiously told amorous adventure and an encounter with an eight-forked serpent in Izumo, and afterwards reappears as the capricious and filthy deity of Hades, who however seems to retain some power over the land of the living, as he invests his descendant of the sixth generation with the sovereignty of Japan. Of this latter personage a whole cycle of stories is told, all centering in Izumo. We learn of his conversations with a hare and with a mouse, of the prowess and cleverness which he displayed on the occasion of a visit to his ancestor in Hades, which is in this cycle of traditions a much less mysterious place than the Hades visited by Izanagi, of his amours, of his triumph over his eighty brethren, of his reconciliation with his jealous empress, and of his numerous descendants, many of whom have names that are particularly difficult of comprehension. We hear too in a tradition, which ends in a pointless manner, of a microscopic deity who comes across the sea to ask this monarch of Izumo to share the sovereignty with him.

This last-mentioned legend repeats itself in the sequel. The Sun Goddess, who on her second appearance is constantly represented as acting in concert with the "High August Producing Wondrous Deity,"—one of the abstractions mentioned at the commencement of the *Records*,—resolves to bestow the sovereignty of Japan on a child of whom it is doubtful whether he were hers or that of her brother the "Impetuous Male Deity." Three embassies are sent from Heaven to Izumo to arrange matters, but it is only a fourth that is successful, the final ambassadors obtaining the submission of the monarch or deity of Izumo, who surrenders his sovereignty and promises to serve the new dynasty (apparently in the under-world), if a palace or temple be built for him and he be appropriately worshiped. Thereupon the child of the deity whom the Sun Goddess had originally wished to make sovereign of Japan, descends to earth,—not to Izumo in the northwest, be it mentioned, as the logical sequence of the story would lead one to expect,—but to the peak of a mountain in the southwestern island of Kyushu.

Here follows a quaint tale accounting for the odd appearance of the bêche-de-mer, and another to account for the shortness of the lives of mortals, after which we are told of the birth under peculiar circumstances of the heaven-descended deity's three sons. Two of these, Ho-deri and Ho-ori, whose names may be Englished as "Fire-Shine" and "Fire-Subside," are the heroes of a very curious legend, which includes an elaborate account of a visit paid by the latter to the palace of the God of Ocean, and of a curse or spell which gained for him the victory over his elder brother, and enabled him to dwell peacefully in his palace at Takachiho for the space of five hundred and eighty years,—the first statement resembling a date which the *Records* contain. This personage's son married his own aunt, and was the father of four children, one of whom "treading on the crest of the waves, crossed over to the Eternal Land," while a second went into the sea plain," and the *two* others moved eastward, fighting with the chiefs of Kibi and Yamato, having adventures with gods both with and without tails, being assisted by a miraculous sword and a gigantic crow, and naming the various places they passed through after incidents in their own career, as "the Impetuous Male" and other divine personages had done before them. One of these brothers was Kamu-Yamato-Iware-Biko, who (the other having died before him) was first given the title of Jin-mu Ten-nō more than fourteen centuries after the date which in the *Chronicles* is assigned as that of his decease.

Henceforth Yamato, which had scarcely been mentioned before, and the provinces adjacent to it become the center of the story, and Izumo again emerges into importance. A very indecent love-tale forms a bridge which unites the two fragments of the mythology; and the "Great Deity of Miwa," who is identified with the deposed monarch of Izumo, appears on the scene. Indeed during the rest of the story this "Great Deity of Miwa," and his colleague the "Small August Deity" (*Sukuna-Mi-Kami*[64]), the deity Izasa-wake, the three Water-Gods of Sumi, and the "Great Deity of Kazuraki," of whom there is so striking a mention in Sect. 158, form, with the Sun Goddess and with a certain divine sword preserved at the temple of Isonokami in Yamato, the only objects of worship specially named, the other gods and goddesses being no more heard of. This portion of the story is closed by an account of the troubles which inaugurated the reign of Jin-mu's successor, Sui-zei, and then occurs a blank of (according to the accepted chronology) five hundred years, during which absolutely nothing is told us excepting dreary genealogies, the place where each sovereign dwelt and where he was buried, and the age to which he lived,—this after the minute details which had previously been given concerning the successive gods or monarchs down to Sui-zei inclusive. It should likewise be noted that the average age of the first seventeen monarchs (counting Jin-mu Ten-nō as the first according to received ideas) is nearly 96 years if we follow the *Records* and over a hundred if we follow the accepted chronology which is based chiefly on the constantly divergent statements contained in the *Chronicles*. The age of several of the monarchs exceeds 120 years.[65]

The above-mentioned lapse of an almost blank period of five centuries brings us to the reign of the Emperor known to history by the name of Su-jin, whose life of one hundred and sixty-eight years (one hundred and twenty according to the *Chronicles*) is supposed to have immediately preceded the Christian era. In this reign the former monarch of Izumo or god of Miwa again appears and produces a pestilence, of the manner of staying which Su-jin is warned in a dream, while a curious but highly indecent episode tells us how a person called Ō-Tata-Ne-Ko was known to be a son of the deity in question, and was therefore appointed high priest of his temple. In the ensuing reign an elaborate legend, involving a variety of circumstances as miraculous as any in the earlier portion of the mythology, again centers in the necessity of pacifying the great god of Izumo; and this, with details of internecine strife in the Imperial family, of the sovereign's amours, and of the importation of the orange from the "Eternal Land," brings us to the cycle of traditions of which Yamato-Take, a son of the Emperor Kei-kō, is the hero. This prince, after slaying one of his brothers in the privy, accomplishes the task of subduing both western and eastern Japan; and, notwithstanding certain details which are unsavory to the European taste, his story, taken as a whole, is one of the most striking in the book. He performs marvels of valor, disguises himself as a woman to slay the brigands, is the possessor of a magic sword and fire-striker, has a devoted wife who stills the fury of the waves by sitting down upon their surface, has encounters with a deer and with a boar who are really gods in disguise, and finally dies on his way westward before he can reach his home in Yamato. His death is followed by a highly mythological account of the laying to rest of the white bird into which he ended by being transformed.

The succeeding reign is a blank, and the next after that transports us without a word of warning to quite another scene. The sovereign's home is now in Tsukushi, the southwestern island of the Japanese archipelago, and four of the gods, through the medium of the sovereign's wife, who is known to history as the Empress Jin-gū, reveal the existence of the land of Korea, of which, however, this is not the first mention. The Emperor disbelieves the divine message, and is punished by death for his incredulity. But the Empress, after a special consultation between her prime minister and the gods, and the performance of various religious ceremonies, marshals her fleet, and, with the assistance of the fishes both great and small and of a miraculous wave, reaches Shiragi[A] (one of the ancient divisions of Korea), and subdues it. She then returns to Japan, the legend ending with a curiously naive tale of how she sat a-fishing one day on a shoal in the river O-gawa in Tsukushi with threads picked out of her skirt for lines.

The next section shows her going up by sea to Yamato,—another joint in the story, by means of which the Yamato cycle of legends and the Tsukushi cycle are brought into apparent unity. The *Chronicles of Japan* have even improved upon this by making Jin-gū's husband dwell in Yamato at the commencement of his reign and only remove to Tsukushi later, so that if the less elaborated *Records* had not been preserved, the two threads of the tradition would have been still more difficult to unravel. The Empress's army defeats the troops raised by the native kings or princes, who are represented as her stepsons; and from that time forward the story runs on in a single channel and always centers in Yamato. China likewise is now first mentioned, books are said to have been brought over from the mainland, and we hear of the gradual introduction of various useful arts. Even the annals of the reign of Ō-jin however, during which this civilizing impulse from abroad is said to have commenced, are not free from details as miraculous as any in the earlier portions of the book. Indeed Sects. 114–116 of the following translation, which form part of the narrative of his reign, are occupied with the recital of one of the most fanciful tales of the whole

[A] 新羅. [Shiragi is the Japanese word for the Kingdom of Silla. —M.F.]

mythology. The monarch himself is said to have lived a hundred and thirty years, while his successor lived eighty-three (according to the *Chronicles* Ō-jin lived a hundred and ten and his successor Nin-toku reigned eighty-seven years). It is not till the next reign that the miraculous ceases, a fact which significantly coincides with the reign in which, according to a statement in the *Chronicles*, "historiographers were first appointed to all the provinces to record words and events, and forward archives from all directions." This brings us to the commencement of the fifth century of our era, just three centuries before the compilation of our histories, but only two centuries before the compilation of the first history of which mention has been preserved. From that time the story in the *Records*, though not well told, gives us some very curious pictures, and reads as if it were reliable. It is tolerably full for a few reigns, after which it again dwindles into mere genealogies, carrying us down to the commencement of the seventh century. The *Chronicles*, on the contrary, give us full details down to 701 CE, that is to within nineteen years of the date of their compilation.

The reader who has followed this summary, or who will take the trouble to read through the whole text for himself, will perceive that there is no break in the story,—at least no chronological break,—and no break between the fabulous and the real, unless indeed it be at the commencement of the fifth century of our era, *i.e.* more than a thousand years later than the date usually accepted as the commencement of genuine Japanese history. The only breaks are,—not chronological,—but topographical.

This fact of the continuity of the Japanese mythology and history has been fully recognized by the leading native commentators, whose opinions are those considered orthodox by modern Shintoists; and they draw from it the conclusion that everything in the standard national histories must be equally accepted as literal truth. All persons however cannot force their minds into the limits of such a belief; and early in the eighteenth century a celebrated writer and thinker, Arai Hakuseki, published a work in which, while accepting the native mythology as an authentic chronicle of events, he did so with the reservation of proving to his own satisfaction that all the miraculous portions thereof were allegories, and the gods only men under another name. In this particular, the elasticity of the Japanese word for "deity," *kami,* which has already been noticed, stood the eastern Euhemerus in good stead. Some of his explanations are however extremely comical, and it is evident that such a system enables the person who uses it to prove whatever he has a mind to.[66] In the nineteenth century a diluted form of the same theory was adopted by Tachibana Moribe, who, although endeavoring to remain an orthodox Shintoist, yet decided that some of the (so to speak) uselessly miraculous incidents need not be believed in as revealed truth. Such, for instance, are the story of the speaking mouse, and that of Izanagi's headdress turning into a bunch of grapes. He accounts for many of these details by the supposition that they are what he calls *osana-goto,* i.e. "child-like words," and thinks that they were invented for the sake of fixing the story in the minds of children, and are not binding on modern adults as articles of faith. He is also willing to allow that some passages show traces of Chinese influence, and he blames Norinaga's uncompromising championship of every iota of the existing text of the *Records of Ancient Matters.* As belonging to this same school of what may perhaps be termed "rationalistic believers" in Japanese mythology, a contemporary Christian writer, Mr. Takahashi Goro, must also be mentioned. Treading in the foot-steps of Arai Hakuseki, but bringing to bear on the legends of his own country some knowledge of the mythology of other lands, he for instance explains the traditions of the Sun Goddess and of the Eight-Forked Serpent of Yamada by postulating the existence of an ancient queen called Sun, whose brother, after having been banished from her realm for his improper behavior, killed an enemy whose name was Serpent, etc., while such statements as that the microscopic deity who came over the waves to share the sovereignty of Izumo would not tell his name, are explained by the assertion that, being a foreigner, he was unintelligible for some time until he had learnt the language. It is certainly strange that such theorists should not see that they are undermining with one hand that which they endeavor to prop up with the other, and that their own individual fancy is made by them the sole standard of historic truth. Yet Mr. Takahashi confidently asserts that "his explanations have nothing forced or fanciful" in them, and "that they cannot fail to solve the doubts even of the greatest of doubters."[67]

The general habit of the more skeptical Japanese of the present day,—*i.e.* of ninety-nine out of every hundred of the educated,—seems to be to reject, or at least to ignore, the history of the gods, while implicitly accepting the history of the emperors from Jin-mu downwards; and in so doing they have been followed with but little reserve by most Europeans,—almanacs, histories and encyclopedias all continuing to repeat on the antiquated authority of such writers as Kaempfer and Titsingh, that Japan possesses an authentic history covering more than two thousand years, while Siebold and Hoffman even go the length of discussing the *hour* of Jin-mu's accession in the year 660 BCE! This is the attitude of mind now sanctioned by the governing class. Thus, in the historical compilations used as text-books in the schools, the stories of the gods,—that is to say the Japanese traditions down to Jin-mu exclusive,—are either passed over in silence or dismissed in a few sentences, while the annals of the human sovereigns,—that is to say the Japanese traditions from Jin-mu inclusive,—are treated precisely as if the events therein related had happened yesterday, and were as incontrovertibly historical as later statements for which there is contemporary evidence. The same plan is pursued elsewhere in official publications. Thus, to take but one example among many, the Imperial Commissioners to the Vienna Exhibition, in their *Notes on the Empire of Japan*, tell us that

> The history of the imperial dynasty goes back quite far. Its origins are surrounded by obscurity, given the absence of regular documents or a perfect calendar. The first Emperor of the present dynasty for whom trustworthy annals remain is Jin-mou-ten-nō, who organized an uprising in the province of Hiuga, marched to the east with his companions, founded his capital in the valley of Kashi-hara in Yamato, and took the throne as Emperor. It is from this Emperor that the present ruling family of Japan is descended, through regular succession. It is from the year of the accession of Jin-mou-ten-nō that the Japanese era (Years 1–660 before Jesus Christ) dates.[68]

As for the *ère Japonaise [Japanese era]* mentioned by the commissioners, it may be pertinent to observe that it was only introduced by an edict dated 15th Dec., 1872,[69] that is to say just a fortnight before the publication of their report. *And this era, this accession, is confidently placed thirteen or fourteen centuries before the first history which records it was written, nine centuries before (at the earliest computation) the art of writing was introduced into the country, and on the sole authority of books teeming with miraculous legends!!* Does such a proceeding need any comment after once being formulated in precise terms, and can any unprejudiced person continue to accept the early Japanese chronology and the first thousand years of the so-called history of Japan?

Leaving this discussion, let us now see whether any information relative to the early religious and political state of the Japanese can be gleaned from the pages of the *Records* and of the *Chronicles*. There are fragments of information,—fragments of two sorts,—some namely of clear import, others which are rather a matter for inference and for argument. Let us take the positive fragments first—the notices as to cosmological ideas, dreams, prayers, etc.

The first thing that strikes the student is that what, for want of a more appropriate name, we must call the religion of the Early Japanese, was not an organized religion. We can discover in it nothing corresponding to the body of dogma, the code of morals, and the sacred book authoritatively enforcing both, with which we are familiar in civilized religions, such as Buddhism, Christianity, and Islam. What we find is a bundle of miscellaneous superstitions rather than a coordinated system. Dreams evidently were credited with great importance, the future being supposed to be foretold in them, and the will of the gods made known. Sometimes even an actual object, such as a wonderful sword, was sent down in a dream, thus to our ideas mixing the material with the spiritual. The subject did not, however, present itself in that light to the Early Japanese, to whom there was evidently but one order of phenomena,—what we should call the natural order. Heaven, or rather the Sky, was an actual place,—not more ethereal than earth, nor thought of as the abode of the blessed after death—but simply a "high plain" situated above Japan and communicating with Japan by a bridge or ladder, and forming the residence of some of those powerful personages called *kami,*—a word which we must make shift to translate by "god" or "goddess," or "deity." An arrow shot from earth could reach Heaven, and make a hole in it. There was at least one mountain in Heaven, and one river with a broad stony bed like those with which the traveler in Japan becomes familiar, one or two caves, one or more wells, and animals, and trees. There is, however, some confusion as to the mountain,—the celebrated Mount Kagu,—for there is one of that name in the province of Yamato.

Some of the gods dwelt here on earth, or descended hither from Heaven, and had children by human women. Such, for instance, was the Emperor Jin-mu's great-grandfather. Some few gods had tails or were otherwise personally remarkable; and "savage deities" are often mentioned as inhabiting certain portions of Japan, both in the so-called "Divine Age" and during the reigns of the human emperors down to a time corresponding, according to the generally received chronology, with the first or second century of the Christian era. The human emperors themselves, moreover, were sometimes spoken of as deities, and even made personal use of that designation. The gods occasionally transformed themselves into animals, and at other times simple tangible objects were called gods,—or at least they were called *kami;* for the gulf separating the Japanese from the English term can never be too often recalled to mind. The word *kami,* as previously mentioned, properly signifies "superior," and it would be putting more into it than it really implies to say that the Early Japanese "deified,"—in our sense of the verb to "deify,"—the peaches which Izanagi used to pelt his assailants with, or any other natural objects whatsoever. It would, indeed, be to attribute to them a flight of imagination of which they were not capable, and a habit of personification not in accordance with the genius of their language. Some of the gods are mentioned collectively as "bad Deities like unto the flies in the fifth moon"; but there is nothing approaching a systematic division into good spirits and bad spirits. In fact the word "spirit" itself is not applicable at all to the gods of Archaic Japan. They were, like the gods of Greece, conceived of only as more powerful human beings. They were born, and some of them died, though here again there is inconsistency, as the death of some of them is mentioned in a manner leading one to suppose that they were conceived of as being then at an end, whereas in other cases such death seems simply to denote transference to Hades, or to what is called "the One Road," which is believed to be a synonym for Hades. Sometimes, again, a journey to Hades is undertaken by a god without any reference to his death. Nothing, indeed, could be less consistent than the various details.

Hades[70] itself is another instance of this inconsistency. In the legend of Ō-Kuni-Nushi (the "Master of the Great Land"),—one of the Izumo cycle of legends,—Hades is described exactly as if it were part of the land of the living, or exactly as if it were Heaven, which indeed comes to the same thing. It has its trees, its houses, its family quarrels, etc., etc. In the legend of Izanagi, on the other hand, Hades means simply the abode of horrible putrefaction and of the vindictive dead, and is fitly described by the god himself who had ventured thither as "a hideous and polluted land." The only point in which the legends agree is in placing between the upper earth and Hades a barrier called the "Even Pass (or Hill) of Hades." The state of the dead in general is nowhere alluded to, nor are the dying ever made to refer to a future world, whether good or evil.

The objects of worship were of course the gods, or some of them. It has already been stated that during the later portions of the story, whose scene is laid almost exclusively on earth, the Sun Goddess, the deity Izasa-wake, the Divine Sword of Iso-no-kami, the Small August Deity (*Sukuna-Mi-Kami)*, the "Great Gods" of Miwa and of Kazuraki and the three Water-Deities of Sumi, alone are mentioned as having been specially worshiped. Of these the first and the last appear together, forming a sort of quaternion, while the other five appear singly and have no connection with each other. The deities of the mountains, the deities of the rivers, the deities of the sea, etc., are also mentioned in the aggregate, as are likewise the heavenly deities and the earthly deities; and the Empress Jin-gū is represented as conciliating them all previous to her departure for Korea by "putting into a gourd the ashes of a *maki* tree,[71] and likewise making a quantity of chopsticks and also of leaf-platters, and scattering them all on the waves."

This brings us to the subject of religious rites,—a subject on which we long for fuller information than the texts afford.[72] That the conciliatory offerings made to the gods were of a miscellaneous nature will be expected from the quotation just made. Nevertheless, a very natural method was in the main followed; for the people offered the things by which they themselves set most store, as we hear at a later period of the poet Tsurayuki, when in a storm at sea, flinging his mirror into the waves because he had but one. The Early Japanese made offerings of two kinds of cloth, one being hempen cloth and the other cloth manufactured from the bark of the paper-mulberry, —offerings very precious in their eyes, but which have in modern times been allowed to degenerate into useless strips of paper. They likewise offered shields, spears, and other things. Food was offered both to the gods and to the dead; indeed, the palace or tomb of the dead monarch and the temple of the god cannot always be distinguished from each other, and, as has already been mentioned, the Japanese use the same word *miya* for "palace" and for "temple." Etymologically signifying "august house," it is naturally susceptible of what are to us two distinct meanings.

With but one exception,[73] the *Records* do not give us the words of any prayers (or, as the Japanese term *norito* has elsewhere been translated, "rituals"). Conversations with the gods are indeed detailed, but no devotional utterances. Fortunately however a number of very ancient prayers have been preserved in other books, and translations of some of them by Mr. Satow will be found scattered through the volumes of the *Transactions* of this society. They consist mostly of declarations of praise and statements of offerings made, either in return for favors received or conditionally on favors being granted. They are all in prose, and hymns do not seem to have been in use. Indeed of the hundred and eleven Songs preserved in the *Records*, not one has any religious reference.

The sacred rite of which most frequent mention is made is purification by water. Trial by hot water is also alluded to in both histories, but not till a time confessedly posterior to the commencement of intercourse with the mainland. We likewise hear of compacts occasionally entered into with a god, and somewhat resembling our European wager, oath, or curse. Priests are spoken of in a few passages, but without any details. We do not hear of their functions being in any way mediatorial, and the impression conveyed is that they did not exist in very early times as a separate class.[74] When they did come into existence, the profession soon became hereditary, according to the general tendency in Japan towards the hereditability of offices and occupations.

Miscellaneous superstitions crop up in many places. Some of these were evidently obsolescent or unintelligible at the time when the legends crystallized into their present shape, and stories are told purporting to give their origin. Thus we learn either in the *Records* or in the *Chronicles*, or in both works, why it is unlucky to use only one light, to break off the teeth of a comb at night-time, and to enter the house with straw hat and rain-coat on. The world-wide dread of going against the sun is connected with the Jin-mu legend, and recurs elsewhere.[75] We also hear of charms,—for instance, of the wondrous "Herb-Quelling Saber" found by Susa-no-o (the "Impetuous Male Deity") inside a serpent's tail, and still preserved as one or the Imperial *regalia.* Other such charms were the "tide-flowing jewel" and "tide-ebbing jewel," that obtained for Jin-mu's grandfather the victory over his elder brother, together with the fishhook which figures so largely in the same legend.[76] Divination by means of the shoulder-blade of a stag was a favorite means of ascertaining the will of the gods. Sometimes also human beings seem to have been credited in a vague manner with the power of prophetic utterance. Earthenware pots were buried at the point of his departure by an intending traveler. In a fight the initial arrow was regarded with superstitious awe. The great precautions with which the Empress Jin-gū is said to have set out on her expedition to Korea have already been alluded to, and indeed the commencement of any action or enterprise seems to have had special importance attributed to it.

To conclude this survey of the religious beliefs of the Early Japanese by referring, as was done in the case of the arts of life, to certain notable features which are conspicuous by their absence, attention may be called to the fact that there is no tradition of a deluge, no testimony to any effect produced on the imagination by the earthquakes from which the Japanese islanders suffer such constant alarms, no trace of star-worship, no notion of incarnation or of transmigration. This last remark goes to show that the Japanese mythology had assumed its present shape before the first echo of Buddhism reverberated on these shores. But the absence of any tradition of a deluge or inundation is still more remarkable, both because such catastrophes are likely to occur occasionally in all lands, and because the imagination of most nations seems to have been greatly impressed by their occurrence. Moreover what is specifically known to us as *the* Deluge has been lately claimed as an ancient Altaic myth. Yet here we have the oldest of the *undoubtedly* Altaic nations without any legend of the kind. As for the neglect of the stars, round whose names the imagination of other races has twined such fanciful conceits, it is as characteristic of Modern as of Archaic Japan. The Chinese designations of the constellations, and some few Chinese legends relating to them, have been borrowed in historic times; but no Japanese writer has ever thought of looking in the stars for "the poetry of heaven." Another detail worthy of mention is that the number seven, which in so many countries has been considered sacred, is here not prominent in any way, its place being taken by eight. Thus we have eight Great Islands, an Eight-forked Serpent, a beard Eighty Handbreadths long, a God named "Eight-Thousand Spears," Eighty or Eight Hundred Myriads of Deities, etc., etc. The commentators think it necessary to tell us that all these eights and eighties need not be taken literally, as they simply mean a great number. The fact remains that the number eight had, for some unknown reason, a special significance attached to it; and as the documents which mention eight also mention nine and ten, besides higher numbers, and as in some test cases, such as that of the Eight Great Islands, each of the eight is separately enumerated, it is plain that when the Early Japanese said eight they meant eight, though they may doubtless have used that number in a vague manner, as we do a dozen, a hundred, and a thousand.

How glaringly different all this is from the fanciful accounts of Shinto that have been given by some recent popular writers calls for no comment. Thus one of them, whom another quotes as an authority,[77] tells us that Shinto "consists in the belief that the productive ethereal spirit being expanded through the whole universe, every part is in some degree impregnated with it, and therefore every part is in some measure the seat of the deity; whence local gods and goddesses are everywhere worshiped, and consequently multiplied without end. Like the ancient Romans and the Greeks, they acknowledge a Supreme Being, the first, the supreme, the intellectual, by which men have been reclaimed from rudeness and barbarism to elegance and refinement, and been taught through privileged men and women, not only to live with more comfort, but to die with better hopes."(!) Truly, when one peruses such utterly groundless assertions,—for that here quoted is but one among many,—one is tempted to believe that the nineteenth century must form part of the early mythopoeic age.

With regard to the question of government, we learn little beyond such vague statements as that to so-and-so was yielded by his eighty brethren the sovereignty of the land of Izumo, or that Izanagi divided the dominion over all things between his three children, bestowing on one the "Plain of High Heaven," on another the "Dominion of the Night," and on the third the "Sea-Plain." But we do not in the earlier legends see such sovereignty actually administered. The heavenly gods seem rather to have been conceived as forming a sort of commonwealth, who decided things by meeting together in council in the stony bed of the "River of Heaven," and taking the advice of the shrewdest of their number. Indeed the various divine assemblies, to which the story in the *Records* and *Chronicles* introduces us, remind us of nothing so much as of the village assemblies of primitive tribes in many parts of the world, where the cleverness of one and the general willingness to follow his suggestions fill the place of the more definite organization of later times.

Descending from heaven to earth, we find little during the so-called "Divine Age" but stories of isolated individuals and families; and it is not till the narrative of the wars of the earlier Emperors commences, that any kind of political organization comes into view. Then at once we hear of chieftains in every locality, who lead their men to battle, and are seemingly the sole depositories of power, each in his microscopic sphere. The legend of Jin-mu itself, however, is sufficient to show that autocracy, as we understand it, was not characteristic of the government of the Tsukushi tribes; for Jin-mu and his brother, until the latter's death, are represented as joint chieftains of their host. Similarly we find that the "Territorial Owners" of Yamato, and the "Rulers" of Izumo, whom Jin-mu or his successors are said to have subjugated, are constantly spoken of in the Plural, as if to intimate that they exercised a divided sovereignty. During the whole of the so-called "Human Age" we meet, both in parts of the country which were already subject to the Imperial rule and in others which were not yet annexed, with local magnates bearing these same titles of "Territorial Owners," "Rulers," "Chiefs," etc.; and the impression left on the mind is that in early historical times the sovereign's power was not exercised directly over all parts of Japan, but that in many cases the local chieftains continued to hold sway though owning some sort of allegiance to the emperor in Yamato, while in others the emperor was strong enough to depose these local rulers, and to put in their place his own kindred or retainers, who however exercised unlimited authority in their own districts, and used the same titles as had been borne by the former native rulers,—that, in fact, the government was feudal rather than centralized. This characteristic of the political organization of Early Japan has not altogether escaped the attention of the native commentators. Indeed the great Shinto scholar Atsutane not only recognizes the fact, but endeavors to prove that the system of centralization which obtained during the eighth, ninth, tenth, eleventh, and part of the twelfth centuries, and which has been revived in our own day, is nothing but an imitation of the Chinese bureaucratic system; and he asserts that an organized feudalism, similar to that which existed from the twelfth century down to the year 1867, was the sole really ancient and national Japanese form of government. The translator cannot follow Atsutane to such lengths, as he sees no evidence in the early histories of the intricate organization of medieval Japan. But that, beyond the immediate limits of the Imperial domain, the government *resembled* feudalism rather than centralization seems indisputable. It is also true that the seventh century witnessed a sudden move in the direction of bureaucratic organization, many of the titles which had up till that time denoted actual provincial chieftains being then either suppressed, or else allowed to sink into mere "gentile names." Another remark which is suggested by a careful perusal of the two ancient histories is that the Imperial succession was in early historical times very irregular. Strange gaps occur as late as the sixth century of our era; and even when it was one of the children who inherited his father's throne, that child was rarely the eldest son.

What now are we to gather from this analysis of the religious and political features revealed to us by a study of the books containing the Early Japanese traditions as to the still remoter history and tribal divisions of Japan, and as to the origin of the Japanese legends? Very little that is certain, perhaps; but, in the opinion of the present writer, two or three interesting probabilities.

In view of the multiplicity of gods and the complications of the so-called historical traditions, he thinks that it would be *à priori* difficult to believe that the development of Japanese civilization should have run on in a single stream broken only in the third century by the commencement of intercourse with the mainland of Asia. We are, however, not left to such a merely theoretical consideration. There are clear indications of there having been three centers of legendary cycles, three streams which mixed together to form the Japan which meets us at the dawn of authentic history in the fifth century of our era. One of these centers,—the most important in the mythology,—is Izumo; the second is Yamato; the third is Tsukushi, called in modern times Kyushu. Eastern and northern Japan count for nothing; indeed, much of the northeast and north was, down to comparatively recent times, occupied by the barbarous Ainu or, as they are called by the Japanese Emishi, Ebisu or Ezo. That the legends or traditions derived from the three parts of the country here mentioned accord but imperfectly together is an opinion which has already been alluded to, and upon which light may perhaps be thrown by a more thorough sifting of the myths and beliefs classified according to this three-fold system. The question of the ancient division of Japan into several independent states is, however, not completely a matter of opinion. For we nave in the *Shanhai jing*[78] a positive statement concerning a Northern and a Southern Yamato (倭), and the Chinese annals of both the Han dynasties tell us of the division of the country into a much larger number of kingdoms, of which, according to the annals of the later Han dynasty, Yamato (邪馬台) was the most powerful. A later official Chinese historian also tells us that *Jih-pên* (日本, our *Japan*) and Yamato had been two different states, and that *Jih-pên* was reported to have swallowed up Yamato. By *Jih-pên* the author evidently meant to speak of the island of Tsukushi or of part of it. That the Chinese were fairly well acquainted with Japan is shown by the fact of there being in the old Chinese literature more than one mention of "the country of the hairy people beyond the mountains in the east and north,"—that is of the Emishi or Ainu. No Chinese book would seem to mention Izumo as having formed a separate country; and this evidence must be allowed its full weight. It is possible, of course, that Izumo may have been incorporated with Yamato before the conquest of the latter by the Tsukushi people, and in this case some of the inconsistencies of the history may be traceable to a confusion of the traditions concerning the conquest of Izumo by Yamato and of those concerning the conquest of Yamato by Tsukushi. Perhaps too (for so almost impossible a task is it to reconstruct history out of legend) there may not, after all, be sufficient warrant for believing in the former existence of Izumo as a separate state, though it certainly seems hard to account otherwise for the peculiar place that Izumo occupies in mythic story. In any case, and whatever light may hereafter be thrown on this very obscure question, it must be remembered that, so far as clear native documentary evidence reaches, 400 CE is approximately the highest limit of reliable[79] Japanese history. Beyond that date we are at once confronted with the miraculous; and if any facts relative to earlier Japan are to be extracted from the pages of the *Records* and *Chronicles*, it must be by a process very different from that of simply reading and taking their assertions upon trust.

With regard to the origin, or rather to the significance, of the clearly fanciful portions of the Japanese legends, the question here mooted as to the probability of the Japanese mythology being a mixed one warns us to exercise more than usual caution in endeavoring to interpret it. In fact it bids us wait to interpret it until such time as further research shall have shown which legends belong together. For if they are of heterogeneous origin, it is hopeless to attempt to establish a genealogical tree of the gods, and the very phrase so often heard in discussions on this subject,—"the original religious beliefs of the Japanese,"—ceases to have any precise meaning; for different beliefs may have been equally ancient and original, but distinguished geographically by belonging to different parts of the country. Furthermore it may not be superfluous to call attention to the fact that the gods who are mentioned in the opening phrases of the histories as we now have them are not therefore necessarily the gods that were most anciently worshiped. Surely in religions, as in books, it is not often the preface that is written first. And yet this simple consideration has been constantly neglected, and, one after another, European writers having a tincture of knowledge of Japanese mythology, tell us of original Dualities, Trinities, and Supreme Deities, without so much as pausing to notice that the only two authorities in the matter,—viz., the *Records* and the *Chronicles*,—differ most gravely in the lists they furnish of primary gods. If the present writer ventured to throw out a suggestion where so many random assertions have been made, it would be to the effect that the various abstractions which figure at the commencement of the *Records* and of the *Chronicles* were probably later growths, and perhaps indeed mere inventions or individual priests. There is nothing either in the histories or in the *Shinto Rituals* to show that these gods, or some one or more of them, were in early days, as has been sometimes supposed, the objects of a purer worship which was afterwards obscured by the legends of Izanagi, Izanami, and their numerous descendants. On the contrary, with the exception of the deity Taka-Mi-Musu-Bi,[80] they are no sooner mentioned than they vanish into space.

Whether it is intrinsically likely that so rude a race as the Early Japanese, and a race so little given to metaphysical speculation as the Japanese at all times of their history, should have commenced by a highly abstract worship which they afterwards completely abandoned, is a question which may better be left to those whose general knowledge of early peoples and early religious beliefs entitles their decisions to respect. Their assistance, likewise, even after the resolution of the Japanese mythology into its several component parts, must be called in by the specialist to help in deciding how much of this mythology should be interpreted according to the "solar" method now so popular in England, how much should be accepted as history more or less perverted, how much should be regarded as embodying attempts at explaining facts in nature, and what residue may be rejected as simple fabrication of the priesthood in comparatively late times.[81] Those who are personally acquainted with the Japanese character will probably incline to enlarge the area of the three latter divisions more than would be prudent in the case of the highly imaginative Aryans, and to point out that, though some few Japanese legends or portions of legends can be traced to false etymologies invented to account for names of places, and are therefore true myths in the strictest acceptation of the term, yet the kindred process whereby personality is ascribed to inanimate objects,—a process which lies at the very root of Aryan mythology,—is altogether alien to the Japanese genius, and indeed to the Far-Eastern mind in general. Mythology thus originated has been aptly described as a "disease of language." But all persons are not liable to catch the same disease, neither presumably are all languages; and it is hard to see how a linguistic disease which consists in mistaking a metaphor for a reality can attack a tongue to which metaphor, even in its tamest shape, is an almost total stranger. Thus not only have Japanese nouns no genders and Japanese verbs no persons, but the names of inanimate objects cannot even be used as the subjects of transitive verbs. Nowhere for instance in Japanese, whether Archaic, Classical, or Modern, do we meet with such metaphorical,—mythological,—phrases as "the hot wind melts the ice," or "his conversation delights me," where the words "wind" and "conversation" are spoken of as if they were personal agents. No, the idea is invariably rendered in some other and impersonal way. Yet what a distance separates such statements, in which the ordinary European reader unacquainted with any Altaic tongue would scarcely recognize the existence of any personification at all, from the bolder flights of Aryan metaphor! Indeed, though Altaic Asia has produced very few wise men, the words of its languages closely correspond to the definition of words as "the wise man's counters"; for they are colorless and matter of fact, and rarely if ever carry him who speaks them above the level of sober reality. At the same time, it is patent that the sun plays *some* part in the Japanese mythology; and even the legend of Prince Yamato-Take, which has hitherto been generally accepted as historical or semi-historical, bears such close resemblance to legends in other countries which have been pronounced to be solar by great authorities that it may at least be worthwhile to subject it to investigation from that point of view.[82] The present writer has already expressed his conviction that this matter is not one for the specialist to decide alone. He would only, from the Japanese point of view, suggest very particular caution in the application to Japanese legend of a method or interpretation which has elsewhere been fruitful of great results.

A further particular which is deserving of notice is the almost certain fact of a recension of the various traditions at a comparatively late date. This is partly shown by the amount of geographical knowledge displayed in the enumeration of the various islands supposed to have been given birth to by Izanagi and Izanami (the "Male who Invites" and the "Female who Invites"),—an amount and an exactness of knowledge unattainable at a time prior to the union under one rule of all the provinces mentioned, and significantly not extending much beyond those provinces. Such a recension may likewise be inferred,—if the opinion of the manifold origin of the Japanese traditions be accepted,—from the fairly ingenious manner in which their component parts have generally been welded together. The way in which one or two legends,—for instance, that of the curious curse pronounced by the younger brother Ho-ori on the elder Ho-deri—are repeated more than once exemplifies a less intelligent revision.[83] Under this heading may, perhaps, be included the legends of the conquest of Yamato by the Emperor Jin-mu and of the conquest of the same country by the Empress Jin-gū, which certainly bear a suspicious likeness to each other. Of the subjection of Korea by this last-named personage it should be observed that the Chinese and Korean histories, so far as they are known to us, make no mention, and indeed the dates, as more specifically given in the *Chronicles*, clearly show the inconsistency of the whole story; for Jin-gū's husband, the Emperor Chū-ai, is said to have been born in the 19th year of the reign of Sei-mu, *i.e.* in 149 CE, while his father, Prince Yamato-Take, is said to have died in the 43rd year of Kei-kō, *i.e.* in 113 CE, so that there is an interval of thirty-six years between the death of the father and the birth of the son![84]

One peculiarly interesting piece of information to be derived from a careful study of the *Records* and *Chronicles* (though it is one on which the patriotic Japanese commentators preserve complete silence) is that, at the very earliest period to which the twilight of legend stretches back, Chinese influence had already begun to make itself felt in these islands, communicating to the inhabitants both implements and ideas. This is surely a fact of very particular importance, lending, as it does, its weight to the mass of evidence which goes to prove that in almost all known cases culture has been introduced from abroad, and has not been spontaneously developed. The traces of Chinese influence are indeed not numerous, but they are unmistakable. Thus we find chopsticks mentioned both in the Izumo and in the Kyushu legendary cycle. The legend of the birth of the Sun Goddess and Moon-God from Izanagi's eyes is a scarcely altered fragment of the Chinese myth of Pangu; the superstition that peaches had assisted Izanagi to repel the hosts of Hades can almost certainly be traced to a Chinese source, and the hand-maidens of the Japanese Sun Goddess are mentioned under the exact title of the Spinning Damsel of Chinese myth (天衣織女), while the River of Heaven (天河), which figures in the same legend, is equally Chinese,—for surely both names cannot be mere coincidences. A like remark applies to the name of the Deity of the Kitchen, and to the way in which that deity is mentioned.[85] The art of making an intoxicating liquor is referred to in the very earliest Japanese legends. Are we to believe that its invention here was independent of its invention on the continent? In this instance moreover the old histories bear witness against themselves; for they mention this same liquor in terms showing that it was a curious rarity in what, according to the accepted chronology, corresponds to the century immediately preceding the Christian era, and again in the third century of that era. The whole story of the Sea God's palace has a Chinese ring about it, and "cassia tree" (桂) mentioned in it is certainly Chinese, as are the crocodiles. That the so-called *maga-tama*, or "curved jewels," which figure so largely in the Japanese mythology, and with which the Early Japanese adorned themselves, were derived from China was already suspected by Mr. Henry von Siebold; and quite latterly Mr. Milne has thrown light on this subject from an altogether unexpected quarter. He has remarked, namely, that jade or the jade-like stone of which many of the *maga-tama* are made, is a mineral which has never yet been met with in Japan. We therefore know that *some* at least of the "curved jewels" or of the material for them came from the mainland, and the probability that the idea of curving these very oddly shaped ornaments was likewise imported thence gains in probability. The peculiar kind of arrow called *narikabura* (鳴摘) is another trace of Chinese influence in the material order, and a thorough search by a competent Chinese scholar would perhaps reveal others. But enough at least has been said to show the indisputable existence of that influence. From other sources we know that the more recent mythic fancy of Japan has shown itself as little impenetrable to such influence as have the manners and customs of the people. The only difference is that assimilation has of late proceeded with much greater rapidity.

In this, language is another guide; for, though the discoverable traces of Chinese influence are comparatively few in the Archaic Dialect, yet they are there. This is a subject which has as yet scarcely been touched. Two Japanese authors of an elder generation, Kaibara and Arai Hakuseki, did indeed point out the existence of some such traces. But they drew no inference from them, they did not set to work to discover new ones, and their indications, except in one or two obvious cases, have received little attention from later writers whether native or foreign. But when we compare such words as *kane, kume, kuni, saka, tana, uma,* and many others with the pronunciation now given, or with that which the phonetic laws of the language in its earlier stage would have caused to be given, to their Chinese equivalents 金. 軍, 群, 尺, 壇, 馬, etc., the idea forces way that such coincidences of sound and sense cannot all be purely accidental; and when moreover we find that the great majority of the words in question denote things or ideas that were almost certainly imported, we perceive that a more thorough sifting of Archaic Japanese (especially of botanical and zoological names and of the names of implements and manufactures) would probably be the best means of discovering at least the negative features of an antiquity remoter than all written documents, remoter even than the crystallization of the legends which those documents have preserved. In dealing with Korean words found in Archaic Japanese we tread on more delicate ground; for there we have a language which, unlike Chinese, stands to Japanese in the closest family relationship, making it plain that many coincidences of sound and sense should be ascribed to radical affinity rather than to later intercourse. At the same time it appears more probable that, for instance, such seemingly indigenous Japanese terms as *Hotoke,* "Buddha," and *tera,* "Buddhist temple," should have been in fact borrowed from the corresponding Korean words *Puchhö* and *chöl* than that both nations should have independently chosen homonyms to denote the same foreign ideas. Indeed, it will perhaps, not be too bold to assume that in the case of *Hotoke,* "Buddha," we have before us a word whose journeyings consist of many stages, it having been first brought from India to China, then from China to Korea, and thirdly from Korea to Japan, where finally the ingenuity of philologists has discovered for it a Japanese etymology *(hito ke,* "human spirit") with which in reality it has nothing whatever to do.

These introductory remarks have already extended to such a length that a reference to the strikingly parallel case of borrowed customs and ideas which is presented by the Ainu in this same archipelago must be left undeveloped. In conclusion, it need only be remarked that a simple translation of one book, such as is here given, does not nearly exhaust the work which might be expended even on the elucidation of that single book, and much less can it fill the gap which still lies between us and a proper knowledge of Japanese antiquity. To do this, the cooperation of the archaeologist must be obtained, while even in the field of the critical investigation of documents there is an immense deal still to be done. Not only must all the available Japanese sources be made to yield up the information which they contain, but the assistance of Chinese and Korean records must be called in. A large quantity of Chinese literature has already been ransacked for a similar purpose by Matsushita Ken-rin, a translation of part of whose very useful compilation entitled *An Exposition of the Foreign Notices of Japan* (異稱日本伝) would be one of the greatest helps towards the desired knowledge. In fact there still remains to be done for Japanese antiquity from our standpoint what Atsutane has done for it from the standpoint of a Japanese Shintoist. Except in some of Mr. Satow's papers published in these *Transactions,* the subject has scarcely yet been studied in this spirit, and it is possible that the Japanese members of our Society may be somewhat alarmed at the idea of their national history being treated with so little reverence. Perhaps, however, the discovery of the interest of the field of study thus only waiting to be investigated may reconcile them to the view here propounded. In any case if the early history of Japan is not all true, no amount of make-believe can make it so. What we would like to do is to sift the true from the false. As an eminent writer on anthropology[86] has recently said, "Historical criticism, that is, judgment, is practiced not for the purpose of disbelieving, but of believing. Its object is not to find fault with the author, but to ascertain how much of what he says may be reasonably taken as true." Moreover, even in what is not to be accepted as historic fact there is often much that is valuable from other points of view. If, therefore, we lose a thousand years of so-called Japanese history, it must not be forgotten that Japanese mythology remains as the oldest existing product of the Altaic mind.

The following is a list of all the Japanese works quoted in this Introduction and in the Notes to the Translation. For the sake of convenience to the English reader all the titles have been translated excepting some few which, mostly on account of their embodying a recondite allusion, do not admit of translation:

Catalogue of Family Names, 姓氏録, by Prince Mata.[87]

Chronicles of Japan (generally quoted as the *Chronicles*), 日本紀 or 日本書紀, by Prince Toneri and others.

Chronicles of Japan Continued, 続日本紀, by Sugano Ason Mamichi, Fujiwara no Ason Tsugunawa and others.

Chronicles of Japan Explained, 釈日本紀, by Urabe no Yasukata.

Chronicles of the Old Matters of Former Ages, 先代旧事本紀, authorship uncertain.

Collection of a Myriad Leaves, 万葉集, by Tachibana no Moroe (probably).

Collection of Japanese Songs Ancient and Modern, 古今和歌集, by Ki no Tsurayuki and others.

Commentary on the Collection of a Myriad Leaves, 万葉考, by Kamo no Mabuchi.

Commentary on the Lyric Dramas, 謡曲拾葉抄, by Jin-ko.

Commentary on the Ritual of the General Purification, 大葉詞後釋, by Motoori Norinaga.

Correct Account of the Divine Age, 神代正語, by Motoori Norinaga.

Dictionary of Pillow-Words, 冠辞考, by Kamo no Mabuchi.

Digest of the Imperial Genealogies, 纂輯御系図, by Yokoyama Yoshikiyo and Kurokawa Saneyori.

Discussion of the Objections to the Inquiry into the True Chronology, 真暦不審考, by Motoori Norinaga.

Examination of Difficult Words, 難語考, by Tachibana Moribe.

Examination of the Synonyms for Japan, 国号考, by Motoori Norinaga.

Explanation of Japanese Names, 日本釈名, by Kaibara Tokushin.

Explanation of the Songs in the Chronicles of Japan, 日本紀歌猶解, by Arakida no Hisaoi.

Exposition of the Ancient Histories, 古史伝, by Hirata Atsutane.

Exposition of the Foreign Notices of Japan, 異稱日本伝, by Matsushita Ken-rin.

Exposition of the Records of Ancient Matters (usually quoted simply as Norinaga's *Commentary*), 古事記伝, by Motoori Norinaga.

Exposition of the Records of Ancient Matters Criticized (usually quoted as *Moribe's Critique on Norinaga's Commentary*), 難古事記伝, by Tachibana Moribe.

Gleanings from Ancient Story, 古語拾遺, by Inbe no Hironari.

Izu-no-chi-waki, 稜威道別, by Tachibana Moribe.

Izu-no-koto-waki, 稜威言別, by Tachibana Moribe.

Inquiry into the Signification of the Names of All the Provinces (MS.), 諸国名義考, by Fujiwara Hikomaro.

Inquiry into the True Chronology, 真暦考, by Motoori Norinaga.

Japanese Words Classified and Explained, 和名類聚鈔, by Minamoto No Shitagō

Ko-Shi Tsu, 古史通, by Arai Hakuseki.

Kō-Gan Shō (MS.), 厚顔抄, by Kei-Chū.

Perpetual Commentary on the Chronicles of Japan (usually quoted as Tanikawa Kotosuga's *Commentary*), 日本書記通證, by Tanikawa Kotosuga.

Records of Ancient Matters (often quoted simply as the *Records*), 古事記, by Futo no Yasumaro.

Records of Ancient Matters in the Divine Character, 神字古事記, by Fujiwara no Masaoki.

Records of Ancient Matters in the Syllabic Character, 名古事記, by Sakata no Kaneyasu.

Records of Ancient Matters Revised, 校正古事記, Anonymous.

Records of Ancient Matters With Marginal Notes (usually quoted as "the Edition of 1687"), 鼇頭古事記, by Deguchi Nobuyoshi.
Records of Ancient Matters With the Ancient Reading, 古訓古事記, by Nagase no Masachi (published with Norinaga's sanction).
Records of Ancient Matters with Marginal Readings, 標註古事記, by Murakami Tadayoshi.
Ritual of the General Purification, 大祓詞, Authorship Uncertain.
Shinto Discussed Afresh, 神道新論, by Takahashi Gorō.
Sources of the Ancient Histories, 古史徵, by Hirata Atsutane.
Tale of a Bamboo-Cutter, 竹取物語, Authorship Uncertain.
Tama-Katsuma, 玉勝間, by Motoori Norinaga.
Tokiwa-Gusa (the full title is *Jin-dai sei-go tokiwa-gusa),* 常盤草 (神代正語常盤草), Hosoda Tominobu.
Topography of Yamashiro, 山城風土記, Authorship Uncertain.
Tō-Ga (MS.), 東雅, by Arai Hakuseki.
Wa-Kun Shiori, 和訓菜, by Tanikawa Kotosuga.
Yamato Tales, 大和物語, Authorship Uncertain.

Besides these, two or three standard Chinese works are referred to, such as the *I jing* or *Book of Changes* (易経), and the *Shanhai jing* or *Mountain and Sea Classic* (山海経); but they are very few, and so easily recognized that it were unnecessary to enumerate them. All Japanese words properly so called are transliterated according to Mr. Satow's "Orthographic System," which, while representing the native spelling, does not in their case differ very greatly from the modern pronunciation. [These have been updated to the Hepburn System. —M.F.] In the case of Sinico-Japanese words, where the divergence between the "Orthographic" spelling and the pronunciation is often considerable, a phonetic spelling has been preferred. With but two or three exceptions, which have been specially noted, Sinico-Japanese words are found only in proper names mentioned in the Preface and in the translator's Introduction, Footnotes, and Sectional Headings. The few Chinese words that occur in the Introduction and Notes are transliterated according to the method introduced by Sir Thomas Wade, and now so widely used by students of Chinese. [These have been updated to the Pinyin System. —M.F.]

Kojiki

RECORDS OF ANCIENT MATTERS

Preface[1]

I[2] Yasumaro[3] say:[4]

Now when chaos had begun to condense, but force and form were not yet manifest, and there was nought named, nought done, who could know its shape?[5] Nevertheless[6] Heaven and Earth first parted, and the Three Deities performed the commencement of creation; the Passive and Active Essences then developed, and the Two Spirits became the ancestors of all things.[A] Therefore[7] did he enter obscurity and emerge into light, and the Sun and Moon were revealed by the washing of his eyes; he floated on and plunged into the sea-water, and Heavenly and Earthly Deities appeared through the ablutions of his person?[B] So in the dimness of the great commencement, we, by relying on the original teaching, learn the time of the conception of the earth and of the birth of islands; in the remoteness of the original beginning, we, by trusting the former sages, perceive the era of the genesis of Deities and of the establishment of men.[8] Truly do we know that a mirror was hung up, that jewels were spat out, and that then a Hundred Kings succeeded each other; that a blade was bitten, and a serpent cut in pieces, so that a Myriad Deities did flourish.[C][9] By deliberations in the

---

[A]This sentence summarizes the first eight Sections of the text of the *Records*. The "three Deities" are the Deity Master-of-the-August-Center-of-Heaven, the High-August-Producing-Wondrous-Deity, and the Divine-Producing-Wondrous-Deity (see Vol. 1, Sect. 1, Notes b, c, d and 42). The two Spirits representing the "Passive and Active Elements" are the creatrix and creator Izanami and Izanagi (the "Female-Who-Invites" and the "Male-Who-Invites,"—see Vol. 1, Sect. 2, Notes i and 52), the procreation by whom of the islands of the Japanese archipelago and of a large number of gods and goddesses forms the subject of Sections 3–7.

[B]This sentence alludes to Izanagi's visit to Hades, and to the purification of his person on his return to the Upper World (see Sects. 9 and 10). It also refers to the birth of the Sun-Goddess and of the Moon-God from his left and from his right eye respectively, and to that of a large number of lesser gods and goddesses, who were produced from every article of his wearing apparel and from every part of his person on the occasion of his performing those ablutions (see Sect. 10).

[C]The mirror here mentioned is that by means of which the Sun-Goddess was

Tranquil River the Empire was pacified; by discussions on the Little Shore the land was purified.[A] Wherefore His Augustness Ho-no-ni-nigi[B] first descended to the Peak of Takachi,[C10] and the Heavenly Sovereign Kamu-Yamato[D] did traverse the Island of the Dragonfly.[E11] A weird[12] bear put forth its claws, and a heavenly saber was obtained at Takakura.[F13] They with tails obstructed the path, and a great crow guided him to Yoshino.[G] Dancing in rows they destroyed[14] the brigands, and listening to a song they vanquished the foemen.[H15] Being instructed in a dream, he was reverent to the Heavenly and Earthly Deities, and was therefore styled the Wise Monarch;[I16] having gazed

allured out of the cave (see Sect. 16); the jewels are those which Susa-no-o (the "Impetuous Male Deity") begged of his sister the Sun-Goddess, and crunched into fragments (see Sect. 8); the blade that was bitten to pieces by the Sun-Goddess figures in the same legend; the serpent is that slain by Susa-no-o after his banishment from Heaven (see Sect. 18); the "Myriad Deities" are supposed by Norinaga to be this same god's numerous descendants (see Sect. 20), who ruled in Izumo.

[A] For the Tranquil River of Heaven, in whose stony bed the gods were wont to meet in council, see Vol. 1, Note 217. The divine deliberations here referred to are those which resulted in the investiture of the sovereignty of Japan in the grandson of the Sun-Goddess (see Sects. 30–33). The "discussions on the Little Shore" allude to the parleys on the beach of Inasa in Izumo which preceded the abdication of the Deity who had held sway over that part of country prior to the descent of the Sun-Goddess' grandson (see Sect. 32).

[B] The abbreviated form of the name of the Sun-Goddess's grandson (see Vol. 1, Notes 566 and 571).

[C] *I.e.*, Mount Takachiho (see Vol. 1, Note 594).

[D] *I.e.*, the first "human emperor" Jin-mu, whose full native Japanese name is Kamu-Yamato-Iware-Biko. For the account of his reign see Sects. 44–52.

[E] *I.e.*, Japan.

[F] For the mention of the bear, whose appearance caused the Emperor Jin-mu and his army to faint away, see commencement of Sect. 45.

[G] For the gods with tails who met and conversed with the Emperor Jin-mu in Yamato, see the latter part of Sect. 46, a perusal of which will however show that the phrase "obstructed the path" which is here used of them, is not exactly applicable. The miraculous crow, which was sent down from Heaven to assist Jin-mu in his conquests, is mentioned at the commencement of the same Section and again at the commencement of Sect. 47. For Yoshino see Vol. 2, Note 56.

[H] The reference is to the song which Jin-mu sang as a signal to his followers to destroy the "earth-spiders" (see Sect. 48), and perhaps also to the songs in Sect. 49.

[I] "The Emperor Su-jin" must be mentally supplied as the logical subject of this clause. For the story of his dream see Sect. 54, and for the origin of the laudatory

on the smoke, he was benevolent to the black-haired people, and is therefore remembered as the Emperor-Sage.[A] Determining the frontiers and civilizing the country, he issued laws from the Nearer Ōmi;[B] reforming the surnames and selecting the gentile names, he held sway at the Further Asuka.[C] Though each differed in caution and in ardor, though all were unlike in accomplishments and in intrinsic worth, yet was there none who did not by contemplating antiquity correct manners that had fallen to ruin, and by illumining modern times repair laws that were approaching dissolution.[17]

In the august reign of the Heavenly Sovereign who governed the Eight Great Islands from the Great Palace of Kiyomihara at Asuka,[D18] the Hidden Dragon put on perfection, the Reiterated[19] Thunder came at the appointed moment. Having heard a song in a dream, he felt that he should continue the succession; having reached the water at night, he knew that he should receive the inheritance. Nevertheless Heaven's time was not yet, and he escaped like the cicada to the Southern Mountains; both men and matters were favorable, and he marched like the tiger to the Eastern Land. Suddenly riding in the Imperial Palanquin, he forced his way across mountains and rivers: the Six Divisions rolled like thunder, the Three Hosts sped like lightning. The erect spears lifted up their might, and the bold warriors arose like smoke: the

---

designation here mentioned see the end of Sect. 57, which is however obscure.

[A] "The Emperor Nin-toku" must be supplied as the logical subject of this clause. The allusion to the smoke and the laudatory designation here mentioned will be understood by reference to Sect. 121. The "black-haired people" is a common Chinese phrase for the peasantry or the people in general.

[B] The Emperor Sei-mu" must be supplied as the logical subject of this clause. His labors are briefly recapitulated in Sect. 94. For the province called Nearer Ōmi (*Chika-tsu-Ōmi*) see Vol. 1, Note 461. Its name is here rhythmically balanced against "Further Asuka" in the following clause.

[C] "The Emperor Ingyō must be supplied as the logical subject of this sentence. This Sovereign's rectification of the names forms the subject of Sect. 139. For Further Asuka (*Tō-tsu-Asuka*) see Vol. 3, Notes 145 and 147.

[D] Viz., the Emperor Ten-mu, whose struggle for the crown in the latter part of the seventh century of our era against the contending claims of Prince Ōtomo is related at great length in the pages of the *Chronicles*, though naturally beyond the scope of these *Records*, which close in 628 CE. The "Eight Great Islands" is one of the synonyms of Japan (see Vol. 1, Note 92).

crimson flags glistened among the weapons, and the ill-omened crew were shattered like tiles. Or ere a day[20] had elapsed, the evil influences were purified: forthwith were the cattle let loose and the horses given repose, as with shouts of victory they returned to the Flowery Summer; the flags were rolled up and the javelins put away, as with dances and chants they came to rest in the capital city. The year was that of the Cock, and it was in the Second Moon.[21] At the Great Palace of Kiyomihara did he ascend to the Heavenly seat: in morality he outstripped the Yellow Emperor, in virtue he surpassed King Wu of Zhou. Having grasped the celestial seals, he was paramount over the Six Cardinal Points; having obtained the heavenly supremacy, he annexed the Eight Wildernesses. He held the mean between the Two Essences,[22] and regulated the order of the Five Elements. He established divine reason wherewith to advance good customs; he disseminated brilliant usages wherewith to make the land great. Moreover the ocean of his wisdom, in its vastness, profoundly investigated the highest antiquity; the mirror of his heart, in its[23] fervor, clearly observed former ages.

Hereupon the Heavenly Sovereign commanded, saying: "I hear that the chronicles of the emperors and likewise the original words in the possession of the various families deviate from exact truth, and are mostly amplified by empty falsehoods. If at the present time these imperfections be not amended, ere many years shall have elapsed, the purport of this, the great basis[24] of the country, the grand foundation of the monarchy, will be destroyed. So now I desire to have the chronicles of the emperors selected and recorded, and the old words examined and ascertained, falsehoods being erased and truth determined in order to transmit [the latter] to after ages."[25] At that time there was a retainer whose surname was Hieda and his personal name Are. He was twenty-eight years old, and of so intelligent a disposition that he could repeat with his mouth whatever met his eyes, and record in his heart whatever struck his ears.[26] Forthwith Are was commanded to learn by heart the genealogies of the emperors, and likewise the words of former ages. Nevertheless time elapsed and the age changed,[A] and

[A] *I.e.*, there was a new reign. —W.G.A.

the thing was not yet carried out.[A]

Prostrate I consider how Her Majesty the Empress, having obtained Unity, illumines the empire—being versed in the Triad, nourishes the people.[27] Ruling from the Purple Palace, Her virtue reaches to the utmost limits of the horses' hoof-marks: dwelling amid the Somber Retinue, Her influence illumines the furthest distance attained to by vessels' prows. The sun rises, and the brightness is increased; the clouds disperse, neither is there smoke. Never cease the historiographers from recording the good omens of connected stalks and double rice-ears; never for a single moon is the treasury without the tribute of continuous beacon-fires and repeated interpretations.[28] In fame She must be pronounced superior to Yu the Great, in virtue more eminent than Tang of Shang.[B29] Hereupon,[30] regretting the errors in the old words, and wishing to correct the misstatements in the former chronicles, She, on the eighteenth day of the ninth moon of the fourth year of Wa-dō,[C] commanded me Yasumaro to select and record the old words learnt by heart by Hieda no Are according to the Imperial Decree, and dutifully to lift them up to Her.[31]

In reverent obedience to the contents of the Decree, I have made a careful choice. But in high antiquity both speech and thought were so simple, that it would be difficult to arrange phrases and compose periods in the characters.[32] To relate everything in ideographic transcription would entail an inadequate expression of the meaning; to write altogether according to the phonetic method would make the story of events unduly lengthy.[33] For this reason have I sometimes in the same sentence used the phonetic and ideographic systems conjointly, and have sometimes in one matter used the ideographic record exclusively. Moreover where the drift of the words was obscure, I have

---

[A] *I.e.*, the Emperor Ten-mu died before the plan of the compilation of these Records had been carried into execution, viz., it may be presumed, before a selection from the various original documents committed to memory by Are had been reduced to writing.

[B] In the above four sentences the compiler expresses his respectful admiration of the Empress Gen-mei, who was on the throne at the time when he wrote, and tells us how wide was her rule and how prosperous her reign.

[C] *I.e.*, 3rd November, 711 CE. Wa-dō (和銅) is the name of a Japanese "year-period" which lasted from 708 to 714 CE. [708–715 CE—M.F.].

by comments elucidated their signification; but need it be said that I have nowhere commented on what was easy?[34] Again, in such cases as calling the surname 日下 Kusaka, and the personal name written with the character 帯 *Tarashi*, I have followed usage without alteration.[35] Altogether the things recorded commence with the separation of Heaven and Earth, and conclude with the august reign at Oharida.[A] So from the Deity Master-of-the-August-Centre-of-Heaven down to His Augustness Prince-Wave-Limit-Cormorant-Thatch-Meeting-Incompletely makes the First Volume; from the Heavenly Sovereign Kamu-Yamato-Iware-Biko down to the august reign of Homuda makes the Second Volume; from the Emperor Ō-Sazaki down to the great palace of Oharida makes the Third Volume.[36] Altogether I have written Three Volumes, which I reverently and respectfully present.[37] I Yasumaro, with true trembling and true fear, bow my head, bow my head.

Reverently presented by the Court Noble[38] Futo no Yasumaro, an Officer of the Upper Division of the First Class of the Fifth Rank and of the Fifth Order of Merit, on the 28th day of the first moon of the fifth year of Wa-dō.[B]

[A] *I.e.*, commence with the creation, and end with the death of the Empress Sui-ko (628 CE), who resided at Oharida.

[B] *i.e.*, 10th March, 712 CE.

Vol. I.[1]

SECT. 1—THE BEGINNING OF HEAVEN AND EARTH

The names of the Deities[2] that were born[3] in the Plain of High Heaven[A] when the Heaven and Earth began were:

the Deity Master-of-the-August-Center-of-Heaven,[B]

next the High-August-Producing-Wondrous-Deity,[C4]

next the Divine-Producing-Wondrous-Deity.[D]

These three Deities were all Deities born alone, and hid their persons.[E]

The names of the Deities that were born next from a thing that sprouted up like unto a reed-shoot when the earth,[5] young and like unto floating oil, drifted about medusa-like, were:

the Pleasant-Reed-Shoot-Prince-Elder -Deity,[F6]

next the Heavenly-Eternally-Standing-Deity.[G7]

These two Deities were likewise born alone, and hid their persons.

The five Deities in the above list are separate Heavenly Deities.[H8]

[A] In Japanese *Takama-no-hara.*

[B] *Ame-no-mi-naka-nushi-no-kami.*

[C] *Taka-mi-musu-bi-no-kami.*

[D] *Kami-musu-bi-no-kami.* This name reappears in later Sections under the lengthened form of *Kami-musu-bi-mi-oya-no-mikoto*, i.e., His Augustness the Deity-Producing-Wondrous-August-Ancestor, and also in abbreviated forms.

[E] *I.e.,* they all came into existence without being procreated in the manner usual with both gods and men, and afterwards disappeared, *i.e.,* died.

[F] *Umashi-ashi-kabi-hiko-ji-no-kami.*

[G] Or, the Deity-Standing-Eternally-in-Heaven, *Ame-no-toko-tachi-no-kami.*

[H] This is a note in the original, where such notes are indented, as has also been done in the translation.

SECT. 2—THE SEVEN DIVINE GENERATIONS

The names of the Deities that were born next were:

the Earthly-Eternally-Standing-Deity,[A]

next the Luxuriant-Integrating-Master-Deity.[B9]

These two Deities were likewise Deities born alone, and hid their persons.

The names of the Deities that were born next were:

the Deity Mud-Earth-Lord,

next his younger sister the Deity Mud-Earth-Lady[C10]

next the Germ-Integrating-Deity,

next his younger sister[D] the Life-Integrating-Deity[E11]

next the Deity Elder-of-the-Great-Place,

next his younger sister the Deity Elder-Lady-of-the-Great-Place[F]

next the Deity Perfect-Exterior,[G]

next his younger sister the Deity Oh-Awful-Lady;[H12]

next the Deity the Male-Who-Invites,[13]

next his younger sister the Deity the Female-Who-Invites.[I14]

From the Earthly-Eternally-Standing Deity down to the Deity the Female-Who-Invites in the previous list are what are termed the Seven Divine Generations. (The two solitary Deities above [-mentioned] are each called one generation. Of the succeeding ten Deities each pair of Deities is called a generation.)

SECT. 3—THE ISLAND OF ONOGORO

Hereupon all the Heavenly Deities commanded the two Deities His Augustness[15] the Male-Who-Invites and Her Augustness the

[A] Or, the Deity-Standing-Eternally-on-Earth, *Kuni-no-toko-tachi-no-kami. Cf.* Vol. 1, Sect. 1, Notes g and 45.

[B] *Toyo-kumo-nu-no-kami.*

[C] *U-hiji-ni-no-kami* and *Su-hiji-ni-no-kami.*

[D] Or young woman.—W.G.A. [Or wife.—M.F.]

[E] "*Tsunu-gui-no-kami* and *Iku-gui-no-kami.*"

[F] *Ō-to-no-ji-no-kami* and *Ō-to-no-be-no-kami.*

[G] *Omo-daru-no-kami.* We might also render *omo-daru* by "perfect-face," *i.e.*, "perfectly beautiful."

[H] *Aya-kashiko-ne-no-kami.* For "awful" we might substitute "venerable."

[I] *Izana-gi-no-kami* and *Izana-mi-no-kami.*

Female-Who-Invites, ordering them to "make, consolidate, and give birth to this drifting land." Granting to them a heavenly jeweled spear,[16] they [thus] deigned to charge them. So the two Deities, standing upon the Floating Bridge of Heaven,[A17] pushed down the jeweled spear and stirred with it, whereupon, when they had stirred the brine till it went curdle-curdle,[B18] and drew [the spear] up, the brine that dripped down from the end of the spear was piled up and became an island. This is the Island of Onogoro.[C]

SECT. 4—COURTSHIP OF THE DEITIES THE MALE-WHO-INVITES AND THE FEMALE-WHO-INVITES

Having descended from Heaven onto this island, they saw to the erection[19] of an heavenly august pillar, they saw to the erection of a hall of eight fathoms.[20] Then he [His Augustness the Male-Who-Invites] asked his younger sister Her Augustness the Female-Who-Invites, "In what manner did your body come to be?"

She responded saying, "My body springing forth, grew up, yet there is one part that has not wholly grown."

Then said His Augustness the Male-Who-Invites, "My body springing forth, grew up, yet there is one part that has grown to excess. Therefore, will it be good for me to insert this part of my body that has grown to excess in the part of your body that has not grown continuously, and procreate the earth?"

Her Augustness the Female-Who-Invites responded saying, "It will be good."

Then said His Augustness the Male-Who-Invites, "That being the case, you and I, circling this heavenly august pillar and meeting each other,[21] will make an august union of august [i.e. private] parts.[22]

Having made this agreement, [His Augustness the Male-Who-Invites] said, "You go around on the right and meet, and I will meet from the left."

When they went around in absolute agreement, Her Augustness

[A] *Ama-no-uki-hashi* or *Ame-no-uki-hashi.*

[B] *I.e.* "till it became thick and glutinous."

[C] *I.e.*, "Self-Curdling," "Self-Condensed." It is supposed to have been one of the islets off the coast of the larger island of Awaji.

the Female-Who-Invites said first, "Ah! Fair and lovely youth!"

Then His Augustness the Male-Who-Invites said, "Ah! Fair and lovely maiden!" After each of them had finished making their speech, [His Augustness the Male-Who-Invites] spoke to his sister, saying, "It is not proper for the woman to speak first." Nevertheless, they began [the act of procreation] in the chamber, and gave birth to a son [named] Leech[23] [actually similar to a leech].[24] This child they placed in a boat of reeds, and let it float away. Next they gave birth to the Island of Awa.[25] This likewise is not reckoned among their children.[26]

SECT. 5—BIRTH OF THE EIGHT GREAT ISLANDS

Hereupon the two Deities took counsel, saying: "The children to whom we have now given birth are not good. It will be best to announce this in the august place[27] of the Heavenly Deities." They ascended forthwith to Heaven and enquired of Their Augustnesses the Heavenly Deities. Then the Heavenly Deities commanded and found out by grand divination,[28] and ordered them, saying: "They were not good because the woman spoke first. Descend back again and amend your words."

So thereupon descending back, they again went round the heavenly august pillar as before. Thereupon his Augustness the Male-Who-Invites spoke first: "Ah! what a fair and lovely maiden!" Afterwards his younger sister Her Augustness the Female-Who-Invites spoke: "Ah! what a fair and lovely youth!" In this manner, they finished making their speeches, augustly united, and gave birth[29] to a child, the Island of Awaji, Ho-no-sa-wake.[30]

Next they gave birth to the Island of Futa-na in Iyo.[31] This island has one body and four faces, and each face has a name. So the Land of Iyo is called Lovely-Princess;[32] the Land of Sanuki[33] is called Prince-Good-Boiled-Rice;[34] the Land of Awa is called the Princess-of-Great-Food;[35] the Land of Tosa[36] is called Brave-Good-Youth.[37]

Next they gave birth to the Islands of Mitsu-go[38] near Oki.[39] another name for which [islands] is Heavenly-Great-Heart-Youth.[40]

Next they gave birth to the island of Tsukushi.[41] This island likewise has one body and four faces,[42] and each face has a name. So the Land of Tsukushi is called White-Sun-Youth;[43] the Land of Toyo[44] is called Luxuriant-Sun-Youth;[45] the Land of Hi is called Brave-Sun-Confronting-Luxuriant-Wondrous-Lord-Youth;[46] the Land of Kumaso is called Brave-Sun-Youth.[47]

Next they gave birth to the Island of Iki,[48] another name for which is Heaven's One-Pillar.[49] Next they gave birth to the Island of Tsu,[50] another name for which is Heavenly-Hand-net-Good-Princess.[51]

Next they gave birth to the Island of Sado.[52]

Next they gave birth to Great-Yamato-the-Luxuriant-Island-of-the-Dragonfly,[53] another name for which is Heavenly-August-Sky-Luxuriant-Dragonfly-Lord-Youth. The name of "Land-of-the-Eight-Great-Islands"[54] therefore originated in these eight islands having been born first.

After that, when they had returned[55] they gave birth to the Island of Ko [-jima][56] in Kibi,[57] another name for which [island] is Brave-Sun-Direction-Youth.

Next they gave birth to the Island of Azuki,[58] another name for which is Ō-Nu-De-Hime.

Next they gave birth to the Island of Oho [-shima],[59] another name for which is Ō-Tamaru-Wake.

Next they gave birth to the Island of Hime,[60] another name for which is Heaven's-One-Root.

Next they gave birth to the Island of Chika,[61] another name for which is Heavenly-Great-Male.

Next they gave birth to the Island[s] of Futa-go,[62] another name for which is Heaven's-Two-Houses. (Six islands in all from the Island of Ko in Kibi to the Island of Heaven's-Two-Houses.)

SECT. 6—BIRTH OF THE VARIOUS DEITIES

When they had finished giving birth to countries, they began afresh giving birth to Deities. So the name of the Deity they gave birth to was:

the Deity Great-Male-of-the-Great-Thing;[63]
next they gave birth to the Deity Rock-Earth-prince;[64]
next they gave birth to the Deity Rock-Nest-Princess;[65]
next they gave birth to the Deity Great-Door-Sun-Youth[66]
next they gave birth to the Deity Heavenly-Blowing- Male;[67]
next they gave birth to the Deity Great-House-Prince;[68]
next they gave birth to the Deity Youth-of-the-Wind-Breath-the-

Great-Male;[69]

next they gave birth to the Sea-Deity, whose name is the Deity Great-Ocean-Possessor;[70]

next they gave birth to the Deity of the Water-Gates,[A] whose name is the Deity Prince-of-Swift-Autumn;[71]

next they gave birth to his younger sister the Deity Princess-of-Swift-Autumn. (Ten Deities in all from the Deity Great-Male-of-the-Great-Thing to the Deity Princess-of-Autumn.[72])

The names of the Deities given birth to by these two Deities Prince-of-Swift-Autumn and Princess-of-Swift-Autumn from their separate dominions of river and sea were:

the Deity Foam-Calm;[73]

next the Deity Foam-Waves;

next the Deity Bubble-Calm;

next the Deity Bubble-Waves;

next the Deity Heavenly-Water-Divider;[74]

next the Deity Earthly-Water-Divider;

next the Deity Heavenly-Water-Drawing-Gourd-Possessor;[75]

next the Deity Earthly-Water-Drawing-Gourd-Possessor. (Eight Deities in all from the Deity Foam-Prince to the Deity Earthly-Water-Drawing-Gourd-Possessor.)

Next they gave birth to the Deity of Wind, whose name is the Deity Prince-of-Long-Wind.[76]

Next they gave birth to the Deity of Trees, whose name is Deity Stem-Elder,[77]

next they gave birth to the Deity of Mountains, whose name is the Deity Great-Mountain-Possessor.[78]

Next they gave birth to the Deity of Moors, whose name is the Deity Thatch-Moor-Princess,[79] another name for whom is the Deity Moor-Elder. (Four Deities in all from the Deity Prince-of-Long-Wind to Moor-Elder.)

The names of the Deities given birth to by these two Deities, the Deity Great-Mountain-Possessor and the Deity Moor-Elder from their separate dominions of mountain and moor were:

[A] I.e., river-mouths, estuaries, or ports. In the original *Minato-no-kami.*

the Deity Heavenly-Elder-of-the-Passes,
next the Deity Earthly-Elder-of-the-Passes;[80]
next the Deity Heavenly-Pass-Boundary,
next the Deity Earthly-Pass- Boundary;[81]
next the Deity Heavenly-Dark-Door,
next the Deity Earthly-Dark-Door;[82]
next the Deity Great-Vale-Prince, next the Deity Great-Vale-Princess.[83] (Eight Deities in all from the Deity Heavenly-Elder-of-the-Passes to the Deity Great-Vale-Princess.)

The name of the Deity they[84] next gave birth to was the Deity Bird's-Rock-Camphor-tree-Boat,[85] another name for whom is the Heavenly-Bird-Boat.

Next they gave birth to the Deity Princess-of-Great-Food.[86]

Next they gave birth to the Fire-Burning-Swift-Male-Deity,[87] another name for whom is the Deity Fire-Shining-Prince, and another name is the Deity Fire-Shining-Elder.

SECT. 7—RETIREMENT OF HER AUGUSTNESS THE PRINCESS-WHO-INVITES

Through giving birth to this child her august private parts were burnt, and she sickened and lay down.[A]

The names of the Deities born from her vomit were the Deity Metal-Mountain-Prince and next the Deity Metal-Mountain-princess.[88]

The names of the Deities that were born from her feces were the Deity Clay-Viscid-Prince and next the Deity Clay-Viscid-Princess.[89]

The names of the Deities that were next born from her urine were the Deity Mitsuhanome[90] and next the Young-Wondrous-Producing-Deity.[91] The child of this Deity was called the Deity Luxuriant-Food-Princess.[92]

So the Deity the Female-Who-Invites, through giving birth to the Deity-of-Fire, at length divinely retired.[B] (Eight Deities in all from

[A] "Lying down" (*koyasu*) is a term often used in the Archaic language in the sense of "dying." But here it must be taken literally, the death ("divine retirement") of the goddess being narrated a few lines further on.

[B] *I.e.*, "died."

the Heavenly-Bird-Boat to the Deity Luxuriant-Food-Princess.[A])

The total number of islands given birth to jointly by the two Deities the Male-Who-Invites and the Female-Who-Invites was fourteen, and of Deities thirty-five. (These are such as were given birth to before the Deity the Princess-Who-Invites divinely retired. Only the Island of Onogoro was not given birth to[B] and moreover the Leech-Child[C] and the Island of Awa are not reckoned among the children.)

So then His Augustness the Male-Who-Invites said: "Oh! Thine Augustness my lovely younger sister! Oh! that I should have exchanged thee for this single child!"[93] And as he crept round her august pillow, and as he crept round her august feet and wept, there was born[94] from his august tears the Deity that dwells at Konomoto near Uneo on Mount Kagu,[95] and whose name is the Crying-Weeping-Female-Deity.[96] So he buried the divinely retired[D] Deity the Female-Who-Invites on Mount Hiba[97] at the boundary of the Land of Izumo[98] and the Land of Hahaki.[99]

SECT. 8—THE SLAYING OF THE FIRE-DEITY

Then His Augustness the Male-Who-Invites, drawing the ten-grasp[E] saber[100] that was augustly girded on him, cut off the head of his child the Deity Shining-Elder. Hereupon the names of the Deities that were born from the blood that stuck to the point of the august sword and bespattered the multitudinous rock-masses were:

The Deity Rock-Splitter,[101]
next the Deity Root-Splitter,

[A]There is here an error in the computation, as *nine* Deities are mentioned. The total of thirty-five Deities given immediately below is still more erroneous, as no less than *forty* are named in the preceding passage. Norinaga makes an ingenious effort to reconcile arithmetic and revelation by supposing the five pairs of brothers and sisters with parallel names to have been considered as each forming but one deity.

[B]See Sect. 3. This island was not *born*, but arose spontaneously from drops of brine.

[C]*Hiru-go*. See the latter part of Sect. 4 for these two names. Hiru-go was not counted among the children of these Deities for the reason that the latter abandoned him as soon as he was born, he being a failure. The reason for omitting Awa from the computation is not so clear.

[D]*I.e.*, dead.

[E]Or ten spans long.—W.G.A.

next the Rock-Possessing-Male-Deity.[102]

The names of the Deities that were next born from the blood that stuck to the upper part[103] of the august sword and again bespattered the multitudinous rock-masses were:

the Awfully-Swift-Deity,[104]

next the Fire-Swift-Deity,[105]

next the Brave-Awful-Possessing-Male-Deity,[106] another name for whom is the Brave-Snapping-Deity,[107] and another name is the Luxuriant-Snapping-Deity.

The names of the Deities that were next born from the blood that collected on the hilt of the august sword and leaked out between his fingers were:

the Deity *Kura-okami* and next

the Deity *Kura-mitsuha.*[108]

All the eight Deities in the above list, from the Deity Rock-Splitter to the Deity *Kura-mitsuha,* are Deities that were born from the august sword.

The name of the Deity that was born from the head of the Deity Shining-Elder who had been slain was the Deity Possessor-of-the-True-Pass-Mountains.[109]

The name of the Deity that was next born from his chest was the Deity Possessor-of-Descent-Mountains.[110]

The name of the Deity that was next born from his belly was the Deity Possessor-of-the-Innermost Mountains.[111]

The name of the Deity that was next born from his private parts was the Deity Possessor-of-the-Dark-Mountains.

The name of the Deity that was next born from his left hand[A] was the Deity Possessor-of-the-Dense[ly-Wooded]-Mountains.

The name of the Deity that was next born from his right hand was the Deity Possessor-of-the-Outlying-Mountains.

The name of the Deity that was next born from his left foot[B] was the Deity Possessor-of-the-Moorland-Mountains.

The name of the Deity that was next born from his right foot was

---

[A] Or "arm."

[B] Or "leg."

the Deity Possessor-of-the-Outer-Mountains. (Eight Deities in all from the Deity Possessor-of-the-True-Pass-Mountains to the Deity Possessor-of-the-Outer-Mountains.)

So the name of the sword with which [the Male-Who-Invites] cut off [his son's head] was Heavenly-Point-Blade-Extended, and another name was Majestic-Point-Blade-Extended.[112]

SECT. 9—THE LAND OF HADES

Thereupon [His Augustness the Male-Who-Invites], wishing to meet and see his younger sister Her Augustness the Female-Who-Invites, followed after her to the Land of Hades.[113] So when from the palace she raised the door and came out to meet him,[114] His Augustness the Male-Who-Invites spoke, saying: "Thine Augustness my lovely younger sister! the lands that I and thou made are not yet finished making; so come back!"

Then Her Augustness the Female-Who-Invites answered, saying: "Lamentable indeed that thou camest not sooner! I have eaten of the furnace of Hades.[A][115] Nevertheless, as I reverence[116] the entry here of Thine Augustness my lovely elder brother, I wish to return.[B] Moreover[117] I will discuss it particularly with the Deities of Hades.[118] Look not at me!" Having thus spoken, she went back inside the palace; and as she tarried there very long, he could not wait.

So having taken and broken off one of the end-teeth[119] of the multitudinous and close-toothed comb stuck in the august left bunch [of his hair], he lit one light[120] and went in and looked. Maggots were swarming, and [she was] rotting, and in her head dwelt the Great-Thunder, in her breast dwelt the Fire-Thunder, in her belly dwelt the Black-Thunder, in her private parts dwelt the Cleaving-Thunder, in her left hand[C] dwelt the Young-Thunder, in her right hand dwelt the Earth-Thunder, in her left foot[D] dwelt the Rumbling-Thunder, in her right foot dwelt the Couchant-Thunder;—altogether eight Thunder-Deities had been born and dwelt there.[121]

[A] *I.e.*, "of the food of Hades."

[B] *Q.d.* "with thee to the land of the living."

[C] Or "arm."

[D] Or "leg."

Hereupon His Augustness the Male-Who-Invites, overawed at the sight, fled back, whereupon his younger sister Her Augustness the Female-Who-Invites said: "Thou hast put me to shame," and at once sent the Ugly-Female-of-Hades[122] to pursue him.

So His Augustness the Male-Who-Invites took his black august head-dress[123] and cast it down, and it instantly turned into[124] grapes. While she picked them up and ate them, he fled on; but as she still pursued him, he took and broke the multitudinous and close-toothed comb in the right bunch [of his hair] and cast it down, and it instantly turned into bamboo-sprouts. While she pulled them up and ate them, he fled on. Again later [his younger sister] sent the eight Thunder-Deities with a thousand and five hundred warriors of Hades to pursue him. So he, drawing the ten-grasp saber that was augustly girded on him, fled forward brandishing it in his back hand;[A] and as they still pursued, he took, on reaching the base of the Even Pass of Hades,[125] three peaches that were growing at its base, and waited and smote [his pursuers therewith], so that they all fled back. Then His Augustness the Male-Who-Invites announced to the peaches: "Like as ye have helped me, so must ye help all living people[126] in the Central Land of Reed-Plains[B][127] when "they shall fall into troublous circumstances and be harassed!"—and he gave [to the peaches] the designation of Their Augustnesses Great-Divine-Fruit.[128]

Last of all his younger sister Her Augustness the Princess-Who-Invites came out herself in pursuit. So he drew a thousand-draught rock,[C] and [with it] blocked up the Even Pass of Hades, and placed the rock in the middle; and they stood opposite to one another and exchanged leave-takings;[129] and Her Augustness the Female-Who-Invites said: "My lovely elder brother, thine Augustness! If thou do like this, I will in one day strangle to death a thousand of the folks of thy land."

Then His Augustness the Male-Who-Invites replied: "My lovely younger sister, Thine Augustness! If *thou* do this *I* will in one day set up a thousand and five hundred parturition-houses.[D] In this manner

[A] *I.e.* brandishing it behind him.

[B] *Ashi-hara-no-naka-tsu-kuni*, a common periphrastic designation of Japan.

[C] *I.e.*, a rock which it would take a thousand men to lift.

[D] *I.e.*, "I will cause fifteen hundred women to bear children." (For the custom of

each day a thousand people would surely die, and each day a thousand and five hundred people would surely be born."

So Her Augustness the Female-Who-Invites is called the Great-Deity-of-Hades.[130] Again it is said that, owing to her having pursued and reached [her elder brother], she is called the Road-Reaching-Great-Deity.[131] Again the rock with which he blocked up the Pass of Hades is called the Great-Deity-of-the-Road-Turning-back;[132] and again it is called the Blocking-Great-Deity-of-the-Door-of-Hades.[133] So what was called the Even-Pass-of-Hades is now called the If-uya-Pass[134] in the Land of Izumo.

SECT. 10—THE PURIFICATION OF THE AUGUST PERSON

Therefore the Great Deity the Male-Who-Invites said: "Nay! hideous! I have come to a hideous and polluted land—I have![135] So I will perform the purification of my august person." So he went out to a plain [covered with] *ahagi*[A] at a small river-mouth near Tachibana[136] in Himuka[137] in [the island of] Tsukushi and purified and cleansed himself. So the name of the Deity that was born from the august staff which he threw down was the Deity Thrust-Erect-Come-Not-Place.[138]

The name of the Deity that was born from the august girdle which he next threw down was the Deity Road-Long-Space.[139]

The name of Deity that was born from the august skirt which he next threw down was the Deity Loosen-Put.[140]

The name of the Deity that was born from the august upper garment which he next threw down was the Deity Master-of-Trouble.[141]

The name of the Deity that was born from the august trousers which he next threw down was the Road-Fork Deity.[142]

The name of the Deity that was born from the august hat which he next threw down was the Deity Master-of-the-Open-Mouth.[143]

The names of the Deities that were born from the bracelet of his august left hand[B] which he next threw down were the Deity Off-

---

erecting a separate hut for a woman about to be delivered see Introduction p. 39.)

[A] This botanical name is identified by Arai Hakuseki and Atsutane with the modern *hagi*, or "bushclover" (*Lespedeza* of various species). The received opinion used to be that the *aoki* (*Aucuba Japonica*) was here intended.

[B] Or "arm."

ing-Distant,[144] next the Deity Wash-Prince-of-the-Offing, next the Deity Intermediate-Direction-of-the-Offing.

The names of the Deities that were born from the bracelet of his august right hand which he next threw down were: the Deity Shore-Distant, next the Deity Wash-Prince-of-the-Shore, next the Deity Intermediate-Direction-of-the-Shore.

The twelve Deities mentioned in the foregoing[145] list from the Deity Come-Not-Place down to the Deity Intermediate-Direction-of-the-Shore are Deities that were born from his taking off the things that were on his person.

Thereupon saying: "The water in the upper reach is [too] rapid; the water in the lower reach is [too] sluggish," he went down and plunged in the middle reach; and, as he washed, there was first born the Wondrous-Deity-of-Eighty-Evils, and next the Wondrous-Deity-of-Great-Evils.[146] These two Deities are the Deities that were born from the filth [he contracted] when he went to that polluted, hideous land.[A]

The names of the Deities that were next born to rectify those evils were:

the Divine-Rectifying-Wondrous-Deity,
next the Great-Rectifying-Wondrous-Deity,[147]
next the Female-Deity-Izu.[148]

The names of the Deities that were next born, as he bathed at the bottom of the water, were the Deity Possessor-of-the-Ocean-Bottom,[149] and next His Augustness Elder-Male-of-the Bottom.

The names of the Deities that were born as he bathed in the middle [of the water] were the Deity Possessor-of-the-Ocean-Middle, and next His Augustness Elder-Male-of-the-Middle.

The names of the Deities that were born as he bathed at the top of the water were the Deity Possessor-of-the-Ocean-Surface, and next His Augustness Elder-Male-of-the-Surface.

These three Ocean-Possessing Deities are the Deities held in reverence as their ancestral Deities by the Chiefs of Azumi.[150] So the Chiefs of Azumi are the descendants of His Augustness *Utsushi-hi-ga-na-saku*,[151] a child of these Ocean-Possessing Deities.[152]

[A] Viz. to Hades.

These three Deities His Augustness Elder-Male-of-the-Bottom, His Augustness Elder-Male-of-the-Middle, and His Augustness Elder-Male-of-the-Surface are the three Great Deities of the Inlet of Sumi.[153]

The name of the Deity that was born as he thereupon washed his left august eye was the Heaven-Shining-Great-August-Deity.[A154]

The name of the Deity that was next born as he washed his right august eye was His Augustness Moon-Night-Possessor.[B155]

The name of the Deity that was next born as he washed his august nose was His Brave-Swift-Impetuous-Male-Augustness.[C156]

The fourteen Deities in the foregoing list from the Wondrous-Deity-of-Eighty-Evils down to His Swift-Impetuous-Male-Augustness are Deities born from the bathing of his august person.

SECT. 11—INVESTITURE OF THE THREE DEITIES THE ILLUSTRIOUS AUGUST CHILDREN

At this time His Augustness the Male-Who-Invites greatly rejoiced, saying: "I, begetting child after child, have at my final begetting gotten three illustrious children," [with which words,] at once jingly taking off and shaking the jewel-string[D] forming his august necklace, he bestowed it on the Heaven-Shining-Great-August-Deity, saying: "Do Thine Augustness rule the Plain-of-High-Heaven." With this charge he bestowed it on her. Now the name of this august necklace was the August-Store-house-Shelf-Deity.[157]

Next he said to His Augustness Moon-Night-Possessor: "Do Thine Augustness rule the Dominion of the Night."[158] Thus he charged him.

Next he said to His-Brave-Swift-Impetuous-Male-Augustness: "Do Thine Augustness rule the Sea-Plain."[159]

SECT. 12—THE CRYING AND WEEPING OF HIS IMPETUOUS-MALE-AUGUSTNESS

So while [the other two Deities] each [assumed his and her] rule

[A] *Ama-terasu-ō-mi-kami* 天照大御神.

[B] *Tsuki-yomi-no-kami.*

[C] *Take-haya-susa-no-o-no-mikoto.* [Usually called Susa-no-o.—M.F.]

[D] *I.e.*," the string of jewels." For these so-called "jewels" see Introduction, p. 75.

according to the command with which [their father] had deigned to charge them, His-Swift-Impetuous-Male-Augustness did not [assume the] rule [of] the dominion with which he had been charged, but cried and wept till his eight-grasp beard[160] reached to the pit of his stomach.[A]

The fashion of his weeping was such as by his weeping to wither the green mountains into withered mountains and by his weeping to dry up all the rivers and seas.[161] For this reason the sound of bad Deities was like unto the flies in the fifth moon[B][162] as they all swarmed,[163] and in all things[164] every portent of woe arose.

So the Great August Deity the Male-Who-Invites said to His Swift-Impetuous-Male-Augustness: "How is it that, instead of ruling the land with which I charged thee, thou dost wail and weep?"

He replied, saying: "I[165] wail because I wish to depart to my deceased mother's[166] land, to the Nether Distant Land."[C]

Then the Great August Deity the Male-Who-Invites was very angry and said: "If that be so, thou shalt not dwell in this land,"[167] and forthwith expelled him with a divine expulsion. So the Great Deity the Male-Who-Invites dwells at Taga[168] in Ōmi.[169]

SECT. 13—THE AUGUST OATH

So thereupon His-Swift-Impetuous-Male-Augustness said: "If that be so, I will take leave[170] of the Heaven-Shining-Great-August-Deity, and depart." [With these words] he forthwith went up to Heaven, whereupon all the mountains and rivers shook, and every land and country quaked.

So the Heaven-Shining-Great-August Deity, alarmed at the noise, said: "The reason of the ascent hither of His Augustness my elder brother[171] is surely no good intent.[D] It is only that he wishes to wrest my land from me." And she forthwith, unbinding her august hair, twisted it into august bunches; and both into the left and into the right august bunch, as likewise into her august head-dress and likewise on to her left

---

[A] Lit, "in front of his heart."

[B] *I.e.*, the fifth month.—M.F.

[C] *I.e.*, Hades. The translation follows Norinaga's explanation of the original term *Ne-no-kata-su-kuni*, which is obscure.

[D] Lit. "heart," here and elsewhere.

and her right august arm,[A] she twisted an augustly complete [string] of curved jewels eight feet [long]—of five hundred jewels,[172] and, slinging on her back a quiver holding a thousand [arrows], and adding [thereto][173] a quiver holding five hundred [arrows], she likewise took and slung at her side a mighty and high [-sounding] elbow-pad,[174] and brandished[175] and stuck her bow upright so that the top[176] shook, and she stamped her feet into the hard ground up to her opposing thighs,[B] kicking away [the earth] like rotten snow,[C] and stood valiantly like unto a mighty man, and waiting, asked: "Wherefore ascendest thou hither?"

Then His-Swift-Impetuous-Male-Augustness replied, saying: "I have no evil intent. It is only that when the Great-August Deity [our father] spoke, deigning to inquire the cause of my wailing and weeping, I said: 'I wail because I wish to go to my deceased mother's land,'– whereupon the Great-August Deity said: 'Thou shalt not dwell in this land,' and deigned to expel me with a divine expulsion. It is therefore solely with the thought of taking leave of thee and departing, that I have ascended hither. I have no strange intentions."

Then the Heaven-Shining-Great-August-Deity said: "If that be so, whereby shall I know the sincerity of thine intentions?"

Thereupon His-Swift-Impetuous-Male-Augustness replied, saying: "Let each of us swear,[D177] and produce children."[178] So as they then swore to each other from the opposite banks of the Tranquil River of Heaven,[179] the august names of the Deities that were born from the mist [of her breath] when, having first begged His-Swift-Impetuous-Male-Augustness to hand her the ten-grasp saber which was girded on him and broken it into three fragments, and with the jewels making a jingling sound[180] having brandished and washed[181] them in the True-Pool-Well of Heaven,[182] and having crunchingly crunched them, the Heaven-Shining-Great-August-Deity blew them away, were:

[A] Or "hand."

[B] *I.e.,*" both legs penetrated into the ground up to the thigh," a proof of the vigor with which she used her limbs in stamping.

[C] Lit. "bubble-snow." [Or the foam-like snow?—W.G.A.]

[D] *I.e.*, "pledge our faith," "bind ourselves," in order to show forth the sincerity of our intentions.

Her Augustness Torrent-Mist-Princess,[183] another august name for whom is Her Augustness Princess-of-the-Island-of-the-Offing;

next Her Augustness Lovely-Island-Princess,[184] another august name for whom is Her Augustness Good-Princess;

next Her Augustness Princess-of-the-Torrent.[185]

The august name of the Deity that was born from the mist [of his breath] when, having begged the Heaven-Shining-Great-August-Deity to hand him the augustly complete [string] of curved jewels eight feet [long]—of five hundred jewels—that was twisted in the left august bunch [of her hair], and with the jewels making a jingling sound having brandished and washed them in the True-Pool-Well of Heaven, and having crunchingly crunched them, His-Swift-Impetuous-Male-Augustness blew them away, was His Augustness Truly-Conqueror-I-Conquer-Conquering-Swift-Heavenly-Great-Great-Ears.[186]

The august name of the Deity that was born from the mist [of his breath] when again, having begged her to hand him the jewels that were twisted in the right august bunch [of her hair], and having crunchingly crunched them, he blew them away, was His Augustness Ame-no-ho-hi.[187]

The august name of the Deity that was born from the mist [of his breath] when again, having begged her to hand him the jewels that were twisted in her august headdress, and having crunchingly crunched them, he blew them away, was His Augustness Prince-Lord-of-Heaven.[188]

The august name of the Deity that was born from the mist [of his breath] when again, having begged her to hand him the jewels that were twisted on her left august arm,[A] and having crunchingly crunched them, he blew them away, was His Augustness Prince-Lord-of-Life.[189]

The august name of the Deity that was born from the mist [of his breath] when again, having begged her to hand him the jewels that were twisted on her right august arm, and having crunchingly crunched them, he blew them away, was His-Wondrous-Augustness-of-Kumanu.[190] (Five Deities in all.)

[A] Or "hand."

SECT. 14—THE AUGUST DECLARATION OF THE DIVISION OF THE AUGUST MALE CHILDREN AND THE AUGUST FEMALE CHILDREN

Hereupon the Heavenly Shining-Great-August-Deity said to His-Swift-Impetuous-Male-Augustness: "As for the seed[A] of the five male Deities born last, their birth was from things of mine; so undoubtedly they are my children. As for the seed of the three female Deities born first; their birth was from a thing of thine; so doubtless they are thy children." Thus did she declare the division.

So Her Augustness Torrent-Mist-Princess, the Deity born first, dwells in the Inner temple of Munakata.[191] The next, Her Augustness Lovely-Island-Princess, dwells in the middle temple of Munakata. The next, Her Augustness Princess-of-the-Torrent, dwells in the outer temple[192] of Munakata These three Deities are the three Great Deities[193] held in reverence by the Dukes of Munakata.[194]

So His Augustness Brave-Rustic-Illuminator, child of His Augustness Ame-no-ho-hi, one of the five children born afterwards ([195]this is the ancestor of the Rulers of the Land of Izumo,[196] of the Rulers of the Land of Musashi,[197] of the Rulers of the Upper Land of Unakami,[198] of the Rulers of the Lower Land of Unakami,[199] of the Rulers of the Land of Ijimu,[200] of the Departmental Suzerains of the Island of Tsu[201] and of the Rulers of the Land of Tō-tsu-Ōmi.[202])

The next, His Augustness Prince-Lord-of-Heaven (is the ancestor of the Rulers of the Land of Ōchi-kōchi,[203] of the Chiefs of Nuka-tabe-no-yue,[204] of the Rulers of the Land of Ki,[205] of the Suzerains of Tanaka[206] in Yamato, of the Rulers of the Land of Yamashiro,[207] of the Rulers of the Land of Umaguta,[208] of the Rulers of the Land of Kihe[209] in Michi-no-Shiri,[210] of the Rulers of the Land of Suwa,[211] of the Rulers of Amuchi,[212] in Yamato, of the Departmental Suzerains of Takechi,[213] of the Territorial Lords of Kamō,[214] and of the Rulers of Sakikusabe[215]).

SECT. 15—THE AUGUST RAVAGES OF HIS-IMPETUOUS-MALE-AUGUSTNESS

Then His-Swift-Impetuous-Male-Augustness said to the Heaven-Shining-Great-August-Deity: "Owing to the sincerity of my in-

[A] *I.e.*, the origin.

tentions I have, in begetting children, gotten delicate females. Judging from this,[216] I have undoubtedly gained the victory." With these words, and impetuous with victory, he broke down the divisions of the rice-fields[217] laid out by the Heaven-Shining-Great-August-Deity, filled up the ditches, and moreover strewed excrements[218] in the palace where she partook of the great food.[219]

So, though he did thus, the Heaven-Shining-Great-August-Deity upbraided him not,[220] but said: "What looks like excrements must be something that His Augustness mine elder brother has vomited through drunkenness. Again, as to his breaking down the divisions of the rice-fields and filling up the ditches, it must be because he grudges the land [they occupy[A]] that His Augustness mine elder brother acts thus."

But notwithstanding these apologetic words, he still continued his evil acts, and was more and more [violent]. As the Heaven-Shining-Great-August-Deity sat in her awful[B221] weaving-hall[222] seeing to the weaving of the august garments of the Deities, he broke a hole in the top[223] of the weaving-hall, and through it let fall a heavenly piebald horse which he had flayed with a backward flaying,[C] at whose sight the women weaving the heavenly garments were so much alarmed that they struck their private parts with the opposing [loom—M.F.] rods and died.[224]

SECT. 16—THE DOOR OF THE HEAVENLY ROCK DWELLING

So thereupon the Heaven-Shining-Great-August-Deity, terrified at the sight, closed [behind her] the door of the Heavenly Rock-Dwelling,[225] made it fast,[226] and retired. Then the whole Plain of High Heaven was obscured[227] and all the Central Land of Reed-Plains darkened. Owing to this, eternal[228] night prevailed. Hereupon the voices of the myriad[229] Deities were like unto the flies in the fifth moon as they swarm and a myriad portents of woe arose.

[A] *I.e.*, he thinks that none of the land should be wasted in ditches and embankments, but should all be devoted to the production of food.

[B] The character used is 忌, "to shun," which in Japanese has approximately the meaning of "sacred."

[C] *I.e.*, it is supposed, beginning at the tail. That this was considered criminal may be seen by comparing Vol. 2, Note 798.

Therefore did the eight hundred myriad[230] Deities assemble in a divine assembly in the bed[231] of the Tranquil River of Heaven, and bid the Deity Thought-Includer,[232] child of the High-August-Producing-Wondrous-Deity think of a plan, assembling the long-singing birds of eternal night[A] and making them sing, taking the hard rocks of Heaven from the river-bed of the Tranquil River of Heaven, and taking the iron[233] from the Heavenly Metal-Mountains,[B] calling in the smith Ama-tsu-ma-ra,[234] charging Her Augustness I-shi-ko-ri-do-me[235] to make a mirror, and charging His Augustness Jewel-Ancestor[236] to make an augustly complete [string] of curved jewels eight feet [long]—of five hundred jewels,[237] —and summoning His Augustness Heavenly-Beckoning-Ancestor-Lord[238] and His Augustness Grand-Jewel,[239] and causing them to pull out with a complete pulling the shoulder [-blade] of a true[C] stag from the Heavenly Mount Kagu,[240] and take cherry-bark[241] from the Heavenly Mount Kagu, and perform divination,[242] and pulling up by pulling its roots a true *Cleyera japonica*[D] with five hundred [branches] from the Heavenly Mount Kagu, and taking and putting upon its upper branches the augustly complete [string] of curved jewels eight feet [long]—of five hundred jewels—and taking and tying to the middle branches[243] the mirror eight feet [long],[244] and taking and hanging upon its lower branches the white pacificatory offerings[245] and the blue pacificatory offerings, His Augustness Grand-Jewel taking these divers things and holding them together with the grand august offerings,[246] and His Augustness Heavenly-Beckoning-Ancestor-Lord prayerfully reciting grand liturgies,[247] and the Heavenly Hand-Strength-Male-Deity[248] standing hidden beside the door, and Her Augustness Heavenly-Alarming-Female[249] hanging [round her] the heavenly club moss from the Heavenly Mount Kagu as a sash,[250] and making the heavenly spindle-tree her head-dress,[E] and binding the leaves of the bamboo-grass of the Heav-

[A] *I.e.*, as is generally believed, the barn door fowl.

[B] *I.e.*, the mines. The original expression is *Ame no kana-yama*.

[C] The word "true" (*ma*) here and below is not much more than an honorific.

[D] In Japanese *saka-ki*. It is commonly planted in the precincts of Shintō temples.

[E] *I.e.*, making for himself a head-dress of spindle-tree leaves. [The club-moss seems a more likely material than the spindle tree for a head-dress—*vide* Norinaga. Later

enly Mount Kagu in a posy for her hands, laying[251] a sounding-board[252] before the door of the Heavenly Rock-Dwelling, and stamping till she made it resound and doing as if possessed by a Deity,[253] and pulling out the nipples of her breasts, pushing down her skirt-string all the way up to the private parts.[254] Then the Plain of High Heaven shook, and the eight hundred myriad Deities laughed together.

Hereupon the Heaven-Shining-Great-August-Deity was amazed, and, slightly opening the door of the Heavenly Rock-Dwelling, spoke thus from the inside: "Methought that owing to my retirement the Plain of Heaven would be dark, and likewise the Central Land of Reed-Plains would all be dark: how then is it that the Heavenly-Alarming-Female makes merry, and that likewise the eight hundred myriad Deities all laugh?"

Then the Heavenly-Alarming-Female spoke, saying: "We rejoice and are glad because there is a Deity more illustrious than Thine Augustness." While she was thus speaking, His Augustness Heavenly-Beckoning-Ancestor-Lord and His Augustness Grand-Jewel pushed forward the mirror and respectfully showed it to the Heaven-Shining-Great-August-Deity, whereupon the Heaven-Shining-Great-August-Deity, more and more astonished, gradually came forth from the door and gazed upon it, whereupon the Heavenly-Hand-Strength-Male-Deity, who was standing hidden, took her august hand and drew her out, and then His Augustness Grand-Jewel drew the bottom-tied rope[255] along at her august back, and spoke, saying: "Thou must not go back further in than this!" So when the Heaven-Shining-Great-August-Deity had come forth, both the Plain of High Heaven and the Central-Land-of-Reed-Plains of course again became light.[256]

SECT. 17—THE AUGUST EXPULSION OF HIS-IMPETUOUS-MALE-AUGUSTNESS

Thereupon the eight hundred myriad Deities took counsel together, and imposed on His-Swift-Impetuous-Male-Augustness a fine of a thousand tables,[A][257] and likewise cut his beard, and even caused the

writers mention a *Hikage-Kazura*, never (?) a *Misaki-Kazura*.—W.G.A.]

[A] *I.e.*, "an immense fine."

nails of his fingers and toes to be pulled out, and expelled him with a divine expulsion.

Again he begged food of the Deity Princess-of-Great-Food.[258] Then the Princess-of-Great-Food took out all sorts of dainty things from her nose, her mouth, and even her fundament, and made them up into all sorts [of dishes], which she offered to him. But His-Swift-Impetuous-Male-Augustness watched her proceedings, considered that she was offering up to him filth, and at once killed the Deity Princess-of-Great-Food.

So the things that were born in the body of the Deity who had been killed were [as follows]: in her head were born silkworms, in her two eyes were born rice-seeds, in her two ears was born millet,[259] in her nose were born small beans,[260] in her private parts was born barley,[261] in her fundament were born large beans.[262] So His Augustness the Deity-Producing-Wondrous-Ancestor[263] caused them to be taken and used as seeds.

SECT. 18—THE EIGHT-FORKED SERPENT

So, having been expelled, [His-Swift-Impetuous-Male-Augustness] descended to a place [called] Tori-kami[264] at the head-waters of the River Hi[265] in the Land of Izumo. At this time some chopsticks[A] came floating down the stream. So His-Swift-Impetuous-Male-Augustness, thinking that there must be people at the head-waters of the river, went up it in quest of them, when he came upon an old man and an old woman— two of them—who had a young girl between them,[266] and were weeping. Then he deigned to ask: "Who are ye?"

So the old man replied, saying: "I[267] am an Earthly Deity,[268] child of the Deity Great-Mountain-Possessor.[269] I am called by the name of Foot-Stroking-Elder,[270] my wife is called by the name of Hand-Stroking-Elder, and my daughter is called by the name of Wondrous-Inada-Princess."[271]

Again he asked: "What is the cause of your crying?"

[The old man] answered, saying: "I had originally eight young girls as daughters. But the eight-forked serpent of Koshi[272] has come every

[A]Or in the singular, "a chopstick."

year and devoured [one], and it is now its time to come, wherefore we weep."

Then he asked him: "What is its form like?"

[The old man] answered, saying: "Its eyes are like *akakagachi*,[273] it has one body with eight heads, and eight tails. Moreover on its body grows moss, and also chamaecyparis[A] and cryptomerias. Its length extends over eight valleys and eight hills, and if one look at its belly, it is all constantly bloody and inflamed." (What is here called *akakagachi* is the modern *hōzuki*[B]).

Then His-Swift-Impetuous-Male-Augustness said to the old man: "If this be thy daughter, wilt thou offer her to me?"

He replied, saying: "With reverence,[274] but I know not thine august name."

Then he replied, saying: "I am elder brother[C] to the Heaven-Shining-Great-August-" Deity. So I have now descended from Heaven."

Then the Deities Foot-Stroking-Elder and Hand-Stroking-Elder said: "If that be so, with reverence will we offer [her to thee]."

So His-Swift-Impetuous-Male-Augustness, at once taking and changing the young girl into a multitudinous and close-toothed comb which he stuck into his august hair-bunch, said to the Deities Foot-Stroking-Elder and Hand-Stroking-Elder: "Do you distill some eight-fold refined liquor.[275] Also make a fence round about, in that fence make eight gates, at each gate tie [together] eight platforms,[276] on each platform put a liquor-vat, and into each vat pour the eight-fold refined liquor, and wait."

So as they waited after having thus prepared everything in accordance with his bidding, the eight-forked serpent came truly as [the old man] had said, and immediately dipped a head into each vat, and drank the liquor. Thereupon it was intoxicated with drinking, and all[277] [the heads] lay down and slept.

Then His-Swift-Impetuous-Male-Augustness drew the ten-grasp saber,[278] that was augustly girded on him, and cut the serpent in piec-

[A] A coniferous tree, the *Chamaecyparis obtsusa*, in Japanese *hi-no-ki*. The cryptomeria is *Cryptomeria japonica*.

[B] The winter-cherry, *Physalis alkekengi*.

[C] He was her younger brother; but see Introduction, p. 41.

es, so that the River Hi flowed on changed into a river of blood. So when he cut the middle tail, the edge of his august sword broke. Then, thinking it strange, he thrust into and split [the flesh] with the point of his august sword and looked, and there was a sharp great sword [within]. So he took this great sword, and, thinking it a strange thing, he respectfully informed the Heaven-Shining-Great-August-Deity.[279] This is the Herb-Quelling Great Sword.[280]

SECT. 19—THE PALACE OF SUGA

So thereupon His-Swift-Impetuous-Male-Augustness sought in the land of Izumo for a place where he might build a palace. Then he arrived at a place [called] Suga,[281] and said: "On coming to this place my august heart is pure,"[A]—and in that place he built a palace to dwell in. So that place is now called Suga. When this Great Deity first built[282] the palace of Suga, clouds rose up thence. Then he made an august song.[283] That song said:[284]

[1] Eight clouds arise. The eight-fold fence
of Izumo makes an eight-fold fence
for the spouses to retire [within]. Oh!
that eight-fold fence.[285]

Then he called the Deity Foot-Stroking-Elder and said: "Thee do I appoint Headman[286] of my palace;" and moreover bestowed on him the name of Master-of-the-Temple-of-Inada Eight-Eared-Deity-of-Suga.[287]

SECT. 20—THE AUGUST ANCESTORS OF THE DEITY-MASTER-OF-THE-GREAT LAND

Why, when he began in the chamber [the work of procreation] with Wondrous-Inada-Princess, he produced a Deity named Eight-Island Ruler.[288] And again, having wedded the Divine-Princess-of-Great-Maj-

---

[A] *I.e.*, "I feel refreshed." The Japanese term used is *suga-sugashi*, whence the origin ascribed to the name of the place Suga. But more probably the name gave rise to this detail of the legend.

esty,[289] daughter of the Deity Great-Mountain-Possessor, he begot children: the Great-Harvest Deity[290] and the August-Spirit-of-Food.[291]

The elder brother the Deity Eight-Island-Ruler wedded Princess-Falling-Like-the-Flowers-of-the-Trees,[292] daughter of the Deity Great-Mountain-Possessor, and begot a child: the Deity Fuwa-no-moji-ku-nu-su-nu.[293]

This Deity wedded Princess Hikawa,[294] daughter of the Deity Okami[295] and begot a child: Water-Spoilt-Blossom-of-Fuka-buchi.[296]

This Deity wedded the Deity Ame-no-tsudoe-chi-ne,[297] and begot a child: the Deity Great-Water-Master.[298]

This Deity wedded the Deity Grand-Ears,[299] daughter of the Deity Funu-zu-nu,[300] and begot a child: the Deity Heavenly-Brandishing-Prince-Lord.[301]

This Deity wedded the Young-Princess-of-the-Small-Country,[302] daughter of the Great-Deity-of-the-Small-Country,[303] and begot a child: the Deity Master-of-the-Great-Land,[A] another name for whom is the Deity Great-Name-Possessor,[B][304] and another name is the Deity-of-the-Reed-Plains,[305] and another name is the Deity of Eight-Thousand-Spears,[306] and another name is the Deity-Spirit-of-the-Living-Land.[307] In all there were five names.[308]

SECT. 21—THE WHITE HARE OF INABA

So this Deity Master-of-the-Great-Land had eighty Deities his brethren; but they all left the land to the Deity Master-of-the-Great-Land. The reason for their leaving it was this: Each of these eighty Deities had in his heart the wish to marry the Princess of Yakami[309] in Inaba,[310] and they went together to Inaba, putting their bag on [the back of] the Deity Great-Name-Possessor, whom they took with them as an attendant.

Hereupon, when they arrived at Cape Keta,[311] [they found] a naked hare lying down. Then the eighty Deities spoke to the hare, saying: "What thou shouldst do is to bathe in the sea-water here, and lie on the slope[312] of a high mountain exposed to the blowing of the wind."

[A] *Ō-kuni-nushi-no-kami.*

[B] *Ō-na-muji-no-kami.*

So the hare followed the instructions of the eighty Deities, and lay down. Then, as the sea-water dried, the skin of its body all split with the blowing of the wind, so that it lay weeping with pain.

But the Deity Great-Name-Possessor, who came last of all, saw the hare, and said: "Why liest thou weeping?"

The hare replied, saying: "I was in the Island of Oki,[313] and wished to cross over to this land, but had no means of crossing over. For this reason I deceived the crocodiles[314] of the sea, saying 'Let you and me compete, and compute the numbers of our [respective] tribes. So do you go and fetch every member of your tribe, and make them all lie in a row across from this island to Cape Keta. Then I will tread on them, and count them as I run across. Hereby shall we know whether it or my tribe is the larger.' Upon my speaking thus, they were deceived and lay down in a row, and I trod on them and counted them as I came across, and was just about to get on land, when I said: 'You have been deceived by me.' As soon as I had finished speaking, the crocodile who lay the last of all seized me and stripped off all my clothing. As I was weeping and lamenting for this reason, the eighty Deities who went by before [thee] commanded and exhorted me, saying: 'Bathe in the salt water, and lie down exposed to the wind.' So, on my doing as they had instructed me, my whole body was hurt."

Thereupon the Deity Great-Name-Possessor instructed the hare, saying: "Go quickly now to the river-mouth, wash thy body with the fresh water, then take the pollen of the sedges [growing] at the river-mouth, spread it about, and roll about upon it, whereupon thy body will certainly be restored to its original state."[A] So [the hare] did as it was instructed, and its body became as it had been originally. This was the White Hare of Inaba.[315] It is now called the Hare Deity.

So the hare said to the Deity Great-Name-Possessor: "These eighty Deities shall certainly not get the Princess of Yakami. Though thou bearest the bag, Thine Augustness shall obtain her."

[A] Lit. "to its original skin"; that is to say that its skin would again be covered with fur.

SECT. 22—MOUNT TEMA

Thereupon the Princess of Yakami answered[A] the eighty Deities, saying: "I will not listen to your words. I mean to marry the Deity Great-Name-Possessor."

So the eighty Deities, being enraged, and wishing to slay the Deity Great-Name-Possessor, took counsel together, on arriving at the foot of Tema[316] in the land of Hahaki, and said [to him]: "On this mountain there is a red boar. So when we drive it down, do thou wait and catch it. If thou do not wait and catch it, we will certainly slay thee." Having [thus] spoken, they took fire, and burnt a large stone like unto a boar, and rolled it down. Then as [they] drove it down and [he] caught it,[317] he got stuck to and burnt by the stone, and died.

Thereupon Her Augustness his august parent[318] cried and lamented, and went up to Heaven, and entreated His Divine-Producing-Wondrous-Augustness,[B] who at once sent Princess Cockle-Shell[319] and Princess Clam[320] to bring him to life. Then Princess Cockle-Shell triturated and scorched[C] [her shell], and Princess Clam carried water and smeared [him] as with mother's[321] milk, whereupon he became a beautiful young man, and wandered off.

Hereupon the eighty Deities, seeing [this], again deceived him, taking him with them into the mountains, where they cut down a large tree, inserted a wedge in the tree,[322] and made him stand in the middle, whereupon they took away the wedge and tortured him to death.[323]

Then on Her Augustness his august parent again seeking him with cries, she perceived him, and at once cleaving the tree, took him out and brought him to life, and said to him:[324] "If thou remain here, thou wilt at last be destroyed by the eighty Deities." Then she sent him swiftly off to the august place of the Deity Great-House-Prince[325] in the land

---

[A]It must be understood that in the meantime they had arrived at her dwelling and begun to court her.

[B]*Kami-musu-bi-no-mikoto.* See Sect. 1, Note D.

[C]The character used is 集, "collected," "gathered together." But the combined authority of Mabuchi, Norinaga and Atsutane obliges us either to consider it a copyist's error for 焦, "scorched," or else to believe that in early times in Japan the two characters were used interchangeably. [A competing explanation suggests that the kami collected or gathered together the bits of the Deity Great-Name-Possessor so he could be put back together and restored to life.—M.F.]

of Ki.[A][326] Then when the eighty Deities searched and pursued till they came up to him, and fixed their arrows [in their bows], he escaped by dipping under the fork of a tree, and disappeared.

SECT. 23—THE NETHER-DISTANT-LAND

[The Deity Great-House-Prince spoke to him[327]], saying: "Thou must set off to the Nether-Distant-Land where dwells His Impetuous-Male-Augustness. That Great Deity will certainly counsel thee."

So on his obeying her commands and arriving at the august place[B] of His Impetuous-Male-Augustness, the latter's daughter the Forward-Princess[328] came out and saw him, and they exchanged glances and were married, and [she] went in again and told her father, saying: "A very beautiful Deity has come."

Then the Great Deity went out and looked, and said: "This is the Ugly-Male-Deity-of-the-Reed-Plains"[329] and at once calling him in, made him sleep in the snake-house.

Hereupon his wife, Her Augustness the Forward-Princess, gave her husband a snake-scarf,[C] saying: "When the snakes are about to bite thee, drive them away by waving this scarf thrice." So, on his doing as she had instructed, the snakes became quiet, so that he came forth after calm slumbers.

Again on the night of the next day [the Impetuous-Male-Deity] put him into the centipede and wasp-house;[330] but as she again gave him a centipede and wasp-scarf, and instructed him as before, he came forth calmly.

Again [the Impetuous-Male-Deity] shot a whizzing barb[D][331] into the middle of a large moor, and sent him to fetch the arrow, and, when he had entered the moor, at once set fire to the moor all round. Thereupon, while he [stood] knowing no place of exit, a mouse[E] came and

[A] *I.e.*, "the land of trees "(木国).

[B] *I.e.*, the Palace.

[C] *I.e.*, "a scarf by waving which he might keep off the snakes." Similarly the "centipede and wasp-scarf" mentioned a little farther on must be understood to mean "a scarf to ward off centipedes and wasps with."

[D] *I.e.*, "arrow."

[E] Or "rat."

said: "The inside is hollow-hollow; the outside is narrow-narrow."[332] Owing to its speaking thus, he trod on the place, whereupon he fell in and hid himself, during which time the fire burnt past. Then the mouse brought out in its mouth and presented to him the whizzing barb. The feathers of the arrow were brought in their mouths by all the mouse's children.

Hereupon his wife the Forward-Princess came bearing mourning-implements,[333] and crying. Her father the great Deity, thinking that [the Deity-Great-Name-Possessor] was already dead and done for, went out and stood on the moor, whereupon [the Deity Great-Name-Possessor] brought the arrow and presented it to him, upon which [the Great Deity], taking him into the house and calling him into an eight-foot spaced large room,[334] made him take the lice off his head. So, on looking at the head, [he saw that] there were many centipedes [there]. Thereupon, as his wife gave to her husband berries of the *muku* tree[A] and red earth, he chewed the berries to pieces, and spat them out with the red earth which he held in his mouth, so that the Great Deity believed him to be chewing up and spitting out the centipedes, and, feeling fond [of him] in his heart, fell asleep.

Then [the Deity Great-Name-Possessor], grasping the Great Deity's hair, tied it fast to the various rafters of the house, and, blocking up the floor of the house with a five hundred draught rock,[B] and taking his wife the Forward-Princess on his back, then carried off the Great Deity's great life-sword[C] and life-bow-and-arrows,[335] as also his heavenly speaking-lute,[336] and ran out. But the heavenly speaking-lute brushed against a tree, and the earth resounded. So the Great Deity, who was sleeping, started at the sound, and pulled down the house. But while he was disentangling his hair which was tied to the rafters, [the Deity Great-Name-Possessor] fled a long way.

So then, pursuing after him to the Even Pass of Hades,[D] and gazing on him from afar, he called out to the Deity Great-Name-Possessor,

---

[A] *Aphananthe aspera*, also sometimes called *Celtis muku*.

[B] *I.e.*, "a rock which it would require five hundred men to lift."

[C] *Iku-tachi* (大刀), supposed by Norinaga to be "a sword having the virtue of conferring long life upon its possessor."

[D] See Vol. 1, Note 163.

saying: "With the great life-sword and the life-bow-and-arrows which thou carriest, pursue thy half-brethren[337] till they crouch on the august slopes of the passes,[A] and pursue them till they are swept into the reaches of the rivers, and do thou, wretch![338] become the Deity Master-of-the- Great-Land;[B] and moreover, becoming the Deity Spirit-of-the-Living-Land, and making my daughter the Forward-Princess thy consort[C] do thou make stout the temple-pillars at the foot of Mount Uka[339] in the nethermost rock-bottom, and make high the cross-beams to the Plain-of-High-Heaven, and dwell [there], thou villain!"[D]

So when, bearing the great sword and bow, he pursued and scattered the eighty Deities, he did pursue them till they crouched on the august slope of every pass,[340] he did pursue them till they were swept into every river, and then he began to make the land.[E341]

Therefore the Princess of Yakami, according to their previous agreement, joined [with him] in the chamber.[342] So he brought her with him; but, fearing his consort the Forward Princess, she stuck into the fork of a tree the child that she had borne, and went back.[F] So the child was called by the name of the Tree-Fork-Deity,[343] and another name was the Deity-of-August-Wells.[344]

[A] Or "hills."

[B] Thus, according to this legend, "Master-of-the-Great-Land" (*Ō-kuni-nushi*) not the original name of the Deity commonly designated by it, and his sovereignty over the Land of the Living (whence the appropriateness of the second name in this context) was derived by investiture from the god of the Land of the Dead.

[C] The characters 嫡妻, which are here used, designate specifically the chief or legitimate wife, as opposed to the lesser wives or concubines.

[D] *I.e.*, "Firmly planting in the rock the pillars forming the foundation of thy palace, and rearing its fabric to the skies, do thou rule therefrom the Land of the Living, thou powerful wretch, who hast so successfully braved me!"

[E] This is taken to mean that he continued the act of creation which had been interrupted by the death of *Izanami* (the "Female Who-Invites"). See Sect 9, p. 35, where her husband Izanagi says to her: "The lands that I and thou made are not yet finished making."

[F] *Q.d.*, to Inaba.

SECT. 24—THE WOOING OF THE DEITY-OF-EIGHT-THOUSAND-SPEARS

This Deity-of-Eight-Thousand-Spears,[A] when he went forth[345] to woo the Princess of Nuna-kawa[346] in the land of Koshi, on arriving at the house of the Princess of Nuna-kawa sang, saying:

[2] [I] His Augustness the Deity-of-Eight-
Thousand-Spears, having been unable to
find a spouse in the Land of the Eight
Islands, and having heard that in the
far-off Land of Koshi there is a wise
maiden, having heard that there is a
beauteous maiden, I am standing [here]
to truly woo her, I am going backwards
and forwards to woo her.

Without having yet untied even the cord of my sword,
without having yet untied even my veil,
I push back the plank-door shut by the
maiden; while I am standing [here], I pull
it forward. While I am standing [here],
the *nue* sings upon the green mountain,
and [the voice of] the true bird of the
moor, the pheasant, resounds; the bird of
the yard, the cock, crows.

Oh! the pity[B] that [the] birds should sing!
Oh! These birds!
Would that I could beat them till
they were sick!
Oh! swiftly-flying heaven-racing messenger,
the tradition of the thing, too, this![347]

[A] In this Section, the Deity Master-of-the-Great-Land is spoken of under this *alias (See Vol. 1, Note 344).*

[B] How annoying! what a nuisance! —W.G.A.

Then the Princess of Nuna-kawa, without yet opening the door, sang from the inside saying:

[3] Thine Augustness the Deity-of-Eight-Thousand-Spears!
Being a maiden like a drooping plant,
my heart is just a bird on a sand-bank by the shore;
it will now indeed be a dotterel.
Afterwards it will be a gentle bird;
so as for thy life,
do not deign to die.
Oh! swiftly-flying heaven-racing messenger!
the tradition of the thing, too, this![348]

[Second Song of the Princess[349]]

When the sun shall hide behind the green mountains,
in the night [black as] the true
jewels of the moor will I come forth.
Coming radiant with smiles like the morning sun,
[thine] arms white as rope of paper-mulberry-bark
shall softly pat [my] breast soft as the melting snow;
and patting [each other] interlaced,
stretching out and pillowing [ourselves] on [each other's] jewel-
arms,
—true jewel-arms—
and with outstretched legs, will we sleep.
So speak not too lovingly,
Thine Augustness the Deity-of-Eight-Thousand-Spears!
The tradition of the thing, too, this![350]

Therefore, they did not meet that night, but augustly united on the night of the following day.[351]

SECT. 25—THE CUP PLEDGE

Again this Deity's Chief Empress,[A] Her Augustness the Forward-Princess, was very jealous. So the Deity her husband, being distressed, was about to go up from Izumo to the Land of Yamato; and as he stood attired, with one august hand on the saddle of his august horse and one august foot in the august stirrup, he sang, saying:

[4] When I take and attire myself so carefully
in my august garments
black as the true jewels of the moor,
and, like the birds of the offing,
look at my breast—
though I raise my fins,
[I say that] these are not good,
and cast them off on the waves on the beach.

When I take and attire myself so carefully
in my august garments
green as the kingfisher,
and, like the birds of the offing, look at my breast—
though I raise my fins,
[I say that] these, too, are not good,
and cast them off on the waves on the beach.
When I take and attire myself so carefully
in my raiment dyed in the sap of the dye-tree,
the pounded madder sought in the mountain fields,
and, like the birds of the offing, look at my breast—
though I raise my fins,
[I say that] they are good.

My dear younger sister, Thine Augustness!
Though thou say that thou wilt not weep—
if like the flocking birds, I flock and depart,
if, like the led birds, I am led away and depart,

[A] *I.e.*, chief wife.

thou wilt hang down thy head
like a single eulalia upon the mountain
and thy weeping shall indeed rise
as the mist of the morning shower.
Thine Augustness [my] spouse like the young herbs!
The tradition of the thing, too, this![352]

Then his Empress, taking a great august liquor-cup, and drawing near and offering it to him, sang, saying:—

[5] Oh! Thine Augustness the Deity-of-Eight-Thousand-Spears!
[Thou], my [dear] Master-of-the-Great-Land
indeed, being a man, probably hast
on the various island-headlands that thou seest,
and on every beach-headland that thou lookest on,
a wife like the young herbs.
But as for me, alas!
being a woman, I have no man except thee;
I have no spouse except thee.
Beneath the fluttering of the ornamented fence,
beneath the softness of the warm coverlet,
beneath the rustling of the cloth coverlet,
[thine] arms white as rope of paper-mulberry bark
softly patting [my] breast soft as the melting snow,
and patting [each other] interlaced,
stretching out and pillowing [ourselves] on [each other's arms],
—true jewel-arms,
and with outstretched legs, will we sleep.
Lift up the luxuriant august liquor![353]

She having thus sung, they at once pledged [each other] by the cup with [their hands] on [each other's] necks,[354] and are at rest till the present time. These are called divine words.[355]

SECT. 26—THE DEITIES THE AUGUST DESCENDANTS OF THE DEITY MASTER-OF-THE-GREAT-LAND

So this Deity Master-of-the-Great-Land wedded Her Augustness Torrent-Mist-Princess, the Deity dwelling in the inner temple of Munakata,[356] and begot children: the Deity Aji-shiki-taka-hiko-ne,[357] next his younger sister Her Augustness High-Princess,[358] another name for whom is Her Augustness Princess Under-Shining.[359] This Deity Aji-shiki-taka-hiko-ne is he who is now called the Great August Deity of Kamo.[360]

Again the Deity Master-of-the-Great-Land wedded Her Augustness Princess Divine-House-Shield[361] and begot a child: the Deity Thing-Sign-Master.[A362]

Again he wedded the Deity Bird-Ears,[363] daughter of the Deity Eight-Island-Possessor,[364] and begot a child: the Deity Bird-Growing-Ears.[365]

This Deity wedded Hina-teri-nakata-bichi-o-ikochini,[366] and begot a child: the Deity Land-Great-Wealth.[367]

This Deity wedded the Deity Ashi-nadaka,[368] another name for whom is Princess-Eight-Rivers-and-Inlets,[369] and begot a child: the Deity Swift-Awful-Brave-Sahaya-Lord-Ruler.[370]

This Deity wedded Princess Luck-Spirit,[371] daughter of the Deity Heavenly-Awful-Master,[372] and begot a child:[373]

This Deity wedded Princess Hina-rashi,[374] daughter of the Deity Okami[375] and begot a child: the Deity Tahiri-kishi-marumi.[376]

This Deity wedded the Deity Princess-Life-Spirit-Luck-Spirit,[377] daughter of the Deity Waiting-to-See-the-Flowers-of-the-Holly,[378] and begot a child: the Deity Miro-na-mi.[379]

This Deity wedded Princess Ao-numa-no-oshi,[380] daughter of the Deity Master-of-Shiki-yama,[381] and begot a child: the Deity Nunoshi-tomi-tori-naru-mi.[382]

This Deity wedded the Young-Day-Female-Deity,[383] and begot a child: the Deity Heavenly-Hibara-Great-Long-Wind-Wealth.[384]

This Deity wedded the Deity Tō-tsu-ma-chi-ne,[385] daughter of

[A] *I.e.*, "the Deity who gave a sign of the thing he did." The Japanese original is *Koto-shiro-nushi-no-kami.*

the Deity Heavenly-Pass Boundary,[386] and begot a child: the Deity Tō-tsu-yama-zaki-tarashi.[387]

From the above-mentioned Deity Eight-Island-Ruler down to the Deity Tō-tsu-yama-zaki-tarashi are called the Deities of seventeen generations.[388]

SECT. 27—THE LITTLE-PRINCE-THE-RENOWNED-DEITY

So when the Deity Master-of-the-Great-Land dwelt at the august cape of Miho[389] in Izumo, there came riding on the crest[390] of the waves in a boat of heavenly *Kagami*[391] a Deity dressed in skins of geese[392] flayed with a complete flaying, who, when asked his name, replied not; moreover the Deities who accompanied him, though asked, all said that they knew not. Then the toad[393] spoke, saying: "As for this, the Crumbling Prince will surely know it."

Thereupon [the Deity Master-of-the-Great-Land] summoned and asked the Crumbling-Prince,[394] who replied, saying: "This is the Little-Prince-the-Renowned-Deity,[395] the august child of the Deity-Producing-Wondrous-Deity."[396] So on their then respectfully informing[397] His Augustness the Deity-Producing-Wondrous-August-Ancestor, he replied, saying: "This is truly my child. He among my children is the child who dipped between the fork of my hand.[A] So do he and thou become brethren, and make and consolidate this land."[398]

So from that time forward the two Deities the Great-Name-Possessor and the Little-Prince-the-Renowned-Deity made and consolidated this land conjointly. But afterwards the Little-Prince-the-Renowned-Deity crossed over to the Eternal Land.[399] So [the Deity here] called the Crumbling Prince, who revealed the Little-Prince-the-Renowned-Deity, is what is now [called] the scarecrow in the mountain fields. This Deity, though his legs do not walk, is a Deity who knows everything in the Empire.[400]

[A] *I.e.*," slipped away between my fingers." In the legend as given in the *Chronicles*, the father explains more particularly that the Little-Prince-the-Renowned-Deity had been a bad boy who ran away.

SECT. 28—THE AUGUST-LUCK-SPIRIT-THE-AUGUST-WONDROUS-SPIRIT[401]

Thereupon the Deity Master-of-the-Great-Land lamented himself, and said: "How shall I alone be able to make this land?[402] Together with what Deity can I make this land?"

At this time there came a Deity illuminating the sea. This Deity said: "If thou wilt lay me to rest[A] well, I can make it together with thee. If not, the land cannot be made."

Then the Deity Master-of-the-Great-Land said: "If that be so, what is the manner of reverently laying thee to rest?"

He replied, saying: "Reverently worship me on Yamato's green fence, the eastern mountain's top."[403] This is the Deity who dwells on the top of Mount Mimoro.[404]

SECT. 29—THE AUGUST CHILDREN OF THE GREAT-HARVEST-DEITY AND OF THE SWIFT-MOUNTAIN-DEITY

So the Great-Harvest-Deity wedded the Princess [of?] Inu,[405] daughter of the Divine-Life-Producing-Wondrous-Deity,[406] and begot children:

the Deity August-Spirit-of-the-Great-Land,[407]
next the Deity of Kara,[408]
next the Deity Sohori,[409]
next the Deity White-Sun,[410]
next the Sage-Deity.[411] (Five Deities.[B])

Again he wedded the Refulgent-Princess,[412] and begot children: the Deity Great-Refulgent-Mountain-Dwelling-Grandee,[413] next the August-Harvest-Deity.[414]

Again he wedded Princess Ame-shiru-karu-mizu,[415] and begot children:

the Deity Oki-tsu-hiko,[416]
next Her Augustness Oki-tsu-hime,[417] another name for whom is the Deity Great Furnace-Princess:[418]–this is the Deity of the Furnace[419] held in reverence by all people.

Next the Deity Great-Mountain-Integrator,[420] another name for

---

[A] *I.e.*, "if thou wilt build me a temple." The original might also be rendered "if thou wilt worship before me," or "at my shrine," or "if thou wilt establish a temple to me."

[B] Viz. from the August-Spirit-of-the-Great-Land to the Sage-Deity inclusive.

whom is the Deity-Great-Master-of-the-Mountain End:[421] this Deity dwells on Mount Hie[422] in the land of Chika-tsu-ōmi,[423] and is likewise the Deity dwelling at Matsu-no-o[424] in Kazuno,[425] who uses the whizzing barb.[A426]

Next the Deity-of-the-Fire-in-the-Yard;[427]
next the Deity Asuha;[428]
next the Deity Hahigi;[429]
next the Deity Refulgent-Mountain-Dwelling-Grandee;[430]
next the Deity Swift-Mountain-Dwelling;[431]
next the High Deity-of-the-Fire-in-the-Yard;[432]
next the Great-Earth-Deity,[433] another name for whom is the Deity August-Ancestor-of-Earth.[434] (Nine Deities.[435])

In the above paragraph the children of the Great-Harvest-Deity, from the Deity August-Spirit-of-the-Great-Land down to the Great-Earth-Deity, are altogether sixteen Deities.

The Deity Swift-Mountain-Dwelling[436] wedded the Deity Princess-of-Great-Food,[437] and begot children:

the Deity Young-Mountain-Integrator;[438]
next the Young-Harvest-Deity;[439]
next his younger sister the Young-Rice-Transplanting-Female-Deity;[440]
next the Water-Sprinkling-Deity;[441]
next the Deity-of-the-High-Sun-of-Summer,[442] another name for whom is the Female-Deity-of-Summer;[443]
next the Autumn-Princess;[444]
next the Deity Stem-Harvest;[445]
next the Deity Lord-Stem-Tree-Young-House-Rope.[446]

In the above paragraph the children of the Deity Swift-Mountain-Dwelling, from the Deity Young-Mountain-Integrator down to the Deity Lord-Young-House-Rope,[447] are altogether eight Deities.

SECT. 30—THE AUGUST DELIBERATION FOR PACIFYING THE LAND

The Heaven-Shining-Great-August-Deity commanded, saying: "The

[A] Why barb and not simply arrow-head? An arrow-head has two barbs.—W.G.A.

Luxuriant-Reed-Plains-the-Land-of-Fresh-Rice-ears-of-a-Thousand-Autumns,–of Long-Five-Hundred-Autumns[448] is the land which my august child His Augustness Truly-Conqueror-I-Conquer-Conquering-Swift-Heavenly-Great-Great-Ears[449] shall govern." Having [thus] deigned to charge him, she sent him down from Heaven.[450]

Hereupon His Augustness Heavenly-Great-Great-Ears, standing on the Floating Bridge of Heaven,[451] said: "The Luxuriant-Reed-Plains-the-Land-of-Fresh-Rice-ears-of-a-Thousand-Autumns—of Long-Five-Hundred-Autumns is painfully uproarious—it is."[452] With this announcement, he immediately re-ascended, and informed the Heaven-Shining-Great-August-Deity.

Then the High-August-Producing-Wondrous-Deity[453] and the Heaven-Shining-Great-August-Deity commanded the eight hundred myriad Deities to assemble in a divine assembly in the bed of the Tranquil River or Heaven,[454] and caused the Deity Thought-Includer[455] to think [of a plan], and said:[456] "This Central Land[457] of Reed-Plains is the land with which we have deigned to charge our august child as the land which he shall govern. So as he deems that violent and savage Earthly Deities[458] are numerous in this land, which Deity shall we send to subdue them?"

Then the deity Thought-Includer and likewise the eight hundred myriad Deities took counsel and said: "The Deity Ame-no-ho-hi;[459] is the one that should be sent." So they sent the Deity Ame-no-ho-hi; but he at once curried favor with the Deity Master-of-the-Great-Land, and for three years brought back no report.

SECT. 31—THE HEAVENLY-YOUNG-PRINCE

Therefore the High-August-Producing-Wondrous-Deity and the Heaven-Shining-Great-August-Deity again asked all the Deities, saying: "The Deity Ame-no-ho-hi, whom we sent down to the Central Land of Reed-Plains, is long of bringing back a report.[460] Which Deity were it best to send on a fresh mission?"[461]

Then the Deity Thought-Includer replied, saying: "The Heavenly-Young-Prince,[462] son of the Deity Heaven's-Earth-Spirit[463] should be sent." So they bestowed on the Heavenly-Young-Prince the heavenly true deer-bow and the heavenly feathered arrows,[464] and sent him.

Thereupon the Heavenly-Young-Prince, descending to that land, at once wedded Princess Under-Shining,[465] daughter of the Deity Master-of-the-Great-Land,[466] and moreover, planning how he might gain [possession of] the land, for eight years brought back no report.

So then the High-August-Producing-Wondrous-Deity and the Heaven-Shining-Great-August-Deity again asked all the Deities, [saying]: "The Heavenly-Young-Prince is long of bringing back a report.[467] Which Deity shall we send on a fresh mission to inquire the cause of the Heavenly-Young-Prince's long tarrying?"

Thereupon all the Deities and likewise the Deity Thought-Includer replied, saying: "The pheasant the Name-Crying-Female should be sent," upon which [the High-August-Producing-Wondrous-Deity and the Heaven-Shining-Great-August-Deity] charged [the pheasant], saying: "What thou shalt go and ask the Heavenly-Young-Prince is this: 'The reason for which thou wast sent to the Central Land of Reed-Plains was to subdue and pacify the savage Deities of that land. Why for eight years bringest thou back no report?'"

So then the Crying-Female, descending from Heaven, and perching on the multitudinous [-ly-branching] cassia-tree[468] at the Heavenly-Young-Prince's gate, told him everything according to the mandate of the Heavenly Deities. Then the Heavenly-Spying-Woman,[469] having heard the bird's words, spoke to the Heavenly-Young-Prince, saying: "The sound of this bird's cry is very bad. So thou shouldest shoot it to death."

On her [thus] urging him, the Heavenly-Young-Prince at once took the heavenly vegetable wax-tree bow and the heavenly deer-arrows bestowed on him by the Heavenly Deities, and shot the pheasant to death. Then the arrow, being shot up upside down[470] through the pheasant's breast, reached the august place where the Heaven-Shining-Great-August-Deity and the High-Integrating-Deity[471] were sitting in the bed of the Tranquil River of Heaven. This "High-Integrating-Deity" is another name for the High-August-Producing-Wondrous-Deity.

So, on the High-Integrating-Deity taking up the arrow and looking at it [he saw that] there was blood adhering to the feathers of the arrow. Thereupon the High-Integrating-Deity, saying: "This arrow is the arrow that was bestowed on the Heavenly-Young-Prince," showed it to all the Deities, and said: "If this be an arrow shot at the evil Deities by the Heavenly-Young-Prince in obedience to our command, let it not hit him. If he has a foul heart, let the Heavenly-Young-Prince perish[472] by this arrow." With these words, he took the arrow and thrust it back down through the arrow's hole,[A] so that it hit the Heavenly-Young-Prince on the top of his breast[473] as he was sleeping on his couch, so that he died. (This is the origin of [the saying] 'Beware of a returning arrow.'"[474]) Moreover the pheasant returned not. So this is the origin of the modern proverb which speaks of "the pheasant as sole messenger."[475]

So the sound of the wailings of the Heavenly-Young-Prince's wife Princess Under-Shining, re-echoing in the wind, reached Heaven. So the Heavenly-Young-Prince's father, the Deity Heaven's-Earth-Spirit, and his wife and children[B] who were in heaven, hearing it, came down with cries and lamentations, and at once built a mourning-house there,[C] and made the wild goose of the river[476] the head-hanging bearer,[477] the heron the broom-bearer, the kingfisher the person of the august food, the sparrow the pounding-woman,[478] the pheasant the weeping woman; and having thus arranged matters, they disported themselves[479] for eight days and eight nights.[480]

At this time the Deity Aji-shiki-taka-hiko-ne[481] came and condoled on the mourning for the Heavenly-Young-Prince, whereupon the Heavenly-Young-Prince's father and wife who had come down from Heaven bewailed themselves,[482] saying: "My child is not dead, no! My lord is not dead, no!" and with these words clung to his hands and feet, and bewailed themselves and lamented. The cause of their mistake was that the two Deities closely resembled each other in countenance: so therefore they made the mistake.

Thereupon the Deity Aji-shiki-taka-hiko-ne was very angry, and said: "It was only because he was my dear friend that I came to con-

---

[A] *I.e.*, through the hole in the bottom of the sky through which the arrow had entered, or which the arrow had made for itself.

[B] *I.e.*, the wife and children of the Heavenly-Young-Prince, who had been left behind by him in Heaven when he went on his embassy to Izumo.

[C] *I.e.*, in the place where he died. The "mourning house" was used to keep the corpse in till it was finally buried.

dole. Why should I be likened to an unclean dead person?"—and with these words he drew the ten-grasp saber[483] that was augustly girded on him, and cut down the mourning-house, and kicked away [the pieces] with his feet. This was on what is called Mount Mourning[484] at the source of the River Aimi[485] in the land of Minu.[486] The great sword with which he cut [the mourning-house to pieces] was called by the name of Great-Blade-Mower,[487] another name by which it was called being the Divine-Keen-Saber[488] So when the Deity Aji-shiki-taka-hiko-ne flew away in his anger, his younger sister Her Augustness the High-Princess in order to reveal his august name, sang, saying:

[6] Oh! 'tis the Deity Aji-shiki-taka-hiko-ne
traversing two august valleys
with the refulgence of august assembled hole-jewels,
of the august assembled jewels
worn round her neck
by the Weaving Maiden in Heaven![489]

This Song is of a Rustie Style.[490]

SECT. 32—ABDICATION OF THE DEITY MASTER-OF-THE-GREAT-LAND

Hereupon the Heaven-Shining-Great-August-Deity said: "Which Deity were it best to send on a fresh mission?"[491] Then the Deity Thought-Includer and likewise all the Deities said: "He who is named the Deity Majestic-Point-Blade-Extended[492] and dwells in the Heavenly Rock-Dwelling by the source of the Tranquil River of Heaven, is the one that should be sent; or if not this Deity, then this Deity's child, the Brave-Awful-Possessing-Male-Deity,[493] might be sent. Moreover,[494] owing to this Deity Heavenly-Point-Blade-Extended having blocked up and turned back the waters of the Tranquil River of Heaven, and to his dwelling with the road blocked up, other Deities cannot go [thither]. So the Heavenly-Deer-Deity[495] should be sent specially to ask him."

So then the Heavenly-Deer -Deity was sent to ask the Deity Heavenly-Point-Blade-Extended, who replied, saying: "I will obey, and will respectfully serve you. Nevertheless on this errand[496] ye should send my[497] child, the Brave-Awful-Possessing-Male-Deity,"[498]—[and with these words] immediately offered [his son to the Heaven-Shining-Great-August-Deity]. So the Deity Heavenly-Bird-Boat[499] was attached to the Brave-Awful-Possessing-Male-Deity, and they were sent off.

Therefore these two Deities, descending to the little shore[500] of Inasa[501] in the land of Izumo, drew their swords ten hand-breadths long,[502] stuck them upside down[503] on the crest of a wave, seated themselves cross-legged[504] on the point of the swords, and asked the Deity Master-of-the-Great-Land, saying: "The Heaven-Shining-Great-August-Deity and the High-Integrating-Deity have charged us and sent us to ask, [saying]: 'We have deigned to charge our august child with thy dominion, the Central Land of Reed-Plains, as the land which he should govern. So how is thy heart?'"[A]

He replied, saying: "I[505] am unable to say. My child the Deity Eight-Fold-Thing- Sign-Master[506] will be the one to tell you; but he is gone to Cape Miho[507] to pursue birds and catch fish, and has not yet returned."

So then the Deity Bird-Boat was sent to summon the Deity Eight-Fold-Thing-Sign-Master, who, on being graciously asked, spoke to the Great Deity his father, saying: "I will obey. [Do thou[508]] respectfully present this land to the august child of the Heavenly Deity";—and thereupon he trod on [the edge of] his boat so as to capsize it, clapped his heavenly departing hands in the fence of green branches, and disappeared.[509]

So then they asked the Deity Master-of-the-Great-Land, saying: "Thy son the Deity Thing-Sign-Master has now spoken thus. Hast thou other sons who should speak?"

Hereupon he spoke again, saying: "There is my other son, the Deity Brave-August-Name-Firm.[510] There is none beside him."

While he was thus speaking, the Deity Brave-August-Name-Firm came up, bearing on the tips of his fingers a thousand-draught rock[B], and said: "Who is it that has come to our land, and thus secretly talks?

[A] *I.e.*, "What sayest thou to this our decree?"

[B] *I.e.*, a rock which it would take a thousand men to lift.

If that be so,[A] I should like to have a trial of strength. So I should like to begin by taking thine august hand." So on his letting him take his august hand, his touch at once turned it into an icicle, and again his touch turned it into a sword-blade[B]. So then he was frightened and drew back.

Then on the Brave-Awful-Possessing-Male-Deity wishing to take the hand of the Deity Brave-August-Name-Firm, and asking permission to take it in return, he grasped and crushed it as if it were taking a young reed, and cast it aside, upon which [the Deity Brave-August-Name-Firm] fled away. So when [the Brave-Awful-Possessing-Male-Deity] pursuing after him, came up with him at the Sea of Suwa[511] in the land of Shi-nanu,[512] and was about to slay him, the Deity Brave-August-Name-Firm said: "I will obey. Slay me not. I will go to no other place but this, neither will I go against the command of my father the Deity Master-of-the-Great-Land. I will not go against the words of the Deity Eight-Fold-Thing-Sign-Master. I will yield up this Central Land of Reed-Plains according to the command of the august child of the Heavenly Deities."

So they returned again, and asked the Deity Master-of-the-Great-Land [saying]: "Thy children the two Deities the Deity Thing-Sign-Master and the Deity Brave-August-Name-Firm have said that they will follow and not go against the commands of the august child of the Heavenly Deities. So how is thy heart?"

Then he replied, saying: "According as the two Deities my children have said, I too will not go against them. In accordance with the [heavenly] command, I will at once yield up this Central Land of Reed-Plains. But as to my place of residence, if ye will make stout the temple-pillars on the nethermost rock-bottom, and make high the cross-beams to the Plain of High Heaven like the rich and perfect august nest where the august child of the Heavenly Deities rules the succession of Heaven's sun, and will deign to establish me, I will

---

[A] This expression seems here, as Norinaga says, to be used in the sense of "Come on!" It has survived in the modern word *saraba*, which sometimes has that meaning.

[B] *I.e.*. the Brave-Awful-Possessing-Male-Deity's hand turned first into an icicle and next into a sword- blade on being touched by the Deity Brave-August-Name-Firm, to the alarm and hurt of the latter.

hide in the eighty (less than a hundred) road-windings, and wait on him. Again, as for my children the hundred and eighty Deities, if the Deity Eight-Fold-Thing-Sign-Master will be the Deities' august rear and van and will respectfully serve them, there will be no disobedient Deities."[513] Having thus spoken [he hid himself.[A]

So in accordance with his word,][514] they built a heavenly august abode on the shore[515] of Tagishi[516] in the land of Izumo; and the Deity Wondrous-Eight-Spirits,[517] grandson of the Deity of Water-Gates,[518] was made butler to offer up the heavenly august banquet, when,[519] having said prayers, the Deity Wondrous-Eight-Spirits turned into a cormorant, went down to the bottom of the sea, took in his mouth red earth from the bottom, made eighty heavenly platters, and, cutting sea-weed[520] stalks, made a fire-drill mortar, and made a fire-drill pestle out of stalks of *komo*,[521] and drilled out fire, saying: "This fire which I have drilled will I burn until, in the Plain of High Heaven, the soot on the heavenly new lattice of the gable of His Augustness the Wondrous-Divine-Producer-the-August-Ancestor[522] hang down eight hand-breadths; and as for what is below the earth, I will bake down to the nethermost rock-bottom, and— the fishing sailors, who spread their thousand-fathom ropes of paper-mulberry and angle, having with many shouts drawn in and landed the large-mouthed small-finned perch—I will offer up the heavenly true fish-food so that the split bamboos bend."[523] So the Brave-Awful-Possessing-Male Deity re-ascended [to Heaven], and reported how he had subdued and pacified the Central Land of Reed-Plains.

SECT. 33—THE AUGUST DESCENT FROM HEAVEN OF HIS AUGUSTNESS THE AUGUST GRANDCHILD

Then the Heaven-Shining-Great-August-Deity and the High-Integrating-Deity[524] commanded and charged the Heir Apparent[525] His Augustness Truly-Conqueror-I-Conquer-Swift-Heavenly-Great-Great-Ears[526] [saying: "The Brave-Awful-Possessing-Male-Deity] says that he has now finished pacifying the Central Land of Reed-Plains. So do thou, in accordance with our gracious charge, descend to and

[A] *I.e.*, disappeared.

dwell in and rule over it."

Then the Heir Apparent His Augustness Truly-Conqueror-I-Conquer-Conquering-Swift-Heavenly-Great-Great-Ears replied, saying: "While I[527] have been getting ready to descend, there has been born [to me] a child whose name is His Augustness Heaven-Plenty-Earth-Plenty-Heaven's-Sun-Height-Prince-Rice-ear-Ruddy-Plenty.[528] This child should be sent down." [[A529]As for this august child,[530] he was augustly joined to Her Augustness Myriad-Looms-Luxuriant-Dragonfly-Island-Princess,[531] daughter of the High-Integrating-Deity, and begot children: His Augustness-Heavenly Rice-ear-Ruddy,[532] and next His Augustness Prince-Rice-ear-Ruddy-Plenty.[533]]

Therefore, in accordance with these words, they laid their command on His Augustness Prince Rice-ear-Ruddy-Plenty, deigning to charge him with these words: "This Luxuriant Reed-Plain-Land-of-Fresh-Rice-ears[534] is the land over which thou shalt rule."

So [he replied]: "I will descend from Heaven according to your commands."

So when His Augustness Prince-ear-Ruddy-Plenty was about to descend from Heaven, there was at the eight-forking road of Heaven a Deity whose refulgence reached upwards to the Plain of High Heaven and downwards to the Central Land of Reed-Plains. So then the Heaven-Shining-Great-August-Deity and the High-Integrating Deity commanded and charged the Heavenly-Alarming-Female-Deity[B] [saying]: "Though thou art but a delicate female, thou art a Deity who conquers in facing Deities.[C] So be thou the one to go and ask thus: 'This being the road by which our august child is about to descend from Heaven, who is it that is thus there?'"[D]

[A]The translator puts this sentence between brackets because it is an evident interruption of the main story. Indeed the edition of 1687 prints it as a note to the text.

[B]*Ame-no-uzu-me-no-kami,* the goddess whose loud, bold merriment was the chief cause of the Sun-Goddess emerging from her retreat in the cavern (see Vol. 1, Note 287).

[C]*I.e.*, "Thy brazen-facedness allows thee to stare others out of countenance, and make them uneasy."

[D]Between this sentence and the next, the Alarming-Female-Deity must be supposed to have gone on her embassy and to have delivered the message with which she had been entrusted.

So to this gracious question he replied, saying "I[535] am an Earthly Deity named the Deity Prince of Saruta.[536] The reason for my coming here is that, having heard of the [intended] descent of the august child of the Heavenly Deities, I have come humbly to meet him and respectfully offer myself as His Augustness's vanguard."[A]

Then joining to him His Augustness Heavenly-Beckoning-Ancestor-Lord, His Augustness Grand-Jewel, Her Augustness Heavenly-Alarming-Female, Her Augustness I-shi-ko-ri-do-me, and His Augustness Jewel-Ancestor,[537] in all five chiefs of companies,[538] they sent him down from Heaven. Thereupon they joined to him the eight-feet [long] curved jewels and mirror that had allured [the Heaven-Shining-Great-August-Deity from the Rock-Dwelling,[539]] and also the Herb-Quelling-Great-Sword,[B] and likewise the Deity Thought-Includer, the Hand-Strength-Male-Deity, and the Deity Heavenly-Rock-Door-Opener[540] of Eternal Night,[541] and charged him thus: "Regard this mirror exactly as if it were our august spirit, and reverence it as if reverencing us."[C][542] Next did they say: "Let the Deity Thought-Includer take in hand our affairs, and carry on the government." These two Deities are worshiped at the temple of Isuzu.[543]

The next, the Deity of Luxuriant-Food,[544] is the Deity dwelling in the outer temple of Watarai.[545] The next, the Deity Heavenly-Rock-Door-Opener, another name for whom is the Wondrous-Rock-True-Gate-Deity, and another name for whom is the Luxuriant-Rock-True-Gate-Deity,[546]–this Deity is the Deity of the August Gate.[D] The next, the Deity Hand-Strength-Male, dwells in Sanagata.[547] Now His Augustness the Heavenly-Beckoning-Ancestor-Lord (is the ancestor of the Nakatomi Chieftains);[548] His Augustness Grand Jewel (is the ancestor of the Imibe Headmen);[549] Her Augustness the Heavenly-Alarming-Female (is the ancestress of the Duchesses of Saru);[550] Her Augustness I-shi-ko-ri-do-me (is the ancestress of the Mirror-Making Chieftains);[551] His Augustness-Jewel-Ancestor (is the ancestor of the Jewel-Ancestor Chieftains).[552]

[A] Or "guide."

[B] Obtained from the tail of the Serpent of Koshi. See the story in Sect. 18.

[C] Or "worshiping before us," or "in our presence."

[D] Viz. of the gate or gates of the Imperial Palace.

SECT. 34—THE AUGUST REIGN IN HIMUKA OF HIS AUGUSTNESS PRINCE RICE-EAR-RUDDY-PLENTY

[553]So then [the Heaven-Shining-Great-August-Deity and the High-Integrating-Deity] commanded[554] His Augustness Heaven's-Prince-Rice-ear-Ruddy-Plenty; and he, leaving the Heavenly Rock-Seat,[A] pushing asunder the eight-fold heavenly spreading clouds, and dividing a road with a mighty road-dividing, set off floating shut up in the Floating Bridge of Heaven,[555] and descended from Heaven on to the peak of Kujifuru which is Takachiho in Tsukushi.[556]

So His Heavenly Great Wondrous Augustness[557] and His Augustness Heaven's-Round-Eyes,[558] both[559] taking on their backs the Heavenly rock-quivers,[560] taking at their side the large mallet-headed swords,[561] taking in their hands the Heavenly vegetable-wax-tree bow,[562] and clasping under their arms the Heavenly true deer-arrows, stood in his august van in respectful attendance. So His Heavenly-Great-Wondrous-Augustness (is the ancestor of the Ōtomo Chieftains);[563] His Augustness Heaven's-Round-Eyes (is the ancestor of the Kume Lords).[564]

Thereupon he said: "This place is opposite to the land of Kara.[B] One comes straight across to the august Cape of Kasasa;[565] and it is a land whereon the morning sun shines straight, a land which the evening sun's sunlight illumines. So this place is an exceedingly good place."[566] Having thus spoken, he made stout the temple-pillars on the nethermost rock-bottom, and made high the cross-beams to the Plain of High Heaven,[C] and dwelt there.

SECT. 35—THE DUCHESS OF SARU

So then he charged Her Augustness the Heavenly-Alarming-Female [saying]: "Do thou, who wast the one to make known this Great Deity Prince of Saruta who respectfully served as my august vanguard,[567] respectfully escort him [back]; and do thou likewise bear the august name of that Deity, and respectfully serve me." Wherefore the Duch-

[A] *I.e.*, his place in Heaven. The original Japanese of the term is *ama-no-iwa-kura*.

[B] Or *Kan* according to the Sinico-Japanese reading. We might render it in English by Korea. The Chinese character Is 韓.

[C] *I.e.*, he built himself a palace to dwell in (Cf. Vol. 1, Note 551).

esses of Saru bear the name of the Male Deity the Prince of Saruta, and the women are Duchesses of Saru.[568]

SECT. 36—THE DEITY PRINCE OF SARUTA AT AZAKA

Now when this Deity Prince of Saruta dwelt at Azaka,[569] he went out fishing, and had his hand caught by a *hirabu* shell-fish,[570] and was drowned in the brine of the sea. So the name by which he was called when he sank to the bottom was the Bottom-Touching-August-Spirit;[571] the name by which he was called when the sea-water gurgled up was the Gurgling-Up-August-Spirit;[572] the name by which he was called when the bubbles formed was the Bubble-Bursting-August-Spirit.[573]

Thereupon [Her Augustness the Heavenly-Alarming-Female], having escorted [back] the Deity Prince of Saruta, came back,[574] and at once drove together all the things broad of fin and the things narrow of fin,[A] and asked them, saying: "Will ye respectfully serve the august son of the Heavenly Deities— upon which all the fishes declared that they would respectfully serve him. Only the bèche-de-mer said nothing. Then Her Augustness the Heavenly-Alarming-Female spoke to the bèche-de-mer, saying: "Ah! this mouth is a mouth that gives no reply!"–and [with these words] slit the mouth with her stiletto.[575] So at the present day the bèche-de-mer has a slit mouth. Wherefore [from august reign to] august reign, when the offerings of the first fruits of Shima[576] are presented [to the Emperor, a portion of them] is granted to the Duchesses of Saru.

SECT. 37—THE CURSE OF THE DEITY GREAT-MOUNTAIN-POSSESSOR

Hereupon His Augustness Heaven's-Sun-Height-Prince-Rice-ear-Ruddy-Plenty met a beautiful person at the august cape of Kasasa, and asked her whose daughter she was. She replied, saying: "I am a daughter of the Deity Great-Mountain-Possessor,[577] and my name is the Divine-Princess-of-Ata,[578] another name by which I am called being Princess-Blossoming-Brilliantly-Like-the-Flowers-of-the-Trees.[579]

[A] *I.e.*, all the fishes both great and small.

Again he asked: "Hast thou any brethren?"[580]

She replied, saying: "There is my elder sister, Princess-Long-as-the-Rocks."[A]

Then he charged her, [saying]: "I am desirous of uniting with you. How does that seem to you?"[581]

She replied, saying: "I[582] am not able to say. My father the Deity Great-Mountain-Possessor will say."

So he sent a request [for her] to her father the Deity Great-Mountain-Possessor, who, greatly delighted, respectfully sent her off, joining to her elder sister Princess Long-as-the-Rocks, and causing merchandise to be carried on tables holding a hundred.[B]

So then, owing to the elder sister being very hideous, [His Augustness Prince-Rice-ear-Ruddy-Plenty] was alarmed at the sight of her, and sent her back, only keeping the younger sister Princess-Blossoming-Brilliantly-Like-the-Flowers-of-the-Trees, whom he wedded for one night. Then the Deity-Great-Mountain-Possessor was covered with shame at Princess Long-as-the-Rocks being sent back, and sent a message [to His Augustness Prince-Rice-ear-Ruddy-Plenty], saying: "My reason for respectfully presenting both my daughters together was that, by sending Princess-Long-as-the-Rocks, the august offspring[583] of the Heavenly Deity,[584] though the snow[585] fall and the wind blow, might live eternally immovable like unto the enduring rocks, and again that by sending Princess-Blossoming-Brilliantly-Like-the-Flowers-of-the-Trees, [they] might live flourishingly like unto the flowering of the blossoms of the trees: to insure this,[586] I offered[587] them. But owing to thy thus sending back[588] Princess Long-as-the-Rocks, and keeping only Princess-Blossoming-Brilliantly-Like-the-Flowers-of-the-Trees, the august offspring of the Heavenly Deity shall be but as frail[589] as the flowers of the trees." So it is for this reason that down to the present day the august lives of Their Augustnesses the Heavenly Sovereigns[590] are not long.

[A] *I.e.*, as enduring as the rocks. The original name is *Iwa-naga-hime*.

[B] *I.e.*, every kind of goods as a dowry for his daughters.

SECT. 38—THE AUGUST CHILD-BEARING OF PRINCESS-BLOSSOMING-BRILLIANTLY-LIKE-THE-FLOWERS-OF-THE-TREES

So later on Princess-Blossoming-Brilliantly-Like-the -Flowers-of-the-Trees waited on[A] [His Augustness Prince Rice-ear-Ruddy-Plenty], and said: "I[591] am pregnant, and now the time for my delivery approaches. It is not fit for me to be delivered of the august offspring of Heaven privately[B] so I tell thee."

Then [His Augustness Prince-Rice-ear-Ruddy-Plenty] said: "Princess-Blossoming-Brilliantly![C] what! pregnant after one night![D] It cannot be my child. It must surely be the child of an Earthly Deity."[592]

Then she replied, saying: "If the child with which I am pregnant be the child of an Earthly Deity, my delivery will not be fortunate. If it be the august child of the Heavenly Deity,[E] it will be fortunate";—and thereupon she built a hall eight fathoms [long] without doors,[F] went inside the hall and plastered up [the entrance] with earth and when the time came for her delivery, she set fire to the hall and was delivered.[G] So the name of the child that was born when the fire was burning most fiercely was His Augustness Fire-Shine[593] (this is the ancestor of the Hayabito, Dukes of Ata)[594] the name of the child born next was His Augustness Fire-Climax[595] the august[596] name of the child born next was His Augustness Fire-Subside,[597] another name for whom is His Augustness Heaven's-Sun-Height-Prince-Great-Rice-ears-Lord-Ears[598] (three Deities[599] [in all]).

[A] More literally "came to" but the character which is employed implies that her visit was to a superior.

[B] *I.e.*, "secretly," "without telling thee."

[C] In this one instance only is the name thus abbreviated. Norinaga supposes it to be on account of the scorn implied in the god's words.

[D] Lit., "one sojourn."

[E] *I.e.*, "thy child and the Sun-Goddess descendant."

[F] That is to say that it remained doorless after she had, as stated immediately below, plastered up the entrance.

[G] Viz. of child, not from the flames. There is no ambiguity in the Japanese expression.

SECT. 39—THE AUGUST EXCHANGE OF LUCK

So His Augustness Fire-Shine was a prince who got his luck[A] on the sea, and caught things broad of fin and things narrow of fin. His Augustness Fire-Subside was a prince who got his luck on the mountains, and caught things rough of hair and things soft of hair. Then His Augustness Fire-Subside said to his elder brother His Augustness Fire-Shine: "Let us mutually exchange, and use each other's luck." [Nevertheless], though he thrice made the request, [his elder brother] would not accede [to it] but at last with difficulty the mutual exchange was obtained.

Then His Augustness Fire-Subside, undertaking the sea-luck, angled for fish, but never got a single fish and moreover he lost the fish-hook in the sea. Thereupon his elder brother His Augustness Fire-Shine asked him for the fish-hook, saying: "A mountain-luck is a luck of its own, and a sea-luck is a luck of its own. Let each of us now restore [to the other] his luck."[B]

To which the younger brother His Augustness Fire-Subside replied, saying: "As for thy fish-hook, I did not get a single fish by angling with it and at last I lost it in the sea" But the elder brother required it of him [the more] urgently.

So the younger brother, breaking his ten grasp saber[600] that was augustly girded on him, made [of the fragments] five hundred fish-hooks as compensation but he would not take them. Again he made a thousand fish-hooks as compensation but he would not receive them, saying: "I still want the real original fish-hook."

[A] For the archaic Japanese word *sachi*, here rendered "luck," there is no satisfactory English equivalent. Its original and most usual signification is "luck," "happiness;" then that which a man is lucky in or skillful at—his *"forte"* and finally that which he procures by his luck or skill and the implements which he uses in procuring it. The exchange negotiated below was doubtless that of the bow and arrows of one deity for the other deity's fish-hook.

[B] *I.e.*, "Some men are naturally good hunters, and others naturally good fishermen. Let us therefore restore to each other the implements necessary to the successful following of our respective avocations." The clause rendered" Let each of us now restore to the other his luck" is a little confused in the original but the *kana* readings both old and new agree in interpreting it as has here been done.

SECT. 40—THE PALACE OF THE OCEAN-POSSESSOR

Hereupon, as the younger brother was weeping and lamenting by the sea-shore, the Deity Salt-Possessor[601] came and asked him, saying: "What is the cause of the Sky's-Sun-Height's[602] weeping and lamentation?"

He replied, saying: "I had exchanged a fish-hook with my elder brother,[A] and have lost that fish-hook and as he asks me for it, I have given him many fish-hooks as compensation but he will not receive them, saying, 'I still want the original fish-hook.' So I weep and lament for this."

Then the Deity Salt-Possessor said: "I will give good counsel to Thine Augustness"—and therewith built a stout little boat without interstices,[B] and set him in the boat, and instructed him, saying: "When I shall have pushed the boat off, go on for some time. There will be a savory august road[C603] and if thou goest in the boat along that road, there will appear a palace built like fishes' scales—which is the palace of the Deity-Ocean-Possessor.[604] When thou readiest the august gate of that deity['s palace], there will be a multitudinous[-ly branching] cassia-tree[605] above the well at its side. So if thou sit on the top of that tree, the Sea-Deity's daughter will see thee, and counsel thee."

So following [these] instructions, [His Augustness Fire-Subside] went a little [way], and everything happened as [the Deity Salt-Possessor] had said and he forthwith climbed the cassia-tree, and sat [there]. Then when the handmaidens of the Sea-Deity's daughter Luxuriant-Jewel-Princess,[606] bearing jeweled vessels, were about to draw water, there was a light in the well.[607] On looking up, there was a beautiful young man. They thought it very strange.

Then His Augustness Fire-Subside saw the handmaidens, and begged to be given some water. The handmaidens at once drew some water, put it into a jeweled vessel, and respectfully presented it to him. Then, without drinking the water, he loosened the jewel at his august

[A] *I.e.,* "I had received a fish-hook from my elder brother in exchange for a bow." The text is here concise to obscurity.

[B] *I.e.,* as is supposed, a punt or tub made of strips of bamboo plaited so tightly that no water could find its way in between them.

[C] *I.e.,* simply "a pleasant road."

neck, took it in his mouth, and spat it into the jeweled vessel. Thereupon the jewel adhered to the vessel, and the handmaidens could not separate the jewel [from the vessel]. So they took it with the jewel adhering to it, and presented it to Her Augustness Luxuriant-Jewel-Princess. Then, seeing the jewel, she asked her handmaidens, saying: "Is there perhaps some one outside the gate?"

They replied, saying: "There is some one sitting on the top of the cassia-tree above our well. It is a very beautiful young man. He is more illustrious even than our king. So, as he begged for water, we respectfully gave him water but, without drinking the water, he spat this jewel into [the vessel]. As we were not able to separate this [from the other],[608] we have brought [the vessel] with [the jewel] in it to present to thee."

Then Her Augustness Luxuriant-Jewel-Princess, thinking it strange, went out to look, and was forthwith delighted[609] at the sight. They exchanged glances, after which she spoke to her father, saying: "There is a beautiful person at our gate."

Then the Sea-Deity himself went out to look, and saying, "This person is the Sky's-Sun-Height, the august child of the Heaven's-Sun-Height,"[610] led him into the interior [of the palace], and spreading eight layers of rugs of sea-asses[A] skins, and spreading on the top other eight layers of silk rugs, and setting him on the top of them, arranged merchandise on tables holding a hundred,[611] made an august banquet, and forthwith gave him his daughter Luxuriant-Jewel-Princess in marriage. So he dwelt in that land for three years.

Hereupon His Augustness Fire-Subside thought of what had gone before,[B] and heaved one[612] deep sigh. So Her Augustness Luxuriant-Jewel-Princess, hearing the sigh, informed her father, saying: "Though he has dwelt three years [with us], he had never sighed but this night he heaved one deep sigh. What may be the cause of it?"

The Great Deity her father asked his son-in-law, saying: "This morning I hear my daughter speak, saying: 'Though he has dwelt

[A] This is a literal translation of the Chinese character 海驢, by which the Archaic word *michi,* here written phonetically, is elsewhere represented. Perhaps the sea-lion (*Otaria arsina)* or a species of seal may be intended.

[B] Lit., "thought of the first things."

three years [with us], he had never sighed but this night he heaved one deep sigh. What may the cause be?' Moreover what was the cause of thy coming here?" Then [His Augustness Fire-Subside] told the Great Deity exactly how his elder brother had pressed him for the lost fish-hook.

Thereupon the Sea-Deity summoned together all the fishes of the sea, great and small, and asked them, saying: "Is there perchance any fish that has taken this fish-hook?"

So all the fishes replied: "Lately the *tai*[613] has complained of something sticking in its throat[A] preventing it from eating so it doubtless has taken [the hook]." On the throat of the *tai* being thereupon examined, there was the fish-hook [in it].

Being forthwith taken, it was washed and respectfully presented to His Augustness Fire-Subside, whom the Deity Great-Ocean-Possessor then instructed, saying: "What thou shalt say when thou grantest this fish-hook to thine elder brother [is as follows]. 'This fish-hook is a big hook, an eager hook, a poor hook, a silly hook.'[614] Having [thus] spoken, bestow it with thy back hand.[B] Having done thus, if thine elder brother make high fields,[C] do Thine Augustness make low fields and if thine elder brother make low fields, do Thine Augustness make high fields. If thou do thus, thine elder brother will certainly be impoverished in the space of three years, owing to my ruling the water. If thine elder brother, incensed at thy doing thus, should attack thee, put forth the tide-flowing jewel[615] to drown him. If he express grief, put forth the tide-ebbing jewel to let him live. Thus shalt thou harass him."

With these words, [the Sea-Deity] gave [to His Augustness Fire-Subside] the tide-flowing jewel and the tide-ebbing jewel—two in all—and forthwith summoned together all the crocodiles,[616] and asked

[A] Or, "of a fish-bone in its throat."

[B] *I.e.,* "with thy hand behind thy back." This is supposed by the commentators to have been a sort of charm by which evil was averted from the person of him who practiced it, and they point out that Izanagi (the "Male-Who-Invites") brandished his sword behind him when he was pursued by the hosts of Hades (see Sect. 9, Note c).

[C] By "high fields" and "low fields" are meant respectively upland rice-fields where the rice is planted in the dry, and "paddy-fields" properly so called, where the rice perpetually stands in the water. Different varieties of rice are used for these different methods of culture.

them, saying: "The Sky's-Sun-Height, august child of the Heaven's-Sun-Height, is now about to proceed out to the Upper-Land.[617] Who will in how many days respectfully escort him, and bring back a report."[A]

So each according to the length of his body in fathoms spoke, fixing [a certain number of] days—one of them, a crocodile one fathom [long], saying: "I[618] will escort him, and come back in one day." So then [the Sea-Deity] said to the crocodile one fathom [long]: "If that be so, do thou respectfully escort him. While crossing the middle of the sea, do not alarm him.[619] Forthwith he seated him upon the crocodile's head, and saw him off. So [the crocodile] respectfully escorted him home in one day, as he had promised. When the crocodile was about to return, [His Augustness Fire-Subside] untied the stiletto[620] which was girded on him, and, setting it on the crocodile's neck,[B] sent [the latter] back. So the crocodile one fathom [long] is now called the Deity Blade-Possessor.[621]

SECT. 41—SUBMISSION OF HIS AUGUSTNESS FIRE-SHINE

Hereupon [His Augustness Fire-Subside] gave the fish-hook [to his elder brother], exactly according to the Sea-Deity's words of instruction. So thenceforward [the elder brother] became poorer and poorer, and, with renewed savage intentions, came to attack him. When he was about to attack [His Augustness Fire-Subside, the latter] put forth the tide-flowing jewel to drown him; on his expressing grief, he put forth the tide-ebbing jewel to save him. When he had thus been harassed, he bowed his head,[C] saying: "I[622] henceforward will be Thine Augustness's guard by day and night, and respectfully serve thee." So down to the present day his various posturings when drowning are ceaselessly served up.[D623]

[A] *I.e.,* "Which of you will most speedily escort him home to the upper world, and bring back news of his safe arrival there?"

[B] *I.e.,* probably, tying it round the crocodile's neck.

[C] *I.e.,* "did humble obeisance by prostrating himself on the ground." The Old Printed Edition has 稽白 instead of 稽首白, and the *kana* gloss *kamugae-mōsu i.e.,* "reflected and said": but this reading, though interesting, is less good.

[D] *I.e.,* "Prince Fire-Shine's descendants the *Hayabito* (see Vol. 1, Note 632) still constantly perform before the Court dances and posturings symbolical of the antics which their divine ancestor went through for the amusement of his younger brother,

SECT. 42—THE PARTURITION-HOUSE OF CORMORANTS' FEATHERS

Hereupon the Sea-Deity's daughter Her Augustness Luxuriant-Jewel-Princess herself waited on[624] [His Augustness Fire-Subside], and said: "I[625] am already with child, and the time for my delivery now approaches. But methought that the august child of a Heavenly Deity[A] ought not to be born in the Sea-Plain.[B] So I have waited on thee here."[C]

Then forthwith on the limit of the waves upon the seashore she built a parturition-hall,[626] using cormorants' feathers for thatch. Hereupon, before the thatch was completed,[D] she was unable to restrain the urgency of her august womb. So she entered the parturition-hall. Then, when she was about to be delivered, she spoke to her husband,[627] [saying]: "Whenever a foreigner is about to be delivered, she takes the shape of her native land to be delivered.[E] So I now will take my native shape to be delivered. Pray look not upon me!"

Hereupon [His Augustness Fire-Subside], thinking these words strange, stealthily peeped at the very moment of delivery, when she turned into a crocodile[628] eight fathoms [long], and crawled and writhed about and he forthwith, terrified at the sight, fled away. Then her Augustness Luxuriant-Jewel-Princess knew that he had peeped and she felt ashamed, and, straightway leaving the august child which she had borne, she said: "I had wished always to come and go across the sea-path.[629] But thy having peeped at my [real] shape [makes me] very shamefaced,"[630]—and she forthwith closed the sea-boundary,[F] and went down again.[G]

Therefore the name by which the august child whom she had borne was called His Augustness Heaven's-Sun-Height-Prince-Wave-lim-

after the latter had saved him from drowning."

[A] Or "of *the* Heavenly Deity," *i.e.*, "thyself." But it seems better to understand the speaker to intimate that it would be unfitting for one who properly belonged to Heaven to be born in the sea, which was another country or kingdom.

[B] *I.e.*, in the sea.

[C] Lit., "come out and arrived."

[D] Or, completely put on; lit., "thatched [so as] to meet."

[E] *I.e.*, she assumes the shape proper to her in her native land.

[F] *I.e.*, the boundary dividing the dominions of the Sea-God from the world of men.

[G] Viz., to the Sea-God's palace.

it-Brave-Cormorant-Thatch-Meeting-Incompletely.[631] Nevertheless afterwards, although angry at his having wished to peep, she could not restrain her loving heart, and she entrusted to her younger sister Jewel-Good-Princess,[632] on the occasion of her nursing the august child,[A] a Song to be presented [to His Augustness Fire-Subside]. The Song said:

[7] As for red jewels, though even the string
[they are strung on] shines, the aspect of
[my] lord [who is] like unto white jewels
is [more] illustrious.[633]

Then her husband replied by a Song, which said:

[8] As for my younger sister, whom I took to
sleep [with me] on the island where light
the wild-duck, the birds of the offing, I
shall not forget her till the end of my life.[634]

So His Augustness-Prince-Great-Rice-ears-Lord-Ears[635] dwelt in the palace of Takachiho for five hundred and eighty years.[B] His august mausoleum[C] is likewise on the west of Mount Takachiho.

[A] *I.e.,* of Jewel-Good-Princess nursing the child. The mother did not return to the upper world, and so sent this poetic message by her sister, who had consented to act as the child's nurse.

[B] Probably the writer means us to understand that the total age reached by this deity was five hundred and eighty years. This is the first mention in these Records of anything approaching a date. The way in which it is recorded resembles that in which the chronicle of each Emperor's reign is brought to a close in the later volumes of the work.

[C] The character 陵 might also be rendered by the simpler word "grave." But neither it nor its Japanese reading *misasaki* are ever used except honorifically of the Imperial tombs, and "mausoleum" seems therefore a more suitable English equivalent.

SECT. 43—THE AUGUST CHILDREN OF HIS AUGUSTNESS CORMORANT-THATCH-MEETING-INCOMPLETELY

His Augustness Heaven's-Sun-Height-Prince Wave-limit-Brave-Cormorant-Thatch-Meeting-Incompletely wedded his maternal aunt Her Augustness Jewel-Good-Princess, and begot august children named: His Augustness Five-Reaches;[636] next His Augustness Boiled-Rice;[637] next His Augustness August-Food-Master;[638] next His Augustness Young-August-Food-Master,[639] another name for whom is His Augustness Luxuriant-August-Food-Master,[640] and another name is His Augustness Divine-Yamato-Iware-Prince.[A]

So His Augustness August-Food-Master, treading on the crest of the waves, crossed over to the Eternal Land.[641] His Augustness Boiled-Rice went into the Sea-Plain, it being his deceased mother's[642] land.

[A] *Kamu-yamato-iware-biko-no-mikoto.* Yamato being the name of the province where this prince, the first Emperor of the so-called "human age," fixed his capital, it appropriately forms part of his name. For a discussion of the etymology of the word Yamato, see Vol. 1, Note 91. *Iware,* a word which is said to signify "assembling," is the name of a village in that province. [Four Deities.—W.G.A.] [This figure is commonly known as Jinmu, the mythical first emperor of Japan.—M.F.]

Vol. 2.[1]

SECT. 44—REIGN OF THE EMPEROR JIN-MU[A] (PART 1—HIS PROGRESS EASTWARD, AND DEATH OF HIS ELDER BROTHER)

The two Deities His Augustness Kamu-yamato-iware-biko[2] and his elder brother His Augustness Itsu-se, dwelling in the palace of Takachiho,[3] took counsel, saying: "By dwelling in what place shall we [most] quietly carry on the government of the Empire?[4] It were probably best to go east."

Forthwith they left Himuka[5] on their progress[B] to Tsukushi.[6] So when they arrived at Usa[7] in the land of Toyo,[8] two of the natives, whose names were Usa-tsu-hiko and Usa-tsu-hime[C] built a palace raised on one foot,[9] and offered them a great august banquet. Removing thence, they dwelt for one year at the palace of Okada[10] in Tsukushi. Again making a progress up[D] from that land, they dwelt seven years at the palace of Takeri[11] in the land of Agi.[12] Again removing, and making a progress up from that land, they dwelt eight years at the palace of Takashima[13] in Kibi.[14]

So when they made their progress up from that land, they met in the Hayasui[15] Channel a person riding towards them on the carapace of a tortoise, and raising his wings[16] as he angled. Then they called to him to approach, and asked him, saying: "Who art thou?"

[A] *Jin-mu* signifies "divine valor." It is the "canonical name" of the Emperor *Kamu-yamato-iware-biko* (see Introduction, p. 27).

[B] The Japanese expression here used is one which exclusively denotes an Imperial Progress, and not the movements of lesser people. It recurs perpetually in this and the following Volume.

[C] *I.e.*, Prince of Usa and Princess of Usa.

[D] *Q.d.*, towards Yamato, the province where the capital was eventually fixed. [Nara Prefecture.— M.F.] In Japanese, as in English, people are said to go *up* to the capital and *down* to the country.

He replied, saying: "I[17] am an Earthly Deity."[18]

Again they asked him, saying: "Knowest thou the sea-path?"

He replied, saying: "I know it well."

Again they asked him, saying: "Wilt thou follow and respectfully serve us?"

He replied, saying: "I will respectfully serve you." So they pushed a pole[19] across to him, drew him into the august vessel, and forthwith conferred on him the designation of Sao-ne-tsu-hiko.[A] (This is the ancestor of the Rulers of the land of Yamato)[20]

So when they went up from that land they passed the Nami-haya[21] Crossing, and brought up at the haven of Shirakata.[22] At this time Nagasune-hiko[23] of Tomi[24] raised an army, and waited to go out to fight [against them]. Then they took the shields that had been put in the august vessel, and disembarked. So they called that place by the name of Tate-zu.[25] It is what is now called the Tadetsu of Kusaka.[26]

Therefore when fighting with the Prince of Tomi,[B] His Augustness Itsu-se was pierced in his august hand by the Prince of Tomi's hurtful arrow.[27] So then he said: "It is not right for me, an august child of the Sun-Deity, to fight facing the sun. It is for this reason that I am stricken by the wretched villain's[28] hurtful hand. I will henceforward turn round, and smite him with my back to the sun." Having [thus] decided, he, on making a progress round from the southern side, reached the sea of Chinu,[29] and washed the blood on his august hand: so it is called the sea of Chinu.[30] Making a progress round from thence, and arriving at the river-mouth of O[31] in the land of Ki,[32] he said: "Ah! That I should die stricken by the wretched villain's hand!" and expired[33] as a valiant man.[34] So that river-mouth was called the river-mouth of O.[35] The mausoleum, too, is on Mount Kama[36] in the land of Ki.

SECT. 45—EMPEROR JIN-MU (PART 2—THE CROSS-SWORD SENT DOWN FROM HEAVEN)

So when His Augustness Kamu-yamato-iware-biko made progress round from thence, and reached the village of Kumano,[37] a large bear

---

[A] *I.e.*, if we suppress the syllable *ne*, which seems to be either expletive or honorific, the "prince of the pole."

[B] Viz., *Nagasune-biko*.

came out of the mountain,[38] and forthwith disappeared into it.[39] Then His Augustness Kamu-yamato-iware-biko suddenly fainted away, and his august army likewise all fainted and fell prostrate.

At this time Takakuraji[40] (this is the name of a person)[41] of Kumano came bearing one cross-sword[42] to the place where the august child of the Deity was lying prostrate, and presented it to him, upon which the august child of the Heavenly Deity forthwith rose up, and said: "How long I have slept!" So when he accepted the cross-sword, the savage Deities of the mountains of Kumano all spontaneously fell cut down.[A] Then the whole august army, that had been bewildered and had fallen prostrate, awoke and rose up.

So the august child of the Heavenly Deity asked him how he had got the cross-sword. Takakuraji replied, saying: "I was told in a dream that the two Deities the Heaven-Shining-Great-Deity[43] and the High Integrating Deity[44] commanded and summoned the Brave-Awful-Possessing-Male-Deity,[45] and charged, him [thus]: 'The Central Land of Reed-Plains[46] is painfully uproarious, —it is.[47] Our august children must be ill at ease. As [therefore] the Central Land of Reed-Plains is a land which thou specially subduest, thou the Brave-Awful-Possessing-Male-Deity shalt descend [thither].'

"Then he replied, saying: 'I[48] will not descend [myself], but I have the cross-sword wherewith I specially subdued the land. (The name by which this sword is called is the Deity Thrust-Snap;[49] another name by which it is called is the Deity Awful-Snap,[50] and another name for it is the August-Snap-Spirit.[51] This sword dwells in the temple of the Deity of Isonokami.)[52] The manner in which I will send this sword down will be to perforate the ridge of [the roof of] Takakuraji's store-house,[53] and drop it through!'

"[So the Brave-Awful-Possessing-Male-Deity instructed me, saying: 'I will perforate the ridge of (the roof of) thy store-house, and drop this sword through.][B] So do thou, with the good eyes of morning,[54] take it and present it to the august child of the Heavenly Deity.'

[A] *I.e.,* they fell down cut to pieces before they had even been cut at with this wonderful sword.

[B] The sentence here placed between braces is proposed by Norinaga to supplement an evident lacuna in the text.

"So on my searching my store-house early next morning in accordance with the instructions of the dream, there really was a cross-sword there. So I just present this cross-sword to thee."

SECT. 46—EMPEROR JIN-MU (PART 3—THE GIGANTIC CROW AND GODS WITH TAILS)

"Then His[A] Augustness the Great-High-Integrating-Deity again commanded and taught, saying: 'August son of the Heavenly Deity! Make no progress hence into the interior. The savage Deities are very numerous. I will now send from Heaven a crow eight feet [long].[55] So that crow eight feet [long] shall guide thee. Thou must make thy progress following after it as it goes.'"

So on [His Augustness Kamu-yamato-iware-biko] making his progress following after the crow eight feet [long] in obedience to the Deity's instructions, he reached the lower course of the Yoshino[56] river where there was a person catching fish in a weir.[57] Then the august child of the Heavenly Deity asked, saying: "Who art thou?"

He replied, saying: "I[58] am an Earthly Deity[59] and am called by the name of Nie-motsu no Ko."[60] (This is the ancestor of the Cormorant-Keepers of Ada).[61]

On [His Augustness Kamu-yamato-iware-biko] making his progress thence, a person with a tail[62] came out of a well. The well shone. Then [His Augustness] asked: "Who art thou?"

He replied, saying: "I am an Earthly Deity, and my name is I-hika.[B]" (This is the ancestor of the Headmen of Yoshino).[63]

On his forthwith entering the mountains,[C] His Augustness Kamu-yamato-iware-biko again met a person with a tail. This person came forth pushing the cliffs apart. Then [His Augustness Kamu-yamato-iware-biko] asked: "Who art thou?"

He replied, saying: "I am an Earthly Deity, and my name is Iwa-oshi-waku no Ko. I heard [just] now that the august son of the Heavenly

---

[A] The intention of the writer is here obscure, but he probably meant the following passage to form part of the dream, as is the case in the parallel passage of the *Chronicles*. The inverted commas are therefore continued in the translation.

[B] *I.e.,* "Well-Shine."

[C] *I.e.,* disappearing among the mountains.

Deity was making his progress. So it is for that that I have come to meet thee." (This is the ancestor of the Territorial Owners of Yoshino)[64]

Thence [His Augustness Kamu-yamato-iware-biko] penetrated over on foot to Uda.[65] So they say: "The Ugachi of Uda."[66]

SECT. 47—EMPEROR JIN-MU (PART 4—THE UKASHI BRETHREN)

So then there were in Uda two persons, Ukashi the Elder Brother and Ukashi the Younger Brother.[67] So [His Augustness Kamu-yamato-iware-biko] sent the crow eight feet [long] in advance to ask these persons, saying: "The august child of the Heavenly Deity has made a progress [hither]. Will ye respectfully serve him?"

Hereupon Ukashi the Elder Brother waited for and shot at the messenger with a whizzing barb[A] to make him turn back. So the place where the whizzing barb fell is called Kabura-zaki.[68] Saying that he intended to wait for and smite [His Augustness Kamu-yamato-iware-biko], he [tried to] collect an army. But being unable to collect an army, he said deceitfully that he would respectfully serve [His Augustness Kamu-yamato-iware-biko], and built a great palace,[B] and in that palace set a pitfall, and waited.

Then Ukashi the Younger Brother came out to[69] [His Augustness Kamu-yamato-iware-biko] beforehand, and made obeisance, saying: "Mine[70] elder brother Ukashi the Elder Brother has shot at and turned back the messenger of the august child of the Heavenly Deity, and, intending to wait for and attack thee, has [tried to] collect an army; but, being unable to collect it, he has built a great palace, and set[C] a gin within it, intending to wait for and catch thee. So I have come out to inform [thee of this]."

Then the two persons His Augustness Michi-no-Omi,[D] ancestor of the Ōtomo Chieftains,[71] and His Augustness Ōkume,[72] ancestor of

[A] Arrow. —W.G.A.

[B] Or, hall.

[C] Lit., "spread." This gin is supposed to have been of the kind whose top closes down after the man or animal has fallen into it.

[D] *I.e.*, "Grandee of the Way." This "gentile name" is said in the *Chronicles* to have been bestowed on this worthy in consideration of his services as a guide to his master the Emperor on the occasion of the latter's progress eastward.

the Kume Lords,[73] summoned Ukashi the Elder Brother and reviled him, saying: "Into the great palace which thou[74] hast built to respectfully serve [His Augustness Kamu-yamato-iware-biko], be thou[75] the first to enter, and declare plainly the manner in which thou intendest respectfully to serve him;"—and forthwith grasping the hilts of their cross-swords, playing with their spears,[76] and fixing arrows [in their bows], they drove him in, whereupon he was caught in[A] the gin which he himself had set, and died. So they forthwith pulled him out, and cut him in pieces. So the place is called Uda-no-Chihara.[77]

Having done thus, [His Augustness Kamu-yamato-iware-biko] bestowed on his august army the whole of the great banquet presented [to him] by Ukashi the Younger Brother. At this time he sang, saying:

[9] The woodcock, for which I laid a woodcock-snare
and waited in the high castle of Uda,
strikes not against it;
but a valiant whale strikes against it.

If the elder wife ask for fish,
slice off a little like the berries of the standing *soba*;
if the younger wife ask for fish,
slice off a quantity like the berries of the vigorous *sakaki*.[78]

Ugh![79] pfui! dolt!
This is saying thou rascal.
Ah! pfui! dolt!
This is laughing [him] to scorn.

So Ukashi the Younger Brother (is the ancestor of the Water-Directors of Uda).[80]

SECT. 48—EMPEROR JIN-MU (PART 5—THE EARTH-SPIDERS OF THE CAVE OF OSAKA)

When [His Augustness Kamu-yamato-iware-biko] made his prog-

[A] Lit. "struck by."

ress, and reached the great cave of Osaka,[81] earth-spiders[A82] with tails, [namely] eighty bravoes,[83] were in the cave[84] awaiting him. So then the august son of the Heavenly Deity commanded that a banquet be bestowed on the eighty bravoes. Thereupon he set eighty butlers, one for each of the eighty bravoes, and girded each of them with a sword, and instructed the butlers, saying: "When ye hear me sing, cut [them down] simultaneously." So the Song by which he made clear to them to set about smiting the earth-spiders said:

[10] Into the great cave of Osaka
people have entered in abundance,
and are [there].
Though people have entered in abundance,
and are [there],
the children of the augustly powerful warriors
will smite and finish them
with [their] mallet-headed [swords],
[their] stone-mallet [swords]:
the children of the augustly powerful warriors,
with [their] mallet-headed [swords],
[their] stone-mallet [swords],
would now do well to smite.[85]

Having thus sung, they drew their swords, and simultaneously smote them to death.

SECT. 49—EMPEROR JIN-MU (PART 6—THE PRINCE OF TOMI AND THE SHIKI BRETHREN)

After this, when about to smite the Prince of Tomi,[86] he sang, saying:

[11] The children of the augustly powerful army
will smite and finish

[A] There is little doubt that by this well-known name, which has given rise to much conjecture, a race of cave-dwelling savages or a class of cave-dwelling robbers is intended.

the one stem of smelly chive in the millet-field,
—the stem of its root, both its root and shoots.[87]

Again he sang:

[12] The ginger,
which the children of the augustly powerful army
planted near the hedge,
resounds[88] in the mouth.
I shall not forget it.
I will smite and finish it.[89]

Again he sang, saying:

[13] Like the *turbinidoe*
creeping round the great rock in the sea of Ise
[on which blows] the divine wind,
[so] will we creep round,
and smite and finish them.[90]

Again when he smote Shiki the Elder Brother and Shiki the Younger Brother,[91] the august army was temporarily exhausted. Then he sang, saying:

[14] As we fight placing our shields in a row,
going and watching from between the trees
on Mount Inasa,
Oh! We are famished.
Ye keepers of cormorants,
the birds of the island,
come now to our rescue![92]

SECT. 50—EMPEROR JIN-MU (PART 7—THE EMPIRE PACIFIED)

So then His Augustness Nigi-hayabi[93] waited on and said to the august child of the Heavenly Deity: "As I heard that [thou], the august child of the Heavenly Deity, hadst descended from Heaven, I have followed down to wait on thee." Forthwith presenting to him the heavenly symbols,[A] he respectfully served him.

So His Augustness Nigi-hayabi wedded the Princess of Tomi,[94] sister of the Prince of Tomi, and begot a child, His Augustness Uma-shi-ma-ji.[95] (He was the ancestor of the Chief of the Warrior-Clan,[96] of the Grandees of Hozumi[97] and of the Grandees of the Neck-Clan.)[98]

So having thus subdued and pacified the savage Deities, and extirpated the unsubmissive people, [His Augustness Kamu-yamato-iware-biko] dwelt at the palace of Kashibara[99] near Unebi,[100] and ruled the Empire.[B]

SECT. 51—EMPEROR JIN-MU (PART 8—HE WEDS I-SUKE-YORI-HIME)

So when he dwelt in Himuka, [His Augustness Kamu-yamato-iware-biko] wedded[C] Princess Ahira,[101] younger sister of the Duke of Obashi[102] in Ata,[103] and begot children: there were two,[104] —

His Augustness Tagishi-mimi,[105]
next His Augustness Kisu-mimi.[106]

But when he sought for a beautiful maiden to make her his Chief Empress,[107] His Augustness Ō-kume said: "There is here a beauteous maiden who is called the august child of a Deity. The reason why she is called the august child of a Deity is that the Princess Seya-datara,[108] daughter of Mizokui[109] of Mishima,[110] was admired on account of her beauty by the Great-Master-of-Things the Deity of Miwa,[111] who, when the fair maiden was defecating, turned into an arrow painted red, and pierced the private parts of the maiden from the lower part of the sewer [for use in] defecating. Then the fair maiden was startled, and rose up, and fled in alarm. She immediately brought the arrow, and placed it in her chamber. Suddenly [the arrow] became a handsome young man, who quickly married the beautiful girl, and she gave birth

[A] *I.e.*, the swords, quivers, bows, and arrows mentioned in Sect. 33, as having been brought down from Heaven by the divine attendants of the Emperor Jin-mu's grandfather.

[B] *I.e.*, "ruled the Empire from his palace of Kashibara near Unebi." For the expression 天下 (lit. "[all] beneath Heaven"), here rendered "Empire," see Vol. 1, Note 438.

[C] Or, "*had* wedded;" for the episode here related must be supposed to have taken place before Jin-mu and his army started eastward on their career of conquest.

to a daughter named Hoto-tatara-i-susugi-hime and her alternative name is Hime-tatara-i-suke-yori-hime. (That is a later change of name, since they were loathe to mention private parts).[112] So therefore she is called the august child of a Deity."

Hereupon seven beauteous maidens were out playing on the moor of Takasaji,[113] and I-suke-yori-hime[114] was among them. His Augustness Ōkume, seeing I-suke-yori-hime, spoke to the Heavenly Sovereign in a Song, saying:

[15] Seven maidens on the moor of Takasaji
in Yamato:—which shall be interlaced?[115]

Then I-suke-yori-hime was standing first among the beauteous maidens. Forthwith the Heavenly Sovereign, having looked at the beauteous maidens, and knowing in his august heart[A] that I-suke-yori-hime was standing in the very front, replied by a song, saying:

[16] Even [after nought but] a fragment[-ary glimpse],
I will intertwine the lovely [one]
standing in the very front.[116]

Then His Augustness Ōkume informed I-suke-yori-hime of the Heavenly Sovereign's decree, whereupon she, seeing the slit sharp eyes[117] of His Augustness Ōkume, sang in her astonishment, saying:

[17] Wherefore the slit sharp eyes?"[B][118]

Then His Augustness Ōkume replied by a Song, saying:

[18] My slit sharp eyes [are] in order to find
the maiden immediately.[119]

[A] *I.e.*, "having a presentiment."

[B] The first lines of this short poem are so hopelessly unintelligible that the commentators are not even agreed as to how the syllables composing them should be divided into words.

So the maiden said that she would respectfully serve [the Heavenly Sovereign].[120] Hereupon[121] the house of Her Augustness[A] I-suke-yori-hime was on [the bank of] the River Sai.[122] The Heavenly Sovereign made a progress to the abode of I-suke-yori-hime, and augustly slept [there] one night.[123] (The reason why that river was called the River Sai was that on the river's banks the mountain-lily-plant grew in abundance. So the name of the mountain-lily-plant was taken, and the designation of River Sai [bestowed]. The name by which the mountain-lily-plant was originally called was *sai).* Afterwards, when I-suke-yori-hime came and entered into the palace, the Heavenly Sovereign sang augustly saying:

[19] In a damp hut on the reed-moor
having spread layer upon layer of sedge mats,
we two slept![124]

The names of the august children thus born were:
His Augustness Hiko-ya-i[125]
next His Augustness Kamu-ya-i-mimi,[126]
next His Augustness Kamu-nuna-kawa-mimi,[127] (Three Deities).[128]

SECT. 52—EMPEROR JIN-MU (PART 9—TROUBLES WHICH FOLLOWED HIS DECEASE)

So when, after the decease of the Heavenly Sovereign,[129] the[B] elder half-brother, His Augustness Tagishi-mimi,[C] wedded[130] the Empress I-suke-yori-hime, he plotted how he might slay his three younger brethren, pending which their august[131] parent I-suke-yori-hime lamented, and made [the plot] known to her august children by a song. The Song said:

[A]Having become the Emperor's consort, this Honorific title is now prefixed for the first time to her name.

[B]The Japanese is *sono* which looks as if it was Jin-mu Tennō's elder brother who was intended. Perhaps 兄 is a mistake for 子. —W.G.A.

[C]Who was the deceased Emperor's son by Princess Ahira (see Vol. 2, Note 105), and consequently stepson to the Empress and half-brother to her three sons.

[20] From the River Sai
the clouds have risen across,
and the leaves of the trees
have rustled on Mount Unebi:
the wind is about to blow.[132]

Again she sang, saying:

[21] Ah! What rests on Mount Unebi
as clouds in the daytime,
will surely blow
as wind at nightfall,
[whence] the rustling of the leaves![133]

When hereupon her august children, hearing and knowing [of the danger], were alarmed and forthwith were about to slay Tagishi-mimi, His Augustness Kamu-nuna-kawa-mimi said to his elder brother His Augustness Kamu-ya-i-mimi: "Thy dear Augustness, [do thou] take a weapon, and go in and slay Tagishi-mimi." So he took a weapon and went in, and was about to slay him. But his arms and legs trembled so, that he was unable to slay him.

So then the younger brother His Augustness Kamu-nuna-kawa-mimi begged [to be allowed] to take the weapon which his elder brother held, and went in and slew Tagishi-mimi. So again, in praise of his august name, he was called His Augustness Take-nuna-kawa-mimi.[134]

Then His Augustness Kamu-ya-i-mimi resigned [in favor of] the younger brother His Augustness Take-nuna-kawa-mimi, saying: "I could not slay the foeman; but Thine Augustness was at once able to slay him. So, though I be the elder brother, it is not right that I should be the superior.[135] Wherefore do Thine Augustness be the superior, and rule [all] beneath the Heaven. I[136] will assist Thine Augustness, becoming a priest,[137] and respectfully serving thee."

SECT. 53—EMPEROR JIN-MU (PART 10—GENEALOGIES)

So His Augustness Hoko-ya-i (is the ancestor of the Chieftains of Mamuta,[138] and of the Chieftains of Teshima[139]).

His Augustness Kamu-ya-i-mimi (is the ancestor of the Grandees of Ō,[140] of the Chieftains of the Tribe of Chiisako,[141] of the Chieftains of the Tribe of Sakai,[142] of the Dukes of Hi,[143] of the Dukes of Ōkida,[144] of the Dukes of Aso,[145] of the Chieftains of the Granaries of Tsukushi,[146] of the Grandees of the Sazaki Tribe,[147] of the Rulers of the Tribe of Sazaki,[148] of the Rulers of O-Hatsuse,[149] of the Suzerains of Tsuke,[150] of the Rulers of the land of Iyo,[151] of the Rulers of the land of Shinano,[152] of the Rulers of the Land of Iwaki in Michinoku,[153] of the Rulers of the Land of Naka in Hitachi,[154] of the Rulers of the Land of Nagasa,[155] of the Suzerains of Funaki in Ise,[156] of the Grandees of Niwa in Owari,[157] and of the Grandees of Shimada.)[158]

SECT. 54—EMPEROR JIN-MU (PART 11—HIS AGE AND PLACE OF BURIAL)

His Augustness Kamu-nuna-kawa-mimi ruled the Empire. Altogether the august years of this Heavenly Sovereign Kamu-yamato-iware-biko were one hundred and thirty-seven.[A] His august mausoleum is on the top of the Kashi Spur on the northern side of Mount Unebi.[159]

SECT. 55—EMPEROR SUI-ZEI

His Augustness Kamu-nuna-kawa-mimi dwelt at the palace of Taka-oka in Kazuraki,[160] and ruled the Empire. This Heavenly Sovereign wedded Kawa-mata-bime,[161] ancestress of the Departmental Lords of Shiki,[162] and begot an august child:

His Augustness Shiki-tsu-hiko-tama-de-mi[163] (one Deity).

The Heavenly Sovereign's august years were forty-five. His august mausoleum is on the Mound of Tsukida.[164]

SECT. 56—EMPEROR AN-NEI

His Augustness Shiki-tsu-hiko-tama-de-mi dwelt in the palace of Ukiana at Kata-shiwa,[165] and ruled the Empire. This Heavenly Sovereign wedded Akuto-hime,[166] daughter of the Departmental Lord

[A]The author's confused style must not here mislead the student. It is *after* the decease of the Emperor Jin-mu (Kamu-yamato-iware-biko), who attains to the age of a hundred and thirty-seven, that the Emperor Sui-zei (Kamu-nuna-kawa-mimi) begins to rule.

Hae,[167] elder brother of Kawa-mata-bime, and begot august children:

His Augustness Toko-ne-tsu-hiko-irone,[168]

next His Augustness Ō-yamato-hiko-suki-tomo,[169]

next His Augustness Shiki-tsu-hiko.[170]

Of the august children of this Heavenly Sovereign,—three Deities,— His Augustness Ō-yamato-hiko-suki-tomo [was he who afterwards] ruled the Empire.

There were two Kings,[171] children of the next [brother], His Augustness Shiki-tsu-hiko. One child[A] (was the ancestor of the Territorial Lords of Suchi in Iga,[172] of the Territorial Lords of Nabari,[173] and of the Territorial Lords of Mino).[174]

One child,[B] His Augustness Wa-chi-tsumi,[175] dwelt in the palace of Mii in Awaji.[176] So this King had two daughters: the name of the elder was Hae-irone,[177] and another name for her was Her Augustness Princess Ō-yamato-kuni-are[178] the name of the younger was Hae-irodo.[179]

The Heavenly Sovereign's august years were forty-nine. His august mausoleum is on the private parts of Mt. Unebi.[180]

SECT. 57—EMPEROR I-TOKU

His Augustness Ō-yamato-hiko-suki-tomo dwelt in the palace of Sakaio at Karu,[181] and ruled the Empire. This Heavenly Sovereign wedded her Augustness Princess Futo-ma-waka,[182] another name for whom was Her Augustness Princess Ii-bi,[183] ancestress of the Departmental Lords of Shiki,[184] and begot august children:

His Augustness Mi-ma-tsu-hiko-kae-shine,[185]

next His Augustness Tagishi-hiko[186] (two Deities).

So His Augustness Mi-ma-tsu-hiko-kae-shine [was he who afterwards] ruled the Empire.

The next His Augustness Tagishi-hiko (was the ancestor of the Lords of Chinu,[187] of the Lords of Take in Tajima,[188] and of the Territorial Lords of Ashii).[189]

[A] The text has "descendant;" but it must here be corrupt or at least faulty, as may be seen by the omission of the proper name.

[B] *I.e.,* the other child.

The Heavenly Sovereign's august years were forty-five. His august mausoleum is above the Vale of Managō by Mount Unebi.[190]

SECT. 58—EMPEROR KŌ-SHŌ

His Augustness Mi-ma-tsu-hiko-kae-shine dwelt at the palace of Waki-no-kami in Kazuraki,[191] and ruled the Empire. This Heavenly Sovereign wedded Her Augustness Princess Yoso-taho,[192] younger sister of Oki-tsu-yoso,[193] ancestor of the Chiefs of Owari,[194] and begot august children:

His Augustness Ame-oshi-tarashi-hiko,[195]

and next His Augustness Ō-yamato-tarashi-hiko-kuni-oshi-bito[196] (two Deities).

Now the younger brother, His Augustness Tarashi-hiko-kuni-oshi-bito [was he who afterwards] ruled the Empire.

The elder brother His Augustness Ame-oshi-tarashi-hiko (was the ancestor of the Grandees of Kasuga,[197] the Grandees of Ōyake,[198] the Grandees of Awata,[199] the Grandees of Onu,[200] the Grandees of Kaki-no-moto,[201] the Grandees of Ichihii,[202] the Grandees of Ōsaka,[203] the Grandees of Ana,[204] the Grandees of Taki,[205] the Grandees of Haguri,[206] the Grandees of Chita,[207] the Grandees of Muza,[208] the Grandees of Tsunoyama,[209] the Dukes of Iitaka in Ise,[210] the Dukes of Ichishi,[211] and the Rulers of the Land of Chika-tsu-Ōmi).[212]

The Heavenly Sovereign's august years were ninety-three. His august mausoleum is on Mount Hakata[213] at Waki-no-kami.

SECT. 59—EMPEROR KŌ-AN

His Augustness Ō-yamato-tarashi-hiko-kuni-oshi-bito dwelt in the palace of Akizushima at Muro[214] in Kazuraki, and ruled the Empire. This Heavenly Sovereign wedded his niece Her Augustness Princess Oshika,[215] and begot august children:

His Augustness Ō-kibi-no-moro-susumi,[216]

next His Augustness Ō-yamato-ne-ko-hiko-futo-ni[217] (two Deities).

So His Augustness Ō-yamato-ne-ko-hiko-futo-ni [was he who afterwards] ruled the Empire.

The Heavenly Sovereign's august years were one hundred and twenty-three. His august mausoleum is on the Mound of Tamade.[218]

SECT. 60—EMPEROR KO-REI

His Augustness Ō-yamato-ne-ko-hiko-futo-ni dwelt at the palace of Ioto at Kuruda,[219] and ruled the Empire. This Heavenly Sovereign wedded Her Augustness Princess Kuwashi,[220] daughter of Ōme,[221] ancestor of the Departmental Lords of Tōchi,[222] and begot an august child:

His Augustness Ō-yamato-ne-ko-hiko-kuni-kuru[223] (one Deity).

Again he wedded Princess Chiji-haya-ma-waka of Kasuga,[224] and begot an august child:

Her Augustness Princess Chiji-haya[225] (one Deity).

Again wedding Her Augustness Princess Ō-yamato-kuni-are,[226] he begot august children:

Her Augustness Yamato-to-mo-so-bime;[227]

next His Augustness Hiko-sashi-kata-wake;[228]

next His Augustness Hiko-isa-seri-biko,[229] another name for whom is His Augustness Ō-kibi-tsu-hiko;

next Yamato-to-bi-haya-waka-ya-hime[230] (four Deities).

Again he wedded Hae-irodo,[231] younger sister of Her Augustness Princess Are, and begot august children:

His Augustness Hiko-same-ma;[232]

next His Augustness Waka-hiko-take-kibi-tsu-hiko[233] (two Deities).

The august children of this Heavenly Sovereign [numbered] in all eight Deities (five kings and three queens). So His Augustness Ō-yamato-ne-ko-hiko-kuni-kuru [was he who afterwards] ruled the Empire.

The two Deities His Augustness Ō-kibi-tsu-hiko and His Augustness Waka-take-kibi-tsu-hiko together set sacred jars[234] at the front[235] of the River Hi[236] in Harima;[237] and making Harima the mouth of the road,[238] subdued and pacified the Land of Kibi.

So His Augustness Ō-kibi-tsu-hiko (was the ancestor of the Grandees of Kamu-tsu-michi in Kibi).[239]

The next, His Augustness Waka-hiko-take-kibi-tsu-hiko (was the ancestor of the Grandees of Shimo-tsu-michi in Kibi,[240] and of the Grandees of Kasa).[241]

The next His Augustness Hiko-same-ma (was the ancestor of the Grandees of Ujika in Harima).[242]

The next, His Augustness Hiko-sashi-kata-wake (was the ancestor of the Grandees of Tonami in Koshi,[243] of the Grandees of Kunisaki in the land of Toyo,[244] of the Dukes of Iobara,[245] and of the Maritime Suzerains of Tsunuga).[246]

The Heavenly Sovereign's august years were one hundred and six. His august mausoleum is at Umasaka at Kataoka.[247]

SECT. 61—EMPEROR KŌ-GEN

His Augustness Ō-yamato-ne-ko-hiko-kuni-kuru dwelt in the palace of Sakai-bara at Karu,[248] and ruled the Empire. This Heavenly Sovereign wedded Her Augustness Utsu-shiko-me,[249] younger sister of His Augustness Utsu-shiko-o,[250] ancestor of the Grandees of Hozumi,[251] and begot august children:

His Augustness Ō-biko;[252]

next His Augustness Sukuna-biko-take-i-gokoro;[253]

next His Augustness Waka-yamato-ne-ko-hiko-ō-bibi[254] (three Deities).

Again, wedding Her Augustness I-kaga-shiko-me,[255] daughter of His Augustness Utsu-shiko-o, he begot an august child:

His Augustness Hiko-futsu-oshi-no-makoto.[256]

Again, wedding Princess Haniyasu,[257] daughter of Aotama[258] of Kōchi, he begot an august child:

His Augustness Take-hani-yasu-biko[259] (one Deity).

The august children of this Heavenly Sovereign [numbered in all five Deities]. So His Augustness Waka-yamato-ne-ko-hiko-ō-bibi [was he who afterwards] ruled the Empire.

The children of his elder brother, His Augustness Ō-biko, were His Augustness Take-nuna-kawa-wake[260] (ancestor of the Grandees of Abe);[261] next His Augustness Hiko-inakoshi-wake.[262] (This was the ancestor of the Butler Grandees.)[A]

His Augustness Hiko-futsu-oshi-no-makoto wedded Princess Takachina of Kazuraki,[263] younger sister of Ō-nabi,[264] ancestor of the

[A] *Kashiwade no omi.* This name is traditionally referred to an incident in the reign of the Emperor Kei-kō, who is said to have bestowed it on one of his attendants who served up to him a particularly savory dish of shellfish. "Butlers" (perhaps the word might also be rendered "cooks") have been mentioned towards the end of Sect. 32, and again in the legend of Jin-mu's slaughter of the "earth-spiders" related in Sect. 48.

Chiefs of Owari,[265] and begot a child: the Noble Umashi Uchi.[266] (This was the ancestor of the Grandees of Uchi in Yamashiro.)[267]

Again, wedding Princess Yama-shita-kage,[268] younger sister of Uzu-hiko,[269] ancestor of the Rulers of the Lord of Ki,[270] he begot a child: the Noble Take-uchi.[A]

The children of this Noble Take-uchi [numbered] in all nine (seven males and two females),—[namely] the Noble of Hata-no-Yashiro,[271] [who] (was the ancestor of the Grandees of Hata,[272] of the Grandees of Hayashi,[273] of the Grandees of Hami,[274] of the Grandees of Hoshikawa,[275] of the Grandees of Ōmi,[276] and of the Dukes of the Hatsuse Tribe);[277] next the Noble Kose-no-o-kara[278] [who] (was the ancestor of the Grandees of Kose,[279] of the Grandees of the Sazaki Tribe,[280] and of the Grandees of the Karu Tribe);[281] next the Noble Soga no Ishikawa[282] [who] (was the ancestor of the Grandees of Soga,[283] of the Grandees of Kawanobe[284] of the Grandees of Tanaka,[285] of the Grandees of Takamuko,[286] of the Grandees of Oharida,[287] of the Grandees of Sakurai,[288] and of the Grandees of Kishida);[289] next the Noble Heguri-no-Tsuku,[290] [who] (was the ancestor of the Grandees of Heguri,[291] of the Grandees of Sawara,[292] and of the Uma-mi-kui Chiefs);[293] next the Noble Ki-no-Tsuno[294] [who] (was the ancestor of the Grandees of Ki,[295] of the Grandees of Tsuno,[296] and of the Grandees of Sakamoto);[297] next Princess Mato of Kume,[298] next Princess Nu-no-iro;[299] next Kazuraki-no-nagae-no-sotsu-biko[300] [who] (was the ancestor of the Grandees of Tamade,[301] of the Grandees of Ikuha;[302] of the Grandees of Ikue[303] and of the Grandees of Agina);[304] moreover [there was] the Noble Waku-go[305] (the ancestor of the Grandees of Enuma).[306]

This Heavenly Sovereign's august years were fifty-seven. His august mausoleum is on the mound in the middle of the Pool of Tsurugi.[307]

SECT. 62—EMPEROR KAI-KA

His Augustness Waka-yamato-ne-ko-hiko-ō-bibi dwelt in the palace

[A] *Take-uchi no sukune. Take* signifies "brave," and *Uchi* is the name of a district in Yamato. The common, but erroneous, reading of this name is *Take no uchi no sukune.* This celebrated personage, who may be styled the Methuselah of Japan, is said to have lived during the reigns of five Emperors, who themselves averaged over a hundred years of life each. His own age is variously given as 255, 260, etc., up to 360 years.

of Izakawa at Kasuga,[308] and ruled the Empire. This Heavenly Sovereign wedded the Princess of Takano,[309] daughter of Yugori[310] the Great Departmental Lord of Tanba,[311] and begot an august child:

His Augustness Hiko-yumusumi,[312] (one Deity).

Again he wedded his step-mother, Her Augustness I-kaga-shiko-me,[313] and begot august children:

His Augustness Mima-ki-iri-biko-inie,[314]

next Her Augustness Mima-tsu-hime[315] (two Deities).

Again he wedded Her Augustness Oke-tsu-hime,[316] younger sister of His Augustness Hiko-kuni-oketsu,[317] ancestor of the Grandees of Wani,[318] and begot an august child:

King Hiko-imasu[319] (one Deity).

Again, wedding Princess Washi,[320] daughter of the Noble Kazura-ki-no-tarumi,[321] he begot an august child:

King Take-toyo-hazura-wake[322] (one Deity).

The august children of this Heavenly Sovereign [numbered] in all five Deities (four Kings and one Queen). So His Augustness Mi-maki-iri-biko-inie [was he who afterwards] ruled the Empire.

The children of his elder brother, King Hiko-yumu-sumi were: King Ō-tsutsuki-tari-ne,[323] next King Sanugi-tari-ne[324] (two Kings). There were five Deities daughters of these two Kings.

Next King Hiko-imasu wedded the Princess of Ena in Yamashiro,[325] another name for whom was Kari-bata-tobe,[326] and begot children: King Ō-mata,[327] next King O-mata,[328] next King Noble [of?] Shibu-mi[329] (three Deities). Again, wedding Saho-no-ō-kurami-tome,[330] daughter of Take-kuni-katsu-tome, of Kasuga,[331] he begot children: King Saho-biko;[332] next King O-zao;[333] next Her Augustness Saho-bi-me,[334] another name for whom is Sawaji-hime[335] (Her Augustness Saho-bime here mentioned was consort of the Heavenly Sovereign Ikume);[A] and King Muro-biko[336] (four Deities). Again, wedding Okinaga-no-mizu-yori-hime,[337] daughter of the Heavenly Deity Mi-kage,[338] who is held in reverence by the deacons of Mikami in Chika-tsu-Ōmi,[339] he begot children: King Tatasu-michi-no-ushi, Prince of Tanba[340]; next King Mizuho-no-ma-waka;[341] next King Kamu-ō-ne,[342]

[A] I.e., the Emperor Sui-nin.

another name for whom is King Yatsuri-iri-biko;[343] next Mizuho-no-i-o-yori-hime;[344] next Mimi-tsu-hime[345] (five Deities). Again, wedding his mother's younger sister Her Augustness Oke-tsu-hime,[346] he begot children: King Ma-waka of Ō-tsutsuki in Yamashiro;[347] next King Hi-ko-osu;[348] next King In-ne[349] (three Deities). Altogether the children of King Hiko-imasu [numbered] in all eleven Kings.

So the children of the elder brother King Ō-mata were: King Ake-tatsu;[350] next King Unakami[351] (two Deities). This King Ake-tatsu (was the ancestor of the Dukes of the Homuji Tribe in Ise[352] and of the Rulers of Sana in Ise[353]). King Una-kami (was the ancestor of the Dukes of Himeda[354]).

The next King O-mata (was the ancestor of the Dukes of Magari in Tagima[355]).

The next King Noble Shibumi (was the ancestor of the Dukes of Sasa).[356]

The next King Saho-biko (was the ancestor of the Chiefs of the Kusaka Tribe[357] and of the Rulers of the Land of Kai).[358]

The next, King O-zao (was the ancestor of the Lords of Kazuno[359] and the Lords of Kano in Chika-tsu-Ōmi).[360]

The next King Muro-biko (was the ancestor of the Lords of Mimi in Wakasa).[361]

King Michi-no-ushi wedded the Lady Masu of Kawakami in Tanba[362] and begot children: Her Augustness Princess Hibasu;[363] next Her Augustness Princess Matono;[364] next Her Augustness Ō-hime;[365] next King Mi-kado-wake[366] (four Deities).

This King Mi-kado-wake (was the ancestor of the Lords of Ho in Mikaha).[367]

Prince Mizuho-no-ma-waka, younger brother of this King Michi-no-ushi, (was the ancestor of the Suzerains of Yasu in Chika-tsu-Ōmi).[368]

The next, King Kamu-ō-be (was the ancestor of the [Rulers of] the Land of Mino,[369] of the Rulers of the land of Motosu,[370] and of the Chiefs of the Nagahata Tribe).[371]

The next, King Mawaka of Ō-tsutsuki in Yamashiro wedded Princess Ajisawa of Mone,[372] daughter of his younger brother[373] Iri-ne, and begot a child: King Kani-me-ikazuchi.[374] This King wedded Princess

Takaki,[375] daughter of the Grandee Tōtsu of Tanba;[376] and begot a child: King Noble Okinaga.[377] This King wedded the Princess of Takanuka in Kazuraki,[378] and begot children: Her Augustness Princess Okinaga-tarashi;[A] next Her Augustness Sora-tsu-hime;[379] next King Noble Okinaga.[380] (Three Deities. This King was the ancestor of the Dukes of Homuji in Kibi,[381] and of the Dukes of Aso in Harima).[382]

Again King Noble Okinaga wedded Princess Inayori of Kawamata,[383] and begot a child: King Ō-tamu-saka.[384] (This was the ancestor of the Rulers of the land of Tajima.)[385]

The above-mentioned Take-toyo-hazura-wake (was the ancestor of the Grandees of Chimori,[386] of the Rulers of the Oshinumi Tribe,[387] of the Rulers of the Mina Tribe,[388] of the Oshinumi Tribe in Inaba,[389] of the Lords of Takano in Tanba,[390] and of the Abiko of Yosami).[391]

The Heavenly Sovereign's august years were sixty-three. His august mausoleum is at the top of the hill of Izakawa.[392]

SECT. 63—EMPEROR SU-JIN (PART 1—GENEALOGIES)

His Augustness Mima-ki-iri-biko-inie dwelt at the Palace of Mizu-gaki at Shiki,[393] and ruled the Empire. This Heavenly Sovereign wedded Tōtsu-no-ayu-me-me-kuwashi-hime,[394] daughter of Arakawa-to-be,[395] Ruler of the land of Ki,[396] and begot august children:

His Augustness Toyo-ki-iri-biko,[397]

and next Her Augustness Toyo-suki-iri-bime[398] (two Deities).

Again, wedding the Great Princess of Ama,[399] ancestress of the Chiefs of Owari[400], he begot august children:

His Augustness Ō-iri-ki;[401]

next His Augustness Ya-saka-no-iri-biko;

next Her Augustness Nuna-ki-no-iri-bime;

next Her Augustness Tōchi-no-iri-bime[402] (four Deities).

Again, wedding Her Augustness Princess Mimatsu,[403] daughter of His Augustness Ō-biko, he begot august children:

[A] *Okinaga-tarashi-hime.* Okinaga is the name of a place (see Vol. 2, Note 337). *Tarashi* is an honorific designation, signifying literally "sufficient," *i.e.*, "perfect," and is supposed by Norinaga to have been bestowed after death on this princess, who was the celebrated conqueror of Korea, and is better known to fame by her "canonical name" of Jingū Kōgō.

His Augustness Ikume-iri-biko-isachi;[404]
next His Augustness Iza-no-ma-waka;[405]
next Her Augustness Princess Kuni-kata;[406]
next Her Augustness Princess Chiji-tsuku-yamato;[407]
next Her Augustness Princess Iga;[408]
next His Augustness Yamato-Hiko[409] (six Deities).

The august children of this Heavenly Sovereign [numbered] in all twelve Deities (seven Kings and five Queens). So His Augustness Ikume-iri-biko-isachi [was he who afterwards] ruled the Empire.

The next, His Augustness Toyo-ki-iri-biko (was the ancestor [of the Dukes] of Kami-tsu-ke-no,[410] and the Dukes of Shimo-tsu-ke-no).[411] The younger sister Her Augustness Princess Toyo-Suki (was high-priestess of[412] the temple of the Great Deity of Ise).[413] The next brother, His Augustness Ō-iri-ki (was ancestor of the Grandees of Noto).[414] The next, His Augustness Yamato-hiko,—(in the time of this King a hedge of men was for the first time set at the mausoleum).[A][415]

SECT. 64—EMPEROR SU-JIN (PART 2—A PESTILENCE IS STAID BY Ō-TATA-NE-KO)

In the reign of this Heavenly Sovereign a great pestilence arose, and the people died as if none were to be left.[416] Then the Heavenly Sovereign grieved and lamented, and at night, while on his divine couch,[417] there appeared [to him] in an august dream the Great Deity the Great-Master-of-Things,[418] and said: "This is my august doing.[B] So if thou wilt cause me to be worshiped[C] by Ō-tata-ne-ko,[419] the divine spirit shall not arise,[D] and the land will be tranquillized."

When, therefore, couriers[E] were dispatched in every direction[420] to

[A] The meaning of this imperfectly formed sentence is: "On the occasion of the interment of the next prince, His Augustness Yamato-hiko, the custom of setting a row of the deceased prince's retainers round his grave and burying them alive was first introduced."

[B] Lit. "my august heart."

[C] Or, "cause my shrine to be worshiped at." The import of the god's words is that he wishes Ō-tata-ne-ko to be appointed chief priest of his temple. For the origin of this latter see the second half of Sect. 32 (pp. 103-105).

[D] *I.e.*, "the divine anger shall no longer be kindled."

[E] Mounted couriers are almost certainly intended.

search for the person [named] Ō-tata-ne-ko, he was discovered in the village of Mino[421] in Kōchi, and was respectfully sent [to the Heavenly Sovereign].[422] Then the Heavenly Sovereign deigned to ask: "Whose child art thou?"

He replied, saying: "I[423] am Ō-tata-ne-ko, child of His Augustness Taka-mika-zu-chi[424] [who was] child of His Augustness Ii-gata-sum-i,[425] [who was] child of His Augustness Kushi-mi-gata,[426] [who was] child of the Great Deity the Great-Master-of-Things by his wife Iku-tama-yori-bime,[427] daughter of His Augustness Sue-tsu-mimi."[428]

Hereupon the Heavenly Sovereign, being greatly rejoiced, commanded that the Empire should be tranquil, and the people flourish, and forthwith made His Augustness Ō-tata-ne-ko high-priest[A] to worship[B] the Great Deity of Great Miwa[C] on Mount Mimoro.[429]

Again he ordered His Augustness Igaka-shiko-o[430] to make eighty heavenly platters, and reverently to establish the shrines of the Heavenly Deities and the Earthly Deities;[431] likewise to worship with a red-colored shield and spear the Deity of Sumisaka[432] at Uda, and with a black-colored shield and spear the Deity of Ōsaka;[D] likewise to present august offerings of cloth to all the Deities of the august declivities of the hills and to all the Deities of the reaches of the rivers, without neglecting any.[433] In consequence of this the pestilential vapor ceased altogether, and the country was tranquillized.

SECT. 65—EMPEROR SU-JIN (PART 3—STORY OF Ō-TATA-NE-KO'S BIRTH)

The reason why this person called Ō-tata-ne-ko was known to be a

---

[A] The exact meaning of the characters used to write the word *kamu-nushi* (modern *kannushi*), here rendered "high priest," is "owner of the deity." Though commonly used in modern parlance to denote any Shinto priest, it properly signifies only the chief priest in charge of a temple, whence the odd-sounding name.

[B] Or, "conduct the worship at the shrine of."

[C] Viz the deity Master-of-the-Great-Land. For the traditional etymology of Miwa see the legend in Sect. 55.

[D] Lit. "great hill," or "great pass." It is at the boundary of the provinces of Yamato and Kōchi [Osaka Prefecture. —M.F.]. Neither Norinaga nor Tanikawa Kotosuga sanctions the view of the elder scholars, who fancied they saw in the distinction of red and black some mysterious import connected with the four cardinal points.

Deity's child, was that the above-mentioned Iku-tama-yori-bime was regularly beautiful,[434] whereupon a [divine[A]] youth [who thought] the majesty of her appearance without comparison in the world,[B] came suddenly to her in the middle of the night. So, as they loved each other and lived in matrimony together, the maiden ere long was pregnant. Then the father and mother, astonished at their daughter being pregnant, asked her,[435] saying: "Thou art pregnant by thyself. How art thou with child without [having known] a man?"

She replied, saying: "I have naturally conceived through a beautiful young man, whose name[436] I know not, coming here every evening and staying with me."

Therefore the father and mother, wishing to know the man, instructed their daughter, saying: "Sprinkle red earth in front of the couch,[437] and pass a skein[438] of hemp through a needle, and pierce [therewith] the skirt of his garment."

So she did as they had instructed, and, on looking in the morning, the hemp that had been put in the needle went out through the hole of the door-hook,[439] and all the hemp that remained was three twists[440] only. Then forthwith, knowing how he had gone out by the hook-hole, they went on their quest following the thread, which, reaching Mount Miwa, stopped at the shrine of the Deity. So they knew [that Ō-tata-ne-ko was] the child of the Deity [residing] there. So the place was called by the name of Miwa on account of the three twists of hemp that had remained. (His Augustness Ō-tata-ne-ko, here referred to, was the ancestor of the Dukes of Miwa[441] and of the Dukes of Kamo.)[442]

SECT. 66—EMPEROR SU-JIN (PART 4—WAR WITH KING TAKE-HANI-YASU)

Again in this august reign His Augustness Ō-biko[443] was sent to the circuit of Koshi,[444] and his son, His Augustness Take-nuna-kawa-wake,[445] was sent to the twelve circuits to the eastward to quiet the unsubmissive people. Again Hiko-imasu was sent to the land of Tan-

[A] This word, which is not in most texts, was supplied by the editor of 1687, and is adopted by Norinaga on apparently satisfactory grounds. [I cannot agree with this. And was not the "majestic appearance" that of the youth, not of the maiden? —.]

[B] Lit. "in the time."

ba[446] to slay Kugamimi-no-mikasa[447] (this is the name of a person). So when His Augustness Ō-biko was going away to the land of Koshi, a young girl wearing a loin-skirt[448] stood on the Pass of Hera[449] in Yamashiro, and sang, saying:

[22] Now then! Oh Prince Mima-ki-iri![450]
Oh Prince Mi-ma-ki-iri,
Ignorant that they
to steal and slay one's life,
cross backwards and forwards by the back-door,
cross backwards and forwards by the front door and spy,
—Oh Prince Mima-ki-iri![451]

Hereupon His Augustness Ō-biko, thinking it strange, turned his horse back, and asked the young girl, saying: "These words that thou speakest, what are they?"

The young girl replied, saying: "I said nothing; I was only singing a song,"—and thereupon she suddenly vanished, none could see whither.

So His Augustness Ō-biko returned up again [to the capital] and made a report [of the matter] to the Heavenly Sovereign, who replied and charged him, [saying]: "Methinks this is a sign that my half-brother, King Take-hani-yasu,[452] who dwells in the land of Yamashiro, is planning some foul plot.[A] [Do thou,] uncle, raise an army, and go [after him]." When he forthwith sent him off, joining to him his Augustness Hiko-kuni-buku,[453] ancestor of the Grandees of Wani,[454] they set sacred jars on the Pass of Wani,[455] and went away.

Thereupon, when they reached the River Wakara[456] in Yamashiro, King Take-hani-yasu, who had raised an army, was waiting to intercept [their passage], and [the two hosts] stood confronting and challenging each other with the river between them.[B] So the place was called by the name of Adomi,[457] —what is now called Izumi. Then His Augustness Hiko-kuni-buku spoke, begging the other side[458] to let fly the first arrow.[459]

[A] Lit. "foul heart."

[B] More literally, "each having put the river in the middle, and mutually challenging."

Then King Take-hani-yasu shot, but could not strike. Thereupon, on His Augustness Kuni-buku shooting an arrow, it forthwith struck King Take-hani-yasu dead. So the whole army was routed, and fled in confusion. Then the [Imperial troops pursued] after the fugitive army as far as the ferry of Kusuba, when, harassed by the pursuit, [the enemy's][A] excrement came out, which stuck to their breeches. Wherefore the name Kuso-bakama was applied to this place. In the present it is named Kusu-ba.[B460] Again, on being intercepted in their flight and cut down, [their bodies] floated like cormorants in the river. So the river was called by the name of U-kawa.[C] Again, because the warriors were cut to pieces, the place was called by the name of Hafuri-sono.[D] Having thus finished [the work of] pacification, they went up [to the capital] to make their report [to the Heavenly Sovereign].

SECT. 67—EMPEROR SU-JIN (PART 5—PEACE RESTORED AND TRIBUTE LEVIED)

So His Augustness Ō-biko went away to Koshi in accordance with the previous [Imperial] commands. Then Take-nuna-kawa-wake, who had been sent round by the east, and his father Ō-biko met together in Aizu. So the place was called by the name of Aizu.[E] Wherefore, each of them, having settled the government of the land to which he had been sent, made his report [to the Heavenly Sovereign]. Then the Empire was at peace and the people prosperous.

Thereupon tribute on the arrow-notches[461] of the men and tribute on the finger-tips of the women was first levied.[F] So in praise of this august reign they said: "the Heavenly Sovereign Mima-ki, who ruled the first land."[462] Again, in this august reign the Pool of Yosami[463] was made; moreover the Pool of Sakaori at Karu[464] was made.

[A] Surely their own, from fear.

[B] *I.e.,* "excrementis [foedatae] bracae." [breeches stained with excrement —M.F.]

[C] *I.e.,* "cormorant-river."

[D] *I.e.,* "the garden of cutting-to-pieces."

[E] A district forming the southern part of the modern province of Iwashiro [Fukushima Prefecture —M.F.] in northeastern Japan. The derivation here given, from *ai-zu,* "meeting port," seems fanciful.

[F] *I.e.,* taxes levied on the produce of the chase, by which the men gained their livelihood, and on the domestic handiwork of the women.

SECT. 68—EMPEROR SU-JIN (PART 6—HIS AGE AND PLACE OF BURIAL)

The Heavenly Sovereign's august years were one hundred and sixty-eight. His august mausoleum is on the mound at the corner of the Yamanobe road.[465]

SECT. 69—EMPEROR SUI-NIN (PART 1—GENEALOGIES)

His Augustness Ikume-iri-biko-isachi dwelt at the palace of Tama-kaki in Shiki,[466] and ruled the Empire. This Heavenly Sovereign wedded Her Augustness the Princess Sawaji,[467] younger sister of His Augustness Saho-biko, and begot an august child:

His Augustness Homu-tsu-wake[468] (one Deity).

Again, wedding Her Augustness the Princess Hibasu, daughter of King Tatasu-michi-no-ushi, Prince of Taniwa, he begot august children:

His Augustness Ini-shiki-no iri-biko;[469]

next His Augustness Ō-tarashi-hiko-oshiro-wake;[470]

next His Augustness Ō-naka-tsu-hiko;[471]

next Her Augustness Yamato-hime;[A]

next His Augustness Waka-ki-iri-biko[472] (five Deities).

Again, wedding Her Augustness Nubata-no-iri-biko,[473] younger sister of Her Augustness Princess Hibasu, he begot august children:

His Augustness Nu-tarashi-wake;[474]

next His Augustness Iga-tarashi-hiko[475] (two Deities).

Again, wedding Her Augustness Azami-no-iri-bime,[476] younger sister of Her Augustness Nubata-no-iri-bime,[477] he begot august children:

His Augustness Ikobaya-wake;[478]

next Her Augustness the Princess of Azami[479] (two Deities).

Again, wedding Her Augustness Kagu-ya-hime,[480] daughter of King Ō-tsutsuki-tari-ne, he begot an august child:

King Ozabe[481] (one Deity).

Again, wedding Karibata-tobe daughter of Fuchi of Ōkuni in Yamashiro,[482] he begot august children:

King Ochi-wake;[483]

[A] *I.e.*, "Yamato princess." She is a very celebrated personage in Japanese legendary story,—high priestess of Ise and aunt of the hero Yamato-take. A miraculous tale is related of her birth, and she is supposed to have lived several hundreds of years.

next King Ika-tarashi-hiko;[484]

next King Itoshi-wake.[485]

Again, wedding Oto-karibata-tobe,[486] daughter of Fuchi of Otokuni, he begot august children:

King Iwa-tsuku-wake;[487]

next Her Augustness Iwa-tsuku-bime, another name for whom was Her Augustness Futaji-no-iri-bime[488] (two Deities).

The august children of this Heavenly Sovereign [numbered] altogether sixteen (thirteen Kings and three Queens). So His Augustness Ō-tarashi-hiko-oshiro-wake [was he who afterwards] ruled the Empire. (His august stature was ten feet[A] two inches; the length of his august shank was four feet one inch).

The next, His Augustness Ini-shiki-no-iri-biko made the pool of Chinu;[489] again he made the pool of Sayama;[490] again he made the pool of Takatsu at Kusaka.[491] Again he dwelt at the palace of Kawakami at Totori,[492] and caused a thousand cross-swords[493] to be made, and presented them to the temple of the Deity of Iso-no-kami.[494] Forthwith he dwelt at that palace,[B] and established the Kawakami Tribe.[495]

The next, His Augustness Ō-naka-tsu-hiko, (was the ancestor of the Lords of Yamanobe,[496] of the Lords of Sakikusa,[497] of the Lords of Inaki,[498] of the Lords of Ada,[499] of the Lords of Mino in the Land of Owari;[500] of the Lords of Iwanashi in Kibi,[501] of the Lords of Koromo,[502] of the Lords of Takasuka,[503] of the Dukes of Asuka,[504] and of the Lords of Mure).[505]

The next, Her Augustness Yamato-hime, (was high-priestess of[506] the temple of the Great Deity of Ise).

The next, King Ikobaya-wake (was the ancestor of the Lords of Anahobe at Sao).[507]

The next, Her Augustness the Princess of Azami (was married to King Inase-biko).

The next, King Ochi-wake (was the ancestor of the Mountain Dukes of Otsuki[508] and of the Dukes of Koromo in Mikawa).[509]

The next, King Ika-tarashi-hiko (was the ancestor of the Moun-

---

[A] The actual word "feet" is not in the original, but an equivalent Chinese measure is used.

[B] Or, "in that temple."

tain Dukes of Kasuga,[510] of the Dukes of Ike in Koshi,[511] and of the Dukes of Kasugabe).[512]

The next, King Itoshi-wake (owing to his having no children, made the Itoshi Tribe[513] his proxy).

The next, King Iwa-tsuku-wake, (was the ancestor of the Dukes of Hagui[514] and of the Dukes of Mio).[515]

The next, Her Augustness Futaji-no-iri-bime (became the Empress of His Augustness Yamato-take).

SECT. 70—EMPEROR SUI-NIN (PART 2—CONSPIRACY OF KING SAHO-BIKO AND THE EMPRESS SAHO-BIME)

When this Heavenly Sovereign made Saho-bime his Empress, Her Augustness Saho-bime's elder brother, King Saho-biko, asked his younger sister, saying: "Which is dearer [to thee], thine elder brother or thy husband?"

She replied, saying: "Mine elder brother is dearer."

Then King Saho-biko conspired, saying. "If I be truly the dearer to thee, let me and thee rule the empire," and forthwith he made an eight times tempered stiletto,[516] and handed it to his younger sister, saying: "Slay the Heavenly Sovereign in his sleep with this small knife."

So the Heavenly Sovereign, not knowing of this conspiracy, was augustly sleeping, with the Empress's august knees as his pillow. Then the Empress tried to cut his august throat with the stiletto; but though she lifted it thrice, she could not cut the throat for an irrepressible feeling of sadness, and she wept tears, which fell overflowing[517] onto [the Heavenly Sovereign's] august face.

Straightway the Heavenly Sovereign started up, and asked the Empress, saying: "I have had a strange dream: a violent shower came from the direction of Sao and suddenly wetted my face; again a small damask-colored[518] snake coiled itself round my neck. Of what may such a dream be the omen?"

Then the Empress, thinking it improper to dispute,[A] forthwith informed the Heavenly Sovereign, saying: "Mine elder brother King Saho-biko, asked me,[519] saying, 'Which is dearer [to thee], thy hus-

[A] *I.e.*, seeing that it would be vain to deny the truth.

band or thine elder brother?' So as I was embarrassed by [this] direct question, I replied, saying, 'Oh! mine elder brother is the dearer.' Then he charged[A] me, saying: 'I and thou will together rule the Empire; so the Heavenly Sovereign must be slain;'—and so saying, he made an eight times tempered stiletto, and handed it to me. Therefore I wanted to cut thine august throat; but though I thrice lifted [the weapon], a feeling of regret suddenly arose, so that I could not cut thy throat, and the tears that I wept fell and wetted thine august face. [The dream] was surely the omen of this."

Then the Heavenly Sovereign said: "How nearly have I been betrayed!"—and forthwith he raised an army to smite King Saho-biko, whereupon the King made a rice-castle[520] to await the fray.[B] At this time Her Augustness Saho-bime, unable to forget her elder brother, fled out through the back-gate [of the palace], and came into the rice-castle.

SECT. 71—EMPEROR SUI-NIN (PART 3—BIRTH OF PRINCE HOMU-CHI-WAKE AND DEATH OF THE CONSPIRATORS)

At this time the Empress[C] was pregnant. Thereupon the Heavenly Sovereign could not restrain [his pity for] the Empress, who was pregnant and whom he had loved for now three years. So he turned his army aside, and did not hasten the attack. During this delay, the august child that she had conceived was born. So having put out the august child and set it outside the rice-castle, she caused [these words] to be said to the Heavenly Sovereign: "If this august child be considered to be the Heavenly Sovereign's august child, let him[D][521] deign to undertake[E] it."

Hereupon the Heavenly Sovereign said:[522] "Although detesting the elder brother, I yet cannot repress my love for the Empress," and forthwith planned to secure the Empress. Wherefore, choosing from among his warriors a band of the strongest and deftest,[F] he charged

[A] Or "enticed."
[B] *I.e.*, stood on the defensive."—W.G.A.
[C] *I.e.*, Her Augustness Saho-bime, who was the subject of the preceding sentence.
[D] *I.e.* the Sovereign.
[E] Why not, "take charge of"? —W.G.A.
[F] Nimblest? —W.G.A.

[them, saying]: "When ye take the august child, likewise abduct the queen its mother. Whether by the hair or by the hands, or wherever ye may best lay hold of her, clutch her and drag her out."

Then the Empress, knowing his intention beforehand, shaved off all her hair and covered her head with the hair, and likewise made her jewel-string rotten and wound it thrice round her arm, and moreover made her august garments rotten by means of rice-liquor and put on the garments as if they were whole. Having made these preparations, she took the august child in her arms and pushed it outside the castle. Then the strong men, taking the august child, forthwith clutched at the august parent. Then, on their clutching her august hair, the august hair fell off of itself; on their clutching her august arms, the jewel-string likewise snapped; on their clutching her august garments, the august garments at once tore. Therefore they obtained the august child, but did not get the august parent.

So the warriors came back [to the Sovereign], and reported, saying: "On account of her august hair falling off of itself, of her august garments easily tearing, and moreover of the jewel-string which was wound round her august hand at once snapping, we have not got the august parent; but we have obtained the august child."

Then the Heavenly Sovereign, sorry and angry,[A] hated the people who made the jewels,[523] and deprived them all of their lands.[B] So the proverb says: "Landless jewel-makers."[524] Again did the Heavenly Sovereign cause[525] the Empress to be told, saying: "A child's name must be given by the mother: by what august name shall this child be called?"

Then she replied, saying: "As he was born now at the time of the castle being burnt with fire and in the midst of the fire, it were proper to call him by the august name of Prince[526] Homu-chi-wake."[527]

And again he caused her to be asked: "How shall he be reared?"[C]

She replied, saying: "He must be reared by taking an august mother[D] and fixing on old bathing-women and young bathing-women.[528]" So he

---

[A] Disappointed. —W.G.A.

[B] Or, as Norinaga prefers to read, "deprived them of all their lands."

[C] Lit., "his days be reverently prolonged." The same expression is repeated thrice below.

[D] *I.e.*, foster-mother.

was respectfully reared in accordance with the Empress's instructions.

Again he asked the Empress, saying: "Who shall loosen the fresh small pendant[529] which thou didst make fast?"

She replied, saying: "It were proper that E-hime and Oto-hime,[530] daughters of King Tatasu-michi-no-ushi[531] prince of Tanba, should serve thee, for these two queens are of unsullied parentage."[A][532]

So at last [the Heavenly Sovereign] slew King Saho-biko, and his younger sister followed him.[B]

SECT. 72—EMPEROR SUI-NIN (PART 4—THE DUMB PRINCE HOMU-CHI-WAKE)

So the way they led about and amused the august child was by making a two-forked boat[533] out of a two-forked cryptomeria[C] from Aizu in Owari,[534] bringing it up and floating it on the Pool of Ichishi and on the Pool of Karu[535] in Yamato, [thus] leading about and amusing the august child. Nevertheless the august child spoke never a word, though his eight-grasp beard reached to the pit of his stomach.[D] So[536] it was on hearing the cry of a high-flying swan[537] that he made his first utterance.[538]

Then [the Heavenly Sovereign] sent Yamanobe-no-Ōtaka[539] (this is the name of a person) to catch the bird. So this person, pursuing the swan, arrived in the Land of Harima[540] from the Land of Ki, and again in his pursuit crossed over to the Land of Inaba, then reaching the Land of Tanba and the Land of Tajima; [thence] pursuing round to the eastward, he reached the Land of Ōmi, and thereupon crossed over into the Land of Mino; and, passing along by the Land of Owari, pursued it into the Land of Shinano, and at length, reaching in his pursuit the Land of Koshi, spread a net in the Estuary of Wanami,[541] and, having caught the bird, brought it up [to the capital] and presented it [to the Sovereign]. So that estuary is called the Estuary of Wanami.

It had been thought that, on seeing the bird again, he would speak;

[A] Lit., "are pure subjects."

[B] *I.e.*, was slain with him.

[C] Japanese cedar. —M.F.

[D] Lit., "in front of his heart." This phrase descriptive of a long beard has already occurred at the commencement of Sect. 12.

but he did not speak, as had been thought.[542] Hereupon the Heavenly Sovereign, deigning to be grieved, augustly fell asleep, when, in an august dream, he was instructed, saying: "If thou wilt build my temple like unto thine august abode, the august child shall surely speak."

When he had been thus instructed, [the Heavenly Sovereign] made grand divination to seek what Deity's desire[A] this might be. Then [it was discovered that] the curse was the august doing of the Great Deity of Izumo.[543] So when about to send the august child to worship [at] that Great Deity's temple, [he made divination to discover[544]] by whom it were well to have him attended. Then the lot fell on King Ake-tatsu.[B]

So he made King Ake-tatsu swear,[545] saying: "If there is truly to be an answer[C] to our adoration of this Great Deity, may the heron dwelling on the tree by the Pool of Sagisu[546] here fall [through my] oath." When he thus spoke, the heron that had been sworn by fell to the ground dead. Again on his commanding it to come to life [in answer to his] oath, it then came to life again.[547] Moreover he caused to wither by an oath and again brought to life again by an oath a broad-foliaged bear-oak on Cape Amakashi.[548] Then [the Heavenly Sovereign] granted to Prince Ake-tatsu the name of Prince Yamato-oyu-shiki-tomi-toyo-asakura-ake-tatsu.[549]

So when the august child was sent off with the two Princes, Prince Ake-tatsu and Prince Una-kami,[550] as his attendants, it was divined[D] that [if they went out] by the Nara gate,[551] they would meet a lame person and a blind person;[552] that [if they went out] by the Ōsaka[553] gate, they would likewise meet a lame person and a blind person, and that only the Ki gate,—a side gate,[554]—would be the lucky gate; and when they started off, they established the Homuji clan[555] in every place they arrived at.

So when they had reached Izumo and had finished worshipping the Great Deity, and were returning up [to the capital], they made in the middle of the River Hi[556] a black plaited bridge and respectfully offered a temporary palace [for the august child] to dwell in.[557] Then

[A] Lit. "heart."

[B] Lit., "King Ake-tatsu ate the divination."

[C] Lit., a "sign," a "proof."

[D] *I.e.*, shown by divination.

when the ancestor of the rulers of the Land of Izumo, whose name was Kiisa-tsu-mi,[558] having made an imitation green-leafed mountain,[559] placed [it] in the lower reach of the river, and was about to present the great august food,[560] the august child spoke, saying: "What here resembles a green-leafed mountain in the lower [reach of the] river, looks like a mountain, but is not a mountain. Is it perchance the great court[A] of the deacon[B] who holds in reverence the Great Deity Ugly-Male-of-the-Reed-Plains[561] that dwells in the temple of So at Iwakuma in Izumo?"[562] [Thus] he deigned to ask.

Then the Kings, who had been sent in august attendance [on him], hearing with joy and seeing with delight,[563] set the august child to dwell in the palace of Nagaho at Ajimasa,[564] and dispatched a courier [to inform the Heavenly Sovereign].

Then the august child wedded Princess Hinaga[565] for one night. So, on looking privately at the beautiful maiden, [he found her] to be a serpent, at the sight of which he fled away alarmed. Then Princess Hinaga was vexed, and, illuminating the sea-plain,[566] pursued after them in a ship; and they, more and more alarmed at the sight, pulled the august vessel across the mountain-folds,[C] and went fleeing up [to the capital].

Thereupon they made a report, saying: "We have come up [to the capital] because thy great and august child has become able to speak through worshipping the Great Deity." So the Heavenly Sovereign, delighted, forthwith sent King Una-kami back to build the Deity's temple. Thereupon the Heavenly Sovereign, on account of this august child, established the Totori Clan, the Torikai Clan, the Homuji Clan, the Ōyue and the Wakayue.[567]

SECT. 73—EMPEROR SUI-NIN (PART 5—HIS LATER WIVES)

Again, in accordance with the Empress's words, he summoned Her Augustness Princess Hibasu, next Her Augustness Princess Oto,

[A] Viz., the court in front of, or the approach to, the shrine, which would naturally be planted with the sacred tree, the *saka-ki (Cleyera japonica)*, and thus justify the prince's comparison to it of the artificial grove at which he was looking.

[B] *I.e.*, the priest attached to the worship of, etc. For "deacon" see Vol. 2, Note 339.

[C] *I.e.* the depressions or valleys separating one mountain from another.

next Her August Princess Utakori, next Her Augustness Princess Matono,[568] daughters of Princess Michi-no-ushi, four Deities in all. Now he kept the two Deities Her Augustness Princess Hibasu and Her Augustness Princess Oto; but as for the two Deities the younger queens, he sent them back to their native place on account of their extreme hideousness.

Thereupon Princess Matono said with mortification: "When it is known in the neighboring villages that, among sisters of the same family, we have been sent back on account of our ugliness, it will be extremely mortifying;" and, on reaching Sagaraka[569] in the Land of Yamashiro, she tried to kill herself[A] by hanging herself from a branch of a tree. So that place was called by the name of Sagariki. It is now called Sagaraka. Again, on reaching Otokuni,[B] she at last killed herself by jumping[C] into a deep pool. So that place was called by the name of Ochikuni. It is now called Otokuni.

SECT. 74—EMPEROR SUI-NIN (PART 6—TAJIMA-MORI BRINGS BACK THE ORANGE FROM THE ETERNAL LAND)

Again the Heavenly Sovereign sent Tajima-mori,[570] ancestor of the Chiefs of Miyake,[571] to the Eternal Land[572] to fetch the fruit of the everlasting[573] fragrant tree. So Tajima-mori at last reached that country, plucked the fruit of the tree, and brought of clubmoss eight and of spears eight;[574] but meanwhile the Heavenly Sovereign had died.

Then Tajima-mori set apart of clubmoss four and of spears four, which he presented to the Great Empress,[575] and set up of clubmoss four and of spears four as an offering at the door of the Heavenly Sovereign's august mausoleum, and, raising on high the fruit of the tree, wailed and wept, saying: "Bringing the fruit of the everlasting fragrant tree from the Eternal Land, I have come to serve thee;" and at last he wailed and wept himself to death. This fruit of the everlasting fragrant tree is what is now called the orange.[576]

[A] Lit. "wished to die." Norinaga supposes that her design was frustrated by her attendants.

[B] Written with characters signifying *"younger country,"* but here supposed by the author to be derived from *ochi-kuni*, "falling country," in connection with this legend.

[C] Lit., "died by falling."

SECT. 75—EMPEROR SUI-NIN (PART 7—HIS DEATH AND THAT OF THE EMPRESS HIBASU)

This Heavenly Sovereign's august years were one hundred and fifty-three. His august mausoleum is in the middle of the moor of Mitachi at Sugahara.[577]

Again in the time of the Great Empress Her Augustness Princess Hibasu,[A] the Stone-Coffin-Makers' clan[578] was established, and also the Earthenware-Masters' Clan[579] was established. This Empress was buried in the mausoleum of Terama near Saki.[580]

SECT. 76—EMPEROR KEI-KŌ (PART 1—GENEALOGIES)

The Heavenly Sovereign Ō-tarashi-hiko-oshiro-wake dwelt in the palace of Hishiro at Makimuku,[581] and ruled the Empire. This Heavenly Sovereign wedded the Elder Lady of Inabi in Harima,[582] daughter of Waka-take, Prince of Kibi,[583] ancestor of the Grandees of Kibi,[584] and begot august children:

King Kushi-tsunu-wake;[585]
next His Augustness Ō-usu;[586]
next His Augustness O-usu, another name for whom is His Augustness Yamato-o-guna;[587]
next His Augustness Yamato-ne-ko;[588]
next King Kamu-kushi.[589]

Again wedding Her Augustness Princess Yasaka-no-iri,[590] daughter of His Augustness Prince Yasaka-no-iri, he begot august children:

His Augustness Prince Waka-tarashi;[591]
next His Augustness Prince Io-ki-no-iri;[592]
next His Augustness Oshi-no-wake;[593]
next Her Augustness Princess Io-ki-no-iri.[594]

Children by another concubine were:
King Toyo-to-wake;[595]
next the Lady Nunoshiro.[596]

Children by another concubine were:
the Lady Nunaki;[597]
next Her Augustness Princess Kago-yori;[598]

[A] *I.e.*, at the time of the burial of the great Empress, etc.

next King Prince Waka-ki-no-iri;[599]
next King the Elder Prince of Kibi-no-e;[600]
next Her Augustness Princess Takaki;[601]
next Her Augustness Princess Oto.[602]

Again wedding Princess Mi-hakashi of Himuka,[603] he begot an august child:

King Toyo-kuni-wake.[604]

Again wedding the Younger Lady of Inabi,[605] younger sister of the Elder Lady of Inabi, he begot august children:

King Ma-waka;[606]
next King Hiko-hito-no-ō-e.[607]

Again wedding Princess Ka-guro,[608] daughter of King Prince Sume-iro-ō-naka-tsu-hiko,[609] greatgrandchild of His Augustness Yamato-take,[610] he begot an august child:

King Ō-e.[611]

The august children of this Heavenly Sovereign Ō-tarashi-hiko numbered in all twenty-one kings and queens[612] of whom there is a register, and fifty-nine kings and queens of whom there is no record,—eighty kings and queens altogether, out of whom His Augustness Waka-tarashi-hiko and also His Augustness Yamato-take, and also His Augustness Prince I-o-ki-no-iri,—these three Kings,—bore the name of Heirs Apparent.[613] The seventy-seven kings and queens beside these[614] were all granted Rulerships in the various lands, or else [posts as] Lords, Territorial Lords or Departmental Chiefs.[615] So His Augustness Waka-tarashi-hiko [was he who afterward] ruled the Empire.

His Augustness O-usu subdued the savage Deities and likewise the unsubmissive people in the East and West.

The next, King Kushi-tsuno-wake (w as the ancestor of the chiefs of Mamuta).[616]

The next, His Augustness Ō-usu, (was the ancestor of the Dukes of Mori,[617] of the Dukes of Ōta[618] and of the Dukes of Shimada).[619]

The next, King Kamu-kushi, (was the ancestor of the Sakabe Abiko in the Land of Ki,[620] and of the Sakabe of Uda).[621]

The next, King Toyo-kuni-wake (was the ancestor of the Rulers of the Land of Himuka).[622]

SECT. 77—EMPEROR KEI-KŌ (PART 2—THE MAIDENS E-HIME AND OTO-HIME)

Hereupon the Heavenly Sovereign, to assure himself[623] of what he had heard of the beauty of the two maidens E-hime and Oto-hime,[624] daughters of King Kamu-ō-ne,[625] ancestor of the Rulers of the Land of Mino,[626] sent his august child, His Augustness Ō-usu, to summon them up [to the Capital].

So His Augustness Ō-usu who had been sent, instead of summoning them up, forthwith wedded both the maidens himself, and then sought other women, to whom he falsely gave the maidens' names, and sent them up [to his father]. Hereupon the Heavenly Sovereign, knowing them to be other women, frequently subjected them to his long glances;[A] but, never wedding them, caused them[627] to sorrow.

So the child that His Augustness Ō-usu begot on wedding E-hime, was King Oshi-kuro-no-e-hiko[628] (he was the ancestor of the Lords of Unesu in Mino).[629] Again, the child that he begot on wedding Oto-hime, was King Oshi-kuro-no-oto-hiko (he was the ancestor of the Dukes of Mugetsu).[630]

SECT. 78—EMPEROR KEI-KŌ (PART 3—VARIOUS DEEDS)

In this august reign the Laborers' Tribe[631] was established; again, the port of Awa in the East was established; again, the Great Butlers' Tribe[632] was established; again, the granaries of Yamato were established; again, the Pool of Sakate was made, and bamboos planted on its bank.[633]

SECT. 79—EMPEROR KEI-KŌ (PART 4—YAMATO-TAKE SLAYS HIS ELDER BROTHER)

The Heavenly Sovereign said to His Augustness O-usu: "Why does not thine elder brother come forth to the morning and evening great august repasts?[B] Be thou the one to take the trouble to teach him [his duty]." Thus he commanded; but for five days after, still [the prince] came not forth.

[A] *I.e.*, "gazed at them intently." The Classical word *nagamuru*, "to gaze," is properly a compound of *naga*, "long," and *miru*, "to see."

[B] Viz., to attend on his Imperial father.

Then the Heavenly Sovereign deigned to ask His Augustness O-usu [saying]: "Why is thine elder brother so long of coming? Hast thou perchance not yet taught him [his duty]?"

He replied, saying: "I have been at that trouble."

Again [the Heavenly Sovereign] said: "How didst thou take the trouble?"[A]

He replied, saying: "In the early morning when he went into the privy, I grasped hold of him and crushed him, and, pulling off his limbs,[634] wrapped them in matting and flung them away."[635]

SECT. 80—EMPEROR KEI-KŌ (PART 5—YAMATO-TAKE SLAYS THE KUMASO BRAVOES)

Thereupon the Heavenly Sovereign, alarmed at the valor and ferocity of his august child's disposition, commanded him, saying: "In the West there are two Kumaso bravoes,[636] —unsubmissive and disrespectful men. So take[B] them,"—and [with this command] he sent him off. It happened that at this time his august hair was bound at the brow.[C]

Then His Augustness O-usu was granted by his aunt Her Augustness Yamato-hime[D] her august [upper] garment and august skirt; and, with a saber hidden in his august bosom, he went forth.[637]

So, on reaching the house of the Kumaso bravoes, he saw that near the house there was a three-fold belt of warriors, who had made a cave[638] to[639] dwell in. Hereupon they, noisily discussing a rejoicing for the august cave,[640] were getting food ready. So [Prince O-usu] sauntered about the neighborhood, waiting for the day of the rejoicing.

Then when the day of the rejoicing[641] came, having combed down after the manner of girls his august hair which was bound up,[642] and having put on his aunt's august [upper] garment and august skirt, he looked quite like a young girl, and, standing amidst the women,[643]

[A] *I.e.*, "How didst thou do it?"

[B] Norinaga seems right in interpreting "take" here and elsewhere in the sense of "slay." But "take" is in the text.

[C] *I.e.*, caught up from the brow and tied together on the crown of the head. This being the way in which the hair of boys was dressed, the author thus intimates that His Augustness was still a youth.

[D] Who was high-priestess of the temple of the Great Deity of Ise, as mentioned in Vol. 2, Note 506.

went inside the cave. Then the elder brother and the younger brother, the two Kumaso bravoes, delighted at the sight of the maiden, set her between them, and rejoiced exuberantly.

So, when [the feast was] at its height, [His Augustness O-usu,] drawing the saber from his bosom, and catching Kumaso[A] by the collar of his garment, thrust the saber through his chest, whereupon, alarmed at the sight, the younger bravo ran out. But pursuing after and reaching him at the bottom of the steps[644] of the cave, and catching him by the back,[645] [Prince O-usu] thrust the saber through his buttock.

Then the Kumaso bravo spoke, saying: "Do not move the sword; I[646] have something to say." Then [His Augustness O-usu], respited him for a moment, holding him down [as he lay] prostrate. Hereupon [the bravo] said: "Who is Thine Augustness?"

Then he said: "I am the august child of Ō-tarashi-hiko-oshiro-wake, the Heavenly Sovereign who, dwelling in the palace of Hishiro at Makimuku, rules the Land of the Eight Great Islands; and my name is King Yamato-o-guna. Hearing that you two [fellows[647]], the Kumaso bravoes, were unsubmissive and disrespectful, [the Heavenly Sovereign] sent me with the command to take and slay you."

Then the Kumaso bravo said: "That must be true. There are no persons in the West so brave and strong as we two.[648] Yet in the Land of Great Yamato there is a man braver than we two, —there is.[649] Therefore will I offer thee an august name. From this time forward it is right that thou be praised as the August Child Yamato-take.[B]" As soon as he had finished saying this, [the Prince] ripped him up[650] like a ripe melon,[651] and slew him.[652]

So thenceforward he was praised by being called by the august name of[653] his Augustness Yamato-take. When he returned up [to the capital] after doing this, he subdued and pacified every one of the Deities of the mountains and of the Deities of the rivers and likewise of the Deities of Anado,[654] and then went up to [the capital].

[A] *I.e.*, the elder bravo of Kumaso.

[B] *I.e.*, "Yamato-Brave," *q.d.*, "the Bravest in Yamato." It is by his name that the hero is always commonly spoken of. Remember that "august child" signifies prince.

SECT. 81—EMPEROR KEI-KŌ (PART 6—YAMATO-TAKE SLAYS THE IZUMO BRAVO)

Forthwith entering the Land of Izumo, and wishing to slay the Izumo bravo, he, on arriving, forthwith bound [himself to him in] friendship. So, having secretly made [the wood of] an oak [tree[655]] into a false sword and augustly girded it, he went with the bravo to bathe in the River Hi.[656]

Then, His Augustness Yamato-take, getting out of the river first, and taking and girding on the sword[657] that the Izumo bravo had taken off and laid down, said: "Let us exchange swords!" So afterwards the Izumo bravo, getting out of the river, girded on His Augustness Yamato-take's false sword. Hereupon His Augustness Yamato-take, suggested, saying: "Come on! let us cross[658] swords." Then on drawing his sword, the Izumo bravo could not draw the false sword. Forthwith His Augustness Yamato-take drew his sword and slew the Izumo bravo. Then he sang augustly, saying:

[23] Alas that the sword girded on the Izumo bravo,
and wound round with many a creeper,
should have had no true blade![659]

So having thus extirpated the [bravoes] and made [the land] orderly, he went up [to the capital], and made his report [to the Heavenly Sovereign].

SECT. 82—EMPEROR KEI-KŌ (PART 7—YAMATO-TAKE IS SENT TO SUBDUE THE EAST, AND VISITS HIS AUNT AT ISE)

Then the Heavenly Sovereign again urged a command on His Augustness Yamato-take, saying: "Subdue and pacify the savage Deities and likewise the unsubmissive people of the twelve roads of the East;"[660] and when he sent him off, joining to him Prince Mi-suki-tomo-mimi-take,[661] ancestor of the Grandees of Kibi,[662] he bestowed on him a holly-wood[663] spear eight fathoms [long].

So when he had received the [Imperial] commands and started off, he went into the temple of the Great August Deity of Ise, and worshiped the Deity's court,[664] forthwith speaking to his aunt, Her

Augustness Yamato-hime, saying: "It must surely be that the Heavenly Sovereign thinks[A] I may die quickly; for after sending me to smite the wicked people of the West, I am no sooner come up again [to the capital] than, without bestowing on me an army, he now sends me off afresh to pacify the wicked people of the twelve circuits of the East. Consequently I think that he certainly thinks I shall die quickly."

When he departed with lamentations and tears, Her Augustness Yamato-hime bestowed on him the "Herb-Quelling-Saber,"[B] and likewise bestowed on him an august bag,[C] and said: "If there should be an emergency, open the mouth of the bag."

SECT. 83—EMPEROR KEI-KŌ (PART 8—YAMATO-TAKE SLAYS THE RULERS OF SAGAMI)

So reaching the Land of Owari, he went into the house of Princess Miyazu,[665] ancestress of the Rulers of Owari,[666] and forthwith thought to wed her; but thinking again that he would wed her when he should return up [toward the capital], and having plighted his troth, he went [on] into the Eastern Lands, and subdued and pacified all the savage Deities and unsubmissive people of the mountains and rivers.

So then, when he reached the Land of Sagami,[667] the Ruler of the land lied, saying: "In the middle of this moor is a great lagoon, and the Deity that dwells in the middle of the lagoon is a very violent Deity." Hereupon [Yamato-take] entered the moor to see the Deity. Then the Ruler of the land set fire to the moor.

So, knowing that he had been deceived, he opened the mouth of the bag which his aunt, Her Augustness Yamato-hime had bestowed on him, and saw that inside or it there was a fire-striker.[668] Hereupon he first mowed away the herbage with his august sword, took the fire-striker and struck out fire, and, kindling a counter-fire, burnt [the herbage] and drove back [the other fire], and returned forth, and killed and destroyed all the Rulers[669] of that Land, and forthwith set fire to

---

[A] Here and below, the word "thinks" may be understood to mean "wishes."

[B] *Kusa-nagi no tsurugi.* The discovery of this sword by the deity Susa-no-o ("Impetuous Male") inside one of the tails of the eight-headed serpent which he had slain, is narrated at the end of Sect. 18.

[C] The use of the contents of this bag will be seen in the next Section.

and burnt them. So [that place] is now called Yakizu.[670]

SECT. 84—EMPEROR KEI-KŌ (PART 9—YAMATO-TAKE'S EMPRESS STILLS THE WAVES)

When he thence penetrated on, and crossed the sea of Hashiri-mizu,[671] the Deity of that crossing raised the waves, tossing the ship so that it could not proceed across. Then [Yamato-take's] Empress,[672] whose name was Her Augustness Princess Oto-tachibana[673] said: "I[674] will enter the sea instead of the august child.[A] The august child must complete the service[B] on which he has been sent, and take back a report [to the Heavenly Sovereign]."

When she was about to enter the sea, she spread eight thicknesses of sedge rugs,[675] eight thicknesses of skin rugs and eight thicknesses of silk rugs on the top of the waves, and sat down on the top [of them]. Thereupon the violent waves at once went down, and the august ship was able to proceed. Then the Empress sang, saying:

[24] Ah! thou [whom I] enquired of,
standing in the midst of the flames of the fire
burning on the little moor of Sugamu,
where the true peak pierces.[676]

So seven days afterwards the Empress's august comb drifted onto the sea-beach,—which comb was forthwith taken and placed in an august mausoleum which was made.

SECT. 85—EMPEROR KEI-KŌ (PART 10—YAMATO-TAKE SLAYS THE DEITY OF THE ASHIGARA PASS)

When, having thence penetrated on and subdued all the savage Emishi[677] and likewise pacified all the savage Deities of the mountains and rivers, he was returning up [to the capital], he, on reaching the foot of the Ashigara Pass,[678] was eating his august provisions, when the Deity of the pass, transformed into a white deer, came and stood [before

[A] *I.e.*, "instead of thee, the Prince."

[B] More literally, "finish the government."

him]. Then forthwith, on his waiting[A] and striking [the deer] with a scrap of wild chive,[679] [the deer] was hit in the eye and struck dead. So mounting to the top of the pass, he sighed three times and spoke, saying: "Azuma wa ya!"[B680] So that land is called by the name of Azuma.

SECT. 86 — EMPEROR KEI-KŌ (PART 11 — YAMATO-TAKE DWELLS IN THE PALACE OF SAKAORI)

When, forthwith crossing over from that land out into Kai,[681] he dwelt in the palace of Sakaori,[682] he sang saying:

> [25] How many nights have I slept
> since passing Niibari and Tsukuba?"[683]

Then the old man, who was the lighter of the august fire,[684] completed[685] the august Song, and sang, saying:

> [26] Oh! having put the days in a row,
> there are of nights nine nights,
> and of days ten days![686]

Therefore [Yamato-take] praised the old man, and forthwith bestowed [on him] the Rulership of the Eastern Lands].[687]

SECT. 87—EMPEROR KEI-KŌ (PART 12—YAMATO-TAKE WOOS PRINCESS MIYAZU)

Having crossed over from that land into the land of Shinano[688] and subdued the Deity of the Shinano pass,[689] he came back to the land of Owari, and went to dwell in the house of Princess Miyazu, to whom he had before plighted his troth.

Hereupon, when presenting to him the great august food, princess Miyazu lifted up a great august liquor-cup and presented it to him. Then Princess Miyazu's menses were stuck to the edge of her veil. Wherefore [His Augustness Yamato-take] saw her menses and sang

---

[A] *I.e.*, lying in ambush.

[B] *I.e.*, "Oh! my wife!" *Azuma* is still used as a poetical designation of Eastern Japan.

augustly, saying:

[27] I wanted to rest [my head] delicately
upon a soft arm [yours, which is like] a surrounding fortification,
thrusting a sharp knife on Mt. Kagu
shaped like a gourd in the sky; —I longed
to sleep [with you.] But at the edge of the veil
you are wearing, the moon has risen.[690]

Then Princess Miyazu answered the august song, saying:

[28] August child of the shining sun on high!
My great lord, calmly performing the administration!
As the renewed years come and go,
the renewed moons go by coming and going.
Of course, of course while I impatiently
wait for you, the moon rises on its own
at the edge of the veil that I wear![691]

For this reason then [he] did have intercourse [with her],[692] after which, placing in Princess Miyazu's house his august sword "the Grass-Quelling Saber," he went forth[693] to take the Deity of [Mount] Ibuki.[694]

SECT. 88—EMPEROR KEI-KŌ (PART 13—YAMATO-TAKE MEETS THE DEITY OF MOUNT IBUKI)

Hereupon he said: "As for the Deity of this mountain, I will simply take him empty-handed,"[A]—and was ascending the mountain, when there met him on the mountainside a white boar whose size was like unto that of a bull.[695] Then he lifted up words,[696] and said: "This creature that is transformed into a white boar must be a messenger from the Deity.[697] Though I slay it not now, I will slay it when I return,"—and

[A] *I.e.,* without weapons, and specifically without the magic sword which he had left behind in Princess Miyazu's house.

[so saying,] ascended.

Thereupon the Deity caused heavy ice-rain[698] to fall, striking and perplexing His Augustness Yamato-take. (This creature transformed into a white boar was not a messenger from the Deity, but the very Deity in person. Owing to the lifting up of words, he appeared and misled [Yamato-take.[699]]) So when, on descending back, he reached the fresh spring of Tama-kura-be[700] and rested there, his august heart awoke somewhat.[701] So that fresh spring is called by the name of the fresh spring of I-same.

SECT. 89—EMPEROR KEI-KŌ (PART 14—YAMATO-TAKE SICKENS AND DIES)

When he departed thence and reached the moor of Tagi,[702] he said: "Whereas my heart always felt like flying through the sky, my legs are now unable to walk. They have become rudder-shaped."[703] So that place was called by the name of Tagi.

Owing to his being very weary with progressing a little further beyond that place, he lent upon an august staff to walk a little. So that place is called by the name of the Tsue-tsuki pass.[704]

On arriving at the[705] single pine-tree on Cape Otsu,[706] an august sword, which he had forgotten at that place before when augustly eating,[707] was still [there] not lost. Then he augustly sang, saying:

[29] Oh mine elder brother, the single pine-tree
that art on Cape Otsu which directly
faces Owari! If thou, single pine-tree!
wert a person, I would gird [my] sword
[upon thee], I would clothe thee with
[my] garments,—O mine elder brother,
the single pine-tree!"[708]

When he departed thence and reached the village of Mie,[709] he again said: "My legs are like three-fold crooks,[710] and very weary." So that place was called by the name of Mie.

When he departed thence and reached the Moor of Nobo,[711] he, regretting[712] [his native] land,[713] sang, saying:

[30] As for Yamato, the most secluded of
lands Yamato, retired behind Mount
Aogaki encompassing it with its folds,
is delightful."[714]

Again he sang, saying:

[31] Let those whose life may be complete
stick [in their hair] as a head-dress
the leaves of the bear-oak
from Mount Heguri,—
those children!

This Song is a Land-Regretting Song.[A] Again he sang, saying:

[32] How sweet! Ah!
From the direction of home
clouds are rising and coming!

This is an Incomplete Song.[B]

At this time, his august sickness was very urgent. Then he sang augustly, saying:

[33] The saber-sword which I placed
at the maiden's bedside alas!
That sword![715]

As soon as he had finished singing, he died. Then a courier was dispatched [to the Heavenly Sovereign.]

[A] *I.e.*, a Song of loving regret for his native land.

[B] "Incomplete Song" must be understood as the designation of a poem of a certain number of lines, viz., three, and was probably given by comparison with the greater length of poetical compositions in general. [This seems hardly consistent with the statement on the preceding page that a mutilation of the original poem is implied. —W.G.A.]

SECT. 90—EMPEROR KEI-KŌ (PART 15—YAMATO-TAKE TURNS INTO A WHITE BIRD)

Thereupon [his] Empresses[A] and likewise [his] august children, who dwelt in Yamato, all went down[B] and built an august mausoleum, and, forthwith crawling hither and thither in the rice-fields encompassing [the mausoleum], sobbed out a Song, saying;

[34] The maple-leaved vine crawling hither
and thither among the rice-stubble,
among the rice-stubble in the rice-fields
encompassing [the mausoleum].[716]

Thereupon [the dead prince], turning into a white dotterel[717] eight fathoms [long], and soaring up[C] to Heaven, flew off towards the shore. Then the Empresses and likewise the august children, though they tore their feet treading on the stubble of the bamboo-grass, forgot the pain, and pursued him with lamentations. At that time they sang, saying:

[35] Our loins are impeded in the plain
[overgrown with] short bamboo-grass.
We are not going through the sky,
but oh! we are on foot.[718]

Again when they entered the salt sea,[719] and suffered as they went, they sang, saying:

[36] As we go through the sea, our loins are
impeded,—tottering in the sea like herbs
growing in a great riverbed.[720]

Again when [the bird] flew and perched on the seaside, they sang, saying:

[A] *I.e.*, wives. It will be remembered that the historian habitually mentions Yama-to-take as if he had been Emperor.

[B] *Q.d.*, to the land of Ise.

[C] Across. —W.G.A.

[37] The dotterel of the beach goes not on the
beach, but follows the seaside.[721]

These four Songs were all sung at [Yamato-take's] august interment. So to the present day these Songs are sung at the great august interment of a Heavenly Sovereign. So [the bird] flew off from that country,[722] and stopped at Shiki in the land of Kōchi.[723] So they made an august mausoleum there, and laid [Yamato-take] to rest.[724] Forthwith that august mausoleum was called by the name of the "August Mausoleum of the White-Bird."[725] Nevertheless the bird soared up thence to heaven again, and flew away.

SECT. 91—EMPEROR KEI-KŌ (PART 16—YAMATO-TAKE'S BUTLER)

During all the time that this [Prince] His Augustness Yamato-take went about pacifying countries, Nana-tsuka-hagi,[726] ancestor of the Suzerains of Kume,[727] always followed and respectfully served him as butler.

SECT. 92—EMPEROR KEI-KŌ (PART 17—YAMATO-TAKE'S DESCENDANTS)

This [Prince] His Augustness Yamato-take wedded Her Augustness Princess Futaji-no-iri,[728] daughter of the Heavenly Sovereign Ikume, and begot an august child:

His Augustness Tarashi-naka-tsu-hiko[729] (one Deity).

Again, wedding Her Augustness Princess Oto-tachibana[730] who [afterwards] entered the sea,[731] he begot an august child:

King Waka-take[732] (one Deity).

Again, wedding Princess Futaji,[733] daughter of Ō-tamu-wake,[734] ancestor of the Rulers of the Land of Yasu in Chika-tsu-Ōmi,[735] he begot an august child:

King Ine-yori-wake[736] (one Deity).

Again wedding Princess Ō-kibi-take,[737] younger sister of Take-hiko, [ancestor of the] Grandees of Kibi,[738] he begot an august child:

King Take-kaiko[739] (one Deity).

Again, wedding Princess Kukuma-mori of Yamashiro,[740] he begot an august child,

King Ashi-kagami-wake[741] (one Deity).

A child by another wife was King Okinaga-ta-wake.[742]

Altogether the entire [number] of the august children of His Augustness Yamato-take was six Deities. So His Augustness Tarashi-naka-tsu-hiko [was he who afterwards] ruled the Empire.

The next, King Ine-yori-wake (was the ancestor of the Dukes of Inukami[743] and of the Dukes of Takebe).[744]

The next, King Take-kaiko (was the ancestor of the Dukes of Aya in Sanuki,[745] the Dukes of Wake in Iyo,[746] the Lords of Tō,[747] the Headmen of Masa[748] and the Lords of Miyaji).[749]

King Ashi-kagami-wake (was the ancestor of the Lords of Kamakura,[750] the Dukes of Ozu,[751] the Lords of Iwashiro[752] and the Lords of Fukita).[753]

The child of the next, King Okinaga-ta-wake was King Kui-mata-naga-hiko.[754] This King's children were:

Her Augustness Princess Iino-ma-guro,[755]

next Okinaga-ma-waka-naka-tsu-hime,[756]

next Oto-hime[757] (three Deities).

So the above mentioned King Waka-take wedded Princess Iino-ma-guro, and begot King Sume-iro-ō-naka-tsu-hiko.[758] This King wedded princess Shibanu,[759] daughter of Shibanu-iri-ki[760] of Ōmi, and begot a child, Her Augustness Princess Kaguro.[761]

So the Heavenly Sovereign Ō-tarashi-hiko wedded this [lady] Her Augustness Princess Kaguro, and begot King Ō-e[762] (one Deity). This King wedded his younger half-sister Queen Shiro-kane,[763] and begot children:

King Ō-na-gata,[764]

and next Her Augustness Ō-naka-tsu-hime[765] (two Deities). So this [lady] Her Augustness Ō-naka-tsu-hime was the august mother[A] of King Kagosaka[766] and King Oshikuma.[767]

SECT. 93—EMPEROR KEI-KŌ (PART 18—HIS AGE AND PLACE OF BURIAL)

This Heavenly Sovereign's august years were one hundred and thirty-seven, and his august mausoleum is above the Yamanobe road.[768]

[A] Lit. "ancestress."

SECT. 94—EMPEROR SU-JIN

The Heavenly Sovereign Wata-tarashi-hiko dwelt at the palace of Taka-anaho at Shiga[769] in Chika-tsu-Ōmi and ruled the empire.

This Heavenly Sovereign wedded the Lady Oto-takara,[770] daughter of Take-oshiyama-tari-ne,[771] ancestor of the Grandees of Hozumi,[772] and begot an august child:

King Waka-nuke[773] (one Deity).

So [the Heavenly Sovereign] raised the Noble Take-uchi[774] [to the office of] Prime Minister,[775] deigned to settle the Rulers of the Great Countries and Small Countries,[776] and likewise deigned to settle the boundaries of the various countries, as also the Departmental Lords of the Great Departments and Small Departments.[777]

The Heavenly Sovereign's august years were ninety-five, and his august mausoleum is at Tatanami near Saki.[778]

SECT. 95—EMPEROR CHŪ-AI (PART 1—GENEALOGIES)

The Heavenly Sovereign Tarashi-naka-tsu-hiko dwelt at the palace of Toyora at Anado,[779] and likewise at the palace of Kashihi[780] in Tsukushi, and ruled the Empire. This Heavenly Sovereign wedded Her Augustness Ō-naka-tsu-hime,[781] daughter of King Ō-e, and begot august children: King Kago-saka and King Oshikuma (two Deities).

Again he wedded Her Augustness Princess Okinaga-tarashi. This Empress[782] gave birth to august children:

His Augustness Homu-ya-wake,[783]

and next His Augustness Ō-tomo-wake,[A] another name for whom was His Augustness Homuda-wake.[784] The reason why this Heir Apparent[785] was given the august name of His Augustness Ō-tomo-wake was that when first[786] born, he had on his august arm [a protuberance of] flesh resembling an elbow-pad,[787] whence the august name bestowed on him. By this it was known while he was in the womb that he would rule countries.[788] In this august reign the granaries of Awaji were established.

[A] *I.e.*, "great elbow-pad lord," *tomo* signifying "elbow-pad." The next sentence of the text gives the traditional origin of this curious name.

[SECT. 96—EMPEROR CHŪ-AI (PART 2—THE POSSESSION OF KOREA DIVINELY PROMISED)

This Empress, Her Augustness Princess Okinaga-tarashi, was at that time[A] divinely possessed.[789] So when the Heavenly Sovereign, dwelling at the palace of Kashihi in Tsukushi, was about to smite the Land of Kumaso,[790] the Heavenly Sovereign played on his august lute, and the Prime Minister the Noble Take-uchi, being in the pure court,[791] requested the divine orders.

Hereupon the Empress, divinely possessed, charged him with this instruction and counsel: "There is a land to the Westward, and in that land is abundance of various treasures dazzling to the eye, from gold and silver downwards.[B] I will now bestow this land upon thee."

Then the Heavenly Sovereign replied, saying: "If one ascend to a high place and look Westward, no country is to be seen. There is only the great sea;" and saying,[792] "they are lying Deities,"[793] he pushed away his august lute, did not play on it, and sat silent.

Then the Deities were very angry, and said: "Altogether as for this empire, it is not a land over which thou oughtest to rule. Do thou go to the one road!"[794]

Hereupon the Prime Minister the Noble Take-uchi said: "[I am filled with] awe, my Heavenly Sovereign![C] Continue playing thy great august lute." Then he slowly[D] drew his august lute to him, and languidly played on it. So almost immediately the sound of the august lute became inaudible. On their forthwith lifting a light and looking, [the Heavenly Sovereign] was dead.

SECT. 97—EMPEROR CHŪ-AI (PART 3—PREPARATIONS FOR THE CONQUEST OF KOREA)

Then, astonished and alarmed, they set him in a mortuary palace,[795] and again taking the country's great offerings,[796] seeking out all sorts of crimes,[797] such as flaying alive and flaying backwards,[798] breaking down the divisions of rice-fields, filling up ditches, evacuating excrements

---

[A] At what time, we are not told.

[B] Lit. "making gold and silver the origin."

[C] *I.e.*, "I tremble, Sire, for the consequences of thine impiety."

[D] By and by,—after a little. —W.G.A.

and urine,[799] marriages between superiors and inferiors,[A] marriages with horses, marriages with cattle, marriages with fowls, and marriages with dogs, and having made a great purification of the land,[800] the Noble Take-uchi again stood in the pure court and requested the Deities' commands.

Thereupon the manner of their instruction and counsel was exactly the same as on the former day: "Altogether this land is a land to be ruled over by the august child in Thine Augustness's august womb."[801]

Then the Noble Take-uchi said, "[I am filled with] awe, my Great Deities! The august child in this Deity's womb,[B] what [sort of] child may it be?"

[The Deities] replied, saying: "It is a male child."

Then [the Noble Take-uchi] requested more particularly, [saying]: "I wish to know the august names of the Great Deities whose words have now thus instructed us."

Forthwith [the Deities] replied, saying: "It is the august doing[C] of the Great-August- Heaven-Shining-Deity, likewise it is the three great Deities Bottom-Possessing-Male, Middle-Possessing Male and Surface-Possessing-Male.[802] (At this time the august names of these three great Deities were revealed.[803]) If now thou truly thinkest to seek that land, thou must, after presenting the offerings[804] to every one of the Heavenly Deities and Earthly Deities,[805] and likewise of the Deities of the mountains and also of all the Deities of the river and of the sea, and setting our august spirits[806] on the top of[807] thy vessel, put into gourds[808] the ashes of the *Podocarpus macrophylla* tree,[809] and likewise make a quantity of chopsticks and also of leaf-platters,[D] and must scatter them all on the waves of the great sea, that thou mayest cross over."

So when [she] punctually fulfilled these instructions, equipped an army, marshalled her vessels, and crossed over, the fishes of the

---

[A] *I.e.*, incest between parents and children.

[B] *I.e.*, in the Empress's womb. Norinaga supposes that she is thus spoken of as a deity on account of her being at that moment divinely possessed.

[C] Lit. "heart."

[D] *I.e.*, broad shallow platters made of the leaves of the oak-tree, and used for placing food on.

sea-plain, both great and small, all bore the august vessel[A] across on their backs, and a strong favorable wind arose, and the august vessel followed the billows.

SECT. 98—EMPEROR CHŪ-AI (PART 4—THE EMPRESS JIN-GŪ CONQUERS KOREA)

So the wave[B] of the august vessel pushed up onto the land of Shiragi,[C] reaching to the middle of the country. Thereupon the chieftain[810] of the country, alarmed and trembling, petitioned[811] [the Empress], saying: "From this time forward obedient to the Heavenly Sovereign's commands, I will feed his august horses and will marshal vessels every year, nor ever let the vessels' keels[812] dry or their poles and oars dry, and will respectfully serve him without drawing back while heaven and earth shall last."[813]

So therefore the Land of Shiragi was constituted the feeder of the august horses, and the Land of Kudara[814] was constituted the crossing store.[D] Then the Empress stuck[815] her august staff on the gate of the chieftain of Shiragi, and having made the Rough August Spirits[816] of the Great Deities of the Inlet of Sumi[817] the guardian Deities of the land, she laid them to rest,[E818] and crossed back.

So while this business[F] was yet unconcluded, [the child] with which she was pregnant was about to be born. Forthwith, in order to restrain her august womb, she took a stone and wound it round the waist of her august skirt,[819] and the august child was born after she had crossed [back] to the Land of Tsukushi.[820] So the name by which the

[A] *Viz.,* that in which the Empress herself took passage.

[B] *I.e.,* "the wave on which the august vessel was riding."

[C] In Sinico-Japanese *Shin-ra* (新羅), one of the three states into which Korea was anciently divided, the other two being known in pure Japanese as *Kudara* and *Koma* (in Sinico-Japanese *Hyaku-sai* and *Kō-rai,* 百済 and 高麗). *Shiragi* is evidently a mere corruption of the Sinico-Japanese form, which closely resembles the native Korean *Sil-la.* The origin of the pure Japanese forms of the other two names is obscure.

[D] *I.e.,* "the sea-store." The author means to say that from the Land of Kudara tribute was to be paid with the regularity implied by the King's asseveration to the effect that the keels, poles, and oars of the [tribute-bearing] vessels should never remain dry.

[E] Lit. "established and worshiped."

[F] Lit. "government."

place was called where the august child was born was Umi.[821] Again the stone which she wound round her august skirt is at the village of Ito[822] in the Land of Tsukushi.

SECT. 99[823]—EMPEROR CHŪ-AI (PART 5—THE EMPRESS JIN-GŪ FISHES IN TSUKUSHI)

Again when, having reached the village of Tamashima[824] in the Department of Matsura[825] in Tsukushi, she partook of an august meal on the bank of the river, it being then the first decade of the fourth moon, she then sat on a shoal[826] in the middle of the river, picked out threads from her august skirt, used grains of rice as bait, and hooked the trout[827] in the river. (The name by which the river is called is the O-gawa;[828] again the name by which the shoal is called is Kachi-do-hime.[829])

So down to the present time it is an uninterrupted [custom] for women in the first decade of the fourth moon to pick out threads from their skirts, use grains as bait, and hook trout.

SECT. 100—EMPEROR CHŪ-AI (PART 6—THE EMPRESS JIN-GŪ SUBDUES YAMATO)

Hereupon, when Her Augustness Princess Okinaga-tarashi was returning up to Yamato, she, owing to doubts concerning the disposition[A] of the people, prepared a mourning-vessel,[830] set the august child in that mourning-vessel, and let a report ooze out that the august child was already dead.

While she went up thus, King Kagosaka and King Oshikuma,[831] having heard [of the circumstance], thought to waylay[B] her, went forth to the moor of Toga,[832] and hunted for an omen.[833] Then King Kagosaka climbed up an oak-tree,[834] and then[835] a large and angry boar came forth, dug up the oak-tree, and forthwith devoured King Kagosaka.

His younger brother, King Oshikuma, undaunted by this circumstance,[C] raised an army and lay in wait [for the Empress], to close

[A] Lit., "the hearts."

[B] Lit., "wait for and catch." This "catch" is always taken [Rightly, I think. —W.G.A.] by Norinaga to mean "slay."

[C] *I.e.,* this evil omen. —W.G.A

with the mourning-vessel as being an empty[A] vessel. Then an army was landed from the mourning-vessel,[836] and joined in combat [with the opposing forces].

At this time King Oshikuma made the Noble Isai,[837] ancestor of the Kishi Clan of Naniwa,[838] his generalissimo;[839] and on the august side of the Heir Apparent His Augustness Naniwa-ne-ko-take-furu-kuma,[840] ancestor of the Grandees of Wani,[841] was made generalissimo.

So when [the Empress's troops] had driven [King Oshikuma's troops] as far as Yamashiro, [the latter] turned and made a stand, and both [sides] fought together without retreating. Then His Augustness Take-furu-kuma planned, and caused it to be said that, as Her Augustness Princess Okinaga-tarashi was already dead, there was no need for further fighting,—forthwith snapping his bowstrings and feigning submission.

Therefore King Oshikuma's generalissimo, believing the falsehood, unbent his bows and put away his arms. Then [the Empress's troops] picked out of their topknots some prepared bowstrings (one name [of the bowstrings] was *usa-yu-zuru*,[842]) stretched [their bows] again, and pursued and smote [the enemy]. So [these] fled away to Ōsaka,[843] rallied, and fought again. Then [the Empress's troops] pursued, pressed on, and defeated them, and cut to pieces that army at Sasanami.[844]

Thereupon King Oshikuma, together with the Noble Isai, being pursued and pressed, got on board a vessel and floated on the sea, and sang, saying:

[38] Come on, my lord! Rather than be stricken
by Furu-kuma's hurtful hand,
I will plunge like the grebe
into the Sea of Ōmi,— I will![845]

Forthwith they plunged into the sea, and died together.

[A] *I.e.*, defenseless, not filled with troops.

SECT. 101—EMPEROR CHŪ-AI (PART 7—THE HEIR APPARENT EXCHANGES NAMES WITH THE GREAT DEITY IZASA-WAKE)

So when His Augustness the Noble Take-uchi, taking with him the Heir Apparent for the purpose of purification,[846] passed through the lands of Ōmi and Wakasa,[847] he built a temporary palace at Tsunuga[848] at the mouth of the Road of Koshi[849] [for the Heir Apparent] to dwell in.

Then His Augustness the Great Deity Izasa-wake,[850] who dwelt in that place, appeared at night in a dream,[851] and said: "I wish to exchange my name for the august name of the august child."

Then [the dreamer of the dream] prayed, saying: "[I] am filled with awe! [A] The name shall be respectfully exchanged according to thy command."

Again the Deity charged [him, saying]: "Tomorrow morning [the Heir Apparent] must go out on the beach; I will present my [thank-] offering for the name [given me] in exchange." So when [the Heir Apparent] went out in the morning to the beach, the whole shore was lined with broken-nosed dolphin-fishes.[852]

Thereupon the august child caused the Deity to be addressed, saying: "Thou bestowest on me fish of thine august food."[853] So again his august name was honored by his being called the Great Deity of August Food.[854] So he is now styled the Food-Wondrous-Great-Deity.[855] Again the blood from the noses of the dolphin-fishes stank. So the strand was called by the name of Chiura.[856] It is now styled Tsunuga.

SECT. 102—EMPEROR CHŪ-AI (PART 8—THE EMPRESS JIN-GŪ PRESENTS LIQUOR TO THE HEIR APPARENT)

Hereupon, when the [Heir Apparent] returned up [to the Capital], his august parent, Her Augustness Princess Okinaga-tarashi, distilled some waiting-liquor,[857] and presented it to him. Then his august parent sang augustly, saying:

[39] This august liquor is not my august liquor:
—oh! it is august liquor
respectfully brought as a divine congratulation,

[A] Or, "I reverence [thy commands]."

a repeated congratulation,[858]
a bountiful congratulation,
a reiterated congratulation,
by the Small August Deity,
who dwells eternally, firmly standing.
Partake not shallowly! Go on! go on!"[859]

Having thus sung, she presented to him the great august liquor. Then His Augustness the Noble Take-uchi replied for the august child and sang, saying:

[40] Whatever person distilled[A] this august liquor
must surely have distilled it singing the while
with that drum on the mortar,
—must surely have distilled it dancing the while,
for this august liquor,
august liquor, to be ever more and more joyful.
Go on! go on![860]

These are Drinking Songs.[861]

SECT. 103—EMPEROR CHŪ-AI (PART 9—HIS DEATH AND THAT OF THE EMPRESS JIN-GŪ)

Altogether the august years of this Heavenly Sovereign Tarashi-naka-tsu-hiko[862] were fifty-two. His august mausoleum is at Nagae,[863] near Ega,[864] in Kōchi.

(The Empress died at the august age of one hundred. She was buried in the mausoleum of Tatanami in Saki.[865])

SECT. 104—EMPEROR Ō-JIN[866] (PART 1—GENEALOGIES)

His Augustness Homuda-wake dwelt at the palace of Akira at Karushima,[867] and ruled the Empire. This Heavenly Sovereign wedded three[868] queens, daughters of King Homuda-no-ma-waka,[869] the name of one of whom was Her Augustness Princess Takagi-no-iri;[870] of the next,

[A] Brewed. —W.G.A.

Her Augustness Naka-tsu-hime;[871] and of the next, Her Augustness Oto-hime.[872] (The father of these Queens, King Homuda-no-ma-waka, was the son of His Augustness Prince Io-ki-no-iri[873] by his wife Shiritsuki-tome,[874] daughter of the Noble Take-inada,[875] ancestor of the Chiefs of Owari.)[876] So the august children of Her Augustness Princess Takagi-no-iri were:

His Augustness Nukata-no-ō-waka-tsu-hiko;[877]
next His Augustness Ō-yama-mori;[878]
next His Augustness Iza-no-ma-waka;[879]
next his younger sister the Lady of Ōhara;[880]
next the Lady of Komuku.[881] (Five Deities.)

The august children of Her Augustness Naka-tsu-hime were:
the Lady of Arata in Ki;[882]
next His Augustness Ō-sazaki;[883]
next His Augustness Netori.[884] (Three Deities.)

The august children of Her Augustness Oto-hime were:
the Lady Abe;[885]
next the Lady of Mihara in Awaji;[886]
next the Lady of Uno in Ki;[887]
next the Lady of Mino.[888] (Five Deities.)[889]

Again he wedded the Princess Miya-nushi-ya-kawa-e,[890] daughter of the Grandee Wani-no-Hifure, and begot august children:
Uji-no-waki-iratsuko;[891]
next his younger sister Yata-no-waki-iratsume;[892]
next Queen Medori.[893] (Three Deities.)

Again he wedded O-nabe-no-iratsume,[894] younger sister of Yaka-wa-e-hime, and begot an august child:
Uji-no-waki-iratsume.[895] (One Deity.)

Again he wedded Okinaga-ma-waka-naka-tsu-hime,[896] daughter of King Kuimata-naga-hiko,[897] and begot an august child:
King Waka-nuke-futa-mata[898] (One Deity.)

Again he wedded the Princess of Itoi[899] daughter of Shima-tari-ne,[900] ancestor of the Agricultural Chiefs of Sakurai,[901] and begot an august child:
His Augustness Hayabusa-wake[902] (One Deity.)

Again, he wedded Naga-hime of Izumi in Himuka,[903] and begot august children:

King Ō-hae;[904]

next King O-hae;[905]

next Hata-bi-no-waki-ira-tsume.[906] (Three Deities.)

Again he wedded Princess Ka-guro,[907] and begot august children:

Kawarada-no-iratsume;[908]

next, Tama-no-iratsume;[909]

next, Osaka-no-ō-naka-tsu-hime;[910]

next, Tōshi-no-iratsume;[911]

next, King Kataji.[912] (Five Deities.)

Again, he wedded Nu-iro-me of Kazuraki,[913] and begot an august child:

King Iza-no-ma-waka.[914] (One Deity.)

The august children of this Heavenly Sovereign [numbered] altogether twenty-six (eleven Kings and fifteen Queens). Of these His Augustness Ō-sazaki [was he who afterwards] ruled the Empire.

SECT. 105—EMPEROR Ō-JIN (PART 2—HE DIVIDES THE INHERITANCE BETWEEN HIS THREE SONS)

Hereupon the Heavenly Sovereign asked His Augustness Ō-yama-mori and His Augustness Ō-sazaki,[915] saying: "Which think ye the dearer, an elder child or a younger child?" (The reason why the Heavenly Sovereign propounded this question was because it was his intention[A] to make Uji-no-waki- iratsuko rule the Empire).

Then His Augustness Ō-yama-mori said: "The elder child is the dearer."

Next His Augustness Ō-sazaki, knowing the august feeling which made the Heavenly Sovereign deign to ask [the question], said: "The elder child, having already become a man, gives no trouble; but the younger child, not being yet a man, is the dearer."

Then the Heavenly Sovereign said: "My lord Sazaki's words agree with my thoughts," and forthwith ordained the division [of the inheritance] thus: His Augustness Ō-yama-mori to administer the

[A] Lit. "heart."

government of the mountains and the sea,[A] His Augustness Ō-sazaki to take and deign to report on the government of the realm,[B] and Uji-no-waki-iratsuko to rule the succession of Heaven's sun.[C] So His Augustness Ō-sazaki was not disobedient to the Heavenly Sovereign's commands.[916]

SECT. 106—EMPEROR Ō-JIN (PART 3—HE WOOS PRINCESS MIYA-NUSHI-YA-KAWA-E)

One day[D] the Heavenly Sovereign, when he had crossed over into the land of Ōmi, augustly stood on the moor of Uji, gazed[E] on the moor of Kazu, and sang, saying:

[41] As I look on the Moor of Kazu in Chiba
both the hundred thousand-fold abundant
house-places are visible,
and the land's acme is visible.[917]

So when he reached the village of Kohata,[918] a beautiful maiden met him at a fork in the road. Then the Heavenly Sovereign asked the maiden, saying: "Whose child art thou?"

She replied, saying: "I am the daughter of the Grandee Wani-no-Hifure,[919] and my name is Princess Miya-nushi-ya-kawa-e."[920]

The Heavenly Sovereign forthwith said to the maiden: "When I return on my progress tomorrow, I will enter into thy house." So Princess Ya-kawa-e told her father all that [had happened].

Thereupon her father replied, saying: "Ah! it was the Heavenly Sovereign! [His commands are to be respected. My child, respectfully serve him!"—and so saying, he grandly decorated the house, and awaited [the Heavenly Sovereign's return], whereupon he came in on

[A] *I.e.*, Norinaga thinks, to have control over the guilds of foresters and fishermen.
[B] *I.e.*, to act as regent or minister.
[C] *I.e.*, to inherit the empire. It will be remembered that the Japanese Emperors claim to descend from the Sun-Goddess.
[D] Lit. "one time."
[E] Gazed down. —W.G.A.

the next day.[A]

So when [the father] served [the Heavenly Sovereign] a great august feast, he made his daughter Her Augustness[921] Princess Ya-kawa take the great august liquor-cup and present it. Thereupon, while taking the great august liquor-cup, the Heavenly Sovereign augustly sang, saying:

[42] Oh this crab! whence this crab? [It is]
a crab from far-distant Tsunuga. Whither
reaches its sideward motion? [It has]
come towards Ichiji-shima and Mi-shima.

It must be because, plunging and breathless
like the grebe, I went without stopping
along the up and down road by the wavelets,
that the maiden I met on the Kohata road
has a back oh! like a small shield,
a row of teeth like acorns.

Oh! the earth of the Wani pass at Ichihii!
Owing to the skin of the first earth being ruddy,
to the last earth being of a reddish black,
she, without exposing to the actual sun
that makes one bend one's head
the middle earth like three chestnuts, draws thickly
down her drawn eyebrows;—the woman
I met, the child I saw and wanted in this
way, the child I saw and wanted in that
way, oh! she is opposite to me at the
height of the feast! oh! she is at my side!"[922]

Thus, he augustly united [with her], and begot a son, Uji-no-waki-iratsuko.[923]

[A] I.e., that day having passed by, the Emperor came on the next day according to his promise.

SECT. 107—EMPEROR Ō-JIN (PART 4—HE GRANTS PRINCESS KAMI-NAGA TO HIS SON Ō-SAZAKI)

The Heavenly Sovereign, hearing of the beauty of Princess Kami-naga,[924] daughter of the Duke of Muragata[925] in the land of Himuka, and thinking to employ her,[A] sent down for her,[B] whereupon the Heir Apparent[926] His Augustness Ō-sazaki, having seen the maiden land[C] at the port of Naniwa, and being charmed with the grace of her appearance, forthwith directed the Prime Minister the Noble Take-uchi, to intercede for him in the great august presence of the Heavenly Sovereign, and make [the latter] grant to him Princess Kami-naga, whom he had sent down for.

Then on the Prime Minister the Noble Take-uchi requesting the great commands,[D] the Heavenly Sovereign forthwith granted Princess Kami-naga to his august child. The way he granted her was this:—the Heavenly Sovereign, on a day when he partook of a copious feast,[927] gave Princess Kami-naga the great august liquor oak-[leaf[E][928]] to present to the Heir Apparent. Then he augustly sang, saying:

[43] Come on, children! oh! the fragrant
flowering orange-tree on my way
as I go to pluck the wild garlic,
—to pluck the garlic,—
has its uppermost branches
withered by birds perching on them,
and its lowest branches withered through people
plucking from them. But the budding
fruit on the middle branch, like three
chestnuts,—the ruddy maiden, oh! if
thou lead her off with thee,
it will be good, oh![929]

[A] *I.e.*, wed her.

[B] Lit. "summoned her up." The same phrase occurs immediately below.

[C] Arrive? —W.G.A

[D] *I.e.*, the Emperor's orders.

[E] *I.e.*, an oak-leaf which was used as a cup to sip out of. Leaf-platters for food have already been mentioned.

Again he augustly sang, saying:

[44] Driving the dyke-piles into Lake Yosami
where the water collects, my heart
(ignorant of the pricking of the stumps of the water-caltrop,
ignorant of the creeping[A] of the roots of the watershield),
being more and more laughable,
is now indeed repentant.[930]

Having thus sung, he bestowed [her on the Heir Apparent]. So after having been granted the maiden, the Heir Apparent sang, saying:

[45] Oh! the maiden of Kohada
in the back of the road!
though I heard of her like the thunder,
we mutually intertwine [our arms] as pillows.[931]

Again he sang, saying:

[46] I think lovingly ah!
of how the maiden of Kohada
in the back of the road
sleeps [with me] without disputing.[932]

SECT. 108—EMPEROR Ō-JIN (PART 5—SONGS OF THE TERRITORIAL OWNERS OF YOSHINO)

Again, the Territorial Owners of Yoshino,[933] seeing[B] the august sword which was girded on His Augustness Ō-sazaki, sang, saying:

[47] Sharp is the beginning, freezing is the end
of the sword girded on Ō-sazaki, Ō-sazaki,
the solar august child of Homuda,—

[A] Growing? —W.G.A.

[B] The Chinese character means "look up to," "to reverence," "to revere," "to regard very respectfully." The writer evidently meant this and not simply 見 "see."—W.G.A.

[it is] chilly, chilly like the trees beneath
the trunks of the winter trees.[934]

Again, having made a cross-mortar[935] at Kashifu[936] in Yoshino, and having in that cross-mortar distilled[937] some great august liquor, they, when they presented the great august liquor [to the Heavenly Sovereign], sang as follows, drumming with their mouths:[938]

[48] We have made a side-mortar at Kashinofu,
and in the side-mortar we have distilled
some great august liquor, which do thou
sweetly partake of, oh our lord![939]

This Song is one which it is the custom to chant down to the present day when, from time to time, the Territorial Owners present a great feast [to the Sovereign].

SECT. 109—EMPEROR Ō-JIN (PART 6—VARIOUS DEEDS)

In this august reign were graciously established the Fisher Tribe,[940] the Mountain Tribe,[941] the Mountain Warden Tribe,[942] and the Ise Tribe.[943] Again the Pool of Tsurugi was made. Again there came over [to Japan] some people from Shiragi. Therefore His Augustness the Noble Take-uchi, having taken them with him and set them to labor on pools and embankments, made the Pool of Kudara.[944]

SECT. 110—EMPEROR Ō-JIN (PART 7—TRIBUTE FROM KOREA)

Again King Shō-ko,[945] the Chieftain of the land of Kudara, sent as tribute by Achi-kishi[946] one stallion and one mare. (This Achi-kishi was the ancestor of the Achiki Scribes.[947]) Again he sent as tribute a cross-sword,[948] and likewise a large mirror. Again he was graciously bidden[949] to send as tribute a wise man, if there were any such in the land of Kudara.

Therefore, receiving the [Imperial] commands, he sent as tribute a man named Wani-kishi,[950] and likewise by this man he sent as tribute the Confucian *Analects*[951] in ten volumes and the *Thousand Character Essay*[952] in one volume,—altogether eleven volumes. (This Wani-kishi was the ancestor of the Fumi Grandees.[953])

Again he sent as tribute two artisans,—a smith from Kara named Taku-so[954] and a weaver from Go[955] named Sai-so.[956]

SECT. 111—EMPEROR Ō-JIN (PART 8—THE EMPEROR INTOXICATED)

Again there came over [to Japan] the ancestor of the Hada Rulers,[957] the ancestor of the Aya Suzerains,[958] and likewise a man who knew how to distill liquor, and whose name was Nim-pan,[959] while another name for him was Susukori.[960] So this [man] Susukori distilled[A] some great august liquor, and presented it to the Heavenly Sovereign, who, excited with the great august liquor that had been presented to him, augustly sang, saying:

[49] I have become intoxicated with the august liquor
distilled by Susukori.
I have become intoxicated with the soothing liquor,
with the smiling liquor.[961]

On his walking out singing thus, he hit with his august staff a large stone in the middle of the Ōsaka[962] road, upon which the stone ran away. So the proverb says: "Hard stones get out of a drunkard's way."

SECT. 112—EMPEROR Ō-JIN (PART 9—TROUBLES WHICH FOLLOWED HIS DECEASE)

So after the decease of the Heavenly Sovereign, His Augustness Ō-sazaki, in conformity with the Heavenly Sovereign's commands, ceded[963] the Empire to Uji-no-waki-iratsuko.

Thereupon His Augustness Ō-yama-mori, disobeying the Heavenly Sovereign's commands, and anxious in spite thereof to obtain the Empire, had the design to slay the Prince[964] his younger brother, secretly raised an army, and prepared to attack him. Then His Augustness Ō-sazaki, hearing that his elder brother had prepared an army, forthwith dispatched a messenger to apprise Uji-no-waki-iratsuko.

So, startled at the news, [the latter] set troops in ambush by the

[A] Brewed. —W.G.A.

river-bank, and likewise, after having drawn a fence of curtains and raised a tent on the top of the hill, placed there publicly on a throne[965] one of his retainers to pretend that he was the King,[A] the manner in which all the officials[966] reverentially went and came being just like that [usual] in the King's presence. And moreover, preparing for the time when the King his elder brother[B] should cross the river, he arranged and decorated a boat and oars, and moreover[967] ground[C] [in a mortar] the root of the *Kadsura japonica*, and having taken the slime of its juice, rubbed therewith the grating[968] inside the boat, so as to make any who should tread on it fall down, and then himself[969] put on a cloth coat and trousers, and having assumed the appearance of a common fellow, stood in the boat holding the oar.

Hereupon, when the King his elder brother, having hid his troops in ambush and put on armor beneath his clothes, reached the river-bank and was about to get into the boat, he gazed at the grandly decorated place [on the hill], thought the King his younger brother was sitting on the throne, being altogether ignorant [of the fact] that he was standing in the boat holding the oar, and forthwith asked the fellow who was holding the oar, saying: "It has been reported to me that on this mountain there is a large and angry boar. I wish to take that boar. Shall I peradventure get that boar?"

Then the fellow holding the oar replied, saying: "Thou canst not."

Again he asked, saying: "For what reason?"

[The boat-man] answered, saying: "He is not to be got, however often and in however many places he be chased. Wherefore I say that thou canst not [catch him either]."

When they had crossed as far as the middle of the river, [Prince Uji-no-waki-iratsuko] caused the boat to be tilted over, and [his elder brother] to fall into the water.[D] Then forthwith he rose to the surface and

---

[A] *I.e.*, Uji-no-waki-iratsuko.

[B] *Q.d.*, his Augustness Ō-yama-mori.

[C] Or "pounded."—W.G.A.

[D] It must be understood that Uji-no-waki-iratsuko and his men, having planned to act thus, were on their guard, and did not fall into the water as did Ō-yama-mori, who was taken unawares. [Ō-yama-mori was probably thinking of the *ukei-gari* mentioned above. He wished to judge of his luck from the answer he received.—W.G.A.]

floated down with the current. Forthwith, as he floated, he sang, saying:

[50] Whoever is swiftest among the boatmen
of the Uji ferry will come to me."[970]

Thereupon the troops that had been hidden on the riverbank rose up simultaneously on this side and on that side, and fixing their arrows [in their bows], let him go floating down. So he sank on reaching Kawara Point.[971] So on their searching with hooks[972] the place where he had sunk, [the hooks] struck on the armor inside his clothes, and made a rattling sound.[973] So the place was called by the name of Kawara Point. Then when they hooked up[974] his bones the younger King sang, saying:

[51] Catalpa bow, spindle tree[A]
standing by the ferry-bank of Uji!
My heart had thought to cut [you],
my heart had thought to take [you];
but at the base methought of the lord,
at the extremity methought of the younger sister;
grievously methought of this,
sorrowfully methought of that;
and I come [back] without cutting it,
—the *Catalpa* bow, the *Euonymus*."[975]

So the bones of His Augustness Ō-yama-mori were buried on the Nara[976] mountain. His Augustness Ō-yama-mori (was the ancestor of the Dukes of Hijikata,[977] the Dukes of Heki,[978] and the Dukes of Harihara[979]).

SECT. 113—EMPEROR Ō-JIN (PART 10—PRINCES Ō-SAZAKI AND UJI-NO-WAKI-IRATSUKO CEDE THE EMPIRE TO EACH OTHER)

Thereupon while the two Deities[980] His Augustness Ō-sazaki and Uji-no-waki-iratsuko were, each of them, ceding the Empire to the

[A] Spindle tree refers to the genus *Euonymus*. —M.F.

other,[A] a fisherman[B] came with a great feast as tribute.[C] So they each resigned it to the other. So the elder brother refused it, and caused it to be offered to the younger brother, and the younger brother refused it and caused it to be offered to the elder brother, during which mutual cedings many days elapsed.

As such mutual ceding took place not [only] once or twice, the fisherman wept from the fatigue of going backwards and forwards. So the proverb says: "Ah! the fisherman weeps on account of his own things."[981] Meanwhile Uji-no-waki-iratsuko died early.[982] So His Augustness Ō-sazaki did rule the Empire.

SECT. 114—EMPEROR Ō-JIN (PART 11—AMA-NO-HI-BOKO CROSSES OVER TO JAPAN)

Moreover of old there had been [a man] called by the name of Ama-no-hi-boko,[983] child of the ruler of the land of Shiragi. This person crossed over here [to Japan]. The reason of his crossing over here was [this]:

In the land of Shiragi there was a certain lagoon,[984] called by the name of the Agu Lagoon.[985] On the bank of this lagoon[986] a certain poor girl was [taking her] midday sleep. Then the rays of the sun, like a heavenly bow, struck her private parts.[987] Again there was a certain poor man, who, thinking this occurrence[988] strange, constantly watched the woman's behavior.

So the woman, having conceived from the time of that midday sleep, gave birth to a red jewel. Then the poor man who had watched her begged [to be allowed] to take the jewel, and kept it constantly wrapped up by his side.[D] This person, having planted a rice-field in a valley,[989] had loaded a cow[990] with food for the laborers, and was getting into the middle of the valley, when he met the ruler's son, Ama-no-hi-boko, who thereupon asked him, saying: "Why enterest thou the valley with a load of food upon a cow? Thou wilt surely kill this cow and eat her."

Forthwith he seized the man and was about to put him into prison,

---

[A] Neither being willing to accept the Imperial dignity.

[B] Or, "some fishermen," and similarly in the plural throughout.

[C] *I.e.*, came to present fish to His Majesty.

[D] Lit. "attached to his loins."

when the man replied, saying: "I was not going to kill the cow. I was simply taking food to the people in the fields." But still [the ruler's child] would not let him go. Then he undid the jewel [which hung] at his side, and [therewith] bribed [the ruler's child].

So [the latter] let the poor man go, brought the jewel [home], and placed it beside his couch. Forthwith it was transformed into a beautiful maiden, whom he straightway wedded, and made his chief wife. Then the maiden perpetually prepared all sorts of dainties with which she constantly fed her husband. So the ruler's child [grew] proud in his heart, and reviled his wife.

But the woman said: "I am not a woman who ought to be the wife of such as thou. I will go to the land of my ancestors;"—and forthwith she secretly embarked in a boat, and fled away across here [to Japan], and landed[991] at Naniwa.[992] (This is the Deity called princess Akaru,[993] who dwells in the shrine of Hime-goso[994] at Naniwa.) Thereupon Ama-no-hi-boko, hearing of his wife's flight, forthwith pursued her across hither, and was about to arrive at Naniwa, when the Deity of the passage[A] prevented his entrance. So he went back again, and landed in the country of Tajima.[995]

SECT. 115—EMPEROR Ō-JIN (PART 12—DESCENDANTS OF AMA-NO-HI-BOKO, AND TREASURES BROUGHT BY HIM)

Forthwith staying in that country, he wedded Saki-tsu-mi,[996] daughter of Tajima-no-matao,[997] and begot a child: Tajima-morosuku.[998] The latter's child was Tajima-hi-ne.[999] The latter's child was Tajima-hinara-ki.[1000] The latter's children were Tajima-mori,[1001] next Tajima-hitaka,[1002] next Kiyo-hiko[1003] (three Deities).[1004]

This Kiyo-hiko wedded Tagima-no-mehi,[1005] and begot children: Saga-no-moroo,[1006] next his younger sister Suga-kama-yura-domi.[1007] So the above-mentioned Tajima-hitaka wedded his niece Yura-domi, and begot a child: Her Augustness Princess Takanuka of Kazuraki.[1008] (This was the august parent[1009] of Her Augustness Princess Okina-ga-tarashi.)

So the things which Ama-no-hi-boko brought over here, and which

[A] *I.e.*, the water-god of the portion of the sea near Naniwa.

were called the "precious treasures,"[1010] were: two strings of pearls;[1011] likewise a wave-shaking scarf, a wave-cutting scarf, a wind-shaking scarf, and a wind-cutting scarf;[A] likewise a mirror of the offing and a mirror of the shore;[1012]—eight articles in all. (These are the Eight Great Deities[1013] of Izushi.)

SECT. 116—EMPEROR Ō-JIN (PART 13—THE YOUTH-OF-THE-GLOW-ON-THE-AUTUMN-MOUNTAINS AND THE YOUTH-OF-THE-HAZE-ON-THE-SPRING-MOUNTAINS)

So this Deity had a daughter whose name was the Deity Maiden-of-Izushi.[1014] So eighty Deities wished to obtain this Maiden-of-Izushi in marriage, but none of them could do so.[1015]

Hereupon there were two Deities, brothers, of whom the elder was called the Youth-of-the-Glow-on-the-Autumn-Mountains,[1016] and the younger was named the Youth-of-the-Haze-on-the-Spring-Mountains.[1017] So the elder brother said to the younger brother: "Though I beg for[1018] the Maiden of Izushi, I cannot obtain her in marriage. Wilt thou [be able] to obtain her?"

He answered, saying: "I will easily obtain her."

Then the elder brother said: "If thou shalt obtain this maiden, I will take off my upper and lower garments, and distill liquor in a jar of my own height,[B] and prepare all the things of the mountains and of the rivers,[C1019] [and give them to thee] in payment of the wager."

Then the younger brother told his mother everything that the elder brother had said. Forthwith the mother, having taken wisteria-fiber, wove and sewed in the space of a single night an upper garment and trousers, and also socks and boots, and likewise made a bow and arrow, and clothed him in this upper garment, trousers, etc., made him take the bow and arrows, and sent him to the maiden's house, where both

[A] *I.e*, a scarf to raise the waves and a scarf to still the waves, a scarf to raise the wind and a scarf to still the wind. *Cf.* the magic scarfs mentioned near the beginning of Sect. 23, by waving which the Deity Master-of-the-Great-Land (Ō-kuni-nushi) kept off the snakes, the wasps and the centipedes.

[B] Lit. "compute the height of my person and distill liquor in a jar."

[C] *I.e.*, all the valuable produce of the chase and of the fisheries, such as are perpetually mentioned in the Shintō *Rituals* as being presented to the gods.

his apparel and the bow and arrows all turned into wisteria blossoms.

Thereupon the Youth-of-the-Haze-on-the-Spring-Mountains hung up the bow and arrows in the maiden's privy. Then, when the Maiden-of-Izushi, thinking the blossoms strange, brought them [home, the Youth-of-the-Haze-on-the-Spring-Mountains] followed behind the maiden into the house, and forthwith wedded her. So she gave birth to a child.[1020]

Then he spoke to his elder brother, saying: "I have obtained the Maiden-of-Izushi."

Thereupon the elder brother, vexed that the younger brother should have wedded her, did not pay the things he had wagered. Then when [the younger brother] complained to his mother, his august parent replied, saying: "During my august life the Deities indeed are to be well imitated; moreover it must be because he imitates mortal men[1021] that he does not pay those things."

Forthwith, in her anger with her elder child, she took a jointed bamboo[1022] from an island in the River Izushi, and made a coarse basket with eight holes,[1023] and took stones from the river, and mixing them with brine, wrapped them in the leaves of the bamboo[A] and caused this curse to be spoken:[B] "Like unto the becoming green of these bamboo-leaves,[C] [do thou] become green and wither! Again, like unto the flowing and ebbing of this brine,[1024] [do thou] flow and ebb! Again, like unto the sinking of these stones, [do thou] sink and be prostrate!"

Having caused this curse to be spoken, she placed [the basket] over the smoke.[D] Therefore the elder brother dried up, withered, sickened, and lay prostrate[1025] for the space of eight years. So on the elder brother entreating his august parent with lamentations and tears, she forthwith caused the curse to be reversed.[1026] Thereupon his body became sound[E] as it had been before. (This is the origin of the term "a divine wager-payment."[1027])

[A] *Scil.* of which the basket was woven.
[B] *Scil.* by her younger son.
[C] Like unto the withering of these bamboo leaves. —W.G.A.
[D] *Scil.* of the furnace (kitchen) in the younger brother's house, as Norinaga suggests.
[E] Lit. "was pacified."

SECT. 117—EMPEROR Ō-JIN (PART 14—GENEALOGIES)

Again this Heavenly Sovereign Homuda's[1028] august child King Waka-nuke-futa-mata wedded his mother's younger sister Momo-shiki-iro-be,[1029] another name for whom was Her Augustness Oto-hime-ma-waka-hime,[1030] and begot children:

Ō-ira-tsuko,[1031] another name for whom was King Ō-hodo;[1032]
next Her Augustness Osaka-no-ō-naka-tsu-hime;[1033]
next Tai-no-naka-tsu-hime;[1034]
next Tamiya-no-naka-tsu-hime;[1035]
next Fujiwara-no-koto-fushi-no-iratsume;[1036]
next Queen Torime;[1037]
next King Sane.[1038] (Seven Kings [and Queens].[1039])

So King Ō-hodo (was the ancestor of the Dukes of Mikuni,[1040] the Dukes of Hata,[1041] the Dukes of Okinaga,[1042] the Dukes of Sakabito of Sakata,[1043] the Dukes of Yamaji,[1044] the Dukes of Meta in Tsukushi,[1045] and the Dukes of Fuse).[1046]

Again King Netori wedded his younger half-sister the Lady Mi-hara, and begot children:

King Naka-tsu-hiko;[1047]
next King Iwa-shima.[1048] (Two Kings.)

Again the child of King Katashiwa[1049] was King Kuno.[1050]

SECT. 118—EMPEROR Ō-JIN (PART 15—HIS AGE AND PLACE OF BURIAL)

The august years of this Heavenly Sovereign Homuda were altogether one hundred and thirty. His august mausoleum is on the mound of Mofusu[1051] at Ega in Kōchi.

Vol. 3.[1]

SECT. 119—EMPEROR NIN-TOKU (PART 1—GENEALOGIES)

His Augustness Ō-sazaki dwelt in the palace of Takatsu[2] at Naniwa, and ruled the Empire. This Heavenly Sovereign wedded (the Empress[3]) Her Augustness Iwa-no-hime,[4] daughter of Kazuraki-no-so-tsu-biko,[5] and begot august children:

His Augustness Ōe-no-izaho-wake;[6]

next the Middle King of the Inlet of Sumi;[7]

next His Augustness Mizu-ha-wake of Tajihi;[8]

next His Augustness the Noble O-asazuma-no-waku-go[9] (Four Deities).

Again he wedded Princess Kami-naga, daughter of the Duke of Muragata in Himuka, as mentioned above,[10] and begot august children:

Hatabi-no-ō-iratsuko,[11] another name for whom was the King of Great Kusaka;[12]

next Hatabi-no-waki-iratsume,[13] another name for whom was Her Augustness Princess Nagai,[14] and another name was Her Augustness Waka-kusaka-be.[15] (Two Deities.)

Again he wedded his younger half-sister Yata-no-waki-iratsume.[16] Again he wedded his younger half-sister Uji-no-waki-iratsume. These two Deities had no august children.

Altogether the august children of this Heavenly Sovereign Ō-sazaki [numbered] in all six Deities. (Five Kings and one Queen.) So His Augustness Izaho-wake [was he who afterwards] ruled the Empire. Next His Augustness Tajihi-no-mizu-ha-wake likewise ruled the Empire. Next His Augustness the Noble O-asazuma-no-waku-go likewise ruled the Empire.[17]

SECT. 120—EMPEROR NIN-TOKU (PART 2—VARIOUS DEEDS)

In the august reign of this Heavenly Sovereign the Kazuraki Tribe[18] was established as the august proxy of the Empress, Her Augustness Iwa-no-hime. Again the Mibu Tribe[19] was established as the august proxy of the Heir Apparent, His Augustness Izaho-wake. Again the Tajihi Tribe[20] was established as the august proxy of His Augustness Mizuha-wake. Again the Ō-kusaka Tribe[21] was established as the august proxy of King Ō-kusaka, and the Waka-kusaka Tribe[22] was established as the august proxy of King Waka-kusaka-be.

Again people from Hada were set to labor, and the embankment at Mamuta[23] and also the granaries of Mamuta were made.[24] Again the Pool of Wani[25] and the Pool of Yosami were made. Again the Naniwa Channel[26] was dug, and [the waters of the rivers] led to the sea. Again the Obashi Channel[27] was dug. Again the port of the Inlet of Sumi[28] was established.

SECT. 121—EMPEROR NIN-TOKU (PART 3—HE REMITS THE TAXES)

Thereupon the Heavenly Sovereign, ascending a lofty mountain and looking on the land all round, spoke, saying: "In the whole land there rises no smoke; the land is all poverty-stricken. So I remit[29] all the people's taxes and [forced labor[30]] from now till three years [hence]." Therefore the great palace became dilapidated, and the rain leaked in everywhere; but no repairs were made. The rain that leaked in was caught in troughs,[31] and [the inmates] removed from [its reach] to places where there was no leakage.

When later [the Heavenly Sovereign] looked on all the land, the smoke was abundant in the land. So finding the people rich, he now exacted taxes and forced labor. Therefore the peasantry[32] prospered, and did not suffer from forced labor. So in praise of that august reign, it was called the reign of the Emperor-Sage.[33]

SECT. 122—EMPEROR NIN-TOKU (PART 4—HE LOVES PRINCESS KURO)

His Empress, Her Augustness Iwa-no-hime, was exceedingly jealous. So the concubines employed by the Heavenly Sovereign could not even peep inside[A] the palace; and if anything happened,[34] [the Empress] stamped with jealousy. Then the Heavenly Sovereign, hearing of the regular beauty of Princess Kuro,[35] daughter of the Suzerain of Ama in Kibi,[36] and having sent for her, employed her. But she, afraid of the Empress's jealousy, fled down to her native land. The Heavenly Sovereign, gazing from an upper story upon Princess Kuro's departure by boat upon the sea, sang, saying:

[52] In the offing there are rows of small boats.
My wife Masazuko of Kurozaki goes
down towards her [native] land.[37]

So the Empress was very angry on hearing this august Song, and sent people to the great strand[38] to drive Princess Kuro ashore, and chase her away on foot.[39] Thereupon the Heavenly Sovereign, for love of Princess Kuro, deceived the Empress, saying that he wanted to see the Island of Awaji.[40] And when he made his progress and was in the Island of Awaji, he, gazing afar, sang, saying:

[53] When, having departed from the point of
wave-beaten Naniwa, I look at the country,
the Island of Awa, the island of Onogoro,
and also the Island of Ajimasa are visible.
The Island of Saketsu is visible.[41]

Forthwith passing on from that island, he made a progress to the land of Kibi. Then Her Augustness Princess Kuro made him grandly reside at a place among the mountain-fields,[42] and presented to him great august food. When for this [purpose] she plucked cabbage[B] in that place to boil into great august soup, the Heavenly Sovereign went to the place where the maiden was plucking the cabbage, and sang, saying:

[A] Approach? —W.G.A.
[B] Is not cabbage (*aona*) a little too specific? Pot-herbs? —W.G.A.

[54] Oh! how delightful it is to pluck with a
person of Kibi the cabbage sown in the
mountain fields![43]

When the Heavenly Sovereign made his progress up,[44] Princess Kuro presented an august[45] Song, saying:

[55] Even though the west wind blow up
towards Yamato, and the clouds part, and
we be separated, shall I forget [thee]?[46]

Again she sang, saying:

[56] Whose spouse is it that goes towards
Yamato? Whose spouse is it that creeps
from beneath like hidden water?[47]

SECT. 123—EMPEROR NIN-TOKU (PART 5—THE EMPRESS RETIRES TO YAMASHIRO)

After this time the Empress made a progress to the land of Ki in order to pluck aralia-leaves for a copious feast;[48] and in the meanwhile the Heavenly Sovereign wedded Yata-no-waki-iratsume.

Hereupon, when the Empress was returning in her august vessel loaded full of aralia-leaves, a porter from Kojima[49] in the land of Kibi, who was in the service of the Superintendent of the Water-Directors,[50] being on his way off to his own country, met at the great passage[51] of Naniwa the vessel of a lady of the train[52] who had got behind, and forthwith told her, saying: "The Heavenly Sovereign has recently[53] wedded Yata-no-waki-iratsume, and plays with her day and night. It must probably be because the Empress has not heard of this thing, that she quietly makes progresses for pleasure."

Then the lady of the train, having heard this narrative, forthwith pursued and reached the august vessel, and reported everything exactly as the porter had told it. Hereupon the Empress, greatly vexed and angry, threw away into the sea all the aralia-leaves which she had put on board the august vessel. So the place [where she did so] is called by the name of Cape Mitsu.[54] Forthwith without entering the palace, but taking her august vessel away [from it][55] and ascending the channel[56] against the current, she made a progress up into Yamashiro by the river.[57] At this time she sang, saying:

[57] Oh! the river of Yamashiro
where the seedlings grow in succession!
As I ascend, ascend the river,
oh! on the bank of the river
[there] stands growing a *sashibu*!—
a *sashibu*-tree; below it stands growing a
broad-foliaged five hundred [-fold branching]
true camellia-tree; oh! he who is
brilliant like its blossoms, widely powerful
like its foliage, is the great lord.[58]

Forthwith going round by Yamashiro,[59] and arriving at the entrance of the Nara Mountain,[60] she sang, saying:

[58] Oh! the river of Yamashiro where the
seedlings grow in succession! As I
ascend, ascend to Miya, I pass Nara, I
pass Yamato with its shield of mountains;
and the country I fain would see is Takamiya in Kazuraki,
the neighborhood of my home.[61]

Having sung thus, she returned and entered for some time into the house of a person from Kara[62] named Nurinomi[63] at Tsutsuki.[64]

SECT. 124—EMPEROR NIN-TOKU (PART 6—HE FOLLOWS THE EMPRESS INTO YAMASHIRO)

The Heavenly Sovereign, having heard that the Empress had made a progress up by Yamashiro, made a person,—a retainer called by the name of Toriyama,[65]—give an august Song,[66] which said:

[59] Reach [her] in Yamashiro, Toriyama!
Reach [her]! reach [her]! Ah! wilt thou
reach and meet my beloved spouse?[67]

Again he continued by dispatching Kuchiko, Grandee of Wani,[68] and sang, saying:

[60] Wilt thou be without thinking
even of the heart that is in
the moor of Ōiko,
the moor of Ōiko,
that is by Takaki at Mimoro?[69]

Again he sang, saying:

[61] If indeed I had not
pillowed [my head] on thy white arm
like the whiteness of the roots,
the great roots, that were beaten with wooden hoes
by the women of Yamashiro
where the seedlings grow in succession,
[then] mightest thou say, 'I know [thee] not!'[70]

So when the Grandee of Kuchiko was repeating this august Song [to the Empress], it was raining heavily. Then upon his, without avoiding the rain, coming and prostrating himself at the front door of the palace,[71] she on the contrary went out at the back door; and on his coming and prostrating himself at the back door of the palace, she on the contrary went out at the front door. Then, as he crept backwards and forwards on his knees in the middle of the court, the streams[72] of water[73] reached to his loins. Owing to the grandee being clad in a garment dyed[74] green and with a red cord, the streams of water brushed against the red cord, and the green all changed to red color. Now the Grandee of Kuchiko's younger sister Princess Kuchi[A] was in the service

---

[A] *Kuchi-hime.*

of the Empress.[75] So Princess Kuchi sang, saying:

[62] Oh! how tearful is my lord elder brother,
saying things in the palace
of Tsutsuki in Yamashiro![76]

Then when the Empress asked the reason,[77] she replied, saying: "He is my brother, the Grandee of Kuchiko."

Thereupon the Grandee of Kuchiko and also his younger sister Princess Kuchi and likewise Nurinomi [all] three took counsel [together], and sent to report to the Heavenly Sovereign, saying: "The reason of the Empress's progress is that there are [some] insects reared by Nurinomi,—strange insects changing in three ways,[A] once becoming creeping insects, once becoming cocoons,[78] and once becoming flying birds,[B]—and it is only to go and look at them that she has entered into [Nurinomi's house]. She has no strange intentions."[C]

When they had thus reported, the Heavenly Sovereign said: "That being so, I want to go and see [these insects], as I think [they must be] strange;" [and with these words] he made a progress up from the great palace. When he entered into Nurinomi's house, Nurinomi had already presented to the Empress the three-fold insects reared by him. Then the Heavenly Sovereign augustly stood at the door of the palace where the Empress dwelt and sang, saying:

[63] Pure as the great roots
that were beaten with their wooden hoes
by the women of Yamashiro
where the seedlings grow in succession:
— it is because thou spokest tumultuously
that I come in here
[with my retainers numerous]
as the more and more flourishing trees
that I look across at.[79]

[A] Lit., "colors."

[B] According to another reading, "flying insects."

[C] *I.e.*, "she is not meditating any evil conduct."

These six Songs sung by the Heavenly Sovereign and by the Empress are Changing Songs which are Quiet Songs.[80]

SECT. 125—EMPEROR NIN-TOKU (PART 7—HE LOVES YATA-NO-WAKI-IRATSUME)

The Heavenly Sovereign, loving Yata-no-waki-iratsume, deigned to send her an august Song. That Song said:

[64] Will the one sedge-stem of Yata, having
no children, wither as it stands? Poor
sedge-moor! Sedge-moor indeed is what
I may say—poor pure girl![81]

Then Yata-no-waki-iratsume replied in a Song, saying:

[65] Even though the one sedge-stem of Yata
be alone, if the Great Lord say it is right,
even though it be alone [it is right].[82]

So the Yata Tribe[83] was established as the august proxy of Yata-no-waki-iratsume.

SECT. 126—EMPEROR NIN-TOKU (PART 8—DEATH OF KING HAYABUSA-WAKE AND QUEEN MEDORI)

Again the Heavenly Sovereign begged for his younger half-sister Queen Medori, using as middle-man his younger brother King Hayabusa-wake. Then Queen Medori spoke to King Hayabusa-wake, saying: "Owing to the violence of the Empress, [the Heavenly Sovereign] has not deigned to take Yata-no-waki-iratsume [into the Palace]. So I will not respectfully serve him. I will become the wife of Thine Augustness." Forthwith they wedded each other, wherefore King Hayabusa-wake made no report [to the Heavenly Sovereign[84]].

Then the Heavenly Sovereign, going straight to the place where Queen Medori dwelt, stood on the doorsill of the palace. Hereupon, Queen Medori being at her loom, was weaving garments. Then the Heavenly Sovereign sang, saying:

[66] Oh! for whom may be the garments that
my Great Lady Medori weaves?[85]

Queen Medori replied in a Song, saying:

[67] For an august veil[A] for the nigh-going
Falcon-Lord.[B86]

So the Heavenly Sovereign, perceiving her feelings, returned into the palace. At this time[87] when her husband King Hayabusa-wake came, his wife Queen Medori sang, saying:

[68] The lark flies to heaven. Oh! high-going
Falcon-Lord, catch the wren.[88]

The Heavenly Sovereign, hearing this Song,[89] forthwith raised an army, wishing to slay King Hayabusa and Queen Medori, who then fled away together, and ascended Mount Kurahashi.[90] Thereupon King Hayabusa-wake sang, saying:

[69] Owing to the steepness of ladder-like
Mount Kurahashi, being unable to clamber
[up] the rocks, oh! she takes my hand![91]

Again he sang, saying:

[70] Though ladder-like Mount Kurahashi be
steep, it is not steep when I ascend it
with my younger sister.

So when they fled thence, and reached Soni in Uda,[92] the Imperial[93] army pursued, overtook, and slew them.

[A]Mantle? —W.G.A

[B]There is here a play on the name of the Queen's paramour Hayabusa-wake, which signifies "Falcon-Lord" as in the translation.

SECT. 127—EMPEROR NIN-TOKU (PART 8—QUEEN MEDORI'S ARMLET)

Chief Ōtate of Yamabe,[94] who was the generalissimo of that army, took the jeweled armlet which was wound round Queen Medori's august arm, and gave it to his own wife. After this time, when a copious feast[95] was to be held, the women of the various families all went to court. Then the wife of Chief Ōtate came with that Queen's jeweled armlet wound round her own arm.

Thereupon the Empress, Her Augustness Iwa-no-hime,[96] herself took the oak-leaves[97] [full] of great august liquor and graciously gave them to the women of the various families. Then the Empress, recognizing the jeweled armlet, gave [the wearer] no oak-leaf [-full] of great august liquor, but forthwith sent her away;[98] and sending for the husband, Chief Ōtate, said: "Owing to that King and Queen's impropriety, [the Emperor] deigned to send them away. This was nothing strange. And a slave such as thou despoils of the jeweled armlet that was wound round her august arm the body of his lady [that was still] warm, and gives it to his own wife!"—and forthwith he was condemned to death.[99]

SECT. 128—EMPEROR NIN-TOKU (PART 9—A WILD GOOSE LAYS AN EGG)

Another time, the Heavenly Sovereign, when about to hold a copious feast,[100] made a progress to the Island of Hime,[101] just when a wild goose had laid an egg on that island. Then, sending for His Augustness the Noble Take-uchi, he asked him in a Song about the laying of an egg by a wild goose. This Song said:

[71] Court Noble of Uchi!
thou indeed art a long-lived person.
Hast thou [ever] heard of a wild goose
laying an egg in the land of Yamato?[102]

Hereupon the Noble Take-uchi spoke in a Song, saying:

[72] August Child of the High-Shining Sun,
it is indeed natural

that thou shouldest deign to ask,
it is indeed right that thou shouldest ask.
I indeed am a long-lived person,
[but] have not yet heard of a wild goose
laying an egg in the land of Yamato.[103]

Having thus spoken, he was granted the august[104] lute, and sang, saying:

[73] Oh thou prince!
the wild goose must have
laid the egg because
thou wilt at last rule.[105]

This is a Congratulatory Incomplete Song.[106]

SECT. 129—EMPEROR NIN-TOKU (PART 10—A VESSEL IS MADE INTO A LUTE)

In this august reign there was a tall tree on the west of the river Tsu-ki.[107] The shadow of this tree, on its being struck by the morning sun, reached to the Island of Awaji;[108] and on its being struck by the evening sun, it crossed Mount Taka-yasu.[109] So the tree was cut down and made into a vessel,—and a very swift-going vessel it was. At the time, this vessel was called by the name of Karano.[110]

So with this vessel the water[111] of the Island of Awaji was drawn morning and evening, and presented as the great august water.[A] The broken [pieces] of this vessel were used [as fuel] to burn salt, and the pieces of wood that remained over from the burning were made into a lute, whose sound re-echoed seven miles[112] [off]. So [some one[113]] sang, saying:

[74] Karano was burnt [as fuel] for salt; the
remainder was made into a lute; oh!

[A] *I.e.*, this vessel was used to bring over every morning and evening the water for the Imperial household, which was drawn on the Island of Awaji.

when struck, it sounds like the wet plants
standing rocked on the reefs in the middle
of the harbor,—the harbor of Yura.[114]

This is a Changing Song which is a Quiet song.[115]

SECT. 130—EMPEROR NIN-TOKU (PART 11— HIS AGE AND PLACE OF BURIAL)

The august years of this Heavenly Sovereign were eighty-three. His august mausoleum is on the Ear-Moor of Mozu.[116]

SECT. 131—EMPEROR RI-CHŪ (PART 1— GENEALOGIES)

His Augustness Iza-ho-wake dwelt in the palace of Waka-sakura at Iware,[117] and ruled the Empire. This Heavenly Sovereign wedded Her Augustness Princess Kuro,[118] daughter of the Noble of Ashida,[119] child of So-tsu-biko of Kazuraki,[120] and begot august children:

King Oshiwa of Ichinobe;[121]

next King Mima;[122]

next his younger sister Aomi-no-iratsume,[123] another name for whom was Ii-toyo-no-iratsume.[124]

SECT. 132—EMPEROR RI-CHŪ (PART 2— HE IS TAKEN TO ISO-NO-KAMI)

Originally, when dwelling at the palace of Naniwa, [the Heavenly Sovereign] on holding a copious feast when at the great tasting,[A] was intoxicated with the great august liquor, and fell greatly and augustly asleep. Then his younger brother, King Sumi-no-e-naka-tsu, wishing to take the Heavenly Sovereign, set fire to the great palace.

Thereupon the Suzerain of Achi,[125] ancestor of the Suzerains of Aya[126] in Yamato, having taken him away by stealth, set him on an august horse, and caused him to make a progress into Yamato. So [the Heavenly Sovereign] awoke on reaching the moor of Tajihi,[127] and said: "What place is this?"

[A] *I.e.,* on the occasion of his performing the religious ceremony of tasting the first rice of the season.

Then the Suzerain of Achi said: "King Sumi-no-e-no-naka-tsu set fire to the great palace; so I am fleeing with thee into Yamato."

Then the Heavenly Sovereign sang, saying:

[75] Had I known that I should sleep
on the Moor of Tajihi, oh!
I would have brought
my dividing matting,
—had I known that I should sleep![128]

On reaching the Pass of Hanifu[129] and gazing at the palace of Naniwa, the fire was still bright. Then the Heavenly Sovereign sang again, saying:

[76] The group of houses sparklingly burning,
as I stand and look
from the Pass of Hanifu,
is in the direction of the house of my spouse.[130]

So when they reached the entrance of the Ōsaka mountain,[131] they met one woman. This woman said: "A number of men bearing weapons are barring [the way across] the mountain. Thou shouldst cross it going round by way of Tagima."[132] Then the Heavenly Sovereign sang, saying:

[77] Oh! on asking the way of the maiden
we met at Ōsaka, she tells not [the] direct
[way], but tells of the Tagima way.[133]

So, making his progress up, he dwelt in the temple of the Deity of Isonokami.[134]

SECT. 133—EMPEROR RI-CHŪ (PART 3—HIS REBELLIOUS BROTHER AND THE LATTER'S RETAINER SOBAKARI ARE SLAIN)

Thereupon his younger brother His Augustness Mizu-ha-wake came, and sent [to ask for] an audience.[135] Then the Heavenly Sovereign caused him to be told [these words]: "As I am in doubt whether perhaps

Thine Augustness may [not] be of like mind[136] with King Sumi-no-e-no-naka-tsu, I will not meet and speak with thee."

[His Augustness Mizu-ha-wake] replied, saying: "I have no evil intent. I am not of like mind with King Sumi-no-e-no-naka-tsu."

[The Heavenly Sovereign] again caused him to be told [these words]: "If that be so, [do thou] now return down, and slay King Sumi-no-e-no-naka-tsu, and come up [again hither]. At that time I will surely meet and speak with thee."

So he forthwith returned down to Naniwa, and deceived [a man] named Sobakari,[137] a man-at-arms[138] in the personal service of[139] King Sumi-no-e-no-naka-tsu, saying: "If thou wilt obey my words, I shall become Heavenly Sovereign, and will make thee prime Minister, to rule the Empire.[140] How [would this be]?"

Sobakari replied, saying: "[I will do] according to thy command."

Then plenteously endowing that man-at-arms, he said: "If that be so, slay the King."

Thereupon Sobakari watched for the time when his King went into the privy, and thrust him to death with a spear. So when [His Augustness Mizu-ha-wake] was making his progress to Yamato taking Sobakari with him, he, on reaching the entrance of the Ōsaka mountain, thought [thus]: "Although Sobakari deserves very well of me, he has truly[141] slain his lord. This is unrighteous. Nevertheless if I reward not his deed, I may be called untruthful; and if I quite carry out my promise, his intentions are on the contrary to be feared. So, though recompensing his deed, I will destroy his actual person."

Therefore he said to Sobakari: "I will halt here to-day and bestow on thee the rank of Prime Minister, and to-morrow will [continue my] progress up." So a halt was made at the entrance to the mountain, a temporary palace forthwith built, a copious feast[142] suddenly held, the rank of Prime Minister forthwith bestowed on the man-at-arms, and all the officials[143] made to do obeisance [to him]. The man-at-arms, delighted, thought that he had accomplished his design.

Then [His Augustness Mizu-ha-wake] said to the man-at-arms: "Today I will drink liquor from the same cup as the Prime Minister." And when they drank together, a bowl[144] large [enough] to hide the face was filled with the liquor presented.[145] Hereupon the King's child drank first, and the man-at-arms drank afterwards. So when the man-at-arms was drinking, the great cup covered his face. Then [His Augustness Mizu-ha-wake] drew forth a saber which he had laid under the matting, and cut off the head of the man-at-arms. Forthwith on the morrow he made his progress up. So the place was called by the name of Chika-tsu-Asuka.[146]

Going up and reaching Yamato, he said: "I will halt here today and, having purified myself, will go forth tomorrow and worship at the temple of the Deity."[147] So that place is called by the name of Tō-tsu-Asuka.[148]

So going forth to the temple of the Deity of Iso-no-kami, he sent to report to the Heavenly Sovereign that he had come up to serve him after accomplishing the work [with which he had been entrusted].[149] So [the Heavenly Sovereign] sent for, and met, and spoke with him.

SECT. 134—EMPEROR RI-CHŪ (PART 4—VARIOUS DEEDS)

The Heavenly Sovereign thereupon first appointed the Suzerain of Achi to the office of Treasurer,[150] and likewise bestowed on him domains.[151] Again in this august reign the name of Waka-sakura Tribe[152] was granted to the Grandees of the Waka-sakura Tribe.[153] Again the "gentile name"[154] of Dukes of Himeda[155] was granted to the Dukes of Himeda. Again the Iware Clan[156] was established.

SECT. 135—EMPEROR RI-CHŪ (PART 5—HIS AGE AND PLACE OF BURIAL)

The Heavenly Sovereign's august years were sixty-four. His august mausoleum is at Mozu.[157]

SECT. 136— EMPEROR HAN-ZEI

His Augustness Mizu-ha-wake dwelt in the palace of Shibakaki at Tajihi,[158] and ruled the Empire. The length of this Heavenly Sovereign's august person was nine feet two inches and a half.[159] The length of his august teeth was one inch, and their breadth two lines, and the upper and lower [row] corresponded exactly, like jewels strung [together].

The Heavenly Sovereign wedded the Lady of Tsuno,[160] daughter of Kogoto, Grandee of Wani,[161] and begot august children:

the Lady of Kai;[162]
next the Lady of Tsubura[163] (two Deities).

Again he wedded Oto-hime,[164] daughter of the same Grandee, and begot august children: King Takara;[165] next the Lady of Takabe,[166]—altogether four Kings [and Queens].[167]

The Heavenly Sovereign's august years were sixty. His august mausoleum is on the Moor of Mozu.[168]

SECT. 137—EMPEROR IN-GYŌ[169] (PART 1—GENEALOGIES)

His Augustness O-asazuma-waku-go-no-sukune dwelt in the Palace of Tō-tsu-Asuka,[170] and ruled the Empire. This Heavenly Sovereign wedded Her Augustness Osaka-no-ō-naka-tsu-hime,[171] younger sister of King Ō-hodo, and begot august children:

King Karu of Kinashi;[172]
next Nagata-no-ō-iratsume;[173]
next King Kuro-hiko of Sakai;[174]
next His Augustness Anaho;[175]
next Karu-no-ō-iratsume,[176] another name for whom is So-tōshi-no-iratsume[177] (the reason for her being given the august name of Queen So-tōshi was that the refulgence of her person passed through her garments);
next King Shiro-biko of Yatsuri;[178]
next His Augustness Ō-hatsuse;[179]
next Tachi-bana-no-ō-iratsume;[180]
next Sakami-no-iratsume[181] (nine Deities).

Altogether the Heavenly Sovereign's august children [numbered] nine Deities (five Kings and four Queens). Of these nine Kings and Queens, His Augustness Anaho [was he who afterwards] ruled the Empire. Next his Augustness Ō-hatsuse ruled the Empire.

SECT. 138—EMPEROR IN-GYŌ (PART 2—HIS SICKNESS IS CURED BY A KOREAN PHYSICIAN)

The Heavenly Sovereign, when first about to rule the succession of Heaven's Sun,[182] declined, saying: "I have a long sickness; I cannot rule the sun's succession." Nevertheless, as from the Empress downwards all the magnates strongly urged him, he forthwith ruled the Empire.

At this time the ruler of Shiragi[183] dutifully sent eighty-one vessels with august tribute.[184] Then the chief envoy[185] sent with the august tribute, whose name was Komu-ha-chimu-kamu-ki-mu,[186] was a man deeply versed in the medical art. So he cured the Heavenly Sovereign's august sickness.

SECT. 139—EMPEROR IN-GYŌ (PART 3—HE RECTIFIES THE PEOPLE'S NAMES)

Thereupon the Heavenly Sovereign, lamenting the transgressions in the surnames and "gentile names" of the people of all the surnames and names in the Empire[187] placed jars [for trial by] hot water[188] at the Wondrous Cape of Eighty Evils in Words at Amakashi[189] and deigned to establish the surnames and "gentile names" of the eighty heads of companies.[190]

Again the Karu Tribe[191] was established as the august proxy of King Karu of Ki-nashi; the Osaka Tribe[192] was established as the Empress's august proxy; and the Kawa Tribe[193] was established as the august proxy of the Empres's younger sister Ta-i no Naka-tsu-hime.[194]

SECT. 140—EMPEROR IN-GYŌ (PART 4—HIS AGE AND PLACE OF BURIAL)

The Heavenly Sovereign's august years were seventy-eight. His august mausoleum is at Naga-e near Ega in Kōchi.[195]

SECT. 141—EMPEROR IN-GYŌ (PART 5—PRINCE KARU LOVES HIS SISTER PRINCESS SO-TŌSHI)

After the decease of the Heavenly Sovereign, it was settled that King Karu of Ki-nashi should rule the Sun's succession.[196] But in the interval before his accession, he debauched his younger sister the Great Lady of Karu, and sang, saying:

[78] Making rice-fields on the mountain,
Making hidden conduits run on account
of the mountain's height:—today indeed [my]
body easily touches the younger sister
whom I wooed

with a hidden wooing,
the spouse for whom I wept
with a hidden weeping.[197]

This is a Hind-Lifting Song.[198] Again he sang, saying:

[79] The rattle-rattle of the hail against the bamboo-grass:—
After I shall have certainly slept,
what though I be plotted against by people!
When I shall have slept a good sleep delightfully,
if there is the disorder of the cut *wild rice,*
let there be disorder,
—when I shall have slept a good sleep![199]

This is a Rustic Lifting Song.[200]

SECT. 142—EMPEROR IN-GYŌ (PART 6—WAR BETWEEN PRINCE KARU AND PRINCE ANAHO)

Therefore all the officials[201] and likewise the people of the Empire turned against the Heir Apparent Karu, and towards the August Child Anaho. Then the Heir Apparent Karu, being alarmed, fled into the house of the Grandee the Noble Ō-mae O-mae,[202] and made a provision of implements of war. (The arrows made at this time[A] were provided with copper arrow-insides;[203] so those arrows are called by the name of Karu arrows.) Prince Anaho likewise made implements of war. (The arrows made by this Prince were just the arrows of the present time:[204] they are called Anaho arrows.)

Thereupon Anaho raised an army, and beleaguered the house of the Noble Ō-mae O-mae. Then, when he reached the gate, heavy ice-rain[205] was falling. So he sang, saying:

[80] Come thus under cover of the metal gate
of the Noble Ō-mae O-mae!
We will stand till the rain stops.[206]

[A] *I.e.*, "on this occasion."

Then the Noble Ō-mae O-mae came singing, lifting his hands, striking his knees, dancing, and waving his arms. The Song said:

[81] The courtiers are tumultuous, [saying]
that the small bell of the garter of the
courtiers has fallen off.
Country-people, too, beware![207]

This Song is of a Courtier's Style.[208] Singing thus, he came near and said: "August Child of our Heavenly Sovereign! Come not with arms against the King thine elder brother. If thou shouldst come against him with arms, people will surely laugh. I[209] will secure him and present him to thee."[210] Then Prince Anaho disbanded his troops and went away. So the Noble Ō-mae O-mae secured Prince Karu, and led him forth, and presented him [to Prince Anaho]. The captive Prince sang, saying:

[82] Maiden of heaven-soaring Karu!
if thou cry violently, people will know.
Cry quietly like the doves on Mount Hasa.[211]

Again he sang:

[83] Maiden of heaven-soaring Karu!
Come[212] and sleep, and [then] pass on,
oh maiden of Karu![213]

SECT. 143—EMPEROR IN-GYŌ (PART 7—DEATH OF PRINCE KARU AND PRINCESS SO-TŌSHI)

So Prince Karu was banished to the hot waters of Iyo.[214] Again when about to be banished, he sang, saying:

[84] The heaven-soaring birds, too, are indeed
messengers. When thou hearest the voice
of the crane, ask my name.[215]

These three songs are of a Heaven-Soaring style.[216] Again he sang, saying:

[85] If they banish the Great Lord to an island,
he will indeed make the remaining return
voyage. Beware of my mat! Mat indeed
in words,—beware of my spouse![217]

This Song is of a Partly Lowered Rustic style.[218] Queen So-tōshi presented a Song [to him]. That Song said:

[86] Let not thy feet tread on the oyster-shells
of the shore of Aine
with its summer herbs!
Pass there [after] having made clear.[219]

So when afterwards again, being unable to restrain her love, she went after him, she sang, saying:

[87] Thy going has become long past.
I will go, oh! to meet thee.
Wait! I cannot wait.[220]

(What is here called *yama-tazu* is [what is] now [known by the name of] *tatsuge*.)[221]

So when in her pursuit she reached [the place where Prince Karu was, he, who had been] pensively waiting, sang, saying:

[88] Alas! beloved spouse, who settledst the
whereabouts of our grave,
setting up flags in the great vale,
setting up flags in the little vale of Hatsuse
the hidden castle!
Alas! beloved spouse, whom I see after [our many troubles],
prostrate like an *tsuki* bow,
standing like an *azusa* bow![222]

Again he sang, saying:

[89] Driving sacred piles in the upper reach,
driving true piles in the lower reach
of the river of secluded Hatsuse,
and hanging on the sacrificial piles a mirror,
hanging on the true piles true jewels:—if they said
that the younger sister whom I love like a true jewel,
that the spouse whom I love like a mirror were [there],
I would go home, I would long for my country.[223]

Having thus sung, they forthwith killed themselves together.[224] So these two songs are Reading Songs.[225]

SECT. 144—EMPEROR AN-KŌ (PART 1—HE SLAYS KING Ō-KUSAKA)

The august child[226] Anaho dwelt at the palace of Anaho at Iso-no-kami,[227] and ruled the Empire. The Heavenly Sovereign sent the Grandee of Ne,[228] ancestor of the Grandees of Sakamoto, to the residence of King Ō-kusaka, on behalf of his younger brother Prince Ō-hatsuse to command thus: "I wish Thine Augustness's younger sister Queen Waka-kusaka to wed Prince Ō-hatsuse. So do thou present her."[229]

Then King Ō-kusaka did obeisance four times, and said: "Owing to a supposition that there might be some such Great Commands, I have kept her always indoors.[230] With reverence[231] will I respectfully offer her according to the Great Commands." Nevertheless, thinking it disrespectful [merely] to send a message,[232] he forthwith, as a ceremonial gift[233] from his younger sister, made [the Grandee of Ne] take a pushwood jewel headdress[234] to present [to the Heavenly Sovereign].

The Grandee of Ne forthwith stole the jewel headdress meant as a ceremonial gift, and slandered King Ō-kusaka, saying: "King Ō-kusaka would not receive the Imperial Commands," but said: "Shall my sister likewise become the inferior straw mat of the scion [man]?"[235] and, grasping the hilt of his cross-sword,[236] was angry. So the Heavenly Sovereign, having in his great anger slain King Ō-kusaka, took that King's chief wife Nagata-no-ō-iratsume,[237] and made her Empress.

SECT. 145—EMPEROR AN-KŌ (PART 2—HE IS SLAIN BY KING MA-YOWA)

After this, the Heavenly Sovereign, being on [his] divine couch,[238] was sleeping at midday. Then he spoke to his Empress, saying: "Is there anything on thy mind?"[239]

She replied, saying: "Being the object of the Heavenly Sovereign's generous favor, what can there be on my mind?"

Hereupon the Empress's former child,[240] King Ma-yowa, who was seven years old that year, happened to be just then playing outside the apartment.[241] Then the Heavenly Sovereign, not knowing that the young King was playing outside the apartment, spoke to the Empress, saying: "I have constantly something upon my mind, namely [the fear] that thy child King Ma-yowa, when he comes to man's estate, may, on learning that I slew the King his father, requite me with a foul heart."[242]

Thereupon King Ma-yowa, who had been playing outside the apartment, and whose ear had caught these words, forthwith watched for the Heavenly Sovereign to be augustly asleep, and, taking the great sword [that lay] by his side,[243] forthwith struck off the Heavenly Sovereign's head, and fled into the house of the Grandee Tsubura.[244] The Heavenly Sovereign's august years were fifty-six. His august mausoleum is on the mound of Fushimi at Sugahara.[245]

SECT. 146— EMPEROR AN-KŌ (PART 3— PRINCE Ō-HATSUSE SLAYS PRINCES KURO-BIKO AND SHIRO-BIKO)

Then Prince Ō-hatsuse,[246] who at that time was a lad, was forthwith grieved and furious on hearing of this event, and went forthwith to his elder brother King Kuro-biko,[247] and said: "They have slain[248] the Heavenly Sovereign. What shall be done?" But King Kuro-biko was not startled, and was of unconcerned heart.[249]

Thereupon King Ō-hatsuse reviled his elder brother, saying: "For one thing it being the Heavenly Sovereign, for another thing it being thy brother, how is thy heart without concern?[250] What! Not startled, but unconcerned on hearing that they have slain thine elder brother!"—and forthwith he clutched him by the collar, dragged him out, drew his sword, and slew him.

Again, going to his elder brother King Shiro-biko, he told him the circumstances as before. The unconcernedness again was like [that shown by] King Kuro-biko. [So King Ō-hatsuse,] having forthwith clutched him by the collar, pulled him along, and dug a pit on reaching Oharida,[251] buried him as he stood,[252] so that by the time he had been buried up to the loins, both his eyes burst out, and he died.[253]

SECT. 147—EMPEROR AN-KŌ (PART 4—DEATH OF PRINCE MA-YOWA AND OF THE GRANDEE TSUBURA)

Again he raised an army and beleaguered the house of the Grandee Tsubura. Then [the other side also] raised an army to resist the attack,[254] and the arrows that were shot forth were like unto the falling down of the [ears of the] reeds.[255] Thereupon King Ō-hatsuse, using his spear as a staff, peeped in,[256] and said: "Is perchance the maiden, with whom I spoke, in this house?"[257]

Then the Grandee Tsubura, hearing these commands,[258] came forth himself, and having taken off the weapons with which he was girded, did obeisance eight times, and said: "The maiden Princess Kara, whom anon thou deignedst to woo, is at thy service. Again in addition I will present to thee five granaries. (What are called the five granaries are now the gardeners of the five villages of Kazuraki.[259]) Meanwhile the reason why she does not come out to meet thee in person is that from of old down to the present time grandees and chiefs have been known to hide in the palaces of Kings, but Kings have not yet been known to hide in the houses of grandees.[260] Therefore I think that, though a vile slave of a grandee[261] exerting his utmost strength in the fight can scarcely conquer, yet must he die rather than desert a Prince who, trusting in him, has entered into his house."[262]

Having thus spoken, he again took his weapons and went in again to fight. Then, their strength being exhausted and their arrows finished, he said to the Prince: "My[263] hands are wounded, and our arrows likewise are finished. We cannot now fight. What shall be done?"

The Prince replied, saying: "If that be so, there is nothing more to do. [Do thou] now slay me." So [the Grandee Tsubura] thrust the Prince to death with his sword, and forthwith killed himself by cutting off his own head.

SECT. 148—EMPEROR AN-KŌ (PART 5—PRINCE Ō-HATSUSE SLAYS PRINCE OSHIWA)

After this Kara-fukuro,[264] ancestor of the Dukes of Yama of Sasaki in Ōmi,[265] said [to King Ō-hatsuse]: "At Kuta[266] [and?] on the moor of Kaya at Wata in Ōmi, boars and deer are abundant. Their legs as they stand are like a moor [covered] with *ogi*;[A] the horns they point up are like withered trees."

At this time [King Ō-hatsuse], taking with him King Ichi-no-be-no-oshiwa, made a progress to Ōmi, and on reaching this moor, each of them built a separate temporary palace to lodge in. Then next morning, before the sun had risen, King Oshiwa with a tranquil heart rode along on his august horse, and, reaching and standing beside King Ō-hatsuse's temporary Palace, said to King Ō-hatsuse's august attendants: "Is he not awake yet? He must be told quickly [that I am come]. It is already daylight.[267] He must come to the hunting-ground,"—and forthwith urging his horse, he went forth.

Then the people who served the august person of King Ō-hatsuse said: "As [King Oshiwa] is a violent-spoken[268] Prince, thou shouldst be on thy guard, and likewise it were well to arm thine august person." Forthwith he put on armor underneath his clothes, took and girded on him his bow and arrows, rode off on horseback, and in a sudden interval setting his horse by the side [of the other King's], took out an arrow, shot King Oshiwa down, forthwith moreover cut his body [to pieces], put [them] into a Horse's manger, and buried them level with the earth.[B]

SECT. 149—EMPEROR AN-KŌ (PART 6—FLIGHT OF PRINCES ŌKE AND OKE)

Hereupon King Ichi-no-be's children[269] King Ōke and King Oke (two Deities), having heard of this affray, fled away. So when they reached Karibai[270] in Yamashiro and were eating their august provisions, an old man with a tattooed face came and seized the provisions. Then the two Kings said: "We do not grudge the provisions. But who art thou?"

[A] The *Hedysarum esculeltum*. [Silvergrass. —M.F.]

[B] *I.e.*, without raising a tumulus over them. —W.G.A.

He replied, saying: "I am a boar-herd in Yamashiro."

So they fled across the River Kusuba,[271] reached the land of Harima,[272] entered the house of a native of that country named Shijimu,[273] hid their persons, and worked as grooms and cow-herds.

SECT. 150—EMPEROR YŪ-RYAKU (PART 1—GENEALOGIES)

His Augustness Ō-hatsuse-no-waka-take dwelt in the palace of Asakura at Hatsuse,[274] and ruled the Empire. The Heavenly Sovereign wedded Queen Wake-kusaka-be, younger sister of King Ō-kusaka (no children).

Again he wedded Princess Kara, daughter of the Grandee Tsubura, and begot august children:

His Augustness Shiraka;

next his younger sister Her Augustness Princess Waka-tarashi (two Deities).

SECT. 151—EMPEROR YŪ-RYAKU (PART 2—VARIOUS DEEDS)

So the Shiraka Clan[275] was established as the august proxy of Prince Shiraka. Again the Hatsuse-Clan-Retainers[276] were established. At this time there came over people from Kure. Again the Kawase Retainers[277] were established. These people from Kure[278] were lodged[279] at Kure-hara. So the place was called by the name of Kure-hara.[280]

SECT. 152—EMPEROR YŪ-RYAKU (PART 3—THE ROOF OF THE HOUSE OF THE GREAT DEPARTMENTAL LORD OF SHIKI)

In the beginning, when the Empress[281] dwelt at Kusaka,[282] [the Heavenly Sovereign] made a progress into Kōchi by way of the Tadagoe[283] road at Kusaka. Then, on climbing to the top of the mountain and gazing on the interior of the country, [he perceived that] there was a house built with a raised roof-frame.[284] The Heavenly Sovereign sent to ask [concerning] that house, saying: "Whose roof with a raised frame is that?"

The answer was: "It is the house of the great Departmental Lord of Shiki."[285]

Then the Heavenly Sovereign said: "What! A slave builds his own house in imitation of the august abode of the Heavenly Sovereign!"—

and forthwith he sent men to burn the house [down], when the Great Departmental Lord, with trembling and dread, bowed his head,[286] saying: "Being a slave, I like a slave did not understand, and have built overmuch. I am in great dread."[287] So the thing that he presented as an august offering [in token] of his entreaty was a white dog clothed in cloth,[288] and with a bell hung [round its neck]; and he made a kinsman of his own, named Koshihaki,[289] lead it by a string and present it [to the Heavenly Sovereign]. So the Heavenly Sovereign ordered them to desist from burning [the house].

SECT. 153—EMPEROR YŪ-RYAKU (PART 4—HE WOOS PRINCESS WAKA-KUSAKA-BE)

Forthwith making a progress to the residence of Queen Waka-kusa-ka-be, the Heavenly Sovereign sent the dog as a present with a message, saying: "This thing is a strange thing which I got today on the road. So it is a thing to woo with,"—and so saying, sent it in as a present.

Thereupon Queen Waka-kusaka-be sent to say to the Heavenly Sovereign: "It is very alarming that thou shouldst make a progress with thy back to the sun.[290] So I will come up straight [to the capital], and respectfully serve thee."[291]

When therefore he returned up and dwelt in the palace, he went and stood on the ascent[292] of that mountain, and sang, saying:

[90] In the hollow between the nearer and the
further mountain, this Mount Kusaka-be
and Mount Heguri, [is] growing the
flourishing broad-leafed bear-oak;
at the base grow intertwining bamboos;
on the top grow luxuriant bamboos:
—we sleep not [now] intertwined like the intertwining
bamboos,
we sleep not certainly like the luxuriant bamboos:
[but] oh! my beloved spouse,
with whom [I] shall afterwards sleep intertwined![293]

And he forthwith sent back a messenger with this Song.[294]

SECT. 154—EMPEROR YŪ-RYAKU (PART 5—STORY OF THE WOMAN AKAI-KO)

Again once when the Heavenly Sovereign, going out for amusement, reached the River Miwa,[295] there was a girl, whose aspect was very beautiful, washing clothes by the river-side. The Heavenly Sovereign asked the girl, [saying]: "Whose child art thou?"

She replied, saying: "My name is Akai-ko of the Hiketa Tribe."[296]

Then he caused her to be told, saying: "Do not thou marry a husband. I will send for thee,"—and [with these words] he returned to the palace. So eighty years had already passed while she reverently awaited the Heavenly Sovereign's commands.

Thereupon Akai-ko thought: "As, while looking for the [Imperial] commands, I have already passed many years, and as my face and form are lean and withered, there is no longer any hope. Nevertheless, if I do not show [the Heavenly Sovereign] how truly I have waited, my disappointment will be unbearable;"—and [so saying] she caused merchandise to be carried on tables holding a hundred,[297] and came forth and presented [these gifts as] tribute.

Thereat the Heavenly Sovereign, who had quite forgotten what he had formerly commanded, asked Akai-ko, saying: "What old woman art thou, and why art thou come hither?"

Then Akai-ko replied, saying: "Having in such and such a month of such and such a year received the Heavenly Sovereign's commands, I have been reverently awaiting the great command until this day, and eighty years have past by. Now appearance is quite decrepit, and there is no longer any hope. Nevertheless I have come forth in order to show and declare my faithfulness."

Thereupon the Heavenly Sovereign was greatly startled [and exclaimed]: "I had quite forgotten the former circumstance; and thou meanwhile, ever faithfully awaiting my commands, hast vainly let pass by the years of thy prime. This is very pitiful." In his heart he wished to marry her, but shrank from her extreme age, and could not make the marriage; but he conferred on her an august Song. That Song said:

[91] How awful is the sacred oak-tree,
the oak-tree of the august dwelling!
Maiden of the oak-plain![298]

Again he sang, saying:

[92] The younger chestnut orchard plain of Hiketa:
—Oh, if only I had slept with her in my youth![299]
Oh! how old she has become!"[300]

Then the tears that Akai-ko wept quite drenched the red-dyed sleeve that she had on.[301] In reply to the great august Song, she sang, saying:

[93] Left over from the
piling up of the jewel-wall
piled up round the august dwelling,
—to whom shall the person of the Deity's temple go?[302]

Again she sang, saying:

[94] Oh! how enviable is she
who is in her bloom like the flowering lotus,
—the lotus of the inlet, of the inlet of Kusaka.[303]

Then the old woman was sent back plentifully endowed. So these four Songs are Quiet Songs.[304]

SECT. 155—EMPEROR YŪ-RYAKU (PART 6—HE MAKES A PROGRESS TO YOSHINO)

When the Heavenly Sovereign made a progress to the palace of Yoshino,[305] there was on the bank of the Yoshino river a girl of beautiful appearance. So having wedded this girl, he returned to the Palace. Afterwards, when he again made a progress to Yoshino, he halted where he had met the girl, and in that place raised a great august throne,[306] seated himself on that august throne, played on his august lute, and made the maiden dance. Then he composed an august Song on account of the maiden's good dancing. That Song said:

[95] Oh! that the maiden dancing
to the lute-playing
of the august hand of the Deity
seated on the throne
might continue forever![307]

SECT. 156—EMPEROR YŪ-RYAKU (PART 7—THE HORSEFLY AND THE DRAGONFLY)

When forthwith he made a progress to the Moor of Akizu,[308] and augustly hunted, the Heavenly Sovereign sat on an august throne. Then a horsefly bit his august arm, and forthwith a dragonfly came and ate up[309] the horsefly,[310] and flew [away]. Thereupon he composed an august Song. That Song said:

[96] Who is it tells in the great presence that
game is lying on the peak of Omuro at
Mi-yoshino? Our Great Lord,
who tranquilly carries on the government, being
seated on the throne to await the game, a
horsefly alights on and stings the fleshy
part of his arm fully clad in a sleeve of
white stuff, and a dragonfly quickly eats
up that horsefly. That it might properly
bear its name,[311] the land of Yamato was
called the Island of the Dragonfly.[312]

So from that time that moor was called by the name of Akizu-no.[313]

SECT. 157—EMPEROR YŪ-RYAKU (PART 8—ADVENTURE WITH A WILD BOAR)

Again once the Heavenly Sovereign made a progress up to the summit of Mount Kazuraki.[314] Then a large [wild] boar ran out. When the Heavenly Sovereign forthwith shot the boar with a whizzing barb,[315] the boar, furious, came towards him roaring.[316] So the Heavenly Sovereign, alarmed at the roaring, climbed up to the top of an alder. Then he sang, saying:

[97] The branch of the alder-tree
on the opportune mound which I climbed in my
flight on account of the terribleness of the
roaring of the boar, of the wounded boar,
which our great lord who tranquilly
carries on the government had been
pleased to shoot![317]

SECT. 158—EMPEROR YŪ-RIYAKU (PART 9—REVELATION OF THE GREAT DEITY OF KAZURAKI, LORD OF ONE WORD)

Again once, when the Heavenly Sovereign made a progress up Mount Kazuraki, the various officials[318] were all clothed in green-stained garments with red cords that had been granted to them. At that time there were people ascending the mountain on the opposite mountain acclivity quite similar to the order of the Heavenly Monarch's retinue. Again the style of the habiliments and likewise the people were similar and not distinguishable.[319] Then the Heavenly Sovereign gazed, and sent to ask, saying: "There being no other king in Yamato excepting myself, what person goeth thus?"

The style of the reply again was like unto the commands of a Heavenly Sovereign.

Hereupon the Heavenly Sovereign, being very angry, fixed his arrow [in his bow], and the various officials all fixed their arrows [in their bows].

Then those people also all fixed their arrows [in their bows].

So the Heavenly Sovereign again sent to ask, saying: "Then tell thy name. Then let each of us tell his name, and [then] let fly his arrow."

Thereupon [the other] replied, saying: "As I was the first to be asked, I will be the first to tell my name. I am the Deity who dispels with a word the evil and with a word the good,—the Great Deity of Kazuraki, Lord of One Word."[320]

The Heavenly Sovereign hereupon trembled, and said: "I reverence

[thee], my Great Deity. I understood not that thy great person would be revealed;"[321]—and having thus spoken, he, beginning by his great august sword and likewise his bow and arrows, took off the garments which the hundred officials had on and worshipfully presented them [to the Great Deity].[322]

Then the Great Deity, Lord of One Word, clapping his hands,[323] accepted the offering. So when the Heavenly Sovereign made his progress back, the Great Deity came down the mountain,[324] and respectfully escorted him to the entrance[325] of the Hatsuse mountain. So it was at that time that the Great Deity Lord of One Word was revealed.

SECT. 159—EMPEROR YŪ-RYAKU (PART 10—THE MOUND OF THE METAL SPADE)

Again when the Heavenly Sovereign made a progress to Kasuga to wed Princess Odo,[326] daughter of the Grandee Satsuki of Wani,[327] a maiden met him by the way, and forthwith seeing the imperial progress, ran and hid on the side of a mound. So he composed an august Song. That august Song said:

[98] Oh! the mound where the maiden is hiding!
Oh for five hundred metal spades!
then might [we] dig her out![328]

So that mount was called by the name of the Mound of the Metal Spade.[329]

SECT. 160—EMPEROR YŪ-RYAKU (PART 9—THE LEAF IN THE CUP)

Again when the Heavenly Sovereign made a copious feast under a hundred-branching *tsuki-tree*[330] at Hatsuse, a female attendant from Mie[331] in the land of Ise lifted up the great august cup, and presented it to him.

Then from the hundred-branching *tsuki*-tree there fell a leaf and floated in the great august cup. The female attendant, not knowing that the fallen leaf was floating in the cup, did not desist from presenting[332] the great august liquor to the Heavenly Sovereign, who, perceiving the leaf floating in the cup, knocked the female attendant down,[333] put his sword to her neck, and was about to cut off her head, when the female attendant spoke to the Heavenly Sovereign, saying: "Slay me not! There is something that I must say to thee;" and forthwith she sang, saying:

[99] The palace of Hishiro at Makimuku is a
palace where shines the morning sun,
a palace where glistens the evening sun,
a palace plentifully rooted as the roots of the bamboo,
a palace with spreading roots like the roots of the trees,
a palace pestled with oh! eight hundred [loads of] earth.
As for the branches of the hundred-fold flourishing
tsuki-tree growing by the house of new
licking at the august gate [made of] false cypress [wood],
the uppermost branch has the sky above it,
the middle branch has the east above it,
the lowest branch has the country above it.
A leaf from the tip of the uppermost branch
falls against the middle branch;
a leaf from the tip of the middle branch
falls against the lowest branch;
a leaf from the tip of the lowest branch,
falling into the oil
floating in the fresh jeweled goblet
which the maid of Mie is lifting up,
all [goes] curdle-curdle. Ah! this is very awful,
August Child of the High-Shining Sun!
The tradition of the thing, too, this![334]

So on her presenting this Song, her crime was pardoned. Then the Empress sang. Her Song said:

[100] Present the luxuriant august liquor to the
august child of the high-shining sun,
who is broad like the leaves,
who is brilliant like the blossoms

of the broad-foliaged five
hundred [-fold branching] true camellia-
tree that stands growing by the house of new
licking in this high metropolis of Yamato,
on the high-timbered mound of the metropolis.
The tradition of the thing, too, this![335]

Forthwith the Heavenly Sovereign sang, saying:

[101] The people of the great palace, having put
on scarfs like the quail-birds, having put
their tails together like wagtails, and con-
gregated together like the yard-sparrows,
may perhaps today be truly steeped in
liquor, the people of the palace of the
high-shining sun.
The tradition of the
thing, too, this.[336]

These three Songs are Songs of Heavenly Words.[337] So at this copious feast[338] this female attendant from Mie was praised and plentifully endowed.

SECT. 161—EMPEROR YŪ-RYAKU (PART 12—SONGS BY THE EMPEROR AND PRINCESS ODO)

On the day of this copious feast the Heavenly Sovereign, when Princess Odo of Kasuga[339] presented to him the great august liquor, sang again, saying:

[102] Oh! the grandee's daughter
holding the excellent flagon!
[If] thou hold the excellent flagon,
hold it firmly!
Hold it quite firmly,
more and more firmly,
child holding the excellent flagon.[340]

This is a Cup Song.[341] Then Princess Odo presented a Song. That Song said:

[103] Would that I were [thou,] the lower
board of the armrest
whereon our great lord
who tranquilly carries on the government
stands leaning at morn,
stands leaning at eve!
Oh! mine elder brother![342]

This is a Quiet Song.

SECT. 162—EMPEROR YŪ-RYAKU (PART 13—HIS AGE AND PLACE OF BURIAL)

The Heavenly Sovereign's august years were one hundred and twenty-four. His august mausoleum is at Takawashi in Tajihi[343] in Kōchi.

SECT. 163—EMPEROR SEI-NEI (PART 1—SEARCH FOR A SUCCESSOR TO HIM)

His Augustness Shiraka-no-ō-yamato-ne-ko dwelt at the palace of Mikakuri at Iware,[344] and ruled the Empire. This Heavenly Sovereign had no Empress, and likewise no august children. So the Shiraka Clan[345] was established as his august proxy. So after the Heavenly Sovereign's decease, there was no King to rule the Empire. Thereupon, on enquiry [being made] for a King who should rule the sun's succession, Oshi-numi-no-iratsume,[346] another name for whom was Princess Ii-toyo, younger sister of Prince Ichinobe-oshiwa-wake,[347] [was found to be] residing at the palace of Tsunosashi at Takaki in Oshinumi in Kazuraki.[348]

SECT. 164—EMPEROR SEI-NEI (PART 2—PRINCES ŌKE AND OKE ARE DISCOVERED)

Then Odate, Chief of the Mountain Clan,[349] when appointed governor of the land of Harima, arrived just at [the time of] a rejoicing[A]

[A] House-warming.—W.G.A.

for the new cave[A] of an inhabitant called Shijimu.[350] Hereupon, when the feasting and the drinking were at their height, they all danced in turn. So two young children[351] [employed] to light the fire[B] sat beside the furnace.[352] These young children were made to dance. Then one of the young children said: "Do thou the elder brother dance first."

The elder brother likewise said: "Do thou the younger brother dance first."

When they thus yielded to each other, the people who were met together laughed at their manner of yielding to each other.[353] So at last the elder brother danced, [and when he had] finished, the younger when about to dance chanted, saying:

> [104] Oh! the bamboos on the mountain-slope,
> behind which are hidden as soon as they
> appear my warrior-mate's sword, on whose
> hilt red earth was daubed, for whose cord
> red cloth was cut, and his red flags that
> were set up!—Beggarly descendants of
> King Ichinobe-no-oshiwa, august child of
> the Heavenly Sovereign Izaho-wake, who
> ruled the Empire as it were cutting the
> [bamboos'] roots and bending down their
> extremities, and like playing on an eight-
> stringed lute![354]

Then forthwith Chief Odate, starting at the sound [of these words], and rolling off his couch,[355] drove away the people of the cave; and, having set the two[356] princes [one] on his left knee and [the other] on his right and wept and lamented, he collected the people together, and having built a temporary palace, and set [the two princes] to dwell in that temporary palace, he sent a courier up [to the capital]. Thereupon their aunt, Queen Ii-toyo, delighted to hear [the news], made them come up to palace.

[A] Norinaga interprets this to mean "arrived at the new *muro*" —W.G.A.

[B] Is not *hitaki* rather "attend to the fire" than "light the fire"? —W.G.A.

SECT. 165—EMPEROR SEI-NEI (PART 3—THE GRANDEE SHIBI)[357]

So when the government of the Empire was about to be assumed,[358] the Grandee Shibi,[359] ancestor of the Grandees of Heguri,[360] mixed in the Songs, and took the hand of the beautiful person whom His Augustness Oke was about to wed. This maiden was a daughter of one of the Headmen of Uda,[361] and her name was Ōuo.[362] Then His Augustness Obe likewise mixed in the Song-Hedge.[363] Thereupon the Grandee Shibi sang, saying:

[106] The further fin of the roof of the great
palace is bent down at the corner.[364]

When he had thus sung, and requested the conclusion of the Song, His Augustness Oke sang, saying:

[107] It is on account of the great carpenter's
awkwardness that it is bent down at the corner.[365]

Then the Grandee Shibi sang again, saying:

[107] The great lord, on account of the
magnanimity of his heart, does not enter and
stand in the eight-fold hedge of branches
of the child of a grandee.[366]

Hereupon the Prince sang again, saying:

[108] Looking on the breakers of the briny current, I see my spouse standing by the
fin of the tunny that comes sporting.

Then the Grandee Shibi, getting more and more angry, sang, saying:

[109] [Though] the eight-fold hedge of branches
of the Prince the Great Lord be made fast
at eight places, be made fast all round, 'tis

a hedge that shall be cut, 'tis a hedge
that shall be burnt.[367]

Then the Prince again sang, saying:

[110] Oh fisherman that spearest the tunny,
the great fish! He being [there], thou
must be sad at heart, tunny-spearing fisherman![368]

Having thus sung, the feast was concluded at dawn, and they all retired.[A] Next morning the two Deities,[369] His Augustness Ōke and His Augustness Oke, took counsel, saying: "All the people of the Court go to Court in the morning, and assemble at Shibi's gate at noon. So[370] Shibi must surely now be sleeping, and moreover there will be nobody at the gate. So unless it be now, it were hard to plot against him,"[B] and forthwith they at once raised an army, and beleaguered the house of the Grandee Shibi, and slew him.

SECT. 166—EMPEROR SEI-NEI (PART 4—PRINCE ŌKE CEDES THE EMPIRE TO PRINCE OKE)

Then each of the two Princes ceded the Empire to the other, and His Augustness Ōke [finally] ceded it to the younger brother His Augustness Oke, saying: "Had not Thine Augustness revealed our names when we dwelt in the house of Shijimu in Harima, we should never have arrived at being the lords of the Empire. This is quite owing to Thine Augustness's deed. So, though I be the elder brother, do Thine Augustness rule the Empire first,—and [with these words] he urgently ceded [his claim]. So, being unable to refuse, His Augustness Oke ruled the Empire first.

[A] I do not see sufficient reason for rejecting the reading 鬪 (*tatakau*,—to contend). The meaning would be "contended (in this contest of verse) until the morning." —W.G.A.

[B] *I.e.*, There is no time like the present for plotting against him.

SECT. 167—EMPEROR KEN-ZŌ (PART 1—THE OLD WOMAN OKI-ME)

His Augustness Oke-no-iwasu-wake dwelt at the palace of Chika-tsu-Asuka,[371] and ruled the Empire for eight years. The Heavenly Sovereign wedded the Queen of Naniwa,[372] daughter of the King of Iwaki.[373] He had no children.

At the time when this Heavenly Sovereign was searching for the august bones of the King his father, King Ichinobe,[374] there came out from the land of Ōmi [to the palace] a poor old woman, who said: "The place where the prince's august bones are buried is specially well known to me,[375] and moreover [his skeleton] can be known by his august teeth."[376] (His august teeth were teeth uneven like a lily.)

Then people were set[377] to dig the ground and search for the august bones; and the bones having been forthwith obtained, an august mausoleum was made on the mountain east of the Moor of Kaya,[378] and they were interred, and the children of Kara-fukuro[379] were made to guard the august mausoleum. Afterwards the august bones were brought up [to the Capital].

So having returned up [to the Capital, the Heavenly Sovereign] sent for the old woman, praised her for having, without forgetting, kept the place in mind, and conferred upon her the name of the Old Woman Oki-me:[380] Thus did he send for her into the palace, and deign to treat her with deep and wide kindness. So he built a house for the old woman to dwell in close to the palace, and always sent for her every day. So he hung a bell by the door of the great hall, and always rang it when he wished to call the old woman. So he composed an august Song. That Song said:

[111] Oh! the far-distant bell tinkles when she
has past the moor with its low eulalias
and the little valley. Oh! Oki-me must be coming![381]

Hereupon[382] the old woman said: "I am very aged, and would fain depart to my native land."

So when the Heavenly Sovereign let her depart according to her request, he saw her off and sang, saying:

[112] Ah Okime! Okime from Ōmi! From
tomorrow [onwards] wilt [thou] be hidden
behind the deep mountains, and alas! not seen![383]

SECT. 168—EMPEROR KEN-ZŌ (PART 3—HE SLAYS THE BOAR-HERD)

The Heavenly Sovereign searched for the old boar-herd who had seized his august provisions at the time when he first met with adversity and was fleeing;[384] and, having sought him out, sent for him up [to the Capital], beheaded him in the bed[385] of the River Asuka,[386] and cut the knee-tendons of all his kindred. Wherefore down to the present time his descendants, on the day when[387] they come up to Yamato, always limp of their own accord. So the man's abode had been well seen and divined.[A] So the place was named Shimesu.[388]

SECT. 169—EMPEROR KEN-ZŌ (PART 3—THE EMPEROR YŪ-RYAKU'S MAUSOLEUM IS DISFIGURED)

The Heavenly Sovereign, deeply hating the Heavenly Sovereign Ō-hatsuse, who had slain the King his father, wished to be revenged on his spirit.[389] So when, wishing to destroy the august mausoleum of the Heavenly Sovereign Ō-hatsuse, he [was about to] send people [to execute this design], his elder brother, His Augustness Ōke, addressed[390] him, saying: "To demolish this august mausoleum thou shouldst not send other people. None but myself shall go, and I will demolish it according to the Heavenly Sovereign's august heart."[391]

Then the Heavenly Sovereign commanded: "Make thy progress, then, according to thy decree."

Wherefore His Augustness Ōke, having proceeded down himself, slightly excavated the side of the august mausoleum, and returned up [to the capital], and reported that he had dug up and demolished it. Then the Heavenly Sovereign, astonished at the quickness of his return up, asked how he had demolished it.

He replied, saying: "I slightly excavated the earth at the side of the august mausoleum."[392]

[A] *I.e.*, "discovered by augury" or else simply "found and pointed out,"—by whom does not appear.

The Heavenly Sovereign said: "Wishing to be revenged on the enemy of the King our father, I had counted on the complete demolition of the mausoleum. Why hast thou [only] slightly excavated it?"

He replied, saying: "The reason why I did so was that the wish to be revenged on the spirit of the foe of the King our father is truly just. Nevertheless the Heavenly Sovereign Ō-hatsuse, though he were our father's foe, was still our uncle, and moreover was a Heavenly Sovereign who ruled the Empire. So if we now, simply from the consideration of his having been our father's enemy, were completely to demolish the mausoleum of a Heavenly Sovereign who ruled the Empire, after-generations would surely revile us. Meanwhile the wrongs of the King our father must not be unrevenged. So I slightly excavated the side of the mausoleum. This insult will quite suffice as a token to future ages."

On his thus addressing him, the Heavenly Sovereign said: "This also is very just. Be it as thou sayest."

SECT. 170—EMPEROR KEN-ZŌ (PART 4—HIS AGE AND PLACE OF BURIAL)

So the Heavenly Sovereign died, and His Augustness Ōke ruled the succession of Heaven's sun.[393] The Heavenly Sovereign's august years were thirty-eight, and he ruled the Empire for eight years. His august mausoleum is on the mound of Iwatsuki at Kataoka.[394]

SECT. 171—EMPEROR NIN-KEN[395]

His Augustness Ōke dwelt at the palace of Hirataka at Isonokami, and ruled the Empire. The Heavenly Sovereign wedded Kasuga-no-ō-iratsume, the august daughter of the Heavenly Sovereign Ō-hatsuse-no-waka-take, and begot august children:

Takaki-no-iratsume;
next Takara-no-iratsume;
next Kusubi-no-iratsume;
next Tashiraka-no-iratsume;
next His Grandeur O-hatsuse-no-waka-sazaki;
next Prince Ma-waka.

The child born to him by his next wife Nuka-no-waku-go-no-iratsume, daughter of the Grandee Hitsuma of Wani, was: Kasuga-no-yamada-no-iratsume.

The august children of this Heavenly Monarch numbered seven altogether. Of these His Augustness O-hatsuse-no-waka-sazaki [was he who afterwards] ruled the Empire.

SECT. 172—EMPEROR BU-RETSU

His Grandeur O-hatsuse-no-waka-sazaki dwelt in the palace of Namiki at Hatsuse, and ruled the Empire for eight years. This Heavenly Monarch had no august children. So the O-hatsuse Tribe was established as his august proxy. His august mausoleum is on the mound of Iwatsuki at Kara-oka.

On the death of this Heavenly Monarch there was no prince to inherit the Empire. So His Augustness Ōdo, the fifth descendant of the Heavenly Monarch Homuda, was sent for down to the land of Ōmi, and married to her Augustness Tashiraka, and presented with the Empire.

SECT. 173—EMPEROR KEI-TAI

His Augustness Ōdo dwelt in the Palace of Tamaho at Iware, and ruled the Empire. The (two) august children born to this Heavenly Monarch by Waka-hime, ancestress of the Dukes of Mio, were:

Ō-iratsuko;

next Izumo-no-iratsume.

The (two) august children born to him by his next wife, Meko-no-iratsume, sister of the Chieftain Ofushi, ancestor of the Chieftains of Owari, were:

His Augustness Hiro-kuni-oshi-take-kana-hi;

next His Augustness Take-o-hiro-kuni-oshi-tate.

The (one) august child born to him by his next wife (the Great Empress) Her Augustness Tashiraka, the august daughter of the Heavenly Monarch Ōke, was: His Augustness Ame-kuni-oshi-haruki-hiro-niwa.

The (one) august child born to him by his next wife O-kumi-no-iratsume, daughter of Prince Okinaga-no-ma-de, was: Sasage-no-iratsume.

The three august children born to him by his next wife Kuro-hime, daughter of Prince Sakata-no-ō-mata, were:

Kamu-saki-no-iratsume;

next Mamuta-no-iratsume;

next Umakuta-no-iratsume.

The (three) august children born to him by his next wife Seki-hime, daughter of Omochi Grandee of Mamuta, were:

Mamuta-no-ō-iratsume;

next Shira-saka-no-iku-hi-no iratsume;

next O-nu-no-iratsume, another name for whom is Naga-me-hime.

The (four) children born to him by his next wife Yamato-hime, younger sister of Katabu Duke of Mio, were:

Ō-iratsume;

next Prince Maroko;

next Prince Mimi;

next Aka-hime-no-iratsume.

The (three) children born to him by his next wife Abe-no-hae-hime, were:

Waka-ya-no-iratsume;

next Tsubura-no-iratsume;

next Prince Azu.

The august children of this Heavenly Monarch numbered nineteen in all (seven Kings and twelve Queens). Of these His Augustness Ame-kuni-oshi-haruki-hiro-niwa [was he who afterwards] ruled the Empire; next His Augustness Hiro-kuni-oshi-take-kana-hi ruled the Empire; next His Augustness Take-o-hiro-kuni-oshi-tate ruled the Empire; the next, Queen Sasage, presided at the temple of the Deity of Ise.

In this august reign Iwai, Lord of Tsukushi, was disobedient to the Imperial Decrees, and was exceedingly disrespectful. So the Great Chieftain Mononobe-no-arakai and the Chieftain Ōtomo-no-kanamura were both sent to slay Iwai.[396]

The august years of this Heavenly Monarch were forty-three. His august mausoleum is at Ai in Mishima.

SECT. 174—EMPEROR AN-KAN

His Augustness Hiro-kuni-oshi-take-kana-hi dwelt in the Palace of Kanahashi at Magari, and ruled the Empire. This Heavenly Monarch had no august children. His august grave is at the village of Takaya in Furuchi in Kōchi.

SECT. 175—EMPEROR SEN-KA

His Augustness Take-o-hiro-kuni-oshi-tate dwelt in the Palace of Iorinu at Hinokuma, and ruled the Empire. The august children born to this Heavenly Sovereign by his wife Her Augustness Tachiba-na-no-naka-tsu-hime, the august daughter of the Heavenly Sovereign Ōke, were:

Her Augustness Ishi-hime;
next Her Augustness O-ishi-hime;
next King Kura-no-waka-e.

The august children born to him by his next wife, Kōchi-no-waku-go-hime, were:

King Honō,
next King Eha.

The august children of this Heavenly Sovereign numbered altogether five (three Kings and two Queens). So King Honō (was the ancestor of the Dukes of Shihida). Prince Eha (was the ancestor of the Dukes of Ina and of the Dukes of Tajihi).

SECT. 176—EMPEROR KIN-MEI

The Heavenly Sovereign Ame-kuni-oshi-haruki-hiro-niwa dwelt in the Great Palace of Shikishima, and ruled the Empire. The (three) august children born to this Heavenly Sovereign by his wife, Her Augustness Ishi-hime, the august daughter of the Heavenly Sovereign Hi-no-kuma, were:

King Yata;
next His Augustness Nu-na-kura-tama-shiki;
next King Kasanu.

The (one) august child born to him by his next wife Her Augustness O-ishi-hime, younger sister [of the first one] was: King Kami.

The (three) august children born to him by his next wife Nuka-ko-no-iratsume, daughter of the Grandee Hitsuma of Kasuga, were:

Kasuga-no-yamada-no-iratsume;
next King Maroko;
next King Soga-no-kura.

The (thirteen) children born to him by his next wife Kitashi-hime, daughter of the Prime Minister the Noble Iname of Soga were:

His Augustness Tachibana-no-toyo-hi;
next his younger sister Queen Iwakumo;
next King Atori;
next Her Augustness Toyo-mike-kashiki-ya-hime;
next King Mata-maroko;
next King Ō-yake;
next King Imigako;
next King [of?] Yamashiro;
next his younger sister Queen Ō-tomo;
next King Sakurai-no-yumi-hari;
next King Manu;
next King Tachibana-moto-no-waku-go;
next King Tone.

The five august children born to him by his next wife O-ane-hime, aunt of Her Augustness Kitashi-hime, were:

King Umaki;
next King Kazuraki;
next King Hashi-bito-no-ana-ho-be;
next King Saki-kusa-be-no-ana-ho-be, another name for whom was Sume-irodo;
next His Augustness Hatsuse-be-no-waka-sazaki.

Altogether the august children of this Heavenly Sovereign numbered twenty-five Kings and Queens. Of these His Augustness Nuna-kura-futo-tama-shiki [was he who afterwards] ruled the Empire. Next His Augustness Tachibana-no-toyo-hi ruled the Empire. Next Her Augustness Toyo-mike-kashiki-ya-hime ruled the Empire. Next His Augustness Hatsuse-be-no-waka-sazaki ruled the Empire. In all there were four Kings and Queens that ruled the Empire.

SECT. 177—EMPEROR BI-DATSU

His Augustness Nuna-kura-futo-tama-shiki dwelt in the Palace of Osada, and ruled the Empire for fourteen years. The (eight) children born to this Heavenly Sovereign by his wife, his half-sister Her Augustness Toyo-mike-kashiki-ya-hime, were:

King Shizu-kai, another name for whom was Kai-dako;
next King Takeda, another name for whom was King O-kai;

next King Oharida;
next King Umori;
next King Owari;
next King Tame;
next King Sakurai-no-yumi-hari.

The (two) august children born to him by his next wife O-kuma-ko-no-iratsume, daughter of the Headman Ōka of Ise, were:

Her Augustness Futo-hime;
next Queen Takara, another name for whom was Queen Nu-kade-hime.

The (three) august children born to him by his next wife Her Augustness Hiro-hime, daughter of King Okinaga-no-ma-de, were:

King Osaka-no-hiko-hito, another name for whom was King Maroko;
next King Saka-nobori;
next King Uji.

The (four) august children born to him by his next wife Omina-ko-no-iratsume, daughter of Kasuga-no-naka-tsu-waku-go, were:

King Naniwa;
next King Kuhada;
next King Kasuga;
next King Ō-mata.

Of the august children of this Heavenly Monarch,—seventeen Kings and Queens altogether,—King Hiko-hito begot by his wife his half-sister Queen Tamura, another name for whom was Her Augustness Nukade-hime, (three) august children, namely:

the Heavenly Sovereign that ruled the Empire from the Palace of Okamoto;
next King Naka-tsu;
next King Tara.

The (two) august children born to him by his next wife, Queen Ōmata, younger sister of King Aya, were:

King Chinu
next his younger sister Queen Kuhada.

The (two) august children born to him by his next wife his half-sister Princess Yumi-hari, were:

King Yamashiro;
next Queen Kasanui,—altogether seven Kings and Queens.

The august mausoleum [of the Heavenly Sovereign Nuna-kura-futo-tama-shiki] is at Shinaga in Kōchi.

SECT. 178—EMPEROR YŌ-MEI

His Augustness Tachibana-no-toyo-hi dwelt in the Palace of Ikeno-be, and ruled the Empire for three years. The one august child born to this Heavenly Sovereign by his wife Ō-gitashi-hime, daughter of the Prime Minister the Noble Iname, was: King Tame.

The (four) august children born to him by his next wife, his half-sister Princess Hashi-bito-no-ana-ho-be, were:

His Augustness Ue-no-miya-no-uma-ya-dono-toyo-to-mimi;
next King Kume;
next King E-kuri;
next King Mamuta.

The august children born to him by his next wife Ii-me-no-ko, daughter of Tagima-no-kura-bito-niro, were:

King Tagima,
next his younger sister Sugashiroko-no-iratsume.

The august mausoleum of this Heavenly Sovereign, which had been by the borders of Lake Iware, was afterwards removed to the middle sepulcher of Shinaga.

SECT. 179—EMPEROR SU-JUN

The Heavenly Sovereign Hatsuse-be-no-waka-sazaki[397] dwelt at the Palace of Shibakaki at Kurahashi, and ruled the Empire for four years. His august mausoleum is on the mound of Kurahashi.

SECT. 180—EMPRESS SUI-KO

Her Augustness Toyo-mike-kashiki-ya-hime dwelt at the Palace of Oharida, and ruled the Empire for thirty-seven years. Her august mausoleum, which had been on the mound of Ōnu, was afterwards removed to the great sepulcher at Shinaga.

THE END.

Appendix

THE HITHERTO ACCEPTED CHRONOLOGY OF THE EARLY JAPANESE SOVEREIGNS MENTIONED IN THE *RECORDS OF ANCIENT MATTERS* (*KOJIKI*) AND IN THE *CHRONICLES OF JAPAN (NIHONGI)*

This "Accepted Chronology" is contained in the first three columns of figures, whereof the first two, giving the corresponding dates according to the European reckoning, are transcribed from some *Comparative Chronological Tables* by Mr. Ernest Satow, printed for private distribution in 1874. The ages of the monarchs in the third column are from *The Digest of the Imperial Pedigree*, a work published by the Imperial Japanese Government in 1877, and therefore carrying with it the weight of authority. It might perhaps be too much to say that even its decisions are universally bowed to by the native literati; but the differences between various writers are all slight, and excepting on points that affect only a very few years, the chronology contained in the first three columns may justly be styled the "Accepted Chronology" both as far as natives and as far as foreigners are concerned. It will be seen that it is founded in the main on the statements contained in the *Chronicles of Japan*, though sometimes differing therefrom as well as from the *Records*. The fourth column contains the ages of the monarchs according to the *Records*, and the fifth their ages according to the *Chronicles*. The portion printed in italics, and including a little over a thousand years, is that which has been shown in Section 5 of the Translator's Introduction to be undeserving of credence.

Emperor	Accession	Death	Age	Age, according to *Records*	Age, according to *Chronicles*
Jin-mu	*660 BCE*	*585 BCE*	*127*	*137*	*127*
Suizei	*581*	*549*	*84*	*45*	*80*
An-nei	*548*	*511*	*57*	*49*	*57*
I-toku	*510*	*477*	*77*	*45*	*77*
Kō-shō	*475*	*393*	*114*	*93*	*113*

Kō-an	*392*	*291*	*137*	*123*	*reigned 102 years*
Kō-rei	*290*	*215*	*128*	*106*	*“ 76 “*
Kō-gen	*214*	*158*	*116*	*57*	*“ 57 “*
Kai-ka	*157*	*98*	*111*	*63*	*“ 60 “*
Su-jin	*97*	*30*	*119*	*168*	*120*
Sui-nin	*29*	*70 CE*	*141*	*153*	*140*
Kei-kō	*71 CE*	*130*	*143*	*137*	*106*
Sei-mu	*131*	*190*	*108*	*95*	*107*
Chū-ai	*192*	*200*	*52*	*52*	*52*
Jin-gū[A]	*201*	*269*	*100*	*100*	*100*
Ō-jin	*270*	*310*	*111*	*130*	*110*
Nin-toku	*313*	*399*	*110*	*83*	*reigned 87 years*
Ri-chū	400	405	67	64	70
Han-zei	406	411	60	60	reigned 6 years
In-gyō	412	453	80	78	“ 42 “
An-kō	454	456	56	56	“ 3 “
Yū-ryaku	457	479	age omitted	124	“ 23 “
Sei-nei	480	484	41	not given	“ 5 “
Ken-zō	485	487	age omitted	38	“ 3 “
Nin-ken	488	498	50	not given	“ 11 “
Bu-retsu	499	506	18	reigned 8 years	“ 8 “
Kei-tai	507	531	82	43	82
An-kan	534	535	70	not given	70
Sen-ka	536	539	73	“	73
Kin-mei	510	571	63	“	reigned 32 years
Bi-datsu	572	585	48	reigned 14 years	“ 14 “
Yō-mei	586	587	69	“ 3 “	“ 2 “
Su-jun	588	592	73	“ 4 “	“ 5 “
Sui-ko	593	628	75	“ 37 “	75

[A]The reign of this Empress is in the *Records* not counted separately, but included in that of her son Ō-jin. For the mention of her age in the *Records* cf. Sect. 103, Note 865.

Endnotes

Translator's Introduction

[1]Should the claim of Akkadian to be considered an Altaic language be substantiated, then Archaic Japanese will have to be content with the second place in the Altaic family. Taking the word Altaic in its usual acceptation, viz., as the generic name of all the languages belonging to the Manchu, Mongolian, Turkish and Finnish groups, not only the Archaic, but the Classical, literature of Japan carries us back several centuries beyond the earliest extant documents of any other Altaic tongue.—For a discussion of the age of the most ancient Tamil documents see the Introduction to Bishop Caldwell's *Comparative Grammar of the Dravidian Languages*. p. 91 *et seq.*

[2]Published in Vol. VIII, Part I of these *Transactions*.

[3]The 古道大意 (Kodō Taii) by one of Atsutane's pupils calls Are a woman. Vol. 1, p. 28. —W.G.A.

[4]Unfortunately the portion already printed does not carry the history down even to the close of the "Divine Age." The work is as colossal in extent as it is minute in research, forty-one volumes (including the eleven forming the "Sources") having already appeared. The *Izu-no-chi-waki and Izu-no-koto-waki are still similarly incomplete.*

[5]The translator adopts the term "ideographic" because it is that commonly used and understood, and because this is not the place to demonstrate its inappropriateness. Strictly speaking, "logographic" would be preferable to ideographic, the difference between Chinese characters and alphabetic writing being that the former represent in their entirety the Chinese words for things and ideas, whereas the latter dissects into their component sounds the words of the languages which it is employed to write.

[6]*Grammar of the Japanese Written Language*, Second Edition, Appendix 2, p. 6.

[7]For a special account of the pillow-words, etc., see a paper by the present writer in Vol. 5, Pt. 1, pp. 79 *et seq.* of these *Transactions*, and for a briefer notice, his *Classical Poetry of the Japanese*, pp. 5 and 6.

[8]The practice of bestowing a canonical name (*okurina*) on an emperor after his decease dates from the latter part of the eighth century of our era when, at the command of the emperor Kan-mu, a scholar named Mifune-no-Mahito selected suitable "canonical names" for all the previous sovereigns, from Jin-mu down to Kan-mu's immediate predecessor. From that time forward every emperor has received his "canonical name" soon after death, and it is generally by it alone that he is known to history.

[9]See Sect. 4. of this Introduction and Sect. 14. Note 232 of the Translation.

[10] *Cf. Nihongi*, 7, p. 6. —W.G.A. (page 191 Aston's translation in *Transactions of the Japan Society*, London).

[11] *Cf.* Section 56, Note 171.

[12] See the legend in Sect. 23.

[13] 易経. [*Book of Changes.* —M.F.]

[14] 礼記. [*Book of Rites.* —M.F.]

[15] See Sects. 21, 27 and 23.

[16] Rendered in the English translation by "the Male-Who-Invites."

[17] Yomo-tsu-hira-saka.

[18] 書経. [*Classic of Documents.* —M.F.]

[19] Details as to the adoption by the Japanese of the Chinese system of computing time will be found in the late Mr. Bramsen's *Japanese Chronological Tables*, where that lamented scholar brands "the whole system of fictitious dates applied in the first histories of Japan," as "one of the greatest literary frauds ever perpetrated, from which we may infer how little trust can be placed in the early Japanese historical works." See also Norinaga's *Inquiry into the True Chronology*, pp. 33–36, and his second work on the same subject entitled *Discussion of the Objections to the Inquiry into the True Chronology*, pp. 46 *et seq.*

[20] Confucian *Analects*, Book 7. Chap. 1. Dr. Legge's translation.

[21] It may perhaps be worthwhile to quote this legend in full. It is as follows:

"One account says that the Heaven-Shining Great Deity, being in Heaven, said: 'I hear that in the Central Land of Reed-Plains *(i.e.* Japan) there is a Food-Possessing Deity. Do thou, Thine Augustness Moon-Night-Possessor, go and see.'

His Augustness the Moon-Night-Possessor, having received these orders, descended [to earth], and arrived at the place where the Food-Possessing Deity was. The Food-Possessing Deity forthwith, on turning her head towards the land, produced rice from her mouth; again, on turning to the sea, she also produced from her mouth things broad of fin and things narrow of fin; again, on turning to the mountains, she also produced from her mouth things rough of hair and things soft of hair. Having collected together all these things, she offered them [to the Moon-God] as a feast on a hundred tables.

At this time His Augustness the Moon-Night-Possessor, being angry and coloring up, said: 'How filthy! how vulgar! What! shalt thou dare to feed me with things spat out from thy mouth?, [and with these words,] he drew his saber and slew her. Afterwards he made his report [to the Sun Goddess].

When he told her all the particulars, the Heaven-Shining Great Deity was very angry, and said: 'Thou art a wicked Deity, whom it is not right for me to see'—and forthwith she and His Augustness the Moon-Night-Possessor dwelt separately day and night." The partly parallel legend given in these *Records* forms the subject of Sect. 17 of the Translation.

[22] Compare Mr. Satow's remarks on this subject in Vol. 3, Pt. 1, pp. 21–23 of these *Transactions.*

[23] Wrist pads? —W.G.A.

[24]The quern? —W.G.A.

[25]The two-forked boat was a mere caprice. —W.G.A.

[26]A curious scrap of the history of Japanese civilization is preserved in the word *kaji,* whose exclusive acceptation in the modern tongue is "rudder." In archaic Japanese it meant "oar," a signification which is now expressed by the term *ro,* which has been borrowed from the Chinese. It is a matter of debate whether the ancient Japanese boats possessed such an appliance as a *rudder,* and the word *tagishi* or *taishi* has been credited with that meaning. The more likely opinion seems to be that both the thing and the word were specialized in later times, the early Japanese boatmen having made any oar do duty for a rudder when circumstances necessitated the use of one.

[27]See the end of Sect. 32.

[28]See Vol. 9, Pt. 2, pp. 191–192, of these *Transactions,*

[29]*Yamato Monogatari.*

[30]For a translation of this story see the present writer's *Classical Poetry of the Japanese,* pp 42–44.

[31]See sect. 44, Note 9 and Sect. 72, Note 557.

[32]Mr. Ernest Satow, who in 1878 visited the island of Hachijo, gives the following details concerning the observance down to modern times in that remote corner of the Japanese Empire of the custom mentioned in the text: "In Hachijo women, when about to become mothers, were formerly driven out to the huts on the mountain-side, and according to the accounts of native writers, left to shift for themselves, the result not unfrequently being the death of the newborn infant, or if it survived the rude circumstances under which it first saw the light, the seeds of disease were sown which clung to it throughout its after life. The rule of non-intercourse was so strictly enforced, that the woman was not allowed to leave the hut even to visit her own parents at the point of death, and besides the injurious effects that this solitary confinement must have had on the wives themselves, their prolonged absence was a serious loss to households, where there were elder children and large establishments to be superintended. The rigor of the custom was so far relaxed in modern times, that the huts were no longer built on the hills, but were constructed inside the homestead. It was a subject of wonder to people from other parts of Japan that the senseless practice should still be kept up, and its abolition was often recommended, but the administration of the Shoguns was not animated by a reforming spirit, and it remained for the government of the Mikado to exhort the islanders to abandon this and the previously mentioned custom. They are therefore no longer sanctioned by official authority and the force of social opinion against them is increasing, so that before long these relics of ancient ceremonial religion will in all probability have disappeared from the group of islands." (*Trans. of the Asiat. Soc. of Japan,* Vol. 6, Pt. 3, pp. 455–6.)

[33]See Sect. 70, Note 520. The Japanese term is *ina-ki, ki* being an Archaic term for "castle."

[34]See Sect. 16. Mention of cave-dwellers will also be found in Sects. 48 and 80.

[35]Pits? —W G.A.

[36]See the latter part of Sect. 17.

[37]See Sect. 18, Note 313.

[38]山海経. [*Classic of Mountains and Seas.* —M.F.]

[39]See, however, the legend in Sect. 65.

[40]See beginning of Sect. 27.

[41]Stems? —W.G.A.

[42]For details on this subject and illustrations, see Mr. Henry von Siebold's *Notes on Japanese Archaeology*, p. 15 and Table 11, and a paper by Professor Milne on the "Stone Age in Japan," read before the Anthropological Society of Great Britain on the 25th May 1880, pp. 10 and 11.

[43]The tradition preserved in Sect. 124, shows that in times almost, if not quite, historical (the 4th century of our era) the silkworm was a curious novelty, apparently imported from Korea. It is not only possible, but probable, that silken fabrics were occasionally imported into Japan from the mainland at an earlier period, which would account for the mention of "silk rugs" in Sects 40 and 84.

[44]The (necessarily somewhat arbitrary) line between earlier and later times has been drawn at the epoch of the traditional conquest of Korea by the Empress Jingū at the commencement of the third century of our era, it being then, according to the received opinions, that the Japanese first came in contact with their continental neighbors, and began to borrow from them. (See however the concluding Section of this Introduction for a demonstration of the untrustworthiness of all the so-called history of Japan down to the commencement of the fifth century of the Christian era.)

[45]See Sect. 24, Note 385.

[46]Mr. Satow, in his translation of a passage of the *Records of Ancient Matters* forming part of a note to his third paper on the *Rituals* in Vol. 9, Pt. 2 of these *Transactions*, renders *wani* by "shark." There is perhaps some want of clearness in the old historical books in the details concerning the creature in question, and its fin is mentioned in the *Chronicles*. But the accounts point rather to an amphibious creature, conceived of as being somewhat similar to the serpent, than to a fish, and the Chinese descriptions quoted by the Japanese commentators unmistakably refer to the crocodile. The translator therefore sees no sufficient reason for abandoning the usually accepted interpretation of *wani* (鰐) as "crocodile." It should be noticed that the *wani* is never introduced into any but patently fabulous stories, and that the example of other nations, and indeed of Japan itself, shows that myth-makers have no objection to embellish their tales by the mention of wonders supposed to exist in foreign lands. [May not the *wani* have been a cetacean; perhaps the porpoise? I have translated *wani* by "Sea-monster" —W.G.A.]

[47]Sect. 128 preserves a very early ornithological observation in the shape of the songs composed by the Emperor Nin-toku and his Minister Take-uchi on the subject of a wild-goose laying eggs in central Japan. These birds are not known to breed even so far south as the island of Ezo [Hokkaido. —M.F.].

[48]See the legend in Sect. 74.

[49]Mr. Satow suggests that *ao* ("blue" or "green") means properly any color derived from the *ai* plant (*Polygonum tinectorium*).

[50]Only the footnotes of the original are omitted, as not being essential.

[51]See the story of Prince Karu, which is probably historical, in Sects. 141 *et seq*.

[52]The custom of using surnames was certainly borrowed from China, although the Japanese have not, like the Koreans, gone so far as to adopt the actual surnames in use in that country. The "gentile names" may have sprung up more naturally, though they too show traces of Chinese influence. Those most frequently met with are *Agata-nushi*, *Ason*, *Atae*, *Kimi*, *Miyatsuko*, *Muraji*, *Omi*, *Sukune*, and *Wake*. See above, pp. 28.

[53]See Sect. 25, (the second song in that Section).

[54]See Sect. 71, Note 529.

[55]See Sect. 42.

[56]Representations of these clay images (*tsuchi-nin-gyō*) will be found in Table 12 of Mr. Henry von Siebold's *Notes on Japanese Archaeology*, and in Mr. Satow's paper on "Ancient Sepulchral Mounds in Kaudzuke" published in Vol. 7, Pt. 3, pp. 313 *et scq*. of these *Transactions*.

[57]The Chinese notices of Japan speak of their tattooing themselves thus indicating distinctions of rank —W.G.A.

[58]See Sect. 87.

[59]See Sect. 97.

[60]A translation,—especially a literal prose translation,—is not calculated to show off to best advantage the poetry of an alien race. But even subject to this drawback, the present writer would be surprised if it were not granted that poetic fire and grace are displayed in some of the Love-Songs (for instance the third Song in Sect. 24 and both Songs in Sect. 25), and a quaint pathos in certain others (for instance in Yamato-Take's address to his "elder brother the pine-tree," and in his Death-Songs contained in Sect. 89).

[61]Viz. of the Chinese 文 and 筆 (in the modern Mandarin pronunciation *wen* and *pi*). Mr. Aston would seem to derive both the Japanese term *fude* and the Korean *put* independently from the Chinese 筆. The present writer thinks it more likely that the Japanese *fude* was borrowed mediately through the Korean *put*. In any case, as it regularly corresponds with the latter according to the laws of letter-change subsisting between the two languages, it will be observed that the Japanese term would still have to be considered borrowed, even if the derivation of *put* from 筆 had to be abandoned; for we can hardly suppose Korean and Japanese to have independently selected the same root to denote such a thing as a "pen." As to the correctness of the derivation of *fumi* from 文 there can be little doubt, and it had long ago struck even the Japanese themselves, who are not prompt to acknowledge such loans. They usually derive *fude* from *fumi-te*, "document hand," and thus again we are brought back to the Chinese 文 as the origin of the Japanese word for "pen." [Or "brush," used to write Chinese characters with ink. —M.F.]

[62]The Chinese characters used to write this word are 神道, which signify the "Way of the Gods." The term was adopted in order to distinguish the old native beliefs from Buddhism and Confucianism.

[63]*Cf.* p. 30, last paragraph for the modified sense in which alone the word "deification" can be used in speaking of the Early Japanese worship.

[64]In Sect. 27, where this deity is first mentioned, he is called *Sukuna-Biko-Na-no-Kami*, the "Little Prince the Renowned Deity."

[65]See the Appendix.

[66]As a specimen of the flexibility of his system, the reader to whom the Japanese language and Japanese legend are familiar is recommended to peruse pp. 13–24 of Vol. 1 of Arai Hakuseki's *Ko Shi Tsū* (古史通), where an elaborate rationalistic interpretation is applied to the story of the amours of Izanagi and Izanami. It is amusing in its very gravity, and one finds it difficult to believe that the writer can have been in earnest when he penned it.

[67]Mr. Takahashi Goro's book here alluded to is his *Shinto Discussed Afresh*.

[68]B.H.C. gives this passage in the original French. *Notice sur l'Empire du Japon*, tell us that «L'histoire de la dynastie imperiale remonte très-haut. L'obscurité entoure ses débuts, vu l'absence de documents réguliers ou d'un calendrier parfait. Le premier Empereur de la dynastie présente, dont il reste des annales dignes de confiance, est Jin-mou-ten-nō [*I.e.* the Emperor Jin-mu, —*ten-nō,* written 天皇 being simply the sinico-Japanese word for «emperor."] qui organisa un soulèvement dans la province de Hiuga, marcha à l'Est avec ses compagnons, fonda sa capitale dans la vallee de Kashi-hara dans le Yamato, et monta sur le trône comme Empereur. C'est de cet Empereur que descend, per une succession régulière, la présente famille regnante du Japon. C'est del, année de l'avènement de Jin-mou-ten-nô que date l'ère Japonaise (Année 1-660 avant Jesus-Christ.»)

[69]15th day of 11th moon of 5th year of Meiji.

[70]For the use of this word to represent the Japanese *Yomo* or *Yomi,* see Sect. 9, Note 151.

[71]*Podocarpus macrophylla.*

[72]The least meagre account will be found in Sects. 16 and 32.

[73]To be found at the end of Sect. 32.

[74]The Inbe? —W.G.A.

[75]In the Jin-mu legend we have the more usual form of the superstition, that, viz., which makes it unlucky to go from west to east, which is the contrary of the course pursued by the sun in Sect. 153. On the other hand, the Emperor Yū-ryaku is found fault with for acting in precisely the reverse manner, viz., for going from east to west, *i.e.* with his back to the sun. The idea is the same, though its practical application may thus diametrically differ, the fundamental objection being to going *against* the sun, in whatever manner the word *against,* or some kindred expression, may be interpreted.

[76]See Sects. 39 to 41. For the "Herb-Quelling Saber" see Sects. 18 and 82, *et seq.*

[77]General Le Gendre, quoted by Sir Edward Reed.

[78]山海経. [*Classic of Mountains and Seas.*—M.F.]

[79]Trustworthy —W.G.A.

[80]I.e. the High August Producing Wondrous Deity. He is the second divine personage whose birth is mentioned in the *Records* (see Sect. 1 Notes c and 42). In the story of the creation given in the *Chronicles* he does not appear except in "One account."

[81]Sect. 37 is a good instance of the third of these categories. For an elaborate myth founded on the name of a place see Sect. 65. Lesser instances occur in Sects. 44, 65, and 73.

[82]See Sects. 79–91

[83]See this legend as first given in Sects. 40 and 41, and afterwards in quite another context in Sect. 116. The way in which "One account" of the *Chronicles of Japan* tells the story of the ravages committed on the fields of the Sun Goddess by her brother, the "Impetuous Male Deity," might perhaps justify the opinion that that likewise is but the same tale in another form. The legend is evidently a very important one.

[84]The translator's attention was drawn to the inconsistency of these dates by Mr. Ernest Satow.

[85]See Sect. 29, Note 457.

[86]Dr. Tylor in his *Anthropology*, Chap. 15.

[87]The names in small capitals are those by which the authors (or compilers) are best known, and are mostly either their surname or personal name. Japanese usage is however very fluctuating, and sanctions moreover the use of a variety of *noms de plume.* Thus Motoori is not only often mentioned by his personal name Norinaga, but also by the designation of *Suzunoya no Ushi,* Mabuchi by the designation of *Agatai no Ushi,* etc.

Preface

[1]The peculiar nature of this Preface, which is but a *tour de force* meant to show that the writer could compose in the Chinese style if he chose to do so, has been already hinted at in the Introduction. It is indeed a labored little composition, and, but for the facts stated in its latter portion, has no value except perhaps as a specimen of the manner in which the legends of one country may be made to change aspect by being presented through the medium of the philosophical terminology and set phrases of another. It may be divided into five parts. In the first the writer, in a succession of brief allusions antithetically balanced, summarizes the most striking of the legends that are detailed in the pages of his *Records*, and in a few words paints the exploits of some of the early emperors. In the second the troubles that ushered in the reign of the Emperor Ten-mu and his triumph over Prince Ōtomo are related at greater length in high-flown allusive phrases borrowed from the Chinese historians. The third division gives us the Emperor Ten-mu's decree ordering the compilation of the *Records*, and the fourth tells how the execution of that decree was delayed till the reign of the Empress Gen-mei (708–715 CE),

on whom likewise a panegyric is pronounced. In the fifth and last the compiler enters into some details concerning the style and method which he has adopted.

[2]The First Personal Pronoun is here represented by the humble character 臣, "vassal," used in China by a subject when addressing his sovereign in writing. This number and that in the corner of every succeeding page of the Translation is the number of the Volume of Norinaga's Commentary treating of the Section in question. [This information has been omitted from this edition.—M.F.]

[3]This is the compiler's personal name. His full name and titles, as given at the end of this preface, were 正五位上勳五等太朝臣安萬侶, *i.e.,* the Court Noble Futo no Yasumaro, an Officer of the Upper Division of the First Class of the Fifth Rank and of the Fifth Order of Merit. The family of Futo claimed to descend from His Augustness Kamu-ya-i-mimi, second son of the Emperor Jin-mu. Yasumaro's death is recorded in the *Chronicles of Japan Continued*, under date of 30th August, 723 CE. [The compiler's full name is Ō no Yasumaro.—M.F.]

[4]*I.e.,* I report as follows to Her Majesty the Empress.

[5]*I.e.,* in the primeval void which preceded all phenomena there was neither form nor movement, and it was therefore unnamed and unknowable.

[6]Shikō shite (然して) = The next stage was that.—W.G.A

[7]The word "therefore" is not appropriate in this place, and Norinaga accordingly warns the reader to lay no stress upon it.

[8]The "original teaching" here mentioned means the original traditions of Japanese antiquity. The "former sages"—a term which in China fitly designates such philosophers as Confucius and Mencius, but which it is difficult to invest with any particular sense here in Japan where no sages have ever arisen—may be best taken to mean those unknown persons who transmitted the legends of the gods and early emperors. The "establishment of men" probably alludes to the investiture of the sovereignty of Japan in the human descendants of the Sun-Goddess. The expression is however obscure, and Norinaga himself has nothing satisfactory to tell us about it.

[9]There remains the phrase "a Hundred Kings," which is lacking in clearness. The only rational interpretation of it is as designating the Japanese imperial line, and yet the reference seems to have no special appropriateness in this context.

[10]The final syllable is here apocopated, in order to preserve the rhythmical balance of the sentence by using only three Chinese characters to write this name, the "Island of the Dragonfly" being likewise written with three characters.

[11]For the traditional origin of this poetical synonym of Japan see Vol. 1, Note 91 and also the legend in Sect. 156. The word "traverse" in this sentence alludes to the Emperor Jin-mu's victorious progress from Western Japan to Yamato in the center of the country, which he is said to have subdued, and where it is related that he established his capital (see Sects. 44–50).

[12]化— W.G.A.

[13]Norinaga thinks that the character 刀, "claws," is a copyist's error for 山, "mountain" or 穴, "hole," (*cf.* Vol. 2, Note 38). For the curious legend of the saber

see Section 45, and for the name of Takakura see more especially Vol. 2, Note 40.

[14]Expel?—W.G.A.

[15]The word "dancing" in this sentence must not be too closely pressed, as it is used simply to balance the word "song" in the parallel clause,—which clause itself does but echo the sense of that which precedes it.

[16]Jingo? Norinaga —W.G.A.

[17]*I.e.*, though unlike in character, some of the ancient emperors excelling in caution and others in ardor, some being remarkable for their attainments and others for their native worth, yet was there not one without a claim to greatness, not one who did not regard antiquity as the standard by which modern times should be judged, and repair the deviations from antique perfection that successively arose during the lapse of ages.—How marvellously inapplicable is this rodomontade to the early monarchs of Japan the student of Japanese history need scarcely be told, and Norinaga himself allows that "it is not completely appropriate." Here the first part of the Preface terminates.

[18]The reason for the specially laudatory mention in this place of the Emperor Ten-mu is the fact that it was with him that the idea of compiling these *Records* originated, as is indeed stated a little further on. He is here alluded to by the expressions Hidden Dragon and Reiterated Thunder, metaphorical names borrowed from the *Yi Jing* and denoting the heir apparent, Ten-mu not having ascended the throne till some time after his predecessor's death, as Prince Ōtomo disputed by force of arms his right to the succession. The phrases "put on perfection" and "came at the appointed moment" are attempts at representing the original 體元, and 應期. The meaning is that the Emperor Ten-mu was the man for the age, and that he took his proper and exalted place in it. In the following sentences we have a flowery *résumé* of the story of the successful war by which he obtained the crown. The reference to the "song in a dream" is indeed obscure; but the "water at night" is the River Yoko, which we read of in the *Chronicles* as having been crossed by him. The characters somewhat freely rendered by the English words "succession" and "inheritance" are 業 and 基, which approximate to that sense in this context. The "Southern Mountains" are the Mountains of Yoshino, whither he escaped for a season as a cicada escapes from its cast-off shell; the "Eastern land" denotes the eastern provinces of Japan where he organized his army. The "Six Divisions" and the "Three Hosts" are Chinese designations of the Imperial troops, while the "ill-omened crew" of course refers to Ten-mu's enemies—Prince Ōtomo and his followers. In the ensuing sentence we see peace restored: Ten-mu has returned to the capital (for which the words "Flowery Summer" are a Chinese periphrasis), he has taken in his hands the insignia of office, and reigns supreme over the Six Cardinal Points (North, South, East, West, Above, and Below) and over the "Eight Wildernesses" (*i.e.*, the barbarous regions on all sides). The writer concludes this division of his Preface by a glowing panegyric of the Monarch, who was, he says, superior to Hsüan Hou (軒后 Jap. Ken-Kō) [the Yellow Emperor—M.F.], and Chou Wang (周王 Jap. Shiū-O) [King Wu of Zhou—M.F.], famous Chinese sov-

ereigns of the legendary period. So intelligent were his efforts, so perfect was his conformity with the ways of Heaven as displayed in the workings of the Active and Passive Essences, that the Five Elements (Water, Fire, Wood, Metal, and Earth) all interacted with due regularity, and laudable usages alone prevailed throughout the land. Up to this point the preface may be said to be purely ornamental.

[19]Reverberating—W.G.A.

[20]Why not adopt Norinaga's explanation 12 days.—W.G.A.

[21]*I.e.*, March (20th as the *Chronicles* tell us), 673 CE. The original, to denote the year and the month mentioned, uses the periphrases 歳次大梁 and 月踵夾鍾, but doubtless without any reference to the original proper meaning of those terms.

[22]The text literally reads thus: "He rode in the exactness of the Two Essences." But the author's intention is to tell us that Ten-mu acted according to the golden mean, keeping the balance even, and not inclining unduly either to the Active or the Passive side.

[23]Glowing and luminous.—W.G.A.

[24]Lit. "warp and woof," *i.e.*, canon, standard, mainspring, first necessity.

[25]This is the imperial decree ordering the compilation of the *Records of Ancient Matters*. The expressions "original words" (本辭) and "old words" (舊辭) are curious, and Norinaga is probably right in arguing from the emphatic manner in which they are repeated that the Emperor Ten-mu attached special importance to the actual archaic phraseology in which some at least of the early documents or traditions had been handed down.

[26]*I.e.*, he could repeat the contents of any document that he had once seen and remember all that he had ever heard.

[27]得一光宅通三亭育. For the phrase "obtaining Unity," which is borrowed from *Lao Tzu*, the student should consult Stanislas Julien's *Livre de la Voie et de la Vertu*, pp. 144–149. The "Triad" is the threefold intelligence of Heaven, Earth, and Man. The general meaning of the sentence is that the Empress's perfect virtue, which is in complete accord with the heavenly ordinances, is spread abroad throughout the empire, and that with her all-penetrating insight she nourishes and sustains her people.

[28]Does not 重譯 mean simply "interpreters" cf. *Nihongi* 9. 33 (page 252 Aston's Translation) extract from Tsin book. Also Parker translates so in *Early Japanese History*.—W.G.A.

[29]The "Purple Palace" is one of the ornamental names borrowed from the Chinese to denote the imperial residence. The "Sombre Retinue" (if such indeed is the correct rendering of the original expression. 玄扈 is a phrase on which no authority consulted by the translator throws any light. [Vide Legge's *Annals of the Bamboo Books*. "The characters for Sombre Retinue" are the name of a place where the Emperor Huangdi had his throne, above Luoyang.—W.G.A.] The "utmost limits of the horses' hoof-marks" and the "furthest distance attained to by vessels' prows" are favorite phrases in the old literature of Japan to express extreme distance (see, for instance, Mr. Satow's translation of the "Ritual of the Praying for Harvest,"

Vol. 7, Pt. 2, p. 111 of these *Transactions*, and the present writer's *Classical Poetry of the Japanese*, p. 111). Such unusual phenomena as connected stalks, *i.e.*, trunks springing from the same root and uniting again higher up, and "joint rice-ears," *i.e.*, two rice-ears growing on a single stem, are considered lucky omens by the Chinese, and their appearance is duly chronicled in those Japanese histories that are composed after the Chinese model. The "continuous beacon-fires" and the "repeated interpretations" are phrases alluding to the foreign lands *(i.e.*, the various small Korean states) speaking strange languages, whence tribute was sent to Japan. [*Cf.* passage quoted by Norinaga, but vide Williams *Chinese Dictionary* p. 1094. The phrase is borrowed from China where it is more applicable than in Japan. In Korea nightly signals are made to the capital from the provinces, by beacon fires, to signify that all is well, perhaps some such practice is alluded to. My Chinese beacon customs.—W.G.A.] The text, as it stands, gives the impression that the arrival of the tribute-ships was announced by beacon-fires being lighted. Norinaga however wishes us to understand the author's meaning to be that foreign states which, in the natural course of events, would be inimical, and the approach of whose ships would be signalized by the lighting of beacon-fires, now peacefully sent gifts to the Japanese monarch. It may by added that the whole sentence is borrowed scarcely without alteration from the *Wen Xuan* (文選). Bun-mei is the Japanese pronunciation of the characters 文命, the original name of Yu the Great (禹), a celebrated legendary emperor of China. Ten-Itsu is the Japanese pronunciation of the characters 天乙, the original name of the ancient Emperor Tang (湯), who is said to have founded the Shang dynasty in the eighteenth century BCE.

[30]This word is here used as an initial particle without special significance.

[31]*I.e.*, present them to her. With this sentence ends the fourth division of the preface.

[32]*I.e.*, the simplicity of speech and thought in Early Japan renders it too hard a task to rearrange the old documents committed to memory by Are in such a manner as to make them conform to the rules of Chinese style.

[33]*I.e.*, if I adopted in its entirety the Chinese ideographic method of writing, I should often fail of giving a true impression of the original documents *(*cf. the preceding Note). If, on the other hand, I consistently used the Chinese characters, syllable by syllable, as phonetic symbols for Japanese sounds, this work would attain to inordinate proportions, on account of the great length of the polysyllabic Japanese as compared with the monosyllabic Chinese. The author's meaning may be illustrated by referring to the first clause of the *Records*, 天地初發之時 ("when Heaven and Earth began"), which is thus written ideographically with six Chinese characters, whereas it would require no less than eleven to write it phonetically so as to represent the sound of the Japanese words *ame tsuchi no hajime no toki*, viz., 阿米都知能波士賣能登伎. It should be noticed that in this passage the author employs the technical expressions *on* and *kun* (音 and 訓) in a manner which is the precise reverse of that sanctioned by modern usage, *on* being with him the phonetic, and *kun* the ideographic, acceptation of the Chinese characters.

[34]It will be seen by perusing the following translation that the author can scarcely be said to have vouchsafed as much exegetical matter as this statement would lead us to expect. Indeed his "comments" are mostly confined to information concerning the pronunciation of certain characters. See however Norinaga's remarks on this sentence in Vol. 2 pp. 19–20 of his *Commentary*.

[35]The author here refers to a certain class of Japanese words which offer peculiar difficulties because written neither ideographically nor phonetically, but in a completely arbitrary manner, the result of a freak of usage. His manner of expressing himself is, however, ambiguous. What he meant to say is, as Norinaga points out: "Again in such cases as writing the surname *Kusaka* with the characters 日下, and the personal name *Tarashi* with the character 帶, I have followed usage without alteration." It is his imperfect mastery over the Chinese construction that makes him fall into such errors, errors easily rectifiable, however, by the more widely read modern Japanese *literati*.

[36]For the Deity Master-of-the-August-Centre-of Heaven see Sect. 1, Note b, and for Prince-Wave-Limit, etc., see Vol. 1, Note 669. Kamu-Yamato-Iware-Biko is the proper native Japanese name of the emperor commonly known by the Chinese "canonical name" of Jin-mu. Homuda is part of the native Japanese name of the Emperor Ō-jin (see Sects. 94 to 118). Ō-Sazaki is the native Japanese name of the Emperor Nin-toku (see Sects. 119 to 130).

[37]*Q.d.*, to the Empress.

[38]Norinaga has "Ō" why Futo? And Ō no Ason does not look like *ō* being part of the name. Is it not simply the Great Court Noble? *Ason* is a mean title "Respectfully presented."—W.G.A.

Vol. 1

[1]Lit. "Upper Volume," there being three in all, and it being the common Japanese practice (borrowed from the Chinese) to use the words Upper, Middle, and Lower to denote the First, Second and Third Volumes of a work respectively.

[2]For this rendering of the Japanese word *kami* see Introduction, pp. 30.

[3]Lit., "that became" (成). Such "becoming" is concisely defined by Norinaga as "the birth of that which did not exist before."

[4]It is open to doubt whether the syllable *bi*, instead of signifying "wondrous," may not simply be a verbal termination, in which case the three syllables *musubi* would mean, not "wondrous producing," but simply "producing," *i.e.*, if we adopt the interpretation of the verb *musubu* as "to produce" in the active sense of the word, an interpretation as to whose propriety there is some room for doubt. In the absence of certainty the translator has followed the view expressed by Norinaga and adopted by Atsutane. The same remark applies to the following and other similar names.

[5]Here and elsewhere the character 国, properly "country" *(regio)*, is used where "earth" (*tellus*) better suits the sense. Apparently in the old language the word *kuni* (written 国), which is now restricted to the former meaning, was used ambiguously somewhat like our word "land."

[6]For *hiko* here and elsewhere rendered "prince" see Introduction p. 29; *ji* is rendered "elder" in accordance with the opinion expressed by Norinaga and Atsutane, who say that it is "an honorific designation of males identical with the *ji* meaning old man."

[7]The translation of the name here given follows the natural meaning of the characters composing it, and has the sanction of Tanikawa Kotosuga. Norinaga and Atsutane take *toko* to stand for *soko,* "bottom," and interpret accordingly; but this is probably but one of the many instances in which the Japanese philologists allow themselves to be led by the boldness of their etymological speculations into identifying words radically distinct. [Might not this mean: the Deity by whom Heaven stands forever?— W.G.A.]

[8]The author's obscure phrase is explained by Norinaga to mean that these Heavenly Deities were separate from those who came into existence afterwards, and especially from the Earthly-Eternally-Standing-Deity (*Kuni-no-toko-tachi-no-kami*) who in the *Chronicles* is the first divine being of whom mention in made. These five were, he says, "separate" and had nothing to do with the creation of the world. It should be stated that the sentence will also bear the interpretation "The five Deities in the above list are Deities who divided Heaven" (*i.e.*, presumably from Earth); but this rendering has against it the authority of all the native editors. As the expressions "Heavenly Deity" and "Earthly Deity" (lit., "Country Deity") are of frequent occurrence in these *Records*, it may be as well to state that, according to Norinaga, the "Heavenly Deities" were such as either dwelt in Heaven or had originally descended to Earth from Heaven, whereas the Earthly Deities were those born and dwelling in Japan.

[9]There is much doubt as to the proper interpretation of this name. The characters 雲野 ("cloud-moor"), with which the syllables read *kumo-nu* are written, are almost certainly phonetic, and the translator has followed Norinaga's view as corrected by Atsutane, according to which *kumo* is taken to stand for *kumu*, "integrating," and *nu* is considered to be an apocopated form of *nushi*, "master" (or more vaguely "the person who presides at or does a thing"). Mabuchi in his *Dictionary of Pillow-Words*, article *Sasu-take*, argues that the syllables in question should be interpreted in the sense of "coagulated mud"; but this is less satisfactory.

[10]The names of this pair lend themselves to a variety of interpretations. Norinaga's view of the meaning of the first three syllables in each seems best, as it is founded on the Chinese characters with which they are written in the parallel passage of the *Chronicles*, and it has therefore been adopted here. Atsutane interprets the names thus: First-Mud-Lord and First-Sand-Lady, and takes *ni* to be an alternative form of the honorific *ne* found in so many proper names. This view of the meaning of *ni* has been followed by the translator. On the other hand Mabuchi explains the names to mean respectively Floating-Mud-Earth and Sinking-Mud-Earth. The only thing therefore that is granted by all is that the names in question refer to the mud or slime out of which the world was afterwards made.—The reader will bear in mind that "younger sister" and "wife" are convertible names in

Archaic Japanese. (See Introduction p. 47.)

[11]The interpretation given is one in which the commentators agree, and which has some probability in its favor. It must however only be accepted with reservation.

[12]Atsutane, commentating on this name and the seven which precede it, says: "*U-hiji-ni* and *Su-hiji-ni* are so named from their having contained the germs of what was to become the earth. *Ō-to-no-ji* and *Ō-to-no-be* are so called from the appearance of the incipient earth. *Tsunu-gui* and *Iku-gui* are so called from the united appearance of the earth and the Deities as they came into existence. *Omo-daru* and *Kashiko-ne* are so called from the completion of the august persons of the Deities. Thus their names were given to them from the gradual progress [of creation]."

[13]Incites?—W.G.A.

[14]There is some slight diversity of opinion as to the literal signification of the component parts of the names of these the best-known of the Deities hitherto mentioned, though the gist of the meaning remains unchanged. Norinaga would prefer to read *Iza-na-gi* and *Iza-na-mi*, taking the syllable *na* as the Second Personal Pronoun "thou," and understanding the name thus: "the Prince-Who-Invites-Thee" and the "Princess-Who-Invites-Thee." It seems however more natural to look on *izana* as forming but one word, viz., the root of the verb *izanafu*, "to invite." The older native commentators mean the same thing when they tell us that *na* is an expletive. The syllables *gi* and *mi* are of uncertain etymology, but occur in other Archaic words to denote the male and female of a pair. The appropriateness of the names of these Deities will be seen by referring to Sect 4.

[15]For this rendering of the Japanese title *Mikoto* see Introduction, p. 29, last paragraph.

[16]The characters translated "jeweled spear" are 沼矛, whose proper Chinese signification would be quite different. But the first of the two almost certainly stands phonetically for 瓊 or 玉—the syllable *nu*, which is its sound, having apparently been an ancient word for "jewel" or "bead," the better-known Japanese term being *tama.* In many places the word "jewel" (or "jeweled") seems to be used simply as an adjective expressive of beauty. But Norinaga and Atsutane credit it in this instance with its proper signification, and the translator always renders it literally, leaving the reader to consider it to be used metaphorically if and where he pleases.

[17]The best authorities are at variance as to the nature of this bridge uniting Heaven with Earth. Atsutane identifies it with the Heavenly-Rock-Boat (*Ame-no-iwa-fune*) mentioned in some ancient writings, whereas Norinaga takes it to have been a real bridge, and finds traces of it and of similar bridges in the so-called "Heavenly Stairs" *(Ama-no-hashi-date)* which are found on several points of the coast, forming a kind of natural breakwater just above water-level.

[18]It is not easy to find in English a word which will aptly render the original Japanese onomatopoeia *kōroro-kōroro.* The meaning may also be "till it made a curdling sound." But though the character 鳴, "to make a noise," sanctions this view, it is not the view approved by the commentators, and 鳴 is probably [Yes.—W.G.A.] only written phonetically for a homonymous word signifying "to become," which

we find in the parallel passage of the *Chronicles*.

[19]The original of this quasi-causative phrase, of which there is no other example in Japanese literature so far as the translator's reading goes, is interpreted by Norinaga in the sense of the English locution to which it literally corresponds, and it has here been rendered accordingly, though with considerable hesitation. Atsutane does not approve of Norinaga's view; but then the different text which he here adopts imposes on him the necessity of another interpretation. (See his *Exposition of the Ancient Histories*, Vol. 2, pp. 39–40.)

[20]The original word *hiro* (written 尋) is defined as the distance between the hands when the arms are outstretched. The word rendered "hall" may also be translated "palace"–The text of the parallel passage of the *Chronicles* is "they made the Island of Onogoro the central pillar of the land"–a statement which seems more rational and more in accordance with general tradition than that of these *Records*.

[21]May not *mi tono maguwai* (美斗能麻具波比) mean simply "nuptial-chamber-intercourse" as opposed to irregular chance connection. The author seems to take pains to represent the union of *Izanami* and *Izanagi* as a regular marriage.—W.G.A.

[22]This is Atsutane's view of the import of the somewhat obscure original (see his *Exposition of the Ancient Histories*, Vol. 2, pp. 61–64). Norinaga's interpretation is: "auguste in thalamo coibimus" [we will unite augustly in the chamber].

[23]The name in the original is Hiru-go, an instance of the fortuitous verbal resemblances occasionally found between unrelated languages.

[24]B.H.C. provides this passage in Latin: Tunc quaesivit [Augustus Mas-Qui-Invitat] a minore sorore Augustâ Feminâ-Qui-Invitat: "Tuum corpus quo in modo factum est?" Respondit dicens: "Meum corpus crescens crevit, sed una pars est quae non crevit continua." Tunc dixit Augustus Mas-Qui-Invitat: "Meum corpus crescens crevit, sed est una pars que crevit superflua. Ergo an bonum erit ut hanc corporis mei partem quae crevit superflua in tui corporis partem quas non crevit continua inser-am, et regiones procreem?" Augusta Femina-Quae-Invitat respondit dicens: "Bonum erit." Tunc dixit Augustus Mas-Qui-Invitat: "Quod quum ita sit, ego et tu, hanc coelestem augustam columnam circumeuntes mutuoque occurrentes, augustarum [i.e. privatarum] partium augustam coitionem faciemus." Hâc pactione factâ, dixit [Augustus Mas-Qui-Invitat]: «Tu a dexterâ circumeuns occurre; ego a sinistra occurram." Absolutâ pactione ubi circumierunt, Augusta Femina-Qui-Invitat primum inquit: "O venuste et amabilis adolescens!" Deinde Augustus Mas-Qui-Invitat inquit: «O venusta et amabilis virgo! Postquam singuli orationi finem fecerunt, [Augustus Mas-Qui-Invitat] locutus est sorori, dicens: "Non decet feminam primum verba facere." Nihilominus in thalamo [opus procreationis] inceperunt, et filium [nomine] Hirudinem [vel Hirudini similem] pepererunt.

[25]Lit. "foam." It is supposed to have been an islet near the island of Awaji in the province of Sanuki.

[26]Hiru-go was not so reckoned, because he was a failure.

[27]The characters 御所, here translated "august place" (the proper Chinese signification is "imperial place") are those still in common use to denote the Mikado's palace.

[28]For an elaborate account of the various methods of divination practiced by the Ancient Japanese see Note 5 to Mr. Satow's translation of the "Service of the Gods of Wind at Tatsuta" in the *Transactions of the Asiatic Society of Japan*, Vol. 7, Pt. 4, p. 425 *et seq.* "The most important mode of divination practiced by the primitive Japanese was that of scorching the shoulder-blade of a deer over a clear fire, and finding omens in the cracks produced by the heat."

[29]B.H.C. gives the first part of this sentence in Latin. Tali modo quum orationi finem fecerunt, auguste coierunt et pepererunt

[30]*Awa-ji* signifies "foam-way," *i.e.*, "the way to Foam (Awa)-Island," [I should say Awaji originally meant the millet country, foam being an afterthought. —W.G.A.] on account, it is said, of its intermediate position between the mainland and the province of Awa in what is in modern parlance the Island of Shikoku. The author of the *Chronicles of Old Affairs* fancifully derives the name from *awaji* "my shame." The etymology of Ho-no-sa-wake is disputed; but Atsutane, who in the body of Vol. 3 of his *Exposition of the Ancient Histories* had already expended much ingenuity in discussing it, gives the most satisfactory interpretation that has yet been proposed in a postscript to that volume where he explains it to signify "Rice-ear-True-Youth." *Wake* (sometimes *waki* or *waku*) is a word of frequent occurrence in the names of gods and heroes. Whether it really signifies "youth," as Atsutane believes and as it is most natural to suppose, or whether Norinaga's guess that it is an honorific title corrupted from *wage kimi ye* (lit. "my prince elder brother," more freely "lord") remains undecided. When it is used as a "gentile name," the translator renders it by "lord," as that in such cases is its import apart from the question of derivation. *Sa*, rendered "true," may almost be considered to have dwindled down to a simple honorific.—It is this little island which is said by the author of the *Chronicles* to have been the caul with which the great island of Yamato was born. Awaji and Ho-no-sa-wake must be understood to be alternative names, the latter being what in other cases is prefaced by the phrase "another name for whom."

[31]*Futa-na* is written with characters signifying "two names "and Norinaga's derivation from *futa-narabi*, "two abreast," does not carry conviction. The etymology of Iyo is quite uncertain. It is here taken as the name of the whole island called in modern times Shikoku; but immediately below we find it in its usual modern acceptation of one of the four provinces into which that island is divided. A similar remark applies to Tsukushi a little further on.

[32]*E-hime.* For the rendering of *hiko* and *hime* as "prince" and "princess" see Introduction, p. 29.

[33]Probably derived, as Atsutane shows, from *saho-ki*, "pole-trees," [Shaft trees. —W.G.A.] a tribute of poles [Spear shafts?—W.G.A.] having anciently been paid by that province. Norinaga adopts the unusual reading of the name given in the *Japanese Words Classified and Explained*, viz. Sanugi, with the last syllable

nigori'ed [voiced—M.F.]

[34]*Ii-yori-hiko.* The translator, though with some hesitation, follows Norinaga in looking on *yori* as a contraction of *yoroshi*, "good." The character used for it in the original is 依.

[35]*Ō-ge-tsu-hime.* Remember that *awa* signifies not only "foam" but "millet," so that we need not be astonished to find that the alternative designation of the island so designated is that of a food-goddess.

[36]Etymology uncertain, only fanciful derivations being proposed by the native philologists.

[37]*Take-yori-wake.*

[38]*Mitsu-go* signifies "triplets," lit., "three children." The three islets intended are *Ama-no-shima, Mukō-no-shima* and *Chiburi-no-shima.*

[39]Oki probably here signifies "offing," which is its usual acceptation.

[40]*Ame-no-oshi-koro-wake.* The syllables *oshi,* which recur in the names of many gods and heroes, are rendered "great" in accordance with Norinaga's plausible conjecture that they are an abbreviation of *ōshi* ("great," not "many" as in the later language). The translation of *koro* by "heart" follows a conjecture of Atsutane's (Norinaga acknowledged that he could make nothing of the word), according to which it is taken to be an abbreviated form of *kokoro,* "heart."

[41]None but fanciful derivations of this word are suggested by the native philologists.

[42]A note to the edition of 1687 says: "Should the word 'four' be changed to 'five'?" For most texts enumerate five countries in this passage with slight variations in the names, Himuka (Hyūga), which it certainly seems strange to omit, being the fourth on the list with the alternative name of Toyokuji-hine-wake, while the alternative name Hi is Haya-hi-wake. Norinaga argues that an enumeration of four agrees better with the context, while Moribe in his *Critique on Norinaga's Commentary* decides in favor of the five. There are thus texts and authorities in favor of both views,

[43]*Shira-bi-wake.*

[44]*Toyo* means "luxuriant" or "fertile." *Hi* appears to signify "fire" or "sun." *Kumaso* is properly a compound, *Kuma-so,* as the district is often mentioned by the simple name of *So.* Kuma signifies "bear," and Norinaga suggests that the use of the name of this the fiercest of beasts as a prefix may be traced to the evil reputation of that part of the country for robbers and outlaws. He quotes similar compounds with *kuma* in support of this view.

[45]*Toyo-bi-wake.*

[46]*Take-hi-mukahi-toyo-kuji-hine-wake.* The interpretation of this name follows Norinaga.

[47]*Take-bi-wake.*

[48]Etymology uncertain, but there seems reason to suppose that the name was originally pronounced Iki or Yuki.

[49]*Ame-hito-tsu-bashira.*

[50]*Tsu* (Tsu-shima) means "port," "anchorage," a name probably given to this island on account of its being the midway halting-place for junks plying between Japan and Korea.

[51]*Ame-no-sade-yori-hime.* The interpretation of *sade* (rendered "hand-net") is uncertain. The translator has followed that sanctioned by an ode in Vol. 1 of the *Collection of a Myriad Leaves* and by a passage in the *Japanese Words Classified and Explained.* Atsutane takes *sa* to be an honorific and *te* to be the usual word for "hand," while Norinaga gives up the name in despair.

[52]Etymology uncertain.

[53]*Ō-yamato-toyo-aki-zu-shima* (the original of the alternative personal name is *Ama-no-mi-sora-toyo-aki-zu-ne-wake*). The etymology of Yamato is much disputed. Mabuchi, in his *Addenda to the Commentary on the Collection of a Myriad Leaves,* derives the name from *yama-to,* "mountain-gate." Norinaga, in a learned discussion to be found in his *Examination of the Synonyms of Japan,* pp. 24–27, proposes three other possible derivations, viz. *yama-to,* "mountain-place," *yama-to* (supposed to stand for *yama-tsubo* and to mean "mountain-secluded"), and *yama-utsu* (*utsu* being a supposititious Archaic from of *uchi*), "within the mountains." Other derivations are *yama-to* (山夕), "without the mountains," *yama-ato,* "mountain-traces" and *yama-todomi,*" mountains stopping," *i.e.* (as Moribe, who proposes it, explains), "far as the mountains can be seen." Another disputed point is whether the name of Yamato which here designates the Main Island of the Archipelago, but which in the common parlance of both ancient and modern times is the denomination on the one hand of the single province of Yamato and on the other of the whole Empire of Japan, originally had the wider application or the more restricted one. Norinaga and the author of the *Exposition of the Foreign Notices of Japan* seem to the present writer to make out the case in favor of the latter view. Norinaga supposes the name to have denoted first a village and then a district, before being applied to a large province and finally to the entire country. The "Island of the Dragonfly" is a favorite name for Japan in the language of the Japanese poets. It is traced to a remark of the Emperor Jin-mu, who is said to have compared the shape of the country round Mount Hohoma to "a dragonfly drinking with its tail." Cf. also the tradition forming the subject of Sec. 156 of the present translation.

[54]*Ō-ya-shima-kuni.* A perhaps still more literal English rendering of this name would be "Land of the Grand Eight Islands" or "Grand Land of the Eight Islands," for the word *ō* must be regarded rather as an honorific than as actually meant to convey an idea of size.

[55]"To the Island of Onogoro," [The idea plainly is that the God and Goddess went on a circuit depositing islands on their way.— W.G.A.] says Norinaga; but we are not told that the god and goddess had ever left it.

[56]*Ko* means "infant" or "small." The original of the alternative personal name is *Take-hi-gata-wake. Gata* (or, without the *nigori, kata*) here and in other names offers some difficulty. The translator renders it by the equivalent of the usual Japanese signification of the character 方, "direction," with which it is written.

[57] Etymology uncertain.

[58] *Azuki* is written with the characters 小豆, which signify a kind of bean (the *Phaseolus radiatus*); but it is possible that they represent the sound, and not the sense, of the name. In the alternative personal name *ō* signifies "great," and *hime* "*princess*," while the syllables *nu-de* are of altogether uncertain interpretation. Norinaga suggests that *nu may* mean "moor" and *de* (for *te*) "clapper-bell."

[59] I.e., Great Island. The word *tamaru* in the alternative personal name is so obscure that not even any plausible conjecture concerning it has been ventured and the name is therefore of necessity left untranslated.

[60] *Hime* signifies "princess" or "maiden." The original of the alternative personal name is *Ame-hito-tsu-ne.*

[61] Etymology uncertain. Norinaga would take the name in a plural sense as standing for the modern islands of Hirado and Go-to (Goto). The original of the alternative personal name is *Ame-no-oshi-o*, in which as usual, *oshi* is supposed to represent *ōshi* (大), "great."

[62] *Futa-go* means "twins." The original of the alternative personal name is *Ame-futa-ya.*

[63] *Ō-koto-oshi-o-no-kami.* "The Male-Enduring-Great-Things" would be a possible, but less good rendering. This god is identified by Norinaga with *Koto-toke-no-o* mentioned in "One account" of the *Chronicles of Japan.*

[64] The original *Iwa-tsuchi-biko-no-kami* (石土昆古神) is identified by Norinaga with *Uwa-zutsu-no-o* (上筒之男) mentioned in Vol. 1, Note 187. He would interpret the first *tsu* (*zu*) as the genitive particle and the second as identical with the "honorific appellation *ji* of males," which occurs in such words as *Hiko-ji*, *Ō-to-no-ji*, etc. If this surmise were correct, the entire name would signify Upper-Lord-Prince; but it is safer to be guided by the characters in the text.

[65] *Iwa-zu-bime-no-kami.* Here too Norinaga takes the syllable *zu* to be "connected with" the syllables *tsu-tsu* interpreted as above, forgetting apparently that the second *tsu* (*ji*) is said to occur only in the names of males.

[66] *Ō-to-bi-wake-no-kami*, a name which Norinaga, by supposing corruptions of the text and by making a plentiful use of the pliant and powerful system of derivation with which the Japanese etymologists lay siege to the difficulties of their language, identifies with *Ō-nao-bi-no-kami,* "the Great-Rectifying-Wondrous-Deity," mentioned in Vol. 1, Note 185.

[67] *Ame-no-fuki-o-no-kami.* Identified by Norinaga with *I-buki-do-nushi* mentioned in the *Ritual of the General Purification.* (See his *Commentary* on this Ritual, Vol. 2, pp. 29–32.)

[68] *Ō-ya-biko-no-kami*, identified by Norinaga with *Ō-aya-tsu-bi* mentioned in "One account" of the *Chronicles.*

[69] *Kaza-ge-tsu-wake-no-oshi-o-no-kami.* Norinaga's conjectural interpretation has been followed; but both the reading and the meaning of the original are encompassed with difficulties. Norinaga identifies this deity with *Soko-zutsu-o* mentioned in Vol. 1, Note 187, and with *Haya-sasura-hime* mentioned in the

Ritual of the General Purification.

[70] *Ō-wata-tsu-mi-no-kami.* The interpretation of *mi* as equivalent to *mochi*, "possessor," though not absolutely sure, has for it the weight both of authority and of likelihood.

[71] *Haya-aki-zu-hiko-no-kami. Aki*, whose proper signification is "autumn," might also by metonymy be interpreted to mean "dragonfly" or "Japan." Norinaga, *apropos* of this name, launches forth on very bold derivations and identifications with the names of other gods. The original of the name of the sister-deity is *Haya-aki-zu-hime-no-kami.*

[72] The text here omits the word "Swift" from this name.

[73] The original names of this deity and the three that follow are *Awa-nagi-no-kami, Awa-nami-no-kami, Tsura-nagi-no-kami,* and *Tsura-nami-no-kami.* The interpretation of the component parts is open to doubt, but that here adopted has the authority of Norinaga and Atsutane.

[74] *Ame-no-mi-kumari-no-kami.* The following deity is *Kuni-no-mi-kumari-no-kami.*

[75] This deity and the next are in the original *Ame-no-ku-hiza-mochi-no-kami* and *Kuni-no-ku-hiza-moehi-no-kami.* The etymology is obtained by comparison with a passage in the *Ritual for Averting Fire* (鎮火祭祝詞).

[76] *Shina-tsu-hiko-no-kami.* The original of this name is explained by Norinaga, who founds his view on two passages in the *Collection of a Myriad Leaves*, to signify Prince-of-Long-*Breath.* But the translator feels confident that *shi-na*, by him interpreted in the sense of "long breath" (or rather "long of breath") should be connected with *shi*, an old word for wind which we see in *ara-shi* ("storm-wind"), *ni-shi* ("west-wind"), *hi-gashi* ("east wind"), and perhaps under a slightly altered form in *kaze*, "wind," whereas *shi* nowhere occurs in the sense of "breath." Atsutane notices approvingly this etymology of *shi* (*Exposition of the Ancient Histories*, Vol. 3, p. 63), though without venturing flatly to contradict his predecessor's decision as to the import of the name in question. The difference in the meaning is after all slight. *Na* is to be taken as an apocopated form of *nagaki*, "long." In later times *Shinato* has been used as a name for the north-west wind.

[77] Such seems to be the meaning of the original *Kuku-no-chi-no-kami. [Or simply Tree-Tree-Elder-Deity. Cf. kuki ("stem") vs. ku-ku ("tree-tree").—M.F.]*

[78] *Ō-yama-tsu-mi-no-kami.*

[79] *Kaya-no-hime-no-kami.* The etymology of the alternative personal name (in the original *Nu-zu-chi-no-kami*) is not quite certain. [Probably Moor-Elder-Deity.—M.F.]

[80] The original of these two names is *Ame-no-sa-zu-chi-no-kami* and *Kuni-no-sa-zu-chi-no-kami.* Their signification is obscure, but the translator has, after some hesitation, followed Norinaga's interpretation. The words "heavenly" and "earthly" should probably be considered as qualifying "passes." This word "pass," used here and elsewhere to render the Japanese term *saka* (*sa*) [*Saka* is the Scotch, "brae."—W.G.A.], must be understood to include lesser ascents than those very

arduous ones which are alone denoted by the word "pass" in ordinary English parlance. In the later language of Japan the word *tauge* (*tōge*) generally denotes "passes" properly so called, while *saka* is restricted to the meaning of small ascents or hills. But this distinction is by no means strictly observed.

[81]*Ame-no-sa-giri-no-kami* and *Kuni-no-sa-giri-no-kami. Sa* seems to be rightly considered, as in the two preceding names, to be an archaic form of *saka* (properly *sa-ka*, "hill-place"), and *giri* as an apocopated form of *kagiri*, (properly *ka-giri*, "place cutting"), "limit" or "boundary." Atsutane however, following the Chinese character with which *kiri* is written, interprets it in the sense of "mist."

[82]*Ame-no-kura-do-no-kami* and *Kuni-no-kura-do-no-kami*. Norinaga explains *kura* (闇, "dark") by *tani* (谷, "valley"), and *to* (戸, "door"), by *tokoro* (處, "place").

[83]Such appears to be the proper interpretation of the originals of these two names, *Ō-tomato-hiko-no-kami* and *Ō-tomato-hime-no-kami, tomato* being plausibly referred to *tōmaru*. It is difficult to find an English word to represent exactly the idea, which is rather that of a gentle *fold* in the mountains than of the narrower and steeper hollow which we call a "valley."

[84]*I.e.*, the Prince-Who-Invites and the Princess-Who-Invites (*Izana-gi* and *Izana-mi*).

[85]*Tori-no-iwa-kusa-bune-no-kami*. The alternative name is *Ame-no-tori-bune*, from which the title of Deity is omitted. Norinaga's *Commentary*, Vol. 5, pp. 52–53 should be consulted on the subject of this deity.

[86]Homonymous with the alternative personal name of the Island of Awa. (See Vol. 1, Note 73.)

[87]*Hi-no-haya-yagi-o-no-kami*. If, as seems likely, *yagi* is an incorrect reading for *kagi*, we should have to translate by "shining" the word here rendered "burning." The alternative names are *Hi-no-kaga-biko-no-kami* and *Hi-no-kagu-tsuchi-no-kami*. In "One account" of the *Chronicles* and elsewhere in the *Ritual* this fire-god is called *Ho-musubi, i.e.*, "the Fire-Producer."

[88]*Kana-yama-biko-no-kami* and *Kana-yama-bime-no-kami*. The translation of this pair of names follows the plain sense of the characters 金山 with which they are written, and which seems appropriate enough, coming as they do between the deity of fire and Deities of clay. Norinaga however, declaring both characters to be merely phonetic, derives *kana-yama* from *kare-nayamasu*, "to cause to wither and suffer," and interprets the names accordingly. This is at any rate ingenious.

[89]*Hani-yasu-biko-no-kami* and *Hani-yasu-bime-no-kami.*

[90]The signification of this name is not to be ascertained. In the text it is written phonetically 彌都波倉賣, and two passages in the *Chronicles* where this deity is mentioned as 水神罔象女 and 水名爲嚴罔象女 with directions in each case to read the name with the sounds here given to it, do not help us much, except in so far as they show that Mitsuhanome was conceived of as the deity of water and as a female.

[91]*Waku-musu-bi-no-kami.*

[92]*Toyo-uke-bime-no-kami.*

[93]The text here is very peculiar, the characters rendered "single child" being

子之一木 where we should expect 子之一人 or 子一人. Atsutane proposes to consider 木, "tree," which most scholars agree in reading *ke* instead of *ki* in this place, as phonetic for *ke* (毛) "hair," and to interpret the god's words to signify that he values the child no more than a single hair in comparison with the wife whom that child's birth has lost for him. Moribe, in his *Examination of Difficult Words*, s.v. *Ko no hito-tsu ki* (Vol. 1, p. 8 *et seq.*), ingeniously argues that *ki* was an old native Japanese "auxiliary numeral" for animals, afterwards driven out by the somewhat like-sounding Chinese word *hiki* (匹) which is now in common use, and that the god employs this degrading auxiliary numeral in speaking of his child on account of the resentment which he feels against him. On the other hand we gather from the *Chronicles of Japan Explained* that 木 was used in its natural sense as an "auxiliary numeral" for gods and for men of exalted rank. This seems to the translator the better view to follow and it is supported by the use of 柱, *hashira*, as the regular "auxiliary numeral" for divine personages. The parallel passage in the *Chronicles* has simply 一児 "one infant."

[94]And crept round her august feet and wept, thereupon there was born.—W.G.A.

[95]This reading is but tentative; for it is not certain that Atsutane, whose view has been here adopted, is right in regarding Konomoto and Uneo as names of places. If we followed the older authorities, we should have to translate thus: "The Deity that dwells at the foot of the trees on the slope of the spur of Mount Kagu." The etymology of the name of this celebrated mountain (knows also as *Ame-no-kagu-yama* or *Ama-no-kagu-yama*, i.e., "Heavenly Mount Kagu") is disputed. But Atsutane's view, according to which it should be connected with *kago*, "deer," is the most plausible. If it were established we should be tempted to follow him in rendering by "deer-possessor" the name of the deity *Kagu-tsu-chi*, of whom were born the eight gods of mountains, and whose slaying forms the title of the next section. That the fire-deity should be connected with the mountain-Deities, and thereby with the deer who roam about the mountains and furnish the hunter with a motive for penetrating into their recesses, is of course but natural. The character 香 with which Kagu is written signifies "fragrant"; but it has been suggested that the Japanese word may be connected with an expression signifying "heaven-descended," in allusion to the supposed origin of the mountain as related in an old geographical work (now lost) treating of the Province of Iyo.

[96]*Naki-sawa-me-no-kami*. The sense of the second word of the compound is "marsh" or "stream"; but Norinaga seems right in considering the character 沢 to be here used phonetically as an abbreviation of *isawa* from *isatsu*, "to weep."

[97]Etymology uncertain.

[98]For this name see Vol. 1, Note 323.

[99]Etymology uncertain.

[100]One "grasp" is defined as "the breadth of four fingers when the hand is clenched," so that the meaning intended to be conveyed is of a big saber ten hand-breadths long. The length of sabers and of beards was measured by such "grasps" or "hand-breadths." [The saber is curved, but the ancient Japanese sword

was straight. —W.G.A.]

[101]The original names of this deity and the next are *Iwa-saku-no-kami* and *Ne-saku-no-kami.*

[102]Or the Rock-Elder-Male-Deity, i.e., the Male Deity the Elder of the Rocks, if with Norinaga we regard the second *tsu* of the original name *Iwa-tsutsu-no-o-no-kami* as being equivalent to *chi* or *ji*, supposed to be "the honorific appellation of males," elsewhere rendered "elder." The translation in the text proceeds on the assumption that this *tsu* represents *mochi.* The purport of the name remains much the same whichever of these two views be adopted.

[103]Explained by reference to the parallel passage of the *Chronicles* through a character signifying "the knob at the end of the guard of the sword."— (Williams's *Syllabic Dictionary.*) [I have seen in the Tokio Museum an ancient sword the hilt of which ended in a ring, and a definition of 禪 given in the *Shoki Shūkai* (書紀集解) is "sword-ring."—W.G.A.]

[104]*Mika-haya-bi-no-kami.* Norinaga seems to be right in regarding *mika* as equivalent to *ika*, the root of *ikameshiki*, "stern," "awful," and *bi* as the root of *buru*, a verbalizing suffix.

[105]*Hi-haya-bi-no-kami.* [The character in the Shoki is 集=*Hiru*, to parch, to scorch, to dry in the sun.—W.G.A.]

[106]*Take-mika-zu-chi-no-o-no-kami* written with the characters 建御雷之男神. The translator has without much hesitation followed Norinaga's interpretation.

[107]*Take-futsu-no-kami.* The next name is *Toyo-futsu-no-kami. Futsu* is interpreted in the sense of "the sound of snapping" by reference to a passage in the *Chronicles* where it occurs written both ideographically and phonetically in the name of the deity *Futsu-no-mi-tama.*

[108]The etymology of both these names is obscure. *Kura*, the first element of each compound, signifies "dark." [*Kura* means "valley." *Okami* refers to a kami who controls water. *Mi* means "water." The *tsu* and *ha* remain unclear.—M.F.]

[109]This is the explanation of the original name *Ma-saka-yama-tsu-mi-no-kami* which is given in the *Secret of the Chronicles of Japan*, and is approved by the later commentators.

[110]*Odo-yama-tsu-mi-no-kami.* The English rendering is uncertain, as it rests only on a conjecture of Norinaga's, deriving *odo* from *ori-do* (下處), "descending place," way down.

[111]The original names of this and the following five Deities are: *Oku-yama-tsu-mi-no-kami, Kura-yama-tsu-mi-no-kami, Shigi-yama-tsu-mi-no-kami, Ha-yama-tsu-mi-no-kami, Hara-yama-tsu-mi-no-kami* and *To-yama-tsu-mi-no-kami. Shigi*, here translated "dense," seems to be almost certainly a contraction of *shigeki*, which has that signification. *Ha-yama* is a term for which it is hard to find an exact English equivalent. It denotes the lesser hills or first visibly rising ground forming the approach to an actual mountain-range. The signification of *to* in the last name of the set is disputed. Mabuchi takes it in the sense of "gate." The translator prefers Norinaga's view; but after all, the difference in meaning does not amount to much.

A third derivation proposed by Norinaga is *tawa-yama*, i.e. "mountains with folds." [See the *Nihongi* on this passage. – W.G.A]

[112]These two names are in the original *Ame-no-o-ha-bari* and *Itsu-no-o-ha-bari*. Their import is not absolutely clear, but they seem to designate a weapon broad towards the point, such as is represented in the illustrations given in Vol 1, pp. 19–20 and Vol. 2, pp. 4–5 of the *Tokiwa-Gusa*.

[113]The characters in the original which are here rendered Hades are 黄泉, lit. "Yellow Stream," a Chinese name for the Underworld to which a remark of Mencius and a story in the *Zuo Zhuan* appear to have given rise. They here represent the Japanese word *Yomo* or *Yomi*, which we find phonetically written with the characters 豫母 in the name of *Yomo-tsu-shiko-me* a little further on, and which is defined by Norinaga as "an underworld"..... the habitation of the dead".... the land whither, when they die, go all men, whether noble or mean, virtuous or wicked." The orthodox Japanese derivation of *Yomi* is from *Yoru*, "night," which would give us for *Yomo-tsu-kuni* some such rendering as "the Land of Gloom." A suggestion quoted by Arai Hakuseki ("*Tōga*," art. *Izumi*) that the word may really be but a mispronunciation of Yama, the Sanskrit name of the Buddhist god of hell, is however worthy of consideration; and it seems best on the whole to translate *Yomi* or *Yomo* by "Hades," a term which is itself of uncertain derivation, and the signification attached to which closely resembles the Japanese *Shinto* notion of the world beyond, or rather beneath, the grave.

[114]The original text 爾自殿騰戸出向之時 seems to be corrupt, and Norinaga, unable to make anything of 騰戸, leaves 騰 without any Japanese reading (see the remarks in his *Commentary*, Vol. 6. pp. 5–6). Mr. Aston, in the version of this passage given in the Chrestomathy appended to his *Grammar of the Japanese Written Language*, follows Norinaga in not translating 騰 [This character should I think be read *agari*, a 'temporary burying place,' but this does not remove the whole difficulty. See the *Nihon Shoki* in this passage.—W.G.A.] but does not allude to the difficulty.

[115][A widespread idea that once having eaten of the food of a place one is bound to remain?—W.G.A.] It would be more obvious (following the text) to translate "I have eaten in the doors [*i.e.*, in the house] of Hades"; but the character 戸 in this place stands almost certainly for 竈 [As in the *Nihongi*.—W.G.A.] "a place for cooking," "a furnace."

[116]The word *kashikoshi* (恐), here translated "reverence," exactly corresponds to the modern polite idiom *osore-iri-mashita*, for which there is no precise equivalent in English, but which conveys some such sentiment as "I am overpowered by the honor you do me," "I am sorry you should have taken the trouble."

[117]The original here has the character 且 which signifies "moreover" as in the translation, and Norinaga's proposed emendation to 旦 [dawn, a day.—M.F.] has for it the authority of no manuscript or earlier printed edition. In his *Records of Ancient Matters with the Ancient Reading* he actually substitutes this very *new* reading, accompanying it in *kana* with the Japanese words *ashita ni*, "in the morning." But what is to become of the text if we are at liberty to alter it to suit our

convenience—for there is more than one other passage where 且 is similarly used?

[118]*Yomo-tsu-kami* Both Norinaga and Atsutane take the word "Deities" in the plural, and the translator therefore renders it in that number, though the singular would be at least equally suitable to the text as it stands. Of the Deities of Hades little or nothing is known. Cf. Vol. 1, Note 168.

[119]Lit. "the male pillar," *i.e.* the large tooth of which there is one at each end of the comb.

[120]The use of the expression "lit *one* light," where it would have been more natural to say simply "lit [a] light," is explained by a gloss in the *Chronicles*, which informs us that "at the present day" the lighting of a single light is considered unlucky, as is also the throwing away of a comb at night-time. It is allowed that the gloss is a late addition, and its statement might perhaps be considered a mere invention made to account for the peculiar expression in the text. Norinaga tells us however that "it is said by a native" that these actions are still (latter part of 18th century) considered unlucky in the province of Iwami, and the same superstition also survives, as the translator is assured, in Edo itself. It is to be understood that it was the large tooth broken off from the comb which the god lighted.

[121]The Japanese names of the eight Thunder-Deities are: *Ō-ikazuchi, Ho-no-ikazuchi, Kuro-ikazuchi, Saku-ikazuchi, Waki-ikazuchi, Tsuchi-ikazuchi, Nara-ikazuchi and Fushi-ikazuchi.* Moribe, in his *Critique on Norinaga's Commentary*, has some observations on the appropriateness of each of these names which the student will do well to consult if the work should be published. [The *Nihongi* makes eight of these. —W.G.A]

[122]*Yomo-tsu-shiko-me.*

[123]We might perhaps with equal propriety render by "wreath" the word here translated head-dress—leaves and flowers having been the earliest ornaments for the hair. In later times, however, it has been used to designate any sort of headdress, and that is also the dictionary meaning of the Chinese character with which it is written. The Japanese words for "headdress" and "creeper" are homonymous, and indeed the former is probably but a specialized acceptation of the latter.

[124]Why not "produced"? The *Nihongi* has "changed into."—W.G.A.

[125]Or Flat Hill of Hades, *Yomo-tsu-hira-saka*, said by Norinaga to form the frontier-line between Hades and the World of the Living. See also Vol. 1, Note 172.

[126]The three characters 青人草here rendered "people" are evidently (Norinaga notwithstanding) meant to be equivalent to the common Chinese expression 蒼生, which has that signification. The word translated "living" means literally "present," "visible." [Yes. It is applied to people in this actual visible world as opposed to the gods and spirits who cannot be seen and is the expression used in the corresponding passage of the *Nihongi.*—W.G.A.]

[127]It is better to translate the name thus than to render it by "the Land in the Middle of the Reed-Plains," a forced interpretation which Norinaga and Atsutane would only seem to adopt in order to veil the fact that one of the most ancient and revered names of their native land was imitated from that of China—everything

Chinese being an abomination in the sight of these ardent Shintoists. Yamazaki Ansai, as quoted by Tanikawa Kotosuga, is more sensible when he remarks that each country naturally considers itself central and foreign countries barbarous, and that Japan is not peculiar in being looked on by its inhabitants as the center of the universe. This is also the view taken by the other earlier scholars.

[128] *Ō-kamu-zu-mi-no-mikoto*. The difference between singular and plural is not often present to the Japanese mind, and though there were three peaches, we might just as well render their name by the words "His Augustness, etc.," considering the three as forming together but one divinity. The interpretation of the name here adopted is the simple and natural one which Norinaga borrowed from Tanikawa Kotosuga.

[129]That some kind of leave-taking and separation is intended seems certain; but the precise import of the characters 度事戸 in the text is not to be ascertained. Norinaga's *Commentary*, Vol. 6, pp. 29–30 and Vol. 10, pp. 52–55, should be consulted for an elaborate discussion of the various interpretations which they may be made to bear. Moribe, in his *Critique on this Commentary*, argues that "divorced each other" is the proper signification of the words, and supports his opinion by the parallel passage of the *Chronicles*.

[130] *Yomo-tsu-ō-kami*. On this rather embarrassing statement Norinaga is silent, and Atsutane simply says: It must be supposed that "the 'Deities of Hades' previously mentioned had been its 'Great Deities' up to this time, a position which was henceforward assumed by Her Augustness Izana-mi (the Female-Who-Invites.)" Cf. Vol. 1, Note 156.

[131] *Chi-shiki-no-ō-kami*. [This is Norinaga's reading. We might also read *Michi-shiki-no-ō-kami*.] Norinaga conclusively proves that "reaching" is the signification of the word *shiki* which is here so translated. That it was already obscure at the time of the compilation of these *Records* is however shown by the fact that it is written syllabically in the first instance, and with a "borrowed character" (*i.e.*, a homonymous word) in the second.

[132]Because the goddess was turned back by it on the road where she was pursuing her brother-husband. The original is *Chi-gaeshi* [or *Michi-gaeshi*]*-no-ō-kami*.

[133] *Sayari-masu-yomi-do-no-ō-kami*.

[134] *Ifuya-zaka*. Moribe in his *Izu-no-chi-waki* conjectures that Ifuya may be derived from *Yū-yami*, "evening darkness," an etymology which has at least the merit of suiting the legend.

[135]The words "I have" ["That I have."—W.G.A] thus repeated are an attempt to render the concluding words *ari keri* of the sentence in the original, by which, though they have no particular sense, the author evidently set great store, as he writes them syllabically. They may be considered to emphasize what goes before and, says Norinaga, "convey the idea of lamentation." [Exclamation.—W.G.A.] The idiom occurs some half-dozen times in the course of the present work.

[136]Tachibana is understood to be the general designation of trees of the orange tribe. (See however Vol. 2, Note 576.) Here it is used as a proper name.

[137]This name, which signifies "sun-confronting," was not unnaturally bestowed on a province in the eastern part of the westernmost of the larger Japanese islands, as it might well be conceived as lying "opposite the sun." It has, however, been supposed to have originally denoted the whole of the island in question. In any case the name is not inappropriate, as the island has a long eastern seaboard.

[138]In our text *Tsuki-tatsu-funa-do.* [*Fu* of *funa* may be a verb meaning "to pass" containing the same root as *heru. Funada* and *Kunado* would then have the same signification. Was there a practice of setting up a post to warn people not to approach too closely where a *harai* was being performed?—W.G.A.] But *funa* should almost certainly be *ku-na* and the name (which has here been translated accordingly) is then illustrated by the more extended version of this myth which is given in the *Chronicles*, where we read that the god (probably addressing his sister) threw down his staff with the words: "Come no further." "Stand" must be understood in a transitive sense: the god *stood* his staff up by thrusting it into the sand.

[139]This is Moribe's explanation (*Izu-no-chi-waki,* Vol. 4, p. 44) of the meaning of the original name *Michi-no-naga-chi-ha-no-kami*, the syllable *ha* of which is considered by him to be an alternative form of *ma* (間, "space"). It is however a great crux and Norinaga confesses his inability to explain it satisfactorily. Other views as to the import of the syllable in question will be found in the *Jin-dai no maki Mo-shio-gusa*, Vol. 2, p. 29.

[140]This seems to be the meaning of the original name, if we retain the reading *Toki-okashi-no-kami*. See however Norinaga's remarks *in loco*.

[141] *Wazurai-no-ushi-no-kami.*

[142] *Chi-mata-no-kami.*

[143] *Aki-gui-no-ushi-no-kami.* The English rendering of this obscure name proceeds on the assumption that Norinaga is correct when he proposes to consider *kui* as equivalent in this place to *kuchi*, "mouth." The gaping trousers no longer filled by the deity's legs would perhaps suggest the idea of an open mouth, though it is true that this is not the deity said to have been actually born from that portion of the attire.

[144]The names of this deity and the five who follow are in the original *Oki-zakaru-no-kami, Oki-tsu-nagisa-biko-no-kami, Oki-tsu-kai-bera-no-kami He-zakaru-no-kami, He-tsu-nagisa-biko-no-kami* and *He-tsu-kai-bera-no-kami.* The word "wash," by which for want of a better one the Substantive *nagisa* has been rendered, must be understood to signify the part nearest to the strand of the sea or of a river—the boundary of the waves. The third and sixth of this set of names, in which the syllables *kai-bera* (here represented by "Intermediate Direction") offer a good deal of difficulty, have been translated in accordance with Norinaga's explanation of their probable meaning.

[145]Lit. "right." In Chinese and Japanese compositions the lines follow each other from right to left instead of from top to bottom as with us. "Right" therefore signifies "foregoing," and "left," "following."

[146]The names of these two Deities in the original are *Ya-so-maga-tsu-bi-no-kami*

and *Ō-maga-tsu-bi-no-kami.*

[147]The names of these two Deities in the original are *Kamu-nao-bi-no-kami* and *Ō-nao-bi-no-kami.*

[148]*Izu-ne-me-no-kami.* The word *Izu* is incomprehensible, unless indeed, following Norinaga, we identify this goddess with the god and goddess *Haya-aki-zu-hiko* and *Haya-aki-zu-hime* mentioned in Vol. 1, Note 109, and consider *izu* as standing by apheresis for *ah-zu.* [Perhaps *izu* "solemn, austere, majestic" and *me* "woman" suggesting a woman associated with ceremony, i.e. a shamness.—M.F.]

[149]The original names of this deity and the five who follow are *Soko-tsu-wa-ta-tsu-mi-no-kami, Soko-zutsu-no-o-no-mikoto, Naka-tsu-wata-tsu-mi-no-kami, Naka-zutsu-no-o-no-mikoto, Uwa-tsu-wata-tsu-mi-no-kami* and *Uwa-zutsu-no-o-no-mikoto.* There is the usual doubt as to the signification to be assigned to the syllable *tsu* in the second, fourth and last of these names. If it really means, not "elder" but "possessor," we should be obliged to translate by "the Bottom-*Possessing*-Male," etc.

[150]*Azumi no muraji.* This name is said by Norinaga to be taken from that of a place in the province of Shinano. But Moribe shows that at any rate the etymology of the word may be traced to *ama-tsu-mochi,* "possessors of fishermen."

[151]It is impossible to translate this name which, according to Norinaga, is derived from those of two districts in Shinano to which the word *utsushi* (for *utsutsu,* "present" or "living") is prefixed.

[152]Attention must again be drawn to the vagueness of the Japanese perception of the distinction between singular and plural. As three Deities are particularly and repeatedly mentioned in the foregoing text, we are forced to translate this passage in the plural; and yet how could one child have three fathers?

[153]*Sumi-no-e,* also called *Sumi-yoshi, i.e.,* by a play upon words, "pleasant to dwell in." The real etymology of *sumi* is not certain.—Instead of "the three Great Deities," we might translate by "the Great Deities of the Three Shrines."

[154]The reading *terasu,* which is established by the authority of the *Collection of a Myriad Leaves* and by almost universal usage, must not mislead the student into imagining that the verb, because it is causative in form, has a causative meaning which would require some such English translation as "Heaven-Illuminating." The Causative form is simply Honorific, and the two words *ama terasu* signify, as Norinaga explains, "shining in heaven."

[155]There is no doubt as to a moon-god being intended, but the precise import of the name is disputed. The translator has followed Mabuchi's view as quoted by Norinaga, and which is supported by the fact that, from classical times down to the present day, *tsuku-yo* or *tsuki-yo* has been a word in common use to denote a fine moonlight night. If we were to take *yomi* as one word, we should have to render it either by "Moon-Hades" or by "Moon-Darkness," which seem less appropriate designations, though still of plain enough intent. The characters 月読, 月弓, and 月夜見, with which the name is variously written, seem all phonetic unless we might take the second set 月弓 to mean the crescent (lit. "moon-bow").

[156]Susa, *which is sometimes read* Sosa, is rendered by the word "impetuous" in accordance with Mabuchi's view as quoted by Norinaga. The first member of this compound name is frequently omitted. [But possibly the derivation from *Susamu* may have suggested some features of the myths connected with him. See *Izumo Fudoki* Vol. 3, 77, the Kana edition, from which it may be gathered that *Susa no o* is only a description. *Susa* being the seat of fire worship. —W.G.A.]

[157]*Mi-kura-tana-no-kami*. Norinaga comments on this name by saying that the necklace was doubtless so precious that it was carefully kept by the goddess on a shell in her store-house.

[158]*Yoru-no-osu-kuni*.

[159]*Una-bara*.

[160]See Vol. 1, Note 138.

[161]*Sic* in the original, to the perplexity of commentators. [The God being the Sea-God perhaps it is meant that by his weeping he wasted away his own substance, *i.e.*, the sea, the rivers, and all moisture everywhere so as to leave everything dry.—W.G.A.]

[162]"Flies in the fifth moon" is the received interpretation of the original term *sa-bae*. Cf. *sa-tsuki*, the old native name for the fifth moon.

[163]The text has here the character 滿, "to be full," for which Norinaga somewhat arbitrarily reads 涌, "to bubble up," taking this word in the sense of swarming. The translator has endeavored to preserve the vagueness of the original Japanese, which leaves it doubtful at first sight whether the flies or the Deities should be regarded as the logical subject of the verb. There is an almost identical passage near the beginning of Sect. 16.

[164]Lit. "a myriad things," a Chinese phrase for totality.

[165]The Chinese character for the First-Personal Pronoun used here and below by this deity is the humble one 僕 signifying literally "servant." The commentators read it simply "I."

[166]The Japanese authorities simply read "Mother." But the character 妣, which is used in this place, specially designates a mother who is deceased.

[167]*I.e.*, say the commentators, "in this realm of ocean which I granted to thee as thy domain." Probably, however, this is reading into the text more than it was meant to contain.

[168]Derivation unknown.

[169]From *awa-umi*, "fresh sea," *i.e.*, "lake." The province of Ōmi was doubtless so called from Lake Biwa which occupies a great portion of its surface. It is also known as *Chika-tsu-Ōmi*, *i.e.*, "the Nearer Ōmi, in contradistinction to *Tō-tsu-Ōmi* (in modern pronunciation *Tōtōmi*), *i.e.*, "Distant Ōmi," a province further to the East. The modern pronunciation of *Afumi* is *Omi*. [All other appearances of *Afumi* have been changed to *Ōmi*.—M.F.]

[170]The English locution "to take leave" exactly represents the Chinese character here used which, from having the sense of "asking permission," has come to mean "bidding adieu."

[171]He was her younger brother. [The *Nihongi* has the Chinese character for younger brother, rendered by *nase no mikoto* in the Kana gloss.—W.G.A.] But see what is said on the subject of names expressive of relationship on p. xli of Introduction. The phonetic characters 那勢 are here used to represent 兄, "elder brother."

[172]The original is here obscure, but the translator has, as usual, followed the Chinese characters as far as possible, and has been chiefly guided by Moribe's interpretation. According to this, the "eight feet" (which Moribe takes to mean simply "several feet") must be supposed to refer to the length of the necklace which, he says, probably resembled a Buddhist rosary, only that the beads were somewhat larger. For a discussion of the various interpretations to which this phrase descriptive of the Sun-Goddess's ornaments may be subjected, see Note 4 to Mr. Satow's third paper on the "Rituals" in Vol. 9, Pt. 2, p. 198 of these *Transactions*, and Moribe's *Examination of Difficult Words*, Vol. 2. pp. 4–5, *s.r. Ya-saka-ni no io-tsu no mi sumaru no tama*. Mr. Satow, adopting some of the bolder etymologies of the Japanese commentators, translates thus: the "ever-bright curved (or glittering) jewels, the many assembled jewels," and concludes that "a long string of, perhaps, claw-shaped stone beads" was what the author meant to describe.

[173]Atsutane supposes this additional quiver to have been slung in front.

[174]Norinaga's long note on the expression *taka-tomo*, to be found in Vol. 7, pp. 39–40 of his *Commentary* seems to prove that "high-sounding elbow-pad" (竹 being written phonetically for 高) is the most likely meaning—these pads, of which one was worn on the left elbow, having been made of skin. Arai Hakuseki however takes 竹 in its literal sense of "bamboo," and Moribe suggests the *take* (健) which occurs so often in proper names with the signification of "bold," "brave, "or "stout."

[175]Does this not mean simply that she brandished it top upwards, *i.e.*, in a position for shooting? *furi* being an adverb qualifying *tateru* and indicating a swift motion, cf. *furikaeru* etc.— W.G.A.

[176]The reading *yu-hara*, here rendered "top [of the bow]" is doubtful, and *yu-hazu*, "bow-notch," has been proposed as an emendation.

[177]Atsutane has a long note on the word *ukei*, here rendered "swear" (elsewhere as a substantive, "oath") which the student will do well to consult. It is contained in his *Exposition of the Ancient Histories*, Vol. 7, pp. 61–63.

[178]According to the *Nihon shoki* the oath was to prove the sincerity of his intentions. If the children were male his intentions were to be considered good, but if female, otherwise.—W.G.A.

[179]*Ame-no-yasu-kawa* (according to Norinaga's reading *Ame-no-yasu-no-kawa*), our Milky Way. The *Chronicles of Old Matters of Former Ages* perhaps preserve the true etymology of the word by writing it *Ama no ya-se kawa, i.e.*, "the Heavenly River of eight currents (or reaches)." This would mean simply "a broad river." The text literally says: "having placed the Tranquil River of Heaven in the middle'" etc., but the sense of the clause is that given in the translation.

[180]These words seem, as Norinaga says, to have been erroneously brought in here from the next sentence, where they come in appropriately.

[181]Rinsed *furi* one description of the style of washing.—W.G.A.

[182]*Ame-no-ma-na-i.* The interpretation adopted is that which has the authority of Norinaga and Atsutane. Perhaps only "Heavenly Well" is intended. The above authorities warn us that the word *i*, "well," was not in ancient days restricted to its modern sense, but was used to designate any place at which water could be drawn, and Norinaga thinks that Heaven contained several such. That mentioned in the text seems to have been a pool in the bed of the Tranquil River of Heaven.

[183]This is the interpretation of the original name *Ta-kiri-bime-no-mikoto* which is proposed by Moribe. It is less far-fetched, and agrees better with the name of the sister deity Princess-of-the-Torrent, than do the other explanations that have been attempted. The alternative name is *Oki-tsu-shima-no-mikoto.*

[184]*Ichiki-shima-hime-no-mikoto, ichiki being an unusual form of itsuki.* The island, which is in the Inland Sea, is still celebrated, but bears in common parlance the name of Miya-jima, i.e., "Temple Island." The alternative name is *Sa-yori-bime-no-mikoto*, in which *sa* is an ornamental prefix not calling for translation.

[185]*Tagi-tsu-hime-no-mikoto.*

[186]*Masa-ka-a-katsu-kachi-hayabi-ame-no-oshi-ho-mimi-no-mikoto* The word *mimi* (耳 "ears") forms part of a large number of Ancient Japanese proper names. [*Mimi* is the name given to certain governors of provinces by the Chinese writers quoted in the *Isho Nihon Den.* —W.G.A.] Norinaga, who of course passes over in silence the fact that large ears are considered lucky, not only in Japan, but also in China and Korea, suggests the etymology *hi hi* or *bi bi* (靈々), *i.e.*, the word "wondrous" or "miraculous" repeated. But there are examples of such names in which the interpretation of *mimi* as "ears" is unavoidable. Thus Prince Umayado (commonly called *Shō-toku Tai-shi*) had also the name of *Ya-tsu-mimi no Tai-shi* 八耳太子 bestowed upon him on account of his extraordinary intelligence. Is it not therefore simpler in all cases to allow to the word this its natural meaning? The proper names in *mi* do however undoubtedly offer some difficulty, and Norinaga scarcely seems content with his own derivation of the troublesome syllable. *Oshi*, as in other cases, is taken to represent *ōshi*, "great"; and after much hesitation the translator has followed Norinaga in regarding *ho* likewise as an abbreviated form of that word.

[187]*Ame-no* signifies "of Heaven" or "heavenly." The syllables *hohi* are incomprehensible. [*Ho* means "rice ear." Hi refers to spiritual power.—M.F.]

[188]*Ama-tsu-hiko-ne-no-mikoto.*

[189]*Iku-tsu-hiko-ne-no-mikoto.*

[190]This god does not seem to be known by any other name, but is conjectured by Atsutane to be identical with *Ame-no-ho-hi*, the second of these divine brothers. *Kumanu*, or less archaically *Kumano*, is said to be, not the well-known Kumano in the province of Kii [Wakayama Prefecture—M.F.], but a place in Izumo near Suga (see Vol. 1, Sect. 19, Notes a and 319). The name is written with the characters 熊野, "bear moor." The native commentators however interpret it as a corruption of *Komori-nu*, 隱野, "the moor of retirement," on account of a tradition preserved

in the *Chronicles* of Izanami (the Female-Who-Invites) having been interred at the Kii Province Kumano.

[191] A place in the province of Chikuzen. [Fukuoka Prefecture.—M.F.] The name signifies either "breast-shape" or "body-shape."

[192] Or "seashore temple."

[193] Or "the Great Deities of the three shrines."

[194] *Munakata no kimi*. Remember that all the names in this and similar lists are hereditary "gentile names" (see Introduction, p. 29), and that "Duke" and the other titles used in this translation to designate them must only be regarded as approximations towards giving the force of the Japanese originals, which are themselves by no means always clear, either etymologically or historically. Indeed Norinaga in a chapter entitled "*Kuni no Miyatsuko*" (國造) in his *Tama-Katsuma* Vol. 6, p. 25, remarks that the distinctions obtaining between the various titles of *Kimi, Wake, Muraji*, etc., are no longer to be ascertained, if indeed they were ever sharply drawn, and that *Kuni no Miyatsuko* (here rendered "Rulers of the Land") seems to have been a general term including all the rest, and roughly corresponding to the modern title of *Daimyō*.—It must be well understood that all these names, though properly and originally denoting an office, were inherited as titles, and ended (after the custom of conferring new ones had died out) by being little more than an extra surname appended to the surname proper (*uji*). This kind of quasi-official quasi-titular surname is what is called by the Japanese a *kabane*, which the translator, for want of a better equivalent, renders by "gentile name." Norinaga's learned note in Vol. 39, pp. 14–15 of his *Commentary*, should be consulted for a full exposition of this somewhat intricate subject, on which there has been much misapprehension, chiefly owing to the want of a fitting Chinese character to denote the word *kabane*.

[195] Here and throughout the work passages of this nature containing genealogies are in all the editions printed small, and might therefore be supposed to be either intended as footnotes, or to be later glosses. Norinaga however rightly rejects such an inference. To an English reader the word "this" may seem, by disturbing the grammar of the sentence, to support that inference; but in Japanese construction little importance need be attached to the presence of this double nominative.—The name in the original of the ancestral deity whose children are here enumerated is *Take-Hira-Tori-no-mikoto* and the interpretation thereof in the sense given in the translation is Norinaga's, *Hira-tori* being supposed by him to stand for *Hina-teri*.

[196] *Izumo-no-kuni-no-miyatsuko.*

[197] *Muzashi-no-kuni-no-miyatsuko*. In classical and modern usage *Musashi* does not take the *nigori*. [i.e. Muzashi is now called Musashi.—M.F.]

[198] *Kami-tsu-Unakami-no-kuni-no-miyatsuko*. Unakami was a part of what forms the modern province of Kazusa. [Chiba Prefecture.—M.F.] The name probably signifies "on the sea."

[199] *Shimo-tsu-Unakami-no-kuni-no-miyatsuko.*

[200] *Ijimu-no-kuni-no-miyatsuko*. Ijimu (given in the *Japanese Words Classified and Explained* as *Ijimi*) was a portion of the modern province of Kazusa. The

etymology of the name is unknown.

[201] *Tsushima-no-agata-no-atai.*

[202] *Tō-tsu-ōmi-no-kuni-no-miyatsuko.* In modern times *Tō-tsu-ōmi* has been contracted to *Tōtafumi* and is pronounced *Tōtōmi.* The name signifies "distant fresh sea" (*i.e.*, "distant lake"), the province which bears it being thus designated in reference to a large lagoon which it contains, and in contradistinction to *Chika-tsu-ōmi*, "near fresh sea"' the name of the province in which lies Lake Biwa. In modern times the latter has come to be known simply as Ōmi (pronounced Omi), and the original connection of ideas between its name and that of Tōtōmi is lost sight of.

[203] *Ōchi-kōchi-no-kuni-no-miyatsuko. Ohoshi-kafuchi* (in modern times pronounced *Ōchikōchi*) signifies "within the great rivers."

[204] *Nakatabe-no-yue-no-muraji.* The meaning of this name is not certain, but *yue* seems to be the word for "bathing woman" mentioned in Vol. 2, Note 528. See Norinaga's remarks in Vol. 24, p. 56 of his *Commentary* and the story of the origin of the name given in the *Catalogue of Family Names*, Vol. 2 ,*pp. 8–9 (edit. of 1834.)*

[205] *Ki-no-kuni-no-miyatsuko. Ki* signifies "tree," and the province doubtless received this name from its forests. Norinaga supposes the character 次 to have been lost in this place, and reads *Ubaraki* (the modern *Ibaraki*), a portion of the province of Hitachi. [Ibaraki Prefecture.—M.F.] See Vol. 7, pp. 75–76 of his *Commentary.*

[206] *Tanaka-no-atai.* The word *ta-naka* signifies "in the middle of the ricefields."

[207] *Yamashiro-no-kuni-no-miyatsuko. Yama-shiro* signifies "behind the mountains," though it is now, by a play upon words, written with characters signifying "mountain-castle."

[208] *Umaguta-no-kuni-no-miyatsuko.* Umaguta is a portion of the modern province of Kazusa. [Chiba Prefecture.—M.F.] The etymology of the name is not known.

[209] *Kihe-no-kuni-no-miyatsuko.* The etymology of the name and the position of the place are equally obscure.

[210] The modern province of Echigo, or perhaps any not well defined district in the north of the Main Island. (See Vol. 2, Note 238.)

[211] *Suwa-no-kuni-no-miyatsuko.* The etymology of Suwa is not known; but the name sounds Chinese.

[212] *Amuchi-no-miyatsuko.* The derivation of Amuchi is unknown.

[213] *Takechi-no-agata-nushi.* Takechi means "high market" or "high town."

[214] *Kamō-no-inaki.* Kamō was a portion of Ōmi. Norinaga's suggestion that the name may be derived from *kama* (*gama*), "a bullfrog," does not seem a happy one.

[215] *Sakikusabe-no-miyatsuko. Sakikusa-be* means literally "lily clan," *sakikusa*, the old name for the lily (or one species of lily) being literally "the luckplant." The story of the origin of this cognomen is to be found in the *Catalogue of Family Names*, Vol. 2, p. 9.

[216] Lit. "if one speak from this."

[217] The character used is 田, which in Chinese does not necessarily signify a *rice*-field. But in Japanese it seems to have been always limited to this narrower meaning, to which likewise the context here clearly points.

[218]In the original written 尿麻理, which is partly ideographic and partly phonetic for *kuso-mari*, Norinaga interprets it to signify "excrements and urine"; [What Norinaga says is that *mari* means to pass either excrements or urine.—W.G.A] but the parallel passage of the *Chronicles* which he himself quotes goes to prove that *mari* had not the latter meaning, as does also another well-known passage in the *Tale of a Bamboo-Cutter*. [See the offences enumerated in the Ō-harai norito.— W.G A.(For translation of this norito see T.A.S.J. reprints Vol. 2. 1927.)]

[219]大嘗 read *ō-nie*. The word *nie* now denotes "a sacrifice," and *ō-nie no matsuri* is the religious festival of the tasting of the first new rice of the season.

[220]We might, following classical usage, translate the verb *togamezu*, which is written phonetically, by the words "took no heed" or "made no observation"; but in this passage it certainly seems to have the stronger and more specialized signification of "upbraiding," "scolding," which attaches to it in the colloquial dialect.

[221]Thus a certain family of priests was called by the name of *Imibe*, lit. "the shunning clan," on account of the uncleanness from which they were bound to abstain. [Is it not possible that *Imi* may have meant "taboo," an ancient form of our "No admittance except on business"? —W.G.A.]

[222]Written with characters signifying literally "garment-house," but the meaning, as understood by the native commentators, is that given in the text.

[223]項. This character is taken by the native commentators in the sense of 棟, *mune*, "ridge-pole."

[224]In the parallel passage of the *Chronicles* it is the goddess [Amaterasu.—M.F.] who injures herself with her shuttle, but without dying of the effects of the accident. [B.H.C. gives the last half of this sentence in Latin: impegerunt privatas partes adversis radiis et obierunt.—M.F.]

[225]Norinaga says that the word "rock" need not here be taken literally. But it is always (and the translator thinks rightly) so understood, and the compound considered to mean a cave in the rocks, which is also the expression found in the *Chronicles* (岩窟).

[226]The word *sasu*, which is here used, implies that the goddess made the door fast either by sticking something against it or by bolting it—perhaps with one of the metal hooks of which mention is made in Vol. 2, Note 439.

[227]In my copy the section ends here.—W.G.A.

[228]*Toko-yo*, here properly written 常夜, and a few lines lower down semi-phonetically 常世.

[229]Norinaga supposes "myriad" to be a copyist's error for "evil." This clause is a repetition of one in Sect. 12.

[230]The parallel passage in the *Chronicles* has "eighty myriads."

[231]The Japanese word *kawara*, translated "bed," is thus defined in Dr. Hepburn's *Dictionary*, 2nd Edit. *s.v. kawara*: "That part of the stony bed of a river which is dry except in high water."

[232]*Omoi-kane-no-kami*. "He *included* in his single mind the thoughts and contrivances of many," says Norinaga.

[233]The text has the character 鐵, "iron," which Atsutane reads *ma-gane*, lit. "true metal," the common Japanese term being *kuro-gane*, lit. "black metal." Norinaga prefers to read simply *kane*, "metal" in general. The main text of the parallel passage in the *Chronicles* omits to mention the metal of which the mirror was made; but "One account" has the character 金, "metal" in general, often in Chinese, but rarely if ever in old Japanese, with the specific sense of "gold." The *Chronicles of Old Matters* alone, which are of very doubtful authenticity, say that the mirror was made of copper. (Copper was not discovered in Japan till the eight century of the Christian era, a few years before the discovery of gold.) [But was known. *Hakudo* 白多同, white copper, is frequently mentioned in the *Nihongi*, the Kana reading being *masumi*, "clear." —W.G A.] The best and most obvious course is to adhere to the character in the text, which is, as above stated "iron."

[234]*Ama tsu* signifies "of Heaven," but the rest of this name is not to be explained. Norinaga adopts from the *Chronicles*, the reading *Ama-tsu-ma-ura*, where the character used for *ma* signifies "true," and that for *ura* signifies "seashore." (It should be remarked that the forging of a spear by this personage is referred by the author of the *Chronicles*, not to the "Divine Age" but to the reign of the Emperor Sui-zei.) Norinaga also proposes to supplement after the name the words "to make a spear." Atsutane identifies this god with *Ama-no-ma-hito-tsu-no-mikoto*, His Augustness Heavenly-One-Eye, [Unlikely.—W.G.A.] who is however not mentioned in these *Records*. Obvius hujus nominis sensus foret «Cœlestis Penis» sed nullius commentatoris anctoritate commendatur. [The meaning of this name would be "Heavenly Penis," but this is not recommended by any of the commentators.—M.F.]

[235]This name is written in the *Chronicles* with characters signifying Stone-Coagulating-Old-Woman, which however seem to be as merely phonetic as those in the present text (伊斯許理度売). Norinaga proposes the interpretation of "Again-Forging Old-Woman" (鋳重老女, *I-shikiri-tome*) which is supported by a tradition preserved in the *Gleanings of Ancient Story*, where it is related that the mirror, not having given satisfaction at first, was forged a second time. There is a long note on the subject of this name in Atsutane's *Exposition of the Ancient Histories*, Vol. 9, p. 56, where that author propounds the novel opinion that I-shi-ko-ri-do-me was not a goddess at all, but a god.

[236]*Tama-noya-no-mikoto*. The *Chronicles* write this name with characters signifying "Jewel-House," but such a reading seems less good.

[237]See Vol. 1, Note 144.

[238]*Ame-no-ko-ya-ne-no-mikoto*, also read *Ama-no* etc. and *Ama-tsu* etc. The signification of the syllables *ko-ya*, rendered "beckoning ancestor" in accordance with Norinaga's view connecting the name with the share taken by the god who bore it in the legend here narrated, is obscure. Mr. Satow thinks that Koya may be the name of a place (see these *Transactions* Vol. 7, Pt. 4, p. 400).

[239]*Futo-tama-no-mikoto*. The name is here rendered in accordance with the import of the Chinese characters with which it is written. Norinaga, however, emits a plausible opinion when he proposes to consider *tama* as an abbreviation

of *tamuke*, "holding in the hands as an offering," in connection with what we are told below about this deity and *Ame-no-ko-ya-ne* holding the symbolic offerings.

[240]We might also, though less well, translate by "Mount Kagu in Heaven." This would suit the view of Norinaga, who is naturally averse to the identification of this Mount Kagu with the well-known mountain of that name in Yamato (see Vol. 1, Note 133). But of course a European scholar cannot allow of such a distinction being drawn.

[241]Or perhaps the bark of the common birch is intended. The word in the original is *haha-ka*.

[242]See Mr. Satow's already quoted note in Vol. 7, Pt. 2, p. 425 *et seq*, and more especially pp. 430–432, of these *Transactions*. [In order to roast the shoulder-blade with.—W.G.A.]

[243]We might also translate in the singular "to a middle branch," in order to conform to the rigid distinction which our language draws between singular and plural.

[244]A note to the edition of 1687 proposes to substitute the characters 八咫 for 八尺, and a note in the original tells us to read them not *ya-ta*, [If the reading *yata* is accepted, I prefer the interpretation "8 spans" *ta=te*, "hand," or perhaps "8 cubits."—W.G.A.] but *ya-ata*. Hereupon Norinaga founds his derivation of *ya-ta* from *ya-atama*, "eight heads," and supposes the mirror to have been, not eight feet in length, but octangular, while Moribe, who in the case of the jewels accepts the obvious interpretation "eight feet [long]," thinks that the mirror had "an eight-fold flowery pattern" (*ya-hana-gata*) round its border. But both these etymologies are unsupported by the other cases in which the word *ya-ta* occurs, and are rendered specially untenable by the fact of the mirror and curved beads being spoken of together further on as the 八尺勾璁鏡 (Vol. 1, Note 577).

[245]In rendering the original word *nigi-te* (here written phonetically, but elsewhere with the characters 禾幣) the explanation given by Tanikawa Kotosuga, and indeed suggested by the characters themselves, has been followed. Norinaga's view does not materially differ, but he considers "pacificatory" or "softening" to be equivalent to "soft" applied to the offerings themselves, which consisted of soft cloth, the syllable *te* of *nigi-te* being believed to be a contraction of *tae* which signifies cloth. The white cloth in ancient times was made of the paper mulberry (*Broussonetia papyrifera*), and the blue of hemp.

[246]The original word is written with the same character as the *te* of *nigi-te*, translated "offerings" above.

[247]Or in the Singular "a grand liturgy," or "ritual."

[248]*Ame-no-ta-jikara-o-no-kami.*

[249]*Ame-no-uzume-no-mikoto.* The translator has followed the best authorities in rendering the obscure syllables *uzu* by the word "alarming." Another interpretation quoted in Tanikawa Kotosuga's *Perpetual Commentary on the Chronicles of Japan* and adopted by Moribe in his *Izu-no-chi-waki* is that *uzu* means head-dress, and that the goddess took her name from the head-dress of spindle-tree leaves which she wore. The character 細, with which the syllables in question (here written

phonetically) are rendered ideographically in the *Chronicles*, signifies "metal head-gear," "flowers of gold or silver."

[250] *Tasuki*, "a cord or sash passed over the shoulders, round the back of the neck, and attached to the wrists, to strengthen the hands for the support of weights, whence the name, which means hand-helper. It was thus different both in form and use from the modern *tasuki*, a cord with its two ends joined which is worn behind the neck, under the arms and round the back, to keep the modern loose sleeves out of the way when household duties are being performed." (E. Satow).

[251] And laying bottom upward a sounding-board.—W.G.A.

[252] The original of these words, *uke fusete*, is written phonetically, and the exact meaning of *uke*, here rendered "sounding-board," is open to doubt. The parallel passage in the *Chronicles* has the character 槽, which signifies a "trough," "manger" or "tub," [Why not a tub, *sans* phrase? —W.G.A.] and the commentators seem therefore right in supposing that the meaning intended to be conveyed in both histories is that of some kind of improvised wooden structure used for the purpose of amplifying sound.

[253] Neither the text nor Norinaga's *Commentary* (which Atsutane adopts word for word) is absolutely explicit, but the imitation and not the reality of divine possession appears to be here intended. In the parallel passage of the *Chronicles*, on the other hand, we seem to be reading of genuine possession.

[254] The subject of the verb is not clear in many of the clauses of this immensely long sentence, which does not properly hang together. Some clauses read as if the different Deities who take a part in the action did so of their own free will; but the intention of the author must have been to let a Causative sense be understood throughout, as he begins by telling us that a plan was *devised* by the deity Thought-Includer, which plan must have influenced all the subsequent details. B.H.C. gives the last part of this sentence in Latin. usque ad privatas partes.

[255] *Shiri-kume-nawa*, *i.e.*, rope made of straw drawn up by the roots, which stick out from the end of the rope. Straw-ropes thus manufactured are still used in certain ceremonies and are called *shime-nawa*, a corruption of the Archaic term. Norinaga's explanation shows that this is more likely to be the proper signification of the word than "back-limiting-rope" (*shiri-he-kagiri-me-nawa*), which had been previously suggested by Mabuchi with reference to its supposed origin at the time of the event narrated in this legend.

[256] Norinaga plausibly conjectures the character 得 in the concluding words of this passage to be a copyist's error for 復, and the translator has accordingly rendered it by the English word "again." As it stands, the clause 自得照明, though making sense, does not read like the composition of a Japanese.

[257] The student should consult Norinaga's elaborate note on this passage in Vol. 9, pp. 1–5 of his *Commentary*. Tables of gifts are mentioned in Sect. 37, Note c and Vol. 1, Note 649.

[258] *Ō-ge-tsu-hime-no-kami*. This personage (but without the title of "Deity") has already appeared in Vol. 1, Note 73 as the alternative personal name of the

Island of Awa.

[259] *Panicum italicum.*

[260] *Phaseolus radiaius.*

[261] Or less probably "wheat." [Is the Japanese *O-mugi* really" barley"? Is it not "bearded wheat"—a different thing?—W.G.A.]

[262] *Glycine soja.*

[263] *Kami-musu-bi-mi-oya-no-mikoto*, the same deity as the one mentioned at the beginning of these *Records* under the shorter title of *Kami-musu-bi-no-kami*. (See Sect. 1, Note d.)

[264] Written with the character 鳥髮, "bird's hair"' but these must surely be phonetic. In the *Chronicles* the same name is written 鳥上.

[265] Or Hii, the chief river in Izumo. The name is supposed by some to have been derived from the name of the god *Hi-haya-bi* (see Vol. 1, Note 143).

[266] Lit. "had placed a young girl between them," a similar construction to that in Vol. 1, Note 149.

[267] The humble character 僕 "servant" is used by the old man for the first personal pronoun.

[268] 国神. Being generally used antithetically to 天神, "Heaven Deity," it seems better to translate the characters thus than by "Country Deity" or "Deity of the Land." (See Vol. 1, Sect. 1, Notes h and 46).

[269] *Ō-yama-tsu-mi-no-kami* first mentioned in Vol. 1, Note 116.

[270] *Ashi-nazu-chi*, the wife's name being *Te-nazu-chi*. "One account" in the *Chronicles* gives *Ashi-nazu-te-nazu* (足摩手摩) as the name of the old father alone, while the mother is called *Inada-no-miya-nushi Susa-no-ya-tsu-mimi*. (*Inada-no-miya-nushi* signifies "Mistress of the Temple of Inada; the signification of the second compound, which forms the name properly so called is not clear, but should probably be interpreted to mean "Impetuous-Eight-Ears," the word *susa*, "impetuous," containing an allusion to the name of her divine visitor, and "eight ears" being honorific.)

[271] *Kushi-[I]nada-hime*, Inada (*i.e.*, *ina-da*, "rice-field") being the name of a place. *Kushi* signifies not only "wondrous" but "comb," and is indeed here written with the character for "comb" 櫛, so that there is a play on the word in connection with the incident of her transformation into a comb which is mentioned immediately below, though most authorities agree in considering 櫛 to be here used phonetically for 奇, which is the reading in the *Chronicles*. Moribe, however, in his *Izu-no-chi-waki* suggests the etymology *Kushi-itadaki-hime* (櫛頂姫) *i.e.*, "Princess [used as] a comb [for] the head."

[272] Derivation quite obscure. Norinaga quotes an absurd etymology given in the *Japanese Words Classified and Explained*, which identifies the name of *Koshi* with the past tense of the verb *kuru*," to come"! There is a district (*kōri*) named Koshi in the modern province of Echigo; but Koshi was down to historical times a somewhat vague designation of all the north-western provinces— Echizen, Kaga, Noto, Etchū, and Echigo. A tradition preserved in the *Chronicles* tells us that it

was meant to denote the Island of Ezo (or rather, perhaps, the land of the Ezo, *i.e.*, the Ainu). The expression in the first Song in Sect. 24, and other similar ones in the early literature show that it was not looked upon as a part of Japan proper.

[273] See Note 13.

[274] For the word "reverence" here and a few lines further on, cf. Vol. 1, Note 154.

[275] In Japanese *sake*, and archaically *ki*, written with the character and generally translated "rice-beer," but by Dr. Rein "rice-brandy" (*Reis-brannt-wein*). The modern *sake* resembles the Chinese *huang jiu* (酒). If we translated it by "rice-beer," we should of course have to render by "to brew" the verb *kamu* or *kamosu* (顧) here rendered "to distill." [*Kamu* is surely "brew," not "distill." The process seems to be to add to the malt first water, next fresh malt to the result of this operation, and so on for eight times, the liquor thus gaining in strength every time. A still is too complicated an apparatus for these primitive times, nor have I seen one in a Japanese brewery. —W.G.A.] It should be mentioned that Professor Atkinson who, like Dr. Rein, has studied the subject specially, uses the word "brewing;" but apparently no English term exactly represents the process which the liquor undergoes in the course of preparation. A curious question is suggested by the fact that the old Japanese word for "distilling" or "brewing" liquor is homonymous with the verb "to chew." But there is not, beyond this isolated verbal resemblance, any documentary evidence in favor of the Japanese ever having practiced a method of making liquor which still obtains in some of the South Sea Islands.—"One account" of the *Chronicles of Japan* makes *Susa-no-o* say "Take *all the fruits*, and distill liquor."

[276] The author doubtless intended, as Norinaga suggests, to speak only of eight platforms, [*Azaki*, the modern *sajiki* in a theatre.—W.G.A.]—one at each gate—and not of sixty-four. But what he actually says is as in the translation.

[277] A conjecture of Norinaga.—W.G A.

[278] See Vol. 1, Note 138.

[279] The text is not quite clear, but the above gives the interpretation to which the words most naturally lend themselves. Norinaga, influenced by the parallel passage in the *Chronicles*, which says explicitly that the sword itself was sent up to the Sun-Goddess, reads the passage thus: "thinking it a strange thing, he sent it up with a message to the Heaven-Shining-Great-August-Deity"; and Mr. Satow follows him in thus translating (see Note 4 to Ritual 8, Vol. 9, Pt. 2, pp. 198–200 of these *Transactions*, where the whole of this legend is translated with one or two slight verbal differences from the version here given). In the opinion of the present writer, [I agree.—W.G.A.] Atsutane's arguments in favor of the view here taken are conclusive (see his *Sources of the Ancient Histories*, Section 72, in the second part of Vol. 3. pp. 66–67). That the sword afterwards appears at the temple of the Sun-Goddess in Ise (see end of Section 82), by the high-priestess of which it is bestowed on the legendary hero Yamato-take, is not to the point in this connection, as it is not necessary that all the parts of a myth should be perfectly consistent.

[280] *Kusa-nagi no tachi*. For the applicability of this name see Sect. 83.

[281] The real derivation of Suga is unknown, all the native commentators accept-

ing the statement in the text, and Norinaga supposing that up to the time of the Deity's arrival it had borne the name of Inada. We may perhaps conjecture some connection between *Suga* and *Susa-no-o* ("Impetuous Male," see Norinaga's Commentary, Vol. 9, p. 49), and it may be mentioned that the "Eight-Eared Deity of Suga" is also mentioned as the "Eight-Eared Deity of Susa."

282Or "began to build."

283"Ode" is another rendering of the Japanese term *uta*, which has been used by the present writer and by others. *Uta* being however connected with *utau*, "to sing," it seems more consistent to translate it by the English word "song."

284Or perhaps rather "in that song he said."

285This difficult song has been rather differently rendered by Mr. Aston in the Second Appendix to his *Grammar of the Japanese Written Language* (2nd Edition), and again by Mr. Satow in the note to his translation of the *Ritual* already quoted. Mr. Aston (premising that he follows Norinaga's interpretation) translates it thus:

Many clouds arise:
The clouds which come forth (are) a manifold fence:
For the husband and wife to retire within
They have formed a manifold fence:
Oh! that manifold fence!
Mr. Satow's translation is as follows:
Many clouds arise.
The manifold fence of the forth-issuing clouds
Makes a manifold fence
For the spouses to be within.
Oh! that manifold fence.

[The regularity of this poem as to meter is suspicious; most of the ancient poetry departs from the 5, 7, 5, 7, 7 rule. The punning, too, suggests a late origin. I suggest that Izumo as the name of a place means awful or sacred quarter.—W.G.A.]

In any case the meaning simply is that the multitudinous clouds rose up like a fence or screen behind which the newly-married Deities might retire from public gaze, and Moribe suggests that the repetitions are an after-addition made to bring up to the usual number of thirty-one syllables what were originally but the three lines

Tachi-izuru kumo mo
Tsuma-gome ni
Ya-e-gaki tsukuru yo!
I.e.—
The uprising clouds even, to shut up the
spouses, make an eight-fold fence.

(See his discussion on this song in the *Izu no Kotowaki*, Vol. 1, pp. 1–3)–The present writer has already stated in the Introduction (see p. 67), his reasons for always rendering the native word for "eight "(*ya*) by "eight," instead of by "many" or "numerous," as is done by the two eminent scholars above quoted. With regard to the word *izumo* [While I adhere to the translation given by me, there is no doubt a punning allusion to the name of the province Izumo which is lost in my translation. (A later suggestion: Why not take *Izumo* as the same as *izure mo,* "each," a pun being of course meant?) —W.G.A.*]* which they, in deference to the opinions of the native commentators, render by "clouds which come forth" or "forth-issuing clouds" (the Chinese characters 出雲 with which the word is written having that signification), the present writer cannot persuade himself that such a corruption as *izumo* for *ide-kumo* either retained at the time of the composition of the song, or should now be credited with, the signification which this its supposed etymology assigns to it. The etymology moreover is far from being established, and in this, as in many other cases, the Chinese characters used to write the name of the province of Izumo may well have rested on nothing more than a vague similarity of sound, and probably no European scholar would endorse the opinion of the native commentators, to whom the *Records* are a sacred book, that the province of Izumo received its name from this very poem. On the other hand, we need have no difficulty in conceding that the Pillow-Word *ya-kumo-tatsu,* by which Izumo is preceded in poetical compositions, did probably here originate.–This song is in the *Chronicles* only quoted in a note, for which reason some authorities dispute its antiquity. In the note in question, we find the reading *-gome* (the *Records* have *-gomi*), *i.e.*, the transitive form instead of the intransitive. If this were adopted, the translation would have to run thus:......"The eight-fold "fence of Izumo makes an eight-fold fence to shut up the spouse[s?] in;" and probably "spouse" should be understood in the feminine to mean "wife."

[286] *Obito,* written with the Chinese character 首, while the Japanese word is probably derived from *ō-bito,* great man." When used, as it often is, as a "gentile name," the translator renders it by "Grandee."

[287] *Inada-no-miya-nushi Suga-no ya tsu mimi no-kami.* It should be stated that Norinaga, as usual, objects to the view that *mimi* signifies "ears" (its proper meaning) in this name. But he has no better explanation to offer, and the Chinese characters give us *ya-tsu mimi,* "eight ears." The author of the *Tokiwa-gusa* ingeniously proposes to consider *ya-tsu mimi* as a corruption of *yatsuko mi mi* (奴御身) "servant august body," but this cannot be seriously entertained (Cf. Vol. 1, Note 224).

[288] *Ya-shima-ji-nu-mi. Ya-shima* means "eight islands." The syllables *ji-nu-mi* are obscure, but the translator has little doubt that "ruler" fairly represents their import. Norinaga takes *ji* to be an apocopated and *nigoried* form of *shiru,* "to rule," *nu* to be an apocopated form of *nushi,* "master," and *mi* to be an apocopated form of the "honorific termination *mimi.*" Tanikawa Kotosuga considers *jinu* to stand for *shizumuru,* "to govern," which comes to the same thing so far as the sense is concerned. B.H.C. gives this sentence in Latin: Quare. quum incepit in thalamo [opus procreationis] cum Mirâ-Iierâ-Inadâ, procreavit Deum nomine Eight-Island Ruler.

[289] *Kamu-ō-ichi-hime.* The rendering of *Ō-ichi* as "Great Majesty" rests on a plausible conjecture of Atsutane's, who proposes to identify *ichi* with *izu* (稜威). Norinaga thinks that *Ō-ichi* should be taken as the name of a place; but this

seems less good.

[290] *Ō-toshi-no-kami,* written 大年神, the obvious rendering of which would be "great year." But the Japanese term *toshi* is believed to have originally signified, not "year" in the abstract, but that which was produced each year, viz., the harvest (cf. *toru,* "to take").

[291] *Uka-no-mi-tama.*

[292] *Ko-no-hana-chiru-hime,* so called, says Norinaga, because she probably died young, as a blossom that falls from the tree. We might however perhaps take the Verb *chiru* in a Causative sense, and consider the name to signify "the Princess-Who-Causes-the-Flowers-of-the-Trees-to-Fall." A sister of this goddess appears in the pretty legend narrated in Sect. 37 under the parallel name of the Princess-Blossoming-Brilliantly-Like-the-Flowers-of-the-Trees. See Vol. 1, Note 328.

[293] *Fuwa-no-moji-ku-nu-su-nu-no-kami.* The import of this name is quite uncertain. *Fuwa* however seems to be the name of a place.

[294] *Hi-kawa-hime. Hi-kawa* (lit. "sun-river") is supposed to stand for the name of a place in Musashi, which is however written "ice-river" (水河 and not 日河) the old Japanese words for "ice" and "sun" being homonymous.

[295] See Vol. 1, Note 146, where the name is given as *Kura-okami.*

[296] *Fuka-buchi-no-mizu-yare-hana.* If Fuka-buchi were ascertained to be not, as is supposed, the name of a place, we should have to render it "deep pool," and the whole would mean in English "Water-Spoilt-Blossom-of-the-Deep-Pool."

[297] *Ame-no-tsudoe-chi-ne-no-kami.* In this name nothing is clear but the first three syllables, which signify "heavenly." But if Mabuchi's conjecture as to the meaning of the rest were accepted, we should have to translate the whole by "Heavenly-Assembling-Town-Lady,"

[298] This is the meaning plausibly assigned by Norinaga to the original O-mizu-nu-no-kami.

[299] *Fute-mimi-no-kami,* plausibly conjectured by Tominobu to stand for *Futo-mimi,* etc., which gives the sense here adopted.

[300] *Funu-zu-nu-no-kami.* Norinaga believes Funu to be the name of a place, and interprets the name to signify "Master of Funu." But this seems highly uncertain.

[301] *Ame-no-fuyu-kinu-no-kami* (Norinaga's reading) or *Ama-no,* etc. (Atsutane's reading). The translation of the name follows Atsutane's explanation, which is based on Norinaga's, and according to which the characters 冬衣 ("winter garments") in this text, and 寄根 read *Fuki-ne* in the *Chronicles,* are merely phonetic, while the meaning is derived from a comparison of the sounds given by each. Though himself believing in the soundness of Atsutane's conclusion, the translator must admit that it is not indisputable.

[302] *Sasu-kuni-waka-hime,* or *Sashi-kuni,* etc. The former reading, which Atsutane adopts, seems best. The meaning of *sasu,* here rendered "small," is open to doubt.

[303] *Sasu-kuni-ō-[no-]kami,* or *Sashi,* etc. The syllable *no* in the Japanese reading seems to be a superfluous addition of the modern commentators.

[304] *Ō-na-muji-no-kami,* to which Tominobu proposes to give the sense of "Great

Hole-Possessor," in connection with the story of the mouse-hole in which he took refuge from the fire lit by the Impetuous-Male-Deity (*Susa-no-o*) for his destruction (see Sect. 23). But the interpretation followed in the translation is the most likely as well as the orthodox one, this Deity being entitled the possessor of a Great Name or of Great Names on account of his renown in Japanese mythic story.

[305] *Ashi-hara-shiko-o-no-kami.* The "reed-plains" are doubtless put by metonymy for Japan.

[306] *Ya-chi-hoko-no-kami.*

[307] *Utsushi-kuni-tama-no-kami.* The name must be understood to mean "Spirit of the Land of the Living," and to be antithetical to that of one of his fathers-in-law, the Impetuous Male-Deity (*Susa-no-o*) who became the god of Hades.

[308] Or "he had five names."

[309] *Yakami-hime.* The etymology is uncertain.

[310] The name of a province not far from that of Izumo. The word may possibly, as Norinaga suggests, be derived from *ina-ba,* "rice-leaves."

[311] *Keta-no-saki.* The etymology of the name seems uncertain. The meaning of the word *keta* is "the cross-beams of a roof, the yards of a sail." But perhaps *Keta* and *keta* may be nothing more than homonyms of independent origin.

[312] Spur?—W.G.A.

[313] Not far from the coast of Izumo and of Inaba.

[314] See Translator's Introduction, p. 41, Note 46.

[315] Norinaga and Moribe agree in considering that the word "white" means "bare" in this place, and the latter in his *Critique* of the former's *Commentary* quotes examples which show that their view is probably correct.

[316] Etymology unknown.

[317] The text is here concise to obscurity, but yet there ought not to be much doubt as to the author's intention.

[318] The text has the character signifying properly "grandparent," but frequently used in Archaic Japanese writings in the sense of "mother." It is then read *oya,* which the English word "parent" exactly represents.

[319] *Kisa-gai-hime.* The *kisa-gai* here mentioned is the modern *aka-gai,* a cockle, the *Area inflata.*

[320] *Umugi-hime.* The *umugi* here mentioned is the modern *hama-guri,* a clam of the family *Mactridoe,* the *Cytherea meretrix.*

[321] Or "nurse's." The meaning is that a paste like milk was made of the triturated and calcined shell mixed with water. There is in this passage a play upon words which it is impossible to reproduce in English, the Japanese term for "triturating," *kisage* (which the author has taken care to write phonetically) resembling the name of Princess Kisa-gai, (Cockle-Shell), while *omo,* "mother" or "nurse," similarly recalls that of Princess Umugi (Clam). Norinaga traces the names of the shellfish in question to this exploit of the two goddesses. We shall be justified in applying an inverse interpretation to the legend.

[322] The original of this clause, 茄矢打立其木, or according to another reading 茄

矢, etc. is a great crux to the native commentators, who can make sure neither of the exact sense nor of the Japanese reading of the first two characters, which seem to be ideographic for three others occurring immediately below, 冰目矢, which are themselves of doubtful import. An elaborate discussion of the question will be found in Atsutane's *Exposition of the Ancient Histories*, Vol. 27. pp. 25–27. The general sense at all events is that here given.

[323]The characters 拷殺也, here rendered "tortured him to death" are by the modern commentators read *uchi-koroshiki,* which simply means "killed [him]."

[324]Lit. "to her child."

[325]*Ō-ya-biko-no-kami.* This Deity is identified with the Deity *I-dakeru* mentioned in the *Chronicles* as a son of *Susa-no-o* (the "Impetuous-Male Deity"), and as the introducer into the Island of Tsukushi in particular and into all the "Eight Great Islands" of Japan of the seeds of plants and trees. Norinaga's note on this name in Vol. 10, pp. 28–29, is worth consulting, though his idea of connecting the agricultural and arboricultural renown of the Deity bearing it with the name of the province of Ki [Wakayama Prefecture] is doubtless quite fanciful.

[326]Later the character 木 was replaced by 紀, which in Sinico-Japanese has the same sound *ki*, while a second one, 伊, was added in order to conform to an edict of the Empress Gen-mei (713 CE) to the effect that all names of places were to be written with two Chinese characters, as was usual in China and Korea. The second character in this case simply carried on the *i* sound with which the first ends, so that the name became *Kii.*

[327]Lit., "to the child." The words placed in brackets, and which are not to be found in either of the early printed editions, are supplied in accordance with a suggestion of Moribe's contained in his *Critique* of Norinaga's *Commentary*. Norinaga himself had supplied the words "Her Augustness his august parent spoke to him," which seem less appropriate. It is true that one MS. is quoted by Norinaga as favoring his view; but such authority is insufficient, and the mistake, moreover, peculiarly easy for a copyist to make (*mi oya* for *ō-ya*).

[328]This is Norinaga's view of the import of the original name *Suseri-bime*, which he connects with *susumu*, "to advance," "to press forward," and explains by reference to the bold, forward conduct of the young goddess. [The name may also be related to the "Impetuous" or "Raging" *susa* used in the name *Susa-no-o*, her father.—M.F.]

[329]One of the alternative names of this Deity, who is mostly mentioned by one of his other four designations, for a list of which see Vol. 1, Sect. 20, Notes a, b, 342, 343, 344, and 345.

[330]The word *hachi,* translated "wasp," is a general name including other insects of the family of *Vespidae.*

[331]The original expression is *nari-kabura* (鳴鏑), which has survived in the modern language under the modified form of *kabura-ya,* defined in Dr. Hepburn's Dictionary as "an arrow with a head shaped like turnip, having a hole in it, which causes it to hum as it flies." It was used in China in the time of the Han dynasty.

[332]The translator cannot think of any better English equivalents for the child-

like onomatopoeias *hora-hora* and *subu-subu* of the Japanese original.

[333]The edition of 1687 reads the two characters 喪具 (here translated "mourning implements,") *mo-gari no sonae, i.e.*, "preparations for the funeral." Such preparations are detailed in the latter part of Sect. 31.

[334]This is Mabuchi's interpretation, as quoted by Norinaga, of the expression *ya-ta-ma no ō-muro-ya*. Norinaga's own view it that *ya-ta* stands for *ya-tsu*, which would give us in English "an eight-spaced large room." The character 間, "space" has been in later times used as a measure of length (six Japanese feet). Altogether the precise meaning of the expression is not quite clear, but the general sense is a "large spacious room."

[335]*Iku-yumi-ya* (生弓矢).

[336]*Ame no nori-goto* (天詔琴), so called because, as will be seen in Sect. 96, divine messages were conveyed through a person playing on the lute. Atsutane, in his *Exposition of the Ancient Histories*, invents the reading *ame no nu-goto* (天詔琴), "heavenly jeweled lute."

[337]They were not born of the same mother. The Chinese characters in the text (庶兄弟) imply, properly speaking, that the eighty brethren of the Great-Name-Possessor were the sons of concubines. But Norinaga denies that such is the Japanese usage with regard to the characters in question.

[338]The word in the next is *ore*, an insulting equivalent second personal pronoun. If we were translating into German, we might perhaps approximately represent its force by "*er*."

[339]*Uka-no-yama*. No satisfactory etymology of Uka is forthcoming.

[340]*Q.d.*, to Inaba.

[341]The words *Kuni tsukuri* (作国), here used for "making the land," became a title for "Ruler-of-the-Land" and finally a "gentile name" (*kabane*).

[342]B.H.C. gives this sentence in Latin: Quamobrem Hera Yakami, secundum anterius pactum, [cum eo] in thalamo coivit.

[343]*Ki-no-mata-no-kami*.

[344]*Mi-i-no-kami*. He is supposed to have benefitted the country by digging wells in many places.

[345]The characters 幸行 here, in accordance with the reading of the commentators, rendered by the words "went forth," are Honorific, being only properly applied to the progresses of a sovereign.

[346]*Nuna-kawa-hime*. *Nuna-kawa* or, *Nu-na-kawa* ("lagoon-river") is supposed to be the name of a place in the province of Echigo [Niigata Prefecture.—M.F.].

[347]The drift of this poem needs but little elucidation:—After giving his reasons for coming to woo the Princess of Nuna-kawa, the god declares that he is in such haste to penetrate to her chamber, that he does not even stay to ungird his sword or take off his veil, but tries to push or pull open the door at once. During these vain endeavors, the mountain-side begins to re-echo with the cries of the birds announcing the dawn, when lovers must slink away. Would that he could kill these unwelcome harbingers of day, and bring back the darkness! —The Land of

the Eight Islands (i.e., Japan proper, beyond whose boundaries lay the barbarous northern country of Koshi) is in the original Ya-shima-kuni (Cf. Vol. 1, Note 92).— The *nue* is a bird which must be fabulous if most of the accounts given of it are accepted. The *Commentary on the Lyric Dramas* tells us (with variations) that "it has the head of a monkey, the body of a racoon-faced dog [tanuki—M.F.], the tail of a serpent, and the hands (sic) and feet of a tiger," adding, as the reader will make no difficulty in allowing, that "it is a strange and peculiar creature." The *Wa-Kun Shiori* says that "it is a bird much larger than a pigeon, and having a loud and mournful cry." It is likewise said to come out at nighttime and retire during the day, for which reason doubtless Mabuchi likens it to the owl. A very ancient and curious Chinese book entitled the *Mountain and Sea Classic* (山海経), the modern editions of which contain extremely droll illustrations of fabulous creatures, tells us of a bird called the white *nue* (白鵺), which is "like a pheasant, with markings on its head, white wings, and yellow feet, and whose flesh is a certain cure for the hiccough." The characters 鵼and 鵺 with which, as well as with 鵺, the word *nue* is variously written, seem to be unauthorized.—The line here (following Norinaga and Moribe's view) rendered "Would that I could beat them till they were sick!" will also bear the interpretation formerly proposed by Keichū, "Would that I could beat them till they left off!"— The last five lines, here rendered "Oh! swiftly-flying heaven-racing messenger," etc., are extremely obscure. It is possible that *ishi tafu ya* (rendered "Oh! swiftly flying," in deference to Norinaga's and Moribe's view) may be but a meaningless refrain. [*i shitau ya* is the emphatic particle *i*, the verb *shitau* meaning "pursuit" (and by association, "longing," in modern Japanese), and the exclamatory particle *ya*. The phrase modifies the name of the deity, who "follows" him.—M.F.] "Heaven-racing messenger" is tolerably certain. Of the rest it is not easy to make sense. Norinaga proposes to credit the five lines in question with the following general meaning: "May this song like a messenger, run down to future ages, preserving for them the tradition of this event!" Moribe, in his *Critique* of Norinaga's *Commentary*, supposes the lines in question to be an addition made by the official singers, who in later times sang these songs as an accompaniment to dances. Whatever their origin and proper signification, it is plain that they had come to be used as a refrain, from which the first two lines were sometimes omitted, as we see in some of the songs further on.

[348]The drift of the poem is this: "Being a tender maiden, my heart flutters like the birds on the sandy islets by the beach, and I cannot yet be thine. Yet do not die of despair; for I will soon comply with their desires."—The word *nue-kusa* (here rendered "drooping plant," in accordance with the views of the commentators) is a Pillow-Word of somewhat obscure derivation.—The word *chidori* (rendered "dotterel" throughout this translation) denotes in its modern acceptation, according to Messrs. Blakiston and Pryer, "any kind of sandpiper, plover, or dotterel." Its proper and original signification is, however, greatly debated by the commentators, and some think that it is not the specific name of any kind of bird, but stands simply by apocope for *tachi-dori*, "rising bird," thus designating any kind of small bird

that rises and flies along near the beach.—The word *na-dori* (here, in accordance with Moribe's view, rendered "gentle bird") is taken by Norinaga to mean simply "gentle," "compliant." But both the construction and the context seem to impose on us the interpretation here given. Keichū, in his *Ko-gan Sho* interprets the whole passage differently; but in order to do so he, without sufficient authority, changes the readings of the text into *wa tori*, "my bird," and *na tori*, "thy bird."—The *refrain* is the same as in the previous song.

[349]There is no break in the text; but the commentators rightly consider the following to be a separate poem. [In keeping with the numbering used in the *Shinpen Nihon koten bungaku zenshū* edition of *Kojiki*, these will be considered one poem for the purposes of numbering.—M.F.]

[350]The import of this very plain-spoken poem needs no elucidation.—*Nubatama* (here rendered "true jewels of the moor") is the Pillow-Word for things black or related to darkness. The "true jewels of the moor" are supposed to be the jet-black berries of the *hiafugi* (pron. *hiōgi. Ixia chinensis*). The whole etymology is, however, not absolutely certain.—Of which of the two lovers the words "coming radiant" with "smiles" are spoken, is not clear; but they probably refer to the male deity, as do the white arms, strange though such an expression may appear as applied to a man. The goddess represents herself and her lover as using each other's arms for pillows. The word "jewel-arms" means simply "beautiful arms."

[351]B.H.C. gives this sentence in Latin. Quamobrem eâ nocte non coierunt, sed sequentis diei nocte auguste coierunt.

[352]The meaning of this poem is:—"I start for Yamato, there to search for a better wife, and I carefully array myself for the journey. Black, the color of mourning—is not fair enough—and red is more beautiful than green; so it is on my red garments that my choice rests. And thou, jealous and imperious woman! for all that thou sayest that thou wilt not heed my going, thou wilt weep when I depart with my retainers as departs a flock of birds, and thou wilt bury thy head in thy hands, and thy tears shall be as the misty drops of the morning shower." The words *hata tagi* (rendered in accordance with Norinaga's view by "raise my fins") are supposed to signify "raise my sleeve." If the last syllable were found in any text written with a character not requiring the use of the *nigori* in the Japanese transcription, we should get the more satisfactory reading *ha tataki*, i.e., "beat my wings;" but the syllable in question does not seem to be anywhere so written.—The "madder" is in the original *akane*, here written (but doubtless only through the error of some copyist) *atane*. The words rendered "sought in the mountain fields" might also be translated "sown in the mountain fields," *magishi*, "sought," and *makishi*, "sowed" being thought to be convertible.—The words "my beloved" represent the Japanese *itokoya no*, whose meaning is obscure and much disputed.—The words "when I am led away" must be understood as if they were active instead of passive, signifying as they do "when I lead away my retinue of followers."—The eulalia (*Eulalia japonica*) is a long kind of grass very often alluded to in the later classical poetry. The words "on the mountain" represent the Japanese words *yama-to no*, in accordance with

Norinaga's and Atsutane's view of the meaning of the latter (山處 or 山本). The *prima facie* interpretation of "in the province of Yamato," which Keichū adopts, will not bear investigation.—It is not quite clear whether "the mist of the morning shower" means mist separate from the rain, or is simply a phrase for the rain-drops themselves. Norinaga adopts the former opinion.—"Young herbs," *waka-kusa*, is the Pillow-Word for "spouse,"—newly married youths and maidens being likened to the fresh-grown grass. The refrain is an abbreviated form of that found in the two previous poems.

[353]The import of this poem needs little explanation: —The goddess says to her husband, "Come back and live with me, and quaff this goblet as a sign of reconciliation; for though thou, as a man, mayest have a wife on every shore, I shall be left solitary if thou depart." The "ornamented fence" is supposed to mean "a curtain round the sleeping place."—The latter part of the poem (excepting the concluding phrase) is a repetition of lines that have already occurred in the last ode of Vol. 1, Note 388. The word *tate-matsurase* (here rendered "lift up") occasions some difficulty. It properly signifies "present to a superior;" but here it must be taken to mean "partake of," as the goddess is speaking to her spouse himself, unless indeed we suppose the final words of the song to be a command addressed to one of her attendants to present the cup to their common lord and master.

[354]This is the probable and generally accepted meaning of the original of this clause, which is written phonetically.

[355]Explained by Moribe to mean, with reference to the whole story, "conversation about divine events." Norinaga proposes to supplement the character 歌, "song," to the two (神語) in the text, and to take the three together as designating the nature of the preceding songs, in accordance with the usage in other cases—"Rustic Songs," "Courtiers' Songs," etc. If this view were adopted, we should have to translate by "Divine Converse Songs."

[356]See Vol. 1, Note 150 and Vol. 1, Note 229.

[357]*Aji-shiki-taka-hiko-ne-no-kami*. The meaning of the first two members of this compound name is altogether obscure: *Taka-hiko-ne*, signifies "high-prince lord."

[358]*Taka-hime-no-mikoto*. *Taka-hime* is supposed by Atsutane to be a mutilated form of *Taka-teru-hime*, "High-shining-Princess," which would make the two names of this personage properly complementary.

[359]*Shita-teru-hime-no-mikoto*. This goddess is popularly supposed to have been extremely beautiful, whence perhaps the name, which might be taken to imply that her beauty shone forth from under her garments as in the case of *So-tōri-hime* (see Vol. 3, Note 177).

[360]Because there worshiped. The etymology of Kamo is not clear.

[361]*Kamu-ya-tate-hime-no-mikoto*. The translation here follows the Chinese characters. Another proposal of Norinaga's is to regard the syllables *ya-tate* as a corruption of *iya-taka-teri*, "more and more high shining," which would give us for the whole name in English "Divine-More-and-More-High-Shining-Princess."

[362]The translation of the name here given follows Norinaga's interpretation,

which takes it to contain an allusion to the act by which its bearer symbolized his surrender of the sovereignty of the land to the descendant of the Sun-Goddess. Lengthened forms of the name are *Ya-e-koto-shiro-nushi-no-kami* ("the Deity Eight-Fold-Thing-Sign-Master") and *Tsumi-ba-ya-e-koto-shiro-nushi-no-kami,* the first three syllables of which latter are obscure. Both of the lengthened forms are supposed to contain a reference to the manifold "green branches" mentioned in the legend referred to—that, viz., which forms the subject-matter of Sect. 32.

[363]*Tori-mimi-no-kami.* Norinaga suggests that *tori,* "bird," may be but the name of a place in Yamato.

[364]*Ya-shima-muji-no-kami.* "Possessor" is the probable meaning of *muji,* regarded here and elsewhere as an alternative from of *mochi.* Norinaga suggests that Yashima may be meant for the name of a district in Yamato, in which case both this god and his daughter would have been named from the places of their birth or residence, which are near each other in the same province.

[365]*Tori-naru-mi-no-kami.* The above interpretation, which is proposed by Norinaga, seems more acceptable than "Bird-Sounding-Sea," which the Chinese characters yield. *Tori,* "bird," if taken above to be the name of a place, must be likewise so considered here.–Norinaga reasonably conjectures that a clause to the following effect is here omitted: "He wedded such and such a princess, daughter of such and such a Deity, and begot a child: the Deity *Take-mi-na-gata*" [*i.e.*, probably Brave-August-Name-Firm] (See Sect. 32, Note 21). Atsutane's text, in his *Exposition of the Ancient Histories,*" is 娶高志之沼河比売命而令生給之子謂御穂須美命亦名健御名方神. [He married *Taka-shi-no-nuna-kawa-hime*, who gave birth to a child named *Mi-ho-su-mi-no-mikoto*, also called *Take-mi-na-kata-no-kami.*—M.F.]

[366]The text is here evidently corrupt, and Norinaga proposes to read either *Hina-teri-nukata-bichi-o-no-kami no musume Iko-chini-no-kami,* which would give us in English "the Deity Ikochini, daughter of the male Deity Hina-teri-nukata-bichi," or else to take the whole as the father's name, and to suppose that the name of the daughter has been accidentally omitted. *Hina-teri* means "Rustic Illuminator," and the name resembles that of a deity mentioned in Vol. 1, Note 233. *Nukata* and *Bichi* (or *Hiji,* reversing the position of the *nigori)* are supposed to be names of places. *Ikochini* is altogether obscure.

[367]*Kuni-oshi-tomi-no-kami*, *oshi*, as in other instances, being considered a contraction of *ōshi,* "great."

[368]*Ashi-nadaka-no-kami*. It is not clear whether this is a personal name or, as Norinaga supposes, the name of the place where the goddess resided. He quotes places named Ashidaka and Ashida; but this hardly seems satisfactory. In any case the name remains obscure.

[369]*Ya-kawa-e-hime.* The translation follows the meaning of the Chinese characters with which the name is written. It is, however, also open to us to consider *Yaka-wa-e* as a corruption of *iya-ko-hae,* "more and more flourishing."

[370]*Haya-mika-no-take-sahaya-ji-mi-mi-no-kami.* The syllables *sahaya* are obscure, and Norinaga's proposal to consider them as the name of a place has only

been followed in the translation for want of something more satisfactory.

[371] *Saki-tama-bime.*

[372] *Ame-no-mika-nushi-no-kami.*

[373] *Mika-nushi-hiko-no-kami.*

[374] *Hina-rashi-bime.* Norinaga takes Hina to be the name of a place, and *rashi* to be an apocopated form of *tarashi* or some such word. But this is mere guesswork.

[375] *Okami-no-kami.* See Vol. 1, Note 146.

[376] *Tahiri-kishi-marumi-no-kami.* The meaning of this name is quite obscure. Norinaga throws out the suggestion that *Tahiri* may stand for *Tari-hiri* and *Ri-shi-marumi* for *Kijima-tsu-mi—Tari-hiri* and *Kijima* being names of places, and *tsu-mi,* as usual, being credited with the signification of "possessor."

[377] *Iku-tama-saki-tama-hime.*

[378] *Hihira-gi-no-sono-hana-madzu-mi-no-kami.* The interpretation of the name here given is conjectural as far as the words "waiting to see" (taken on Tominobu's authority to be the most likely meaning of *mazu-mi)* are concerned. Norinaga suggests that *hihira-gi no* may be but a sort of Pillow-Word, and not part of the actual name at all, and the remaining characters corrupted, *Hihira-gi* rendered "holly," is properly the *Olea Aquifolia.*

[379] *Miro-na-mi-no-kami.* Meaning obscure. *Miro* is supposed by Norinaga to be the name of a place, and *na* and *mi* to be Honorific appellations.

[380] *Ao-numa-no-oshi-hime.* Meaning obscure.

[381] *Shiki-yama-nushi-no-kami. Shiki-yama* is supposed to be the name of a place in Echizen [Fukui Prefecture.—M.F.].

[382] *Nunoshi-tomi-tori-naru-mi-no-kami. Nanoshi* is supposed to be the name of a place, and identical with *Nunoshi,* which forms part of the mother's name. Norinaga takes *tomi* to be an honorific, and *Tori,* as previously in the case of the Deities *Tori-mimi* and *Tori-naru-mi* (See Vol. 1, Notes 401 and 403), to be the name of another place. The translator would prefer to take both words in their common signification, and (leaving *nunoshi* aside as incomprehensible) to render the rest of the name thus: "Wealth-Bird-Growing-Ears."

[383] *Waka-hiru-me-no-kami.*

[384] *Ame-no-hibara-ō-shi-na-domi-no-kami.* Norinaga supposes Hibara to be the name of a place, a view which the translator has adopted for want of a better.

[385] *Tō-tsu-ma-chi-ne-no-kami.* Norinaga supposes Tōtsu to be the name of a place, and the remaining syllables to be honorifics.

[386] See Vol. 1, Note 119.

[387] *Tō-tsu-yama-zaki-tarashi-no-kami. Tō-tsu* (lit. "distant") and *yama-zaki* ("mountain-cape") are both considered by Norinaga to be names of places. *Tarashi* signifies "perfect" or "perfection." We might perhaps render the name thus: "Perfection-of-the-Distant-Mountain-Cape."

[388] *I.e.*, "seventeen generations of Deities." But the construction is curious. Norinaga points out that there is here an error in the computation, as the text enumerates but fifteen generations. The names of the gods and goddesses mentioned

in this section offer unusual difficulties. Norinaga says that it is with hesitation that he proposes many of his interpretations, and it is with still greater hesitation that the translator has accepted them.

[389]Not to be confounded with the better known Miho in Suruga [Shizuoka Prefecture.—M.F.]. The derivation of the name seems uncertain.

[390]The character used is 穂, which properly denotes an ear of rice or other grain.

[391]What plant the author intends by this name is not quite certain. The characters 蘿摩 and 簽 are variously used to write it in the native works of reference, where also we learn that it probably corresponds to the plant known in different provinces of modern Japan as *chichi-gusa, tombo-no-chichi, kagarai* and *gaga-imo*. We may best understand the *Ampelopsis serianacefolia* to have been intended, as the plant is described as having a berry three or four inches long shaped like a towel-gourd (*hechima*), so that, if scooped out, it would fairly resemble a boat in miniature. [*Metaplexis japonica* is a relative of milkweed, with the same boat-shaped seed pods. —M.F.]

[392]All the authorities are agreed in considering the character 鶴, "goose," to be a copyist's error; but there is no agreement as to the character which should be substituted for it. Atsutane reads 鶴, "wren" changing the phonetic. "Wren" also is the reading in "One account" of the *Chronicles*, and Moribe, commenting thereon in his *Izu-no-chi-waki*, thinks that "wren" must have been the bird originally intended by the framers of the tradition. Norinaga, following a suggestion of the editor of 1687, prefers to consider the radical for "bird" to have been put by mistake for the radical for "insect," and reads 蛾 which signifies "moth," especially the "silkworm moth." Norinaga, however, proceeds to give to the character in question the Japanese reading of *hi-mushi* (lit. "fire-insect," i.e. "ephemera"), which is not warranted. The proper Japanese reading is *hihiru*. The best would seem to be to adopt the reading 蛾, "moth." [The only reason is that goose-skin is thought too large for such a very small god whose boat is a gourd. This does not seem sufficient. The "moth" seems purely hypothetical. There is really no necessity to make the moth fit the conveyance. Dean Swift does not do so.—W.G.A.]

[393]The original word is *tani-guku*. Its derivation and the name of the species which it denoted are alike unknown. Indeed we might equally well translate by "frog."

[394]*Kue-biko*. The interpretation of the name here adopted is Norinaga's. Tominobu takes *Kue* to be the name of a place, and the personage in question to have been the inventor of scarecrows, whence the tradition connected with his name.

[395]*Sukuna-biko-na-no-kami*, or without the *nigori*, *Sukuna-hiko-na-no-kami*. The interpretation of the name here followed is that proposed by Norinaga, but not followed by Atsutane and Moribe, who prefer to consider it antithetical to that of *Ō-na-muji*, "the Great-Name-Possessor."

[396]First mentioned in Sect. 1, Note d. Immediately below, his name is given in the lengthened form.

[397]Norinaga (who, strange to say, is followed by Atsutane—cf. Vol. 1, Note 316)

interprets the two characters 白上 (here in accordance with general usage taken to signify "respectfully informed") as "informed and took up," thus making it appear that the diminutive deity was personally taken up to Heaven. Surely a recollection of the parallel passage in the *Chronicles*, which says that "a messenger was sent up to inform the Heavenly Deities," should have preserved the commentators from thus offending against both grammar and common sense.

[398]For an explanation of this expression see Vol. 1, Sect. 23, Notes c and 379.

[399]*Toko-yo-no-kuni* (常世国). Some kind of Paradise or Hades is meant, as is proved by innumerable references in the early literature of Japan: and we may suppose the idea to have been borrowed from the Chinese or through them from Buddhism, and to have been afterwards vaguely located in some distant country. In Sect. 74 we are told of the orange having been brought from the "Eternal Land" by Tajima-mori, who is said to have been of Korean extraction. Korea, which is to the west of Japan, and the Buddhist paradise in the west might well be confounded by tradition, though it is equally open to discussion whether Southern China or even the Ryukyu Islands might not have been thus vaguely designated. In any case it was a distant place, imperfectly known, though specifically named. In the *Chronicles*, Tajima-mori is made to say that it is "the retreat of Gods and Fairies, and not to be reached by common men."—Norinaga's immense note on this word (see Vol. 12, pp. 10–13 of his *Commentary*) is a specimen of the specious arguments by which he endeavors to ward off from the Early Japanese the imputation of ever having borrowed any ideas from their neighbors. He would have us believe that *Toko-yo* is derived from *soko yori*. "thence" (!) and that the name simply denotes foreign countries in general. This is on a par with the opinion emitted by Arai Hakuseki in his *Koshi Tsū*, to the effect that the "Eternal Land" was simply a place in the province of Hitachi [Ibaraki Prefecture]. The latter good old commentator apparently founded himself on no better reasons than his general rejection of supernatural or otherwise perplexing details, and the fact that one of the characters with which the name of the province in question is written is 常, which also forms part of the name of *Toko-yo-no-kuni*.

[400]Lit. "everything beneath Heaven." "Beneath Heaven,"(天下), *i.e.*, "all that is beneath the Heavens," is a common Chinese phrase for the Chinese Empire, which was in ancient days not unnaturally supposed by its inhabitants to form the whole civilized world. The expression was borrowed by the Japanese to designate their one country. But its use by them had not the same plea of ignorance of other civilized lands, as they were acquainted with China and Korea, and had thence obtained nearly all the arts of life. [This statement puzzles the commentators.—W.G.A.]

[401]In the *Chronicles*, this is given as the designation of the Deity who came over the sea, and Norinaga therefore adopts it as the heading of this Section.

[402]For an explanation of this expression see Vol. 1, Sect. 23, Notes c and 379.

[403]*I.e.*, on Mount Mimoro which stands as a protecting fence in the eastern part of the province of Yamato. *Ao-kaki-yama*, "green fence mountain," became a proper name used alternatively for Mount Mimoro (or, according to the later

pronunciation, Mimuro). In like manner *Himukashi-yama* (in the later language *Higashi-yama*) "eastern mountain," has by some been considered to be a proper name.

[404] *I.e.*, "august house;" so called probably from the temple of the deity.

[405] *Inu-hime.* Norinaga supposes *Inu* to be the name of a place. The word properly signifies "dog."

[406] *Kamu-iku-musu-bi-no-kami.*

[407] *Ō-kuni-mi-tama-no-kami.*

[408] *Kara-no-kami*, 韓神. *Kara* signifies Korea or China, and the Deity thus named appears in the *Chronicles* under the name of *I-so-takeru* ("Fifty-fold-Valiant"), of whom it is related that he was taken over to Korea by his father *Susa-no-o* (the "Impetuous-Male").

[409] *Sohori-no-kami.* The etymology is not clear. Atsutane derives the name from a verb *soru* "to ride," "to go in a boat," in connection with the story (mentioned in the preceding note) of I-so-takeru having been taken over to Korea. According to this view, *Sohori*, like *Kara-no-kami*, would be an alternative name of *I-so-takeru.* But the derivation is hazardous, to say the least.

[410] *Shira-hi-no-kami.* Norinaga supposes *shira hi* (白日) to be a copyist's error for *mukahi* (向日). The latter, however, does not make satisfactory sense, and Tominobu proposes to invert the characters, thus: 日向, which means "sun-confronting." Norinaga suggests that the word may, after all, be but the name of a place.

[411] *Hijiri-no-kami,* written with the characters 聖神. The first of these is defined as signifying him who is intuitively wise and good, *i.e.,* the perfect sage. But perhaps we should in Archaic Japanese take the term *hijiri* in what is its probable native etymological sense, viz. "sun-governing" *(hi-jiri,* 日知), a title properly applied to the Japanese Emperors as descendants of the Sun-Goddess, and of which the character 聖, which is used of the Chinese Monarchs, is only an equivalent in so far as it, too, is employed as an honorific title.

[412] *Kagayo-hime.*

[413] *Ō-kaga-yama-to-omi-no-kami.* The translation follows Atsutane's interpretation, which nearly agrees with that proposed by Mabuchi.

[414] *Mi-toshi-no-kami.* For the meaning of "harvest" attributed to the word *toshi* see Vol. 1, Note 328.

[415] *Ame-shiru-karu-mizu-hime.* The name might tentatively be translated thus: Heaven-Governing-Fresh-Princess-of-Karu. Norinaga suggests that *ame-shiru* may be but a sort of Pillow-Word for the rest of the name. *Ama-tobu* is, however, the only Pillow-Word for Karu found in the poems. After all, Karu may not here be the name of a place at all.

[416] *Oki-tsu-hiko-no-kami.* The translator ventures to think that the names of this deity and the next might simply be rendered (in accordance with the first character, 奥, entering into their composition) "Inner Prince" and "Inner Princess" or "Prince of the Interior" and "Princess of the Interior." Norinaga however suggests that *Okitsu* may be the name of a place, while Atsutane derives the names from *oki-tsuchi,* "laid earth," finding therein a reference to the furnace (made of clay)

mentioned immediately below.

[417] *Oki-tsu-hime-no-mikoto.*

[418] *Ō-be-hime-no-kami.*

[419] *Kama-no-kami* (竈神). The "furnace" means the "kitchen." Neither Norinaga nor Atsutane informs us that the immense popularity of this Goddess, as well as her name, can clearly be traced to China.

[420] *Ō-yama-kui-no-kami.* The meaning of *kui,* here (as in the case of *Tsunu-gui* and *Iku-gui,* see Vol. 1, Sect. 2, Notes e and 49) rendered by the word "integrator," is open to doubt.

[421] *Yama-sue-no-ō-nushi-no-kami.* Norinaga supposes the word *sue,* "end," to have the signification of "top."

[422] As it stands, the etymology of this name is not clear. In later times the mountain was called *Hie* (比叡). But whether the, to outward appearance, native name *Hie* is but a corruption of this Chinese one, or whether it be true that the latter (on this hypothesis bestowed on account of its likeness in sound to the native designation) was not used till the end of the eighth or beginning of the ninth century, as is commonly stated, is difficult to decide.

[423] *I.e,* "Close-Fresh-Sea." *Afumi* (modern pron. *Ōmi,* for *awa-umi*) alone signifies "fresh sea," *i.e.,* "lake." This province contains the large lake commonly known as Lake Biha (Biwa), but anciently simply called "the Fresh Sea," as being the lake *par excellence* of Japan. When one of the eastern provinces received, on account of a large lagoon or inlet which it contains, the name of *Toho-tsu-Afumi* (in modern pronunciation *Tōtōmi), i.e.,* "Distant-Fresh-Sea," the epithet Close was prefixed to the name of the province nearer to the ancient center of government.

[424] *I.e.,* Pine-tree-Declivity.

[425] *I.e.,* Kudzu-Moor.

[426] This passage (用鳴鏑神者也) must be corrupt. Mabuchi proposes to insert the character 祭 before 神, and to understand the author to have meant to tell us that the deity was worshiped with arrows, that is to say, that arrows were offered at his shrine. Norinaga's proposal to consider 用 as an error for 成 or 化, and to interpret the clause thus: "the Deity who was changed into an arrow" is also worthy of notice. But a further suggestion of his to read 丹 for 用 and to interpret thus: "the Deity of the Red Arrow," seems best of all when taken in connection with the tradition, which he quotes from the "Topography of Yamashiro," to the effect that this god took the shape of a red arrow to gain access to his mistress Tama-yori-hime, such a transformation being one of the commonplaces of Japanese myth.

[427] *Niwa-tsu-hi-no-kami.* The interpretation of this name here adopted is not Norinaga's, who takes *hi* in the sense of "wondrous" but Atsutane's. The latter author makes it clear that this deity (for whom *Niwa-taka-tsu-hi-no-kami, i.e.,* "the High-Deity-of-the-Fire-in-the-Yard" is but a slightly amplified designation) was none other than the above-mentioned Deity of the Kitchen, and his name an inclusive one for the pair of Deities *Oki-tsu-hiko* and *Oki-tsu-hime.*

[428] *Asuha-no-kami.* The signification of this name is obscure, and Norinaga's

proposal to derive it from *ashi-niwa*, "foot-place," because the god in question may be supposed to protect the place on which people stand, is not altogether convincing. In fact he himself only advances it with hesitation. It should be added, however, that Atsutane stamps it with his special approval, as he does also Norinaga's derivation of the following name, *Hahigi.*

[429] *Hahigi-no-kami.* Obscure, but ingeniously derived by Norinaga from *hahi-iri-gimi, i.e.*, "entering prince," the deity in question being supposed to have been the special protector of the entrances to houses, and to have thence received his name. Mr. Satow has translated it in the *Rituals* as "Entrance Limit."

[430] *Kaga-yama-to-omi-no-kami.* The name is almost identical with that in note 10.

[431] *Ha-yama-to-no-kami.* The interpretation of the name is that proposed by Norinaga, and which seems tolerably satisfactory.

[432] *Niwa-taka-tsu-hi-no-kami.* See Vol. 1, Note 465.

[433] *Ō-tsuchi-no-kami.*

[434] *Tsuchi-no-mi-oya-no-kami.*

[435] This number is obtained if (as is perhaps permissible from a Japanese point of view) we consider *Oki-tsu-hiko* and *Oki-tsu-hime* as forming a single deity. Otherwise there are ten. A similar remark applies to the number sixteen mentioned immediately below.

[436] See Vol. 1, Note 469.

[437] See Vol. 1, Note 73. The fact that this goddess is related to have been previously killed (see Sect. 17) causes Norinaga some embarrassment.

[438] *Waka-yama-hahi-no-ami.*

[439] *Waka-toshi-no-kami.* Norinaga proposes (considering this name in connection with the four that follow) to take *waka-toshi* in this place in the signification of "the first sprouting" of the young rice. The five Deities whose birth is here mentioned seem collectively to represent the natural succession of agricultural operations throughout the year.

[440] *Waka-sa-na-me-no-kami.*

[441] *Mizu-maki-no-kami.*

[442] *Natsu-taka-tsu-hi-no-kami.* Norinaga's interpretation of *hi* as "wondrous" is perhaps as good as that here adopted, according to which it signifies "sun." His view would give us in English "the Summer-High-Wondrous-Deity."

[443] *Natsu-no-me-no-kami.*

[444] *Aki-bime-no-kani.*

[445] *Kuku-toshi-no-kami.* The word *kuku*, "stem," seems to allude to the length of the well-grown rice.

[446] *Kuku-ki-waka-muro-tsuna-ne-no-kami.* Norinaga supposes this god to have been the protector of houses, and interprets the name to denote the beams, and the ropes with which the beams were bound together. The word here read *tsuna*, "rope," is written with the character, 葛, and might perhaps be rendered "kudzu." But as in early times the tendrils of such creeping plants formed the only substi-

tute for rope, the two renderings come to have very nearly the same signification.

[447]The name is here abbreviated in the original to *Waka-muro-tsuna-ne-no-kami.*

[448]*Toyo-ashi-hara-no-chi-aki-no-naga-i-ho-aki-no-mizu-ho-no-kuni, i.e.,* freely rendered, "ever fruitful Japan with its reed-covered plains and its luxuriant rice-fields."

[449]See Vol. 1, Note 224. Henceforward this tremendous name is mostly abbreviated to *Ame-no-oshi-ho-mimi* (probably signifying "Heavenly-Great-Great-Ears.")

[450]So in the original. The sense, however, is rather "told him to descend from Heaven;" for he did not actually go further than the top of the "Floating Bridge," and never came down to earth.

[451]See Vol. 1, Sect. 3, Notes k and 55.

[452]The words "it is" stand for *ari keri* in the original. Cf. Vol. 1, Note 173.

[453]*Taka-mi-musu-bi-no-kami,* first mentioned at the very commencement of the work. In this legend this god's name is constantly coupled with that of the Sun-Goddess, who alone, up to this point, had appeared as the ruler of Heaven.

[454]See Vol. 1, Note 217.

[455]See Vol. 1, Note 270.

[456]The meaning must be, as Norinaga suggests, that the story was told first, and the Deity Thought-Includer asked for his advice after he had heard it.

[457]Chinese touch—W.G.A.

[458]See Vol. 1, Sect. 2, Notes h and 46.

[459]See Vol. 1, Note 225.

[460]Lit., "long brings back no report."

[461]Lit., "to send again." The same expression occurs below.

[462]*Ame-waka-hiko.* All the commentators agree that it is in order to express disapprobation of this god's wickedness that the title of Deity or Augustness is never coupled with his name.

[463]*Ama-tsu-kuni-tama-no-kami.*

[464]*Ame-no-kako-yumi* and *ame-no-haha-ya.* In Sect. 34 these weapons are mentioned under the slightly altered names of *ame-no-haji-yumi* ("heavenly vegetable wax-tree bow") and *ame-no-kaku-ya* ("heavenly deer-arrows.") A large bow made of vegetable wax-tree *(Rhus succedanea)* wood, and arrows with broad feathers, are supposed to be intended.

[465]*Shita-teru-hime.* See Vol. 1, Note 397.

[466]*Ō-kuni-nushi-no-kami.* See Sect. 20, Note a.

[467]Lit., "long brings back no report."

[468]*Katsura-no-ki,* variously written 桂,楓, 香木, 杜木, and phonetically 加都羅. Though it is not absolutely certain what tree is intended, the weight of authority and of probability is in favor of its being the cassia, which plays a part in Chinese mythology. In modern parlance the *katsura* is a tree whose Latin name is *Cercidiphyllum japonicum.*

[469]*Ama-no-sagu-me.*

[470]This expression, as Norinaga explains, signifies only that, as the arrow was

shot from below straight up at a pheasant perching on a branch overhead, the feathers, which are properly considered to form the top part of the arrow, were naturally underneath.

[471] *Taka-gi-no-kami.* The name is written with the characters 高木神, which, taken ideographically, would give us in English "High-Tree-Deity." But the translator has little doubt but that Norinaga is correct in considering 木 to be here used phonetically, and the syllable (*gi,* which it represents, to be a contraction of *gui* (for *kui),* itself derived from *kumu,* and best rendered by the verb "to integrate."

[472] In Japanese *magare,* lit. "turn aside," "become crooked," *i.e.,* "come to a bad end."

[473] Lit. "high breast-hill."

[474] The sentence placed between brackets is supposed by Norinaga to be an addition to the text made by some copyist who had in his mind the parallel passage of the *Chronicles.* In the *Records of Ancient Matters Revised* the two characters answering to our word "beware" are omitted, and the resulting meaning is: "This was the origin of the practice of sending back arrows," *i.e.,* of shooting an enemy with the arrow he had himself just used.

[475] The import of the proverb seems to be that an embassy should always consist of more than one person. This is Norinaga's view, based on his interpretation of the character 頓 as *hita*, which he identifies with *hito*, "one"; and it agrees well with the story in the text. Atsutane, who, in his *Exposition of the Ancient Histories*, following the version of the legend given in the *Chronicles*, narrates two pheasant embassies—the male bird being sent first and (as it did not return) the female afterwards—takes the character in the proper sense belonging to it in Chinese, and interprets the words of the proverb to mean "the pheasant's hurried embassy."

[476] Some of the commentators believe this bird to be a separate species, and Moribe, who says that he saw one at the estuary near Kuhana in Ise, describes it as "rather slenderer than an ordinary wild goose, with longer legs and a higher back." If we accepted this, the better English translation would be "river wild goose."

[477] The original of this expression (*kisari-mochi*) is very obscure even in the *Chronicles*, by whose ideographic reading the translator has been guided, and being here written phonetically become more conjectural still. The most likely opinion is that it signifies one bearing on his head the food to be offered to the corpse, though if this view be adopted, the office of the mourner in question may seem to resemble too closely that of the kingfisher. The latter has however been supposed to have brought fish, while the goose may have brought rice. Another proposal is that the goose brought the food and the kingfisher cooked it, while the sparrow, as mentioned below, performed the intermediate operation of pounding the rice. (See Norinaga's elaborate note on this word in Vol. 13, pp. 47–48 of his *Commentary*).

[478] Or simply, "the pounder."

[479] The parallel passage of the *Chronicles* tells us that "they wept and wailed and sang for eight nights." [The words "wail and sing" are probably a compound, they are joined by a line in the Japanese. Sang dirges?—W.G.A.]

[480]See paper on early Japanese history p.54. Mourning lasts for some ten days only, during which time the members of the family weep and lament, while their friends come singing, dancing and making music. —W.G.A.

[481]See Vol. 1, Note 395. He was brother to the Heavenly-Young-Prince's wife.

[482]The author of the *Perpetual Commentary on the Chronicles of Japan* tells us that these tears were tears of joy. Doubtless such is the meaning of the text; yet the repetition of the words "bewailing" and "lamenting" is curious.

[483]See Vol. 1, Note 138.

[484]*Mo-yama.* No such mountain is now known.

[485]*Aimi-gawa.* No such river is now known. According to the characters with which it is written the name signifies "Knot-grass-Seeing River."

[486]Afterwards called Mino [Gifu Prefecture.—M.F.]. This province probably received its name, as the author of the *Explanation of Japanese Names* suggests, from *mi nu*, i.e., "three moors," from the large moors of Kagami, Ao, and Seki-ga-hara which it contains. The modern commentators prefer to derive it from *ma na*, "true moor."

[487]*Ō-ha-kari.* The name might also be rendered "Great-Leaf-Mower." The translator has followed Atsutane in omitting the *nigori* from the syllable *ka.*

[488]*Kamu-do-tsurugi.*

[489]The meaning of the Song is: "Oh! this is *Aji-shiki-taka-hiko-ne*, whose refulgence, similar to that of the jewels worn by the Weaving Maiden in Heaven, shines afar across hills and valleys."— The translator does not follow those commentators who emend *ana-dama*, "hole-jewels" to *aka-dama*, "red," *i.e.*, "resplendent jewels," as the frequent reference in this and the other ancient books to the string on which beads were strung, and the presence in ancient tombs, etc. of numbers of such beads with holes drilled through them (they are now known by the name of *kuda-tama, i.e.*, "tube-jewels,") renders such an emendation unnecessary. The "Weaving Maiden in Heaven" is evidently, notwithstanding Norinaga's endeavor to disprove the fact, the Chinese *Zhi nü, a* personification of a Lyrae, to whom there are countless allusions in Chinese literature, and who also became a frequent theme of the later Japanese poets.

[490]Or, "barbarous style." Norinaga endeavors to explain away the various names of styles of Songs found in the early literature by asserting that they are simply derived from the initial words of the Song in question, and that, for instance, in the present case, the title of Rustic Song was bestowed on the poem only because in the *Chronicles* it is coupled with another which lends itself to such an interpretation. Moribe gives his sanction to this view; but, though it is difficult to explain many of the titles on any other theory, the translator thinks that it cannot be accepted as generally satisfactory in the face of the numerous cases which contradict it, and of which its supporters can give no satisfactory explanation. The whole subject of the titles, of the manner of singing, etc., of the ancient poems is indeed involved in obscurity.

[491]Lit., "to send again."

[492] *Itsu-no-o-ha-bari no kami.* We have already seen (Vol. 1, Note 150) this name (*minus* the title of Deity) as the appellation of the sword with which Izanagi ("the Male-Who-Invites") decapitated his son Kagu-tsu-chi ("Shining Elder") for having by his birth caused the death of Izanami ("the Female-Who-Invites"). This sword's alternative name appears immediately below as the alternative name of this deity— *Ame-no-o-ha-bari-no-kami, i.e.*, "the Deity Heavenly-Point-Blade-Extended." Norinaga's gloss to the effect that the deity was the *spirit* of the sword has no warrant from the text.

[493] *Take-mika-zu-chi-no-o-no-kami.* See Sect. 8, Note 7.

[494] Here, as in Vol. 1, Note 155 the character 且, "moreover," occurs where some other conjunction would seem more appropriate both in Japanese and in English. We may here understand it to be used for "but."

[495] *Ame-no-kaku-no-kami.* The interpretation of *kaku* as "deer" is Atsutane's. See his *Exposition of the Ancient Histories,* Vol. 22, p. 6, and cf.the remarks on Mount Kagu in Vol. 1, Note 133 of this translation.

[496] Lit., "in this road."

[497] The first personal pronoun is here represented by the humble character 僕, "servant."

[498] See Vol. 1, Note 144.

[499] *Tori-bune-no-kami.* See Vol. 1, Note 123.

[500] The word "little" is merely a sort of honorific expletive.

[501] The true etymology of this word is doubtful; for Norinaga's proposal to derive if from *ina se,* supposed to mean "no or yes" (諾否), in allusion to the question here put to the Deity Master-of-the-Great-Land is a mere fancy, and does not provide for the alternative forms *Itasa* and *Isasa,* which occur in other documents.

[502] See Vol. 1, Note 138.

[503] *I.e.,* as Norinaga explains, hilt downwards.

[504] The *Chronicles* say that they "squatted."

[505] Here and below the humble character 僕, "servant," is used for the First Personal Pronoun.

[506] *Ya-e-koto-shiro-nu-shi-no-kami.* For this difficult name see Sect. 36, Note a.

[507] See Vol. 1, Note 427.

[508] Or, "We will."

[509] *I.e.*, He capsized his boat and himself into the sea—the place being one where (as is still done in Japan) a large space of shallow water had been fenced in with posts, and stuck over with branches of trees, a single opening being left for fish to enter by,–then clapped his hands in token of departure, and sank to the bottom.–This is Atsutane's interpretation of the passage, which is a difficult one, and is differently understood by Norinaga, whom Mr. Satow has followed in one of his notes to the *Rituals* (see Vol. 7, Pt 2, p. 122 of these *Transactions*), rendering it thus: "He then trod upon the edge of his boat so as to overturn it, and with his hands crossed back to back (in token of consent), transformed his boat into a green fence of branches, and disappeared." A careful comparison of the remarks

in Norinaga's *Commentary* (Vol. 14, pp. 16–19) with those in Atsutane's *Exposition of the Ancient Histories* (Vol. 22, pp. 50–55) and with the text itself, as also with the text of the parallel passage in the *Chronicles*, has however left no doubt in the mind of the translator that Atsutane's view is the correct one.

[510] *Take-mi-na-gata-no-kami.* The interpretation of the name is that proposed by Norinaga.

[511] *I.e.*, the Lake of Suwa. No satisfactory etymology of the name is forthcoming.

[512] In later times called *Shinano.* [Nagano Prefecture.—M.F.] The usual derivation of the word is that which connects it with *shina-zaka,* "mountainous ascents"–an appropriate enough name for the province in question. It is, however, more probably derived from *shina,* the name of a tree resembling the lime *(Tilia cordata)* and *nu* or *no,* "moor."

[513] *I.e.,* "If ye will build me a temple founded on the nethermost rocks and reaching up to Heaven like unto the august residence of the Heavenly Deity who is coming to replace me as sovereign upon earth, I will vanish to Hades, and serve him there; and as for the Gods my children, none of them will rebel against their new Lord, if the Deity Thing-Sign-Master be accepted as the protector of his escort."—Some of the expressions in the original stand in need of explanation. *Su,* here rendered "nest" in accordance with the character 巣 employed in writing it, may mean "lattice" (簀) and refer to the lattice-work over the hole in the chimney of the roof. The "succession of Heaven's sun" (in Japanese *ama tsu hi-tsugi*) means the inheritance of the sovereignty of Japan, or of Izumo. *Momotarazu* ("less than a hundred") is the Pillow-Word for *ya-so,* "eighty," and for some other words; it must be disregarded in making sense of any sentence in which it occurs. The "eighty road-windings" signify, says Norinaga, "an immensely long way," and are here meant for the long road leading to Hades or for Hades itself (Cf. Vol. 2, Note 794). In rendering the last sentence of the passage (that commencing "Again, as for my children," etc.), which is particularly vague, the translator has been guided by Norinaga's opinion, which seems the most satisfactory one. It must be understood that the Deities whose rear and van the Deity Thing-Sign-Master is to become, are those who are about to escort the new sovereign down from heaven.

[514] The passage placed within brackets is supplied by Norinaga to fill up an evident omission in the text.

[515] Lit. "little shore." See Note 10 to this Section.

[516] The derivation of *Tagishi* is doubtful; but cf. Vol. 2, Note 703. Norinaga remarks that we seem to have here the old name of the place now known only, on account of the temple which it contains, as *Kizuki no Ō-yashiro*, i.e., "the pestle-hardened great shrine."

[517] *Kushi-ya-tama-no-kami.* Norinaga proposes to consider *tama* as a contraction of *tamuke,* "offering," and to take the name to signify "the Deity of Wondrous Increasing Offerings." Atsutane's interpretation, which is followed in the translation, seems better, as the term "eight spirits" or "eight [fold] spirit" accords with the religious role attributed to this Deity without necessitating any hazardous philological

conjectures. The actual character used to write the disputed word is 玉 "jewel."

[518]See Sect. 6, Note a.

[519]The word "when" must be understood resumptively, as signifying that the way in which he carried out his task was by turning into a cormorant, making platters, etc.

[520]It is uncertain whether the word *me* (海布), here rendered seaweed, is a general designation or the name of a particular species.

[521]Supposed to be the same as, or similar to, the modern *hon-dahara (Halochloa macrantha).*

[522]*Kumu-musu-bi-mi-oya-no-kami.*

[523]The translator has followed Moribe in the interpretation of the first part and Atsutane in the interpretation of the latter part of this extremely difficult passage, which is a crux to all the commentators, but whose general sense at least is this: "I will continue drilling fire for the God's kitchen, until the soot hangs down from the roof of the temple of the Ancestral Deity in Heaven above, and until the earth below is baked down to its nethermost rocks; and with the fire thus drilled will I cook for him the fish brought in by the fishermen, and present them to him in baskets woven of split bamboos which will bend beneath their weight."—Another plausible interpretation of the original expression rendered by these last two words is that they are simply the Pillow-Word for *to-o-o-to-o-o ni*, "bending." The rope with which the fishermen are supposed to have angled is described in detail by Atsutane (*Exposition of the Ancient Histories*, Vol. 24. p. 21) as a long rope from which other strings, each with a hook attached, depended, and is said by him to be still in use in the provinces of Shimofusa (Shimōsa) [Chiba and Ibaraki Prefectures.—M.F.] and Hitachi [Ibaraki Prefecture.—M.F.]. The "lattice of the gable" must be understood to mean bamboo lattice covering a hole beneath the gable, which served as a chimney. Norinaga's remarks on this passage will be found in Vol. 14. pp. 39–42 of his *Commentary*, and Moribe's on the words *to-daru ama no nihi-su* (rendered "on the heavenly new lattice of the gable" in his *Examination of Difficult Words*, Vol. 2, pp. 26–29; the latter especially are well worth perusal by the student. Mr. Satow, in one of the notes to his translation of the *Rituals*, (See Vol. 9, Pt. 2, p. 209 of these *Transactions*), gives a somewhat divergent rendering of this passage, following, as he does, the interpretation given by Norinaga. It is as follows: "The fire which I have drilled will I burn until the soot of the rich and sufficing heavenly new nest of the parent Kami-musu-bi in heaven hangs down many hand-breadths long, and the earth below will I bake down to its bottom-most rocks, and stretching a thousand fathoms of paper-mulberry rope, will draw together and bring ashore the fisherman's large-mouthed small-finned *suzuki*, [and] will offer up the heavenly fish-food on bending split bamboos."

[524]*Taka-gi-no-kami.* See Vol. 1, Note 509.

[525]It will be remembered that this god was son of the Sun-goddess (or of her brother *Susa-no-o*, "the Impetuous Male";—see Vol. 1, Note 224, and also the first two sentences of Sect. 14 and the first sentence of Sect. 15). The characters rendered

"Heir Apparent" are 太子, which form the usual Chinese equivalent of that term, and were borrowed by the Japanese. Norinaga's reading of them as *Hi-tsugi no miko*, "Prince of the Sun's Succession," has no authority but his own patriotic fancy.

[526]For this tremendous name see Vol. 1, Note 224.

[527]The humble character 僕, "servant" is used for the first personal pronoun.

[528]*Ame-nigishi-kuni-nigishi-ama-tsu-hi-daka-hiko-ho-no-ni-nigi-no-mikoto*. Excepting as regards the final *gi* of *ni-nigi*, which it is surely better with Atsutane to consider as helping to form the word *nigi*, "plenty," than to take it as a separate word signifying "lord," as Norinaga does, the translation follows Norinaga's interpretation of the various component parts of this tremendous name, which is mostly abbreviated to its latter portion. It is precisely to this latter portion (the syllables *hiko-ho-no-nigi*) that considerable doubt attaches. *Ho* might mean "fire" rather that "rice-ears," and Norinaga himself suggests that *ni-nigi* should perhaps be regarded as a corruption of *nigi-kahi*, "plentiful spikes of grain," rather than as "ruddy plenty." About the meaning of the rest of the name there cannot be much doubt. "Heaven's Sun Height" must be understood as an honorific designation signifying "high as the sun in heaven."

[529]The grammar of it is curious, as, on a first reading, one would be tempted to suppose that "this child," *i.e.*, His Augustness *Ame-nigishi-kuni-nigishi-ama-tsu-hi-daka-hiko-ho-no-ni-nigi*, was the father of *Hiko-ho-no-ni-nigi*. But the latter name is but an abbreviated form of the former, and the god could not be his own father. The meaning rather is (and such a construction is not so forced in Japanese as it sounds in English): "As for the parentage of this child, he was born of the marriage [of His Augustness Truly-Conquerer-etc.] with Her Augustness Myriad-Looms-etc. Princess." There is, however, real confusion in the traditional genealogy, as the *Chronicles* make the deity in question father to His Augustness Heavenly-Rice-ear-Ruddy, instead of younger brother.

[530]Viz. His Augustness Truly-Conqueror-etc.

[531]*Yorozu-hata-toyo-aki-zu-shi-hime-no-mikoto*. Mabuchi, as quoted by Norinaga, suggests that *yorozu*, "myriad," should be connected with the word *yoroshi*" good" as signifying an extreme degree, the *ne plus ultra*. But, though perhaps a good guess at the origin of the word, it need not affect our estimate of its actual signification. The translator has, however, followed Mabuchi in considering the syllable *shi* as an apocopated form of *shima*, "island," and *Aki-zu-shi* [ma] as having its usual signification of "Dragonfly Island" (more literally "Island of the Autumn Insect") rather than accept Norinaga's explanation of *shi* as representing the Verb *chijimu*, "to be puckered," and of the whole compound *aki-zu-shi* as signifying "crape-like dragonflies' wings," Not only is there no mention of crape in other passages of these *Records*, but the derivation does not, to say the least, recommend itself on philological grounds.

[532]*Ame-no-ho-akari no mi koto*. The word rendered "ripe" will bear equally well the interpretation of "red."

[533]*Hiko-ho-no-ni-nigi*, the abbreviated form of the name in Vol. 1, Note 566.

[534] *Toyo-ashi-hara-no-mizu-ho-no-kuni.* This periphrastic synonym of Japan has appeared under a slightly shorter form in Vol. 1, Sect. 9 Notes d and 165.

[535] Written 僕, lit. "servant."

[536] *Saruta-biko no kami.* This is Norinaga's reading. The more usual reading is *Saruda-hiko,* transposing the *nigori*. Atsutane prefers to read *Sada-biko,* and takes *Saruta* or *Sada* to be the name of a place, which indeed seems the most acceptable view. The name actually signifies "monkey field." Norinaga's interpretation of its import is a marvelous example of Japanese etymological gymnastics (see Vol. 15, p. 16 of his *Commentary*). Moribe's derivation from *Sari-hate-hiko* (避果彦) is no better.

[537] For these five names and for the Deity Thought-Includer and the [Heavenly-] Hand-Strength-Male-Deity mentioned a few lines further on, see Vol. 1, Notes 276, 277, 287, 273, 274, 270, and 286 respectively.

[538] *Tomo-no-o.* This expression is here taken to refer to the various offices assumed by the five Deities in question at the time of the withdrawal of the Sun-Goddess into the cave. It signifies properly the head of a company.

[539] The allusion is to the story in Sect. 16. Moribe, in his *Critique* on Norinaga's *Commentary*, points out that it was only the mirror which allured the goddess from the cave. In the Japanese original of this passage, however, even more than in the English translation, the expression "that had allured" is made to refer to both objects.

[540] *Ame-no-iwa-to-wake no kami.* Atsutane observes that this must not be considered as the name of an independent Deity, but be taken simply as an alternative name of *Ame-no-ta-jikara-o-no-kami* (the "Heavenly-Hand-Strength-Male-Deity"). The part taken by this Deity in the legend narrated in Sect. 16 seems a sufficient warrant for such an opinion, though a little lower down in this Section the two are again mentioned separately.

[541] *Toko-yo.* These words, which, according to the rules of Japanese construction, are placed at the commencement of the clause, must be understood to apply either to the three gods collectively or to the first-mentioned (the Deity Thought-Includer) alone.

[542] The strictly logical concordance of an English sentence makes it appear as if the mirror were to be taken to represent the spirit of both Deities whose names are the subjects of the first clause. In Japanese, however, all such concordances are much more loosely observed, and it is only the spirit of the Sun-Goddess that we must understand to be here intended.

[543] *Isuzu* (lit. "fifty bells," or else perhaps the name of a kind of grass with which the neighborhood may originally have been overgrown) is the name of the site of the "Inner Temple" of Ise. It is in the Japanese text preceded by the Pillow-Word *saku-kushiro,* lit. "rent bracelet." See Mabuchi's *Dictionary of Pillow-Words s.v.*

[544] *Toyo-uke-ne-kami,* the same as *Toyo-uke-bime* (see Vol. 1, Note 130). The mention of this goddess in this place is curious, as she would not seem to be connected with the legend. Norinaga, however, supposes that it is through some accidental omission that she does not figure in the list of Deities said to have accompanied

the heaven-descended Sovereign.

[545]This name signifies "meeting when crossing" or "crossing to meet," and is connected by the commentators with an unimportant tradition, for which see Norinaga's Commentary, Vol. 15. p. 48.

[546]These two names are in the original *Kushi-iwa-ma-do-no-kami* and *Toyo-iwa-mado-no-kami*. The tradition in the *Gleanings of Ancient Story* makes them two separate Deities.

[547]Etymology obscure.

[548]*Nakatomi no Muraji. Nakatomi* is taken by Norinaga to be a contraction of *naka-tori-omi,* and by Mabuchi to be a contraction of *naka-tsu-omi,* either of which may be freely rendered "middlemen,""intercessors," referring to the religious functions which were hereditary in this family. (See *Commentary on the Ritual of the General Purification*, Vol. 2. pp. 2–3.)

[549]*Imibe no obito. Imibe* is derived from *imu* "to avoid," *i.e.*, "to abstain from," and *mure*, "a flock" or "collection of persons" "a clan," and refers to the religious duties of this hereditary class of priests, which naturally required their avoidance of all ceremonial uncleanness. The word "priest" would fairly, though freely, represent the meaning of the compound.

[550]*Saru me no kimi.* For the traditional origin of this name see Sect. 35. These "duchesses" were priestesses: but it is a matter of dispute between the commentators whether the title was simply an official one, or hereditary in the female line.

[551]*Kagami-tsukuri no muraji.* Of this family nothing would seem to be known.

[552]*Tama-no-ya (or Tama n'Oya) no muraji.* But the name should probably be *Tama-tsukuri no muraji, i.e.* "Jewel-Making Chieftains," a "gentile name" which is found in the later literature. Perhaps, however, we should understand both this name and the previous one to be simple inventions by means of which divine ancestry was claimed for the hereditary guilds of jewelers and mirror-makers.

[553]Norinaga makes Sect. 34 commence here, and it seems on the whole best to follow him in so doing, as the entire period of the reign on earth of the first of the heaven-descended gods is thus included in one Section. On the other hand, the "Descent from Heaven," which gives its name to the preceding Sect, cannot properly be said to be accomplished until the end of this first sentence of Sect. 34. It will be remembered that the Japanese name of this first deity-king is (in its abbreviated and most commonly used form) *Hiko-ho-no-ni-nigi.*

[554]Norinaga proposes to suppress the character 詔, "commanded," in this clause, and the character 而, "and," at the beginning of the next, and to take the Prince as the subject of the whole sentence. This would be convenient; but the characters 詔 and 而 are in all the texts.

[555]The translator has adopted the interpretation proposed by Atsutane, the only commentator who gives an acceptable view of this extremely difficult clause, which Norinaga admitted that he did not understand. It must be remembered that Atsutane identifies the "Floating Bridge of Heaven" with the "Heavenly Rock-Boat." (For details see his *Exposition of the Ancient Histories*, Vol. 27, pp. 31–32).

[556]Tsukushi [Kyushu.—M.F.], anciently the name of the whole of the large island forming the South-Western corner of Japan, and Himuka [Miyazaki Prefecture.—M.F.] (in modern pronunciation Hyūga), one of the provinces into which that island is divided, have already been mentioned in Vol. 1, Note 79 and Vol. 1, Note 175 respectively. It is uncertain whether the mountain here named is the modern Takachiho-yama or Kirishima-yama, but the latter view is generally preferred. *Kujifuru.* is explained (perhaps somewhat hazardously) as meaning" wondrous," while *Taka-chi-ho* signifies "high-thousand-rice-ears." [Takachiho in Himuka in Tsukushi.—W.G.A]

[557]*Ame-no-oshi-hi no mikoto.* The interpretation is only conjectural.

[558]*Ama-tsu-kume no mikoto.* The traditional origin of this curious name will be found below in the third and fourth Songs of Sect. 51 (see Vol. 2, Sect. 51, Notes b, 118, and 119), where the "sharp slit eyes" of this worthy are specially referred to. But Moribe seems to prove that *kume* is in reality not a personal name at all, but simply the old term for "army," through a misconception of the original import of which has arisen the idea that *Ō-kume* and *Ō-tomo* were two distinct personages. The elaborate and interesting note on this subject in his *Examination of Difficult Words*, Vol. 2, pp. 46–55 is well worth consulting. The only point in which the present writer differs from him is with regard to the etymology of the word *kume*, which Moribe connects with *kumi*, "a company," and *kuma*, "a bravo," whereas in the opinion of the former it is probably nothing more nor less than an ancient mis-pronunciation of the Chinese word *jun* (軍) modern Japanese *gun*, "army," "troops."

[559]The Auxiliary Numeral here used is that properly denoting human beings, not Deities—*futari* (二人), instead of *futa-hashira* (二柱).

[560]*In Japanese ama no iwa-yugi.*

[561]This is the generally received interpretation of the obscure original term *ka-bu tsuchi* (or *kabu-tsutsui*) *no tachi*, the parallel term *ishi-tsutsui* being understood to mean "a mallet-headed sword made of stone." (Both names appear below in the Song at the end of Vol. 2, Note 85). Moribe, however, in his *Izu-no-chi-waki*, rejecting the opinion that any part of the swords were made of stone, explains *kabu-tsutsui* in the sense of "broad-tempered" and *ishi-tsutsui* in that of "hard-tempered."

[562]For the bows and arrows here mentioned see Vol. 1, Note 502.

[563]*Ōtomo no muraji*, a common "gentile name" down to historical times. *Ō-tomo* means "numerous companies" or "large tribe," in allusion, as Moribe supposes, to the force of which the personage here mentioned was the general.

[564]*Kume no atai.* Cf. Vol. 1, *Note 596.*

[565]Etymology uncertain. An alternative form of this name, which is preserved in the *Chronicles*, is *Nagasa,* which Atsutane thinks may stand for *Nagasaki.*

[566]This is the sense of the original Japanese text of this passage as literally as it can be rendered, and so the older editors understood it. Norinaga however, though not daring actually to alter the characters, assumes that they are corrupt, and in his *kana* rendering gives us this instead: "Thereupon, passing searchingly through a bare-backed empty country, be arrived at the august cape of Kasasa, and said:

'This land is a land whereon the morning sun shines straight, etc.'" His evident reason for wishing to alter the reading is simply and solely to conceal the fact that Korea is mentioned, and mentioned in a not unfriendly manner, in the traditional account of the divine age, *i.e.*, long before the epoch of its so-called revelation and conquest by the Empress Jin-gū (see Sects. 96 to 98). That the parallel passage of the *Chronicles* lends some sanction to his view is no excuse for so dishonest a treatment of the text he undertakes to commentate; for the *Records* and the *Chronicles* often differ greatly in the accounts they have preserved. One of Norinaga's arguments is that, as Kasasa is said to have been in the province of Hyūga [Miyazaki Prefecture.—M.F.], it could not have been opposite to Korea, seeing that Hyūga faces east and not west. He here forgets that a little later on in his own same *Commentary* (Vol. 17, p. 86) he asserts that Hyūga in ancient times included the provinces of Ōsumi and Satsuma [both Kagoshima Prefecture.—M.F.], the latter of which does face west.

[567]See Sect. 33 from a little before Note 572 to Note b on p. 42.

[568]*Q.d.*, instead of the men being Dukes, as would be more natural. The title was confined to females (see Vol. 1, Note 588).

[569]Etymology unknown.

[570]What species was denoted by this ancient name is not clear; but one of Norinaga's suggestions, to the effect that it may have been identical with the modern *sarubo-gai* (a shell of the family *Arcade,* probably *Arca subcrenata*), the origin of whose name would thus be traced up to the mythological age, is at least ingenious.

[571]*Soko-doku-mi-tama.*

[572]*Tsubo-tatsu-mi-tama.*

[573]*Awa-saku-mi-tama. Saku* might be translated by "opening," "forming," etc. It is the same word as that used to express the blossoming of a flower.

[574]The characters rendered "came back" are 還到. Norinaga and Atsutane believe 還 to be put erroneously for 罷, which would give the sense of "arrived there," and would thus enable us to locate the episode of the fishes at Ise instead of in Hyūga [Miyazaki Prefecture.—M.F.], which would better suit the concluding clause of this Section narrating the participation of the Duchesses of Saru in the first-fruits of the province of Shima [Mie Prefecture.—M.F.]. If the word Shima however here means, not the province of that name, but simply "islands" in general, there is nothing to be gained by the proposed emendation, which has moreover no sanction from any text; and it may be added that no notice is to be found in any history of the custom here said to have existed.

[575]Lit., "small string-sword," supposed to have been so called from its having been carried inside the garments, attached to the under-belt. [The *tsuchi-ningio* have usually a very short sword not unlike an Ainu knife, which is apparently suspended by one or two cords from the girdle.—W.G.A.]

[576]The smallest of the Japanese provinces, situated to the East of Ise. The name signifies "island," and it is possible that it ought here to be taken in that sense as a common noun.

[577]See Vol. 1, Note 116.

[578]*Kamu-ata-tsu-hime. Ata* is a place in Satsuma [Kagoshima Prefecture.—M.F.].

[579]Or "Tree" *Ko-no-hana-saku-ya-hime.* Perhaps (though there is no native authority for doing so) we might rather understand *saku* as a causative in intention, though not in form, and render the name thus: "Princess-Causing-the-Flowers-of-the-Trees-to-Blossom." The tree alluded to is doubtless the cherry. The deity is now worshiped as the goddess of Mount Fuji (Fushiyama), and in common parlance the last member of the compound forming her name does not receive the *nigori*—*hime* instead of *bime.* The syllable *ya* has no signification in this and similar names. It will be remembered that there was another sister named Princess-Falling-Like-the-Flowers-of-the-Trees. (See Vol. 1, Note 330.)

[580]Or perhaps, though written 兄弟, the original expression were here better rendered by "sisters."

[581]B.H.C. gives this sentence in Latin. Ego sum cupidus coiendi tecum. Tibi quomodo videtur.

[582]The character used here and immediately below for the First Personal Pronoun is 僕, "servant."

[583]The usual word child (子) is employed in the text but it here almost certainly has, as Norinaga suggests, a more extended meaning, and signifies the posterity of the Sun-Goddess or of Prince-Rice-ear-Ruddy-Plenty generally, i.e., the Emperors of Japan. The vaguer term "offspring" is therefore nearer to the author's intention.

[584]*I.e.,* either of the Sun-Goddess or of Prince-Rice-ear-Ruddy-Plenty. There is no difference in the sense, whichever of these two Deities we take the speaker to refer to. The Sun-Goddess was his ancestress, and he was ancestor of the Japanese Emperors.

[585]Or "snow and rain," the reading being uncertain.

[586]Or "having sworn this" or "pledged [myself to the accomplishment of] this."

[587]The Chinese characters used are those properly denoting the presenting of tribute.

[588]Norinaga proposes an emendation in this passage of 此令 to 爾今, which would not materially alter the sense.

[589]The precise meaning of the syllables *a-ma-hi-no-mi,* here rendered by the words "but as frail" in accordance with Norinaga's and Moribe's tentative interpretation, is extremely obscure. The parallel passage in the *Chronicles* is 木華之移落, *i.e.,* "fading and falling like the flowers of the trees."

[590]The characters tendered "Heavenly Sovereign" are 天皇, a common Japanese designation of the Emperor. It would, especially in the later volumes of this work where the expression is repeated on almost every page, be more convenient to translate by the single word "Emperor." But the commentators lay great stress on the high significance of the component portions of the title, which, they contend, was not borrowed from China, but was first used in Japan. It is first met with in Chinese history in the middle of the seventh century of our era, just early enough indeed for it to have been borrowed before the time of the compilation of these

Records. But as there was no difficulty in putting together the two component parts "Heavenly, Sovereign," it is possible that the contention of the Japanese commentators is correct. The ancient pure native term seems to have been *Sumera-mikoto*, for which Mr. Satow has proposed the rendering of "Sovran Augustness."

[591]Written with the character 妾, a "concubine" or "handmaid," a common self-depreciatory equivalent of the first personal pronoun in Chinese, when the speaker is a woman.

[592]See Vol. 1, Sect. 1, Notes h and 46. Here of course one of the gods of the same country-side is meant.

[593]*Ho-deri-no-mikoto*.

[594]*Hayabito-ata-no-kami*. Ata is, as has been already stated in Vol. 1, Note 616, the name of a place in Satsuma [Kagoshima Prefecture.—M.F.]. *Haya-bito* ("swift men, bold men," lit., if we follow the Chinese characters "falcon-men") was an ancient designation of the inhabitants of the south-western corner of Japan which was subsequently divided into the provinces of Satsuma and Ōsumi, and came by metonymy to be used to denote the province of Satsuma itself, for which reason it remained as the Pillow-Word for the word Satsuma even after the exclusive use of this latter name had been established. In after times the *hayabito* (also contracted to *hayato* and *haito)* were chiefly known as forming the Infantry of the Imperial Guard, a curious choice of provincials for which mythological sanction was invoked. They are also said to have furnished the performers of a symbolic dance mentioned at the end of Sect. 41 (see Vol. 1, Sect. 41, Notes d and 661). In later Sections of this work, the translator has ventured to render *hayabito* by "man-at-arms."

[595]*Ho-suseri-no-mikoto*.

[596]The Honorific is doubtless prefixed in this case and not in the others, because it was to this prince or deity that the Imperial House traced its descent. Norinaga's *kana* reading, which prefixes honorifics to all such names indifferently, obliterates this delicate distinction.

[597]*Ho-ori-no-mikoto*. The derivation of this name is less clear than that of his elder brothers. Norinaga's proposal to consider it as a corruption of *ho-yowari*, "fire weakening," is however plausible and as this triad of names is evidently intended to paint the stages in the progress of the conflagration, the import of the third must be something very like what Norinaga suggests, even if his guess at the original form of the word be not quite correct. The names of all three brethren differ more or less in the parallel passage of the *Chronicles*.

[598]*Ama-tsu-hi-daka-hiko-ho-ho-de-mi-no-mikoto*. The interpretation of the last four members of this compound name is extremely doubtful.

[599]The actual word in the text is not *kami*, "deity," but its auxiliary numeral *hashira*.

[600]See Vol. 1, Note 138.

[601]*Shio-tsuchi no kami*. The view of the meaning of this name which has here been taken is founded on the persistent use in all documents of the character 塩, "salt," to write the first element of the compound, and of varying characters to write the

syllables *tsu* and *chi*, an indication that the latter are to be taken phonetically and may therefore be interpreted to signify *tsu mochi* "possessor of," as in numerous other instances. The fact that this god is known as the god of salt-manufacturers (see Tanikawa Kotosuga's *Perpetual Commentary on the Chronicles of Japan* Vol. 7, p. 3) adds another reason for rejecting both Norinaga's far-fetched derivation of the name from *Shiri-ō-tsu-mochi*, "Great Possessor of Knowledge," and his assertion that it denotes no individual deity, but any one gifted with superior wisdom.

[602]*Sora-tsu-hi-daka.* It will be remembered that *Ama-tsu-hi-daka*, "Heaven's-Sun-Height," was the first part of Prince Fire-Subside's alternative name (see Vol. 1, Note 636). The distinction between these two almost identical appellations would seem to be that the former is used of the Heir Apparent, the latter of the reigning sovereign. Both were therefore equally applicable to Prince Fire-Subside; and while that which he eventually bore is mentioned where his names are first given, he is naturally spoken of in this place, when his father may be supposed to have been still living, by that variation of the name properly marking the Heir Apparent. These names, *Ama-tsu-hi-daka* and *Sora-tsu-hi-daka*, will be met with again below applied to other personages.

[603]*Mi chi* "a road" is properly a compound—*mi-chi*, "august road,"—the single syllable *chi* being the most archaic Japanese word for "road." It is in this place written 御路, showing that the etymology was not yet quite forgotten at the time of the compilation of these *Records*. Generally, however, throughout the work we have 路 or 道 alone.

[604]See Vol. 1, Note 108, where the adjective "Great" is prefixed to the name.

[605]See Vol. 1, Note 506.

[606]*Toyo-tama-bime.*

[607]The character 光, properly "light," "refulgence," is here taken by Norinaga in the precisely opposite sense of "shadow" (the parallel passage in the *Chronicles* having 人影, "human shadow"), and his view is absolved from unreasonableness by the fact of the confusion between light and shade which has always existed in Japanese phraseology. Thus *hi-kage* may signify either "sunlight" or "a shadow cast by the sun." It is safest, however, to adhere to the Chinese characters employed by the author and in this special instance we may well suppose him to have intended to say that a celestial light shone from the body of the god in question. Such an idea is not foreign to classical Japanese ways of thought and expression. See also Vol. 2, Notes 62 and 63. [These seem to me quite decisive.—W.G.A.]

[608]Or, taking the character 是 as an initial particle, "So as we were not able to separate [one from the other]."

[609]The Chinese character indicates something more than pleasure.—W.G.A.

[610]See Vol. 1, Note 640.

[611]See Sect. 37, Note c.

[612]As the character for "one" is thrice repeated in this passage, Norinaga is probably right in saying that it should be given its proper signification, and the translator therefore renders it by the numeral "one" rather than by the indefinite article "a."

[613]Pronounced *tai* in modern parlance. Perhaps we should rather read *aka-dai,* "red *tahi,"* as in the parallel passage of the *Chronicles*. Both these fishes belong to the family *Sparidae,* the former being the *Pagrus cardinalis [now identified as Dentex hypselosomus—M.F.]* the latter probably the *P. major. [*Does not the term *tai* include both varieties? The *Chronicles* have 赤女*akame.*—W G.A.]

[614]Tanikawa Kotosuga, quoting from Urabe [Ichijō. —M.F.] no Kaneyoshi, comments thus on the parallel passage in the *Chronicles*, where the whole of this legend is given several times in slightly varying forms: "By *big* hook is meant one that will not serve its purpose [because too big]; *eager* signifies that which [endeavors to, but] cannot advance; *silly* meant unintelligent: hence we have a hook which, not serving its purpose, will be of no use whatever, but rather a road to lead [him who possesses it] to poverty. Poor outwardly, and inwardly silly, he will be the most useless creature in the Empire." It should be noted, however, that Norinaga interprets in the sense of "gloomy," and Moribe in the sense of "drowning," the phonetically written and obscure word *obo* here rendered "great." [The version of the imprecation given in Vol. 2 p. 38 of the *Chronicles* (pp. 97 and 98 Aston's translation) is much more intelligible than this. Cf. also Vol. 2 p. 41 of *Nihongi* (pp. 100 and 101 Aston's translation). —W.G.A.]

[615]*Shio mitsu tama.* The "tide-ebbing jewel" mentioned in the next sentence is in the Japanese *shio hiru tama.*

[616]See Introduction p. 37, Note 46.

[617]*Uwa tsu kuni*, 上国.

[618]Written with the respectful character 僕 "servant."

[619]There is in this sentence a character, 若, which is hard to explain if read *moshi,* "if," as usual in Japanese. Probably, however, it simply stands for "thou," and we might translate thus: "While thou art crossing," etc.

[620]See Vol. 1, Note 613.

[621]*Sai-mochi-no-kami.* "Blade" is the probable signification of *sahi* or *sabi*, though this particular proper name is written in the *Chronicles* with the Chinese character 鋤, "hoe" or "mattock." Here the syllables *sa hi* are written phonetically.

[622]Written with the humble character 僕, "servant."

[623]"One account" in the *Chronicles* relates these antics at full, telling us that they represented the straits to which he was put as the waters gradually rose higher and higher and we learn from other passages in the same work and in the *Chronicles of Japan Continued* that the *Hayabito* did really down to historical times combine the office of Court Jesters with that of Imperial Guardsmen.

[624]For "waited on" see Sect. 38, Note a. The word "herself" (自 *mizukara)* has no particular force or meaning in the Japanese original, where it is simply placed in imitation of the Chinese style.

[625]See Vol. 1, Note 629.

[626]It has been noticed in the Introduction, p. 22, that in Early Japan a parturient woman was expected to build for herself a special hut in which to give birth to her child.

[627]The text here has 日子, "prince," lit. "sun-child," and so the older editors understood the expression. The translator, however, prefers Norinaga's view, according to which the character 遅 should be supplied, and the whole read phonetically as *hikoji,* "husband," a word which occurs again a few lines further on.

[628]According to the parallel passage of the *Chronicles*, she turned into a dragon. "One account" however agrees with our text.

[629]The original of this passage is rather confused but the interpretation here adopted from the Old Printed Edition is more natural than Norinaga's, according to which the verbs are to be taken in a causative sense, to the following effect "I had always wished to let people come and go across the sea-path." Probably it was only in order to make this clause fit in better with the following sentence, in which we are told that the crocodile-princess "closed the sea-boundary," and with the fact that there is at present no path leading to the Sea-God's palace, that Norinaga was induced to sanction such a view of the grammar of this passage.

[630]This is Norinaga's interpretation of the clause, he having emended 作, "action," "doing," which is found in the older editions, to 怍, "shame-faced." (The edition of 1687 mentions 恠, "strange," as an alternative reading.) If we followed the older reading, we should have to translate thus: "thy having peeped at my [real] shape is an outrageous action." [Cf. *Nihongi* Vol. 2. p. 35, (p. 95 Aston's translation).—W.G.A.]

[631]*Ama-tsu-hi-daka-hiko-nagisa-take-u-gaya-fuki-aezu no mikoto.* The older editors read *awasezu* for *aezu*, *i.e.*, "causing to meet," instead of "meeting." Moribe, in his *Critique* on Norinaga's *Commentary*, would have us believe that the name comes from *umi-ga kayoh fuki-aezu* (海陸注來乳養不得) *i.e.*, "going and coming on sea and land and being unable to suckle"!

[632]*Tama-yori-bime.*

[633]"The meaning of the Song," says Norinaga, "is this: 'Although red jewels are so charming that the very string [whereon they are strung] doth shine, the august aspect of my lord, who is like unto white jewels, is still more lovely.' Thus does she express her loving feelings." Moribe supposes the "red jewels" (or "jewel" in the singular) to be meant for the child, than whom her husband is yet dearer to her heart. The word *kimi,* here etymologically rendered "[my] lord," is commonly used in the sense of "thou," especially in poetry.

[634]*I.e.*, "I shall never forget thee who wast my wife in the realm of the Sea-God." The "birds of the offing" are a description of the wild duck, used as a Pillow-Word for their name. In the same manner the whole phrase, "where light the wild-duck, the birds of the offing," may be taken simply as a "Preface" to the word "island." The Sea-God's dwelling is called an island, because it is beyond the sea. The words *yo no koto-goto ni,* here in deference to the views of the best commentators rendered by "till the end of my life," will also bear the interpretation of "night by night."

[635]The alternative name of the deity Fire-Subside.

[636]*Itsu-se-no-mikoto.* The "reaches" are the reaches of a river; at least this seems the most natural view to take of the meaning of the name. Norinaga and Moribe,

however, consider it to be a corruption of *izu-shine,* to which they assign the signification of "powerful rice." Excepting for the fact of its bringing this name into harmony with the three that follow, and which all relate to food, there seems little to recommend so far-fetched a derivation.

[637] *Ina-hi-no-mikoto.* If Norinaga's derivation of the name from *ina-ii* is correct, it might be rendered with greater exactness "Rice-Boiled-rice," *ina* denoting rice in the husk and *ii* the same when boiled.

[638] *Mi-ke-nu-no-mikoto.* This name has been translated in accordance with Norinaga's interpretation of the syllables that compose it.

[639] *Waka-mi-ke-nu-no-mikoto.* Cf. preceding Note.

[640] *Toyo-mi-ke-nu-no-mikoto.* Cf. Vol. 1, Note 676.

[641] See Vol. 1, Note 437.

[642] See Vol. 1, Note 204.

Vol 2

[1] Lit. "Upper Volume," there being three in all, and it being the common Japanese practice (borrowed from the Chinese) to use the words Upper, Middle, and Lower to denote the First, Second and Third Volumes of a work respectively.

[2] In the preceding Section this name was rendered "Divine-Yamato-Iware-Prince." But in the translation of Vols. 2 and 3 of this work, the Japanese proper names are not Englished, unless there be a special reason for so doing. (See Introduction, pp. 20 and 21). [Granting that there is any truth in the story of *Jin-mu Tenno* he could not have been called "Yamato etc.," until he had conquered that part of the country. Why should a Kyushu chieftain have a Yamato in his name? It seems to have been invented by someone who lived in the days when "Yamato" had become a national designation and it was therefore introduced into the name of the national hero. Compare, *Yamato Take no mikoto.* The *Nihongi* says his youthful name was *Sano*, and that *Kamu*, etc., was a title given him after he had conquered Yamato. —W.G.A.]

[3] See Vol. 1, Note 594.

[4] See Vol. 1, Note 438.

[5] See Vol. 1, Note 175.

[6] See Vol. 1, Note 79.

[7] Etymology uncertain.

[8] See Vol. 1, Note 82.

[9] In the original 足一騰宮, read *ashi hito-tsu agari no miya.* The parallel passage of the *Chronicles* has 一柱騰宮 which is directed to be read in the same manner. 柱 (*hashira*) however means, not "foot," but "pillar"; and the commentators understand both passages to allude to a single pillar, which supported the weight of the entire building,—either as being in the middle of it, or (as Norinaga opines) by standing in the water, the edifice, according to this view, being built on a river-bank overhanging the stream.

[10] This name signifies "hillock rice-field."

[11] Etymology uncertain.

[12]Etymology uncertain. This name is better known (without the *nigori* of the second syllable) as Aki. Aki is one of the provinces [now Hiroshima Prefecture. —M.F.] on the northern shore of the Inland Sea.

[13]This name signifies "high island."

[14]Etymology uncertain. Kibi is the name of a province [Okayama Prefecture. —M.F.]

[15]This name signifies "quick sucking."

[16]*I.e.*, as Norinaga supposes, beckoning by waving his sleeve.

[17]The first personal pronoun is represented by the humble character 僕, "servant."

[18]See Vol. 1, Sect. 1, Notes h and 46. Norinaga wishes us here to understand this expression to mean "I am a Deity (*i.e.*, a person) of the countryside." But there is no sufficient reason for departing from the precedent of rendering the characters 国神, which are constantly used antithetically to 天神 by "Earthly Deity" (as opposed to "Heavenly Deity"). Norinaga likewise proposes to append to this sentence the clause "and my name is Uzu-biko," which is found in the *Chronicles*. The name may be taken to signify "precious prince."

[19]The characters 槁機 are evidently, as Norinaga says, meant to represent the Japanese word *sao*, "pole," though they do not properly convey that meaning. Probably they are corrupt. [Cf. *Nihongi*. —W.G.A.]

[20]*Yamato no kuni no Miyatsuko.*

[21]This is the reading of the name preferred by Mabuchi and Norinaga; but the usual from *Naniwa* seems to be at least as well supported by early documentary evidence. The *Chronicles* tell us that the place was called *Nami-haya* 浪速, *i.e.*, "wave-swift," in allusion to the strong current which the Emperor Jin-mu here encountered; and at the present day it is still a dangerous place for navigation. The name properly denotes the water [The water on the bar at the mouth. —W.G.A.] at the mouth of the River Yodo, on which stands the modern town of Ōsaka, for whose name Naniwa is still often used as a poetical synonym. 浪華, "wave-flowers," and 難浪, "dangerous waves," are alternative ways of writing it.

[22]Norinaga says that he cannot explain the etymology of this word; but "white sandbank" would seem a simple and obvious derivation. The Shirakata here mentioned is, according to Norinaga, that situated in the province of Izumo. [Impossible. —W.G.A.] [*Awa-kumo.* Pillow-word? —W.G.A.]

[23]*I.e.*, the Prince of Nagasune. A plausible interpretation of *naga-sune* would be "long-shank," which would give us Prince Long-Shank as the name of the worthy here mentioned; but the *Chronicles* state that Nagasune was properly the name of a place. The characters with which it is written, moreover, signify not exactly "long *shank*," but "long *marrow*," a designation which would have no evident personal applicability.

[24]A legend in the *Chronicles* connects the name of this place with the word *tobi*, "a kite" [bird] it being there related that a miraculous gold-colored kite came and perched on the Emperor Jin-mu's bow, and helped him to the victory. Probably the legend grew out of the name of *Tobi*, which is obscure and may have had nothing

to do with a "kite" originally.

[25] *I.e.*, "shield-haven." But conf. Vol. 2, Note 26.

[26] The real etymology of *Tade-tsu* seems to be "knot-grass-haven," and probably *Taka-tsu* (for *Taketsu*), which is mentioned in Vol. 2, Note 492, is but another form of the same name. Kusaka is a well-known name in the annals of early Japan. Its signification is obscure, and characters (日下), with which it is written, are particularly curious. There were two Kusakas, one in the province of Kōchi and the other in Izumi.

[27] The wording of the original 頁登美比古之痛矢串 [Cf. *Nihongi*.—W.G.A.] is very curious. Norinaga reads it *Tomi-biko ga ita-ya-gushi o ohashiki.* Immediately below we have 負賤奴之痛手.

[28] The character is 奴, properly "slave."

[29] The most likely derivation of this name is from *chi-numa*, "eulalia lagoon," the fact that it will also bear the interpretation of "blood-lagoon" being probably but a coincidence of which the mythopœic faculty took advantage.

[30] Here written with characters signifying "blood-lagoon."

[31] The characters rendered "river-mouth" are 水門, lit. "water-gate;" but here, as elsewhere, "river-mouth" seems to be the signification meant to be conveyed. Rivers in Japan, even at the present day, do not bear one continuous name along their entire course, and there would be nothing unnatural in the fact of the water at the mouth of the river having a special designation. One of the significations of *o* is "man," and the legendary etymology of the name given immediately below rests on the assumption that such is the meaning of *o* in this place. Even Norinaga, however, is not satisfied with it, and it is probably erroneous.

[32] See Vol. 1, Sect. 22, Note a and 364.

[33] The Chinese character 崩, which is here used, is one that specially denotes the demise of an Emperor.

[34] Probably the sense meant to be conveyed is that he expired with a gesture of anger and defiance.

[35] Here written 男, "man." *Cf.*, Vol. 2, Note 31.

[36] *Kama-yama, i.e.*, "furnace-mountain."

[37] This name signifies "bear-moor." The name is now generally pronounced *Kumano.*

[38] Norinaga ingeniously conjectures the text of this passage 大熊髪出, which makes no sense, to be a copyist's error for 大熊從山出, which gives the meaning rendered in the translation. The running hand form of 從山 might well be mistaken for that of the character 髪. The editor of 1687 is less happy in his conjecture that the character intended may be 鰐, "crocodile." This incident of the bear was thought important enough by the compiler for a mention of it to be inserted in his Preface. (See p. 6.)

[39] The mention a few lines further on of *Arafura Kami* savage Deities as the enemies of Jin-mu Tenno, on this occasion would point to a different emendation of the term. *Kuma* is perhaps an epithet of a savage tribe. Cf. *Kumaso*. Even

the present reading "Great Bear-plain," as the name of a tribe of hairy men is not wholly preposterous. *Kuma* means savage sometimes. —W.G.A.

[40]The signification of this name is not clear. Taking *ji* as an apocopated *nigori*'ed form of the postposition *shita,* we might suppose *taka-kura-ji* to signify "under the high store-house" in allusion to the legend which forms the subject of this Section. There are, however, reasons for doubting this etymology (see Norinaga's Commentary, Vol 18, p. 48). In the Preface we have simply *Takakura,* without the final syllable *ji*; but the omission of *ji* in that place is almost certainly to be accounted for on euphonic grounds.

[41]This note to the original is believed to be an interpolation.

[42]横力. Norinaga avers the character 横, "cross," has no importance, and should be neglected in reading. But this assertion seems gratuitous in the face of, for instance, such a Chinese locution as 横磨剣. We may be justified, perhaps, in paying no special heed to the numeral "one" in this place, which Norinaga neglects in his *kana* reading of the text.

[43]The character 御, "august," which should form the penultimate member of this compound name, is here omitted.

[44]See Vol. 1, Sect. 1, Notes c and 42.

[45]See Vol. 1, Note 144.

[46]See Vol. 1, Sect. 9, Notes d and 165.

[47]*Cf.* Vol. 1, Note 173.

[48]The humble character 僕, "servant," is here used.

[49]*Saji-futsu no kami.* The translator follows Tanikawa Kotosuga in considering *saji* (Tanikawa Kotosuga in his *Perpetual Commentary* reads *sashi* without the *nigori*) to mean "thrust." For the rendering of *futsu* as "snap" in this and the two following names *cf.* Vol. 1, Note 145. Moribe, however, in his *Izu-no-chi-waki* asserts that *futsu* is but an alternative form of *futo*, "broad," "thick," or "vast," as shown by the existence of the phrase *ma-futsu no kagami,* "a true vast mirror."

[50]*Mika-futsu no kami.*

[51]*Futsu no mi tama.*

[52]The name of this place, which is in the province or Yamato, seems to signify "above the rock." It is well known as the pillow-word for the syllables *furu.*

[53]Properly what is known to Anglo-Orientals as a "godown." [Warehouse. —M.F.]

[54]Or, "luckily with morning eyes." Norinaga remarks that, even in modern times, special joy is felt at a good discovery made in the morning.

[55]The characters 八咫烏 [*Vide— Wamyōshō* beginning 陽鳥. —WGA] *(ya-ta-garasu),* with which the original of this expression is written, combined with the mention in the Preface of the "great crow," have determined the translator to adopt the interpretation favored by Tanikawa Kotosuga, viz., a "crow eight feet [long]." Norinaga understands the expression to mean "an eight-headed crow." For the arguments on both sides see the *Perpetual Commentary on the Chronicles of Japan*, Vol. 8, p. 16, and Norinaga's *Commentary*, Vol. 18, pp. 60–62, and Vol. 8, pp. 34–38.

See also for the translation of a parallel passage Vol. 1, Note 282.

[56]Yeshinu, better known by the classical and modern form of the name, Yoshino. It seems to signify "good moor." Yoshino, which is in the province of Yamato [Nara Prefecture. —M.F.], has from the earliest times been renowned for the beauty of its cherry-blossoms, and also figures largely in the early and medieval history. Norinaga points out geographical difficulties in the Imperial progress as here detailed. In the *Chronicles*, the verisimilitudes of the journey are better observed.

[57]The character, here rendered "weir" for want of a better word, is defined as signifying "a bamboo trap for catching fish." [Fish-trap? —W.G.A.]

[58]The first personal pronoun is here represented by the humble character 僕, "servant." The other tailed deity mentioned immediately below uses the same expression.

[59]See Vol. 1, Sect. 1, Notes h and 46 and Vol. 2, Note 430, for the considerations that make it better to translate thus than to render by "I am a Deity of the Land."

[60]*I.e.*, "Offering-Bearing Child." Here and elsewhere the word *ko*, "child," as part of a proper name, should be understood as a kind of honorific, employed probably in imitation of Chinese usage.

[61]*Ada no U-kai*. This must be understood to be a "gentile name" *(kabane)*. The etymology of Ada is uncertain. The practice of fishing with the help of cormorants, though now almost obsolete, seems to have been very common in Japan down to the Middle Ages.

[62]Commenting on a similar passage a little further on, Norinaga naively remarks: "It appears that in very ancient times such persons were occasionally to be met with." It should be added that they are also mentioned in Chinese literature.

[63]*Yoshino no obito*. For Yoshino see Vol. 2, Note 56.

[64]*Yoshino no kuzu*. *Kuzu* is a contraction of *kuni-nushi* (properly 国主, with which characters the name is found written at the commencement of Sect. 108, though elsewhere the semi-phonetic rendering 国巣or 国栖 is employed).

[65]Etymology obscure.

[66]*Uda no ugachi*. The meaning of the sentence is: "Hence the name of the Ugachi of Uda." *Ugachi* signifies "to penetrate." But the etymology seems a forced one, and Norinaga is probably correct in identifying this "gentile name" with that of Ukashi, mentioned in the next sentence.

[67]*E-ukashi* and *Oto-ukashi*. Ukashi, as in the other compounds where it occurs, is probably in reality the name of a place. Its etymology is doubtful.

[68]*I.e.*, Barb Point or Cape.

[69]The original has a respectful expression, which is elsewhere translated "waited on."

[70]The first personal pronoun is represented by the respectful character 僕, "servant."

[71]See Vol. 1, Note 601.

[72]*I.e.*, perhaps "Great Round Eyes," supposed to be a descendant of His Augustness *Ama-tsu-kume* (see however Vol. 1, Note 596 for a discussion of the

etymology of *Kume*).

[73]See Vol. 1, Note 602.

[74]The expression *i ga,* here rendered "thou," is, as Norinaga remarks, "extremely hard to understand," and its interpretation as an insulting form of the second personal pronoun is merely tentative. Perhaps the text is corrupt.

[75]The insulting second personal pronoun *ore* is here employed.

[76]Here again we have an expression written phonetically and of uncertain import. The translator has followed Norinaga in tentatively rendering it according to the ideographic reading of the parallel passage of the *Chronicles*.

[77]*I.e.,* Uda's Blood-Plain.

[78]This Song is unusually difficult of comprehension: and the latest important commentator, Moribe, seems to show satisfactorily that all his predecessors, Norinaga included, more or less misunderstood it. He had at least the advantage of coming after them, and the translator has followed his interpretation excepting with regard to *isukuwashi*, the pillow-word for "whale," which is here rendered "valiant," in accordance with the traditional view of its signification. The *soba* tree is identified by Norinaga with the *kaname-mochi, Photinia glabra.* The *saka-ki,* taken together with its prefix *ichi* (here rendered "vigorous") is supposed in this place to signify, not the usual *Cleyera japonica,* but another species popularly known as the *bishiya-gaki,* whose English or Latin name the translator has failed to ascertain. It has a large berry, whereas the *soba* has a small one. [Here *saka-ki* likely refers to a variety of evergreen, perhaps the Japanese stone oak (*Lithocarpus edulis*), an evergreen with edible nuts. —M.F.] —The following is the gist of Moribe's exposition of the general signification of the Song: "If for Ukashi's mean design to kill the Emperor in a gin there be sought a term of comparison in the whales and woodcock forming the Imperial banquet, then in lieu of the woodcock that he expected to catch in the trap that he set, that great whale, the Imperial host, has rushed up against it. Again if, as the fishermen's wives might do, your (*i.e.,* you soldiers') wives ask you for fish, then let each of you give to his elder wife, of whom he must have grown weary, only a small and bony portion, and to his younger wife, who is doubtless his heart's favorite, a good fleshy piece. So jocular a guess at the penchants of the young warriors excites their ardor, which they give vent to in the following shouts."

[79]Some of the Japanese originals of this string of interjections are of uncertain import. The translator has been guided by Norinaga's conjectures, with which Moribe mostly agrees. The exclamations are supposed not to form part of the actual Song, but to proceed from the mouths of the Imperial soldiers. The words rendered "this is saying thou rascal" (such is apparently their meaning) and those rendered "this is laughing [him] to scorn" seem to be glosses as old as the text, which had already become obscure in the eighth century. They are not written altogether phonetically. [Omitted in the *Nihongi* —W.G.A.]

[80]Uda no Moitori. This tribe or guild of "water-directors" was entrusted with the charge of the water, the ice, and the gruel used in the Imperial household. In

later times the word Moitori was corrupted to Mondo.

[81]The etymology of this name is not clear, but readers will of course not confound it with that of the modern town of Ōsaka. The character rendered "cave" is 室, which signifies simply "apartment" but the traditional reading is *muro,* which means a cave or pit dug in the earth. That the latter is the idea which the author wishes to convey becomes clear by comparison with a great number of passages in the older literature. For a more particular discussion of this subject see Mr. Milne's paper entitled "Notes on Stone Implements from Otaru and Hakodate," published in Vol. 8, Part I of these *Transactions*, p. 76 *et seq.*, where a number of passages relative to the "earth-spiders" are likewise brought together.

[82]*Tsuchi-gumo*, generally written 土蜘蛛, but here semi-phonetically 土雲. Norinaga supposes that their name had its origin in a comparison of their habits with those of the spider. But it were surely more rational to regard it as a corruption of *tsuchi-gomori "earth-hiders"* [But is not *kumo* really the same word, "the hider."? —W.G.A.] a designation as obvious as it is appropriate. The *Chronicles* describe one tribe of them as "being short in stature, and having long arms and legs like pigmies." For a further discussion of the subject see Norinaga's Commentary, Vol. 19, pp. 30–31, the *Perpetual Commentary on the Chronicles of Japan*, Vol. 8, p. 35, the *Tō-ga* Vol. 20, *s.v. kumo* and the *Examination of Difficult Words*, Vol. 2, pp. 55 *et seq.*

[83]The original term is *takeru* (梟帥), which might also be rendered "bandit," or "robber chief."

[84]Pit-dwelling. *Muro* can hardly be both "cave" and "pits," the latter only, I think, is the correct word. I have seen at Oyama a pit about four feet deep and perhaps 12 feet square, roofed with thatch on a wooden framework, for the accommodation of pilgrims; also in Korea I have seen a smaller pit used as a dwelling, strong oil-paper taking the place of thatch, *vide* Satow and Hawes' *Guide Book*, 1884 edition, p. 207, where the ladder necessary to go down into such a pit is mentioned. The *muro* of gardeners at the present day are pits covered with a roof —W.G.A.

[85]The import of this poem is too clear to stand in need of explanation. The word *mitsumitsuai,* here rendered "augustly powerful" in accordance with Moribe's view, is understood by Norinaga to mean "perfectly full," in allusion to the fully or perfectly round eyes of the deity *Kume,* to whose name he supposes there to be a reference. Mabuchi, on the other hand, explains the word to signify "young and flourishing." But Moribe's view both of this and of the import of *kume* as "warriors" seems so greatly preferable to any other, that the translator has not hesitated to follow him (*conf.* Vol. 1, Note 596). The "*children* of the warriors" are of course the warriors themselves. With regard to the signification of the two kinds of swords here mentioned it has, however, been thought best to adhere to the usual view, and Vol. 1, Note 599 should be referred to.

[86]See Vol. 2, Notes 23 *et seq.* The apparent want of sequence in this portion of the narrative is not noticed by Norinaga. We might endeavor to harmonize it by supposing that after having slain the "earth-spiders," etc., the Emperor Jin-mu turned round again to fight with the Prince of Tomi, who had harassed him in

the earlier portion of his career as conqueror of Central Japan.

[87]The wild chive growing among the millet is of course the enemy, the Prince of Tomi and his host; and the gist of the Song is that the Imperial troops will smite and destroy them root and branch. The commentators suppose the simile to have been taken from the fields of millet which Jin-mu's troops planted for their subsistence during the long-drawn-out campaigns of early days.—The "stem of its root," *so ne ga moto,* is a curious expression, which is perhaps best accounted for by Moribe's supposition that we have here a pun on *Sune ga moto,* "Sune's house," *Sune* being a natural abbreviation of *Nagasune,* the name of the Prince of Tomi (see Vol. 2, Note 23).

[88]*I.e.,* makes the mouth to tingle, cf. the use of the word *chindo* in speaking of a perfume. —W.G.A.

[89]The sense of this Song is: "I shall not forget the bitterness of seeing my brother slain by Prince Nagasune's arrow (see the latter part of Sect. 44). The word *hajikami,* here rendered ginger in accordance with Norinaga's dictum, is taken by Moribe to signify the xanthoxylon. [*Zanthoxylum piperitum*, the Japanese pepper, a species of Sichuan pepper whose numbing feeling remains in the mouth after eating. —M.F.] "Resounding in the mouth" is a curious phrase here used to express bitterness.

[90]Norinaga thus paraphrases this Song: "As the innumerable *turbinidae* [-shells] creep round the great rock, [The "great rock" may well be the Moto-seki known to ancient legend. *Vide* Satow and Hawes' *Handbook of Japan* p. 176. Also Ise Meisho near end of Vol. 5. —W.G.A.] so will I with the myriads of the Imperial host encompass the Prince of Tomi on every side, that there may be no outlet whereby he can escape." The shell here mentioned is a kind of small conch [Whelk? —W.G.A.]. *Kumu-kaze no*, lit. "of divine wind," is the pillow-word for Ise, and is of disputed derivation, as is the word Ise itself. The curious reader should refer to Fujiwara no Hikomaro's *Inquiry into the Meaning of the Names of All the Provinces s.v.* for the legend to which the name of Ise and its pillow-word were anciently traced and other conjectures on the point. The "great rock" here mentioned is not otherwise known.

[91]*E-shiki* and *Otoshiki.* Shiki is the name of a district in the province of Yamato.

[92]This Song is a request for provisions made by the Emperor to some fishermen, who were working their cormorants along the mountain-streams. Moribe refers it to an incident, not in the war, but in the hunt, and interprets differently the word here, in accordance with its usual meaning and with older authority, rendered "as we fight." He attributes to it the sense of "as we put our shields together," and thinks that the poet may have compared to shields the trunks of the trees. According to this view, the Song should be viewed rather as a joke. It may be mentioned that there is good authority for considering the words *tata namete,* "placing shields in a row," as a punning preface or pillow-word for words commencing with *i* (*i* being the root of *iru,* "to shoot"), so that Moribe's explanation need not involve any tautology. It seems however somewhat far-fetched.—The position of mount Inasa is uncertain, and the name itself of obscure derivation. [Compare *Nihongi* Vol. 3, p.

15 (p. 119 Aston's translation): "Then skirting the river, he proceeded westward, when there appeared a man who had made a fish-trap and was catching fish. On the Emperor enquiring of him, he answered and said: 'Thy servant is the son of Niemotsu.' He it is who was the first ancestor of the clan of U-kai cormorant keepers of Ada." Or above p. 166. —W.G.A.]

[93]The component parts of this name, rendered according to the analogy of that in Vol. 1, Note 566, may be interpreted to signify "Plenty-Swift." The genealogy of this god is not known.

[94]*Tomi-ya-bime.* The syllable *ya* [Cf. *Kagu-ya-hime* and others. —W.G.A.] is inexplicable, but perhaps merely an expletive.

[95]The signification of this name is by no means clear but, rendered according to the characters with which it is written in the *Chronicles*, it would mean "Savory-True-Hand."

[96]*Mononobe no muraji.* This and the two following are of course "gentile names."

[97]*Hozumi no omi.* Hozumi, which is the name of a place, signifies "'rice-ears piled up."

[98]*Une-be no omi.* The interpretation of this name is given according to Norinaga, who explains that the members of this family,—in particular the female members,—waited at the Emperor's table, and wore veils over their necks when so employed. The name is commonly corrupted to *uneme.* [Seems very improbable. —W.G.A.]

[99]Better known as Kashihabara. The name signifies "oak-moor," or rather "a place planted with oaks." This is usually, though without sufficient foundation, reckoned the earliest of the historical capitals of Japan. It is in Yamato.

[100]Unebi is the name of a hill in Yamato. The etymology of the word is obscure.

[101]*Ahira-hime.* Ahira is supposed by Norinaga to be the name of a place in Satsuma. Its etymology is quite obscure.

[102]*Obashi no kimi.* Obashi is supposed by Norinaga to be the name of a place in Satsuma. The characters with which it is generally written mean "small bridge."

[103]Ata is a place in Satsuma.

[104]Or, "there were two Deities." The character employed is not that which itself actually signifies "deity," but is the auxiliary numeral for divine beings.

[105]*I.e.,* perhaps "rudder-ears." [*Vide Early Japanese History*, p. 57, where *Mimi* is an official title. *Kikoshimesu* meaning "to govern," why should not *mimi* be "governor"? *Ō-mimi*= Governor-General. —W.G.A.]

[106]Norinaga adduces good reasons for believing this name to be but a slightly altered form of the preceding one, and for holding that in the original form of the tradition there was but one child mentioned.

[107]See Norinaga's Commentary, Vol. 20, pp. 10–13, for the reasons for thus interpreting the characters 大后 in the text. Elsewhere it has generally, for the sake of convenience, been simply rendered "Empress."

[108]*Seya-datara-hime.* This signification of the name is obscure. Norinaga supposes *Seya* to be a place and *tatara (nigori*'ed to *datara)* perhaps a plant written

with the Chinese character 莘, said by Dr. Williams in his *Syllabic Dictionary* to be possibly a species of *Heterotropa.*

[109]It is uncertain whether this name should, or should not, be regarded as properly that of a place. The meaning is equally obscure. The Chinese characters with which it is here written signify "ditch-eater," whereas those employed in the *Chronicles* signify "ditch-stake." Perhaps both transcriptions are simply phonetic.

[110]A district in the province of Tsu (Settsu) [SE Hyōgo and northern Osaka Prefectures. —M.F.]. The name signifies "three islands."

[111]*Miwa-no-ō-mono-nushi-no-kami.* This god is supposed to be identical with Ō-kuni-nushi (the "Master of the Great Land," see end of Sect. 20 and following Sects.) The rigidly literal rendering of the name as here given would be "the Deity Great Master of Things of Miwa" but the more intelligible version here given represents the Japanese author's meaning. For the traditional etymology of Miwa see the story related in Sect. 65.

[112]B.H.C gives this passage in Latin. qui, quum pulchra puella oletum fecit, in sagittam rubro [colore] fucatam se convertit, et ab inferiori parte cloacæ [ad usum] faciendi oleti virginis privatas partes transfixit. Tunc pulchra virgo consternata est, et surrexit, et trepide fugit. Statim sagittam attulit, et juxta thalamum posuit. Subito [sagitta] formosus adolescens facta est, qui cito pulchram puellam sibi in matrimonio junxit, et filiam procreavit nomine Hoto-tatara-i-susugi-hime et est nomen alternativum Hime-tatara-i-suke-yori-hime. (Id est posterior mutatio nominis, quoniam abhorruit facere mentionem privatarum partium).

[113]Etymology obscure.

[114]An abbreviated form of the princess' alternative name.

[115]The meaning of this Song is: "To which of the seven maidens now disporting themselves on the moor of Takasaji shall I convey the Emperor's command to come that he may make her his consort, and sleep with his arms intertwined in hers?"—Norinaga, overlooking the difference between *maku* which is the word in the text, and the *nigori*'ed form *magu* met with in some other passages, misinterprets the last clause thus: "Which shall be sought?" He makes the same mistake in his explanation of the next Song.

[116]The translation of this Song follows Moribe's exegesis. Norinaga interprets it thus: "Well, well! I will seek the lovely one standing in the very front." As here rendered, the little poem is quite clear,—simply a declaration on the Emperor's part that he will make the girl standing in front his wife.

[117]*Sakeru-to-me,* the original of the phrase here rendered "slit sharp eyes," is obscure and variously understood by the commentators. Moribe supposes the god to have worn a casque with a vizor, and the slit to have been made in the latter, and not actually in, or rather near, the eyes. It should however be observed that, though the Japanese word *saku* means "to slit," the Chinese character in the text properly signifies "to tattoo (or brand) with ink," and is used with that meaning at the end of Sect. 149, and elsewhere in the ancient books. The present writer, after comparing various passages in which the term occurs, thinks that we may

understand a tattooing of the outer corners of the eyes, which would give to the latter the appearance of being long and sharp, or, if the tattooing were very dark, of being actually slit.

[118]For the straits to which Norinaga and his predecessors were driven in their efforts to obtain some plausible signification, see his *Commentary*, Vol. 20, pp. 27–29, and for Moribe's totally divergent interpretation see *Izu-no-koto-waki*, Vol. 2, pp. 30–31. It is not worthwhile to quote here such mere conjectures.—For the doubt attaching to the precise signification of the words rendered by "slit sharp eyes," see Vol. 2, Note 117.

[119]The signification of this Song is as plain as that of the preceding one is obscure.

[120]*Q.d.*, as his wife.

[121]This initial expression is meaningless.

[122]*Sai-gawa. Sai,* as we learn from the compiler's note below, was the name of a kind of lily.

[123]Lit., "one sojourn."

[124]The signification of this Song is: "Now indeed thou comest to share the majesty of the palace. But the beginning of our intimacy was on that night when I came to thy humble dwelling on the reed-grown moor where, when we slept together, we had to pile mat upon mat to keep out the damp." —The translator has followed Moribe's interpretation throughout. Norinaga takes in the sense of "ugly" the word here rendered "damp," and he and all previous commentators give a different explanation of the words *iyasaya shikite,* here translated by "spreading layer upon layer." They take them to mean "spreading more and more cleanlily."

[125]This name may signify "prince eight-wells." But the interpretation of *ya i* as "eight wells" in this and the following name is doubtful.

[126]This name may signify "divine-eight-wells-ears." But see preceding Note.

[127]This name may signify "divine-lagoon-river-ears." But perhaps Nana-kawa is the name of a place.

[128]The character in the next is not actually "Deity," but 柱, *hashira,* the auxiliary numeral for Deities, which is constantly throughout these *Records* used in speaking of members of the Imperial family.

[129]*I.e.,* the Emperor Jin-mu. His decease is not otherwise specially mentioned but a formula at the end of the Section, which is repeated *mutatis mutandis* in the case of each Emperor, tells us the number of years he lived or reigned, and the place of his sepulture. Throughout these *Records*, much matter is often placed in the reign of a Monarch already deceased, and which, according to our ideas, would more naturally be narrated under the heading of his successor.

[130]This is the meaning of the Chinese character in the text. Norinaga tries to save the Empress-Dowager's reputation for conjugal fidelity by rendering it in his *kana* reading by a word signifying "raped." [*Tawakuru* is more comprehensive than "raped"; it would also include "seduced," "had illicit intercourse with." Vol. 30, p. 36, verse last line *"Tawake wa aumajiki hito ni au nari."* But Norinaga does speak of "rape" in the *Commentary*. —W.G.A.]

[131]See Vol. 1, Note 356.

[132]The import of this metaphorical poem, taken in its context, is too clear to need much comment. The rising of the clouds and the rustling of the leaves may be supposed to represent the murderer's preparations, and the blowing of the wind his actual onslaught.

[133]The meaning of this Song is: "The would-be murderer remains quiet during the daytime like the clouds hanging to the mountain-side but at night he will burst upon you like the storm-wind. Already I hear the leaves begin to rustle; already he is gathering his men together."

[134]The word *take* prefixed to the name of this prince signifies "brave."

[135]*I.e.,* either "superior to thee," or as Norinaga understands the phrase, "*the* superior of all," *scil.* the Emperor. [I prefer Norinaga's view. In Korea the single character 上(상) is constantly used for the king. —W.G.A]

[136]Though the elder brother, he here uses the humble character 僕, "servant," to show his respect and deference.

[137]Lit., "a person who shuns," *q.d.* who shuns all pollution, and avoids certain food at certain seasons. *Conf.* the "gentile name" *Inbe* commented on in Vol. 1, Note 587.

[138]*Mamuta no muraji.* Mamuta is said to have been a place in the province of Kōchi. The etymology of the name is obscure.

[139]*Teshima no muraji.* Teshima is said to have been a place in the province of Tsu (Settsu). The name may signify "luxuriant island."

[140]*Ō no omi.* Ō is said to have been a place in the province of Yamato. The name is mostly written with characters signifying "vast" or numerous."

[141]*Chiisako-be no muraji.* Chiisako is said to have been a place in the province of Etchū [Toyama Prefecture —M.F.]. But the name of this family has also been traced to an incident mentioned in the *Newly Selected Catalogue of Family Names* as having occurred in the reign of the Emperor Yū-ryaku, when, owing to a verbal error, a tax was collected in children instead of in cocoons. The monarch, amused at the mistake, is said to have granted to the tax-collector the "gentile name" of *Chiisa-ko, i.e.,* "Little Child."

[142]*Sakai-be no muraji. Sakai* signifies "boundary," and this "gentile name" is traced to the fact, mentioned in the *Newly Selected Catalogue of Family Names*, that the founder of the family distinguished himself by setting up boundary-marks on the frontiers of different provinces in the reign of the Emperor In-gyō (first half of the fifth century of the Christian era).

[143]*Hi no kimi.* Hi (肥) is the name of a province (now two provinces) [Saga, Nagasaki, and Kumamoto Prefectures. —M.F.] in the south-western island of Tsukushi. It is first mentioned in Vol. 1, Note 82.

[144]*Ōkida no Kimi.* Ōkida is the name of a district in the province of Toyo [Ōita Prefecture. —M.F.].

[145]*Aso no kimi.* Aso is the name of a district in Higo [Kumamoto Prefecture. —M.F.], containing a celebrated volcano.

[146]*Tsukushi no miyake no muraji.*

[147] *Sazaki-be no omi.* This name is connected by the compiler of the *Newly Selected Catalogue of Family Names* with that of the Emperor Nin-toku (Ō-sazaki no Mikoto), for which see Vol. 2, Note 883.

[148] *Sazaki-be no miyatsuko.*

[149] *O-hatsuse no miyatsuko.* This name is connected with that of the Emperor Bu-retsu, whose name was O-Hatsuse no Waka-Sazaki.

[150] *Tsue no atae.* Tsuke is the name of a place in Yamato.

[151] *Iyo no kuni no miyatsuko.* For the province of Iyo [Ehime Prefecture. —M.F.] see Vol. 1, Note 69.

[152] *Shinano no kuni no miyatsuko.* For the province of Shinano [Nagano Prefecture. —M.F.] see Vol. 1, Note 550.

[153] *Michinoku no Iwaki no kuni no miyatsuko.* A popular derivation of *Michinoku* is from *michi no kuni,* "the country of the road;" but a more likely one, sanctioned by Norinaga, is from *michi no oku,* the furthest or most distant part of the road" (for the word "road," as here used, *cf.* Sect. 65, Note e). It was for many centuries, and is still in poetry, a vague name for the entire north of Japan. Iwaki, sometimes considered a province, and at others only ranking as a district, formed its southeastern portion along the Pacific seaboard. The name seems to signify "rock (or hard) castle."

[154] *Hitachi no Naka no kuni no miyatsuko.* Hitachi is a province to the south of Iwaki. Norinaga quotes more than one traditional derivation of its name, the best of which, taken from the old topography of the province, is *hita-michi,* "plain road," referring to the level nature of that part of the country. *Naka* is the name of a district. The word signifies "middle," and may have arisen from the fact of the district bearing it being situated between two considerable rivers.

[155] *Nagasa no kuni no miyatsuko. Nagasa* is a district in that portion of the old province of Kazusa [Chiba Prefecture. —M.F.] which was in very early historical times cut off to form the little province of Awa [Southern Chiba Prefecture. —M.F.]. The import of the name is not clear.

[156] *Ise no Funaki no atae.* For Ise see Vol. 2, Note 90. Of Funaki nothing is known. The characters with which the name is written signify "boat-tree."

[157] *Owari no Niwa no omi.* Owari is one of the central provinces of Japan [Aichi Prefecture. —M.F.]. The name is of uncertain origin. Niwa is the name of a district, and is of uncertain origin.

[158] *Shimada no omi.* Shimada is the name of a district in Owari, and signifies "island rice-fields."

[159] For *Unebi* see Vol. 2, Note 118. *Kashi* signifies "oak." The word rendered "spur" is *o.*

[160] In the province of Yamato. *Taka-oka* signifies "high mound." *Kazura-ki* means "kudzu castle," a name accounted for by a legend in the *Chronicles,* which relates how an earth-spider was caught in this place by means of a net made of kudzu tendrils. Kazuraki was the name, not only of a town, but of a district.

[161] *I.e.,* the Princess of Kawamata, a place in Kōchi. The name signifies "river

fork." For the omission in this and a few other places of the words "daughter of," etc., which might be expected instead of "ancestress," see Norinaga's *Commentary*, Vol. 21, p. 4.

[162] *Shiki no agata-nushi.* Shiki is in Yamato. The signification of the name seems to be "stone castle."

[163] *Shiki-tsu-hiko* signifies "Prince of Shiki." Norinaga believes Tamade to be in like manner the name of a place, while he interprets *mi* as the common abbreviation of the Honorific(?) *mimi.*

[164] A place in Yamato. Norinaga derives the name from *tsuki* (modern *toki*), the "ibis," and *ta,* "rice-field."

[165] In Kōchi: *uki-ana* signifies "floating hole." *Kata-shiwa* is said to signify "hard rock" (*kata-iwa*) but this seems doubtful, and the reading given by the characters in the text is not *Kata-shiwa,* but *Kata-shio.*

[166] *I.e.,* Princess of Akuto, or Akuta,—for the latter form of the name is more common. There exists a place thus called in Settsu. The derivation of the word is obscure.

[167] *Agata-nushi Hae.* The reading of this name is obscure, and its derivation uncertain.

[168] *Irone* signifies "elder brother" or "elder sister." The rest of the compound is obscure.

[169] The first three elements of the compound signify "Great Yamato Prince." The last two are obscure, but Norinaga identifies *suki* with *shiki* (see Vol. 2, Note 162).

[170] *I.e.,* "Prince of Shiki" so called, it is supposed, with reference to the place of residence of his grandfather.

[171] The character thus translated is 王, of which "King" is the original and proper signification. To judge by some other passages in the ancient histories, it had not yet in the 8th century altogether paled to the lesser meaning of "prince," which has belonged to it in later times when denoting Japanese personages. It is still, as far as possible, used to denote the rulers of all countries excepting Japan, the zealous admirers of the native literature and institutions even designating by it the Emperor of China, who, one would have thought, had a special right to the more Honorific title of Emperor, which his own subjects were the first to invent. On the whole, therefore, "King" seems to be the most appropriate rendering. The characters 女王 are, by analogy, rendered "Queen."

[172] *Iga no Suchi no inaki.* The etymology of *Iga* and that of *Suchi* are alike obscure. See however Norinaga's *Commentary*, Vol. 21, p. 13, for the traditional derivation of the former. It is the name of a small province, which in very ancient times formed part of the province of Ise [Mie Prefecture. —M.F.].

[173] *Nabari no inaki.* Nabari is in Iga. The name signifies "hiding."

[174] *Mino no inaki.* Mino, not to be confounded with the province of the same name, is a place in Iga [Western Mie Prefecture. —M.F.]. The name probably signifies "three moors."

[175] Norinaga reads *Chichitsumi.* In any case, the name remains obscure.

[176]For Awaji see Vol. 1, Note 103. *Mi-i* signifies "august well," and the name is traced to the custom of bringing water from the Island of Awaji for use in the Imperial Palace, as mentioned in Sect. 129 of the present work, and elsewhere in the early literature.

[177]*Irone* means "elder sister." *Hae* is of uncertain import, it being written with completely different characters in the two histories.

[178]*Ō-yamato-kuni-are-hime-no-mikoto. Ō- yamato-kuni* signifies "the land of Great Yamato," and *hime* signifies "princess" or "maiden." Norinaga suggests that *are*, which is an obscure word, may signify "pure."

[179]*Irodo* signifies "younger sister." For *hae conf.* Vol. 2, Note 177.

[180]B.H.C. gives this sentence and the accompanying note in Latin. Augustum mausoleum est in privatis partibus [Vagina, womb, English good enough. —W.G.A.] Montis Unebi. The note reads: *Scil.* in interiori parte montis, *e.g.* in spelunca. [that is to say in the interior part of the mountain, for example in a cave.] Norinaga explains the use of the term by reference to such words as foot where the name of a portion of the human body is applied to a mountain. In Japanese there are others besides *ashi* ("foot"), such as *itadaki, hara,* and *koshi.*

[181]Karu, which still remains as a village in the province of Yamato, was famous down to the early historical days of Japan, being often mentioned by the poets. The derivation of the name is quite uncertain. *Sakai-o* probably signifies boundary mound.

[182]*Futo-ma-waka-hime-no-mikoto,* The compound signifies "vast, true, and young princess."

[183]*Ii-bi-hime-no-mikoto.* The name seems to signify "rice-sun-princess."

[184]See Vol. 2, Note 162.

[185]The import of this name is obscure.

[186]*I.e.,* perhaps "rudder prince."

[187]*Chinu no wake.* For Chinu see Vol. 2, Notes 29 and 30.

[188]*Tajima no Take no wake.* Norinaga tells us that no mention of any place called Take in the province of Tajima [Northern Hyōgo Prefecture. —M.F.] is to be found in any other book.

[189]*Ashii no inaki.* The same remark applies to this name as to the last. The two "gentile names" here mentioned are equally unknown except from this passage.

[190]*Unebi-yama no Manago-dani.* It is in Yamato, and is now called *Masago.* The name signifies "a sandy place, or desert."

[191]In Yamato. The name of Waki-no-kami is of uncertain derivation. In the *Chronicles* the Emperor Kō-shō is said to have "dwelt at the palace of Ikegokoro at Waki-no-kami." For Kazuraki see Vol. 2, Note 160.

[192]*Yoso-taho-bime-no-mikoto.* Here written phonetically, this name appears in the *Chronicles* written with characters according to which the signification of "perfectly ornamented princess" should be attributed to it.

[193]The signification of this name is obscure, but it seems to be connected in some way with that of the other sister.

[194] *Owari no muraji.*

[195] *I.e.,* "heavenly great perfect prince."

[196] *I.e.,* "great Yamato perfect prince, country great man." This name appears in an abbreviated form in the next sentence.

[197] *Kasuga no omi.* Kasuga is a celebrated place in the province of Yamato. The name is of uncertain origin, though the *Catalogue of Family Names* gives a story referring it to *Kasu-gaki* (糟垣), *i.e.,* "lees fence." The curious combination of characters with which Kasuga is written,—春日,—may be traced to the pillow-word *haru hi no* (春日之) which was not unnaturally prefixed to a name which so much resembled the verb *kasumu,* "to be misty."

[198] *Ōyake no omi.* Ōyake is a place in Yamato. The name signifies "great granary."

[199] *Awata no omi.* Awata is a place in Yamashiro. The name signifies "millet-field."

[200] *Onu no omi.* Onu is a place in Ōmi. The name signifies "little moor."

[201] *Kakinomoto-no-omi. Kaki-no-moto* signifies "at the bottom of the persimmon-tree," and the name is said by the compiler of the *Catalogue of Family Names* to have been granted to this family in allusion to a persimmon-tree which grew near their gate. This name was rendered illustrious in the eighth century by the poet Kakinomoto Hitomaro (see the present writer's *Classical Poetry of the Japanese,* p. 217 *et seq.).*

[202] *Ichihii no omi.* Ichihii is in Yamato. The name may signify "oak-well."

[203] *Ōsaka no omi.* Ōsaka is a place in Bingo [Eastern Hiroshima Prefecture. —M.F.]. The name signifies "great hill, or pass."

[204] *Ana no omi.* Ana is a department in Bingo. The name signifies "hole" or "cave."

[205] *Taki no omi.* Taki is a district in Tanba [Kyoto Prefecture. —M.F.]. The name, which is a common one in Japan, means "waterfall"

[206] *Haguri no omi.* Haguri is a district in Owari. The signification of the name is obscure.

[207] *Chita no omi.* Chita is a district in Owari. The signification of the name is obscure.

[208] *Muza no omi.* Muza is a district in Kazusa. The name seems to be a corruption of the Chinese words 武射, "warlike archer."

[209] *Tsunoyama no omi.* The family, the place, and the signification of the name are alike obscure.

[210] *Ise no Iitaka no kimi.* Iitaka is the name of a district, and is traced to the signification of "abundant rice."

[211] *Ichishi no kimi.* Ichishi is a district in Ise. The signification of the name is obscure.

[212] *Chika-tsu-Ōmi no kuni-no-miyatsuko.* For Chika-tsu-Ōmi see Vol. 1, Note 461.

[213] In Yamato. The signification of the name is obscure.

[214] In Yamato. *Muro* signifies "cave" or "pit." *Akizu-shima,* "the Island of the Dragonfly," is frequently used as an alternative name of Japan (see Vol. 1, Note 91). See also the Emperor Yū-ryaku's song given in Sect. 156.

[215] *Oshika-hime-no-mikoto.* The name *Oshika,* which is obscure, appears in the

Chronicles under the form of *Oshi,* which has generally been interpreted by Norinaga (whom the translator follows) as a corruption of *ōshi,* "great." This version of the name makes it harmonize with that of the Princess's father.

[216]See Vol. 2, Note 229.

[217]This name seems to signify "Great Yamato's Lord Prince, the Vast Jewel."

[218]*Tamade no oka.* In Yamato. For this name see Norinaga's *Commentary,* Vol. 21, pp. 37–38.

[219]In Yamato. *Io-to* signifies "hut door." *Kuru-da* (*Kuro-da* would be the more natural reading) signifies "black rice-field."

[220]*Kuwashi-hime-no-mikoto.* The name signifies "beautiful princess."

[221]This seems to have been originally not a personal name, but the name of a place in Owari.

[222]*Tōchi no agata-nushi.* Tōchi is a district in Yamato. The name seems to signify "ten marts."

[223]This name signifies "great Yamato's lord prince who rules the land."

[224]*Kasuga-no-chiji-haya-ma-waka-hime.* This name probably signifies "the thousand-fold brilliant truly young princess of Kasuga." For Kasuga see Vol. 2, Note 197.

[225]*Chiji-haya-hime-no-mikoto, i.e.,* probably "thousand-fold brilliant princess."

[226]*Ō-yamato-kuni-are-hime-no-mikoto.* See Vol. 2, Note 178.

[227]Norinaga assigns to this name the signification of "Yamato's hundred thousand-fold illustrious princess," and has a very long note on the subject in Vol. 21, p. 42, *et. seq.*

[228]The signification of this name is not clear.

[229]*I.e.,* "prince valorously advancing prince." The alternative name signifies "Great Prince of Kibi," and both refer to his conquest of the province of Kibi as related a little further on in this Section. Norinaga gives good reasons for supposing that *Ō-kibi-no-moro-susumi, i.e.,* "He Who Completely Advances in Great Kibi," is but another form of the same name, erroneously inserted in the account of the preceding reign (see Vol. 2, Note 216).

[230]*I.e.,* perhaps "Yamato's hundred-fold wondrous brilliant young ornamental princess." The name resembles that of the elder sister.

[231]For this and the next following names see Vol. 2, Notes 179 and 178 respectively.

[232]This name is obscure, and differs from that given in the parallel passage of the *Chronicles,* where we read Sashima. The latter sounds more authentic.

[233]*I.e.,* "the young prince the brave prince of Kibi." This name refers to his conquest of Kibi, as related a few lines further on.

[234]*I.e.,* earthenware jars of a moderate size, probably intended to hold the rice-liquor offered to the gods. Being easily broken, they were planted in the ground up to a certain height. [The ancient jars had in very many cases rounded bottoms, so that to make them stand upright it would be necessary to plant them in the ground. —W.G.A.]

[235]The probable meaning of this peculiar expression is "a bend in the river."

[236]Written with the character, 氷, "ice," which may however be only phonetic. No river of this name is anywhere else mentioned as flowing through the province of Harima [Southwest Hyōgo Prefecture. —M.F.], and one is tempted to suppose that there is some confusion with the celebrated river Hi, which figures so frequently in the Izumo cycle of legends.

[237]One of the central provinces of Japan, on the northern shores of the Inland Sea. Some derive the name from *hagi-hara*, "lespedeza moor," ["bush clover moor" —M.F] while others connect it with *hari*, a "needle." Neither etymology has much to recommend it.

[238]*I.e.,* "their point of departure." It must also be remembered that "road" came to have the sense of "circuit" or "province," so that we might translate this phrase by "the commencement of the circuit." *Cf.* such denominations as *Koshi no michi no kuchi*, *Koshi no michi no naka*, and *Koshi no michi no shiri* for what are in modern parlance the provinces of Echizen, Etchū and Echigo [Northern Fukui, Toyama, and Niigata Prefectures. —M.F.]. The region nearest to the capital was called the mouth, while equally graphic designations were bestowed on the more remote districts. It was, as we learn by comparison with a passage in the history of the reign of the Emperor Sū-jin (see Vol. 2, Note 455), customary thus to plant earthenware jars in the earth at the point whence an army started on an expedition, this being considered a means of invoking upon it the blessing of the gods. Not only so, but down to the Middle Ages travelers in general were in the habit of worshipping at the shrine of the god of roads. For "road" in the sense of "circuit," "province," or "administrative division" see Vol. 2, Note 444.

[239]*Kibi no kamu-tsu-michi no omi. Kamu-tsu-michi, i.e.*, "the Upper Road" or "Circuit," was the ancient name of the province of Bizen [Eastern Okayama Prefecture —M.F.] (or of a portion of it), which formerly was a part of the land of Kibi.

[240]*Kibi no shimo-tsu-michi no omi. Shimo-tsu-michi* means "the lower road," and was the ancient name of a portion of the province of Bitchū [Western Okayama Prefecture —M.F.], which formerly was a part of the land of Kibi.

[241]*Kasa no omi, i.e.*, "Grandees of the Hat," a "gentile name" which is referred by the compiler of the *Catalogue of Family Names* to an incident in the reign of the Emperor Ō-jin, which he however by no means clearly relates (see Norinaga's *Commentary*, Vol. 21, pp. 57–58).

[242]*Harima no Ujika no omi.* Ujika is the name of a place. It is written with characters signifying "cow and deer," but the true derivation is quite uncertain.

[243]*Koshi no Tonami no omi.* Tonami is a district in Etchū. The signification of the name is uncertain.

[244]*Toyo-kuni no Kunisaki no omi.* Kunisaki is a district in Bungo. The name seems to signify "land's end."

[245]*Iobara no kimi.* Iobara is a district in Suruga [Central Shizuoka Prefecture —M.F.]. The signification of the name is obscure.

[246]*Tsunuga no ama no atae.* For Tsunuga see Vol. 2, Notes 848 and 856. Perhaps the name should rather be rendered "the Suzerains of Ama in Tsunuga," as Ama

may, after all, as Norinaga suggests, be here the name of a place.

[247]In the province of Yamato. Kata-oka signifies "side-mound" or "incomplete mound." *Uma-saka* signifies "horse-hill" or "horse-pass." Umasaka should perhaps be understood as the particular designation of a portion of the ascent of Kataoka, which is mentioned in the *Chronicles* as the name of a mountain.

[248]In Yamato. For Kuru see Vol. 2, Note 181. *Sakai -bara* signifies "boundary moor."

[249]*I.e.,* perhaps, "the beautiful but alarming female."

[250]*I.e.,* perhaps, "the beautiful but alarming male."

[251]*Hozumi no omi.* There are several places called Hozumi in various provinces. The name appears to signify piling up rice-ears.

[252]*I.e.,* "great prince."

[253]*I.e.,* "little prince-fierce-boar-heart," the boar being known for its savage disposition.

[254]Excluding the last member of the compound, this name signifies "young-Yamato-lord-prince-great." *Bibi* is identified by Norinaga with the word *mimi*, which so often recurs in proper names (see Vol. 1, Note 224).

[255]Norinaga explains this name in the sense of "brilliant-alarming-female," but some doubt must attach to it.

[256]*I.e.,* perhaps, "prince vast-great-truth."

[257]*Hani-yasu-bime,* This name has already been met with in Vol. 1, Note 127. Norinaga however supposes that in this place Haniyasu should be considered to be the name of a place in Yamato.

[258]*I.e.,* a man called "green jewel" who lived in the province of Kōchi.

[259]*Take* signifies "brave." For the rest of the name see Vol. 2, Note 257.

[260]*Take* signifies "brave." *Wake* is either "young" or "lord." For *Nuna-kawa* see Vol. 2, Note 127.

[261]*Abe no omi.* There are several places called Abe, and it is doubtful to which of them the text here refers.

[262]The signification of *inakoshi* seems to be "rice-chariot." *Hiko* is "prince," and *wake* either "young" or "lord."

[263]*Kazuraki-no-takachina-bime-no-mikoto.* The signification of *Takachina* is obscure.

[264]By aphaeresis for *Ō-inabi*, the form of the name given in the *Chronicles of Old Matters of Former Ages,* itself perhaps standing by apocope for *Ō-ina-biko,* which would signify "great rice-prince."

[265]*Owari no muraji.*

[266]*Umashi Uchi no sukune. Umashi* signifies "sweet," and *Uchi* is the name of a place in Yamashiro.

[267]*Yamashiro no Uchi no omi.*

[268]This name may be rendered literally "the shade beneath the mountains"; but the signification is "the glow from the autumn leaves on the mountain-side."

[269]*I.e.,* probably "wonderful (or precious) prince."

[270] *Ki no kuni no miyatsuko no oya.*

[271] *Hata no Yashiro no sukune. Hata* and *Yashiro* are supposed by Norinaga to be the names of places in Yamato. *Yashiro* signifies "shrine." *Hata* is of uncertain derivation.

[272] *Hata no omi.*

[273] *Hayashi no omi.* Hayashi is the name of a place in Kōchi, and signifies "forest."

[274] *Hami no omi.* There is a Hami in Ōmi and another in Tanba. The signification of the name is obscure.

[275] *Hoshikawa no omi.* Hoshikawa is a place in Yamato. The name signifies "star river."

[276] *Ōmi no omi.* For Ōmi see Vol. 1, Note 461.

[277] *Hatsuse-be no Kimi.* For Hatsuse see Vol. 3, Note 222.

[278] *Kose no O-kara no sukune.* Kose is the name of a place in Yamato. The meaning of O-kara is obscure.

[279] *Kose no omi.*

[280] *Sazakibe no omi.* See Vol. 2, Note 147.

[281] *Kurube no omi.*

[282] *Soga no Ishikawa no sukune.* Soga is a place in Yamato, and Ishikawa a district in Kōchi. In cases like this it must generally be presumed that the family had two seats, or was divided into two branches residing in different places. Sometimes, however, the original seat and that to which the family afterwards removed are meant to be indicated.

[283] *Soga no omi.* The signification of Soga is obscure.

[284] *Kawanobe no omi.* Kawanobe is the name of a district in Settsu, and signifies "river-bank."

[285] *Tanaka no omi.* Tanaka is the name of a place in Yamato, and signifies "among the rice-fields."

[286] *Takamuko no omi.* Takamuko seems to be the name of a place in Echizen. Its signification is uncertain.

[287] *Oharida no omi.* Oharida is a place in Yamato. The name seems to mean "little ploughed field."

[288] *Sakurai no omi.* Sakurai is the name of a place in Kōchi, and signifies "cherry-tree well."

[289] *Kishida no omi.* Kishida is a place in Yamato. The signification of the name is not clear.

[290] *Heguri no Tsuku no sukune.* Heguri is the name of a district in Yamato, and is of uncertain signification. *Tsuku* (modern *zuku*), "owl," is a name which is referred to a tradition that will be found in Norinaga's Commentary, Vol. 22, p. 29.

[291] *Heguri no omi.*

[292] *Sawara no omi.* Sawara was perhaps a district in Chikuzen [Fukuoka Prefecture. —M.F.]. The signification of the name is obscure.

[293] *Uma-mi-kui no muraji.* The literal significance of the characters with which *Uma-mi-kui* is written is "horse august post." But whether this name had any relation to horses, or whether it should simply be regarded as the name of a place

is quite uncertain.

[294]*Ki no Tsuno no sukune.* Ki is the name of a province, and Tsuno that of a district in another province, the province of Suhau (Suō) [Eastern Yamaguchi Prefecture. —M.F.]. *Cf.* Vol. 2, Note 282.

[295]*Ki no omi.*

[296]*Tsuno no omi.*

[297]*Sakamoto no omi.* Sakamoto is the name of a place in Izumi, and signifies "base of the hill."

[298]*Kume no Ma-ito-hime. Kume* may be, as Norinaga says, the name of a place. But see Vol. 1, Note 596. In any case the place, if it existed, was probably called after some person of the name of Kume. The signification of Ma-ito is obscure.

[299]*Nu-no-iro-hime.* The meaning of this name is obscure.

[300]Kazuraki is the already frequently mentioned name of a district in Yamato, and Nagae is likewise the name of a place,—whether in Yamato or in Kōchi is not certain. It signifies "long inlet." Norinaga thinks that the syllable *so* in this place is the same as the *so* of *kuma-so,* and signifies "valiant" or "fierce."

[301]*Tamade no omi.* There is a Tamade in Yamato and another in Kōchi. The signification of the name is uncertain.

[302]*Ikuha ito omi.* The *Chronicles of Japan* tell us that the original form of this name *Ikuha* was *uki-ha, i.e.,* "floating leaf," and give a story to account for it. See Norinaga's *Commentary*, Vol. 22, pp. 36–37, where the reason traditionally given to explain the fact of the name Ikuha being written with the character 的 is also mentioned at length.

[303]*Ikue no omi.* Ikue must have been the name of a place; but nothing is known of it.

[304]*Agina no omi.* The same observation applies to this as to the preceding name.

[305]*Waku-go no sukune. Waku-go* signifies "young child or "youth," an honorific designation.

[306]*Enuma no omi.* Enuma is the name of a district in Kaga [Southwest Ishikawa Prefecture. —M.F.], and signifies. "inlet-lagoon."

[307]In Yamato. This pool or lake is often mentioned in the poems of the *Collection of a Myriad Leaves* and was celebrated for its lotus-flowers. We hear of it in the *Chronicles of Japan*, as having been dug in the reign of the Emperor Ō-Jin, but it was probably, like many others, a natural pool or marsh, which was afterwards improved. The name signifies "saber." [Most of the old *misasagi* are surrounded by an artificial lake. —W.G.A.]

[308]For Kasuga see Vol. 2, Note 197. Izakawa is a place in Yamato. The signification of the name is uncertain.

[309]*Takano-hime.* Takano is the name of a district in Tango [Northern Kyoto Prefecture. —M.F.], and signifies "bamboo moor."

[310]The signification of this name is quite obscure

[311]*Taniwa no ō-agata-nushi. Taniwa* (modern *Tanba*) is the name of a province (formerly including the province of Tango) in central Japan. It is supposed to

mean "the place of rice-fields," the rice offered at the shrine of the Sun-Goddess in Ise being brought thence.

[312] *Hiko* signifies "prince." The other syllables of the name are obscure.

[313] See Vol. 2, Note 255.

[314] Biko (*hiko*) signifies "prince." The other elements of this compound are obscure.

[315] One is tempted to render this name by Princess of Mima. But there is no authority for regarding Mima either in this or in the preceding personal name as originally the name of a place.

[316] Norinaga has no explanation to offer of the syllables *Oke-tsu*. *Hime* means "princess."

[317] *Hiko* means "prince" and *kuni* means "country."

[318] *Wani no omi*. *Wani* is a place in Yamato, and there is a pass or hill of that name (*Wani-zaka*). The only signification belonging to the word *wani* is "crocodile."

[319] *Hiko-imasu no miko*. Signification obscure.

[320] Or "the Princess of Washi" or "the Eagle Princess." In Japanese *Washi-hime*.

[321] *Kazuraki* is the name of a district in Yamato, and Norinaga believes Tarumi to be the name of a place in Settsu. [There is a Tarumi near Akashi. —W.G.A.]

[322] *Take-toyo-hazura-wake no miko*. The first two elements of the compound signify respectively "brave" and "luxuriant," while the last probably means "lord." The signification of *hazura* is obscure.

[323] *Ō-tsutsuki-tari-ne no miko*. Tsutsuki being the name of a district in Yamashiro, the whole compound signifies "prince great sufficing lord of Tsutsuki" or "prince sufficing lord of great Tsutsuki."

[324] *Sanugi-tari-ne no miko, i.e.*, "prince sufficing lord of Sanugi" (Sanuki,—see Vol. 1, Note 71).

[325] *Yamashiro no Ena tsu Hime*. Yamashiro is the name of a province, and Ena that of a place in Settsu. The signification of the latter name is obscure.

[326] Norinaga believes *Karibata* to be the name of a place, and *tobe* (*to-me*) to signify "old woman," as in the name *I-shi-ko-ri-do-me*, which latter is however extremely obscure (see Vol. 1, Note 273).

[327] *Ō-mata no miko*. The signification of this name and of the parallel name of the younger brother is obscure.

[328] *O-mata no miko*.

[329] *Shibumi no Sukune no miko*. Shibumi is probably the name of a place, there being a Shibumi in Ise.

[330] *Saho* is the name of a well-known place in Yamato, and Kurami is supposed by Norinaga to be the name of a place in Wakasa. Both names are obscure. *Ō* means "great," and *tome,* according to Norinaga, means "old woman" or simply "female." *Cf.* Vol. 2, Note 326.

[331] *Kasuga no Take-kuni-katsu-tome*. Norinaga supposes this to be the name, not of the father, but the mother of the princess just mentioned. *Take* signifies "brave," and *kuni* "land." The meaning of *katsu* is obscure.

[332]*Saho-biko no miko, i.e.*, "prince of Saho."

[333]*O-zaho no miko, i.e.* "little (*q.d.* 'younger') prince of Saho."

[334]*I.e.*, the princess of Saho.

[335]It is uncertain whether we should understand this name to signify "princess Sawaji" or "the princess of Sawaji," but the latter seems the more probable.

[336]*Muro-biko no miko. Muro-biko* signifies "Prince of Muro," Muro being a place in Yamato. It signifies "dwelling" and specifically cave."

[337]*i.e.*, "flourishing and good princess of Okinaga," the latter being the name of a place in Ōmi. Its signification is not clear.

[338]*Ame no Mikage no kami.* The signification of *Mikage* is obscure, as is also the connection between this deity and the deacons of Mikami.

[339]The signification of the name Mikami is obscure. The word rendered "deacon" is *hafuri,* the name of an inferior class of Shintō priests. See for a discussion of the etymology of the word, etc., Mr. Satow's remarks on p. 112 of Vol. 7, Pt. 3, of these *Transactions.* For Chika-tsu-Ōmi see Vol. 1, Note 461.

[340]*Taniwa no hiko Tatasu-michi-no-ushi no miko.* The signification of *Tatasu* is obscure, but we may accept it as the personal name of the worthy here mentioned. *Michi-no-ushi.* means "master of the road," *i.e.*, "lord of the province."

[341]*Mizuho no ma-waka no miko, i.e.,* "the True Young King of Mizuho, "Mizuho being the name of a place in Ōmi. It probably means "fresh young rice-ears."

[342]*Kamu-ō-ne no miko, i.e.,* probably, "prince divine great lord."

[343]*Yatsuri-iri-boko no miko.* Yatsuri is the name of a village in Yamato, and is of uncertain origin. The signification of *iri* is obscure.

[344]*I-o* signifies "five hundred" and *yori* probably signifies "good." The compound may therefore be taken to mean "manifoldly excellent princess of Mizuho."

[345]*I.e.,* probably "the Princess Mii" (*Mi-i*-dera in Ōmi). *Mi-i* signifies "three wells."

[346]This name is parallel to that which has been commented on in Vol. 2, Note 316.

[347]*Yamashiro-no-ō-Tsutsuki no ma-waka no miko.* All the elements of this compound have already appeared in this Section.

[348]*Hiko-osu no miko.* The signification of *osu* is obscure.

[349]*Iri-ne no miko.* Signification obscure.

[350]*Ake-tatsu no miko.* See Vol. 2, Note 549.

[351]*Unakami no miko.* See Vol. 2, Note 548.

[352]*Ise no Homuji-be no kimi.* See the mention of the establishment of this Clan at the end of Sect. 72.

[353]*Ise no Sana no miyatsuko.* The etymology of Sana is obscure.

[354]*Himeda no kimi.* Himeda is a place in Ōmi. The signification of the name is obscure.

[355]*Tagima no Magari no kimi.* Tagima is the name of a district in Yamato, and is of uncertain origin. Magari is the name of a place, and means "crook" or "bend."

[356]*Sasa no kimi.* Sasa is the name of a place in Iga [Western Mie Prefecture.

—M.F.], and is of uncertain signification.

[357] *Kusaka-be no muraji.*

[358] *Kai no kuni no miyatsuko.* For Kai see Vol. 2, Note 681.

[359] *Kazuno no wake.* Kazuno is the name of a district in Yamashiro [Kyoto Prefecture. —M.F.], and signifies "kudzu moor."

[360] *Chika-tsu-Ōmi no Kami no wake.* Kano is a village in Ōmi. The name is written with characters signifying "mosquito moor."

[361] *Wakasa no Mimi no wake.* Mimi is the name of a village, and is of uncertain signification.

[362] *Taniwa no Kawakami no Masu no iratsume.* Masu is of uncertain derivation. Kawakami is the name of a village, now comprised in the province of Tango. It signifies "river-head."

[363] *Hibasu-hime.* The signification of this name is obscure.

[364] *Matomi-hime.* The signification of this name is obscure.

[365] *I.e.,* "the younger princess."

[366] This name, which is written 朝廷別王, is curious, and Norinaga has no suggestion to make touching its interpretation.

[367] *Mikawa no Ho no wake.* Ho is the name of a district, and is of obscure derivation. Mikawa is the name of a maritime province [Eastern Aichi Prefecture. —M.F.]. It signifies "three rivers," with reference to two large rivers which flow through it and to another which forms the boundary between it and the province of Owari.

[368] *Chika-tsu-Ōmi no Yasu no atae.* Yasu is the name of a district, and is of uncertain origin.

[369] *Mino no kuni no [miyatsuko].* The word *miyatsuko,* which is not in the text, is supplied in Norinaga's *kana* reading.

[370] *Motosu no kuni no miyatsuko.* Motosu is the name of a district in Mino, and seems to signify "original dwelling-place."

[371] *Nagahata-be no muraji.* Nagahata is the name of a place in Hitachi [Ibaraki Prefecture. —M.F.], and seems to signify "long loom."

[372] *Mone no Ajisawa-bime.* This name is particularly obscure, and Mone probably corrupt.

[373] By the same mother. —W.G.A.

[374] *Kani-me-ikazuchi no miko.* Norinaga thinks that this name signifies "fierce like a crab's eye," with reference perhaps to some personal peculiarity of the prince who bore it.

[375] *Takaki-hime.* This name is obscure and perhaps corrupt.

[376] *Taniwa no Tōtsu omi.* This name is obscure.

[377] *Okinaga no sukune no miko.* For Okinaga see Vol. 2, Note 337.

[378] *Kazuraki no Takanuka-hime.* Takanuka is the name of a place in Yamato. It is written with characters signifying "high brow."

[379] *I.e.,* "the princess of the sky."

[380] *Okinaga-hiko no miko.*

[381]*Kibi no Homuji no kimi.* Homuji is the name of a district in the modern province of Bingo, and may perhaps be of Chinese origin.

[382]*Harima no Aso no kimi.* Aso is the name of a place, and is of uncertain origin.

[383]*Kawamata no Ina-yori-bime.* Kawamata ("river-fork") is the name of a place in Kōchi. *Ina* signifies "rice," and *yori* probably signifies "good" in this and numerous other proper names.

[384]*Ō-tamu-saka no miko.* This name is obscure. Norinaga thinks that Tamu-saka may be the name of a place, and signifying "winding ascent."

[385]*Tajima no kuni no miyatsuko.* For Tajima see Vol. 2, Note 570.

[386]*Chimori no omi. Chimori* signifies "road-keeper," and perhaps we should translate this "gentile name" by "road-keeping grandees," and suppose that anciently they may have performed some function in which the bestowal of it originated.

[387]*Oshinumi-be no miyatsuko.* Oshinumi is the name of a district in Yamato, and is of uncertain import.

[388]*Mina-be no miyatsuko.* Perhaps we should rather translate thus, "the Rulers of Minabe," for the name is altogether obscure.

[389]*Inaba no Oshinumi-be.* Norinaga supposes a branch of this family, which was originally established in Yamato, to have removed to the province of Inaba [Eastern Tottori Prefecture. —M.F.].

[390]*Taniwa no Takano wake.* Takano is the name of a district in the modern province of Tango. It signifies "high moor."

[391]*Yosami no abiko.* Yosami is the name of a place in Kōchi, and is of uncertain origin, though the legends connect it with the word *ami*, "a net" (see Norinaga's *Commentary*, Vol. 22, pp. 81). It is chiefly known on account of its lake or pool, which is often mentioned in the early poetry. Abiko is a very rare "gentile name," which in the *Catalogue of Family Names* is written with the characters 我孫, but is derived by Norinaga from 吾孫, *i.e.*, "my grandchildren."

[392]In Yamato. The name is of uncertain origin.

[393]In Yamato. *Shiki* probably signifies "stone castle" (*ishi-ki*). *Mizugaki* signifies "fresh young hedge,"—an honorific designation of the hedge round the Emperor's abode, which passed into a proper name.

[394]According to Norinaga's exegesis, this name is a rather remarkable instance of verbal usage, *ayu-me* ("trout-eyes") being not properly part of the name at all, but only a pillow-word for what follows, viz., *Me-kuwashi-hime, i.e.,* "Princess Beautiful Eyes." *Tōtsu* is the name of a place in the province of Ki [Wakayama Prefecture. —M.F.], signifying "far harbor."

[395]*Arakawa* is the name of a place in Ki, and signifies "rough (*i.e.,* impetuous and dangerous) river." The syllables *to-be* are of uncertain import. [*Tobe*, this shows that Tobe is not confined to women. —W.G.A.]

[396]*Ki no kuni no miyatsuko.*

[397]*Toyo* signifies "luxuriant" and *biko (hiko)* "prince." The other elements of the compound are obscure.

[398]*Bime (hime)* signifies "princess," and *suki* is identified by Norinaga with Shi-

ki, the name of the residence of the monarch whose daughter this princess was.

[399] *Ō-ama-hime.* Ama is the name of a district in Owari, and probably signifies "fisherman."

[400] *Owari no muraji.*

[401] The signification of this and the two following names is uncertain.

[402] *Tōchi* is the name of a district in Yamato.

[403] *Mimatsu-hime.* Signification uncertain.

[404] Signification uncertain.

[405] The syllables *ma* and *waka,* lit. "true and young or "truly young," are honorific. *Iza* is of doubtful signification.

[406] *Kuni-kata-hime. Kuni* means "country" and kata here probably signifies "hard" or "firm."

[407] *Chiji-tsuku-yamato-hime. Chiji* probably means "a thousand," and *Yamato* is the name of a province. *Tsuku* is obscure.

[408] *Iga-hime. Iga* is the name of a district and of a province (see Vol. 2, Note 172).

[409] *I.e.,* "Yamato Prince."

[410] *Kami-tsu-ke-no [no kimi]. The character* 君 (Dukes) is supplied by Norinaga. This is the ancient form of the name now pronounced Kōzuke [Gunma Prefecture. —M.F.] (*cf. Shimo-tsu-ke-nu* corrupted to *Shimotsuke*). The author of the *Inquiry into the Meaning of the Names of All the Provinces* draws attention to the curious fact that, whereas the final syllable *no* of the original word is dropped in speaking, it is the *ke* which is dropped in writing the original form of the name, as written, being 上毛野, whereas now only the first two of these three characters are used. Its signification is supposed to be "upper vegetation-moor," *ke* (毛) being regarded as an archaic general term for trees and grasses, identical with the *ke* that means "hairs," vegetation having struck the early speakers of the language as being similar to the hairs on the bodies of men and beasts.

[411] *Shimo-tsu-ke-no no kimi. Shimo* means "lower." For the rest of the name see preceding Note. Both names are those of provinces [Shimotsuke Province is Tochigi Prefecture. —M.F.] in Eastern Japan.

[412] Or more literally, "worshiped and celebrated the festivals at," etc.

[413] *Viz.,* of the Sun-Goddess (Ama-terasu).

[414] *Noto no omi.* Noto [Northern Ishikawa Prefecture. —M.F.], formerly a part of the province of Echizen, is the name of the peninsula that juts out into the Sea of Japan on the western coast of Honshu. The etymology of the name is obscure.

[415] For a further notice of this custom see Vol. 2, Note 579. According to the *Chronicles*, the "ancient" custom of burying retainers up to their necks in the neighborhood of their lord's grave was abolished after this very same interment. Norinaga endeavors to reconcile the two statements by supposing that the custom was really an old one, but that on the occasion here mentioned the number of victims was increased to an unprecedented degree, [So that for the first time they formed a hedge. But there is something to be said for the reading which asserts "this custom first ceased at the death of this prince."—W.G.A.] so that, as related

in the *Chronicles*, their cries, while their heads were being pulled to pieces by the crows and dogs, filled the Emperor with commiseration.

[416]Lit., "about to be exhausted."

[417]This expression, which recurs at the commencement of Sect. 145, is difficult to explain. See Norinaga's remarks in Vol. 23, pp. 24–25, and again in Vol. 40. pp. 14–15, of his *Commentary*.

[418]See Vol. 2, Note 111.

[419]*Ō* signifies "great," *Tata* (or *Tada*) is taken to be the name of a place, and the syllables *ne* and *ko* are regarded as Honorifics. The whole name may therefore, though with some hesitation, be interpreted to mean "the Lord of the Great [Shrine of] Tata."

[420]Lit., "distributed to the four sides,"—"four sides" being a Chinese phrase for every direction.

[421]This name may signify either "three moors" or "august moor." The village of Mino must not be confounded with the province of Mino.

[422]The characters used are those which properly denote the presenting of tribute to the Monarch.

[423]Here and below the First Personal Pronoun is represented by the respectful character 僕, "servant."

[424]See Vol. 1, Note 144, for the explanation of this name. But probably the deity here intended is another.

[425]The etymology and signification of this name are alike obscure.

[426]Norinaga interprets *kushi* in the sense of "wondrous," and *Migata* as the name of a place, which also occurs under the form of Higata.

[427]*I.e.*, "life-jewel-good-princess."

[428]The precise signification of this name is obscure. Norinaga supposes *Sue* to be the name of a place; *tsu* is the genitive particle, and *mimi* the honorific of doubtful import, whose meaning has been discussed in Vol. 1, Note 224.

[429]See Vol. 1, Notes 441 and 442.

[430]Or *Ikaga-shiko-o*. The probable meaning of this name, proposed by Norinaga, is (neglecting the initial letter *i* as expletive) "the refulgent ugly male."

[431]See Vol. 1, Sect. 1, Notes h and 46.

[432]*Sumisaka* probably signifies "charcoal-hill." Uda, which has already been mentioned in Sect. 46, is in Yamato. This passage may equally well be rendered thus: "to present a red-colored shield and spear to the deity of Sumisaka," and similarly in the following clause. The meaning comes nearly to the same.

[433]In the *Old Printed Edition* the text of this passage differs slightly from that adopted by Norinaga; but the meaning is exactly the same. A large lacuna here occurs in the *Old Printed Edition*, in which the four hundred and forty-five Chinese characters forming the original of the following part of the translation, from the words, "In consequence of this" down to the words immediately preceding "Methinks this is a sign" on p. 217 are missing. Both the editor of 1687 and Norinaga are silent as to the manner in which they supplied the deficiency; but it may

be presumed from their silence that the manuscript authorities furnished them with what had accidentally been omitted from the printed text.

434 It is not easy to render literally into English the force of the characters 容姿端正, containing this description of the maiden's beauty, and of 形姿威儀 in the next clause. But it is hoped that at least the translation represents them better than do Norinaga's readings *kao yokariki* and *kao sugata*.

435 The text places the word "daughter" here, instead of in the preceding clause. For the sake of clearness, the translator has taken the liberty of transposing it.

436 The Chinese characters are 姓名, *i.e.,* "surname and personal (what we should call 'Christian') name." But Norinaga's simple reading *na*, "name," approves itself as probably nearer to the author's intention.

437 Norinaga indulges in several conjectures as to the meaning of this detail, which, it will be seen, is not referred to in the sequel, and is therefore pointless.

438 *Heso* is "ball." *Vide* Hepburn. Probably from its shape with a hole through it.—W.G.A.

439 The same Japanese word *kagi*, which is used as the equivalent of the Chinese characters 鉤, "hook," came in later times to denote a key. [I have seen ancient keys shaped thus [Typesetter please add the symbol in Note 7, p. 215 of the previous edition], nearly a "hook." Kagi always included both key and hook. —W.G.A.]

440 "Three threads" [Rounds of the ball. —W.G.A.] are in Japanese *mi wa*, whence the etymology of the name of Miwa given below in the text. The real derivation is altogether doubtful. The shrine of Miwa was in very early times regarded with such extraordinary reverence, that the term *Ō-gami,* "Great deity," unless otherwise qualified, was commonly understood to refer to the god of Miwa.

441 *Miwa no kimi*, written simply 神君 (lit., "Divine Dukes"), another sign of the estimation in which the shrine of Miwa was held.

442 *Kamo no kimi.*

443 See Se Vol. 2, Note 252.

444 Lit., "to the road of Koshi" *i.e.*, "to the land of Koshi." Which provinces are intended by the "twelve circuits to the eastward" mentioned immediately below is uncertain; but Norinaga hazards the guess that we should understand Ise (including Iga and Shima), Owari, Mikawa, Tōtōmi, Suruga, Kai, Izu, Sagami, Musashi, Fusa (the modern Kazusa, Shimōsa, and Awa), Hitachi, and Michinoku (a vague name for the northeastern portions of Honshu). This would include the whole east and northeast of the country. He likewise supposes the use of the word "road" for circuit or province to have had its origin in the "road" along which the Imperial officers dispatched to the outlying provinces had to travel to reach their post, and remarks very pertinently in another passage of his *Commentary* that the term "road" denotes a province more especially from the point of view of its subjugation or government. His explanation is, however, rendered untenable by the fact that the division of the country into such" roads" or "circuits" was an idea evidently borrowed from the neighboring peninsula of Korea. At first, as in this passage, somewhat vaguely used in the sense of "province," it settled down into the designation of "a set of

adjacent provinces." Thus the Tō-kai-dō, or "Eastern Maritime Circuit," includes fifteen provinces, the Hoku-riku-dō or "Northern Land Circuit," includes seven provinces, and so on. *Cf.* Vol. 2, Note 238.

445 *I.e.*, "brave-lagoon-river-youth."

446 See Vol. 2, Note 311.

447 Norinaga is unable to help us to any understanding of this name, or names, —for he suggests that the character 之, *no*, may be an error for 又, *mata* ("also"), and that two individuals may be intended. The note in the original telling us that "this in the name of a person" might equally well be translated in the plural,—"these are the names of persons."

448 The nature of this garment is not known. One would suppose, from the way it is mentioned in the text, that there was perhaps something contrary to custom in its use by a young girl. [Perhaps the unusual thing was that she had nothing else on, very young girls were perhaps dressed so. —W.G.A.] The parallel passage in the *Chronicles* does not mention it.

449 Or, "Hill of Hera,"—*Hera-zaka*. The *Chronicles* write this name with the characters 平坂 *Hira-zaka*, *i.e.* "Even Pass" or "Hill."

450 From this poem it would appear that Mima-ki-iri was not a posthumous name. —W.G.A.

451 The meaning of this poem, which must be considered as one prolonged exclamation, is: "Oh my sovereign! oh my sovereign!" Heedless or ignorant of the plots hatched against thy life near the very precincts of thy palace, thou sendest away thy soldiers to fight in distant parts. Oh my sovereign!"—It will be remembered that Prince Mima-ki-iri was the (abbreviated) native name of the reigning monarch, commonly known to posterity by his "canonical name" of Sūjin. The word rendered "life" is literally "thread," and the impersonal pronoun "one's," used in the translation, must be understood to refer to the Emperor.

452 See Vol. 2, Notes 259 and 257.

453 *I.e.* probably, "prince land-pacifier." The first element of the compound is sometimes omitted.

454 *Wani no omi*. Wani ("crocodile") is the name of a place in the province of Yamato.

455 *Wani-saka*. For the setting of jars conf. Vol. 2, Note 238.

456 *Wakara-gawa*. It is what is now called the Izumi-gawa. Of Wakara we have nothing but an altogether untenable etymology given in the parallel passage of the *Chronicles*.

457 *I.e.*, "challenging." The more likely etymology of Izumi, which is written with the character 泉, is "source" or "spring."

458 The original has the very curious expression 廂人, lit., "people of the side-building," which was a great crux to the early editors. Norinaga is probably right in interpreting it in the sense of "the other side," *i.e.*, "the enemy."

459 忌矢, lit. "the arrow to be shunned, or avoided,"—but rather, in accordance with Archaic Japanese parlance, "the sacred arrow." Norinaga says: "At the com-

mencement of a battle it was the custom for each side to let fly an initial arrow. Being the commencement of the affair, this arrow was considered specially important, and was shot off reverently with prayers to the Gods,—whence its name."

[460]But it is not at all probable that this is the correct etymology of the name. The stream is a small one in the eastern part of the province of Kōchi. B.H.C. gives this passage in Latin: exierunt [hostium] excrementa, quae bracis adhaeserunt. Quare isti loco impositum est nomen Kuso-bakama. In proesenti nomi-natur Kusu-ba.

[461]"Bow-tips" seems a preferable rendering, the Chinese character is 弓.—W.G.A.

[462]Norinaga has a not particularly satisfactory note, in which he endeavors to explain this obscure phrase. The word "first" should evidently qualify the verb "ruled," and not the substantive "land," and the applicability of the saying to a sovereign, of whom it is not recorded that he initiated anything save the taxes, is not apparent. [Compare *Chronicles* V. 16. (p. 161, Aston's Translation). —W.G.A.] The author of the *Chronicles* observes the verisimilitudes better by applying a synonymous designation to the first "Earthly Emperor" Jin-mu.

[463]See Vol. 2, Note 391.

[464]Reference to the parallel passage of the *Chronicles* shows that probably a couple of words are here omitted from the text, which should read "the Pool of Karu and the Pool of Sakaori" (*Karu no ike, Sakaori no ike*). Karu is the celebrated ancient capital mentioned in Vol. 2, Note 181. Sakaori is quite unknown except from this notice of it, and the derivation of the name is uncertain.

[465]This place, where the Emperor Kei-kō is likewise said to have been interred, was in the province of Yamato, and the road mentioned is supposed by Norinaga to have been the highway from Hatsuse into the province of Yamashiro. The word Yamanobe signifies "in the neighborhood of the mountain" *(yama no be).*

[466]For Shiki see Vol. 2, Note 393. *Tama-kaki* signifies "jewel (*i.e.*, beautiful) hedge."

[467]This name and the next have already been met with in Sect. 62, as have those of Princess Hibasu, King Tatasu-michi, King Ō-tsutsuki-tari- ne, Princess Kari-bata-tobe, and King Inase-biko.

[468]See Vol. 2, Note 527.

[469]The signification of this name is not clear, but Norinaga identifies Shiki with the place of the same name.

[470]This name seems to be a string of honorifics signifying "great perfect prince ruling lord."

[471]*I.e.*, "great middle prince," he being the third of five children.

[472]The signification of this name is obscure.

[473]The signification of this name is obscure.

[474]Norinaga's conjectural interpretation of this name is "jewel-perfect-lord."

[475]The signification of *iga* is obscure. The other two elements of the compound signify "perfect prince."

[476]Signification obscure.

[477]Signification obscure.

[478] Signification obscure. The *Chronicles* read this name *Ike-baya.*

[479] *Azami-tsu-hime.* Signification obscure.

[480] *I.e.*, probably "the refulgent princess," the syllable *ya* being void of signification as in *Ko-no-hana-saku-ya-hime* (see Vol. 1, Note 617). This name is celebrated as that of the heroine of the fairytale entitled *Tale of a Bamboo-Cutter*, though there is no reason for identifying the two personages.

[481] This name is obscure, and Norinaga suspects it of being corrupt.

[482] *Yamashiro no ōkuni no fuchi.* Yamashiro is the name of a province, and Ōkuni ("great land") that of a village, while Fuchi is a personal name written with a character signifying "deep pool."

[483] *Ochiwake no miko.* Norinaga derives *ochi* from *ō*, "great," and *chi;* supposed to be an honorific, while *wake* is taken to mean "lord." After all, the signification of the name remains obscure.

[484] *Ika-tarashi-hiko no miko.* The name probably signifies "severe (or dignified) perfect prince."

[485] This name is obscure.

[486] *I.e.*, Karibata-tobe, the younger sister.

[487] This name and the next are obscure. The first of the two is not in the older editions, but Norinaga supplies what appears to be a lacuna in the text by adding the five characters 石衝別王次.

[488] Signification obscure.

[489] *Chinu no ike.* The "Sea of Chinu" in the province of Izumi, which is the same as the "Pool" here mentioned, has been mentioned in Vol. 2, Note 30.

[490] *Sayama no ike,* in the province of Kōchi. The name probably signifies a "gorge" or "defile."

[491] See above Vol. 2, Note 26.

[492] *Totori* (lit. "bird-catching") was in the province of Izumi, and the name is said to have been derived from the place having been one of those through which Ōtaka of Yamanobe passed when pursuing the bird whose sight was to make Prince Homuchi-wake obtain the power of speech. (See the story as given at the beginning of the next Section.) The name of Kawa-kami ("head-waters of the river"), as we learn by comparison with the parallel passage of the *Chronicles*, is to be traced to the River Udo, near whose headwaters the palace in question is said to have been situated.

[493] See Vol. 2, Note 42.

[494] See Vol. 2, Note 52.

[495] *Kawakami-be.*

[496] *Yamanobe no wake.* Yamanobe (or Yamabe) is the name of a district in Yamato and signifies "mountain-slope."

[497] *Sakikusa no wake.* Of Sakikusa nothing is known. The word means "lily."

[498] *Inaki no wake.* Which Inaki is meant is not known, there being several places of that name in Japan. The name is connected with the word *ine*, "rice."

[499] *Ada no wake.* Of Ada nothing is known.

[500]*Owari no kuni no Mino no wake.* Mino is the name of a village, and signifies "three moors."

[501]*Kibi no Iwanashi no wake.* Iwanashi is the name of a district forming part of the modern province of Bizen, and seems to signify "rockless."

[502]*Koromo no wake.* Norinaga supposes this name to be corrupt. Koromo is the name of a village in Mikawa.

[503]*Takasuka no wake.* Nothing is known either of the place or of the family.

[504]*Asuka no kimi.* It is not known where was this Asuka, which must not be confounded with the famous Asuka mentioned in Vol. 3, Note 145.

[505]*Mure no wake.* There are several places called Mure. The signification of the name is obscure.

[506]Or more literally, "worshiped and celebrated the festivals at," etc.

[507]*Saho no Anahobe-wake.* The name Anahobe is derived from Anaho, the name of the Emperor Yū-ryaku, and *be* "a tribe;" it being related in the *Chronicles* that the tribe which was established as his "name-proxy" was so called.

[508]*Otsuki no yama no kimi.* Otsuki is the name of a place in Ōmi. The family name must be interpreted to signify that they were wardens of the mountain.

[509]*Mikawa no Koromo no kimi. Cf.* the name in Vol. 2, Note 502, with which this is probably identical. Norinaga suspects an error in the text.

[510]*Kasuga no yama no kimi. Cf.* the name in Vol. 2, Note 508.

[511]*Koshi no ike no kimi.* Nothing is known of the place or of the family, Koshi may or may not be the northern province of that name.

[512]*Kasugabe no kimi.* There were two places of the name of Kasugabe (*i.e.*, "Kasuga Clan," so called perhaps after a family that had resided there). It is not known which is here alluded to.

[513]*Itoshi-be.* The name, which is thus restored by Norinaga, is variously mutilated in the older editions. This is the first mention of adoption, lit. in Japanese "child-proxy making" or "name-proxy making." The custom is perpetually referred to in the later portion of these *Records*.

[514]*Hagui no kimi.* Hagui is the name of a district in Noto. The derivation is obscure.

[515]*Mio no kimi,* Mio is the name of a place in Ōmi. It probably means "three mountain-folds."

[516]For stiletto see above, Vol. 1, Note 613. The curious word *ya-shio-ori* (八塩折) in the text seems to have the sense of "eight times tempered," *i.e.*, tempered over and over again, which Norinaga assigns to it. The same expression is used in Vol. 1, Note 313 to denote the refining of rice-liquor.

[517]This word "overflowing" is more appropriately placed in the version of the story given in the *Chronicles*, where the author makes her tears first fill her sleeve (a common Japanese figure of speech), and thence overflow onto the sleeping Monarch's face.

[518]Brocade? Hepburn speaks of a *nisihki hebi* as a kind of mottled snake. —W.G.A.

[519]The first personal pronoun is written with the self-depreciatory character 妾, "concubine."

[520]This expression, which is repeated elsewhere, is one which has given rise to a considerable amount of discussion. The *Chronicles* tell us expressly that "rice [-stalks] were piled up to make a castle,"—an assertion which, as Norinaga remarks, is simply incredible. He therefore adopts Mabuchi's suggestion that a castle *like* a rice-castle [Rice-castle also mentioned in Yū-ryaku, year 14, where a hasty construction is rather implied. *Nihongi*. —W.G.A.] is what is intended,—"rice-castle" being taken to mean "rice-store" or "granary," such granaries having probably been stoutly built in order to protect them from thieves. [I cannot see the likelihood of this. Sheaves of rice piled up might very well make a bulwark. The story shows that it was a hastily prepared work, not at all of the nature of a rice granary. The *Nihongi* says the Empress crossed over it in coming out. —W.G.A.] The historian of the Tang dynasty quoted in the *Exposition of the Foreign Notices of Japan* says that the Japanese had no castles, but only palisades of timber. The latter might well however have been called castles by the Japanese, though they would not have been accounted such by the Chinese, who already built theirs of stone.

[521]The import of this passage is, according to Norinaga, that the Empress imagined that her own conduct might perhaps influence the Emperor to refuse to give to the child she bore him its proper rank,—not from doubts as to its legitimacy, but as having a rebel mother. By "undertaking" the child is of course meant "undertaking" the care and education of it.

[522]Norinaga supposes the Chinese character rendered "said" to be an error, and prefers to consider this clause as containing not the words, but the thought of the Monarch. It would certainly be more convenient to adopt this view, if it were sanctioned by any text.

[523]Seems rather hard on the jewel-makers, who cannot have been in the rice-castle, and could not have been responsible. —W.G.A.

[524]There is nowhere else any reference to this saying. Norinaga supposes it to point to those who, hoping for reward, get punishment instead, these jewelers having doubtless rotted the string on which the beads were strung by special desire of the Empress, whereas they ended by getting nothing but confiscation for their pains.

[525]Norinaga (following Mabuchi) is evidently correct in supposing the character 命 in this place, and again a little further on, to be a copyist's error for 令, "caused," and the translator has rendered it accordingly.

[526]"Prince" is here written 御子.

[527]This name may also be read *Ho-muchi-wake*, and is in the *Chronicles* given as *Ho-mutsu-wake* while it appears as *Homu-tsu-wake* at the commencement of Sect. 69. The first two elements apparently signify "fire-possessing" while *wake* is the frequently recurring honorific signifying either "lord" or "young and flourishing."

[528]The characters 大湯坐若湯生 used in the original of this passage would, if they stood alone, be of difficult interpretation. But a comparison with the passage in

"One account" of the *Chronicles*, which relates the nursing of Fuki-aezu-no-mikoto, the father of the first "Earthly Emperor" Jin-mu, leaves no doubt that the author intended to speak of bathing-women attached to the service of the Imperial infant.

529 [Why not "girdle"? —W.G.A.] The words *mizu no o-himo,* literally rendered "fresh small pendant," call for some explanation. Mizu, which includes in a single term the ideas of youth, freshness, and beauty, is here used as an honorific. The "small pendant" is interpreted by Mabuchi and Norinaga to signify the "inner girdle," which held together the under-garment of either sex. The old literature of Japan teems with allusions to the custom of lovers or spouses making fast each other's inner girdle, which might not be untied till they met again, and the poets perpetually make a lover ask some such question as "When I am far from thee, who shall loosen my girdle?" The translator cannot refrain from here quoting, for the benefit of the lover of Japanese verse (though he will not attempt to translate them), the two most graceful of the many stanzas from the *Collection of a Myriad Leaves* brought together by Norinaga to illustrate this passage:

Wagimoko ga
Yuiteshi himo o
Tokame ya mo:
Toeba tayu to mo
Tada ni au made ni.

Una-bara o
Tōku watarite
Toshi fu to mo:
Ko-ra ga musuberu
Himo toku na yume.

Tanikawa Kotosuga also appropriately quotes the following:

Futari shite
Mitsubishi himo o
Hitori shite
Ware wa toi-miji
Tada ni au made wa.

A literal rendering of which would run thus: "I will not, till we meet face to face, loosen alone the girdle which we two tied together."

530 *I.e.*, the "Elder Princess and the Younger Princess."

531 Norinaga is probably right in explaining *tatasu* as the honorific causative of *tatsu*, "to stand" and *michi no ushi* as *michi-nushi* or *kuni-nushi, i.e.*, "owner of the province," "ruler."

532 What about the character 公? —W.G.A. [The character clarifies that the two women are pure and "loyal," unlike Saho-bime. —M.F.]

533 From a comparison with a passage in the *Chronicles*, where the same expression occurs, one is led to suppose that the craft here mentioned was a sort of double boat, in each half of which passengers could sit.

[534]Nothing is known of any place called Aizu in the province of Owari.

[535]Karu has been mentioned in Vol. 2, Note 181. The Pool of Ichishi (*Ichishi-no ike*) is supposed by Norinaga to be identical with the better known Pool of Iware.

[536]Norinaga reasonably supposes the character 今 in this sentence to be a copyist's error for the emphatic 爾, and the translation has been made accordingly.

[537]The original has the character 鵠, which is now applied to a small species of swan (*Cygnus minor,* Pallas; *Cygnus Bewickii*, Yarrel). But it is uncertain what bird is intended by the author.

[538]A more or less inarticulate utterance is probably meant; but the expression in the original is obscure.

[539]Norinaga supposes the Note in the original to refer only to the word Ōtaka, while he takes Yamanobe to be the name of a place (already mentioned in Se Vol. 2, Note 465). The surname of Ōtaka, signifying "great hawk" was, according to the same commentator, given to the worthy here mentioned in consequence of the incident related in the text. As the bird was not a hawk, this does not seem very convincing, and Norinaga's apparent idea that the man was likened to a hawk because he pursued the other bird as a hawk would do, is extremely far-fetched. It is moreover doubtful whether the name should not be read *Ō-washi* (this is Mabuchi's reading), "great eagle." The *Chronicles* give an altogether different name, viz., *Ame-no-yukawa-tana*.

[540]The *Chronicles* say that the swan was caught in the land of Izumo, and makes no mention of the other places. —W.G.A.

[541]No such place is now known. The name may be interpreted to mean "snare-net" in allusion to this story, as stated in the next sentence of the text.

[542]The various texts and printed editions all differ slightly in their reading of this passage, and from some it might be gathered that the prince did indeed speak as it had been thought that he would do, but could not speak freely. The translation follows Norinaga's emended text.

[543]*I.e.*, *Ō-kuni-nushi* (the Master of the Great Land), the aboriginal monarch of Izumo, the descendant of the Sun-Goddess, whose abdication of the sovereignty of Japan in favor of the descendant of the Sun-Goddess forms the subject-matter of Sect. 32. The word *tatari*, here written with the Chinese character 祟 and rendered "curse," signifies properly the vengeance of a spirit, *i.e.*, either of a deity or of the ghost of a dead man. The word translated "doing" is literally "heart."

[544]That some such words must be supplied is evident, and the translator has followed Mabuchi and Norinaga in supplying them.

[545]Remember that the original word *ukei* combines the meanings of our words "wager" "oath," "pledge," curse," etc,—being in fact a general name for all words to which any mysterious importance attaches.

[546]*Sagisu no ike*, a pool in Yamato. *Sagi-su* signifies "heron's nest."

[547]The reading of the characters 爾者 (rendered "then") in this passage has been a crux to all the editors. Fortunately they make no difference to the sense.

[548]*Amakashi no saki*. Perhaps "Amakashi Point" would be a better rendering if, as

Norinaga supposes, an inland place in the province of Yamato is meant. It might be the point or extremity of a hill or bluff. *Ama-kashi* signifies literally "sweet oak." The "broad-foliaged bear-oak" mentioned immediately above is supposed by Norinaga to be the usual evergreen oak, and not any special kind. The epithet "broad-foliaged" is not, as he remarks, specially appropriate, and he moreover supposes the word *kuma*, "bear," to be a corruption of *kumi* or *komori*, words which would refer to the thick luxuriance of the foliage. The dictionaries do not help us much to a decision on the point.

[549]The component parts of this tremendous name, which is happily abbreviated to Ake-tatsu in the subsequent portions of the text, are somewhat obscure, especially the word *oyu*, which reading rests only on a conjecture of Norinaga's, who emends the evidently erroneous character 者 to 老 (*oyu*), "old." *Toyo*, "luxuriant," is an honorific, *ake* and *tatsu* signify respectively "dawn" and "rise," while the rest seem to be names of places of which this Prince may be supposed to have been the possessor.

[550]Or, the Prince of Unakami, as Unakami is the name of a place in Kazusa.

[551]Nara in Yamato, which is here mentioned for the first time, was the capital of Japan from 710 to 784 C.E., and has always been famous in Japanese history and literature. The name is derived by the author of the *Chronicles* from the verb *narasu*, "to cause to resound," the hosts of the Emperor Sū-jin having, it is said, caused the earth to resound with their trampling when they went out to do battle with Hani-yasu. A more probable derivation is from *nara*, the name of a kind of deciduous oak, the *Quercus glandulifera*. [konara oak —MF] The word rendered "gate" should possibly be taken simply in the sense of "exit" or "approach."

[552]Or, "lame people and blind people," a peculiarly unlucky omen for travelers, to whom, as Norinaga remarks, sound feet and good eyesight are indispensable to carry them on their way.

[553]See Sect. 64, Note d.

[554]In the text the word "gate" is here, by a copyist's error, written "moon." When the author says that the Ki gate, *i.e.* gate or exit leading to the province of Ki, is a "side-gate," he means that it was not the one by which travelers would naturally have left the town:—the province of Ki, indeed, is to the south of Yamato where the capital was, whereas the province of Izumo, whither they were bound, was to the northwest. This road into Ki over Matsuchi-yama is one famous in the classical poetry of Japan.

[555]*Homuji-be*. The meaning of the clause is that they granted the surname of Homuji to persons in every important locality through which they passed on their journey.

[556]See Vol. 1, Note 303.

[557]The signification of this passage is: "They built as a temporary abode for the prince a house in the River Hi (whether with its foundations actually in the water or on an island is left undetermined), connecting it with the main land by a bridge made of branches of trees twisted together and with their bark left on

them" (this is here the import of the word "black"). Such bridges have been met with by the translator in the remote northern province of Dewa [Yamagata and Akita Prefectures. —M.F.], where the country people call them *shiba-bashi* (or, rather, in their patois *suba-bashi* [Hurdle-bridge. —W.G.A.] *i.e.*, "twig-bridges"). The traveler is so likely to fall through interstices into the stream below, that it is not to be wondered at that they should now be confined to the rudest localities.

558 Norinaga supposes *Kiisa* to be the name of a place, and *tsu-mi* to stand as usual for *tsu mochi*, "possessor," according to which view the name would mean "lord" or "possessor" of Kiisa.

559 No book of reference with which the translator is acquainted throws any light on this curious expression, and there is no parallel passage in the *Chronicles* to which to look for help.

560 Viz., to the Prince ("the august child"). The preparations which *Kiisa-tsu-mi* is here said to have made are supposed by Norinaga to have been prompted by a desire to add beauty to the feast. But the whole passage is very obscure.

561 *Ashi-hara-shiko-o,* one of the many names of the deity Ō-kuni-nushi ("Master of the Great Land," see Vol. 1, Note 343), the deity whom the Prince and his followers had just been worshipping.

562 These names cannot now be identified, and are of uncertain etymology. Iwakuma seems, however, to mean "curve in the rock." One would have expected in this place, instead of these unknown names, to find a reference to the main temple of the deity, which was styled *Kizuki no ō-yashiro, i.e.*, "the great shrine of Kizuki."

563 Some such words as "the changed and more intelligent appearance of the Prince, and his attainment of the power of speech" must be mentally supplied in order to bring out the sense which the author intends to convey.

564 These names cannot be identified. *Nagaho* signifies "long rice-ear," while *ajimasa* in modern usage is the name of a palm (the *Levistona chinensis*); but Norinaga supposes that it formerly designated the palmetto or some cognate tree.

565 *Hi-naga-hime*. The signification of the name is obscure, but it would seem most natural to suppose it connected with the River Hi which figures in the Izumo cycle of legends. A proposal of Norinaga's to read *Koe-naga* instead of the traditional *Hi-naga* seems scarcely to be meant in earnest. If accepted, it would give us the meaning of "fat and long princess," with reference to the story of her being a serpent.

566 It will be remembered that the Province of Izumo is a maritime one, and that the fugitives might be supposed to reach the sea-shore in their flight. It is true that this is exactly the reverse of the direction which they would be obliged to take in travelling up to the capital, which was in Yamato.

567 In the original *Totori-be, Torikai-be, Homuji-be, Ō-yue* and *Waka-yue.* All these "gentile names" have a meaning connecting them either really or apparently with the story above related, *to-tori* signifying "bird-catcher" and *tori-kai* "bird-feeder," while the name of the *Homuji* Clan is of course derived from that of the prince (Homuchi or Homuji), and *Ō-yue* and *Waka-yue* signify respectively "elder bather"

and "younger bather."

[568]*Hibasu-hime, Oto-hime* and *Matono-hime*. The first two of these names have already appeared above, where the etymology of *Hibasu* was said to be doubtful, while Oto signifies "younger sister." *Matono* has likewise already appeared, and is of uncertain derivation. Norinaga supposes this last name to be in this place but an alias for *Utakori*, which he explains in the sense of "sad heart," with reference to the story of this princess as here told. In any case there is confusion in the legend, for in the parallel passage of the *Chronicles* five princesses are mentioned, whereas at the end of Sect. 71 of these *Records* the Empress is made to speak of only two. The father's name has been already there explained.

[569]The real derivation of this name is obscure. The ancient (perhaps here and elsewhere supposititious ancient) form *Sagari-ki* signifies "hanging-tree." *Saga-ra-ka* is written 相樂, a good example of the free manner in which some Chinese characters were anciently used for phonetic purposes. *Sō-raku, Sa-raku* or *Sa-gara* would be the only readings possible in the modern tongue.

[570]The meaning of this name, which is written phonetically both here and in the *Chronicles*, has given rise to differences of opinion, some deriving it from the name of the province of Tajima (itself of obscure origin) and from the word *mori* "keeper," while others think it comes from *tachibana*, the Japanese word for orange [*Tachibana* is a small, fragrant citrus fruit native to Japan. —MF], with reference to the story here told. The supporters of the former view, on the other hand, derive the word *tachibana* from *Tajima-mori*.

[571]*Miyake no muraji*. Whether *miyake* is simply the name of a place or whether it should be taken in the sense of "store" or "granary," is uncertain. If the latter view be adopted, it would be natural to suppose that this family had originally furnished the superintendents of the Imperial granaries. In any case it traced its origin to a Korean source (see the *Catalogue of Family Names*, and the genealogies in Sect. 115).

[572]See Vol. 1, Note 437.

[573]Written in the parallel passage of the *Chronicles* with characters signifying literally "timeless." The whole of this circumlocution for the orange has indeed to be interpreted by the help of the *Chronicles*, it being here written phonetically and offering some difficulties as it stands.

[574]This corrupt and obscure passage seems to be well restored by Norinaga, whose explanation of it is likewise as convincing as it is ingenious. The expression "club-moss-oranges" signifies oranges as they grow on the branch surrounded by leaves, while "spear-oranges" are the same divested of leaves and hanging to the bare twig. Thus the words "clubmoss" and "spear" came to be used as "auxiliary numerals" for oranges plucked in these two different manners. [I have my doubts. —W.G.A.]

[575]Viz., says Norinaga, Princess Hibasu, who however, according to the account in the *Chronicles*, was already dead at this time.

[576]The word *tachibana* (written 橘) in the text should probably be taken as a specific and not as a general term. In modern usage it designates the *Citrus tachibana* (wild mandarin). But it is a matter of dispute whether the application of the term

has not altered since ancient times, and whether we should not understand by it one of the other kinds of orange now to be found in Japan,—perhaps the *Citrus nobilis*.

[577]Both the locality and the etymology of Mitachi are obscure. Sugahara ("sedge-moor") is known to be in the province of Yamato.

[578]The character 祝 ("to pray") in the text is indubitably a copyist's error for 棺, "coffin." These stone coffins are described by Mr. Henry von Siebold in his *Notes on Japanese Archaeology* p. 5. It must be understood that, from being the name of an office, Stone-Coffin-Maker (*Ishi-hi-tsukuri*) became a "gentile name."

[579]*Hanishi-be*. The meaning of this expression becomes clear by reference to the parallel passage of the *Chronicles*, which it may be worthwhile to quote at length from Mr. Satow's translation in pp. 329–330 of Vol. 8, Pt. 3, of these *Transactions*: "In 14 the autumn of the 32nd year, on the *tsuchi no to u* day of the moon, which rose on the *ki no e inu* day, the empress Hi-ba-su hime no Mikoto (in another source called Hi-ba-su ne no Mikoto) died, and they were several days going to bury her. The Mikado commanded all his high officers, saying: 'We knew before that the practice of following the dead is not good. In the case of the present burying, what shall be done?' Thereupon Nomi no Sukune advanced and said: 'It is not good to bury living men standing at the sepulcher of a prince, and this cannot be handed down to posterity. I pray leave now to propose a convenient plan, and to lay this before the sovereign.' And he sent messengers to summon up a hundred of the clay-workers' tribe of the country of Izumo, and he himself directed the men of the clay-workers' tribe in taking clay and forming shapes of men, horses and various things, and presented them to the Mikado, saying: 'From now and henceforward let it be the law for posterity to exchange things of clay for living men, and set them up at sepulchers.' Thereupon the Mikado rejoiced, and commended Nomi no Sukune, saying: 'Thy expedient plan has truly pleased Our heart;' and the things of clay were for the first time set up at the tomb of Hi-ba-su hime no Mikoto. Wherefore these things were called *haniwa* (a circle of clay). Then he sent down an order, saying: 'From now and henceforward, be sure to set up these things of clay at sepulchers, and let not men be slain.' The Mikado bountifully praised Nomi no Sukune, bestowed on him a kneading-place, and appointed him to the charge of the clay-workers' tribe."

[580]In the province of Yamato. In the old poetry there are many plays on this word *Saki*, which is homonymous with the verb "to blossom." But whether that be its real derivation, it were hard to say. *Terama* appears to signify "Buddhist temple-space," an etymology which is embarrassing to the Shintō commentators who, accepting every word of our text as authentic history, are hard-driven to explain how Buddhist temples could have existed in Japan before the date assigned for the introduction of Buddhism. [Tera is a Chinese word which came to Japan through the Korean 설. —W.G.A.]

[581]In the province of Yamato. The etymology of *Makimuku* is obscure. *Hi-shiro* is tentatively derived by Norinaga from *hi*, the *Chamaecyparis obtusa* (a kind of conifer) [hinoki cypress. —M.F.] , and *shiro*, "an enclosure."

[582] *Harima no inabi no ō-iratsume.* Inabi is also known under the alternative form of *Inami*: etymology uncertain.

[583] *Waka-take Kibi tsu hiko. Waka-take* signifies "young brave."

[584] *Kibi no omi.*

[585] *Kushi* signifies "wondrous," and *wake* either "young" or "lord." The meaning of *tsunu* is obscure.

[586] The names of this prince and the next signify respectively "great foot-pestle" [Is it not *usu*, the "mortar"? See note in the *Chronicles* where it is thought the upper and lower stones of the quern or hand-mill are meant. —W.G A.] and "little foot-pestle," the origin of the bestowal of which singular designations is thus related in the parallel passage of the *Chronicles*: "The Imperial child Ō-usu and His Augustness O-usu were born together the same day as twins. The Heavenly Sovereign, astonished, informed the foot-pestle. So the two Kings were called Great Foot-pestle and Little Foot-pestle." What the import of this passage may be is, however, a mystery both to Tanikawa Kotosuga and to Norinaga.

[587] Norinaga supposes *o-guna* to have been an archaic word for "boy," *me-gima* signifying "girl." *Yamato o-guna* would thus signify "*the* boy of Japan," a not inappropriate designation for this prince, who under his later name of Yamato-take (Japan Brave, *i.e.*, "*the* brave man of Japan") has remained as the chief legendary type of the martial prowess of his native land.

[588] *I.e.*, Yamato Prince.

[589] *Kamu-kushi no mikoto*, "divine wondrous."

[590] *Ya-saka no iri-bime no mikoto.* The signification of this name and of the next (*Ya-saka no iri-biko no mikoto*) is obscure. [Saka from the Chinese Shaku? —W.G.A.]

[591] *Waka-tarashi-hiko no mikoto, i.e.*, "young and perfect prince."

[592] *I-o-ki no iri-biko no mikoto.* Signification obscure.

[593] Or, *Oshi-wake, i.e.*, perhaps "Great Lord."

[594] *I-o-ki no iri-bime no mikoto.* Signification obscure.

[595] *Toyo-to-wake no mikoto, i.e.*, perhaps "luxuriant swift prince."

[596] *Nunoshiro no iratsume.* Signification obscure.

[597] *Nunaki no iratsume.* Signification obscure.

[598] *Kago-yori-hime no mikoto. Yori-hime* probably means "good princess." The sense of *Kago* is very doubtful, for it may either be the name of a place, or else identical with the verb *kagayaku* "to shine," or with *kago*, "a stag."

[599] *Waka-ki no iri-biko no mikoto.* The signification of this name is obscure.

[600] *Kibi no e-hiko no mikoto.*

[601] *Takaki-hime no mikoto.* The meaning of *takaki* in this place is not certain.

[602] *Oto-hime no mikoto, i.e.*, "the younger princess."

[603] *Himuka no Mi-hakashi-bime. Mi hakashi* signifies "august saber." See Norinaga's *Commentary*, Vol. 26 p. 11, for a gloss on this curious name.

[604] *Toyo-kuni-wake no miko, i.e.*, perhaps "lord of the luxuriant land," or else "lord of the land of Toyo," the Emperor Kei-kō having, according to the account in the

Chronicles, spent some years fighting in southwestern Japan, where the province of Toyo is situated.

[605] *Inabi no waki-iratsume*. See Vol. 2, Note 582.

[606] *Ma-waka no miko, i.e.*, "truly young prince."

[607] *Hiko-hito no ō-e no miko. Hiko* signifies "prince," *hito* is "person" (or here, according to Norinaga, "headman"), and *ō-e* is "great elder brother."

[608] *Ka-guro-hime, i.e.*, probably "the black-haired princess."

[609] *Sume-iro-ō-naka-tsu-hiko-no-mikoto*. The signification of this name is not clear. Norinaga identifies *sume* with the like-sounding verb signifying "to be supreme." *Ō-naka-tsu-hiko* may signify "great middle prince," referring to the comparative ages of this prince and his brethren.

[610] There is here an evident error in the genealogy, as it would make the emperor marry his own great-great-grand daughter! A guess of the editor of 1687 that for Yamato-take we should read Waka-take (a son of the Emperor Kō-rei) is approved by Norinaga, and may be adopted as probably correct,—*i.e.* (what is but little likely) if this portion of the *Records* should eventually be proved to be historically trustworthy. The question is discussed by Norinaga in Vol. 26, pp. 12–14, of his *Commentary*.

[611] *Ō-e no miko*. This name would, as Norinaga remarks, appear to have erroneously crept in here through the influence of the name mentioned in Note 27, the whole account of this union with Princess Ka-guro being corrupt.

[612] The Japanese term (王 *miko*) includes both males and females.

[613] 太子.

[614] As above remarked, the Japanese term includes both males and females, and moreover some of the female children are specially mentioned. The difficulty as to how females could have been appointed to the offices here mentioned is not solved by Norinaga, whose note on this passage is evasive.

[615] The four names of offices (also used as "gentile names") here mentioned are in the original Japanese *Kuni no Miyatsuko, Wake, Inaki* and *Agata-nushi*. (See Introduction, p. 16.)

[616] *Mamuta no muraji*. (See Vol. 2, Note 138.)

[617] *Mori no kimi. Mori* seems to be the name of a place (perhaps in Mino); but nothing is known of this family.

[618] *Ōta no kimi. Ōta* is the name of a place in Mino, and signifies "great rice-fields."

[619] *Shimada no kimi. Shimada* is perhaps the name of a place in Owari. It signifies "island rice-field."

[620] *Ki no kuni no sakabe no abiko*. For *abiko* see Sect. 72, Note 85. *Sakabe* seems to signify "liquor tribe," this family and the next having been entrusted with the management of the Imperial feasts.

[621] *Uda no Sakabe, i.e.*, the "Liquor Tribe of Uda" (in Yamato).

[622] *Himuka no kuni no miyatsuko*.

[623] This is Norinaga, but is hardly satisfactory. Probably the text is corrupt. —W.G.A.

[624] *I.e.*, the elder princess and the younger princess.

[625] See Vol. 2, Note 342.

[626] *Mino no kuni no miyatsuko.*

[627] There is no causative in the Chinese, and the "sorrow" might be the emperor's. The causative form given by Norinaga is probably meant to be honorific only. —W.G.A.

[628] The meaning of the syllables *oshi* in this name and the companion one (*Oshi-kuro no oto-hiko*) immediately below is probably "great"; *kuro* is obscure; *e-hiko* signifies "elder prince" and *oto-hiko* "younger prince."

[629] *Mino no Unesu no wake.* Of Unesu nothing is known.

[630] *Mugetsu no himi.* Mugetsu or Muge was in the province of Minu (Mino).

[631] Such is the reasonable explanation of the original term *tabe* (田部) given by Norinaga. It seems to have become a "gentile name."

[632] *Kashiwade no ō-tomo-be.* This "gentile name" originally denoted one who was butler, steward, or cook, in the Emperor's household. The tradition of its origin is preserved in the *Chronicles.*

[633] Norinaga supposes that the mention both is this history and in the *Chronicles of Japan* of the planting of bamboos on the banks of this pool or lake should be attributed to the rarity of such a proceeding in ancient times.

[634] Lit., "branches."

[635] Norinaga thinks he may have survived this treatment! —W.G.A.

[636] *I.e.*, presumably "bravoes at Kumaso"; but it is to be remarked that in this and like compounds with *takeru* ("bravo") the Japanese language uses no post-position. For Kumaso see Vol. 1, Note 82.

[637] The characters used for these last two words are those properly restricted to the mention of an Imperial progress, but Yamato-take is constantly spoken of as if he had actually sat on the throne.

[638] The character used is 室, which simply means apartment; but see Vol. 2, Note 81.

[639] Were they not actually dwelling in it? —W.G.A.

[640] Norinaga reads "*New* cave," but the word "august" is in the text. At the same time we see that this feast was intended as a house-warming. *Cf.* the commencement of Sect. 164.

[641] Merry-making? "Rejoicing" a little too comprehensive. —W.G.A.

[642] The parallel passage of the *Chronicles* puts the same meaning into plainer words. It says: "He undid his hair, and made it appear like a girl's."

[643] Or, according to the old reading, "mixing with the concubines."

[644] The word rendered "steps" is of doubtful interpretation.

[645] Or perhaps "the skin of his back" or "the [beast's?] skin on his back." But Norinaga is probably right [Yes. —W.G.A.] in supposing the character 皮, "skin" to be an error for 以, "with," to be construed with the word "saber." (In the English idiom this particle falls away.)

[646] Written with the humble character 僕, "servant."

[647]The contemptuous second personal pronoun *ore* is used here and in the next clause.

[648]There is Norinaga's authority for thus understanding the bravo's words. Taken still more literally, they would seem to imply that there were no brave and strong men in the West *excepting* himself and his brother.

[649]The words "there is" are an attempt at rendering the termination *keri* of the original. See Vol. 1, Note 173. [The force of *Keri* here is somewhat like: "Yet in the land," etc.—"it has appeared that,"—"it has turned out that,"—"it would seem that"—"it has come to pass that,"—"I find that." —W.G.A.]

[650]折, "broke," in the text is, as the commentators observe, an evident error for 析, "ripped."

[651]Or specifically, the "muskmelon."

[652]The translator has followed Norinaga's restoration of this passage, in which, by the transposition of the characters 也 and 故, the end of this sentence and the beginning of the next were mixed together in the older editions.

[653]Lit., "[they] praised the august name, calling him," etc.

[654]Or, "of the Ana passage" (lit. door), the modern Strait of Shimonoseki. The word *ana* signifies "hole," and there is a tradition (which Norinaga quotes in his note on this name in Vol. 27, pp. 26–29 of his *Commentary*) to the effect that formerly the Main Island and the island of Kyūshū were continuous at this point, there being only a sort of natural tunnel, through which junks could pass.

[655]The species mentioned (*chihi*) is the *Quercuts gilva* [red-bark oak. —M.F.]

[656]See Vol. 1, Note 303.

[657]Cross-sword —W.G.A.

[658]Lit., "let us join swords." The word "suggested" (誂) in this sentence is an emendation of Norinaga's, the text having 誹, "slandered." The older printed editions, while retaining the character 誹, read it *azamukite*, "deceived."

[659]In its position in the present text, this Song must be taken as an ironical lament of the Prince for the dead bravo. In the *Chronicles* the time and the heroes of the episode, and the singers of the Song are all different, and in that context the lament sounds like a genuine one. The reader will remember what was said in the Introduction as to the use of creepers for string. That mentioned in the text is supposed to be the *Cocculus thunbergi* [Probably refers to a relative of kudzu. —M.F.].

[660]See Vol. 2, Note 444.

[661]*Mi-suki-tomo-mimi-take-hiko*. *Mi* is an honorific, *mimi* probably signifies "ears," and *take* means "brave." The words *suki* and *tomo* are obscure.

[662]*Kibi no omi*.

[663]Properly the *Olea aquifolium* [false holly or holly olive. —M.F.], which resembles holly. Norinaga supposes that an entirely wooden spear or stick is here meant to be spoken of, and not the weapon with a metal point which is commonly understood by the word "spear" (*hoko*).

[664]Perhaps we should write "august court," for the characters 朝廷 in the text are evidently intended for the homonymous 御門. The court in front of the deity's

temple is what is here alluded to, and it would perhaps be a not unpardonable departure from the text to insert the preposition "at" or "in," [*Cf. mi-mae.*—W.G.A.] and translate thus: "worshiped *in* the Deity's court."

[665]*Miyazu-hime* (in the *Chronicles* and in the printed editions of these *Records* previous to Norinaga's written *Miyasu-hime* without the *nigori*). Neither Norinaga nor Tanikawa Kotosuga makes any suggestion as to the signification of this name.

[666]*Owari no miyatsuko.*

[667]In later times *Sagami.* No authority great or small has given a satisfactory etymology of this name, though numerous and elaborate attempts have been made to explain it.

[668]In the original *hi-uchi* (火打). Mr. Satow, who has given a translation of this passage in a note to his third paper on the *Rituals* to be found in Vol. 9, Pt. 2, p. 202 of these *Transactions*, renders this word by "steel." The present writer prefers not to prejudge the question as to whether the "fire-striker" [The word "strike" seems hardly applicable to a fire-drill. —W.G.A.] intended by the author was a steel, or a wooden fire-drill. Norinaga would seem to have held the latter view, as in his gloss on this passage he refers to the previous passage near the end of Sect. 32, where the fire-drill is explicitly mentioned. He also quotes an ancient ode in which "a fire-striker of metal" is specially referred to, so that it would seem that all fire-strikers were not of that material.

[669]Remember that this word "Ruler" (*Miyatsuko*) had the acceptation of a "gentile name," as well as of the name of an office, so that we may understand the author to mean that Yamato-take destroyed the whole Ruling Family of Sagami. The parallel passage of the *Chronicles* has "he burnt all that rebel band, and destroyed them."

[670]The words rendered "that place" are supplied by Norinaga, their omission being evidently a copyist's error. *Yaki-zu* signifies "the port of burning."

[671]*I.e.*, "running water."

[672]*I.e.*, his consort. Conf. Vol. 2, Note 637.

[673]*Oto-tachibana-hime no mikoto.* (See Vol. 2, Note 730.)

[674]Written with the humble character 妾, lit. "concubine."

[675]Or "mats." But the same word is used as that which must be translated "rugs" immediately below.

[676]This Song gives much trouble to the commentators, whose remarks (to be found in Norinaga's *Commentary*, Vol. 27, pp. 67–69, and Moribe's *Izumo Koto-ai,* Vol. 3, pp. 6–9) should be consulted by the student desirous of forming an opinion of his own. The general purport of the poem is of course to allude to Yamato-take's adventure on the burning moor, and at the same time to the love which bound him and his consort together; but almost each individual line offers matter for doubt. Thus it is not certain whether the verb *toishi*, here rendered "enquired of" (*i.e.,* attended upon *q.d.*, by the Empress), should not rather be given the word "thou" as subject, in which case the signification would be "thou who enquiredst of [*i.e.,* wooedst]." The word used for "thou" is the honorific equivalent of that pronoun, signifying literally "prince." Moribe disputes the propriety of considering Sagamu

in this place as the name of a province; and the word *sanesashi,* here translated "where the true peak pierces" (Mt. Fuji being by some supposed to be thus alluded to) is of very doubtful interpretation. Norinaga tells us that the final particles *wa mo*, rendered by the initial interjection "Oh," should here be understood as an exclamation of grief, [*Nageki-kotoba* is simply an interjection,—not necessarily of grief. —W.G.A.] a signification more forcible than that which usually belongs to them. Finally Moribe points out that the Song does not suit the context in which it is found, and has probably been erroneously inserted here instead of in an earlier portion of the text.

[677]This is the traditional ancient reading of what is according to the modern pronunciation *Ezo,* while the Chinese characters 蝦夷, with which the name is written, signify "Prawn Barbarians," in allusion (if Norinaga may be trusted) to the long beards which make their faces resemble a prawn's head. The hairy barbarians known to English readers as *Ainu,* and whose name of *Ezo* is applied by the Japanese to the northernmost large island of the Japanese Archipelago, which is still chiefly tenanted by them, are almost certainly here referred to. In ancient times they inhabited a great part of the Main Island of Japan. The translator may add that the genuineness of the so-called ancient reading *"Emishi"* appears to him doubtful. The name known to the people themselves, and which apparently can be traced as far as Kamchatka, is *Ezo.*

[678]*Ashigara-zaka,* one of the passes from Sagami into Suruga leading towards Mount Fuji.

[679]*Nira,* the *Allium odorum.* [With a scrap of the wild chive which was left over from his meal. —W.G.A.]

[680]The translator doubts the correctness of the derivation of Azuma given in the text, although it is universally accepted and certainly fits in well with the graceful legend by which it is here accounted for.

[681]This name is identified by the native etymologists with a homonymous substantive signifying "a place between mountains."

[682]The etymology of this name is uncertain. But the most likely opinion is that it signifies "a zigzag road down a pass."

[683]*I.e.,* since leaving the province of Hitachi, of which Tsukuha (in modern parlance Tsukuba, with the last syllable *nigori'*ed) and Niibari (modern Niiharu) are two districts. In the later poetry *Niibari no* is often used as a pillow-word for the name of Mount Tsukuba. The etymology of both names is uncertain, but "newly tilled" seems to be the most probable etymology of the first of the two.

[684]Not necessarily a fire kindled for the sake of obtaining warmth, but fire in general, including, as Norinaga suggests, torches and fires lit to drive away mosquitoes. There are frequent mentions in the classical literature of this latter sort of fire, which may indeed still be met with in some districts where mosquito-nets are not yet in common use.

[685]Continued. —W.G.A.

[686]The meaning is: "On counting up, I find that we have been ten days and nine

nights."—Previous to Norinaga the expression *ka-ga nabete,* "having put in a row (*i.e.,* counted) the days" was curiously misunderstood, and subjected to various far-fetched interpretations. There can however be no doubt but that Norinaga is right.—The reason why the old man is said to have "completed" [Continued. —W.G.A.] the Prince's song is that the former taken alone is of incomplete rhythm. [Meter; but with the old man's verse added, no verse of any recognized meter is produced. —W.G.A.]

[687]Or, as Norinaga would prefer to consider it, "the Rulership of *an* Eastern Land," viz., one out of the twelve Eastern provinces.

[688]See Vol. 1, Note 550.

[689]*Shinano no saka,* a pass between the provinces of Shinano and Mino which is no longer used.

[690]Even taken apart from its immediate context, the import of this Song is plain, notwithstanding Moribe's efforts to explain away its indelicacy. The details of the first part, however, require some comment in order to make them comprehensible to the European reader, the words in question being those which might in English be rendered "thy fragile, slender, delicate arm [which resembles] a post striking against the sharp sickle on Mount Kagu of the gourd-shaped heaven." In Japanese they run thus:

Hisa-kata no
Ame no Kagu-yama
To-kama ni
Sa-wataru kubi:—
Hiha-boso
Ta-waya-gaina o, etc.

It will be remarked that the first four lines form a punning preface to the fifth. Such punning prefaces have not necessarily any logical connection with what follows, as has been explained by the present writer in a paper "On the Use of Pillow-Words and Plays upon Words in Japanese Poetry," to be found in Vol. 5, Pt. 1, pp. 79 et seq. of these *Transactions.* In this particular case, however, there is sufficient continuity of sense to warrant the continuous translation above given. The word "post," though such a use of it is very curious, must be understood to denote not a dead, but a living trunk, or rather the stem of some delicate plant or grass which falls beneath the sickle of the mower on Mount Kagu in Heaven, or, as it may better be understood, on the Heavenly Mount Kagu [in Yamato]. "Gourd-shaped" is the translation of *hisa-kata no* or *hisa-gata no*, the pillow-word for "heaven." Its meaning is disputed, but Mabuchi in his *Dictionary of Pillow-Words* and Norinaga agree in giving to it the sense here adopted (see the above-mentioned paper "On the Use of Pillow-Words, etc.," p. 81).

[691]The total sense of this Song is quite plain.—In the first lines of it the Prince is addressed as if he were the reigning sovereign. The words *placidè administrationem faciens* [perform the administration calmly —M.F.] represent the Japanese *yasumishishi,* the pillow-word for *wa ga ō-kimi,* "my great lord." Elsewhere the

English rendering "who tranquilly carries on the government" has been adopted. The word *aratama no*, rendered by the adjective *renovatis* [renewed —M.F.], is the pillow-word for "sun," "moon," and "year," and is of not quite certain import. The interpretation here adopted has, however, for it the weight of probability and of native authority, Mabuchi in his *Dictionary of Pillow-Words* deriving it from the verb *aratamaru*, "to be renewed."

[692]B.H.C. gives the preceding passage and poem in Latin: Tunc Heræ Miyazu veli oræ adhæserunt menstrua. Quare [Augustus Yamato-take] ilia menstrua vidit et auguste cecinit, dicens:

Ego volui reclinare [caput] in fragili,
molli brachiolo [tuo, quod est simile] vallo
impingenti acutæ falci in Monti Kagu in
cœlo formato quasi cucurbita;—ego de-
sideravi dormire [tecum]. Sed in orâ veli
quod induis luna surrexit."
Tunc Hera Miyazu augusto cantui respondit, dicens:
Altè resplendentis solis auguste puer!
Placidè administrationem faciens mî magne
domine! Renovatis annis venientibus et
effluentibus, renovatæ lunæ eunt veniendo
et effluendo. Sane, sane, dum te im-
patienter exspecto, luna suâpte surgit in
orâ veli quod ego induo»!

Quare tunc [ille] coivit [cum illâ],

[693]The characters in the text might also be rendered "he made a progress," as they are those only properly applied to the movements of a reigning sovereign. Here and elsewhere, however, they are used in speaking of Yamato-take. (*Cf.* Sect. 80, Note 5.)

[694]On the frontier of Ōmi and Mino. *Ibuki* seems to signify "blowing," in allusion, it is said, to the pestilential breath or influence of the god by whom the place was tenanted. The word rendered "Mount" is supplied by the editor of 1687.

[695]Or "ox"' or "cow," the original word not distinguishing between the sexes.

[696]The Japanese expression *koto-age shite*, here rendered "lifted up words," very frequently has the signification of "lifting up a prayer" to some superhuman being. In this passage, however, it conveys no more than its proper etymological meaning,

[697]Viz., the god of Mount Ibuki.

[698]Perhaps "hail" may be intended by this expression, and so Norinaga decides. But this interpretation of the term seems to agree less well with the Song in Sect. 142.

[699]The commentators disagree as to whether this note should or should not be considered to form part of the original text. Norinaga so considers it. He however, in the opinion of the translator, is not happy in his alteration of the *kana* reading

given by the editor of 1687, which latter has accordingly been followed in the English version.

[700]The literal meaning of this name is "jewel-store-tribe"; but complete uncertainty attaches both to the etymology of the word and to the position of the place. The first printed edition has *Tama-kui-be.*

[701]He had been misled and dazed, but now came to himself again. Thence, according to the etymology of our author, the name of *I-same,* which signifies "dwelling (resting) and awaking," given to the spring.

[702]*Tagi-no.* We might, following the Chinese characters, translate thus: "and arrived on the Moor of Tagi." But the character 上 has in this context scarcely any meaning. The real etymology of *Tagi* (in classical and modern parlance *taki* without the *nigori)* is "rapid "or "waterfall," the cascade formed by the River Yō-rō in Mino being alluded to. The derivation in the next sentence of the text from *tagishi,* supposed to mean "a rudder," is a mere fancy.

[703]The word here rendered "rudder" is *tagishi,* which is written phonetically and does not occur elsewhere, except in a few Proper Names of doubtful import. There is however some probability in favor of the meaning assigned to it by the native commentators.

[704]*Tsue-tsuki-zaka, i.e.,* "the pass of leaning on a staff." It is in the province of Ise between Yokaichi and Ishi-yakushi.

[705]Norinaga says *mote mae* means "post," so that the translation should be "at the post of the single pine-tree."—W.G.A.

[706]Otsu-no-saki, in the province of Ise. The name probably signifies "harbor of the mountain declivity."

[707]The former portion of the text tells us nothing either of the meal or of the sword here mentioned.

[708]This quaintly simple and apparently very ancient poem needs no elucidation.

[709]In Ise. *Mi-e* signifies "three-fold."

[710]This is the literal rendering of the text. Norinaga thinks, however, that we should understand that there were various swellings on his legs, such as would be produced if the limb were tightly tied round with cord in three places.

[711]*Nobo-no* in the province of Ise. The name seems to signify "the moor of mounting."

[712]The Chinese character here used signifies simply "thinking of;" but in such a context its common Japanese interpretation is" loving or regretting," [Longing for. —W.G.A.] and so Norinaga means us to understand it when he reads *shinuhashite.*

[713]Viz., Yamato.

[714]This Song and the two following form but one in the pages of the *Chronicles,* where they appear with several verbal differences, and are attributed, not to the Prince, but to his father the Emperor. Moribe decides that in the latter particular the text of these *Records* gives the preferable account, but that the *Chronicles* are right in making the three Songs one continuous poem. The expression "this Song is a Land-Regretting Song" strongly supports this view; for though we might also

render in the plural "these Songs are, etc.," such a translation would be less natural, as in similar cases the numeral is used, thus "these *two* Songs are, etc." The expression "this is an Incomplete Song" points as decidedly to some mutilation of the original document, from which the compiler of the *Records* copied this passage. Taking then the three Songs as one, the entire drift is that of a paean on Yamato, the poet's native land, which he could not hope ever to see again:—Commencing by praising its still seclusion as it lies there behind its barrier of protecting mountains, he goes on to mention the rural pleasures enjoyed by those who, wandering over the hillsides, deck their hair with garlands of leaves and flowers. For himself indeed these delights are no more; "but," says he, "do you, ye children full of health and happiness! pursue your innocent enjoyment!" In conclusion he lovingly apostrophizes the clouds which, rising up from the southwest, are, as it were, messengers from home. The word *mahoroba*, rendered "secluded," is a great crux to the commentators, and Norinaga's *Examination of the Synonyms of Japan*, pp. 17–18, and Moribe's *Izu no Koto Waki*, Vol. 3, p. 31, should be consulted by the student desirous of forming his own opinion on the point. Another apparent difficulty is the word *gomoreru,* whose position in the sentence Norinaga seems to have misunderstood. By following Moribe, and taking it as compounded with the word *Aogaki-yama* into *Aogaki-yama-gomoreru* the difficulty vanishes, and we are likewise relieved from the necessity of supposing anything so highly improbable as that the verb *komoreru,* when not compounded, should have commenced with a *nigori*ed syllable. "Complete" signifies "healthy." Mount Heguri is preceded in the original by *tatamikomo* (Moribe reads *tatamigomo* with the *nigori*), a pillow-word whose import is disputed. In any case, being a punning one, it cannot be translated. For the "bear-oak" see Vol. 2, Note 548. Moribe labors, but without success, to prove that "come," the last word of the translation, signifies "go," and imagines that the prince is expressing his envy of the clouds which are rising and going off in the direction of the home which he will never revisit.

[715]This poem is an exclamation of distress at the thought of the sword which he had left with his mistress Princess Miyazu and which, if he had had it with him, would doubtless have preserved him from the evil influences of the god of Mount Ibuki, which were the beginning of his end.—"Saber-sword" (*tsurugi no tachi*) is a curious expression, which Norinaga interprets as signifying "sharp sword," while Moribe thinks it means "double-edged sword."

[716]The drift of the Song is a comparison of the helpless wanderings of the mourners in the neighborhood of the tomb to the convolutions of the *Dioscorea quinqueloba* (a creeping plant) growing among the rice in the adjacent fields. But there are evidently some lines omitted. If we were to adopt the elegant verses conjecturally supplied by Moribe, the entire translation would run thus: "The *Dioscorea quinqueloba* crawls hither and thither among the rice stubble, among the rice stubble in the rice fields encompassing [the mausoleum]; but though, like it, we crawl hither and thither and weep and speak to thee, thou answerest not a word"—Moribe supposes this poem to be the Empress's composition, and the

following three to have proceeded from the children.

[717]As usual when the word *chidori* (defined as "any kind of dotterel, plover or sandpiper") is used, it is doubtful what bird is really intended. At the end of this Section we are told that the Mausoleum was called the "Mausoleum of the White Bird (白鳥)." Specifically, however, these characters are used with their Sinico-Japanese pronunciation of *haku-chō* as the name of the swan. But as swans are nowhere else mentioned is these *Records*, and as moreover their habits are not such as to accord with the legend here narrated, it will perhaps be safer to retain "dotterel" in the translation. "Heron" [I have observed that several of the *misasagi* are favorite haunts of the white egret (paddy bird) for roosting at night and for nesting. They are usually overgrown with trees, and are protected by a moat and also by their sacred character. Compare *Nihongi* 8, 2, (pp. 217–218 Aston's translation.) —W.G.A.] also has been suggested.

[718]The signification of this Song is: "It is easy enough for thee, thou bird-spirit! to fly through the air. But remember that we are on foot, and that our feet are getting torn by the short stubble of the bamboo-grass (sasa, a genus of dwarf bamboo —MF)."

[719]When the bird flew over the sea, they too waded after it through the waves.

[720]The signification of the Song is: "As we pursue thee through the sea, we sink in the waves up to our middles, and totter like the water-plants against which strikes the current of a great river."— The word *ue-gusa*, lit. "herbs planted," is curious; but it simply means "herbs growing," as in the translation (*cf.* our word "plant"). The latter part of the poem is in the original highly elliptical.

[721]The point of this Song seems to rest on a delicate distinction between the words *hama*, "beach" and *iso* "seaside," [*Iso* seems related to *ishi* and *iwa*. The Chinese character also contains the element 石 "stone." Could *iso* therefore be "a rocky beach," *hama* corresponding rather to our word "strand"? The dotterel is fond of sandy places close to the sea rather than of stones and rocks. —W.G.A.] which does not obtain in the later Japanese language any more than it does in English. Both *hama* and *iso*, "beach" and "seaside," denote the boundary-line between sea and land; but we must suppose with the commentators that, while the former was used with special reference to the land, the latter considered the idea (so to speak) from the point of view of the sea. The import of the Song is therefore to upbraid the bird for flying over the waves instead of flying along the adjacent shore.

[722]*I.e.,* says Norinaga, from Ise.

[723]Not to be confounded with the Shiki in Yamato, which is written with different phonetic characters.

[724]The Verb used in the original is *shizumeru,* "to repress," "to quiet," "to lay," to establish," hence "to build a temple to a god," "to worship." The grammatical vagueness of the Japanese language helps in all this passage to preserve the connection of ideas in a manner which it is difficult to render in an English translation. Using no pronouns, it does not require to specialize in each instance whether it is the bird that is meant, or Yamato-take, but the two are confounded together in

language as they were in thought.

[725] *Shira-tori no misasaki.* According to the parallel passage of the *Chronicles*, it was not only this tomb in Kōchi, but the previously mentioned tomb at Nobonu, and also another in Yamato, which were severally known by this designation.

[726] The name signifies "seven-grasp shins," implying that the worthy here mentioned was so big and strong as to have shins seven hand-breadths [Spans? —W.G.A.] in length. For the use of the word "grasp" as a measure of length, see Vol. 1, Note 138.

[727] This family has already been mentioned at the end of Sect. 34, as descended from Ama-tsu-kume no Mikoto, one of the companions of the Emperor Jin-mu's grandfather on the occasion of his descent from Heaven. But see Vol. 1, Note 596, for the probable mistake with regard to this origin of the name.

[728] For this name see Vol. 2, Note 488.

[729] *I.e.*, "the perfect middle prince," a name which is justified by the genealogy as given in the *Chronicles*, where he is mentioned as the second of three sons borne by this princess.

[730] *Oto-tachibana-hime no mikoto. Oto* signifies "younger [sister]," and *tachibana* is the name of the orange [wild mandarin. —M.F.].

[731] See the story in Sect. 84.

[732] *Waka-take no miko.* This name signifies "young brave."

[733] *Futaji-hime.* Signification obscure. Futaji may be the name of a place. [The *Nihongi* [*Chronicles* —M.F.] makes her the same person as the princess of that name. —W.G.A.]

[734] If *Tamu* is, as Norinaga surmises, the name of a place, this personal name signifies "Great Lord of Tamu."

[735] *Chika-tsu-Ōmi no Yasu no kuni no miyatsuko.* For *Yasu* see Vol. 2, Note 368.

[736] *Ine-yori-wake no miko.* This name probably signifies "rice-good-lord."

[737] *Ō-kibi-take-hime. Ō* signifies "great." For the other two elements of the compound see Vol. 2, Note 738.

[738] The text has *Kibi no omi Take-hiko,* if this worthy had been himself the "Grandee of Kibi." Norinaga however compares the commencement of Vol. 2, Notes 661 and 662, and supplies the words "ancestor of." *Kibi* is of course the province of that name (the modern Bizen, Bitchū, and Bingo), and *take* signifies "brave."

[739] *Take-kaiko no miko. Take* signifies brave," *kaiko* is either "egg" or "cocoon," or else perhaps a corruption of some other word.

[740] *Yamashiro no Kukuma-mori-hime.* This name is obscure. Norinaga identifies *Kukuma* with a place called *Kurikuma,* and *mori* is probably the verb "to guard."

[741] *Ashi-kagami-wake no miko.* This name is written with characters signifying "foot-mirror-[lord]." [Or *kagami* is "bent,"—"club-foot"? —W.G.A.]

[742] *Okinaga-ta-wake no miko.* This name is obscure. Norinaga believes Okinaga to be the name of a place in Ōmi, but has no explanation to offer of *ta.*

[743] *Inukami no kimi.* Inukami is the name of a district in Ōmi. Its signification is not clear.

744 *Takebe no kimi. Takebe* became the name of a place in Izumo, but it originally signified "brave tribe," the family having, as in so many other cases, given its name to the place of its residence, instead of being called after the latter. See the origin of the name, given in Norinaga's *Commentary*, Vol. 29, pp. 35–36.

745 *Sanugi no Aya no kimi.* For *Sanugi* see Vol. 1, Note 71. *Aya* is a district in the province; the name is of doubtful origin.

746 *Iyo no wake no kimi.* For *Iyo* see Vol. 1, Note 69. (The text here has Ise for Iyo, and the word wake is missing, but Norinaga's emendation may be accepted.) Wake is the name of a district in Iyo.

747 *Tō no wake.* Of *Tō* nothing is known.

748 *Masa no obito.* Of *Masa* nothing is known.

749 *Miyaji* (宮道) *no wake.* This is Norinaga's ingenious emendation of the characters in the text, 宮首, out of which it is impossible to make a family name. Miyaji is the name of a place in the province of Mikawa, and signifies "temple road."

750 *Kamakura no wake.* Kamakura is the name of a district in the province of Sagami, which became famous during the Middle Ages as the site of an immense town,—the capital of the Shōguns, and the center of the feudalism which then ruled Japan. The import of the name (lit. "sickle-store") is not clear, though it has been fancifully explained by native etymologists.

751 *Ozu no kimi.* The words *no kimi* are supplied by Norinaga, this name and the next being in the text run into one. Ozu seems to be the name of a place in Ōmi, and signifies "little mart."

752 *Iwashiro no wake.* Norinaga says that this Iwashiro is not the province of that name, but a place in Kyūshū. The meaning of the name is obscure.

753 *Fukita no wake.* This is but Norinaga's conjectural restoration (founded on a statement in the *Chronicles of Old Matters of Former Ages*) of the name as given in the text, 漁田.

754 *Kuimata-naga-hiko no miko. Kuimata* (modern *Kumata*) is the name of a place in Settsu. The signification is obscure. *Naga-hiko* means "long prince."

755 *Iino-ma-guro-hime, i.e.*, "quite black princess of Iino," the blackness [Where everybody's hair is black this is not much of a distinction. —W.G.A.] being doubtless predicated of her hair. *Iino* is the name of a district in Ise, and is written with characters signifying "boiled-rice-moor."

756 For *Okinaga* see Vol. 2, Note 742. *Ma-waka* means "truly young." *Naka-tsu-hime* means "middle princess," referring to her being the second of three.

757 *I.e.*, "younger princess."

758 See Vol. 2, Note 609.

759 *Shibanu-hime.* This name is obscure.

760 *Shibanu iri-ko.* This name is obscure

761 *Ka-guro-hime,* see Vol. 2, Note 608.

762 For the confusion in this portion of the genealogy see Vol. 2, Note 610.

763 *Shiro-kane no miko, Shiro-kane* means "silver," but Norinaga suspects corruption in the text.

[764] *Ō-nagata no miko, i.e.*, "great prince of Nagata," the latter being the name of a place in Settsu, signifying "long rice-field."

[765] *I.e.*, "great middle princess."

[766] Or, "the King of Kagosaka," for it is uncertain whether Kago-saka should or should not be regarded as the name of a place. The etymology of the name may be *kago*, "a stag" and *saka*, "an ascent." The original form of the name and title is *Kagosaka no miko.*

[767] Or, "the King of Oshikuma," *Oshikuma no miko. Oshikuma* is a word of doubtful etymology.

[768] See Vol. 2, Note 465.

[769] *Shiga no Taka-anaho. Shiga* is the name of a well known district, and is of uncertain signification, as is also *Taka-anaho.* For *Chika-tsu-Ōmi* see Vol. 1, Note 461.

[770] *Oto-takari no iratsume. Oto* signifies "younger [sister]," and *takara* is "treasure."

[771] *Oshiyama* is the name of a place in Ise, *take* signifies "brave," and *tari* and *ne* are honorifics of frequent occurrence.

[772] *Hozumi no omi.* See Vol. 2, Note 251.

[773] *Waka-nuke no miko.* This name is of doubtful signification, and Norinaga suspects that it is corrupt, and that the true reading would be *Waka-take,* "young-brave."

[774] See Sect. 61, Note b.

[775] 大臣. Norinaga tries to prove that in the earliest times this official title was simply an honorific surname formed by prefixing the adjective 大, "great" to 臣, a surname read *Omi* (the character signifies properly "attendant," "subject"). Probably like other "gentile names" it combined both characters, and had a tendency to become hereditary.

[776] *Ō-kuni o-kuni no kuni no miyatsuko.*

[777] *Ō-agata o-agata no agata nushi* (大縣小縣之,縣主). Their duties are supposed to have consisted in supervising the government farms.

[778] For *Saki* see Vol. 2, Note 580. *Tatanami* may perhaps signify "putting shields is a row."

[779] For *Anado* see Vol. 2, Note 654. *Toyora* (for *Toyo-ura)* signifies "fertile shore."

[780] This name seems to be derived from that of the evergreen oak. It will be noticed that both these capitals are in the South-Western Island of Kyūshū, whereas, from Jin-mu downwards, the capitals of all the Emperors previously mentioned are either in Yamato or in one of the adjacent central provinces.

[781] For this and the three following names see Sect. 92, and for *Okinaga tarashi* Sect. 62, Note b.

[782] Written 大后. It is she who is celebrated in Japanese history under the name of Jin-gū Kō-gō, and in the *Chronicles* her reign is counted separately. In these *Records*, however, the period of her rule is considered as forming part of the reign of her son Ō-jin.

[783] The signification of this name is obscure.

[784] *I.e.*, lord of Homuda. *Homuda* is supposed by Norinaga and Moribe to be the

name of a place, they (apparently with reason) rejecting as a late addition a note to the *Chronicles*, which states that *homuda* was synonymous with *tomo* "elbow-pad."

[785]For "heir apparent" see Vol. 1, Note 563.

[786]This word, says Norinaga, is redundant.

[787]For the use of elbow-pads in war see Vol. 1, Note 212.

[788]The word rendered "rule" *(shiru,* 知) is supplied by the editor of 1687. Norinaga supplies the evident lacuna in the text by the word "establish" (*sadamuru* 定); but this seems less good. Norinaga's reasons for taking the word *kuni* ("country") in the plural are, however, convincing,—the three countries into which Korea was anciently divided, and which are appropriately designated by the title of San kan (三韓) being evidently designated by the expression in the text, as may be seen both by reference to the parallel passage in the *Chronicles*, and also by considering that in this manner that warlike implement the elbow-pad, with the semblance of which the young Emperor was born, obtains its proper significance. This Emperor (for it is he who is known as Ō-jin Ten-nō) is sometimes designated by the name of the "Emperor in the Womb"(胎中天皇).

[789]Himeko in the Chinese historical notices of Japan was skilled in magic, with which she deluded the people. Compare the Biblical expression "to be in the spirit," with *Ki-Shin* —W.G.A.

[790]See Vol. 1, Note 82.

[791]This is Norinaga's interpretation of the obscure original word *sa-niwa,* [*Sa* is phonetic, but not *niwa.* See Notes on this word in *Nihongi* 9, 2, (p. 255 Aston's translation.) —W.G.A.] which is written phonetically. He supposes it to have been so called as being a place used for enquiring the will of the gods, and therefore kept clean and held in reverence. "Place" would perhaps represent the Japanese word *niwa* as well as "court," though "court" has been its usual acceptation in later times.

[792]Norinaga tells us to understand "saying" in the sense of "thinking."

[793]As already frequently remarked, the Japanese mind does not occupy itself much with the distinction (to us all-important) of singular and plural. The reason why the translator renders the word *kami* by the plural "Deities" throughout this passage is because we learn later on that four divine personages were intended by the author.

[794]With the commentators we must accept this as an alternative name of Hades, without being able satisfactorily to explain it. The expression "eighty road-windings" *(yaso kumade)* in Vol. 1, Note 551 may be compared with this one.

[795]A temporary resting-place for the corpse before interment. (See Sect. 31, Note a). [Chapel? —W.G.A]

[796]Or if, with Norinaga, we take country in the plural, "the great offerings of the countries," *i.e.,* of the various countries or provinces of Japan or of Kyūshū. These "offerings" *(musa)* are the same as those mentioned in Vol. 1, Notes 283 and 284, under the names *nigi-te* and *mitegura.* They consisted of cloth, for which in later times paper has been substituted.

[797]Norinaga well observes that *tsumi* includes *kegare* (pollutions) *ashiki waza* (ill

deeds) and *wazawa* (calamities). But in this passage it is unnecessary to take the word in its widest sense. —W.G.A.

[798]There are different views as to the exact bearing of this curious expression. *Cf.* Sect. 15, Note c. [Norinaga thinks the live flaying is the same as the *sakahagi* which I suppose he understands to be "wrongful" flaying. —W.G.A.]

[799]Urine is not mentioned. See page 63 of this translation, and compare with the *Ō-harai norito* translation in T.A.S.J. reprints Vol. 2, 1927. Would it not be possible to take the last of these two characters 尿戸 as an ideograph? The meaning would them be committing a nuisance in a house or at a door. A comparison of the doings of Susa-no-o favors the former of the two suppositions. —W.G.A.

[800]*I.e.,* a general purification.

[801]The Deities now speak to, as well as through, the Empress. Before the quotation marks announcing their words we must understand some such clause as "and they added this divine charge." It would also be possible to translate the whole passage thus: "Thereupon the manner of their instruction and counsel was '[Things] being exactly as on the former day, altogether this land,'" etc.

[802]*Soko-zutsu-no-o, Naka-zutsu-no-o* and *Uwa-zutsu-no-o,* three of the Deities born at the time of the purification of Izanagi (the "Male-Who-Invites") on his return from Hades, and known collectively as the Deities of the Inlet of Sumi. (See Vol. 1, Notes 187 and 191.) The grammar of this sentence is, as Norinaga remarks, not lucid. One would expect the author to say that it was "the august doing" of all the four Deities mentioned.

[803]*I.e.,* says Norinaga, they then first informed Take-uchi who they were. Up to that time, it had not been known by what Deities the Empress was possessed. Mabuchi, however, rejected this gloss as a later addition.

[804]*I.e.,* the sacred offerings of white and blue cloth.

[805]Here written with the Chinese locution 天神地祇, by some rendered "the Spirits of Heaven and Earth." *Cf.* Vol. 1, Sect. 1, Notes h and 46.

[806]Here, as before, the singular would be at least as natural an interpretation as the plural. The three ocean-Deities are supposed to be specially referred to, and in that case, the three being easily conceived as one (like the deified peaches mentioned in Vol. 1, Note 166) owing to the want of discrimination in Japanese between singular and plural, we might retain the singular in English. Altogether the Sun-Goddess seems out of place in this passage, and it would be satisfactory to have some authority for expunging from it the mention of her name.

[807]In, on, on board of? —W.G.A.

[808]Or, "into a gourd."

[809]In the original *maki* (真木). In modern parlance *ma-ki* signifies the *Podocarpus macrophylla*, as in the translation. It is however uncertain whether that or the *Chamaecyparis obtusa* [Japanese cypress. —M.F.] (both being conifers), or simply any "true *(i.e.,* good) tree" is here intended by the author.

[810]The editions previous to Norinaga's have "King" (王 instead of 主) but as the latter character is used in all parallel passages of this work, we must attribute the

occurrence of the former in this single place to a copyist's error, and accuse the author rather than his commentator of the ill-natured degradation of the Korean King into a mere chieftain (more literally a "master").

[811]The character 奏, which is here used, is that employed in speaking of a subject addressing his sovereign.

[812]Lit. "bellies."

[813]Lit., "with heaven and earth."

[814]See Sect. 98, Note e.

[815]Planted her august staff at the gate, etc. *Cf.* the *Nihongi* version. —W.G.A.

[816]*Ara-mi-tama,* the antithetical term to which is *Nigi-mi-tama,* "Gentle August Spirit." We also find *Saki-mi-tama,* and *Kushi-mi-tama,* which signify respectively "August Luck-Spirit" and "Wondrous August Spirit." In this passage it must be understood that the spirits which floated above the Imperial junk to protect it were the "Gentle August Spirits," while the "Rough August Spirits" presided at the Empress's feats of arms and kept the enemy in subjection. Norinaga warns us not to fall into the mistake of supposing that the Rough and Gentle Spirits of a god were separate individualities, they being only, according to him, various manifestations of the same individuality. The student is advised to consult his beautifully written note on the subject of these spirits in Vol. 30, pp. 72–75 of his *Commentary.*

[817]See Vol. 1, Note 191.

[818]Norinaga says that this mention of their being laid to rest is made with an implied reference to the journey on which the Deities in question had accompanied the Imperial army. He also tries to prove that this laying to rest of the Deities must have occurred after the return of the Empress to Japan, as it is not possible to suppose that the gods could find a home in a foreign land (!). But the wording of the text is against him.

[819]*I.e.,* as Norinaga suggests, "she wrapped the stone up, and tied it onto the waist of her skirt in something resembling a sash."

[820]In southwestern Japan.

[821]*I.e.,* "bearing." The word, however, also signifies "sea." According to the *Chronicles* the original name of the village was Kada.

[822]This word signifies "thread," and would therefore, one might think, find a more appropriate place in the legend next narrated, where the "threads" of the Empress's garment are specially mentioned.

[823]The *Nihongi* places this section before the Korean expedition. —W.G.A.

[824]*I.e.,* "jewel-island."

[825]*Matsura-gata.* The *Chronicles* give an absurd derivation of Matsura from the adjective *mezurashi*, "astonishing," which the Empress is supposed to have ejaculated on finding a trout hooked to her line! The obvious etymology is *matsu-ura*, "pine-beach."

[826]The character in the original is 礒 (for 磯), in Japanese *iso,* which may or may not be connected with the word *ishi,* "stone." In any case Norinaga is not justified in saying that it must be understood to mean "stone" in this place, as *iso* means

rather a sandy than a stony place, rising above the water level.

[827]In Japanese *ayu,* a small species of the salmon family *(Plecoglossus altivelis)* [Ayu sweetfish. —M.F.].

[828]*I.e.,* "little river."

[829]*I.e.,* "princess of the gate of victory." But though the words lend themselves to this interpretation, it can hardly be supposed that such is their real etymology, and indeed the editor of 1687 draws attention in a Note to the difficulty of accepting the statement in the text.

[830]*I.e.,* a boat or junk containing a coffin. We might also (adopting the interpretation given by the older editors to the character in this passage) translate by "specially prepared a mourning-vessel." [*I.e.,* ship. —W.G.A.]

[831]These two princes, who are first mentioned at the end of Vol. 2 (Notes 766 and 767), were, according to the story, elder sons of the late monarch Chū-ai, and therefore step-sons of the Empress Jin-gū and half-brothers to the young Emperor Ō-jin.

[832]*Toga-no.* It was in the province of Settsu. The etymology of the name is obscure.

[833]Meaning, I suppose, that they hunted wild beasts in order to judge of their fortune by the results of the chase. —W.G.A.

[834]The species mentioned in the text in the *Quercus serrata* [Jolcham oak. —M.F.].

[835]Norinaga's conjecture that the character 是, "then," is a copyist's error for 見, "saw" or "looked," seems hardly called for, and the translator has therefore not departed from the traditional reading.

[836]Which of course was in reality no mourning-vessel, but full of the soldiers who had just returned from conquering Korea.

[837]*Isai no Sukune. Isai* or *Isachi* is supposed to mean "leading elder."

[838]*Naniwa no Kishi-be.* Naniwa is the old name of the sea and river-shore on which now stands the town of Ōsaka. The name Kishi is said by Norinaga to be properly a Korean official designation (吉士), but it is one whose origin is to be sought in China.

[839]將軍, *Shōgun.* This is the earliest mention of this office, which, passing from the military to the political sphere, played such a great part in the medieval and modern history of Japan.

[840]The signification of all the elements of this compound name is not clear, but it is partly honorific and descriptive of the bravery of its bearer.

[841]*Wani no omi* (see Vol. 2, Note 318).

[842]The text is here somewhat obscure, and the note in small print is of doubtful authenticity. If we retain it, we must understand it to mean that *usa-yu-zuru,* a term whose derivation is by no means clear, was an alternative name of the *make-zuru i.e.,* "prepared bowstrings," such as they had brought with them concealed in their top-knots.

[843]*I.e.,* "the pass [or hill] of meeting." It was on the boundaries of the provinces

of Yamashiro and Ōmi [The railway now passes under it in a tunnel. —W.G.A.]. The modern pronunciation is *Ōsaka* (not to be confounded with the like-sounding name of a well-known town in Central Japan).

[844] *I.e.*, in Ōmi. Mabuchi, in his *Dictionary of Pillow-Words*, explains this name to mean "bamboo-grass bending." Norinaga, following the *Shinpuku-ji* manuscript., alters the character 於 before the word *Sasanami* to 出, but without sufficient warrant.

[845] The meaning of the poem is: "Rather than fall beneath the attacks of the enemy, let us drown ourselves in the Sea of Ōmi" (Lake Biwa).—For the expression "stricken by a hurtful hand" see Vol. 2, Note 27.

[846] Viz., by water, as described in Sect. 10.

[847] Etymology obscure.

[848] The marvelous etymology of this name which the author seems to adopt will be found at the end of this Section (Note 12). The compiler of the *Chronicles* is probably nearer the truth when he derives it from *tsuno-ga*, "horned stag."

[849] For the meaning of this curious expression see Vol. 2, Note 238.

[850] The commentators give no explanation of this one of the three names of the deity in question. It would appear to be made up of a word expressive of solicitation and of a portion of the Heir Apparent's name, thus signifying perhaps "Come on, Wake, [give me thy name]" with reference to the legend here narrated.

[851] To which of the two personages of the legend is not clear. Norinaga, however, prefers to suppose that it was to Take-uchi, as, if the prince himself were intended, the word "dream" would probably receive the honorific 御.

[852] Norinaga supposes that they were caught by being speared in the nose.

[853] *Ie.*, "fish that would naturally have formed part of thine august food." It is less good to translate by "fish for *mine* august food." As usual, the original Japanese text has no personal pronouns to guide the reader but, though Emperors are sometimes made to use the honorific in speaking of themselves, this is not the custom in the case of princes, and Ō-jin is supposed to have not yet assumed the Imperial dignity.

[854] *Mi-ke-tsu-ō-kami.* Norinaga mentions several Deities of this name, who were, according to him, separate beings.

[855] *Kehi no ō-kami.* The meaning of the syllable *hi*, rendered by "wondrous" in accordance with Norinaga's suggestion, is not certain.

[856] *I.e.*, "the strand of blood." From *chi-ura* Norinaga is obliged to derive Tsunuga as well as he can in order not to throw discredit on the implied assertion of the author that the latter is but a mispronunciation of the former. The true derivation of Tsunuga is is probably from *tsuno-ga* "horned stag," as already stated in Vol. 2, Note 848.

[857] *Machi-sake.* This expression, which recurs in the poems of the *Collection of a Myriad Leaves*, signifies liquor distilled for an absent friend by those who are awaiting his return.

[858] How would it do to take *Kamu hogi* and *Toyo hogi* as accusatives governed by the verbs of the succeeding clauses? —W.G.A.

[859]The general signification of the Song is: "Think not that this liquor was made by me. Tis a present from the small August Deity *(Sukuna-biko-na),* who dwells forever in unshaken power and who sends it to thee with endless congratulations. Come on! Come on! Drink deeply!"—Some of the expressions in this Song are a subject of debate among the commentators. Excepting the clause "partake not shallowly," in which the translator has adopted the opinion of the author of the *Explanation of the Songs in the Chronicles of Japan*, Moribe's interpretation has been followed throughout. The latter critic would identify *asazu* ("not shallowly") with *amasazu* ("without leaving anything"). But there seems no warrant for supposing such an elision of the syllable *sa.* The use of the expressions *kuruhoshi* and *motohoshi* to express reiteration is worthy of notice. It will be remembered that the Deity here mentioned was the microsopic personage who came riding over the waves to share the sovereignty of Izumo with the Deity Master-of-the-Great-Land (see Sect. 27). [where does *Kushi no Kami* come in? —W.G.A.]

[860]This Song signifies: "Such a joyful feast must surely have been preceded by joyful distilling of the liquor for it. Continue to drink, oh Prince!"—The commentators disagree on the subject of one or two of the words of this Song, in which the translator has followed Norinaga's interpretation throughout. The words "that drum" are the chief difficulty. Norinaga supposes that drums, being originally unknown in Japan, where first seen by the Japanese on the occasion of the conquest of Korea in this very reign, and thinks that the drum would be placed by the side of the mortar during the pounding of the rice out of which the liquor was to be made. "That drum" means the drum belonging to the pounder of the rice. The original words *so no,* "that," might also be rendered by "his."

[861]Lit., "liquor-rejoicing songs."

[862]The Emperor Chū-ai. The author of these *Records*, not recognizing, as does the author of the *Chronicles*, the time during which the Empress Jin-gū held sway as a separate reign, Chū-ai is by a fiction supposed to have reigned down to the moment when his posthumous son Ō-jin mounted the throne after the conquest of Korea and of Yamato.

[863]*I.e.,* "long branch," or perhaps "long inlet."

[864]Etymology obscure.

[865]Mabuchi and Norinaga seem right in supposing the sentence in small type to be an addition to the text, copied from the *Chronicles*. But as all the manuscripts and printed editions previous to Norinaga's contain it, it has been retained in the translation.

[866]Son of the Emperor Chū-ai and the Empress Jin-gū.

[867]In Yamato. *Akira* signifies "brilliant." *Karushima* seems to mean "the neighborhood of Karu," Karu being the often mentioned place of that name in Yamato.

[868]The auxiliary numeral for Deities is here used.

[869]*Homuda-no-ma-waka no miko.* Homuda has already been met with as the name of a place in Kōchi. *Ma-waka* signifies "truly young." The name might therefore be rendered "truly young king of Homuda."

[870] *Takagi no iri-bime no mikoto.* Norinaga identifies this princess with the *Taka-ki-hime* of Vol. 2, Note 601.

[871] *I.e.,* "middle princess," she being the second of three sisters.

[872] *I.e.,* "younger princess," she being the youngest of the sisters.

[873] *I-o-ki-no-iri-biko no mikoto.* See Vol. 2, Note 592.

[874] *I.e.,* probably "old woman of Shiritsuki." But it is not certain that Shiritsuki is the name of a place.

[875] *Take-inada no sukune.* In the *Chronicles of Old Matters of Former Ages* the name is written *Take-ina-dane,* and it may therefore mean "brave-rice-seed."

[876] *Owari no muraji.*

[877] *I.e.,* "great middle prince of Nukata," the latter being the name of a place in Yamato. It is of uncertain signification.

[878] *I.e.,* "great mountain-warden." For the appropriateness of this name *cf.* Sect. 105.

[879] The same name has appeared in Vol. 2, Note 405.

[880] *Ōhara no iratsume.* Ōhara is the name of a place in Yamato. It signifies "great moor."

[881] *Komuku no iratsume.* This name is written 高目, and its reading as *Komuku* is somewhat hypothetical. It is the name of a place in Kōchi, and probably signifies "an overflowing pool of water."

[882] *Ki no Arata no iratsume. Ki* is the province of that name, and Arata is a place in it. The latter name probably means "uncultivated fields."

[883] This name signifies "Great Wren," and is thus accounted for by the author of the *Chronicles*: "On the day when the Emperor [this Prince became the Emperor Nin-toku] was born, an owl flew into the parturition-hall. Next morning early, the Heavenly Sovereign Homuda [*i.e.*, the Emperor Ō-jin] sent for the Prime Minister the Noble Take-uchi, and asked him whereof this might be a sign. The Prime Minister replied, saying: 'It is a good omen. Moreover yesterday, when thy servant's wife was delivered of child, a wren flew into the parturition-house, likewise a strange thing.' Then the Heavenly Sovereign said: 'It is a portent from Heaven that my child and thine should he born on the same day, and both be attended by a good omen. So let the names of the birds be taken, and each used for the name of the other [*i.e.,* the name of the owl for him into whose parturition-house the wren flew, and vice-versa], as a covenant for the future.' So the wren's name was bestowed on the Heir Apparent, who was called Great-Wren Prince, and the owl's name was given to the Prime Minister's child, who was called the Noble Owl." [The modern form of this word is *sasagi.* —W.G.A.]

[884] This name is obscure.

[885] *Abe no iratsume.* Abe is the name of several places in different provinces, and is of obscure derivation and import.

[886] *Awaji no Mihara no iratsume.* The text properly has *Ayuchi,* but Norinaga emends this to *Awaji* on the authority of the *Chronicles*. Mihara is the name of a district in the island of Awaji, and probably signifies "three moors."

[887] *Ki no Uno no iratsume. Ki* is the province of that name, and *Uno* a place in it. The latter name is of uncertain import.

[888] *Mino no iratsume. Minu (Mino)* is the province of that name.

[889] "Five" must here be a mistake for "four."

[890] For this name and the next see Vol. 2, Notes 920 and 919.

[891] *I.e.,* "the young lord of Uji." Uji is the name of a district in Yamashiro, famous in classical and modern times for its tea. The etymology is obscure.

[892] *I.e.,* "the young lady of Yata." Yata is the name of a place in Yamato. The etymology is obscure.

[893] *Medori no miko. Medori* signifies "hen-bird" but the reason for the application of so strange a name to this princess, whose fortunes are related at some length in Sects. 126 and 127, does not appear. A similar remark applies to the next name.

[894] *I.e.,* probably "the lady of the little kettle."

[895] *I.e.,* "the young lady of Uji."

[896] *I.e.,* "the truly young middle princess of Okinaga."

[897] See Vol. 2, Note 754.

[898] *Waka-nuke-futa-mata no miko.* This name is obscure.

[899] *Itoi-hime.* Itoi is the name of a place in Yamato, and is of uncertain origin.

[900] *Shima* is probably the name of a place, while *tari* and *ne* are the frequently recurring honorifics rendered respectively "perfect" and "lord" in former parts of this translation.

[901] *Sakurai no ta-be no muraji. Ta-be,* rendered "agricultural," is literally "rice-field tribe." *Sakurai* ("cherry-well") is the name of a place in Kōchi.

[902] *I.e.,* falcon-lord.

[903] *Himuka no Izumi no Naga-hime.* Himuka is the name of a province, and Izumi that of a district now comprised within the limits of Satsuma. *Naga-hime,* lit. "long princess," probably signifies "elder princess."

[904] *Ō-hae no miko.* Signification obscure.

[905] *O-hae no miko.* Signification obscure. The antithesis of the adjectives *ō* and *o* ("great" and "small") shows however that the names partly served to distinguish the elder from the younger brother.

[906] *Waki-iratsume* is "young lady." *Hata-bi* is incomprehensible.

[907] See Vol. 2, Note 608.

[908] *I.e.,* probably "the lady of Kawarada." The latter name (lit. "rice-field on the border of a river") is often met with.

[909] *I.e.,* "the jewel lady."

[910] *I.e.,* "the great middle lady of Osaka," the latter being the name of a place in Yamato (see Vol. 2, Note 81).

[911] Norinaga identifies this name with that of *Koto-fushi no iratsume* in Sect. 117, *q.v.*, and thinks that both this and the preceding name have only crept into this Section by mistake.

[912] *Kataji no miko.* Signification obscure.

[913] *Kazuraki no Nu-iro-me.* All the elements of this name have already been met

with several times.

[914]This child has already appeared early in this Section, and the name is here doubtless only repeated through some copyist's error.

[915]Satow's chronology has Ō-sasagi. —W.G.A.

[916]This statement refers proleptically to the contrary course which was taken by the elder Ō-yama-mori.

[917]According to Moribe, whose interpretation has been followed throughout, this Song signifies: "As I gaze across from Uji to the Moor of Toba, I see the numerous and prosperous homesteads of the people, I see the most fertile portion of the country."—On this view Chiba is identified with Toba, the name of a district; and the word *ho,* rendered "acme," is taken to mean the best, highest, most showy part of anything. For Norinaga's opinion, which is that of the older commentators as well, that *chi-ba* is a pillow-word, there is much to be said, and if we followed it, we should have to render the first two lines thus: "As I look on the thousand-leafed kudzu-moor," etc. (*kuzu* signifying "kudzu.") Norinaga's explanation of *momo-chi-daru* (here rendered by "hundred thousand-fold abundant") as referring to the soot of the peasant's roofs, and of *ho* as signifying "a plain surrounded by mountains" seems much less good than Moribe's interpretation of those difficult expressions.

[918]In the district of Uji in the province of Yamashiro. The characters with which the name is written signify "tree-flag."

[919]*Wani no Hifure no omi.* For *Wani no omi* see Vol. 2, Note 318. The meaning of *Hifure* is obscure.

[920]*Miya-nushi-ya-kawa-hime. Miya-nushi* is "priestess," or more literally "temple-guardian." For the rest of the name see Vol. 1, Note 407, though the personages are of course meant to be different.

[921]Norinaga supposes with apparent reason that the character 命, "Augustness," has only crept into the text through the attraction of the following character 令 "made," which it resembles in appearance.

[922][I should be pleased to think that the text of the bulk of the middle part of this Song is corrupt. —W.G.A.] It must be understood that in this Song the Imperial singer commences by referring to what doubtless formed part of the feast, a crab, and thence passes on by an imperceptible transition to allude to his own adventure with the maiden. As the crab when alive walked sideways, so was the Emperor zigzagging up and down the road that lines the shore of Lake Biwa, pursuing his breathless course like that of the busy grebe that perpetually plunges into the water, when the maiden met him near Kohata. Beautiful indeed was she: her back straight as a shield, her teeth like a row of acorns, and the artificial eyebrows painted a dark color on her forehead drawn low down in a perfect crescent-shape. She had been careful in selecting the clay to make the paint, rejecting the upper layer of earth, for that was of too bright a red, rejecting likewise the lower layer, for that was too dark, but taking the middle, which was of the correct blue tint, and drying it, not in the fierce, but in a mildly tempered, sunlight. And now this maiden, for whom

his heart had been panting and turning this way and that ever since the previous day, is actually seated opposite to him, nay! at his very side, and he is feasting in her sweet company.—Tsunuga is the name of a place in the province of Echizen. "Far-distant" is an imperfect attempt at rendering the force of the pillow-word *momo-zutō*, which implies that the traveler must pass through a hundred other places before reaching his destination. "Whither reaches its sideward motion?" signifies "whither is it going with its sideward motion?" Ichiji-shima and Mishima are places of which nothing is known, so that the allusion to them is obscure. At this point Norinaga's interpretation diverges from that of Moribe, which has been followed throughout. *Sasanami*, here rendered "wavelets," is taken by him, as by the older commentators, as the name of a place, and the description of the maiden's teeth is misunderstood to signify that she had a beak filled with a row of teeth like the water-caltrop! Norinaga also would here divide the Song in two, a proceeding for which there is not sufficient warrant. On other minor points, too, his decisions do not seem so happy as Moribe's. The views of both commentators will be found at length in Norinaga's Commentary, Vol. 32, pp. 33–51, and in Moribe's *Izu-no-koto-waki," in loco.* "Three chestnuts" (*mitsuguri no*) is a common pillow-word for *naka*, "middle," founded on the fact, real or supposed, that one burr always contains three nuts, whereof one of course is in the middle, between the other two.

[923]B.H.C. gives this sentence in Latin: Ita auguste coivit [cum illâ], et procreavit filium Uji-no-waki-iratsuko.

[924]*Kami-naga-hime.* The name signifies "the long-haired princess."

[925]*Muragata no kimi. Muragata* seems to signify "many towns."

[926]太子. Mabuchi thinks that 御子, "august child," should be substituted for the reading in the text. But Norinaga insists that the title translated Heir Apparent was anciently borne by all the sons of an Emperor, and that consequently no emendation is called for.

[927]The native term translated "copious feast" is *toyo no akari*, variously written with the characters 豊明,豊樂,宴樂, etc., etc. It literally signifies "copious brightness," in allusion to the ruddy glow which wine gives to the faces of the revelers, and henceforward perpetually recurs in this history. In later times it specifically denoted the festival of the tasting of the first rice, but anciently its meaning was not thus limited. Norinaga's note on the subject, in Vol. 32, pp. 57–59 of his *Commentary*, may be consulted with advantage.

[928]Norinaga says that the word *kashiwa* (properly the name of a deciduous oak, the *Quercus dentata*) was employed to denote any kind of leaf thus used. [Has not the *kashiwa* a smallish leaf,—too small for this purpose? If the authorities were not against it, I should have understood a cup made of the wood of the *kashiwa.* —W.G.A.]

[929]The whole gist of this Song is contained in the last three lines. "The ruddy maiden, oh! if thou lead her off with thee, it will be good,"—*i.e.*, "thou and the maiden will form a fitting couple." All that goes before is what is technically called a "Preface," though its bearing is so clear as to admit of translation, and even in

English to form an appropriate introduction to the Song:—It is not the stinking garlic, but the fragrant orange that the singer has met by the way, and it is the choicest young fruit in the very middle of the tree that forms a suitable comparison for the lovely young girl.—With the favorite allusion to upper, middle, and lower the reader is already familiar, and the pillow-word "three chestnuts" was explained in the note on the preceding Song (Vol. 2, Note 922).

[930]The gist of the Song is: [The *Nihongi* makes this song a reply by the young Prince to the previous one. I prefer the *Nihongi*.—W.G.A.] "I knew not that thou, my son, hadst conceived a secret passion for the maiden; but I am now conscious of my own mistake, and my foolish old heart is ashamed of itself." With this explanation the elaborate comparison between the state of the monarch's mind and the condition of the peasant driving piles for the foundation of a dyke, and having his feet either lacerated by the stumps of the water-caltrop, or made slimy by brushing against the roots of the watershield. at the bottom of the water, becomes intelligible and appropriate.—The word *kuri,* rendered "roots," perplexed Norinaga, who suggests that it may be but a second name of the *Brasenia,* appended to the first; but Moribe's suggestion that it is to be identified with *kori,* and taken in the signification of "roots," though not quite convincing, is at least more plausible. The text of this Song is corrupt in these *Records* and has to be corrected by a comparison with that of the *Chronicles*. Moribe goes into an amusing ecstasy over the picture of ancient manners which it presents, and lauds the simplicity of days when a father and son could so peacefully woo the same maiden without mutual concealment or disastrous consequences!

[931]The meaning of this Song is: "At first I heard of the maiden of Kohada in the furthest parts of Himuka as one hears the distant thunder; but now she is mine, and we sleep locked in each other's arms."—This Kohada in Himuka must not be confounded [Or else there is some confusion in the text,—not unlikely. —W.G.A.] with the Kohata in Yamashiro mentioned in the preceding Section. The "back of the road" means the remotest portion (conf. Vol. 2, Note 238). The thunder must be understood to refer to a very faint and distant sound: the Prince had first heard of the maiden vaguely, but now she is his and has been his for some time; for this Song must be supposed to have been composed after the occasion of the feast with the story of which it is here connected.

[932]The meaning of this Song is: "I love this maiden of Kohada in Himuka, who disputed not my desire and my father's grant, but willingly became my wife."—It is hard to render in English the force of the string of particles *o shi zo mo* in the penultimate line.

[933]Yeshinu is the modern Yoshino, in the province of Yamato (see Vol. 2, Note 56). For the title of kudzu [Where it is spelt *kuzu*.—W.G.A.] see Vol. 2, Note 64, where it also occurs in connection with Yoshino.

[934]According to Moribe, whose interpretation seems best to the translator, the signification of this difficult poem is: "The sword worn by Prince Ō-sazaki, son of the Emperor Homuda (Ō-jin) is double-edged at its upper part, and like

glistening ice towards its point;—oh! 'tis like the icicles on the plants that cluster about the trunks of the dead trees in winter!" Almost every line, however (excepting those giving the name and title of the Prince), is a subject of controversy, and the *Kō-gan Shō in loco* and Norinaga's *Commentary*, Vol. 33, pp. 2–5, should be consulted for Keichiū's, Mabuchi's and Norinaga's views on the disputed point.—The expression "solar august child" signifies sun-descended prince, in allusion to the supposed descent of the Japanese monarchs from the Sun-Goddess. [If this poem were composed at the time stated, it would negate the supposition that Ōsasagi is a posthumous name. It proves at any rate that the author of the *Kojiki* did not consider it so. —W.G.A.]

[935]*Yoko-usu* or *yokusu* (横臼). It is not plain what sort of mortar the author intended to designate by this term. Norinaga supposes it to mean a broad flat mortar in contradistinction to a high and narrow one. Keichū's view, which he quotes, to the effect that it was a mortar that had been carved out of the block against the grain of the wood, seems an equally good guess, where all is guess-work.

[936]In the Song this same name is read *Kashinofu;* but the commentators tell us that the genitive particle *no* ("of") is simply inserted for the sake of rhythm, and it is not unlikely that they are right. The name seems to signify "[a place where] oak-trees grow."

[937]See Vol. 1, Note 313. The character 醸, rendered by "distil" or "brew," according to the view which one may take of the resulting liquor, would seem to be here used in the sense of "to pound." [You cannot distil a thing in a mortar. —W.G.A.]

[938]*Waza o noshite*, "and making gestures." —W.G.A.

[939]In this simple Song the Territorial Owners of Yoshino beg the Monarch to deign to partake of the *sake* which they have made.

[940]*Ama-be* (written 海部 and read *Una-be* in the Old Printed Edition and in the edition of 1687, and perhaps better rendered "Sea-Tribe") The name of this guild or clan does not seem to have remained, like the two mentioned together with it, as a "gentile name."

[941]*Yama-be*. Norinaga thinks that this word has crept into the text erroneously through the influence of that next mentioned, as the functions of the tribes or guilds thus separately named were identical. The differentiation may have taken place after the terms had come to be used as "gentile names."

[942]*Yama-mori-be.*

[943]*Ise-be*. Nothing is known of this tribe or guild.

[944]Doubtless so named after the Korean laborers employed upon it,—Kudara and Shiragi, as different parts of the same peninsula, being confounded in thought. [Called, in the *Nihongi*, "the pool of the Han men." —W.G.A.]

[945]照古王, according to the Japanese kana spelling, Shō-ko. [King Awa it was,—not Shō-ko. —W.G.A.]

[946]阿知吉師. Other forms of the name are Ajiki and Atogi, and all three are but attempts at transcribing phonetically into Japanese a Korean name, the proper characters for which are not given. 吉士 is not properly part of the name, but is

simply an official title (師 here stands for 士).

[947] *Achiki no fumi-bito. Fumi-bito* abbreviated to *Fubito*) became a "gentile name."

[948] See Vol. 2, Note 42.

[949] *Q.d.*, by the Japanese Emperor.

[950] Here written phonetically 和邇吉師, but properly 王仁吉士 *i.e.*, "the Official Wang-In." He is generally spoken of simply as Wani.

[951] 論語- (*Lun Yu* or according to the Japanese pronunciation "Ron-go.") [*Analects*. —M.F.]

[952] 千字文. (Qian Zi Wen, "or according to the Japanese pronunciation "Sen-ji-mon.") [*Thousand Character Classic*. —M.F.] See the translator' remarks on this subject in the Introduction, p. 49. The *Chronicles* more prudently mention only "various classics."

[953] *Fumi no obito. Fumi* signifies "any written document," so that this "gentile name" is equivalent to our word "scribe."

[954] 卓 素. The transliteration of this, as of all other such names here occurring, is the Sinico-Japanese transliteration. *Kara* (Korea) is written 韓.

[955] 呉 (*Wu*, Jp. *Go*), one of the states into which China was divided during the third century of our era. A draper's shop is still called *go-fuku-ya, i.e.*, "Wu-garments-house" in memory of the introduction of wearing apparel from that country.

[956] 西素.

[957] *Hada no miyatsuko* 秦造, a "gentile name." Hada is the native Japanese word used as the equivalent of the Chinese name 秦, *Qin*. Its origin is uncertain.

[958] *Aya no atae* 漢直, a "gentile name." The use of Aya to represent the Chinese name 漢, *Han*, is as difficult to account for as is that of Hada mentioned in the preceding Note.

[959] 仁番. Another and more Japanese-like reading, *Niho* is invented by Norinaga; but the older editors read *Nin-pan* according to the usual Sinico-Japanese sound of the characters. The modern Korean reading would be In Pŏn.

[960] Written phonetically 須須許理.

[961] Thus translated, this Song is too clear to need any explanation. The lines, however, which are rendered by "with the soothing liquor, with the smiling liquor,"—in Japanese *koto nagu shi e-gushi-ni*, are in reality extremely obscure, and Moribe understands them to signify, "Oh! how difficult it is for me to speak! Oh! how ill at ease I am!" In order to do so he has, however, to change and add to the text: and the translator, though not sure of being in the right path, has preferred to follow Norinaga, whose interpretation, without requiring any such extreme measures, yet gives a very plausible sense.

[962] See Sect. 64, Note d.

[963] I don't dispute the translation, but how could he cede what he had not? —W.G.A.

[964] 皇子. This is the only passage in the work where this expression occurs. *Uji-no-waki-iratsuko* is the personage thus designated.

[965] The same expression has been in Sect. 31 (near Note 511) rendered "couch."

The characters in the original are 呉床 or 胡床.

[966]The Chinese phrase 百官, "the hundred officials," is here used.

[967]The text has the character 者, which, in combination with the preceding word "oars," gives the sense of "oarsman," "boatman." But Norinaga reasonably suggests that it is an error for 亦, the grass-hand forms of the two characters closely resembling each other, and 亦 making much better sense; for who would talk of "decorating an oarsman?"

[968]A bamboo grating.

[969]Lit. "that king's son."

[970]This is Norinaga's view of the meaning of the Song, which he interprets as a request for help to some friendly boatman. Moribe adopts quite a different view, and thinks that the drowning prince is rather giving vent to sentiments of pride and defiance. He says (speaking in the Prince's name): "It is not that I have been capsized out of the boat into the river, but that I am swimming off after a pole which has fallen into the water. If there be any strong and willing fellows among my partisans, let them swim after me!" It must be explained that the word rendered "boatmen" in the translation is literally "pole-takers" (or, according to Moribe's view, "to take a pole"). Norinaga's interpretation seems to do less violence to the wording of the original, and Moribe's has not even the merit of accounting for the use of the future *konzu* where the imperative *kome* would be what we should naturally expect.—*Uji* is preceded by the, in this context, untranslatable pillow-word *chihayaburu* (see *Dictionary of Pillow-Words, s.v.*).

[971]*Kawara no saki.* The author, in the next sentence, derives this name from the rattling sound made by the hooks as they struck on the armor. But there seems a great deal to be said in favor of Arai Hakuseki's view that *kawara* is an old word itself signifying "armor."

[972]The word *kagi* here used occurs elsewhere to denote the hooks

[973]Lit., "sounded *kawara*"

[974]The text has the characters 掛出. But Norinaga says that 掛 stands for 掻, and that we must interpret the passage to mean that they scratched [about to find] and take out [his corpse].

[975]The signification of this Song is: "I came here meaning to kill thee as I might cut down and kill that *Catalpa* tree, that *Euonymus*, growing on the river-bank. But the thought of our father and of thy sister (or wife) touched me with pity, and I return without having drawn my bow at thee."—Uji is preceded by the untranslatable pillow-word *chihayabito* (see *Dictionary of Pillow-Words s.v*; —Norinaga reads it *chihaya-hito* without the *nigori*).—The words *azusa-yumi mayumi,* here respectively rendered "*Catalpa* bow" and "*Euonymus*" are difficult, and the doubt as to whether we should understand the prince to be speaking simply of the trees, or to intend likewise to allude to his bow which was made of the wood of one of those trees, is probably not to be settled, as the words in question have always oscillated between the two meanings, and here evidently contain a double allusion. Norinaga thinks that the first of the two forms only a sort of pillow-word for the

second.—The word rendered "bank" in accordance with Moribe's suggestion, is literally "reach."—No special importance must be attached to the expressions "base" (or "main part") and "extremity," though they may doubtless be thought to allude to the father and sister, the recollection of whom softened the victorious younger brother's heart. The word *iranakeku*, rendered "grievously," is of not quite certain interpretation. —It must be understood that though, by overturning the boat, Uji-no-waki-iratsuko did constructively cause Ō-yamamori's death, he did not actually shoot at and slay him when in the water, but followed down the river-side lamenting over what had happened.—This Song is singled out by Moribe for special praise.

[976]See Vol. 2, Note 551.

[977]In Tōtōmi. In the original *Hijikata no kimi*.

[978]*Heki no kimi*. Of Heki nothing is known.

[979]*Harihara no kimi*. In Tōtōmi. *Harihara* signifies "alder plantation."

[980]It is not actually the word *kami*, "Deity," that is here used in the original, but *hashira*, which is the auxiliary numeral for Deities. [Not exclusively. —W.G.A.]

[981]Norinaga is probably right in saying that the point of this proverb lies in the consideration that, whereas people in general weep for that which they have not, this fisherman wept on account of the trouble which was caused to him by the fish which he had. [And which he could not get rid of. —W.G.A.]

[982]Or, "died first." The use in this place of the character, properly confined to the meaning of the "death of an Emperor," is remarkable. See Norinaga's observations on the point in Vol. 33, pp. 78–80.

[983]Or, according to Norinaga's reading, *Ame-no-hi-boko*. The characters in the text, 大日矛,signify "heavenly sun-spear." But the homonymous characters 海檜槍, with which the name is written in the *Gleanings from Ancient Story*, and which are approved of both by Norinaga and by Tanigawa Kotosuga, signify "fisherman's *Chamaecyparis* spear."

[984]Apparently nothing more is meant than that there was "*a* lagoon;" but still the *one* (一) in this context is curious, and Norinaga retains it as *hito-tsu no* in the Japanese reading. "A certain" seems best to render its force in English, as again in the following sentences, where Norinaga interprets it by the character 或. It is of strangely frequent recurrence in the opening sentences of this Section, which are altogether peculiar in style. [Curiously it is in accordance with Korean idiom to use "one" (—) for the indefinite article "a." —W.G.A.]

[985]*Agu-numa*. The meaning of this name is unknown.

[986]The Old Printed Edition has the word "mud" instead of "lagoon."

[987]B.H.C. gives this sentence in Latin: Tunc solis radii, caelesti arcui similes, in privatas partes impegerunt.

[988]Lit., "this appearance."

[989]The words rendered "in a valley" are in the text 山谷之間, of which the commentators find it difficult to make proper Japanese. The translator has followed them in neglecting the character 山, "mountain."

[990]Or bull, or bullock; for Japanese does not distinguish genders.

[991]Lit., "stopped."

[992]See Vol. 2, Note 21.

[993]*Akaru-hime i.e.*, "Brilliant Princess."

[994]The signification of this name is obscure. Norinaga identifies the place with the modern Kōzu (高津).

[995]See Vol. 2, Note 570.

[996]This name may mean "lucky ears," or "possessor of luck"; but it is obscure, and is moreover in the *Chronicles* (where it is given as the name, not of the daughter, but of the father) read *Mae-tsu-mi*—a reading which will not bear either of these interpretations.

[997]*Matao* seems to signify "complete (*i.e.* healthy or vigorous) male." Observe that the word Tajima enters into the designations of most of his descendants.

[998]In the *Chronicles Morosuke,* and elsewhere *Morosugi.* The etymology of these names is obscure except that of the last-mentioned, which signifies "many *Cryptomerias.*"

[999]*Hi-ne* may perhaps signify "wondrous lord."

[1000]The meaning of this name is obscure, but that of *Hina-rashi-bime* in Vol. 1, Note 412. may be compared.

[1001]See S Vol. 2, Note 570.

[1002]*Hi-taka* may signify either "sun-height" or "wondrous height."

[1003]This name signifies "pure prince."

[1004]As usual, it is not the actual word Deity that is used, but the Auxiliary Numeral for Deities.

[1005]*Tagima* is the name of a place, not to be confounded with the province of Tajima. The signification of *mehi* is quite obscure.

[1006]*Suga* may either be the name of place in Tajima, as proposed by Norinaga, or identical with the Suga of Sect. 19. The meaning of *Moroo* is obscure.

[1007]The signification of this name is obscure. But Suga, Kama, and Yura are apparently the names of places.

[1008]*Kazuraki no Takanuka-tame.* Kazuraki is the name of a department, and Takanuka that of a place in that department, in the province of Yamato.

[1009]Lit., "ancestress." But see Vol. 1, Note 356. It will be remembered that *Okina-ga-tarashi-hime* was the Empress Jin-gū.

[1010]Lit., "treasures of jewels."

[1011]Or, "beads."

[1012]This seems to be the signification of the original terms *oki tsu kagami hi* and *he tsu kagami,* but we are not hereby helped to a very clear understanding of the nature of the articles which the author meant to describe. The parallel passage of the *Chronicles* tells us of a "sun-mirror." Indeed it enumerates the "eight precious treasures" in a manner that diverges a great deal from the account given in these *Records.*

[1013]Or, the "Eight-fold Great Deity." As has already frequently been remarked, the distinction which we so rigorously draw between singular and plural does not occupy the Japanese mind, and "eight" and "eight-fold" are taken to mean much the same thing. In the following sentence we find these eight Deities (or this eight-fold Deity) spoken of in such a manner as to necessitate the use of the singular number in the translation. Norinaga supposes that they (or he) took the form of a young man (as in several other legends) to become the father of the Goddess mentioned in the text. —*Izushi* seems to signify wonderful stone. [Sacred? Fetish? —W.G.A.]

1014 *Izushi-otome no kami.*

1015 Lit. "eighty Deities wished to obtain this Maiden-of-Izushi, but none could wed [her]." But the sense is that given in the translation.

1016 *Aki-yama no shita-bi-otoko.* The explanation of the name is that given by Norinaga (following Mabuchi), who sees in it a reference to the ruddy brilliance of the leaves, which is so marked a feature of the Japanese woods in autumn. The Chinese characters used have, indeed, the signification of the lower ice of the autumn mountains; but "lower ice" may well be simply phonetic in this case.

1017 *Haru-yama no kasumi-otoko.*

1018 In Japanese *koedomo,* written with the characters 雖乞. Perhaps Norinaga is right in supposing this verb to have been originally identical with *kofuru*, "to love" (恋), whose corresponding form is *kofuredomo*. If so, the author may have meant to make his hero say, "though I love the maiden, etc." But it is better to be guided by the characters, and to suppose that he referred to the request made to her mother to grant her to him.

1019 Thus in the *Service of the Goddess of Food* (see Mr. Satow's translation in Vol. 7, Pt. 4, p. 414 of these *Transactions*,) we read that the worshipper offered: "as to things which dwell in the mountains—things soft of hair and things rough of hair; as to things which grow in the great-field-plain— sweet herbs and bitter herbs; as to things which dwell in the blue-sea-plain—things wide of fin and things narrow of fin, down to weeds of the offing and weeds of the shore."

1020 Lit., "one child."

1021 The Japanese original of the words here unavoidably rendered by "mortal men" in order to mark the antithesis to the word "Deities," has been more literally translated by "living people" in an earlier passage of the work (see Vol. 2, Note 164). The signification of the entire sentence is: "During my lifetime, thy brother should be careful to imitate the upright conduct of the gods. For if, instead of doing so, he be dishonest and untruthful as are the sons of men, it will be at his own peril." [So long as I live, he might behave as a gentleman, and not refuse to pay, like a cad. —W.G.A.]

1022 Or, according to the more usual reading, "a one-jointed bamboo;" but in either case the meaning is obscure. Norinaga, who adopts the reading that has been followed in the translation, suggests that the expression may simply be a periphrasis for the bamboo in general. [Why not plural? —W.G.A.]

1023 八目荒籠. Norinaga remarks that the word "eight" in this place (where, to indicate a considerable number, we should rather expect "eighty") is curious, and he surmises that 八 may be an error for 大 "large." The word "coarse" itself is sufficient to show that the apertures left in the plaiting of the basket were large.

[1024]In this case, as Norinaga remarks, it is the sea-water that is intended to be spoken of, whereas the allusion in the previous sentence is to hard salt. But the Japanese language uses the same word for both, and the same Chinese character is here also used in both contexts. For this curse *cf.* Vol. 1, Sect. 40 (Note 652 *et. seq.*) and Sect. 41.

[1025]The text has the character 枯, which signifies "to wither" or "dry up" (spoken of trees). But the translator agrees with Norinaga in considering it to be in all probability an error for 臥, "to lie prostrate"; and in any case it could not here be rendered by either of the verbs "dry up" or "wither" without introducing into the English version a tautology which does not exist in the Japanese original.

[1026]Such seems to be the meaning of the obscure original *sono tokohi-do o kae-sashimeki* (令返其詛戸) Norinaga would understand it in a rather more specialized sense to signify that "she caused the implement of the curse (*i.e* the basket) to be taken away."

[1027]Or, if we take 言 in the text as equivalent to 事, "this is the origin of divine wager-payments."

[1028]*I.e.*, the Emperor Ō-jin's.

[1029]The import of this compound is not clear.

[1030]*I.e.*, "the younger princess, the truly young princess."

[1031]*I.e.*, "the great lord."

[1032]*Ō-hodo no miko*. The signification of *Ō-hodo* is obscure. Norinaga surmises it to have been originally the name of a place.

[1033]*I.e.*, "the great middle princess of Osaka." Osaka is the name of a place in Yamato. The word "middle" should by the analogy of other such genealogies indicate the fact that this princess was the fourth child out of seven. Here however she is mentioned second, and the same designation is applied to the two next daughters. There is evidently some confusion in the tradition.

[1034]*I.e.*, "the middle princess of Tai,"—a place in Kōchi.

[1035]*I.e.*, "the middle princess of Tamiya,"—a place in Kōchi.

[1036]*I.e.*, "the lady Koto-fushi of Fujiwara." But the meaning of *Koto-fushi is* obscure, and Norinaga surmises it to be an alternative or corrupt form of *Sotōshi*. (For the celebrated princess of the latter name see Vol. 3, Note 177). Fujiwara is the name of a place in Yamato, and signifies "wisteria-moor."

[1037]*Torime no miko*. This name is obscure.

[1038]*Sane no miko*. Norinaga believes *sane* to stand erroneously for *Hami;* but both forms are obscure.

[1039]The Japanese word includes both genders.

[1040]*Mikuni no kimi. Mikuni* is the name of a well-known place in the province of Echizen. It signifies "three countries."

[1041]*Hata no kimi*. There are several places called Hata, and it is not known which of them is here intended. The signification of the name is also uncertain.

[1042] *Okinaga no kimi.* See Vol. 2, Note 337.

[1043] *Sakata no Saka-bito no kimi.* This is Norinaga's restoration of an apparently corrupt text. Sakata and Sakabito are both taken to be names of places, the first of a district in Ōmi, the second of a place in Settsu. *Sakabito* (酒人) seems a very curious compound for the name of a place. Moreover the double title is unusual, and it may be thought that the word "Dukes" has fallen out of the text, and that in reality two families were intended to be spoken of.

[1044] *Yamaji no kami. Yamaji* ("mountain road") is supposed by Norinaga to be the name of a place,—perhaps in the province of Higo.

[1045] *Tsukushi no Meta no kimi.* Tsukushi is the old name of the whole of the Southwestern island of the Japanese archipelago and Meta the name of a place in the province of Hizen in that island. The etymology of Meta is uncertain.

[1046] *Fuse no kimi.* Fuse is a name of uncertain import found in several provinces. It is not known which is meant to be here designated.

[1047] *Naka-tsu-hiko no miko, i.e.,* "the middle prince," a designation which would lead one to expect to find mention of an elder brother.

[1048] *Iwashima no miko.* Iwashima seems to be the name of a place, but the signification of Iwa (not to be confounded with *iwa*, "stone" or "rock") is altogether obscure.

[1049] *Katashiwa no miko.* This prince has not been mentioned in the previous genealogies, which is curious. Katashiwa is the name of a place in Chikuzen, and signifies "hard rock."

[1050] *Kuno no miko. Kuno* is altogether obscure.

[1051] Or as Norinaga reads it, *Mofushi.* The etymology is uncertain. *Ega* has already appeared in Vol. 2, Note 864. The Old Printed Edition and some manuscripts have at the conclusion of this volume the following note: 百舌鳥陵也. "It is the mausoleum of Mozu." But Mozu is in the province of Izumi, and all the later editions discard this note as an interpolation.

Vol. 3

[1] Lit., "lower volume" (there being three in all). See Vol. 1, Note 1.

[2] *I.e.,* "high port."

[3] Norinaga surmises that the reason why the characters signifying "Empress" are in all the texts here written in small characters is on account of this personage not having been of Imperial birth. [The same characters applied to the same person are written full size in the next chapter. Here it is probably only a note which has crept into the text suggested by its occurrence lower down. —W.G.A.]

[4] *I.e.,* "the rock princess." Norinaga supposes the name to be indicative of prosperity and long life.

[5] See Vol. 2, Note 300.

[6] *I.e.,* "the elder brother lord Izaho," the latter name being of uncertain import.

[7] *Sumi-no-e-no-naka-tsu-miko.* Both the phrase "middle king" and the Inlet of Sumi have been already commented on.

[8] *Tajihi no mizu-ha-wake.* Tajihi is the name of a place in Kōchi. The traditional origin of its application to this will be found in Norinaga's Commentary, Vol. 35, p. 6. *Mizu-ha-wake* probably means "the lord with the beautiful teeth."

[9] O-*asazuma-no-waku-go no sukune.* Asazuma is the name of a place in Yamato, and *o* (though written 男) seems to be the slightly honorific prefix *o* (小) whose proper signification is "small." *Waku-go* means "younger child."

[10] See Sect. 107.

[11] *I.e.,* "the great lord of *Hatabi.*" *Hatabi* is altogether obscure

[12] *Ō-kusaka no miko.*

[13] *I.e.,* "the young lady of Hatabi." *Cf.* Note 11.

[14] *Nagai-hime.* This name it obscure.

[15] *Kusaka-be* is an alternative form of *Kusaka.* The compound therefore signifies "young princess of Kusaka."

[16] This name and the following have already appeared in the genealogies of the preceding reign (Sect. 104).

[17] These were the Emperors Ri-chū, Han-zei, and In-gyō.

[18] *Kazuraki-be.* For Kazuraki see Vol. 2, Note 160.

[19] *Mibu-be.* Norinaga quotes approvingly a derivation of the "gentile name" of Mibu from *Bi-fuku-mon* (美福門), the name of a gate which the first bearer of the name is related to have constructed. Taking into account the letter-changes which occurred in older times in the passage of words from Chinese into Japanese, the etymology is plausible enough.

[20] *Tajihi-be,* Tajihi is the name of a place in Kōchi, and is of uncertain origin

[21] *Ō-kusaka-be.* This tribe of course took its name simply from that of Prince Ō-kusaka.

[22] *Waka-kusaka-be.* A similar observation to that in the last applies to this name.

[23] See Vol. 2, Note 138.

[24] This is suspiciously like some of the works of the ancient Chinese Emperors. —W.G.A.

[25] *Wani no ike,* in the province of Kōchi. *Wani* signifies "crocodile," and it was also the name of the Korean personage mentioned in Vol. 2, Note 950. But the reason why the Pool here spoken of was so called does not appear. The Pool of Yosami has already been mentioned in Vol. 2, Note 391. Norinaga supposes that it must have dried up during the interim.

[26] *Naniwa no hori-e.* Norinaga tells us that the regularization of the channels of the Yodo and Yamato Rivers, whose mouths nearly meet at this point with various intersecting branches, is what is here intended to be referred to.

[27] *Obashi no e. O-bashi* ("little bridge") is the name of a village in the province of Settsu.

[28] *Suminoe no tsu.* Close to Naniwa; it is the modern *Sumiyoshi, Cf.* Vol. 1, Note 191.

[29] Norinaga's reading of this Verb in the Imperative Mood (as if containing an order addressed by the monarch to his ministers) seems less natural than the older

reading in the indicative, which accordingly the translator has followed.

[30]Why in brackets? —W.G.A.

[31]There is uncertainty as to the exact character in the original. But the older editions read it as the Japanese word *hako*, "boxes," while Norinaga prefers *hi*, "tubes." "Troughs" seems to conciliate both views, and to be also appropriate to the use mentioned in the text.

[32]Or simply, "the people" But the expression 百姓 is generally used in Japanese of the peasantry only.

[33]聖帝. If, following most texts, we omitted the final character 世, "reign," the English translation would be "in praise of that august reign, [the Heavenly Sovereign] was called the Emperor-Sage."

[34]Norinaga shows by collating various passages in other ancient works that this is the probable signification of the curious expression in the original, *koto-dateba* (言立者 for 事立者). The reference of course is to the occurrence of anything noteworthy among the concubines, such as the birth of a son, etc.

[35]*Kuro-hime, i.e.,* "black princess," probably meaning "black-haired princess."

[36]*Kibi no Ama no atae*. Of this family nothing is known. *Ama* signifies "fisherman." *Kibi* is the name of a province.

[37]Thus interpreted (according to Moribe), the general sense of the Song is quite clear. The word *Masazuko,* considered by Moribe to be one of the names of Princess Kuro, is however not so understood by Norinaga, who is inclined to see in it rather an honorific description of her. *Kurozaki* likewise *(i.e.,* "black cape," the word *kuro* seemingly containing an allusion to the name of the Princess) is but the best of many emendations of the name as it stands in the text, viz., Furozaya. See Norinaga's Commentary, Vol. 35, p. 33, for all the possible emendations proposed by him or his predecessors.

[38]*Scil.* of the neighborhood of Naniwa. Or possibly *Ō-ura* ("Great Strand") should be taken as the name of a place, though Norinaga does not suggest such a view.

[39]*I.e.,* to make her perform the journey on foot.

[40]See Vol. 1, Note 68.

[41]Moribe, commenting on the import of this Song, says: "Though the alleged reason was a tour of inspection, it was truly out of love for Princess Kuro that the Monarch had undertaken the journey. When her vessel could no longer be descried, he could still, alas! see the islands that remained behind,—the Island of Awa and the Island of Ajimasa; he could still, alas! see the Islands of Ono-goro and Saketsu. Alas for him left alone, parted from his love! Though he spoke not openly, yet those around him understood the undercurrent of his words." [This seems rather nonsensical. There is perhaps an allusion intended by the names of the places. *Naniwa*, which he has left, may refer to his stormy domestic life. *Awa* may be for *awamu*, "will meet," *i.e.*, the Princess Kurohime, who may also be intended by the *Ono go* (*Ono ko* "our child") of Onogoro Shima. *Ajimasa*, "taste preferable," may be a compliment to her, and *saketsu* may suggest *sakebu*, "to shout" (with delight

when he meets her). But this is doubtless fantastic and far-fetched.—W.G.A.] —"Wave-beaten" is the accepted interpretation of *oshiteru ya* (or *oshiteru*), the pillow-word for Naniwa. For the Islands of Awa and Onogoro see respectively Vol. 1, Note 63 and Sect. 3, Note b. Of the Islands of Ajimasa and Saketsu nothing is known. *Ajimasa* is the name of a species of palm, the *Livistona chinensis*, and Norinaga supposes that one of the islands in that neighborhood may anciently have received its name from the palm-trees growing on it. Palms of any kind are, however, not very common in Japan, and seem only to grow when specially cultivated.

[42]Norinaga thinks we should in this place understand the word *yamagata* (for *yama-agata*) as the name of a place. But in the Song which immediately follows, it must certainly be taken in its etymological sense of "mountain-fields," and it seems therefore quite inconsistent to translate it differently here. Moreover it is allowed that no such place as Yamagata in Kibi is anywhere made mention of. [I don't feel quite clear about this. —W.G.A.]

[43]The import of this Song is perfectly clear, "the person of Kibi" being of course the Imperial poet's lady-love.

[44]*I.e.*, was about to start back to the capital, which was in the province of Settsu.

[45]This Honorific seems so out of place (seeing that it is not applied to the Emperor's own Songs given in this section), that it is supposed by the Commentators to be an erroneous addition to the text.

[46]We might also translate thus: "Even though we be separated, [*Kumo-banare*: I fancy this phrase must be taken twice, once with what precedes in the sense given above, and a second time as a fuller equivalent of and introductory to the words *soki-ori* "separated." It might then be translated "under different skies." *Kumo* has this meaning in the compound *Ao-kumo*, "blue skies," *banare*, "skies divided." —W.G.A.] as the clouds that part owing to the west wind blowing up towards Yamato, etc.;—for the initial lines of the poem which contain the allusion to the wind and to the clouds are simply a preface, and their import may therefore at will be either considered separately, or else made continuous with that of the rest of the poem.

[47]The meaning of this Song is: "Whose spouse is it that returns to Yamato? Whose spouse is it that comes thus secretly to make love to me, like a stream flowing underground?"—The allusion contained in the twice repeated words "whose spouse" is of course to the Empress. The poetess, full of tenderness for the Emperor, regrets for his sake, as well as for her own, that he should he the husband of so jealous a wife. "Hidden water" is the accepted interpretation of the pillow-word *komorizu no*, which is with apparent reason supposed to be a contraction of *komori-mizu no*.

[48]See Vol. 2, Note 927.

[49]*I.e.*, "small island." It is first mentioned in Vol. 1, Note 94.

[50]See Vol. 2, Note 80.

[51]*Ō-watari*. The mouth of the River Yodo is meant to be designated by this name.

[52]The original expression *kura-bito-me* (倉人女) is obscure, being met with no-

where else in Japanese literature. Norinaga conjectures that the function exercised by this lady was one connected with the Empress's privy purse.

[53]The text has the character 皆, "all," which makes no sense; and Norinaga (following Mabuchi) reasonably emends it to 比日, "recently," "just now."

[54]*Mitsu no saki. Mitsu*, signifying "three," is supposed by the author to refer to the three-cornered leaves of the aralia (the name of the latter being *mi-tsuna-gashiha*); but a more likely opinion is that which would have us take *mitsu* as two words, in the sense of "august harbor." In the parallel passage of the *Chronicles*, we are told that the place was called *Kashiwa no watari, i.e.*," Oak passage."

[55]*I.e.,* going on up the river without stopping at Naniwa where the palace was.

[56]*I.e.,* the artificial bed of the river mentioned in Vol. 3, Note 26.

[57]*I.e.,* the River Yodo.

[58]The meaning of this Song is: "As I make my way up the river by boat, I see a *sashibu* (the name of a tree which cannot now be identified), below which,—that is to say nearer to the water,—there grows a camellia-tree, wide-spreading and full of blossoms. Ah! how the sight of the sturdy brilliant beauty of this camellia-tree brings back my lord and master to my mind!"—It must be remembered that in Japan the camellia-trees grow to a size far superior to that reached by their representatives in Europe. *Tsuginefu*, rendered according to the view taken by Norinaga and Moribe by the phrase "where the seedlings grow in succession," is the pillow-word for Yamashiro, and its import is disputed. The interpretation here adopted considers it to refer to the regular succession of young trees planted on a mountain side when a tract of older timber has been cut down. Mabuchi, in his *Dictionary of Pillow-Words*, sees in it, on the contrary, a reference to the rising of peak upon peak in a mountainous district (*tsugi-ne fu*= 次經). Both interpretations rest on the connection between this term and *yama*, the first half of the name of the province of Yamashiro, which it qualifies. "Five hundred" ⌊-fold branching⌋ and "true" are ornamental epithets applied by the poetess to the camellia-tree. Moribe would take the syllable *ma*, "true," in the sense of *ha*, "leaf;" but this seems less good.

[59]For the straight road from Naniwa in Settsu to Nara in Yamato would have taken her through the province of Kōchi, and not through Yamashiro.

[60]*I.e.,* the pass or hill leading from the district of Sagara in Yamashiro to Nara in Yamato. For Nara see Vol. 2, Note 551.

[61]This Song expresses the Empress's desire to return to her parental house at Takamiya in the district of Kazuraki, a desire which, however, her restless frame of mind did not allow her to fulfil.—The pillow-word for Yamashiro, which here recurs, has already been discussed in Vol. 3, Note 58. There are two other pillow-words in this Song,—*aoniyoshi*, which is prefixed to Nara, and *o-date* (or *o-date-yama* according to the old reading, or *o-date tatsu* according to another reading), which is prefixed to Yamato. The former of these is so obscure that, rather than attempt to render it into English, the translator prefers to refer the student to the remarks of the various commentators,—Mabuchi s.v. in his *Dictionary of Pillow-Words*, Norinaga in his *Commentary* Vol. 36, pp. 22–24, and Moribe *in loco.*

Odate [*-yama*] seems to refer undoubtedly to the circle of mountains that guard the approach to the province of Yamato, and it has been rendered accordingly. The great difficulty of the Song lies in the line rendered "ascend to Miya," and the commentators from Keichū downwards make all sorts of efforts to explain it. Moribe's view, according to which the word should be regarded as a familiar abbreviation of Takamiya, naturally used by one whose native place it was, seems the most acceptable. Norinaga takes the line to signify: "When I ascend past the palace [of Naniwa];"

[62]韓, *i.e.*, Korea.

[63]For *Nuri no omi, i.e.*, "the Grandee of Nuri." Nuri is probably a corrupt form of some Korean name. [누리 *(nuri)* in Korean is a kind of caterpillar. —W.G.A.]

[64]Or Tsuzuki, in Yamashiro. Etymology obscure.

[65]This name signifies "bird-mountain." The commentators presume that it contains an allusion to the fact of its bearer being an Imperial courier.

[66]This is the actual sense conveyed by the original 使舍人名謂鳥山人送御歌, and we naturally infer that Toriyama was made the bearer to the Empress of the following Song. The Song itself, however, is addressed not to her, but to Toriyama on his departure. On the other hand, the two poems which follow are evidently for the Empress, and it is impossible to suppose that the first messenger was not likewise intended to convey to her some poetic missive. All that we can do is to render the text as it stands, and to suppose it corrupt.

[67]The meaning of this Song is: "Oh Toriyama! pursue her into Yamashiro! I tremble at the thought of the possibility of thy not finding her."

[68]*Wani no omi Kuchiko* (further on he is mentioned as *Kuchiko no omi*, *i.e.*, "the Grandee [of] Kuchiko"). *Kuchi-ko* may be interpreted to mean "mouth-child," and Moribe thinks that this personage was so called on account of the verbal messages of which he was made the bearer. The translator would prefer to consider *ko* as an abbreviation of *hiko*, "prince," especially as the sister's name is *Kuchi-hime*, where the word *hime* must mean "princess."

[69]This Song is so obscure that Norinaga and Moribe differ completely as to its interpretation. The translator has followed Moribe, though by no means persuaded that the latter has hit on the proper signification. According to this view, the Emperor makes a pun on the word "heart," which is supposed to have been the name of a pool situated on the moor of Ōiko near Takaki at Mimoro,—all names of places with which the Empress was familiar,—and reproaches her for having no thought of *his* heart which beats so lovingly for her. Norinaga, on the other hand, thinks that the poem proper consists only of its last two lines (in the English translation they necessarily come first): "Wilt thou be without thinking even of the heart?" —and that all the rest is a "Preface" to the pillow-word *ki-mo-mukō* by which the word *kokoro*, "heart," is preceded. As for *ō-i-ko* and *takaki*, they are taken, not as names of places, but as common nouns. According to this view of the structure of the Song, it ceases (with the exception of its last two lines) to have any rational signification, and it is needless to attempt to translate it for the

English reader. Persons familiar with Japanese are therefore referred to Norinaga's *Commentary*, Vol. 36, pp. 34–36.

[70]The meaning of this Song is: "If thou and I had not so long been spouses, then indeed mightest thou break with me, and declare that thou knowest me not. But how canst thou so far forget our wedded life as to desert me now?"—The "great root'" *ō-ne*, is the modern *daikon (Raphanus sativus)*, a kind of radish which is a favorite vegetable with the Japanese and is distinguished by its brilliantly white appearance. "Beaten" here signifies "dug up." The use of the past tense is curious. *Ko-guwa*, here in accordance with Norinaga's view rendered "wooden hoes," is interpreted by Moribe to mean "little hoes." "Where the seedlings grow in succession" is the English rendering of *tsugi-ne fu*, the pillow-word for Yamashiro (see Vol. 3, Note 58).

[71]The Empress was lodging with a private individual, but her presence warrants the application of the term "palace" [It is *tono*, not *miya*. The *Nihongi* says she built herself a palace at Tsutsuki. —W.G.A.] to his house.

[72]"Puddle" is the translation given by Williams. —W.G.A.

[73]It was raining too hard for the water to stop on the surface in the shape of puddles, so it streamed off in little rivulets.

[74]Lit., "rubbed." See Introduction p. 30. Instead of "green," we might equally well translate by "blue." The garment intended must be the upper garment or coat.

[75]Lit., "respectfully served the Empress."

[76]The meaning of these lines, which can only be called poetry because they are in meter, is plain: in them the speaker draws the Empress's attention to the pitiful condition of the messenger who is doing his best to deliver to her the Emperor's message. Probably the reading in our text has been corrupted; for that in the *Chronicles*, which may be translated thus: "Oh! how tearful am I when I see my lord elder brother," etc., is much preferable. [But will not the *Kojiki* version bear this meaning? *Vide* Norinaga's commentary. —W.G.A.]

[77]*Scil.* of her attendant thus taking the messenger's part.

[78]This is Norinaga's conjectural restoration of the reading of this word, which in all the texts is hopelessly corrupt.

[79]This Song consists of two divisions, the first of which is but a Preface for the second, the pivot being formed by the word *sawa-sawa ni*, which has the meaning of "pure," "cool," or "refreshing," with reference to what precedes it, and the meaning of "tumultuously" (*sawa-sawa ni=sawagashiku*) when taken together with what follows. The difficulties which present themselves in the first division have all been explained in Vol. 3, Note 58 and Vol. 3, Note 70. The general sense of the second division is plain enough; but the precise application of the comparison to the "more and more flourishing trees" is obscure. Norinaga's view has been adopted by the translator, and the words in brackets supplemented accordingly. Moribe prefers to consider that the reference is to the repeated visits first of the Emperor's messengers and afterwards of the Emperor himself. The words "look across at" must be explained by supposing that the trees were in the neighborhood

of Nurinomi's house; they were shoots springing up from roots that had been cut down close to the ground.

[80]The commentators thus explain these obscure expressions: "A Quiet Song is one which is sung to a tranquil tune. A Changing Song is one temporarily [Or could *kaeshi-uta* mean "sung as a duet"? —W.G.A.] sung while the tone (mode?) [Key? —W.G.A.] is changing." The six Songs in question must be supposed to have combined both characteristics.

[81]In this Song the Emperor condoles with his mistress on her childlessness: "Will the single sedge on the moor of Yata die without leaving any offspring? Sedge, indeed! Yes, sedge is the term I use for my metaphor, but what is in my thoughts is the girl I love." There is in the original a *jeu-de-mots*, not capable of translation into English, between *suge* or *suga*, "sedge," and *sugashi*, "pure."

[82]The girl replies: "Even though I be childless, I care not if my lord cares not."

[83]*Yata-be.*

[84]*Scil.* of the success of his mediation.

[85]Or, "for whom is the loom [employed], with which my Great Lady Medori weaves?"—The word *hata* in Archaic Japanese signifies both "garment" and the instrument which is used to weave a garment, *i.e.*, a "loom" (服 and 機). In later times the second meaning has prevailed to the exclusion of the first.

[86]The parallel passage of the *Chronicles* gives these two Songs as a single one which is put into the mouth of Queen Medori's handmaidens,—a more acceptable version of the incident.

[87]Norinaga suspects that there is here an error in the text, which should, according to him, read: "After this."

[88]The gist of this Song is an instigation to murder the Emperor (whose name was *Ō-sazaki, i.e.*, "Great Wren" Cf. Vol. 2, Note 883), [If there is any truth in this story, it would contradict the conjecture that *Ōsazaki* or *sasagi* is a posthumous name.—W.G.A.] addressed to the singer's husband (whose name was *Haya-bu-sa-wake, i.e.*, "Falcon Lord"). But the allusion to the lark remains obscure. Keichū suggests that it is simply mentioned as a term of comparison for the falcon's power of flight, while Norinaga opines that the meaning rather is: "The lark flies so high up to heaven that it would be hard to catch it; but the wren is an easy prey." [A different version in the *Nihongi*, in which there is no lark. —W.G.A.]

[89]Viz., as may be supposed, repeated by some fourth person.

[90]*Kurahashi-yama,* in Yamato.

[91]This Song, like the next, is too clear to stand in need of explanation. "Ladder-like" is an attempt to render the force of the pillow-word *hashi-tate.* See Mabuchi's *Dictionary of Pillow-Words*, *s.v.*, for the exact force attributed to it by Mabuchi.

[92]For Uda see Vol. 2, Note 65. The etymology of Soni is equally obscure.

[93]*The character* 御, though read by the commentators with the usual Japanese honorific *mi,* "august," has here its proper Chinese signification of "Imperial."

[94]*Yamabe no Ōtate no muraji.* The "gentile name" was *Yamabe no muraji*, and the personal name *Ōtate*, though the confused wording of this passage does not make

it appear so. *Yama-be* signifies mountain (*i.e.*, hunters') tribe. *Ō-tate* is "big shield."

[95]See Vol. 2, Note 927.

[96]*Iwa-no-hime* was dead at this time, according to the *Nihongi*. —W.G.A.

[97]Or, perhaps rather "aralia-leaves" (*Cf.* Sect. 123).

[98]Or, "had her dragged away."

[99]Lit., "was granted the punishment of death," or "[the Emperor] deigned to condemn him to death." [Executed? —W.G.A.]

[100]See Vol. 2, Note 927.

[101]*Hime-shima, i.e.*, "Princess Island." The name is supposed to be connected with that of the goddess of Himegoso mentioned near the end of Sect. 114, and first occurs in Vol. 1, Note 98.

[102]The wild goose goes far north at the approach of spring, and the translator is informed by Capt. Blakiston that the latter has not known of any breeding even on the island of Ezo. The Emperor was therefore naturally astonished at so strange an occurrence as that of a wild goose laying an egg in Yamato, and asks the Noble Take-uchi whether he had ever heard of the like of it before, Take-uchi being at that time more than two hundred years old (!) according to the chronology of the *Chronicles*, and therefore the oldest and most experienced man in the Empire.—"Court Noble" represents the Japanese word *Aso* (for *Asomi*, believed by Norinaga and Moribe to be derived from *a se omi* 吾兄臣, lit. "my elder brother minister" but used simply as a title). [*Ason* is a Korean title. —W.G.A.] The words *Uchi* and *Yamato* are preceded in the original by their respective pillow-words *tamaki-haru* and *sora-mitsu* whose force it is impossible to render in English, and whose origin indeed is obscure. The words rendered "laying an egg" are literally "giving birth to a child."

[103]This Song is too clear to need explanation. As in the preceding one, Yamato is accompanied by the pillow-word *sora-mitsu*.

[104]Or, "Imperial."

[105]*I.e.*, say Norinaga and Moribe, who refer this episode to a time previous to Nin-toku's accession, "The wild-goose has laid an egg in token of thy future accession to the throne." The translator prefers the view expressed by Keichū in his *Kō-Gan Shō* and adopted in the *Explanation of the Songs in the Chronicles of Japan*, that the words *tsui ni*, "at last," must here be taken in the sense of "long," and the Song interpreted to mean "The wild goose lays an egg as an omen that thy reign will be a long one." This view is supported by the story in the *Chronicles*, which places the Song in the Emperor's fiftieth year and gives him thirty-six years of subsequent existence, thus making the prophecy amply fulfil itself, as one would expect that it should do in the pages of such a work. According to the other view, the text of the *Chronicles* calls for emendation.

[106]*Hogi-Uta no kata-uta.* For "Incomplete Song" See Sect. 89, Note a.

[107]This is Moribe's reading (given without any comment) of the original characters 免寸. Norinaga pronounces them corrupt; but, having no emendation to propose, simply leaves them without any *kana* reading.

[108]See Vol. 1, Note 68.

[109]*Takayasu no yama*, in the province of Kōchi. The characters with which the name is written signify "high and easy."

[110]The significance of this name, written 枯野, remains obscure notwithstanding the efforts of the commentators to explain it.

[111]Scarcely full enough for 寒泉—W.G.A.

[112]里, the Chinese *li*, Japanese *ri*. The length of the *ri* has varied greatly at different times and in different parts of the country. The modern standard Japanese *ri* is equivalent to about 2.44 English statute miles; but Norinaga supposes the *ri* of the epoch mentioned in our text to have been less than one-seventh of that distance.

[113]In the *Chronicles* this story is placed in the reign of the Emperor Ō-jin, and the Song is attributed to that monarch.

[114]In this Song the sound of the twanging of the lute that had been made from the remnant of the boat Karano is compared to the rustling of the plants standing half out of water on the reefs in the harbor of Yura.—The compound word *kaki-hiku*, rendered by "struck," signifies literally "scratched and struck," the lute being struck with the nail. The onomatopoetic word *saya-saya*, of which "sound" is but a colorless equivalent, represents both the delightful ring of the lute and the rustling of the sea-plants. What plants are intended by the expression "wet plants" (*nazu no ki*) is a point that has been much disputed. Moribe even thinks that the term is meant for the name of a particular species of (apparently) coral now found in the island of Hachijō. Yura is in the Island of Awaji.

[115]See Vol. 3, Note 80.

[116]*Mozu no mimi-hara*. The origin of this singular name is thus explained in the *Chronicles* (Emperor Nin-toku, 67th year, Winter, 10th Moon): "[The Emperor] made a progress to the moor of Ishizu in Kōchi to fix the site of his mausoleum. On the day when the construction of his mausoleum was begun, a deer suddenly ran out from the middle of the moor, rushed into the midst of the porters, fell down, and died. The suddenness of its death causing astonishment, its wound was looked for, whereupon a shrike came out of its ear, and flew away. So on looking into the ear, it was found to be all eaten away. So that is the reason why the place is called *Mozu no mimi-hara* (the 'Shrike's Ear-Moor')."

[117]For *Iware* see Sect. 43, Note c. *Waka-sakura* signifies "young cherry-tree." The origin of the name is traced, rightly or wrongly, to an incident mentioned in the *Chronicles* under the reign of this Emperor, 3rd year.

[118]*Kuro-hime, i.e.,* "black princess." The same name occurs several times, and has reference to the black hair [But all Japanese hair is black. I should rather say complexion. —W.G.A.] of the person so designated.

[119]*Ashida no sukune*. *Ashi-da* signifies "reed-moor." It is the name of a place in Yamato.

[120]*Kazuraki no So-tsu-biko*. For this name, which is here abbreviated, see Vol. 2, Note 300.

[121]*Ichinobe no Oshiwa no miko*. Ichinobe is in the province of Yamashiro, and the

name seems to mean "near the market." The name of *Oshiwa* refers to the "uneven teeth" of this personage which are mentioned in Sect. 167 (near Note 375).

[122] *Mima no miko.* The signification of this name is quite obscure.

[123] *Aomi no iratsume. Aomi* is supposed by Norinaga to be the name of a place.

[124] *Iitoyo no iratsume. Iitoyo* is supposed by Norinaga to be the name of a bird, perhaps a kind of owl.

[125] *Achi no atae,* supposed to be of Korean origin, and to be a descendant of 阿知, great grandson of the Chinese Emperor 霊帝.

[126] *Aya no atae.* This family was of continental origin, Aya being the Japanese reading of the character 漢; see Vol. 2, Note 958.

[127] *Tajihi no no,* in the province of Kōchi. The signification of the name is obscure.

[128] This Song expresses the Monarch's regret at not having brought his mats with him.—From the expression used in the text (*tatsu-gomo,* the commentators suppose that such mats were used as a sort of screen to avert draughts. One proposal is to consider *tatsu* as the verb *tatsuru,* "to set up," because these mats must have been "set up" round the room. But it agrees better with grammatical usage to take it in its other sense of "cutting," or "dividing," and to suppose that the mats were so called because they "cut off" the draught from the person sitting behind them.

[129] Or "Hill of Hanifu," *Hanifu-zaka,* in the province of Kōchi.

[130] The meaning of this Song is perfectly clear.

[131] See Sect. 64, Note d. The word rendered "entrance" here and below in the same context is literally "mouth."

[132] See Vol. 2, Note 355.

[133] Moribe thus paraphrases this Song; "If the maiden whom I met at Ōsaka and whom I sought direction of had been a common mortal, she would have simply told me the shortest road. But now I see why it was that she bid me go round by way of Tagima: it was to preserve me from danger. Ah! she must have been a Goddess."—The words *tada ni* generally have the sense of "directly," "immediately," and are indeed here so understood by Norinaga. Moribe's interpretation, which has been followed by the translator, does but little violence to the text, and suits the general meaning better.

[134] See Sect. 45, Note c.

[135] The original of this clause is very elliptical, consisting only of the two characters 令謁. The old reading joins thereto the characters 爾天皇. which according to Norinaga form the commencement of the next sentence. The meaning is not affected by the change.

[136] Lit., "heart." Similarly below, where the word "intent" is used in the translation.

[137] The signification of this name is quite obscure.

[138] *Hayabito.* The reader should compare Vol. 1, Note 632.

[139] Lit., "closely accustomed to."

[140] The original leaves it uncertain whether the words "to rule the Empire" should be applied to the speaker, to Sobakari, or to both; and the ambiguous application has therefore been preserved in the translation.

[141]Lit., "already."

[142]See Vol. 2, Note 927.

[143]Laterally, "the hundred officials," a Chinese phrase, which has been met with before.

[144]The character 宛 used in the text implies by its radical that the bowl was of metal. It is an unauthorized form of 椀 or 盌.

[145]*Scil.* by the prince to the man-at-arms.

[146]*I.e.*, Nearer Asuka. The name is written 近飛鳥. The student should consult Norinaga's note on this passage in Vol. 38, pp. 38–39 of his *Commentary*, to see what can be done towards reconciling the name, the characters it is written with, and the origin ascribed to it, all of which are so apparently incongruous.

[147]*Scil.* of *Isonokami*. This deity was the sword forming the subject of the legend narrated in Sect. 45.

[148]遠飛鳥, *i.e.*, Further Asuka. *Cf.* Vol. 3, Note 145.

[149]This is the gist of the original phrase, which will not bear literal translation into English: 政既平訖参上侍之.

[150]In Japanese the same word is used for a "storehouse" and for the "treasury." But the appointment here mentioned would seem really to correspond to what we should call Lord of the Treasury or Minister of Finance. The characters in the original are 藏官.

[151]Lit., "ration grounds."

[152]*Waka-sakura-be.*

[153]*Waka-sakura-be no omi*. Cf. Vol. 3, Note 117.

[154]All the editors agree in here reading as *kabane* ("gentile name," see Vol. 1, Note 232) the character 姓, which signifies properly" family name."

[155]*Himeda no kimi*. Nothing is known of this family.

[156]*Iware-be*. For Iware see Sect. 43, Note c. It will be remembered that the Emperor of whose reign the present Section forms part held his court at Iware.

[157]See Vol. 3, Note 116.

[158]For Tajihi see Vol. 3, Note 127. *Shiba-kaki* (or *Shiba-gaki*) signifies "a fence of brushwood."

[159]As to the ancient Japanese measures we have no accurate information, and the English equivalents used in this passage correspond but approximately to the modern Japanese standards. The character rendered "line" is 分 which denotes the tenth part of a 寸 or "inch." Norinaga remarks that the dimensions of the teeth are not anything extraordinary judged by the present standard, and supposes that anciently the measures of length must have been smaller than at present.

[160]*Tsuno no iratsume*. The signification of this name is obscure.

[161]*Wani no kogoto no omi.* The meaning of Kogoto is obscure. Wani has already often appeared.

[162]*Kai no iratsume.* Kai is the name of a province, but it cannot be said for certain that it is from it that this Princess derived her name.

[163]*Tsubura no iratsume.* The meaning of *Tsubura* is obscure.

[164]*I.e.*, "the younger princess."

[165]*Takara no miko. Takara signifies "treasure."*

[166]*Takabe no iratsume. Takabe* seems to be the name of a place, unless it be considered to be connected with the word *taka*, "hawk."

[167]Remember that the single character 王 includes both sexes.

[168]See Vol. 3, Note 116.

[169]Also pronounced *In-kyō*.

[170]See Vol. 3, Note 147.

[171]This name and the next have already appeared in Sect. 117.

[172]*Kinashi no Karu no miko.* Karu is properly the name of a place in Yamato which has already often appeared in the text. It is uncertain whether *kinashi* is likewise the name of a place or of a particular kind of pear; but Norinaga inclines to the former view.

[173]*I.e.*, "the great lord of Nagata." There are many places of this name (lit. "long rice-field"), and it is not known which is here intended.

[174]*I.e.*, "the black prince of Sakai." The latter word signifies "frontier." It is not known where Sakai is, neither is the reason for the name of "black prince" applied to this personage known (*Cf.* the "white prince" mentioned a little further on).

[175]Or, "of Anaho," for Anaho is properly the name of a place in Yamato. Its import is not clear.

[176]*I.e.*, "the great lady of Karu."

[177]Written 衣通郎女, *i.e.*, "the garment-passing lady." *So-tōshi is Norinaga's reading of the characters, the usual reading being So-tōri* (the intransitive instead of the transitive form of the verb). He likewise identifies Koto-fushi (see Vol. 2, Note 1036) with this celebrated princess, who is commonly worshiped as Goddess of Poetry. There is much confusion in the traditions concerning her, and Norinaga's notes on the subject in Vol. 34, pp. 53–54 and in Vol. 39 of his *Commentary*, p. 3, should be consulted.

[178]*Yatsuri no shiro-biko no miko, i.e.*, "the white prince of Yatsuri." Yatsuri is the name of a place in Yamato. It is written with characters signifying "eight melons."

[179]*I.e.*, "great Hatsuse," so called from Hatsuse, a celebrated place in Yamato, which has already been mentioned.

[180]*I.e.*, "the great lady of Tachibana," the latter being the name of a place in Yamato. The word signifies "orange."

[181]*I.e.*, "the lady of Sakami," the latter being apparently the name of a place either in Harima or in Owari. Its derivation is not clear.

[182]For this expression see Vol. 1, Note 551. The story of the refusal of this monarch to accept the crown which was offered to him by the magnates of the nation is told at considerable length in the parallel passage of the *Chronicles*. According to the same authority he belonged to a collateral branch of the Imperial family, and was therefore not in the regular line of succession.

[183]See Sect. 98, Note e.

[184]The *Nihongi* makes the 80 vessels sent after his death. Vide Ingyō, 42nd Year

of his reign, (pp. 323–324 Aston's translation). —W.G.A.

[185]Lit., "great messenger."

[186]金波鎮漢紀武. Norinaga decides that 金 is the surname, 波鎮 an official title, 漢紀 an official designation of the kinsmen of the Korean King, and 武 the personal name.

[187]*The original is:* 天下氏氏名名人等之氏姓, *which Norinaga reads ame no shita no uji-uji na-na no hito-domo no uji kabane.*

[188]We learn from the *Chronicles* that he whose hand was injured in the process of dipping it into the jar of boiling water was pronounced a deceiver, while those who stood the trial unhurt were considered to be telling the truth.

[189]*Amakashi no koto-ya-so-maga-tsu-hi no saki.* Norinaga truly observes that this does not sound like an actual geographical name, but was rather, it may be supposed, a new designation given to Cape Amakashi (see Vol. 2, Note 548) on account of the incident here mentioned. The name reminds us of that of one of the deities born from the purification of the person of the creator Izanagi after his return from Hades (see Vol. 1, Note 184).

[190]*Ya-so tomo-no-o.* See Vol. 1, Note 576.

[191]*Karu-be.*

[192]*Osaka-be*, so called after the Empress's native place (see Vol. 3, Note 171, and Vol. 2, Note 1033). The reading of *Otaka-be* is given in all the editions to the characters in the text, 刑部, where we should expect 忍坂部. Norinaga's explanation of the reason why the name was thus written will be found in Vol. 39, p. 19, of his *Commentary*.

[193]*Kawa-be.* Norinaga supposes that there is here some corruption of the text, as no connection can be discovered between the name of this Tribe and that of the Princess whose proxy the tribe became.

[194]See Vol. 2, Note 1034.

[195]See Vol. 2, Notes 863 and 864.

[196]See Vol. 1, Note 551. The wording of this sentence would make it appear that it was only after the Emperor In-gyō's death that King Karu was chosen to succeed him. But probably King Karu had been appointed Heir Apparent (皇太子) during his father's life-time, as is indeed expressly stated in the *Chronicles*, and is implied in later passages of this work; and what our author meant to say was: "It was settled that King Karu should rule the Empire after the former Sovereign's decease," etc.

[197]The meaning of the Song is: "The sister, the mistress, whom I wooed with such difficulty, is now easily mine."—The first phrase, down to "mountain's height," is but a "Preface" to the poem properly so called, serving to introduce by a *jeu-de-mots* the word *shita-doi*, which means not only "hidden conduit," but "hidden wooing." At the same time the implied comparison of the poet's secret love of one so difficult to obtain as his own sister, to the course of the water in hidden conduits which is carried up the mountain's side to irrigate a field perched in a spot almost inaccessible, is by no means devoid of aptness. The word "mountain" (*yama*) is in the original preceded by the pillow-word *ashihiki* (or *ashibiki*) *no*,

whose signification is obscure and much disputed.

[198] *Shirage-uta* (written phonetically). The interpretation of the term here adopted is that which has the sanction of Norinaga and Moribe. They explain it to signify that the voice rose gradually towards the latter part of the Song.

[199] As in the case of the preceding Song, the first phrase is but a preface, which plays on the coincidence in sound between the words *tashi-dashi*, "rattling," and *tashika*, "certainly," *i.e.*, undisturbedly." The signification of the Song proper is: "If I shall but have gratified my passion, what care I however men may plot against me?" If I can but press my beloved to my bosom, let all things go to "rack and ruin, like the wild rice (*Hydropyrum latifolium*), a grass which, when cut, falls into disorder!"— Of the sentiment of the Song, the less said the better; but viewed simply from a literary point of view, it is certainly one of the most fascinating little productions of the early Japanese muse, and the literal rendering of it into English does it woeful injustice. Moribe rightly rejects Norinaga's proposal to divide the poem in two after the words *hito hakayu to mo*, "plotted against by people." *Kari-komo no*, of the wild rice, is a pillow-word.

[200] *Hinaburi no age-uta.* The commentators have nothing more precise to tell us concerning the expression "Lifting-Song" than that "it refers to the lifting of the voice in singing."

[201] See Vol. 2, Note 966.

[202] *Ō-mae O-mae sukune no omi* (according to the old reading *Ō-saki O-saki,* etc.). Norinaga considers this double name to denote two brothers, the words *ō* and *o* ("great" and "small") naturally lending themselves to the interpretation of "elder" and "younger." Moribe, on the contrary, thinks that there was but one, and is supported both by the authority of the *Chronicles of Japan* and by the fact that, except in the *Chronicles of Old Matters of Former Ages*, which is believed to be a forgery, no second brother is anywhere mentioned. He explains the use of the double name in the prose text as having crept in through the influence of the text of the following Song (see Note 206 below). This seems to the translator the better view.

[203] There is here an evident corruption of the text, and Norinaga aptly conjectures that arrow-*heads*, or, as they are called in Japanese, arrow-*points*, are intended. He adds that up till then arrowheads had always been made of iron.

[204] The author's style is here rather at fault; for he apparently wishes to say that the arrows employed by Prince Anaho were those which had been used in ancient times and were still the most universally employed—that, in fact, they were the usual style of arrow in contradistinction to those of Prince Karu's invention.

[205] See Vol. 2, Note 698.

[206] The prince, in the Song, bids his troops follow his example, and take refuge from the rain under cover of the gate of Ō-mae's house. Such, at least, is the actual sense of the words used; but Norinaga sees in them nothing less than a slightly veiled exhortation to his followers to attack the castle, while Moribe, on the other hand, thinks they were meant to convey to Ō-mae a hint of his presence, and enable the beleaguered prince, for whom (as being his elder brother) Prince Anaho

retained a great affection and respect, to devise some method of escape. This seems extremely far-fetched.—The word "metal" probably refers only to the fastenings of the gate, and not to its whole structure.

[207]The exact purport and application of this Song is disputed, but this much seems clear: that the composer of it seeks to quiet both the besieging army (out of politeness called courtiers), and the peasants who had joined the fray, by making light of the whole occurrence, which he compares to so trivial an accident as the falling of a bell from a man's "garter" or "leggings." The custom of ornamenting this article of dress with a small bell is, however, not mentioned elsewhere. [Norinaga does not say so. —W.G.A.] The word *yume*, which concludes the Song and is here rendered "beware," is identified by Norinaga and Moribe with the imperative of the ierb *imu* "to avoid," "to shun," "not to do."

[208]*Miya-hito-buri.* This is one of the cases which lend support to Norinaga's view that the names of the so-called styles of Songs are derived from their initial words.

[209]Written with the humble character 僕, "servant."

[210]The word used in the Text, here and also in the next sentence, is that which properly denotes the presenting of tribute.

[211]Another reading gives this sense:

> As, if the maiden of heaven-soaring Karu cried
> violently, people would know, she cries quietly
> like the doves on Mount Hasa.

According to this reading, the poet simply explains the reason of the undemonstrativeness of his mistress's grief; according to that in the text, he implores her not to weep too passionately.—*Amadamu* or *amatobu ya*, "heaven-soaring," is the pillow-word for Karu, applied to it punningly on account of its similarity in sound to the word *kari*, "a wild-goose," which well deserves the epithet "heaven-soaring." Of Mount Hasa nothing is known.

[212]*Shitata ni. —W.G.A.*

[213]Rendered thus according to Moribe's exegesis, which quite approves itself to the translator's mind, this Song signifies: "Oh! maiden of Karu! come and sleep with me but once, before my impending banishment renders it hard for us to meet again." Norinaga chooses to interpret *nete* as a crasis of *naete*, "bending," and sees in the Song an invitation to the maiden to come quietly bending her head and passing along quietly so as not to attract observation.—The final word, translated "maiden," is *otome-domo*, properly a plural, but here used in a singular sense, as *watakushi-domo*, "I" (properly "we"), so constantly is in the modern colloquial dialect. For the pillow-word "heaven-soaring" see Vol. 3, Note 212.

[214]For Iyo see Vol. 1, Note 69. Its hot springs are often mentioned in early documents. Norinaga identifies them with a place now called Dō-go (道後).

[215]The meaning of this Song is: "I go where perchance no messengers will reach me. But thou must ask tidings of me from the birds."

[216]*Ama-da-buri.* The title seems to be derived from the initial pillow-word of these three Songs.

[217]The meaning of this Song seems to the translator to be: "Even if they dare to banish me now, I shall someday return again. Respect my mat during my absence. Mat, indeed! It is my wife that must be respected." The commentators consider the concluding words to be a command addressed to the wife, and interpret the phrase to mean, "My spouse, beware!" But surely this makes less good sense, and moreover fails to suit the exactly parallel passage in the first Song of Sect. 125. By the words "Great Lord" the princely poet denotes himself,—perhaps with a touch of anger at the indignity to which he is subjected. The difficult expression *funa-amari* is here, in accordance with Moribe's view, rendered by the words "remaining voyage," *i.e.*, "the voyage homeward," which is that part of a voyage that may be said to remain over for an outward-bound vessel when she has reached her destination. Norinaga's *Commentary*, Vol. 39, pp. 50–51, should be consulted for older views of the meaning of the term. The expression "beware of my mat" reminds us that in early days the entire floor of a Japanese room was not matted according to the modern custom, but that each individual had his own mat on which to sit and sleep. Great care was always taken not to defile another's mat. *Cf.* an elegy from the *Collection of a Myriad Leaves* translated by the present writer in his *Classical Poetry of the Japanese*, p. 79.

[218]*Hina-buri no kata-oroshi.* Like most of the names of styles of Songs, this one is extremely obscure. The commentators suppose that one part was sung in a lower voice than the rest. But they are merely guessing.

[219]The actual words of the Song signify: "Lacerate not thy feet by walking on the unseen oyster-shells of the shore of Ahine that is covered with the summer herbs; but walk there after dawn." (This is Keichū's interpretation of the word *akashite*, "having made clear," and is the best in the present writer's opinion; the later commentators see in it a recommendation to the exiled prince to clear the grass away on either side.) The word *Ahine* calls, however, for special explanation in order that the full import of the poem may be brought out. It properly signifies "sleeping together" or "lying on each other," and is therefore applicable either to the two spouses or to the summer grass. Indeed it is doubtful if it be the name of any real place at all. The word *natsu-kusa* may also be taken simply as a pillow-word for Ahine.—The total gist of the Song is in any case a warning from the maiden to her lover to guard himself against the perils of the journey.

[220]Norinaga's rendering of *ke* here seems unsatisfactory.—W.G.A.

[221]The meaning of this Song is: "It is too long since thy departure. I can wait no longer, but will go and meet thee."—The verb "to meet" (*mukake*) is in the original preceded by the pillow-word *yama-tazu*, which forms the subject of the note appended to the poem by the compiler. The commentators are not agreed as to the precise nature of the instrument intended; but it seems to have been some kind of axe. The cause of its use as a pillow-word for "meeting" is equally disputed. It only occurs written phonetically. The term *tatsu-ge*, by which it is explained in the text, is there written 造木, which does not help us much towards understanding what is meant to be designated.

[222]So obscure is this Song in the original, that Norinaga confesses himself unable to make any sense of it. The translator has adopted Moribe's interpretation, according to which the gist of it is this: "Alas! my dear wife, who wast so willing to be forever united to me that thou didst even fix on the spot in the funereal vale of Hatsuse where we should one day be buried together! Alas for thee, whom at last I now see again!"—In order to arrive at this meaning, Moribe is obliged to prove more or less satisfactorily that the thrice repeated word *o* signifies "vale" or "mountain-fold" the first two times that it occurs, and "grave" the third, and that *komo-riku no hatsuse,* usually interpreted as secluded "Hatsuse," means "the hidden castle," the" final place," *i.e.*, "the tomb." It is also necessary to suppose, without authority, that the flags mentioned by the poet are meant for funeral flags, and that the words "prostrate" like a *tsuki* bow," etc., which, according to the laws of Japanese construction, precede instead of following the phrase "alas! beloved spouse," etc., are but a preface for the latter.—It will be seen that the foundation on which Moribe's interpretation rests is slight, and that Norinaga was scarcely to be blamed for pronouncing the Song incomprehensible. At the same time the translator has thought it better, by following Moribe, to give some translation of it than to leave the passage blank. With this warning, the student may search for other possible meanings if he pleases.—Hatsuse is a still existent and celebrated place among the mountains of Yamato. The etymology of the name, unless we accept Moribe's mentioned above, is obscure. It is now usually pronounced Hase. The *tsuki* is said to be almost indistinguishable from the *keyaki* tree (*Zelkova serrata*). The *azusa* seems to be the *Catalpa kaempferi*, but some believe it to be the cherry-tree.

[223]The first half of this Song down to the words "hanging on the true piles true jewels" is a Preface for what follows. The signification of the rest is: "If my dearly loved sister-wife were still at Hatsuse in Yamato, I would fly to her either in thought or deed; but now that she has followed me into exile, the land of exile is good enough."—Moribe, while allowing the first half of the Song to be a Preface for the rest, contends that it also should be credited with a signification bearing on the subject-matter of the main part of the Song. He supposes, namely, the religious ceremony, whatever it was, of driving piles into the bed or bank of the river and of decorating them with beads and a mirror, to have been one really performed by Princess So-tōshi to compass her lover's return. In the translator's opinion, it is more elegant and more in accordance with archaic usage to consider the Preface as having no special significance or connection (otherwise than verbal) with the rest of the poem. The word *i-kui or i-gui*, rendered "sacred piles," occasions some difficulty; for it is not certain whether Norinaga is right in giving to the initial syllable *i* the meaning of "sacred." It may be simply what has been termed an "ornamental prefix," devoid of meaning. Norinaga however points out that this usage of it is restricted to verbs, and does not occur with substantives. *Komoriku no*, the pillow-word for Hatsuse, is rendered by "secluded" in accordance with Mabuchi's usually accepted derivation from *komori-kuni*, "retired land." Moribe, notwithstanding what he has said in his exegesis of the preceding poem (Note

8), is willing to allow that, though perhaps not its original, this was its common meaning even in ancient times.

[224] *I.e.,* committed suicide together.

[225] This expression is interpreted to mean that these Songs were recited in monotone, as one would read a book or tell a tale.

[226] *I.e.,* Prince. In all other cases we find the word *mikoto*, "Augustness," as the title by which the Sovereign is mentioned at the commencement of his reign.

[227] See Vol. 2, Note 52.

[228] *Ne no omi.* The etymology of *ne* is obscure.

[229] Lit., as "tribute."

[230] More literally, "I have kept her without putting her out of doors."

[231] *Cf.* Vol. 1, Note 154 and Vol. 1, Note 312.

[232] Norinaga surmises that 其 may be an error for 希 in the original of this clause 然言以白事其思無礼.

[233] 礼物. The term corresponds to the modern 結納, the name by which the presents which are exchanged at the time of betrothal are designated.

[234] The original term *oshi-ki no tama-kazura* is extremely obscure. One of Norinaga's conjectures is that the "push-wood" was a kind of frame by which the jewels or beads, strung on an erect stem of some hard material, were kept firmly attached to the head. Perhaps some notion of the *coiffure* intended may be gathered from the plate opposite p. 354 of Part 3 of Vol. 8 of these *Transactions*, (Mr. J. Conder's paper on "The History of Japanese Costume").

[235] B.H.C. gives this passage in Latin: 'An soror mea fiet easdem stirpis [viri] inferior storea'?. B.H.C. adds in a note, *I.e.,* "An soror mea, cujus pater Imperator Nin-toku, fiet uxor praisentis Imperatoris?"—Hujus similitudinis rusticitas et ipsis Japonicis commentatoribus pudori est. [That is, "Shall my sister, whose father is the Emperor Nin-toku, become the wife of the present Emperor?" The barbarity of this simile is shameful even to the Japanese commentators. —M.F.]

[236] See Vol. 2, Note 42.

[237] See Vol. 3, Note 173.

[238] *Cf.* Vol. 2, Note 417.

[239] Lit., "Hast thou anything to think about?" The same construction is used in the next sentence.

[240] *I.e.,* her son by her former husband King Ō-kusaka.

[241] Lit., "below the palace." The same expression recurs further on. The parallel passage in the *Chronicles* has "below the upper story" *i.e.,* in the court or garden of a two-storied house. With the small proportions assumed by Japanese architecture, conversation could well be overheard under these conditions.

[242] *I.e.,* "take vengeance upon me.

[243] *Scil.* by the Emperor's side.

[244] *Tsubura omi.* The etymology of Tsubura is obscure.

[245] For Sugahara see Vol. 2, Note 577. The Fushimi here mentioned, which is in Yamato, must not be confounded with the better known Fushimi in Yamashiro.

The popular etymology of this name (and it is to be found in many books) traces it to *fushi-mi*, i.e., "lying three," in connection with the story of a man who "lay on the mound for three years." Probably *fuse-mizu*, "water laid on," a name perhaps given on account of an aqueduct or of water-pipes, was the original designation, which has been corrupted.

[246]See Vol. 3, Note 179.

[247]See Vol. 2, Note 174.

[248]Lit., "taken"

[249]*I.e.,* treated the matter with indifference.

[250]Lit., "without relying," as if the speaker meant to say that the dead man could not rely on him for vengeance.

[251]In Yamato. The name seems to mean "new tilled field."

[252]Written 随立 in the text followed by Norinaga. The other reading 墮立 is untenable.

[253]In order to account for such an effect from so apparently insufficient a cause, Norinaga supposes that after the prince had been made to stand up to the height of his loins in the pit, the latter was filled by having stones thrown into it, whereby his feet and legs would be crushed.

[254]Lit., "to wait and fight."

[255]The character 来, "to come" (here in accordance with English idiom rendered by "down") is supposed to be an error. One conjectural emendation of it, viz., 盛, would suggest the "plentiful" falling of the flowers of the reeds.

[256]*I.e.*, he lifted himself on tiptoe by leaning on his spear, so as to be able to peep in.

[257]The maiden thus suddenly introduced into the story is Tsubura's daughter Kara, whom it must be supposed that the Prince had previously been wooing.

[258]Or rather, "Imperial words." The application of the characters 詔命 to the words of one who was not yet actually Emperor is curious.

[259]*I.e.,* the places where the five granaries originally were are now the five villages inhabited by the men who cultivate the Imperial gardens. For Kazuraki see Vol. 2, Note 160.

[260]Or we may, following Norinaga's proposal, take the character 臣 in this clause in its slightly different acceptation of "subject," which better suits the sense. The partly phonetic wording of the next sentence 賤奴意富美者 shows how the writer was perplexed by the double use of the term.

[261]*Q.d.*, in comparison with a prince of the Imperial family, even a grandee was but a vile slave.

[262]The character 随 in the original of this passage 入坐于随家 is corrupt. But the sense remains clear, and it is scarcely worthwhile looking about for a probable emendation. Norinaga has no satisfactory proposal to make.

[263]The humble character 僕, "servant" is here used for the first personal pronoun. The expression 僕者手悉傷 here literally rendered "my hands are all wounded," is very curious. Norinaga reads it *ita-te oinu*, *i.e.*, "I have received (or suffered from)

hurtful hands," and compares two somewhat similar expressions found in Sect. 44 (see Vol. 2, Note 27). The translator may however point out that the similarity is much more apparent in Norinaga's *kana* reading than it is in the Chinese text itself. May not the sense of the present passage rather be: "All our men are wounded?" for the word *te* (手) "hand," is frequently used in Japanese,—in compounds at least,—in the sense of "man," somewhat as it is in English naval, mining, and other technical parlance.

[264]This name has the curious signification of "Korean (or Chinese) bag." [There was also a *Yamato bukuro (no sukune)*, or Japanese bag. —W.G.A]

[265]*Ōmi no Sasaki no yama no kimi. Cf.* Vol. 2, *Note 508.*

[266]This and the following names are altogether obscure, neither is it evident whether two places are meant, or only one. The present passage reads as if two were intended, but a little further down the author seems to be speaking of but one.

[267]Lit., "the night has already finished dawning."

[268]Norinaga endeavors, not very successfully, to explain the use of this epithet by Prince Ō-Hatsuse's attendants. As the sequel shows, the violence was all on the other side.

[269]Lit. "prince" (王子). Their names apparently signify "big basket" and "little basket."

[270]Known in later times as Kaniha and Kabai. The name signifies (if the characters with which it is written may be relied on) "the well where the leaves were cut."

[271]See Vol. 2, Sect. 66, Notes c and 460.

[272]See Vol. 2, Note 237.

[273]Or Shijimi. Properly the name of a village, it is here used as the name of a man. The etymology is obscure.

[274]For Hatsuse see Vol. 3, Note 222. Several Asakuras are named in the pages of these *Records*. That here named is in Yamato. The name seems to mean "morning store-house."

[275]*Shiraka-be.*

[276]*Hatsuse-be no toneri*. This Clan was called after the reigning Emperor. Remember that the word "Retainers" is here a "gentile name."

[277]*Kawase no toneri. Kawa-se signifies* "river-reach," and the *Chronicles*, under date of the eleventh year of this reign, tell a story of the appearance of a white cormorant, to commemorate which this family was established. Cormorants, it will be remembered, were used for catching fish in rivers: hence the appropriateness of the name bestowed on the family in question.

[278]The name given by the Early Japanese to Wu (呉), an ancient state in Eastern China to the South of the Yangtze River. In Japanese it however, like other names of portions of China, often denotes the whole of that country in a somewhat vague manner The derivation of the word *Kure* is obscure. The most acceptable proposition is that which would see in it corruption of the original Chinese term *Wu*, of which *Go* is the Sinico-Japanese pronunciation. But what of the second syllable *re?*

[279]The phrase 安置 is in this place used for "lodged." [Settled?" —W.G.A.]

[280] *Ie.,* Kure Moor. It is in Yamato. According to the *Chronicles*, the former name of the place had been *Himokuma-no.*

[281] *I.e., Waka-kusaka-be.*

[282] See Vol. 2, Note 26. The Kusaka here mentioned is that in Kōchi.

[283] From *tada*, "straight" and *koeru* "to cross," this being a short cut over the mountains.

[284] The original of this clause is 有上堅魚作舍屋之家 which is read *katsuo o agete ya o tsukureru ie ari.* The *katsuo* (properly *katsuo-gi* 堅魚木) is the name of the uppermost portion of the roof in modern Shintō temples, and apparently in ancient times also in houses that were not devoted to religious purposes. The difficulty is not with the sense, but with the derivation of the word *katsuo-gi*. Following the characters with which it is here and elsewhere written, Norinaga sees in it a reference to the shape of the blocks of wood resembling "dried bonitos," which is the modem signification of *katsuo*. But Moribe, in his *Examination of Difficult Words*, proposes a derivation which approves itself more to the present writer's mind, viz., *kazuku o-gi* (戴小木), "small timbers atop" (see his *Examination of Difficult Words, s.v.*). Norinaga's *Commentary*, Vol. 41, pp. 11–14, should be consulted for a discussion of the whole question of the use of these frames in ancient times, and for the special force to be attributed to the word "raised" (上) in this passage.

[285] *Shiki no ō-agata-nushi.* For Shiki see Vol. 2, Note 393.

[286] *I.e.,* did humble obeisance by prostrating himself on the ground.

[287] Or, according to the older reading. "This (*i.e.*, thy command) [is to be received with] awe."

[288] Or, "tied with [a string of] cloth." The translation follows Norinaga's interpretation.

[289] The name signifies "loin-girded," *i.e.*, as may be presumed, "wearing a sword."

[290] For he had come from Yamato in the East to Kōchi in the West.

[291] The meaning is: "Thy Majesty must not come to woo me here, as the direction is unlucky. But I will myself come up straightway to the palace to be thine Empress."

[292] The ascent or way up here mentioned is, says Norinaga, the Tadagoe Road, and the mountain is Mount Kusaka. See Vol. 3, Note 282 and 283.

[293] In this Song the Emperor consoles himself for the delay in his union with Princess Waka-kusaka-be by reflecting that after all she will soon be his.—The first half of the poem down to the colon and dash is a preface to the rest. Most of the difficult words occurring in it have been explained in previous notes: for the "broad-leafed bear-oak" see Vol. 2, Note 548; for *tatami-komo*, the pillow-word by which Heguri is preceded in the Japanese text, see Vol. 2, Note 714. *Kusaka-be* is curious, for whereas it properly signifies Kusaka-Tribe,—this tribe or family being called after the place where they resided,—the place itself came to be renamed after them when the fact of the posterior origin of the family designation had been forgotten. The reason for the mention in the Preface of the oak-tree, which is not referred to in the main text of the poem, is difficult to ascertain. Moribe thinks, however, that it is on account of the luxuriance of its foliage which, as if it were

a preface within the preface, paves the way for the mention of the thick-growing bamboos. The punning connection between *tashimi-dake*, "luxuriant bamboos," and *tashi ni wa i-nezu*, "we sleep not certainly," is necessarily obliterated in the English translation. "Certainly" must be taken in the sense of "undisturbedly."

[294] *I.e.,* as may be conjectured, a messenger dispatched to him by his mistress. It seems best to suppose the author to represent the Emperor as not having actually gone to her house at all, but as having only communicated with her by messenger.

[295] *Miwa-gawa.* It is the stream which flows past Hatsuse. For Miwa see Vol. 2, Note 440.

[296] *Hiketa-be no Akai-ko. Hiketa* is in Yamato. The etymology of the word is obscure. Akai-ko signifies "red boar child;" but the appropriateness of the name to the woman in the story is not made to appear.

[297] See Sect. 37, Note c.

[298] Moribe says that, in this Song, the forgetful Monarch calls to mind the majestic and awful appearance of the sacred tree in the temple-grounds, and is moved by this religious thought to repent of his neglectful treatment of her who had so patiently waited for him through so many years. Norinaga, on the contrary, sees in the words nothing more than a comparison of the old woman to some sacred tree of immemorial age, and the aversion felt by the monarch to a union with her.—The oak mentioned (the *Kashi, Quercus myrsinifolia*) is an evergreen species. Both Norinaga and Moribe consider that *mimoro* in the original Japanese of this Song should be taken, not as a proper name (see Vol. 1, Notes 441 and 442), but simply as signifying "a sacred dwelling." As Miwa is mentioned in the earlier part of the story, it might seem more natural to regard *mimoro* as likewise being a proper name. But the word *mimoro* itself signifying "sacred spot," the difference between the two views does not amount to much, and it is best to follow native authority. "Oak-plain" (*kashi-hara*) means "a place planted with oak trees."The first sentence of the Song must be looked on as a sort of preface to the second.

[299] B.H.C. gives this line in Latin: –o si dormivissem cum illâ in juventâ! –MF

[300] The first words of this Song down to the colon and dash are a preface to the Song proper, whose meaning stands in need of no explanation.—Moribe surmises that the word *kuri*, "chestnut," was formerly a general name for all sorts of fruits, somewhat like our English word "berry."

[301] The drenching of the sleeve with tears is a common figure in Japanese poetry.

[302] Or we might (following Moribe) render thus: "Left over from the guarding of the jewel-grove guarded at the august dwelling," etc. The wording of this Song is far from clear. While Norinaga sees in it a reference to the construction of a wall round the grounds of a temple, the overplus of the materials for which sacred wall could not, it may be presumed, be applied to any profane purpose, Moribe disputes the propriety of such an interpretation of the word *kaki* which, according to him, denotes the grove planted in temple-grounds, temples never having been surrounded by walls such as Norinaga assumes the existence of, nor even by "hedges" or "fences," which is the more usual acceptation of the term. He thinks,

therefore, that the superficial signification of the actual words of the Song is that the priest, who has all his life been in the service of one particular shrine, cannot desert it for the adoration of some other deity. The underlying deeper significance of the little poem is in either case the same: Akai-ko had, during her long waiting of eighty years, remained true to her first love the Emperor. For her very reason it had been impossible for her ever to give her affections to another, and she had now come up to the capital to demonstrate to him who had forgotten her the unchangeable nature of her feelings.

[303]This pretty little poem is too clear to need any comment. Moribe supposes that some lotuses brought from Kusaka may have been among the presents made by Akai-ko to the Emperor. In the original Japanese the reference to the lotuses comes first, as a sort of preface to the rest of the poem. The laws of English construction necessitate its being put last in the translation.

[304]See Vol. 3, Note 80.

[305]See Vol. 2, Note 56.

[306]See Vol. 2, Note 965.

[307]This Song presents no difficulties. In it the Emperor speaks of himself as a Deity, and is enthusiastically praised by the commentator Moribe for so doing.

[308]*Akizu-no*. See Vol. 3, Note 313.

[309]Or "bit."

[310]Is the *abu* not the gadfly? I thought the horsefly was a somewhat smaller insect, but I may be mistaken. —W.G.A.

[311]*Na ni ō* means "to be famous."The meaning is "in order to render the dragonfly famous its name was given to the country of Japan." —W.G.A.

[312]The signification of the greater portion of this Song is clear enough, and is sufficiently explained by the context. The word "who" however admits of two interpretations, Norinaga taking it to signify "someone," whereas Moribe, keeping the literal meaning of "who?" ,sees in it an angry exclamation of the monarch's at having been brought out to the hunt under exaggerated promises of game. *O-muro* means "little cave"' but is here a proper name. *Mi-yoshino* is a form of the word Yoshino which is frequently met with in poetry, the syllable *mi* being probably, as Mabuchi tells us in his *Commentary on the Collection of a Myriad Leaves*, equivalent to *ma*, and therefore simply an "ornamental prefix." The phrase "tranquilly carries on the government" represents the Japanese *yasumi-shishi*, the pillow-word for *wa ga ō-kimi*, "our Great Lord," which latter phrase descriptive of the Sovereign is here put into the Sovereign's own mouth. "Of white stuff," *shiro-tae no,* is another pillow-word. The only real difficulty in this Song meets us in the interpretation of its concluding sentence. The meaning apparently intended to be conveyed is that it was in order to prove itself worthy of its name that the dragonfly performed the loyal deed which forms the subject of the tale. But if so, the author forgets that it was not the dragonfly that was called after Japan, but Japan that was called after the dragonfly (Akizu-shima, "Dragon-fly-Island," from *akizu*, "dragonfly"). What should be the point of the whole poem therefore fails of application. The name

"Island of the Dragonfly" has already appeared in Vol. 1, Note 91.

[313]*I.e.,* Dragonfly Moor. See Norinaga's remarks in his *Examination of the Synonyms for Japan*, p. 26.

[314]See Vol. 2, Note 160.

[315]See Vol. 1, Sect. 23, Notes d and 369. [Arrow? —W.G A.]

[316]This is the sense attributed by the commentators to the obscure word *utaki*, which seems to be only found written phonetically. [Grunting? Snorting? —W.G.A.]

[317]Our author cannot be right in attributing this Song to the Emperor, and we need not hesitate to accept the different version of the story given in the parallel passage of the *Chronicles*, where the Monarch, as might be expected from all the other details that have been preserved concerning him, bravely faces the boar, while it is one of his attendants who runs away and climbs a tree to be out of danger, and afterwards composes these lines. This Song is a good instance of what Mr. Aston (in his *Grammar of the Japanese Written Language*, 2nd Edit., p. 194) has said concerning some of the short poems of a later date: "These sentences are not statements of fact; they merely picture to the mind a state of things without making any assertion respecting it." Here we, as it were, simply see the frightened courtier sitting breathless and terrified amid the branches of the alder, and the whole verse has but the meaning of an exclamation. The term *ari-o* rendered "opportune mound," is the only word in the text which raises any difficulties of interpretation. Moribe's exegesis has here been followed. According to the older view it signifies "barren mound." For the words "our great lord who tranquilly carries on the government" see Vol. 3, Note 312. [Norinaga sticks to the *Kojiki* version and understands the poem accordingly. The addition of one word *toneri* after Heavenly Sovereign would make all right. The *Kojiki* puts Yūryaku's proceedings always in the most favorable light and it is impossible to accept the ordinary text as correct. —W.G.A.]

[318]Lit., "the hundred officials." This Chinese phrase has been met with before in the *Records*, and recurs in this Section.

[319]The original has the character 傾, out of which it is hard to make sense. Norinaga's proposal to consider it put by error for 頒 has therefore been adopted, though the translator feels by no means sure that it is a happy one. According to the strict Chinese sense of 頒, it would not fit with this passage any better than 傾; but in Japanese we may be justified in understanding 小頒 to mean "not distinguishable."

[320]In the original: 吾者雖悪事而一言雖善事而一言言離之神葛城之一言主之大神者也. The import of the obscure expression "dispelling with a word the good" is not rendered much more intelligible by Norinaga's attempt to explain it. For Kazuraki see Vol. 2, Note 160.

[321]Lit., "that there would be a present (or manifest) great person."

[322]*I.e.,* he kept nothing for himself, but from his own sword and bow and arrows down to the ceremonial garments in which his followers were clad, gave everything to the god.

[323]In token of joy, says Norinaga.

[324]The characters 満山末, rendered by "came down the mountain," are evidently the result of a copyist's carelessness. The translation follows Norinaga's proposal to emend the text to 降山来.

[325]Lit. "mouth."

[326]*Odo-hime.* The signification of this name is obscure.

[327]*Wani no Satsuki no omi.* For *Wani* see Vol. 2, Note 318. *Satsuki* is the old Japanese name of the fifth moon.

[328]Moribe thus paraphrases this Song: "The Monarch had met a girl carrying a spade in her hand, and, as she was beautiful, wished to address her; but she ran off and hid on the hillside, leaving her spade behind her. His words express a desire for five hundred spades like hers, with which to break down the hill-side and dig her out… It is in joke that he talks of the maiden who was on the *other side* of the hill as being *inside* it." That in ancient times all digging implements were not made of metal will be seen by reference to Vol. 3, Note 70.

[329]*Kanasuki no waka*

[330]Said to be scarcely distinguishable from the *keyaki (Zelhova serrata).*

[331]See Vol. 2, Note 709.

[332]Lit., "still presented"

[333]On her face. —W.G.A.

[334]To understand the allusion at the beginning of this Song to the palace of Hishiro at Makimuku, which had been the residence of the Emperor Kei-kō (see Vol. 2, Note 581), it must be known that in the account of the reign of that monarch as given in the *Chronicles* there is a story which, like that in the text, turns on carelessness in dealing with a goblet,—carelessness which Kei-kō graciously pardoned. Moreover the scene of the incident here related was in the immediate neighborhood of the old palace of Hishiro. There was therefore a double reason for referring to that place; and the under-current of insinuation is that, as Kei-kō in the olden time forgave the courtiers who forgot his goblet, wilt not the present Sovereign forgive the maid of Mie for letting a leaf fall into his? The poetess, after describing the splendor and solidity of the Imperial abode, passes on to a mention of the luxuriant and many-branching *tsuki*-tree growing near "the house of new licking," *i.e.,* the sacred hall where the Sovereign performed each year the ceremony of tasting the first fruits of the harvest. The "gate" may either be taken in its literal acceptation, or else regarded as used by metonymy for the palace itself. The description of that which the middle and lowest branches "have above them" is somewhat obscure, and perhaps the words should not be too strictly pressed for perfectly rational meaning, their chief use being as metrical parallelisms. The supposition of the commentators is however that the poetess, in speaking of this immense tree, meant to say that the middle branch (or branches) spread eastward, and the lowest branches westward. Next we are told of the fall of the fatal leaf into the oil, i.e., into the liquor, contained in the Imperial goblet; and the poetess, before acknowledging the awfulness of her misdemeanor, skillfully brings in an

allusion to the Japanese account of the creation, when the drops that fell from the spear used by the creator and creatrix Izanagi and Izanami to make the brine "go curdle-curdle" did very good work indeed; for they were piled up and became the first-formed island of the Japanese archipelago (see Sect. 3): for drops to fall down, or for leaves to fall into drops (of wine), must therefore surely be a good omen rather than a crime. Conformably with the hesitating nature of her allusion, the maiden leaves it quite uncertain what is conceived of as going curdle-curdle, in the present instance. In fact, neither must the thought be pressed too far, nor the sentence searched too rigorously from a grammatical point of view. Such intentional vagueness is one of the specific characteristics of a great deal of the poetry of Japan. The words "the tradition of the thing, too, this!" which conclude the poem, are obscure in another and more usual sense; but, having been already treated of in Vol. 1, Note 385, they need not detain us here. They do not affect the sense of the rest of the poem. Two points more remain to be noticed: one is that the words *Mie* and *hi no mi kado* "august gate of false cypress (*chamæcyparis*)") are respectively preceded by the pillow-words *ariginu no*, whose signification is disputed, and *maki-saku*, which signifies "splitting true trees"; the other, that the original of the word "glistens" near the commencement of the poem only has that sense if, following Moribe, we identify *hi-gakeru* with *hi-kagayakeru*. As it stands, the word *kakeru* lends itself more naturally to the interpretation of "sets." But the logical difficulty of accepting the phrase "where the sun sets" in such a context, where on the contrary some phrase of good omen is alone appropriate, seems greater than the philological difficulty of deriving *hi-gakera* by a process of contraction from *hi-kagayakera*. The designation of the Emperor or Heir Apparent by the title of "august child of the high-shining sun" has been met with before, and needs no explanation when the solar ancestry claimed by the Japanese monarchs is called to mind.

[335]The gist of this Song, which must be supposed to be addressed to the female attendant, is simply: "Present the goblet full of liquor to the Emperor."—In accordance with the rules of Japanese construction, the Imperative "present," which is the chief Verb of the sentence, comes last, and is preceded by the comparison of the Monarch to the leaves and flowers of the camellia-tree, while the comparatively unimportant words describing the position of the tree come at the beginning. Thus in a literal English translation the climax is necessarily spoilt through the reversal of the order of the words. The "broad-leafed camellia" has already appeared in Vol. 3, Note 58, the "house of new licking" has been explained in the note immediately preceding the present one, and the incomprehensible concluding exclamation has been discussed in Vol. 1, Note 385. The "high metropolis" of Yamato is of course the then capital. There is however some doubt whether the word *takechi*, which is here thus rendered, should not rather be considered as a proper name. The expression *ko-dakaru*, rendered "high-timbered," is also doubtful. Norinaga interprets it simply as slightly high. Moribe seems right in explaining the word *tsukasa* to mean "a mound."

[336]This Song is here out of place, and is supposed by Norinaga to have been

composed not by the Emperor, but by some court lady who was absent from the feast. The meaning simply is: "Ah yes, 'tis today that the court ladies are drinking their fill of rice-liquor [—and would that I were with them]!"—The picture here presented of the manners of the court is not attractive; but the comparison of the ladies' appearance with that of various birds is quaint. The commentators tell us that the appropriateness of the use of the word "scarfs" as applied to the quail lies in the peculiar plumage of that bird, which makes it look as if it had a scarf on. "Having put their tails together" means "standing with their trains in a row." The epithet "yard" applied to the sparrows paints the habits of that bird. The words "great palace" are in the original preceded by the pillow-word *momoshiki no*, whose signification is disputed. After the lines

Kyō mo ka mo
Saka-mi-zuku-rashi,

rendered "may perhaps today be truly steeped in liquor," Moribe would like to consider the lines

Asu mo ka mo
Saka-mi-zuku-rashi

i.e., "may perhaps tomorrow be truly steeped in liquor" to have been accidentally omitted. There is no doubt but that their insertion would add to the effect of the poem from the point of view of style.

337 大語歌, read *ama-koto-uta*. This expression is altogether obscure, and the commentators differ in their interpretations of it. Mabuchi, following the characters, sees in them an allusion to the words "august child of the high-shining sun," which recurs in each of the three Songs thus bracketed together. Norinaga thinks that *ama-koto* should be regarded as standing for *amari-goto* (餘言吾) "surplus words," in allusion to the meaningless *refrain* with which the Songs in question terminate. Other Songs, however, which end in the same manner, are not thus designated. Moribe's exegesis, though founded on Norinaga's, is preferable to it. Accepting *ama-koto* as a contraction of *amari-goto*, he would take the second half of the compound in the sense of "things," not "words" (事 not 語), and regard the whole as signifying that the Songs were composed or sung after the conclusion of the actual feast. Against this view must be set the fact that the Chinese characters lend it no support. The translator, has, as usual when in doubt, preferred to adhere to the sense given by the characters.

338 Banquet. —W.G.A.

339 *Kasuga no Odo-hime.* See Vol. 3, Note 326.

340 This Song is simply a reiterated and playful injunction to the maiden to hold firmly the flagon containing the intoxicating liquor; and Norinaga is, as Moribe remarks, putting more into the words than they are really meant to convey, when he says that they imply praise on the Monarch's part.—The English words "grandee's daughter" represent the Japanese *omi no omina*, a somewhat remarkable expression, which is interpreted by Norinaga to signify "attendant maiden." The translator prefers the view propounded in Moribe's comment on this Song, and

has therefore adopted it. The expression in question is in the original preceded by the untranslatable pillow-word *minasosoku* (Moribe reads the last syllable with the *nigori,—gu*). The word rendered "excellent flagon" is *ho-dari,* the first element of the compound being explained by the commentators in the sense of "excellent," *i.e.*, "big," while the second is the same as the modern word *taru*, "a cask." In ancient times, however, the signification of *tari* or *taru* was that of a vessel to pour liquor from, not to store liquor in,—*i.e.*, a flagon, not a cask. The words "quite firmly, more and more firmly" represent the Japanese *shita-gataku ya-gataku* according to Moribe's exegesis. Norinaga's interpretation of them in the sense of "[take the] bottom firmly and the top firmly" is less acceptable.

[341]Thus does the editor of 1687, who is followed by Moribe, understand the original expression *uki-uta*. Norinaga's interpretation, "Floating Song," seems less good.

[342]So enamored is the maiden of the Sovereign that she would fain be even the board of the armrest on which he leans.—The expression "lower board" is misleading, for it refers simply to the self-evident fact that the board forming the top of the little low table used as an armrest by one squatting on his mat is below the arm, as whose support it serves. The words "stands leaning" must probably be understood to signify "sits" or "squats leaning." The expression "our great lord who tranquilly carries on the government" is a frequently recurring periphrasis for the word "Emperor," and has been explained in Vol. 2, Note 691. The words "at morn" and "at eve" are literally in the original "at morning doors" and "at evening doors," the reference being to the fact that the doors of a house are respectively opened and closed in the early morning and at nightfall. The exclamation "Oh! mine elder brother" is addressed to the board of the armrest. *Cf*, the first Song in Sect. 39, where Yamato-take apostrophizes a pine-tree in the same terms.

[343]For Tajihi see Vol. 3, Note 127. *Taka-washi* signifies "high eagle."

[344]For Iware see Sect. 43, Note c. *Mika-kuri* signifies "jar-chestnut."

[345]*Shiraka-be.*

[346]In Vol. 3, Note 123, this name appears as *Aomi-no-iratsume*. Both *Aomi* and *Oshinumi* are supposed to be names of places. The latter is the name of a district in Yamato. Its etymology is obscure. For *Ii-toyo* see Vol. 3, Note 124.

[347]See Vol. 3, Note 121, where however the title of *wake* ("Lord") is omitted.

[348]For *Kazuraki* see Vol. 2, Note 160, and for *Oshinumi* see Vol. 3, Note 346. *Takaki* seems to signify "high castle," while *Tsunosashi* is obscure. (See Norinaga's remarks on these two names in Vol. 43, p. 3. of his *Commentary*.)

[349]*Yama-be no muraji odate. Yama-be* has already appeared. *O-date* signifies "small shield."

[350]For this name see Vol. 3, Note 273. A similar festival at the inauguration of a new cave is mentioned in Sect. 80.

[351]Norinaga's vain attempts to reconcile the dates with this statement of Princes Ōke and Oke being "young children" at this time, after an interval of two reigns since the death of their father, will be found in Vol. 43, pp. 10–11, of his *Commentary.*

[352]*I.e.*, as the commentators suppose, a place or vessel holding a light with which to kindle other lights for the feast. The word can scarcely here have its common signification of a "kitchen-range."

[353]*I.e.*, at the fact of their being so courteous to each other.

[354][The *Nihongi* and the *Kujiki* give different speeches.—W.G.A] This so-called "chant,"—it is not a Song, because not in meter, and is accordingly not transcribed syllabically,—is at first sight so difficult as to seem to defy translation, and to make the student apply to the whole of his interpretation Norinaga's closing remark on his exegesis of one of the phrases contained in it,— "this is mere guesswork, and the text demands further consideration." A little inspection shows, however, that the drift of the words is by no means so inscrutable as its partly ideographic and partly phonetic transcription makes it appear. The first part down to the colon and dash is a preface to the second, the "pivot" joining the two parts in the original Japanese being the word "bamboos." The laws of English construction unfortunately do not admit of the force of the original, which entirely depends on the position of the words, being rendered into our language. The appropriateness of the preface to the body of the chant rests on the consideration that the *bright* articles mentioned in it, viz., the sword painted and decorated with red streamers (or perhaps tied on with a red sash) and also the red banners are easily *hidden* behind the thick leaves of a bamboo-grove, just as the Imperial origin of the two young Princes was hidden beneath the vile office which they filled in Shijimu's household. The clause "cutting the [bamboos'] roots and bending down their extremities" forms the chief difficulty. Indeed the word "roots" is supplied by Norinaga, and his interpretation of the phrase is merely tentative. We may, however, until some better explanation is offered, see in it a reference to the energetic manner in which the Empire was ruled by the young princes' grandfather, the Emperor Izaho-wake (Ri-chū), or else perhaps by their father Ichibe-no-oshiwa. This latter view is preferred by Norinaga, though according to the history Ichinobe-no-oshiwa never actually ascended the throne. The position of the verb "ruled" in the Japanese text permits of either interpretation. The comparison of the government of the Empire to playing on a lute is poetical and appropriate. It should be noticed that in the Japanese text the construction of the sentence forming the main body of the chant is the reverse of what it is made to appear to be in the translation. The words "beggarly descendants," by which, as a climax, the singer reveals his own and his brother's illustrious descent, therefore come last of all and produce on Odate the startling effect which we read of in the next sentence.

[355]Or, "seat." In ancient times each person in a room sat on a special mat, and it is that small mat which is here meant.

[356]The numeral is accompanied by the auxiliary *hashira*, properly used for gods and goddesses.

[357]The student should compare the version of the story in this Sect, with that given in the *Chronicles of Japan*, where it is placed some year later at the commencement of the reign of the Emperor Bu-retsu, and not only do many of the details

disagree, but the arrangement and number of the Songs is different. It is impossible to make a consistent whole out of the story as here given; so, while noticing the linguistic peculiarities of each of the Songs in the order in which they appear in the present text, the translator has thought tn advisable, following Moribe, to give in Vol. 3, Note 368 a consistent scheme of interpretation for the whole. The small Roman numbers placed in brackets at the commencement of each Song indicate its place in the text as restored by Moribe [These have been converted to the Arabic numerals now used to number all the Songs in these *Records*. —M.F.].

[358]By one or other of the two Princes Ōke and Oke. "Each," we are afterwards told "ceded the Empire to the other," and it therefore remained for some time uncertain which was to be the Sovereign.

[359]*Shibi no omi.* In some of the Songs that follow there is a play on the identity of this name with that of the tunny-fish (*shibi*). But whether that be really the derivation it is difficult to ascertain.

[360]*Heguri no omi. Cf.* Vol. 2, Note 290.

[361]*Uda no obito-ra. Uda* is the name of a place in Yamato.

[362]*I.e.*, "big fish." But see the remark on this name in Vol. 3, Note 368.

[363]*Uta-gaki.* The derivation of this curious expression is disputed; but the meaning seems to be" strophic" or "choric song," or "a place where singing in which more than one takes part is going on."

[364]In this Song the "further fin" (*oto tsu hata-de*, explained by the characters 彼鰭手 or 彼端手) is supposed to signify a pent-roof, or the eaves of the roof, or else an out-house connected by a slanting roof with the main building. The "great palace" is the palace of Prince Oke.

[365]The "great carpenter" is the carpenter employed to build the roof above-mentioned.

[366]The "eight-fold hedge of branches" is simply a "hedge," and the "child of a grandee" the Grandee Shibi himself.

[367]The words "made fast" refer to the tying of the fence at certain places to give it strength. If we accepted Moribe's emendation of the final verb *yakemu*, "burn," to *yaremu*, we should have to translate the last clause thus: "tis a fence that shall be broken."

[368]"The great fish" (*ōuo yo shi*) is the pillow-word for *shibi*, "tunny." The word "he" (which might also be rendered "*it*," —the original being *so*) must be taken to refer both to the fish itself and to the Grandee Shibi (*i.e.*, the grandee Tunny), who bore its name.—Following Moribe's acceptable restoration of the original story, which is founded on a comparison of the text of these *Records* with that of the *Chronicles of Japan*, we find that in the first Song of the series the young Prince half-jokingly remarks on the fact of the Grandee Shibi appearing in public with the damsel who was to have been his (the Prince's) bride. Shibi's name, which, as already stated, signifies "tunny," furnishes the occasion for the marine metaphors borrowed from the currents and the breakers. Shibi's answer (Song 2,—in the *Records* wrongly ascribed to the prince), takes up the same strain, but in a more

taunting tone: the prince is likened to a fisherman who would fain make a futile attempt to spear the great tunny, and his (the tunny's, *i.e.*, the Grandee Shibi's) presence must indeed be pain and grief to him. In a third Song, which is given in the *Chronicles*, but not in the *Records*, the prince retorts that he relies on his good sword to win the girl for him in the end, and in Song 4 the Grandee jeers at the dilapidated condition of his palace, and by implication at the sorry state of his fortunes,—a taunt to which the prince replies in Song 5 by saying that if the palace is dilapidated, and the Empire in disorder, the fault belongs to none other than to the Grandee himself. Songs 6 and 7, which are not found in the *Records*, only serve to continue the growing war of words, which in Song 8 (in the *Records* wrongly attributed to the Grandee) comes to a climax by the prince exclaiming that if he does not force his way into the Grandee's mansion to seize his ladylove, it is only on account of the magnanimity of his disposition. To this the Grandee replies in Song 9 (in the *Records* erroneously attributed to the prince) by a sort of *tu quoque*, vowing that he will cut and burn his way into the prince's palace. This is not the end of the dispute in the pages of the *Chronicles*, but it is all that need detain the reader of the *Records*. It should, however, be mentioned that in the *Chronicles* the name of the girl is *Kage-hime*: *Ōuo*, "Big Fish," which is here given, would seem to be nothing more than a nickname, which perhaps arose from the incidents of this metrical war of words.

[369]The word used in the original is *hashira*, the Auxiliary Numeral for Deities. It recurs at the commencement of the next Section, where however it is not convenient to translate it.

[370]The original here has the character 亦, "again" or "moreover." But this must be, as Norinaga points out, a copyist's error. Almost immediately below the same character recurs where it is equally out of place. The translator has followed Norinaga in rendering it the first time by "so," and the second by "surely."

[371]See Vol. 3, Note 145.

[372]*Naniwa no miko*. For Naniwa see Vol. 2, Note 21.

[373]*Iwaki no miko.*

[374]Who had been treacherously slain by the Emperor Yū-ryaku (see Sect. 148).

[375]*I.e.*, says Norinaga, "it is known to me, and to none besides."

[376]The *Nihongi* says the skeleton of the Prince was distinguished from that of a retainer who was buried with him, by the latter having lost his upper teeth. —W.G.A.

[377]The character used is 起, which is more applicable to the raising of troops than to the *setting to work* of peasants. It seems however here to be used in the latter sense; or perhaps we should consider it to mean that people *were got together*.

[378]See Vol. 3, Note 266. Possibly the "mountain east" should be a proper name, Eastern Mountain, but it is not taken as such by Norinaga.

[379]See Vol. 3, Note 264.

[380]*I e.*, "keeping an eye," *q.d.*, on the place of burial of the Emperor's father. Grammar would lead us to expect the order of the words forming the name to be

reversed thus, *Me-oki*; but see Norinaga's remarks in Vol. 43, p. 56.

[381]This Song is not comprehensible except by reference to the text of the *Chronicles*, whose author gives a somewhat varying version of the story. He tells us that, as a support of the infirm old lady, the Emperor had a string or rope stretched as a sort of hand-rest along the way she was obliged to pass in order to reach the Imperial apartments, and that at the end of the rope was a bell whose tinkling notified the Emperor of her approach. The conjectural exclamation which closes the little poem has therefore an obvious sense, which would be wanting if the bell were at the other end, as in the version here given; for the Emperor would not give expression to surprise at her approach, if he had himself just rung for her to come.—"Far-distant" is an imperfect attempt to represent the pillow-word *momo-zatafu*, which here alludes to the stages along which the old woman may be supposed to be travelling. The valley and the moor overgrown with short grass form an allusion to the way, long and arduous for her,—which Oki-me had to traverse to reach the Imperial apartments, and they contain possibly a further allusion to her original journey to the capital.

[382]The *Nihongi* allows a more reasonable interval. —W.G.A.

[383]The meaning of this Song is quite clear.—The second time the name *Oki-me* occurs, it might, instead of being as here taken as an exclamation, be made the subject of the sentence, thus: "Oki-me from Ōmi will by tomorrow, etc." The words "wilt [thou]," which represent *ka* of the original Japanese may be taken either as an exclamation properly so-called, or as a sort of rhetorical interrogation whose force is simply exclamatory. The meaning comes to the same in either case, and is literally rendered by the same English words; but according to the latter view, we should have to replace the point of exclamation by a point of interrogation.

[384]See Sect. 149.

[385]Norinaga would have us understand the text to mean "in the neighborhood of the river." There is, however, no difficulty in accepting the author's statement literally, as anyone who is acquainted with the broad, stony beds of Japanese rivers will readily admit.

[386]*Asuka-gawa.* For Asuka see Vol. 3, Note 145.

[387]*I.e.*, probably "whenever."

[388]The real etymology of this name is obscure but the author's intention is to connect it with the "divining" or "pointing out" mentioned in the preceding sentence, which is given phonetically as [*mi*] *shimeki*.

[389]霊 read *mi tama* or *tamashihi*. We might also translate it by the word "ghost."

[390]The respectful character 奏 is used for this word, and again below we have the first personal pronoun represented by 僕, "servant."

[391]This sentence ends in the original with the characters 以参出, which it is not necessary to render into English. They imply that the speaker will come back, and report on what he has done.

[392]It is curious that the tumulus of *Yū-ryaku Tenno* is very considerably mutilated. Here is a copy of a note taken after a visit to this tumulus. "This mausoleum is at

the present day a round single mound encircled by a moat, but there are sufficient remains of the second mound and of the original moat to show that it was once a double-topped *misasagi* of the ordinary type. A large quantity of earth must have been removed to deprive this tomb of its distinctive character as an Imperial mausoleum and to give it the appearance of the tomb of a mere subject." —W.G.A.

[393]See Vol. 1, Note 551.

[394]For *Kataoka* see Vol. 2, Note 247. *Iwa-tsuki* probably means "rock-platter," and seems to have been the name of a little plateau.

[395]For the discontinuance of explanatory footnotes in this concluding portion of the translation see Translator's Introduction, Sect. 2, near the top of the page xv.

[396]Details of this struggle and its causes are given in the *Chronicles of Japan*, and are discussed at length in Norinaga's *Commentary*, Vol. 44, pp. 15–20. They are of no special interest..

[397]I am afraid I must abandon my suggestion that Osazaki was a posthumous name. —W.G.A.

Index

"Books to Span the East and West"

Tuttle Publishing was founded in 1832 in the small New England town of Rutland, Vermont [USA]. Our core values remain as strong today as they were then—to publish best-in-class books which bring people together one page at a time. In 1948, we established a publishing outpost in Japan—and Tuttle is now a leader in publishing English-language books about the arts, languages and cultures of Asia. The world has become a much smaller place today and Asia's economic and cultural influence has grown. Yet the need for meaningful dialogue and information about this diverse region has never been greater. Over the past seven decades, Tuttle has published thousands of books on subjects ranging from martial arts and paper crafts to language learning and literature—and our talented authors, illustrators, designers and photographers have won many prestigious awards. We welcome you to explore the wealth of information available on Asia at **www.tuttlepublishing.com.**

Published by Tuttle Publishing, an imprint of Periplus Editions (HK) Ltd.

www.tuttlepublishing.com

Library of Congress Catalog Card No. 2025931603

ISBN 978-4-8053-1833-1

First Tuttle edition published 1982
29 28 27 26 25
10 9 8 7 6 5 4 3 2 1 2503TP
Printed in Singapore

Distributed by:
North America, Latin America & Europe
Tuttle Publishing
364 Innovation Drive, North Clarendon
VT 05759-9436 U.S.A.
Tel: 1 (802) 773-8930
Fax: 1 (802) 773-6993
info@tuttlepublishing.com
www.tuttlepublishing.com

Japan
Tuttle Publishing
Yaekari Building, 3rd Floor,
5-4-12 Osaki, Shinagawa-ku
Tokyo 141-0032
Tel: (81) 3 5437-0171
Fax: (81) 3 5437-0755
sales@tuttle.co.jp
www.tuttle.co.jp

Asia Pacific
Berkeley Books Pte. Ltd.
3 Kallang Sector #04-01
Singapore 349278
Tel: (65) 6741-2178
Fax: (65) 6741-2179
inquiries@periplus.com.sg
www.tuttlepublishing.com